MAX BRAND

FIVE COMPLETE NOVELS

About the Author

MAX BRAND is the pen name of Frederick Faust. An American poet and novelist, he published two books of poetry under his own name: *The Village Street and Other Poems* and *Dionysus in Hades*. He was most famous, however, for his powerful Western novels. *The Untamed* was the first of his long series, and *Destry Rides Again* is the most famous. All told, he published more than seventy-five Westerns.

In addition, he wrote the Dr. Kildare books that were the basis for the popular films.

MAX BRAND

FIVE COMPLETE NOVELS

Destry Rides Again

Six-Gun Country

Trouble Trail

Flaming Irons

The Man from Mustang

AVENEL BOOKS
New York

This omnibus edition was previously published in separate volumes
under the titles:

Destry Rides Again Copyright MCMXXX by Dodd, Mead & Company, Inc.,
Copyright renewed MCMLVIII by Dorothy Faust.

Six-Gun Country Copyright MCMXXV by Street & Smith Corporation,
Copyright renewed MCMLIII by Dorothy Faust.

Trouble Trail Copyright MCMXXVI by Frederick Faust, Copyright renewed
MCMLIV by Dorothy Faust.

Flaming Irons Copyright MCMXXVII by the Estate of Frederick
Faust, Copyright renewed MCMLV by Dorothy Faust.

The Man from Mustang Copyright MCMXXXIII by Frederick Faust,
Copyright renewed MCMLXI by Jane F. Easton, Judith Faust, and John
Frederick Faust.

Six-Gun Country was originally published in *Western Story Magazine* in two
installments: "The Outlaw Redeemer" and "His Fight for a Pardon."

Flaming Irons was first published in magazine serial form in 1927.

This 1982 edition is published by Avenel Books
distributed by Crown Publishers, Inc., by arrangement with
Dodd, Mead & Company.

Manufactured in the United States of America

Library of Congress Cataloging in Publication Data

Brand, Max, 1892–1944.
    Max Brand, five complete novels.

    Contents: Destry rides again—Six-gun country—Trouble
trail—[etc.]
    I. Title.
PS3511.A87A6   1982   813'.52   82-1698
ISBN: 0-517-379457   AACR2

h g f e d c b a

CONTENTS

DESTRY RIDES AGAIN

1

"LIL' ol' town, you don't amount to much," said Harry Destry. "You never done nothin' an' you ain't gunna come to no good. Doggone me if you ain't pretty much like me!"

So said Destry as he came from the swinging doors of the First Chance and now leaned against one of the slim, horse-eaten pillars that supported the shelter roof in front of the saloon. The main street of the town of Wham stretched before him, until it wound itself, snakelike, out of view. It had gained its title in yet earlier days when it was little more than a crossroads store and saloon where the cowpunchers foregathered from east and west and south and north; and meeting from all those directions, often their encounters were so explosive that "wham!" was a really descriptive word. It had grown to some prosperity, and it was yet growing, for the cattlemen still came in, and, in addition, long sixteen-mule teams pulled high wheeled freight wagons out of Wham and lugged them up the dusty slopes to the gold mines of the Crystal Mountains.

But still Wham had not grown too fast for the knowledge of Destry to follow it. It was held in the cup of his memory; it was mapped in his mind; he knew every street sign, and the men behind the signs, from the blacksmiths to the lawyers, for Destry had grown up with the place. He had squirmed his bare toes in the hot dust of the main street; he had fought in the vacant lots; and many a house or store was built over some scene of his grandeur. For the one star in the crown of Harry Destry, the one jewel in his purse, the one song in his story, was that he fought; and when he battled, he was never conquered.

His wars were not for money, and neither were they for fame; but for the pure sake of combat in itself, he used his fists, and never wearied or shifted with ambidexterity to knives or guns, and still was at home with his talents. To him, Wham was a good and proper name for a city; it expressed his own character, and he loved the town as much as he esteemed it little.

Having surveyed it now, he took note of a new roof, white with fresh shingles, as yet unpainted, and went strolling down the street to examine the newcomer. He had turned the first bend of the way when he met Chester Bent.

"Why, doggone my eyes," said Destry gently, "if here ain't lil' ol' Chet Bent, all dressed up pretty and goin' to Sunday school agin. How are you, Chet, and how you gettin' on? Where you get them soft hands of yours all manicured?"

Chester Bent was by no means "little"; he had a spare pair of inches from which he could look down at Destry and twenty-five pounds to give weight to his objections, but in the younger days he had fallen before the rhythmic fury of Destry's two-fisted attack. It had been no easy victory, for under the seal-like sleekness of Chester Bent there was ample strength, and behind his habitual smile was the will of a fighter. Three times they met, and twice they were parted with blood on their hands; but the third time they had battled on the shore of the swimming pool until Chester fell on his back and gasped that he had enough. Therefore, having conquered him, the hard hands of Destry were averted from him, and he became one to whom Destry spoke with a sort of affectionate contempt.

It made no difference that Chester Bent was a rising man in the town, owning a store and two houses, or that he had stretched his interests to include a share in a mine of dubious value; to Harry Destry he remained "lil' old Chet" because of the glory of that day by the swimming pool. And in this, Destry was at fault, since he failed to understand that, while many things are forgotten by many men, there is one thing that never is forgiven, and that is the black moment when man or boy is forced to say: "Enough!"

Chester Bent merely smiled at the greeting of the cowpuncher.

"What you-all doin' here in front of the shoe shop?" went on Destry. "Waitin' for a pair of shoes, Chet?"

"I'm driving out the west road," said Bent, "and I promised Dangerfield to take Charlie out and deliver her; she's in collecting a pair of shoes."

"Is Charlie in there? I'm gunna go in and see her," announced Destry. "You come along and hold my coat, will you?"

He marched into the shoe store, and found a perspiring clerk laboring over a pair of patent leather dancing slippers which he was trying to work onto the foot of a pretty sixteen-year-old girl whose hair was down her back, and the end of the pigtail sun-faded to straw color.

"Why, hullo, Charlie," said Destry. "How you been, and whacha done with your freckles?"

"I bleached 'em out," said Charlie Dangerfield. "Whacha done with your spurs?"

"I left 'em in the First Chance," said Destry, "which they're gunna hang 'em on the wall by token that a man has been there and likkered."

"You lost 'em at poker," said she.

"Who told you that so quick?" asked Destry.

"It don't have to be told, or wrote either," said the girl, "and it don't take any mind reader to tell where you've been. Did you spend your whole six dollars, too?"

"It was five and a half," said Destry. "Who told you that?"

"I know you been out at the Circle Y about six days, that's all."

"I tell you how it was, Charlie. It was a pretty hand as you ever see; it was four sevens pat; and I stand, and Sim Harper draws three, and doggone me if he didn't raise me out of a right good slicker, and my old gun, and a set of silver conchos, and a brand new bandana, nearly, and my spurs, and then he lays down four ladies to smile at me. D'you hear of such luck?"

"You can get all kinds of luck off the bottom of the pack," said Charlie Dangerfield. "That's where Sim mostly keeps his."

"I wasn't watchin' too close," said Destry. "I gotta admit that when I seen the four of a kind it looked to me like a hoss and a saddle, and a pack and a fishin' rod, and a month of fishin' up the Crystal Mountains. I was feelin' the trout sock the fly, and how come I could watch Sim's hands at the same time?"

"Did you lose your hoss and saddle, too?"

"Would I of got to my spurs without that?" asked Destry. "You've kind of slowed up in the head, Charlie, since you lost your freckles. Freckles was always a sign of brains, ain't they, Chet?"

Chester Bent was idly running his glance over the names on the rows of shoe boxes, and he shrugged his shoulders for an answer.

"Lil' ol' Chet is day dreamin' and raisin' his interest rates to nine per cent," suggested Destry. "Look here, George"—this to the shoe clerk—"tell me what's the size of that shoe?"

"Five, Harry," said the clerk.

"D'you aim to get that slipper onto that there foot?" asked Destry, "or are you just wrestlin' for the sake of the exercise?"

"Fives ain't a bit too small," said the girl. "The last time I——"

"You musta been to the Camp Meeting and got saved," declared Destry, "and swallered the miracles down and everything, because you sure are askin' for a tidy little miracle right along about now!"

"You ain't amusin', Harry," she told him. "You're jes' plain rude, and ignorant!"

"About most things, I certainly am, but feet is a thing that I can understand, and shoein'. Fetch down a pair of number sevens, George, because I ain't gunna send this here child home with blistered heels."

He reached down and took the stockinged foot in his hand. The foot jerked violently.

"Whoa, girl," said Destry. "Steady, you sun-fishin', eye-rollin', wo'thless bronc, you! Don't you kick me in the face!"

"You're ticklin' my foot," said the girl. "Leave me be, Harry Destry, and you go and run along about your business. I don't want to waste no time on you, and Mr. Bent is plumb hurried, too."

"I'm aimin' to save the time of *Mister* Bent," said Destry. "George, you go and fetch down them number sevens. But look here what she's been doin' to herself, and crampin' up her toes, and raisin' corns on the tops of the second joints. Doggone me if this old hoss ain't gunna be spoiled for me."

"For you?" asked Bent, now standing by to listen.

"Sure," said Destry. "When she gets filled out to these here feet, I'm gunna marry her. Ain't I, ol' hoss?"

"Bah!" said the girl, and wriggled with mental discomfort, because she felt her face growing hot. "You jus' talk and talk, Harry Destry, and you never say nothin'!"

"Hello, Chet!" called the store owner, letting the door slam as he walked in. "You seen the sheriff?"

"Have I seen what?" asked Chester Bent, without raising his eyes.

"He's been lookin' for you mighty busy. He's just down the street."

"Ah," said Chester absently, "he'll maybe find me, by and by! Are you gunna marry him, Charlie?"

"Why for should I marry such a lazy, shiftless thing?" she asked, looking at Destry with indignation.

"Because I plumb love you, honey," said Destry. "And don't forget that you're all promised to me."

"I ain't any such thing," she declared.

"Are you forgettin' that day that I carried you across the Thunder Creek——"

"Chet!" she exclaimed in furious protest. "Listen at how he carries on, teasin' a poor girl. He wouldn't take me all the way over till I said I'd marry him."

"And you kissed me, honey, and sure said you'd always love old wo'thless Harry!"

"Harry Destry," said the girl, "I wasn't no more'n hardly a baby. I wasn't more'n twelve or thirteen years old. I'd like to beat you, Harry, you wretched thing!"

"You were never a baby," said he. "You were born old, and knowin' more than any man would ever know. Now there, you see how neat that fits?"

The number seven, in fact, fitted like a glove on the long, slender foot. Tears came up in the eyes of Charlie.

"Oh, Harry," she said, "ain't it monstrous big? I'm gunna grow up six feet high, I guess!"

"I mighty sure hope you do," said Destry. "Because it looks like I'm gunna be a tolerable ailin' man the most of my days, and never take kindly to work."

"How come you lost that Circle Y job?" she asked him, forgetting his illimitable personalities. "I'll tell you how. You been fightin' again!"

"Why, how you talk!" said Destry innocently. "Who would I be fightin' with over to the Circle Y, where they ain't had nothin' but scared greasers and broke-down nigger help for years?"

"They gotta rawboned Swede over there lately," she said, "that looks like he could lift a thousand pound. I bet it was him."

"Oh, Charlie," said Destry, "you was born old and wise! What a hell of a life I'm gunna lead with you, honey!"

"How's the Swede?" she snapped.

"Tolerable sick," said Destry. "Tolerable sick and run down. Which his stomach is kind of out of order, and that's got his eyes all involved up, so's he's hardly able to see. He ain't got no appetite, neither, and if he had, he ain't got the teeth left to bite with. But the doctor is gunna get him a new set of celluloid, and pretty soon he'll be better than new!"

"If I had you," said the girl, "I'd keep you muzzled and on a leash. I'd never loose you excepting at loafer wolves and such. That's what I'd do, if I had you!"

"Oh, you're gunna have me, honey!" said he. "Lemme help you out the door, will you?"

"You run along and help yourself," she advised him, "but don't you help yourself to no more redeye!"

"Why, Charlie, I ain't hardly had no taste of it!"

"You do your tastin' by the quart," she observed, "but even if you can fool the bottle, you can't fool me! Come on, Chet! Mighty sorry that I've kept you so long!"

They went out to the hitching rack, where Bent's span of matched bays were hitched in silver bound harness to a rubber tired buggy whose blue spokes were set off with dainty stripes of red.

"I'm gunna drive," said the girl, and leaped into the driver's place.

"You ain't gunna kiss me good-by, Charlie?"

"I'd slap you, you impident thing!" she said, grinning at him. "Listen at him talk, Chet!"

"Say, Chet," said Destry, "now you're gunna take my honey away from me, mightn't you leave me something in her place?"

Chet Bent looked up the street with a nod.

"There's Pike's bull terrier loose again," he said. "He'll leave another dead dog along his trail before the day's out!"

"Will he? He will!" said Destry, turning to watch, and as the wind blew open the flap of his coat, and as the girl sat up to watch the white streak across the street, neither Destry nor she saw the swift hand of Bent slip a thin package into the inside pocket of the cowpuncher's coat.

"About leavin' something—even trade rats do that!" said Destry.

"They leave rocks and stones," said Bent, smiling.

"And gold, I heard tell once!"

"Did you hear tell? Well, here's something. Make it last, Harry, will you?"

Destry was counting it, entranced.

"Forty—fifty—I'm gettin' plain dizzy, Chet!—sixty—seventy—this ain't real, but all sort of dreamlike!—seventy-five—eighty—who's put the new heart in, Bent? Is it your fault, honey?—ninety—a hundred—a hundred dollars——"

"You better start a bank account," suggested the girl.

"Wait a minute, Chet!" cried Destry. "What've you done that you wanta repent it as hard as all of this? Have you got religion, Chet? Have you sold a salted mine?"

He followed them a few steps along the sidewalk as Bent, laughing, started up his team.

Then Destry turned back to survey the town, which had taken on a new aspect.

"I'm gunna buy me a bronc and a saddle and git," said Destry. "Cowboy, buy yourself some spurs, and hump! Because money don't rain down every day, nor ham and eggs don't grow on the cactus, nor Chester Bent unlimber his wallet wide open like this! I'm gunna get reformed and start to work!"

So he said, frowning with resolution, but at this point he saw the swinging doors of the Second Chance saloon, and he felt that no atmosphere was so conducive to serious thought and planning as the damp coolness of that barroom.

So he passed inside.

2

IF alcohol is a mental poison, at least it did not show in Harry Destry by thickness of speech, or uncertainty of hand and foot. His eye grew brighter, wilder, his head was higher; his hand was more swift and restless before he ended the first fifty that Bent had given to him.

A hundred dollars, in those days, could be spread thick over many slices of good time, and Destry was both spreading and eating, and taking friends with him. No one knew how trouble started; they rarely did, when Harry Destry went on the warpath, but already there was a commotion in Donovan's Saloon when the sheriff rode up beside the whirling, flashing wheels of Chester Bent's buggy and raised his hand. Bent drew the horses back to a walk, and they went on, switching their tails, stretching their necks out against the uneasy restraint of the bits, and eager to be off again at full trot.

The sheriff brushed some of the dust from his black moustache, of whose sheen and length and thickness he was inordinately proud; then he said: "Chet, I wanta ask you a coupla questions. Where was you Wednesday night?"

"Wednesday night?" said Chester Bent, calmly thoughtful. "Let me see! I was doing accounts, most of the evening. Why d'you ask?"

"Because the express was held up that night, and the mail was robbed," said the sheriff.

He looked earnestly into the face of the younger man to see if there was not some change of expression. In fact, Chester Bent grew pale, with purple spots faintly outlined on his sleek cheeks.

"And seventy-two thousand dollars was taken," said the sheriff, "as maybe you know!"

"Great Lord!" murmured young Bent, aghast, and added in a rapid muttering: "And poor Harry Destry spending money like wildfire all over town——"

He checked himself, and glanced guiltily at the sheriff.

"Whacha say?" asked the sheriff, his voice high and sharp.

"Nothing, nothing!" said Chester Bent. "I didn't say anything at all. I wonder if you're suspecting me of anything, sheriff?"

"I'm not suspectin' nobody. I'm askin' questions, as the law and my job tells me to do. That's all!"

It was perfectly apparent, however, that he had heard the remark of Bent, as indeed that gentleman expected him to do, and now, with a mere wave of his hand in farewell, he spurred his horse into a gallop up the road, and every clot of sand and dust which the mustang's hoofs flicked upwards, like little hanging birds in the air, spelled mischief for Destry.

Of course all things went wrong at once, for as the sheriff came swiftly down the main street of Wham, he heard loud shouts, frightened yells, gunshots before him, and then he saw a hurried crowd pouring out from the mouth of the Donovan Saloon.

He stopped one frenzied fugitive, who ran at full speed, and made a spy-hop every few strides as though he expected that some danger might fly harmlessly past him under his heels.

The sheriff reached from his horse and caught the shoulder of the other, spinning him around and staggering him.

"What's wrong in there?"

"Destry's wild again!" said the other, and shot ahead at full speed.

The sheriff did not rush at once into the saloon. He was as brave a man as one would find in a hundred mile ride, but still he knew the place for valor and the place for discretion. He halted, therefore, at the swinging door, and called out: "Destry!"

"Wow!" yelled Destry. "Come on in!"

And a forty-five calibre bullet split a panel of the door.

The sheriff stepped a little farther to the side.

"Who's there?" asked the sheriff. "Who's raisin' hell and busting the laws in this here community?"

"I'm the Big Muddy," answered the whooping voice within. "I got snow on my head, and stones on my feet, and the snows are meltin', and I'm gunna overflow my banks. Come on in and take a ride!"

"Is that you, Destry?"

"I'm the Big Muddy," Destry assured him. "Can't you hear me roar? I'm beginnin' to flow, and I ain't gunna stop! I'm rarin' to bust my banks, and I wanta know what kinda levees you got to hold me back. Wow!"

Another shot exploded, and there was a crash of breaking glass.

At this, the man of the law gripped both hands hard.

"Harry Destry," said he, "come out in the name of the law!"

"The only law I know," said Destry, "is to run down hill. Look out, because I'm fast on the corners. I'm the Big Muddy River, and I'm runnin' all the way to the sea!"

The sheriff deliberately turned on his heel and departed. He merely explained in a casual way to bystanders that there was nothing to be done with fools of this calibre except to let them run down and go to sleep. And Wham, though it was a reasonably tough town, agreed. It had experienced the flow of the "Big Muddy" many a time before this and knew what to expect from Destry.

So, when Destry wakened in the raw of the chilly morning, with an alkaline thirst eating at his soul, he found that he was resting peacefully in jail, with the sheriff drowsing comfortably in the chair beside him. A guard was near by, with a grim look and a riot gun. Said the sheriff, while the eyes of Destry were still hardly half open:

"Destry, you robbed the Express!"

"Sure," said Destry, "but gimme a drink, will you?"

"You robbed the Express?"

"I did if I get that drink. If I don't get that drink, I never seen the damn Express."

"Give him a drink," said the sheriff.

The drink was given and disappeared.

At this, Destry sat up and shrugged his shoulders.

"You know you're under arrest," warned the sheriff, who was an honest man, "and whatever you say may be used against you. But you've confessed to robbing the Express!"

"Did I?" said Destry. "I'll rob another for another drink. Who's got the makings?"

He was furnished with Bull Durham and brown wheat-straw papers.

"Now then," said the sheriff, "you better tell me just what you did! How'd you go about it?"

"How do I know?" replied Destry, inhaling smoke deep into his lungs. "If I robbed the Express, all right, I done it. But I don't remember nothin' about it!"

"Look here," said the sheriff. "You recognize this?"

He presented that small packet which he had taken from the inside pocket of Destry's coat.

"How can I recognize it when I ain't seen what's inside of it?"

"You know mighty well," declared the sheriff, "what's in this here! Confess up, young man. It's gunna make everything easier for you in front of the judge and the jury. And even if you don't confess, they'll snag you, anyway!"

"Let 'em snag," said Destry. "I been workin' too hard, and I need a good rest, anyways! Was the Express robbed last night?"

"You know mighty well that the night was Wednesday!"

"Do I? All right. I just wanted to be sure what night it was that I done that robbin'. So long, sheriff. I'm gunna sleep agin."

He dropped the cigarette butt to the floor and allowed it to fume there, while he impolitely turned his back upon the sheriff and instantly was snoring again.

3

". . . that Harrison Destry, residing in, near, or in the region about Wham, in the state of Texas, did on the night of Wednesday, May the eleventh, at or about fifteen minutes past ten o'clock, wilfully, feloniously, and injuriously delay, deter, and cause to stop the train entitled . . ."

Harrison Destry raised his head again and became lost in the labors of the big spider which was at work in the corner above the desk of the judge. The sun struck a mirror so placed against the wall that a bright beam was deflected into this very corner, and there the spider, unseasonable as the time was, busily pursued the work of constructing his net for flying insects. So distinct did the work appear in the bright light, and so keen was the eye of Destry, that he saw every glistening cable as it was laid, all threaded with globules of glue. He lost the voice that was reading.

Presently he was recalled to himself by the voice of the judge asking if he had selected a lawyer to represent him. When he answered no, he was briefly informed that it was well to have the advice of counsel from the first; that already he had been informed of this several times, and that it was specially valuable before the selection of a jury.

"I'm broke," said Destry. "What's your honor got on hand in the way of a good second-rate, up-and-comin' lawyer for me?"

His Honor was none other than Judge Alexander Pearson, whom perhaps six people in the world were permitted to address as Alec. The rest were kept at arm's length, and through all that range he was respected and dreaded for his justice, which he doled out with an equal hand, and for his knowledge of every individual, and of every individual's eccentricities and history almost from birth. It was possible to make promises about future conduct to some judges, but Alexander Pearson was too well able to tell of the future by the past.

"Counsellor Steven Eastwick," said the judge, "is here at hand, and I am sure is capable of giving your case a scholarly and careful handling. Counsellor Eastwick is newly a member of the bar, but I am sure——"

"Hello, Steve," said the prisoner. "Poker, sure, but not courtroom cards, if you play my hand! Thanks, your honor. I'll handle this deal better than Steve, to suit myself."

The judge went on in his even voiced way: "Counsellor Rodman Wayne is also newly one of us. Mr. Wayne, I am sure, would also be adequate and if——"

"Roddie never learned how to swim, till he was chucked into the water off of the dam by Clacky Fisher and me," said the prisoner. "And this here water is a pile too deep and fast for Roddie to look good in it, your honor. Got anybody else?"

"I think that in the hall there is——"

"Gimme the gent in the hall," said the prisoner. "He looks good to me!"

The judge overlooked this sanguine carelessness and gravely asked that Counsellor Christian McDermott be asked to step into the court if he was in the adjoining hall.

"Good old Chris!" said young Mr. Destry. "He'll help me a lot!"

He turned toward Chester Bent, who sat on the first bench among the spectators, and said aloud: "Chris is so nearsighted that he never seen a joke till he got double lenses, and then the first thing he laughed at was himself in a mirror!"

"Mr. Destry," said the judge quietly, "there are certain rules of decorum which must be observed in a courtroom. Here is Mr. McDermott. Counsellor, are you willing to undertake this case?"

Mr. McDermott was. He had really almost given up the practice of law, and spent his time pottering around forty acres of apple trees up the valley toward the mountains. His one real labor of the week was to scrub the food spots from his large expanse of vest on Sunday mornings so that he could go spotless to church at noon. But for the sake of dignity, he occasionally appeared at the court and picked up a small case here and there.

He now came in, looked over his glasses at the judge, under them at the prisoner, and through them at the faces in the crowd, to several individuals among which he nodded greetings. So the selection of the jury began.

It proceeded with amazing swiftness. The only objections were those made by the assistant district attorney, Terence Anson, who was usually called Doc, for no good reason at all. His peremptory challenges did not need to be used often. He objected to Clarence Olsen, because the latter was known to have been pulled out of the creek by Destry years ago, and therefore he might be presumed to have some prejudice in favor of the prisoner, and three other men, one of whom had taken shooting lessons from Destry, and two others had been partners in the cattle business and were helped by Destry in trailing down a band of rustlers who had run off a number of cows. Aside from these four, he also used several peremptory challenges, but none were made by McDermott. He turned in each instance, anxiously, toward his client, but every time Destry merely shrugged his shoulders.

"It ain't much use to try for anybody better," said Destry.

And in a brief half hour, twelve men were sitting in the jury box. There was this remarkable feature which they possessed in common—they were all old inhabitants of Wham, and had known the prisoner for years, and all of them looked toward him with a singular directness.

Mr. McDermott regarded them with anxiety.

"D'you know," he said to his client, "that just from a glance at their expressions, I'd say that not a one of them is particularly a friend of yours?"

"There ain't one of 'em," said Destry, "that wouldn't skin half his hide off if he could put me in jail for life. But that don't matter. In this here town, Chris, I got nothin' but enemies and friends. Less friends than enemies, though. And I wouldn't have it no other way. What good is a hoss to ride that don't have kinks to be took out of its back of a morning? I got the chance, Chris, of a grit stone in a mill race. But what's the difference? I been needin' a rest for a long time, and a chance to think! But let's see what they got agin me?"

He soon learned. The trial proceeded headlong, for the ways of the judge did not admit of great delays. First Terence Anson in a dry, barking voice—he was a man who was continually talking himself out of breath—and having coughing fits while he recovered it—touched not too lightly on the past of Destry, and announced that he was going to prove that Mr. Destry was a man likely to have committed this offense, capable of having committed it, and in need of the money which it would bring in to him. After probabilities, he was going to prove that Harrison Destry did in person stop the Express, hold up the messengers, take their weapons from them, and, passing on through the train, remove the valuables from the entire list of the passengers, escaping with their personal property and the contents of the mail!

Mr. McDermott, when he made his own opening address, was somewhat handicapped for lack of material. He could not very well disprove the known fact that Harrison Destry was a trouble maker and a fighter by taste, cultivation, and habit. But he launched into certain vague generalities which had obscure references to the rights of the individual and the uncertainty of circumstantial evidence, and sat down with his case as well ruined as it could have been by any given number of spoken words. So, puffing and snorting, he waited in his chair and observed the opening examinations of the witnesses.

They were very few.

The engineer of the train was called, and stated that the person who had held up the train had been about the size of the prisoner—or perhaps a little larger. And the voice of the robber had been very much like that of the prisoner, except that it was perhaps a little higher. The two guards who had protected the mail delivered similar testimony.

Then there was the evidence of the owner and bartender of the First Chance saloon to the effect that Mr. Destry had come into his place equipped with very little cash, had lost that, lost even his gun and spurs, and had gone on down the street stripped of available cash. Yet when he had been loaned more money by Mr. Bent, instead of spending it with some caution, he had thrown away the fresh supply with more recklessness than ever! What did this prove, if not that he was confident of a reserve supply of negotiable securities which he could realize upon so soon as he left the town? In fact, a package of those securities had been found in his pocket, and what else could be desired as proof that he was the man?

There was no testimony which the defense could offer against this damning array, except when young Charlotte testified that as a matter of fact, she had seen Bent give the prisoner a hundred dollars. And the inference to be drawn by a very imaginative jury might be that the package of securities had been placed in the pocket of the accused man by someone with malicious intent to shift the burden of the blame upon the shoulders of Destry and so draw a herring across his own trail.

The jury, however, did not appear to be particularly imaginative. It looked upon the prisoner with a cold eye, and retired with an ominous lack of gravity, talking to one another before they were out of the courtroom.

As for Destry himself, he had no doubt at all of what would happen.

"What'll he do, McDermott?" said he. "Will he run me up for ninety days, or will he string me a whole year, d'you think?"

McDermott shrugged his shoulders.

"First offenders usually receive mercy, in some form or another," he declared.

"A year would be the limit, wouldn't you say?"

McDermott grew red and scratched his head.

"Otherwise," said Destry, "I would have bashed my way out of their fool jail and never have stood for the trial at all!"

He gripped the arm of his impromptu lawyer.

"They wouldn't soak me for any more than that?" he asked.

Said McDermott: "The verdict's in charge of the jury, and the penalty must be assessed by the judge. I can't alter the law in your behalf, young man. But," he went on, "if you'll tell me where you've put away the rest of the stolen money and other properties, and make a clean breast of the whole affair, no doubt the judge would reduce the sentence that he now has in contemplation."

"You fat-faced, long-eared jackass," said Destry mildly. "D'you think that I've done this job? Or, if I'd done it, d'you dream that I'd come back here to Wham to spend what I'd made? Wouldn't I barge away for Manhattan, where I could get rid of such stuff for a commission? Of course I would! McDermott, go out and ask for a new set of brains. You make me tired."

He turned his back on McDermott as the jury entered. It had been out for two and a half minutes. He rose at the order of the judge. He stood guarded on both sides, and he heard Philip Barker, the foreman of the twelve good men and true say the fatal word: "Guilty!"

4

AT this point, there was a sudden leaning forward of all within the courtroom. The spectators leaned forward. The twelve good men and true themselves leaned forward in their chairs and watched the face of the judge with a hungry interest. Granted that the prisoner was guilty, what now would be done to him?

It was impossible to guess how hard the judge would strike, for sometimes he was unaccountably severe, and sometimes he was bewilderingly merciful. His very first sentence, however, put all doubts at rest.

He said: "Harrison Destry, you have been found guilty by a jury of twelve of your peers, and it is now my duty to pronounce sentence upon you, not for a first offense, in my estimation, but for the culminating act of a life of violence, indolence, and worthlessness!"

Here a clear, strong young voice cried out: "It's not true! He ain't any of those things!"

The judge should have ordered the disturbing element ejected from the courtroom, but he merely lifted a placid hand toward Charlotte Dangerfield, who had so far exceeded the proprieties of the courtroom, and continued as follows:

"I believe that I am not alone in having followed the events of your career with a fascinated interest since the days of your boyhood, Harrison Destry. You were not very old before I noticed that it was a rare thing to see you on the street without blood on your hands or on your face! If I passed youngsters of your age with discolored eyes, puffed and bleeding mouths, and battered faces, I could take it for granted that Harrison Destry was not far away. And usually I saw you, lingering in the rear of the defeated enemy.

"Such things are not taken seriously in a boy of ten. The ability to fight, after all, is perhaps the most prized of all the talents of man. And if I were to pick out the one cardinal virtue to be desired in a son of mine, I should name courage first, but that is not all!

"What is still a virtue at ten becomes a nuisance at fifteen. And when your hands were stronger, and you struck harder, there were more serious tales about your petty wars in the town, and on the range, as you began to work out as a cowpuncher and find men there as hard as yourself. In the iron school of the range you were molded. There you found men older and stronger than yourself, and almost as fierce. Now and again we had word that Harrison Destry had been beaten horribly. But before the next year rolled around we were sure to learn that he had gone far out on the trail of his conqueror and found him—in Canada—in Mexico—and defeated the former victor.

"At the end of each serious encounter, you usually returned to Wham, in order, one might say, to bask in the admiration of your fellow citizens, and it did not occur to you that it was not unmixed admiration with which they looked upon you. To be sure, they respected your bravery and envied your power of hand and quickness of eye, but when a man begins to use mortal weapons, as you did so young, it becomes less a matter for admiration than for fear, less of envy than of horror.

"And, from that moment, there were voices which announced that Harrison Destry would before the end have taken a human life! Some would not believe it, but eventually belief was forced in upon us.

"They were not entirely reprehensible affairs. The criminal, the brutal, the wasted and vicious lives were those who crossed you, and were those who fell. All seemed fair fight. And yet the time came when men shrank before you, Harrison Destry. In one word, the message went out that you were a 'killer' and all that that ominous term implies. That is to say, one who takes life for the pleasure he gains by the taking! Many a man has begun in that way, keeping within the bounds of the law; few have continued so to the end! They overstep, and an innocent life is taken.

"However, there was another change in you. You began as an industrious boy; you ended as a man who scorned any tool other than a Bowie knife or a Colt's six-shooter. You gambled for a living and fought for amusement. Your visits to the town became an often repeated plague. You roistered in the saloons. You cast a shadow over a community which has never been too peaceful!

"Consider the picture of yourself as at last it was presented to us! The proud, active, hard working boy is changed into the lazy, careless, shiftless, indifferent and tigerish sluggard! Now at last you have discovered a means of making a short cut to a fortune on which you could live for some time. You have taken that short cut. You have violently laid your hands upon the moneys of other people. You have interfered with a mail train. You have robbed the mail itself. For these acts the jury, composed of twelve of your peers, has found you guilty, and I heartily agree with the verdict. Under the circumstances, nothing but intolerable prejudice in your favor could have induced a single man among them to return any other verdict than this one.

"It is now my duty to lay on you a sentence in accordance with the nature of your crime and of your character. And after duly considering all of these things, I have decided that you must be sentenced to ten years of penal confinement at hard labor, in the honest trust that during that time you may have an opportunity to reflect upon your past and prepare yourself for a different future.

"If you have any remarks to make to qualify this judgment, I am ready to hear them, particularly since your legal adviser was summoned at the last moment and has had no fitting opportunity to work on your case."

It seemed that Destry hesitated, and considered for a moment what he should say, if anything. At length he drawled:

"What might be the meaning of 'peer,' your honor?"

"The meaning of peer," said the judge, "is equal. It is a portion of the law, Destry, that an accused man shall not be tried by those who are socially not his equal. That may be held to hark back to other times, when some men were free, and others serfs."

"And serfs, what might they be?"

"A serf was a man attached to the soil, or, more properly speaking, a man subordinated and tied to some social regulation which limited his freedom. But, on the whole, you may say that a serf is a man who is not free."

"These gents," said the prisoner, "you've said a coupla times are my peers. Is that right?"

"I take it there is no man among them who is not your social equal, Destry. At least, they are all free men!"

"Are they?" said Destry.

He turned toward the jury and made a few paces forward, and the guard followed him on either side, anxiously.

"You dunno these here gents," said Destry. "I'll tell you. That one on the far left in the front row, that's Jimmy Clifton—that little narrer shouldered feller with the flower in his buttonhole, as though he was walkin' out on Sunday with his best girl. Free? He's tied up worse than a slave and the thing that he's tied to is the women, I tell you! He can't walk out without feelin' their eyes after him, and the reason that he hates me—look at it in his eyes!—is because a girl that he wanted once turned him down to dance with me. If I lie, Jimmy, you tell the judge!

"Next to him, there's Hank Cleeves. By the look of his face, you'd never think that he'd ever been a boy, but he was. To be on top of the heap is his game and his main idea, and he's a slave to that. He's a serf. He's no free man, I tell you! This here Cleeves, I once socked him on the nose, and sat him down flat and quick. He said 'enough' that day, and that's why he says guilty this day.

"There's Bud Williams, too, him with the thick neck and the little head, that come down here aimin' to become the champion wrestler of the whole world. But you can't fight and you can't wrestle with the strength of your hands, because it's the strength of your heart that tells in the long run!

And after him and me had it out on the gravel at the edge of the road, and his face was rubbed raw in the stones, he started hatin' me, and he never stopped from that day to this. Serf? There never was a worse serf than him! He envies the mules on the road, because of their muscle. He'd turn himself into a steam engine, for the sake of havin' so many hoss power!

"Next to him, I want you to look at Sam Warren, with his long neck, and his long fingers that are square at their tips. Look at him, will you? He could take any gun apart in the dark, and jump the pieces together again without no light. He loved to figger that he had every man's life inside the curl of his forefinger. He felt free and grand so long as he thought that was true. But when him and me had a little tangle, and he was sliced through the leg with the first shot, he sure was fed up quick and lay down to think things over. Your honor, he's a serf to the gun that he packs, and that's draggin' down under his left armpit, right this minute!"

Sam Warren raised his narrow length from his chair, in such an attitude that it looked for a moment as though he would hurl himself out of the jury box and at the throat of the other. And the prisoner said calmly: "If it ain't so, call me a liar. You set that gun up and worship it. You never get it well out of your mind. You dream about it at night, and when you look at your best friend, you pick out the button on his coat that you'll shoot at!"

"Mr. Destry," said the judge, in his quiet way, "you've insulted enough of this jury, I think. Have you finished?"

"I'll finish quick," said Destry. "Only, I wanta finish up first with these twelve peers of mine, as you call 'em. I want you to look at Jerry Wendell, whose God is his tailor, and Clyde Orrin, the handshaker, and Lefty Turnbull that's always hated my heart since I broke his record from Wham to the Crystal Mountains, and there's Phil Barker, too! How many times did Phil raise hell with his practical jokes, until along comes a letter askin' him to call on a girl after dark, and he found the dogs waitin' for him instead of her? He ain't forgot that I wrote that letter to him, and he'd hang me up by the neck today, if his vote would do it! There's the Ogdens, too, that took money for my scalp and cornered me to get it; they lost their blood and their money, that day, and they want to see me holler now. Then there's Bud Truckman and Bull Hewitt. I dunno why they want to stick me, but maybe I've give them a dirty look, some time."

He turned back to the judge.

"Twelve peers?" said Destry. "Twelve half-bred pups. If peers is equals, I'd rather be tried by twelve bullfrogs in a marsh than by them twelve in that jury box! But let 'em set down and think this here over! When my ten years has come up, I'm gunna call on all of these here, and if they ain't in, I'm gunna leave my card, anyway!"

"Destry," said the judge drily, "you'd better finish, here."

The jury sat back, trying to look scornful, but obviously worried, in spite of themselves.

"Here's the last thing," said Destry. "What you've said is plumb true. I been a waster, a lazy loafer, a fighter, a no-good citizen, but what I'm gettin' the whip for now is a lie! I never robbed the Express!"

5

SHORT speeches linger a long time in some memories; and the final speech of the prisoner remained in the mind of the townsfolk long after he was sent away to stripes and bars for ten years. There was one other detail of that day in the courtroom about which men and women and children talked, and that was how young Charlie Dangerfield slipped through the crowd and got to Destry as he was being led away toward the cell from which he would depart to the prison. There before the crowd she threw her arms around his neck.

"I believe in you, Harry!" she cried. "And I'll wait for you, too!"

Wham smiled when it heard this story, for Charlie Dangerfield was only sixteen, but as the years went by and it was noted that, though she would laugh and talk with any man, and dance with the first comer on Saturday nights, yet she discouraged all tokens of a serious interest; and when she grew up from pretty child to beautiful woman, and still preserved the integrity of the fence around her, then Wham scratched its chin and shook its head.

It respected her the more; the more worthless the man to whom a woman is devoted, the more she is admired and beloved by all other men. Their own self-esteem and their right to expect the affection of a wife is thereby, as it were, given a groundwork and an assurance.

More than this: The very girls of Wham, the unmarried ones, the green and hopeful virgins, found it possible to have an actual affection for beautiful Charlie Dangerfield, since, no matter how attractive she might be, or how she dimmed their stars in passing, she was no more than a passing moon, and never interfered with their affairs. The established youth of Wham quickly learned to waste no hopes on Charlie; only the strangers who arrived, attracted by her face and her father's rapidly increasing fortune, flocked for a moment around the flame, singed their wings, and flew lamely away.

Therefore, when the news came to the town that Destry had been allowed to leave the prison, and that his ten years had been shortened to six by good behavior, the first thought of everyone was for Charlie Dangerfield. How would she take this second coming of her hero, now aged from the penitentiary?

Now, on computation, they figured that, if he was twenty-five when he was committed, he could only be thirty-one now. Old in shame, then, if not in actual years—a jail-bird, a refugee still from society. He who has been through the fire must bear the mark on his face!

On the evening of that same day, however, on which the news came to the town of Wham, there was a secret meeting to which came Jerry Wendell, and Clyde Orrin, and the Ogden brothers, and Cleeves, Sam Warren, Bull Hewitt and Bud Williams.

Sam Warren, being the most celebrated shot in the town, presided at the meeting, sitting at the head of the table and regulating the discussion. They talked frankly, as only those talk who are faced by a common danger.

The first suggestion was made by Jerry Wendell, who urged that they should hire a gunman for the work of clearing Mr. Destry permanently from the slate.

It was not waved aside, this murderous thought, but seriously taken in hand, and only after some moments of talk was it decided that it was probably foolish to kill a man who would soon have himself in jail again. Clyde Orrin summed up the verdict on this point.

"Prison never makes a gent better; it always makes him worse! He'll raise the devil before he's been in Wham a day, and the sheriff will be waiting for him with both hands full of irons!"

This being taken for granted, it was decided at once that all eight of them should leave the town of Wham for a little hunting excursion into the mountains. Before they returned, doubtless Destry would be again in the hands of the law!

This proposal hardly had been concluded before there was a rap at the door of the hotel room in which they were sitting, and Chester Bent walked in.

They looked on him without pleasure, but Chester Bent, leaning on the end of the table, a little out of breath, and hat still in hand, smiled on them all.

"My friends," said he, "I know you're surprised to see me here. I wasn't a member of the jury that called Destry guilty and sent him to prison. You know that I was his friend then, and am his friend now, and I suppose that he'll come to stay at my house when he returns. Now, I want to assure you all that I shall do my best to keep Destry from taking any steps that are too rash and bold. But I also want to say that I doubt my ability to keep him in order. I hope that you won't misconstrue what I have to say. I give you my word, I'm your friend, as well as his. I'm here to ask how I can serve you, because I take it for granted that you all realize that you will be in danger from the instant that Destry arrives this evening!"

This was putting the cards on the table with a vengeance, and the eight sitters at that table looked on Mr. Bent with a real enthusiasm, at once. He was a man worth attention in Wham, by this time. For one thing, he had increased his wealth at least sixfold in the time during which unlucky Destry had been in jail. Indeed, it was at about the same time that Destry was taken away that Wham received proof of the business talent of Bent by the amount of cash which he had on hand ready for investment; and, by placing it well in mines, in the buying of shares in a lumber company that operated in the Crystal range, and by picking up random bits of real estate here and there, Chester Bent had now established himself in a position which was hardly second to that occupied by any man in the town or the range around it. He had not piled up such a huge fortune as Benjamin Dangerfield, to be sure, nor as a few of the great cattle barons and the mining millionaires, but Chester Bent was rich, and he was among the few influential men who had to be called in for consultation whenever any important move was made by the controlling spirits of the community.

For all of these reasons, the eight men at the table listened greedily to all that he had to say. Destry, singlehanded, was bad enough, if he were even a ghost of his old self. Destry, backed by such a man as this, would be the equivalent of ruin to them all.

They told him with equal frankness that they had determined to withdraw from the town, and he received the suggestion with pleasure. He would send them word, he assured them, of the time when it was safe for them to return to Wham!

That afternoon they left; that evening, Chester Bent was walking up and down the platform of the station waiting for the westbound train. It drew up, stopped, and half a dozen passengers dismounted; baggage and mails were thrown off, train lanterns swung, and the long line of cars started away, the observation platform swaying out of sight at high speed around the next curve in another moment.

But no Harry Destry!

Then a hand fell lightly on the arm of Bent, a tentative and timid touch, and the young man turned and looked down into a face as sickly white as the belly of a frog.

It was Harry Destry at last, but Bent had to look at him twice before he could recognize the former gunman of Wham, the cynical, reckless warrior whose exploits had broken heads and glassware in every saloon up and down the main street of the town. He seemed both thinner and smaller, like one who has diminished from a great reputation of the past and grown down to a lesser size, a lesser fact.

Such was the Harry Destry who returned to Wham!

A strange gleam of joy appeared in the eye of Chester Bent, and it was not all the pleasure of welcoming home an old friend. Yet he wrung the hand of Destry with a feverish eagerness.

"You're coming home to live with me," said Bent. "I've fixed up a room for you——"

"I've got no claim on you, Chet," said the other. "I reckon I jus' better slide on out of the town and——"

"What are you talking about?" said Bent. "Look yonder—that phaeton under the pepper trees, yonder. There's Charlie Dangerfield waiting for you, man. She would have come up and met you; she wasn't afraid of doing that in front of everyone, y'understand?—but I thought it would be better if she met you quietly. You know how the papers pick up such things? Richest rancher's daughter greets return of ex-convict—you know what I mean, old fellow!"

He was half leading and half pressing his companion forward as he spoke. He had taken in his left hand the little satchel that contained the total possessions of Destry; his right was in the small of the convict's back, forcing him on. But here Destry paused.

"Rich?" said he. "Has Ben Dangerfield gone and got himself rich? Charlie never told me nothing about that in her letters!"

"I guess Charlie didn't want you to know what was waiting for you when you come home," said Bent, losing some of the polish of his higher school education in the excitement of the moment. "Because that's just what Ben Dangerfield has done nothin' else but do! He's gone and got himself to be the richest man on this range! The Dangerfield mine is so doggone rich that you could break a year's income for most men right off the lode and drop it into your pockets an' not weigh uncomfortable much when you walked home with it. Rich? They're made of money, now, and that means that you'll be made of money! Go ahead, there, and see Charlie, and kiss her. She's been waitin' six years for this minute, Harry!"

He paused when he was a few paces from the carriage, so as to let Destry have some privacy, but the instant that the support of his hand was withdrawn, it seemed as though the latter hardly could move forward. Slowly he drifted towards the phaeton; he stole his way along beneath the shadow of the thin branched pepper trees, through which the stars were gleaming. And, at the last, he stood fixed to the ground.

Charlotte Dangerfield was out of the carriage in a flash and had her arms around him.

"Harry, Harry, Harry!" she cried, her voice rising from a whisper to a moan. "What have they-all been doin' to you? What have they done to you, Harry?"

She kissed his white face, luminous in the shadows, and cold to the touch of her warm lips.

He did not stir in her arms, nor raise a hand to her.

"It's been six years of pretty much trouble, Charlotte," he told her.

And she thought that even his voice was changed, lowered to keep any other ear from hearing what he had to say.

At this, she fell into a bustle of activity, making plans, managing a good deal of excited laughter, as she turned him over to the hands of Chester Bent. He was to come out in the morning to the Dangerfield ranch; her father was wild to see him; in the meantime, he needed a good night's sleep.

But before she left, Chester Bent had one opportunity to look into her eyes and see the horror there. It was no effort for Chester to be cheerful on the drive home to his house!

6

HE was anxious to have Destry under the steady light of a lamp when he got to the house, but it was not easy to get Destry into the light. In the dining room, he managed to turn his chair a little, apparently to give more attention to his host, but really so that he threw a shadow over his features, and with repeated and humble bowings of his head, he listened to all that Chester Bent had to say.

For his own part, Destry spoke little, and generally preluded every remark with an apology: "If you don't mind me sayin' "—or "Excuse me, Chet, but"—or "Of course what I say don't count—" And Chester Bent saw more and more literally how the heavy hand of the law had broken and hammered what had seemed such unmalleable metal.

They were in the library after dinner, that library which was the latest crown upon the life of Chester Bent, where dark ranges of volumes mounted in tier on tier toward the shadowy ceiling, where two or three large tomes generally could be seen opened face downward, as though the student had just been called from their perusal, and where the face of the desk was littered with papers, the token of the busy man. Enthroned against such a background, Chester Bent drew out his guest a little more, but it was difficult to go far. It was ten o'clock before the truth came out.

Destry wished to leave Wham!

There had once been a happy hunting ground for him in this village, but now he dreaded the familiar field. He sat with his head slightly canted to the side, listening to the booming chorus of the bullfrogs that saddened the marsh like the drone of bass viols. The longer he listened, the more uneasy Destry appeared.

"I've gotta go," he said to Bent. "I dunno why you should be so extra kind to me, Chet. But I couldn't stay here. I got piles of enemies in this here town!"

"You have friends, too, old timer!"

"I got friends. But friends, they don't catch bullets out of the air! They can't do that, Chet! I'm gunna go on. I wanta be a peaceful man; I don't want no trouble in the world, no more!"

He shivered as he said it, and Chester Bent had to glance slyly down to the floor to keep the flame of exultation in his eyes from being seen. Immediately afterward he allowed Destry to go to bed, but the big chamber

which had been prepared for his accommodation was totally unsatisfactory
to the new guest. In place of that, he preferred a little attic room, with one
small window hardly a foot square.

He called the attention of Bent to it cautiously.

"What would you say, Chet? That a man could squirm through that in
the middle of the night?"

"A man? Hardly a frog could get through there, a frog-sized frog, I
mean to say!"

Destry sighed with relief, and went straightaway to bed; Bent returned
to the library and there wrote the following letter to Jerry Wendell:

> Dear Jerry,
>   Harry Destry is back, but so changed that you wouldn't
> know him! He has just gone to bed in an attic room, because
> it has a window so small that a man couldn't climb through
> it in the middle of the night.
>   His eyes are sunk in his head, and he has the look of a
> dog that's been over-disciplined. He's white and thin, and
> seems to have lost a few inches in height, which I suppose
> is simply another way of saying that he's not the man he
> used to be!
>   I don't think that you need be afraid of coming back to
> town, you and the rest; though perhaps you'd better send
> back a couple of the roughest of you to break the ground
> and make sure that he's really as harmless as he seems.
>   You can observe from this that I am trying to be your
> friend and a friend to all the rest, while I'm also trying to
> make poor Destry happy.
>   He hasn't said much about his prison life, but I gathered
> up a few references to dark cells, etc. I presume that he
> was pretty roughly handled at first, and it's broken his
> spirit.
>   I pity him from my heart, and so will you, when you see
> him.
>
>   Yours cordially,
>   CHET BENT.

He left the house to mail this letter at once, and, walking slowly home
beneath the stars, he looked up to them and thought they burned more
bright and beautiful on this night than ever before. When he opened the
door of his house again, he stood for a moment staring into the dark, and
conjuring up in it the picture of Charlie Dangerfield's lovely smile, and
Ben Dangerfield's still more lovely millions! Then he went back to his
library.

He curled up on the couch and went to sleep, but he kept the light burning, for it did well for the inhabitants of Wham, returning late at night, to see the lighted study windows of that rising young man. They then could tell one another that Chester Bent was a genius, but that genius was nine-tenths work! It increased their respect for him, but it diminished their envy!

It was after one before he put out the light, stumbled sleepily up the stairs to his room, and there fell at once into a profounder slumber, and into the arms of yet happier dreams.

In the morning, he took Destry out to see Benjamin Dangerfield. He walked with Charlie under the trees while Destry talked to his prospective father-in-law; all they heard of the interview was the loud voice of Ben Dangerfield exclaiming: "Whacha lookin' behind the doors for, Harry? Dust?"

Charlotte wanted to talk about Destry continually, but Bent dexterously shied at that subject and finally managed to keep it out of sight. In half an hour they heard Dangerfield shouting for them, and went back to find Destry standing with lowered head, tracing invisible patterns on the floor with the toe of his shoe. Bent heard the caught breath of Charlie, but even he dared not look at her.

Dangerfield himself was gritting his teeth, and he said in the presence of his daughter and Bent: "My daughter's old enough to run her own business. If she wants you, she'll take you, I reckon, and let her have you; it ain't no more affair of mine!"

Chester Bent did not need to look far back to a time when not even Dangerfield, no matter what his years or his millions, would have dared to speak in such a manner to Destry.

But that time was gone. He took Harry Destry back to the town, and the latter bit his lip continually, looking down into the heat haze that obscured the distant vistas of the roadway. Not one word passed between them until they came to the edge of the town, and there Destry asked to be let out, because he wished to saunter through Wham. His wish was obeyed, and Bent drove on back to his office.

All was well with him. He plunged into his affairs for that day, but as he worked, he dreamed, and his dreams were all of Charlotte Dangerfield.

A slice of gingerbread and a glass or two of milk made his lunch, so that he had not left his office since morning, when Charlotte herself came to see him late that afternoon, bursting impetuously into his office.

She had ridden at high speed all the way from the ranch. The flush of the gallop was high in her brown cheeks and the dust was in her hair as she stood before him, kneading the handle of her quirt in her gloved hands. But her eyes were desperate and sick as they had been the night before at the station.

"I can't go on, Chet!" she told him. "I'm mighty miserable; I'm fair done up about it; but I can't go on after this day!"

He asked her what had happened.

"You don't know?" she cried. "The whole of Wham knows! Everybody's shrugging shoulders! Don't try to make me tell over again what's happened!"

He could guess; a prophetic foresight had told him everything when he let his companion out of the buggy that morning and drove softly on through the velvet dust of the main street; but he told her now that he had not left the office.

She had to take a turn up and down the room before she could speak again; and then she faced half away from him, looking out the window.

"He went into the Second Chance," she said, speaking rapidly to get through the thing. "He asked for a lemon sour——"

"I'm glad he's stopped drinking, if that's what it means," said Bent.

She risked one glance at him over her shoulder.

"Oh, Chet," said she, "it means something else; you must know that it does, in spite of all this mighty fine loyalty of yours! Dud Cross came in. You know that wo'thless boy of Dikkon Cross? And Dud was full of redeye. He bumped against Harry, and when he saw who he'd nudged, he jumped half way across the barroom, they say. Then he saw that Harry didn't resent it; just stood there smilin', lookin' a little white and sick——"

She stopped here, but getting a fresher grip on her quirt she went on with a savage determination.

"That Dud Cross seemed to guess everything at one glance. He came back and—and damned Harry for running into *him!* Damned him! And—Harry—took it!"

She gasped in a breath.

"Dud Cross said he wasn't fit to drink with white men, real men, and told him to get out. And Harry went and—"

It was much even for Bent to hear, and he wiped his face with his handkerchief.

"Cross kicked him into the street. Kicked him! And Harry picked himself up and went home to your house. I suppose that he's there now! Chet, I want to do the right thing; but what *is* the right thing?"

It had come so swiftly that Bent could hardly believe in his good fortune, but he had sense enough not to appear to jump at the opening.

"I suppose I understand everything," he said slowly. "It won't do, of course. You'll have to see him and tell him that it can't go on!"

"How can I see him and strike him in the face—a—a thing like that?"

"You don't have to see him. I think he knows, too. He expects it, surely, if he has any speck of manhood left in him. No, Charlie, you just sit down there at my desk and write him a letter. It will do perfectly. I'll tell you what. I'll take the letter along to him, and do any necessary explaining."

"Will you do that?" she asked.

She swung about and dropped her quirt and caught at his hands. "When I see what a noble way you have about you, Chet, standing by him, true to him—out of the whole town the only one that's standing by him, I feel pretty small and low. It's beautiful, the way you're acting! But oh, Chet, tell him very gentle and careful about how things stand. I wouldn't of let him down—only—only—he's *not* a man!"

7

CHESTER BENT took home this letter in the evening and gave it to Destry to puzzle out in the dusk of the library.

> Dear old Harry,
>   It just can't go on. I would have crossed the ocean for you, for the old Harry Destry, but I guess you can see that you've changed a good bit. I don't blame you. Six terrible years have gone by for you. You'll be your old self one day, after you've ridden on the range again for a while; and when you are, come back to see me. If you don't hate me too much, try to think of me as a friend. That's what I want to be, always.
>   CHARLIE DANGERFIELD.

Bent waited on the opposite side of the table.

"She didn't know what to do. She was afraid to see you, Harry. So she gave me this letter to take to you. I'm mighty sorry, because I can guess what it's all about!"

Destry, carefully thumbing the creases of the letter after refolding it, fell into a brown study, out of which he spoke, surprisingly, not of Charlotte Dangerfield at all. He merely said in a worried, depressed voice:

"The Ogden boys are in town, now, Chet. And I hear that Sam Warren and Clyde Orrin are back from the hills, too. You remember? They was all on the jury! They might think that I would do them some harm, and—and try to get at me first! Chet, I guess I better leave town!"

It was of course the wish which of all others lay closest to the heart of Bent; for now that the girl had broken with Destry, it was by all means best to get him away from the range of her impulsive pity, which might undo all that already had been accomplished.

"Perhaps you're right," said Bent. "Perhaps Wham is a bit dangerous for you. You know in the old days your gun was fitted into a mighty loose holster, Harry, and people don't forget that. You'd better go; I'll handle all the financing. I tell you what, old fellow, I'm not going to let you down, no matter what the rest of the world may do and say!"

He was not even thanked! Destry, as one stunned, fumbled still with his thoughts.

"Somebody said that more of them were coming back. I mean, Bud Williams, and Jerry Wendell. Eight of them, all together. Eight that used to be on the jury that sent me away to prison!"

"It might be a bad climate for you here," admitted Bent again. "Look here, old son. Leave right now, if you want. I have a bang-up good horse in my stable this moment. I'll fix you up with a pack, and you can be out and away—with a full wallet, mind you—and fifty miles over the hills before the day breaks!"

At this, Destry groaned aloud.

"Oh, Chet," he said, "what'd I be doin' outside in the open, where so many of 'em could be followin' me? What would I be doin' away in the hills, I'd ask you? They can read trail. They'd run me down. I'd be alone! Oh, God! Think of ridin' the hills and seein' the same buzzards circlin' in the sky that'll eat the eyes out of your head, before long!"

Even Chester Bent was a little aroused with pity.

He said sharply: "What in hell did they do to you in the penitentiary, man?"

"I'd rather not to talk!" said he, and Bent wisely did not press him to speak, for he felt that a hysterical outburst was close at hand.

In his own room, he scratched another note to dapper Jerry Wendell.

Destry is badly broken up, and shaken. You fellows will handle him with gloves, I'm sure. He's helpless and harmless, and you'd pity him if you saw him. Charlie Dangerfield has broken her engagement with him—that's a secret that you're sure to find out by tomorrow—and he hasn't the spirit even to regret the loss of her! He can only think about his personal danger from you and the rest of the boys who served on the jury. I think it may be months before he becomes his old self again!

CHET.

He added that last line after much deliberation, for it would not fit in with his plans to allow Destry to be considered permanently harmless. Harmless he never could be, in the eye of Bent. Not that the latter feared that Destry ever could become his old self, but because he once had read that women truly love once, and once only, and the line had sunk into his heart. At this moment, Bent felt that he was closer than ever to Charlie Dangerfield, simply because she admired the manner in which he stood by the fallen man. If his dream was realized, and she became his wife, what would happen in her heart of hearts if she again met a partially recovered Destry on some future day? The mind of Bent was logical and sure. There must be no future for his guest!

He sent a house mozo to carry the message; then he went down to find Destry and take him to the dinner table.

Destry was not there. He had gone out, Bent was told, to take a little air; but he was not in the back garden, nor in the front.

He had gone into the town, perhaps, tormented by fear, tormented even more by the fascination of lights under which other men were drinking and enjoying themselves. No doubt he wanted to see careless faces, and therein strive to forget his mental burden!

Whatever the reason, Harry Destry had gone down the main street, avoiding the lighted places, slipping from one dark side of the way to the other, until he came to the region of the saloons, and into the Last Chance he started to make his way when fate, which works with a cruel insistence in our lives, placed Dud Cross once more in his path, for Dud came reeling out as Destry approached the swinging door.

"The yaller dog's out and around agin!" shouted Cross. "Get back home and ask your boss to tie you up! Or you're likely to get et up here in Wham!"

He acted as he spoke. The wide-swinging palm of his hand cracked against the cheek of Destry and sent him staggering back against a hitching post. There he leaned, one side of his white face turning crimson, his eyes staring vacantly at his persecutor, and drunken Dud Cross lurched forward to rout his victim.

It was only luck that brought the sheriff there. Ding Slater stepped before Cross and pointed a forefinger like a gun in the face of the bully.

"You get yourse'f home!" said he, and Dud Cross disappeared like a bubble into the night.

The sheriff turned back to Destry with compassion and disgust equally troubling him.

"Harry," he said, "don't you go bein' a fool and showin' your face around the streets. You take my advice. You better go home. You hear me?"

"Yeah," said Destry faintly. "Yeah, I hear you."

And he looked into the face of the sheriff with eyes so blank, so wide, so helpless, that Ding Slater could not endure the weight of them. He turned without pressing his point and hurried down the street damning impartially the stars in the sky and the penal system of that sovereign state.

Destry, as one drawn by powers beyond him, slowly went forward, pushed open the doors of the saloon, and entered.

It was a busy evening. A dozen men were lined up at the bar, and there was a gleam of eyes, a flash of faces as they looked toward the door and the newcomer. Then all backs became rigid and were turned squarely upon him!

He did not seem to understand but, taking his place at the farthest end of the long bar, he half cowered against the wall, ordered a drink, and then forgot to taste it, but looked aimlessly into nothing, while the subdued talk along the bar was picked up again, and carried on in its former tone.

Half of those men had drunk and roistered with him in the old days; their pity and their self-respect kept them from noticing the fallen hero now. Religiously their eyes dodged when they chanced to fall upon the face of Destry in the midst of laughter or in the midst of narrative.

The gay minutes went on; but shortly a pair of them departed. And then another pair, and another. There were other places to drink in Wham, where the depressing influence of Destry would not be felt, and the horror to which a brave man could descend be witnessed!

The bartender was not a callous man, but he was naturally irritated when he saw an evening fairly blasted before it had begun to blossom. He took the first occasion to say behind his hand to Destry: "You better finish your drink and move on!"

"Sure," said Destry, and looked at him with the same humble, but uncomprehending stare.

A man at the far end of the bar growled to the saloon keeper: "Leave him be, will you? He ain't right in the head!"

"He makes me sick," said the bartender, with more ferocity than he felt, and took three fingers for himself, and paid for it with a vicious punch at the cash register. However, the big man at the farther end resolutely moved down beside Destry and found himself at once embarked in conversation.

"I hear that Wendell's in town?" said Destry. "Where might he be livin', now?"

"Down two blocks, in the big house with the fir hedge in front."

"Yeah? Orrin's place is just opposite, ain't it?"

"No. Orrin's moved. He's down by the river, just left of the bridge. Cleeves has the opposite house."

"Yeah? Cleeves was a great pal of Williams."

"They used to be thick."

"Is Williams in town, too? Still here?"

"Still here. He's got a room in the Darlington Hotel where——"

He paused with his glass at his lips.

Destry turned to follow the direction of his companion's glance, and he saw just passing through the swinging door as dark a picture as he could have wished to see. For the Ogden brothers were at that moment kicking the door wide and stalking into the place, and the object on which their eyes fell and stayed was the face of Destry himself.

Some things are obvious as day. When the moose is bogged down in snow, and the wolves sit in a circle with red, lolling tongues, it does not need a prophet to tell that they will soon eat red meat. And it was perfectly apparent from the solemn entrance of the Ogden brothers that they had come for Destry and meant to have his life!

8

AFTER that first glance, they paid no heed to Destry, but strode to the bar and ordered whiskey, and Destry remained in the corner, silent, looking at his dreams with open, empty eyes. The bartender, who had been through many phases of this mortal coil, observed him with the eye of a physician who sees symptoms of a fatal disease, against the progress of which there is no remedy. There were still five men in the room, and these drew back from the bar, not hastily, but by slow degrees, conversing with one another, as though their business required greater privacy than could be found under the bright light of the two kerosene lamps which flooded the bar and its vicinity.

Out of the chatter of conversation which had preceded the entry of the Ogden brothers, an approximate silence fell upon the room, as when, before a prizefight, the voices of the spectators are gradually hushed, and there remains a dead moment in which even the most casual murmur is audible, surprisingly, over several rows and the speakers grow embarrassed and glance about in the hope that no one has overheard their profanity.

So it was now in the barroom after the Ogden brothers had come in. They were two of a kind. That kind originates somewhere in the middle West, instantly understood by all who have been in that region, and understood by no others.

They were tall, but they were not awkwardly built. Their shoulders were broad, but their chests were not shallow. They stood straight, and their heads were high, and yet there was a trail of the eternal slime upon them. It appeared in their greasy complexions, their overbright eyes, wrinkled too much at the corners, as though by continual laughter, though the practiced observer knew that laughter had nothing to do with those lines. They had a way of smiling secretly, one to the other, conscious of a jest which was not apparent to the rest of the world, and they fortified themselves with this laughter; for laughter is a two-edged sword, and all of those who do not understand it are bound in the course of nature to be ill at ease.

At this very moment, they were smiling sourly at each other as they raised their glasses. They did not pledge the bartender with the accustomed nod and tilt of the glass; they did not turn the usual good-natured grin towards the others at the bar, but, instead, they raised their liquor swiftly, and swiftly they disposed of it. Then they put down the glasses with a clink upon the varnished wood of the bar and considered the thing that was before them.

They had come to kill Harrison Destry. That much was plain to themselves and to all observers; but they needed a bridge by which to pass from the commonplace to the greatly desired event. It would hardly do to turn on their heels and lay the new born coward dead!

With secrecy, with some shame, with great embarrassment, indeed, they looked slyly at each other and considered the means by which they would approach this fatal climax of the evening's work.

And still Destry gave them no excuse, no finger's hold, no faintest sham of a pretense to attack him. He stood with the same considerate gaze steadily upon vacancy, and spoke not a word, invited no comment, asked for no opinion. At last he said, timidly: "I'll take another."

The bartender noted with a real amaze that the glass of Destry was empty. He spun out the bottle, and when Destry had poured a moderate measure, the saloon keeper filled a glass for himself to the brim, for once more he needed a stimulant.

There was no conversation at all. One man had slipped noiselessly through the swinging door; the remainder stayed for the obvious purpose of seeing the killing of Harry Destry. Not that he was important now, but that he once had been a man of note.

Suddenly Jud Ogden said: "Destry?"

The latter raised his head with a faint smile.

"Yes?" he said.

No one could see his face, at that moment, except the bartender, and he underwent a strange convulsion that caused the liquor to tilt in his raised glass and to spill upon the floor half of the contents. Still under the influence of the same shock, whatever it could have been, he replaced his glass upon the bar, then changed his mind and tossed off the contents with a single gesture.

He coughed hard, but he did not take a chaser. With both hands gripping the edge of the bar, he remained frozen in place, looking not at the Ogden brothers, but at Destry, as though from him the important act was now to come.

"Destry," said Clarence Ogden, taking up the speech where his brother had left off, "they was a time when you done us wrong, you—Destry!"

"I done you wrong?" said Destry, as contemplative as ever. "*I* done you wrong?"

"You done us wrong," broke in Jud Ogden brutally.

Silence once more fell over the barroom, and the spectators, secure within their shadow, looked at one another, knowing that the time had almost come.

"Well," said Destry, "I'd be powerful sorry to think that I'd made anybody in this town unhappy! I'd sure hate to think of that!"

He turned from the bar as he spoke, a shrill laughter forced and unconvinced, breaking from his lips.

The bystanders winced, and their lips curled. As for the Ogdens, they looked secretly at each other, as much as to say that they had expected this. Then Clarence Ogden turned bodily upon Destry.

"You lousy rat!" he said.

But Destry did nothing, neither did he stir a hand!

"That's a hard name," he said.

But, as he spoke, it became suddenly apparent to all who listened that he was not afraid! He, the coward, the nameless thing, turned a little from the bar so that he faced the Ogdens, and as he spoke, his voice was like a caress.

"That's a hard name," said Destry.

And his voice was unafraid!

It was as though a masked battery had broken out from a screen of shrubbery. The greasy faces of the Ogdens lost color; the spectators by instinct drew closer together, shoulder to shoulder, and stood wedged in a row.

And Destry went on: "What for d'you call me that, boys?"

The Ogdens in their turn were silenced.

They had come expecting to find a wild cat whose teeth and claws were drawn. It appeared that beyond all belief they might be wrong!

"I hear a mighty bad word from the pair of you," said Destry. "It sure hurts my feelings. Here I come in, askin' for a little quiet drink, and along comes the Ogdens. Brave men. Big men. Pretty well known. They call me a yaller skunk, as you might say, for why?"

He smiled at the pair, and the pair did not smile back.

"It ain't possible," said Destry, continuing in the same subdued manner, "that you come here lookin' for a whipped pup and found a real dog in his place?"

His smile grew broader, and as he smiled, it appeared that the stature of Destry grew taller, that his chest expanded, his eye grew brighter.

"It ain't possible," said he, "that the Ogdens are gunna prove themselves to be a pair of mangy rats that wouldn't live up to what they said?"

He made a single light step toward them, and they drew back instinctively before him.

"It ain't possible that they're a pair of lousy fakers," said Destry. "It ain't possible," he added, in a louder tone, "that they're walkin' up and down the town in the attitude of great men and great killers without the heart to back up what they wanta seem to be?"

Fear? In this man?

The white face was lighted; the nostrils flared; the eyes of Destry gleamed with fire, and the audience shrank closer against the wall. If there was sympathy now, it was not for the one man but for the pair.

So action hung suspended until Clarence Ogden yelled, with a voice like that of a screeching old woman: "I'll take you, you——"

He yanked at his gun as he cried; he was dead in the middle of a curse; for out of the flap of his coat Destry had drawn a revolver, long barreled, gleaming blue; a fire spat from its mouth.

Clarence Ogden made a blundering step forward.

"I'd—" he began in a subdued tone, as though about to make an explanation, then sank slowly to the floor, a lifeless heap.

No one noticed his word at the end. His brother had reached for a weapon at the same instant, and fired. Only by a breath was he too late. By less time than it takes for an eye to wink, the second shot of Destry beat the bullet from his own weapon, and Jud Ogden spun in a circle and fell with a crash against the wall. Still he struggled to regain the weapon which he had let drop, sprawling forward like a frog on dry land.

Destry struck him across the head with the barrel of his Colt and leaned above him. Jud lay still. His great hand was fixed on the floor, seeming to grip at it as though anxious to rip up a board and reveal a secret. But all his powerful body lay helpless and unnerved upon the floor.

Destry stood up above his victim.

He said to the gaping row of witnesses along the wall: "I guess you boys all seen that I couldn't do anything to stop this here. I was tolerable helpless. They jus' nacherally insisted on havin' my scalp, as you might say! Terrible sorry!"

He stepped to the end man of the row, nearest to the door.

"Wendell, Jerry Wendell, you know him?"

"Yes," gasped the man.

"Where does he live? Tell me that! I've heard before, and forgot!"

He was told in a stammer, and started for the door.

When he reached it, he turned again toward the others and surveyed the two motionless forms upon the floor; and he laughed! Never to their death day would they forget the sound of that laughter. Then Destry was gone into the night.

It was the bartender who roused himself before any of the others, and running to the telephone, which stood at the end of the bar, he jerked off the receiver.

"One—nine—eight, quick, for God's sake!"

No man stirred among the frozen audience.

Then, finally the saloon keeper was crying:

"Is that you, Wendell? This is the Last Chance Saloon. You hear? The Ogden boys both jumped Destry in my place. They're both dead, I think, or dying! He's started for your house! Get out of town! Get out of town! He's been shammin'. It ain't the old Destry that's back here with us, but a devil that's ten times worse! Wendell, get yourself out of town!"

9

THERE was one habit of industry which Benjamin Dangerfield had clung to all his life, and that was rising at an early hour. To him the entire day was sick unless he saw the night turn gray and the pink of the dawn begin to blossom in the east. It was still not sun-up when he sat at his breakfast table with his daughter.

"I ain't showed you my new coat," said he, and rose and turned before her, a piece of ham poised at his lips on the end of a fork. "How does it look?"

"Mighty grand," said Charlotte. "Down to the knees you look pretty near as fine as a gambler."

For he had on common blue jeans beneath the coat, and the overall legs were stuffed into heavy riding boots, which never had seen a touch of polish or of other care than a liberal greasing in the winter of the year.

Mr. Dangerfield sat down again.

"How I look below the table don't matter; what I look above it is the thing that counts."

He patted his necktie as he spoke and brushed his moustache with his finger tips, sensitively.

"Sure," said the girl. "Anything that's comfortable is right, I guess. The dogs under the table wouldn't be comfortable if they had to go sashayin' around among broadcloth trousers. Neither would the cats."

"Suppose," said the father, "that you wanted to go and set on the corral fence and look at a hoss—would fancy trousers be any good for that?"

"They wouldn't," she answered. "They's just get all full of splinters."

"Or suppose that you got tired of walkin' and wanted to rest, would you go and set down on the ground in fancy pants?"

"No, sir, you most certainly wouldn't."

"Which you're laughin' at me the same," said he. "Speakin' of dogs, where's that brindle hound? I ain't seen him yet this mornin'."

"He's on the foot of your bed, most like," she answered. "You must of throwed the covers over him when you got up."

"I reckon I did," said he. "Mose, go upstairs and see if you can find me that wo'thless Major dog, will you?"

Mose disappeared.

"You look fair to middlin' miserable," observed Mr. Dangerfield. "Help yourself to some of that corn bread and pass it to me. It's cold! I'm gunna kill me a nigger out yonder in the kitchen, one of these days, if you don't bring 'em to time pretty quick!"

"How can I bring 'em to time?" asked the girl. "I've fired that good-for-nothin' Elijah six times, and you always take him back again!"

"In this family," said Dangerfield, "niggers ain't fired, I thank God!"

"Then don't you raise a ruction because you got indigestion. You can thank God for that, too!"

"It ain't the men in the kitchen, it's the women there that makes the trouble. I've fired that useless Maria, too," declared Charlotte, "but bless my soul if she don't start howlin' like a dog at the moon. Last time, she set outside my door three hours and give me nightmares with her carryin's on."

"You oughta cut down their pay," said Dangerfield. "I never seen anything like the way you throw money away on them niggers, the wo'thless good-for-nothin's!"

"Why, how you carry on!" said his daughter. "What diff'ence does it make to them, the money? Didn't they all keep on workin' all them years when they didn't get nothin' at all for pay?"

"Money is no good for niggers," said Dangerfield. "Money and votes ain't no good for them. Pass me some of that fish. They ain't hardly a thing on this table fit to pass a man's lips!"

"You've got a sight particular," said she, "since you've blundered into a few pennies; I seen the day many a time when we was glad to have just the corn bread on the breakfast table, without no eggs, nor ham, nor fish, nor milk, nor coffee neither."

"It ain't true!" said the father. "They never was a time, even when my fortune ebbed its lowest, when I didn't have coffee on my table."

"Yeah," drawled Charlotte. "But it was second and third boilin' most of the time, and I had to flavor it up with molasses to make it taste like something at all!"

"You gotta disposition," said her father, "like a handful of tacks. You got the nacheral sweetness of a tangle of barbed wire, Charlie. I ain't gunna talk to you no more this mornin'."

"Which I never asked you to," said she.

"Why don't you run along and leave me to finish my breakfast, then?"

"Because then I wouldn't have nothin' but niggers to bother," she replied, her chin in her hand.

"Charlie, if you're gunna be so downhearted about it, why don't you go and take him back, then?"

"There ain't anything to take back," said she. "He's only a handful of bubbles."

"Then why for are you sorrowin' so much?" he asked.

"Because I've lost my man," she said, "and only his ghost come back."

"You'll get yourself fixed up with another right now," said he. "You ain't never had no trouble collectin' young nuisances around you. That tribe of young boys has et up a drove of hogs for me, and a herd of cattle, and a trainload of apples and such; they've drunk enough of my whiskey to irrigate a thousand acres of corn; and all because you're close onto half as good lookin' as your mother used to be, Charlie."

"Thanks," said she. "You wanta see me tied up in one of these love-me-little-love-me-long marriages. But the fact is that I ain't gunna marry, never."

"If you ain't gunna get yourself a husband," said he, "you might get yourself some grammar; which a man would think that you never been to school, to listen at you talk!"

"I only dress up my talk once a week," said she, "and the rest of the time I'd rather go around comfortable and let the pronunciation take care of itself. What difference does it make to an adjective if it's used for an adverb?

It don't give the word no pain; it's easier for me; the niggers understand me better, and everybody's happy all around."

"I've seen young Chester Bent look kind of odd at some of your language, though," observed Dangerfield.

"Young Chester Bent," she mocked, "wouldn't mind the language of a red Comanche if she had the Dangerfield money."

"There you go," said he, "puttin' low motives into high minds! That boy is all right!"

"Yeah?" she queried. "Who's that comin' across the field?"

"I don't care who it is," said her father. "What I want to say is that Chester Bent is about the best——"

"It's somebody tryin' to catch something or tryin' to keep from bein' caught," said Charlotte.

Her father leaned to look through a gap in the trees that surrounded the ranchhouse, and he saw across the hill a rider flogging forward a horse so tired that its head bobbed like a cork in rough water.

"He's lookin' back," remarked the girl, "and the fact is that he's scared pretty bad. He's comin' here like a gopher scootin' for a hole in the ground."

"Who is it?" asked Dangerfield.

"Some boy from town," she replied, "because no puncher that's worth his salt ever rode so slantin' as that."

"Which Harrison Destry sure could fork a hoss," remarked her father.

The rider disappeared behind the trees, but almost immediately afterward an excited negress appeared at the kitchen door saying: "They's a young gent here that wants powerful to see you, Colonel Dangerfield!"

It was the family title for him; it was a title that was spreading abroad, now that he was able to lend money instead of "borrowing" it.

He had no chance to invite the stranger to enter and share the hospitality of his house, for the man that instant appeared, shouldering past the fat cook. He was very dusty. Dust was thick in the wrinkles of his sleeve and on his shoulders. His hat was off, and his hair blown into a rat's nest; he walked with a stagger of exhaustion; his face was drawn, and his eyes sunken. Yet it was a handsome face; some said he was the finest looking fellow on the entire range, for it was Jerry Wendell.

He fell into a chair, gasping: "Lock the doors, Colonel! He's not three jumps behind me! He means murder! He's killed two men already, this night. He's hounded me across the hills. I've gone a complete circle around Wham, and he's been after me every minute!"

"Lock the doors and the windows, Charlie," said the Colonel with composure. "Hand me that riot gun, too. I loaded it fresh with buckshot yesterday. How many of them is there, Jerry, and who are they, and what the devil do they mean by chasing you right onto my ranch? There ain't anything to be afraid of. My niggers will fight for me. How many are there, though? Charlie, give the alarm——"

"There's only one," said Jerry Wendell. "*Only* one, but he's the devil. I'm not ashamed of running! You know who it is! You must have heard!"

"Nothing!"

"It's Harry Destry running amok!"

The riot gun crashed to the floor from the hands of the girl.

Jerry Wendell, his eyes rolling wildly at the windows, was crowding himself back into the most obscure corner of the room, as he continued, his voice shaking as violently as his body:

"It was all a sham! You see? Pretending to be afraid! Oh, what fools we were to think that Destry ever could be afraid of anything! He wanted to trap us all—every man that sat on that jury—oh God, how I wish I never had seen that courtroom or listened to that judge! He'll kill the judge. I hope he kills the judge."

"Straighten up," said Dangerfield slowly. "I've seen Destry actin' like a yellow hound dog with his sneakin' tail between its legs, and you tell me that he's runnin' wild?"

"That's it! He waited till all of us were back in town. Then he trapped the Ogdens in the Last Chance. He—he—killed them both. He killed them both!"

Dangerfield stepped closer to him.

"Murder?" he asked.

"Murder? What else? What else?" screamed Jerry Wendell. "What else is it when a killer like him starts after an ordinary man, like me? Murder, murder, I tell you! And he'll never stop till he's got me here and slaughtered me under your eyes in your own house!"

10

SHAME, after all, is a human invention; the animals know no touch of it. The elephant feels no shame when it flees from the mouse, and the lion runs from the rhinoceros without a twinge of conscience, for shame was unknown until man created it out of the whole cloth of his desire to be godlike, though the gods themselves were divorced from such small scruples on sunny Olympus. Poor Jerry Wendell in his paroxysm quite forgot the thing that he should be; fifty thousand years of inherited dignity were shaken out of him and he acted as a caveman might have done if a bear were tearing down the barricade at the mouth of the dwelling, and the points of all the spears inside were broken.

Every moment he was starting, his pupils distending as he looked at the doors or the windows. He was oblivious of the scorn of the Dangerfields, which they were covering as well as they could under an air of kind concern.

"Have you got a man at that door?" asked Jerry. "And that?"

"Yes."

"And that?"

"That leads down into the cellar. He won't try to come that way."

"No matter what you do, he'll be here!" said Wendell, wringing his hands. "*I* thought I could stop him, too. I had the message from the saloon in time; I had three good men posted; I was telephoning across the way for more help, and then I heard a step on the stairs—a step on the stairs——"

The memory strangled him.

"I ran for the back steps and jumped down 'em. I locked the kitchen door as I went out. I tore across the garden and vaulted the street fence, and as I jumped, I looked back and saw a shadow slide through the kitchen window.

"Then I found a horse on the street. I didn't stop to ask whose it was. I jumped into the saddle, thanking God, and started for the lights in the middle of the town.

"But he gained on me. I had to cut down a side alley. He was hard after me on a runt of a mustang.

"I got out of the town. Luckily my horse would jump. I put it over fences and got into fields. There was no sight of him behind me then, and at last I decided to circle back into Wham.

"Then I saw him again, coming over a hill—just a glance of the outline of him against the stars—and he's been on my heels ever since—ever since! He'll——"

"Sit down to breakfast," urged Dangerfield. "The corn bread's still warm. You look—hungry!"

"Breakfast?" said the other. And he laughed hysterically. "Breakfast!" he repeated. "At a time like this! Well, why not?"

He allowed himself to be put into a chair, but his hands shook horribly when he tried to eat. His soul and nerves were in as great disarray as his clothes; his hair stood wildly on end; his necktie was jerked about beneath one ear; in a word, no one would have taken him for that Handsome Jerry who had broken hearts in Wham for many a day.

He spilled half his coffee on his coat and on the tablecloth, but the rest he managed to get down his throat, and his eye became a little less wild. Instantly the buried conscience came to life again. He clutched at his tie and straightened it; he made a pass at his hair, and then noticed for the first time the downward glance of the girl.

He could read in that many a thing which had been scourged out of his frightened brain all during his flight. Ostracism, ridicule would follow him to the ends of his days, unless he actually met Harrison Destry, gun in hand. And that he knew that he dared not do. The cruel cowpunchers and the wags of the town would never be at the end of this tale; they would tell of the mad ride of Jerry Wendell to the end of time!

He said, faltering as he spoke: "I would have stopped and faced him, but what chance would I have against that jailbird? And why should a law-abiding man dirty his hands with such a fellow? It's the sheriff's duty to take charge of such people. Ought to keep an eye on them. I said at the time, I always said that Destry was only shamming. He drew us all back, and then he clicked the trap! He clicked the trap! And——"

Here he was interrupted by another voice inside the room, saying: "Hullo, Colonel! Morning, Charlie. I was afraid that I'd be too late for breakfast, but I'm glad to see that they's still some steam comin' out of that corn bread. Can I sit down with you-all?"

It was Destry, coming towards them with a smile from the cellar door, which he had opened and shut behind him silently before saying a word.

The three reacted very differently to this entrance. The Colonel caught up the sawed-off shotgun that had been brought to him; his daughter started up from her chair, and then instantly steadied herself; while Jerry Wendell was frozen in his place. He could not even face about toward the danger behind him, but remained fixed shivering violently.

Charlotte Dangerfield was the first to find her voice, saying with a good deal of calmness:

"Sit down over here. I'll get in some eggs and some hot ham. I guess the coffee's still warm enough."

"Thanks," said Destry. "Don't you go puttin' yourself out. I been trying to get up with Jerry, here, and give him a watch that he dropped along the road. But he's been schoolin' his hoss across country so mighty fast that I couldn't catch him. How are you, Jerry?"

He laid the watch on the table in front of the other, and Jerry accepted it with a stir of lips which brought forth no sound. Destry sat down opposite him. The host and hostess were likewise in place in a cold silence, which Destry presently filled by saying: "You remember how the water used to flood in the cellar when a rainy winter come along? I had an idea about fixin' of that, Colonel, so I stopped in and looked at the cellar on the way in, but they wasn't quite enough light this early in the day to see anything. You didn't mind me comin' up from the cellar door that way?"

Dangerfield swore softly, beneath his breath.

"You're gunna come to a bad end, boy," he said. "You leave your talkin' be, and eat your breakfast. Why you been gallivantin' around the hills all night?"

"Why," said Destry, "you take a mighty fine gold watch like that, and I guess a man wouldn't like to think that he'd lost it, but the harder I tried to catch up with Jerry, there, the harder he rode away from me. He must of thought that he was havin' a race with big stakes up, but I'm mighty sure that I didn't have money on my mind!"

His smile faded a little as he spoke, and there was a glint in his eyes which turned Jerry Wendell from the crimson of sudden shame, to blanched white.

"What you-all been doin' this while I been away?" Destry asked politely of Wendell.

"Me?" said Wendell. "Why, nothing much. The same things."

"Ah?" said Destry. "You alluz found Wham a pretty interestin' sort of a town. I was kind of surprised when I heard that you was gunna leave it."

"Leave it?" asked Wendell, blank with surprise. "Leave Wham? What would I do, leaving Wham?"

"That's what I said to myself, when I heard it," said Destry gently. "Here you are, with a house, and a business, and money in the mines and in lumber. Jiminy! How could Jerry leave Wham where everybody knows him, and he knows everybody? But him that told me said he reckoned you got tired of a lot of things in Wham, like all the dances that you gotta go to, and the dust from the street in summer blowin' plumb into your office, and all such!"

Wendell, confident that something was hidden behind this casual conversation, said not a word, but moistened his purplish lips and never budged his eyes from the terrible right hand of the gunman.

"Him that told me," went on Destry, "said that you'd got so you preferred a quiet life. Here where everybody knows you, you're always bein' called upon for something or other. They work you even on juries, he says, and that's enough to make any man hot."

Wendell shrank lower in his chair, but Destry, buttering a large slice of corn bread, did not appear to see. He put away at least half the slice and talked with some difficulty around the edge of the mouthful.

"Because them that work on a jury," he explained to his own satisfaction, "they gotta decide a case on the up and up and not let any of their own feelin' take control. Take a gent like you, you'd have an opinion about pretty nigh everybody in town even before the trial come off. And you might make a mistake!"

"There's twelve men on a jury!" said Jerry Wendell hoarsely.

"Sure there is," nodded Destry. "You seem to know all about juries— numbers and everything! There's twelve men, but any single one of 'em is able to hang the rest! One man could stop a decision from comin' through!"

Wendell pushed back his chair a little. He was incapable, at the moment, of retorting to the subtle tortures of Destry.

At last he said:

"I'd better be goin' back."

"To Wham?"

"Yes, of course."

"Well," said Destry, "that's up to you. Go ahead. I think they might be somebody waiting for you along the road, though. But a gent of your kind, old feller, he wouldn't pay no attention to such things."

Wendell stood up.

"I'm leaving now," he replied, with a question and an appeal in his voice that made the girl look up at him as at a new man.

"Good trip to you," said Destry.

"But first I'd like to see you alone, for a minute."

"Don't you do it," said Destry. "I know just what it must be like to cut loose from an old home, the way that Wham has been to you. Well, good luck to you!"

"I'll never come back," said the other, unnerved at the prospect.

"Likely you won't—till the talk dies down a mite."

"Destry!" shouted the tormented man suddenly. "Will you tell me why you've grounds to hate me the way that you do?"

"No hate, old fellow. No hate at all. Don't mix that up in the job. But suppose that we let it drop there? You have your watch back, I have a cigarette in this hand and a forkful of ham in that and a lot of information that I would like to use, one day."

11

WENDELL left that room like a man entranced, and behind him he would have left a silence, if it had not been for the cheerful talk of Destry.

"I come by the Minniver place, last night, lyin' snug under its trees, with the moon standin' like a half face just over the gully, where it splits the hills behind, and doggone me if it wasn't strange to see the old house all lit up, and, off of the veranda, I could hear the whangin' of the banjos, soft and easy, and the tinkle of a girl laughin', like moonshine fingerin' its way across a lake. But we had to go on past that, though it looked like Jerry would of wanted me to stay there, he seemed so bent on turnin' in. But I edged him away from it. Only, when we went by, I recalled that that was the first time that I see you, Charlie. You was fifteen, and your dad, he'd let you go out to that dance. D'you recollect?"

She looked at him, her lips twisting a little with pain and with pleasure.

"I remember, perfectly," said she.

"You can remember the party," said Destry, "but you can't re-member——"

"Harry!" she cried at him. "Will you talk on like this about just nothing, when there's poor Jerry Wendell being driven out from Wham and cut away from everything that he ever was? Wouldn't it be more merciful to murder him, than to do that?"

"Why, look at you, Charlie!" said Destry, pleased and surprised. "How you talk up right out of a school book, when you ain't thinkin'!"

"Sure," said Dangerfield. "If Charlie wasn't always watchin' herself, the boys would think that she was tryin' to have a good influence on 'em, and educate 'em, or something. Now and then I pick up a little grammar from her myself!"

"You can both make light of it," said the girl, too troubled to smile at their words, "but I really think that killing would be more merciful to Jerry!"

"So do I," answered Destry.

It shocked the others to a full pause, but Destry went on: "There ain't much pain in a forty-five calibre bullet tappin' on your forehead and askin' your life to come outdoors and play. I used often to figger how easy dyin' was, when I was in prison. Ten years is a long time!"

They listened to him, grimly enchanted.

"It was only six," said the Colonel.

"Time has a taste to it," said Destry. "Like the ozone that comes from electricity, sometimes, and sometimes like the ozone that the pine trees make. But time has a taste, and it was flavored with iron for me. What good was the six years? I thought it'd be ten, of course. I've seen seconds, Charlie, that didn't tick on a watch, but that was counted off by pickin' at my nerves—thrum, thrum!—like a banjo, d'you see?"

He smiled at them both, and buttered another slice of corn bread.

"This is something like!" said Destry. "I hope I ain't keepin' you from nothin', Colonel?"

The Colonel did not answer; neither did the girl speak, and Destry went on: "Nerves, d'you see, they ain't so pleasant as you might think. I thought jail wouldn't be so bad, and for six months I just sort of relaxed and took it easy, and slept, and never bothered about nothin'. 'It'll get you' says the others at the rock pile. 'Pretty soon it'll get you in a heap!' Well, I used to laugh at 'em. But all at once I woke up out of a dream, one night.

"In that dream, where d'you think that I was? Why, I was at the party in the old Minniver house, and there was all the faces as real as lamplight ever had made 'em, and there was sweet Charlie Dangerfield, with her hair hangin' down her back—and her face half scared, and half mad, and half happy, too, like it was when I kissed her for luck.

"There I lay, wrigglin' my toes again the sheet, and smilin' at the blackness and sort of feelin' around for the stars, as you might say, when all at once I realized that there was nine layers of concrete and steel cells between me and them stars, and in every cot there was a poor crook lyin' awake and hungerin', and sweatin'. Why, just then it seemed to me like death was nothin' at all. I'll tell you a funny thing. I got out of my cot right then and went over to the knob of the door and figgered how I could tie a pillow case onto it and around my neck and then hang myself on that."

"Harry, Harry!" cried the girl. "It's not true! You're making it up to torture me!"

He looked at her; he smiled his way through her.

"I didn't do it, even then when I figgered on nine years and six months more of the prison smell. I didn't do it, honey, even when I seen then that death is only one pulse of life, even if it's the last one. Even when I seen then that every other pulse of life can be as almighty great as the second we die in—and here I was cut off from livin'—but I didn't hang myself,

Charlie—not because I hadn't the nerve, but because I still seen you on the Minniver veranda, slappin' my face!"

He laughed, with his teeth close together.

"I laid there for five and a half years more, thinkin', and that's why I didn't kill Jerry Wendell, seein' that death is only a touch, but shame is a thing that'll lie like a lump of ice under your ribs all the days of your life. So Jerry's alive! You wanted to know, and now I've told you. Could I have another shot of that coffee, Colonel? You got the outcookingest nigger in that kitchen of yours that I ever ate after!"

It was Charlotte, however, who went to the coffee pot and poured his cup steaming full.

"Ah," said Dangerfield, "you had a long wait, there. What busted into you to rob that mail, son?"

Destry laughed again.

"There's the joke, Colonel. It would of been pretty easy to lie close in jail, thinkin' of the good time I'd of had with stolen money the rest of my days, when I got out; but the joke was that I didn't steal the money. I was only framed!"

The Colonel suddenly believed, and, believing, he swore violently and terribly.

"All at once, I know you mean it!" said he.

"Thanks," said Destry, "but there was twelve peers, d'you understand, that wouldn't believe. They wouldn't believe, because they didn't want to. Twelve peers of what? Chinamen?"

The humor had died out of his eyes; they blazed at Dangerfield until the latter actually pushed back his chair with a nervous gesture.

"It's all over now, Harry," he said in consolation. "You're able to forget it, now!"

"I'll tell you," answered Destry. "You know how they say a gent with his arm cut off still feels the arm? Gets twinges in the hand that's dead, and pains in the buried elbows, like you might say! And it's the same way with me; I got five dead years, but a nervous system that's still spread all through 'em!"

"Are you fixed and final on that?" asked the Colonel.

"Fixed as them hills," said Destry. "You gunna leave us, Charlie?"

"I reckon that I better had," said she, standing up. He rose with her.

"You gotta headache, Charlie," said her father. "Maybe you better lie down."

At this, she broke out: "I ain't gunna be dignified, Harry. I'm not gunna put on a sweet smile and go out soft and slow, like funeral music. I'm gunna fight!"

"All right," said Destry. "You're the fightin' kind. But what you gunna fight about, and who with?"

"I'm gunna fight with you!"

"We've had a lot of practice," said Destry, grinning. "Fact is, we've had so much practice that we know how to block most of the punches that the other fellow starts heavin' at us!"

"Oh, Harry," said she, with a subtle change of voice, "I can't block this! It hurts me a powerful lot."

"Look at her!" said the Colonel. "Why, doggone me if she ain't about cryin'! Kiss her, Harry, and make a fuss over her, because if she's cryin' over you, I'll have to use the riot gun on you, after all!"

She waved that suggestion aside.

"What are you gunna do, Harry? Are you gunna take after them all, the way you promised them in the courtroom?"

"Look what they done!" he argued with her. "All the days of six years, one by one, they loaded onto my shoulders, and as the days dropped off, the load got heavier! I tell you what day was the worst—the last day, from noon to noon. That day was made up of sixty seconds in every minute, and sixty minutes in every hour, and the hours, they started each one like spring and ended each one like winter. I was a tolerable young man, up to that last day!"

He added hastily:

"Speakin' of time, I better be goin' along! I got a lot of riding to do today. I better be goin' along."

He turned to the host.

"Good-by, Colonel."

"Wait a minute, Harry! They's a lot of things to talk about——"

"I can't stay now. Some other time. So long, Charlie. You be takin' care of yourself, will you?"

He leaned and touched her forehead with his lips.

"So long again, Colonel!"

He was through the door at once, and instantly they heard a chorus of voices from the negroes hailing him, for he was a prime favorite among them. His own laughing voice was clearly distinguishable.

"Is that a way," said the Colonel, "for a young gent to kiss a girl good-by, when it's a girl like you, and he loves her, like he does you? He pecked at you like a chicken at a grain that turns out to be sand and not corn! Hey, Charlie! God a'mighty, what's possessin' you?"

"Leave me be!" said she, as he overtook her at the door.

He held her shoulders firmly.

"What's the matter? What's the matter?" asked the Colonel.

"You'll make me cry in about a half a minute," said she. "Will you lemme go, dad?"

"Hold on," said the Colonel, his eyes brooding upon her with a real and deep pain. "Has _he_ got something to do with this all? If he has——"

"Hush up," said the girl.

"But there ain't any call for carryin' on the way you are, Charlie. Everything's all right. He's busy. He's got his mind on the road. Everything's all right; ain't he come and started where you and him left off?"

"What makes you think so?" she asked.

"Why, he wouldn't of showed up here at all, except that he wanted to show you that he didn't keep your letter in his mind."

"He came here for Jerry Wendell, and that's all," said the girl.

"But he kissed you, Charlie. He wouldn't of done that!"

"Oh, don't you see?" said she. "He was only kissing me good-by."

12

IT was not yet prime of the day when Destry jogged his tired mustang down the main street of Wham again. He rode with his eyes fixed straight before him, but from their corners, he was able to feel the attention which followed him. The little, light rumor, which rises faster than dead leaves on the wind, which is more penetrating than desert dust, had whispered before him so rapidly that he was aware of faces at windows, at doors, always glimpsed and then disappearing.

Already they knew him thoroughly, and this made him sigh. For, if he could have gone about his work secretly enough, he might have struck them all, one by one, in this same town. But three were gone, in a breath, and nine remained. He looked forward to their trails with a drowsy, almost a dull content, like a wolf that trots on the track of a tiring moose, and knows that there is no hurry.

Sheriff Ding Slater came up to him at a gallop, turning a corner in the fine old slanting style, and raising a huge cloud of dust, like a gunpowder explosion, when he jerked his mustang to a halt. That dust, settling, powdered the moustaches of the sheriff a fine white. He shook his gauntleted hand at Destry.

"Young man," he said, "you been at it fine and early! You clear out of Wham. You ride right on through, and I'll see you out of town!"

"Come along, sheriff," said Destry. "It's a long time since last night, when I talked to you last!"

The sheriff fell in at his side.

"It's a dead man and a mighty sick man besides, since last night," said Ding Slater. "Six years ain't taught you nothin', Harry, and I ain't gunna expose my town no more to you. You're worse'n smallpox!"

"Thanks," said Destry, "because I can feel the compliment behind what you say. Thanks a lot, old timer. Have the makin's?"

"A dead man! Clarence Ogden dead!" said the sheriff. "And here I ride alongside of the killer! What would they think in the East about that?"

"Eastern thinkin' never raised Western crops," observed Destry. "But about the Ogdens, you know them that live by the gun shall die by the gun. That's Bible, or oughta be!"

"You sashay right on outa Wham," said the sheriff.

"Not me," answered Destry, "except that my game ain't here any longer, I guess. All the birds have seen the hunter, and they all have flown, I reckon?"

The sheriff looked grimly at him.

"D'you mean to take 'em all?" he said. "One by one?"

"I mean it!"

"I can use that agin you, young feller, if this comes up in court, as it's sure gunna do!"

"The law'll never get to the wind of me again," replied Destry. "I'm like a good dog. I've had the whip on my back, and I don't need two thrashin's to make me remember the feel of doin' wrong!"

"Of doin' wrong!" cried the sheriff. "Is it doin' right to shoot men down?"

"Self-defense ain't a crime, even in a Sunday School," said Destry.

"Ay," growled Ding Slater. "I can't answer back to that, especial when it was two to one——"

"And they'd hunted me down!"

"They was huntin' a calf. They didn't know that a wild cat was under the skin. But leave the Ogdens out of the picture. What about the rest? Are they likely to come at you?"

"Them and their hired men," said Destry. "But let's not get down to particulars. Everything that I do, it's gunna be inside the law—plumb inside of the laws. You'll be helpin' me out, before long. You'll——"

"You got plenty of brass in you," complained the sheriff. "Help you out? I'll be hanged first!"

"I'm a sort of a special investigatin' agent," said Destry. "I'm gunna open locked doors and let in the light, like the parson said one Sunday in the prison. I'm gunna unlock a lot of private doors and let in the light, sheriff."

"Now, whacha mean by that?"

"There ain't a man on earth," said Destry, "that don't need to wear clothes. They's some part of his life that's a naked shame, and I'm gunna find that part. I'm gunna punish them the way that I was punished, only worse."

"You kinda interest me," said the sheriff thoughtfully.

"I bet I do," replied Destry. "If they was a fine-toothed comb run through your past, what would come of you, son?"

"There ain't a thing for me to cover up, hardly," said the sheriff. "But every man's a fool some time or other. But to get back to the others——"

"Sure," said Destry, smiling.

"I always wished you well, Harry."

"I guess you did."

"But whacha mean about punishing the others the way that you were punished?"

"Why, I was shut off from life behind bars. I'm gunna shut off the rest of 'em, but not behind the bars. They'll have life in the hand, but it'll taste like sand and cactus thorns when they try to eat it."

"You're talkin' right in the middle of the street," noted the sheriff.

"I figger on you tellin' them," replied Destry. "Murder is all that they're lookin' for now, though the case of Jerry Wendell might show 'em different. You go tell 'em all, Ding. The more doors they gotta watch and guard, the worse they'll be able to guard 'em. So long. You'll be wantin' to get to work sendin' out letters. You know the names! I gotta turn in here to see Chester Bent."

He halted his horse and looked fondly at the house.

"He's stood by you fine," agreed the sheriff.

"I wish that his house was ten times as big," said Destry with emotion. "I wish that they was marble columns walkin' down the front, and a hundred niggers waitin' for the bell to ring, and a hundred hosses standin' in his stable, and a hundred towns like Wham in his pocketbook. God never made no finer man than him!"

The sheriff went back down the street, and Destry turned down the short drive that led to the barn behind the house. There, with two other men in a green field behind the house, was Chester Bent, looking at a tall bay mare which one of the others was leading up and down. Bent came hurrying to meet his friend, and wrung his hand.

"I've heard about Jerry!" he said. "Ah, Harry, you've pulled the wool over my eyes, as well as over the eyes of the rest of the town. Wendell's come in, and gone again, looking like a ghost."

"If I'd told you," answered Destry, embarrassed, which was a strange mood in him, "you would have started to talk me out of it!"

He laid his hand on the other's shoulder.

"I know you, man! Good for evil is what you'd say, and turn the other cheek, and all that kind of thing. But it ain't in my nacher. God didn't make me that way, and you could give me a bad time, but you couldn't change me. Not even you!"

"What is it now?" asked Bent, overlooking both the apology and the praise.

"They've scattered like birds. I'm gunna follow down one trail."

"You're set on that?"

"Out yonder I can spot one of 'em. That's Clyde Orrin, the great politician, the risin' man in the state, the honest young legislator, the maker of clean laws—him with the soft hands that are never more'n a half hour away from soap and water! I'm gunna call on Clyde's dark closet and look for spooks. Are you buyin' that mare?"

"I think so. Come and look at her. But about my friend Orrin—a perfectly harmless fellow, and a good man, you know——"

"Listen to me," said Destry. "A man can't live on bread alone. He's gotta have words, too. I can talk to you, old timer, but I don't wanta listen. Understand?"

Chester Bent took a handkerchief from his upper coat pocket and passed it gingerly over his face. Then he nodded.

"I'll stop thinking about you, Harry," said he, "and only remember that whatever my friend does must be right! Now come look at the mare for me. They want nine hundred dollars. And of course that's too much."

"Lemme try her," said Destry.

He took her from the hands of the dealers and swung into the saddle without a glance at her points. Down the pasture he galloped her, jumped a ditch, turned, took a wire fence, jumped back over it, and cantered her back to the group.

He dismounted with an unchanged face.

"You tried her over wire!" exclaimed Bent. "You might have ruined her, man!"

"Look at the old cuts," said Destry calmly. "If she ain't been able to learn wire from that much trouble, she ain't worth her looks!"

Bent drew him aside.

"What you say? Not nine hundred, Harry!"

"Listen," said Destry. "What would you pay for a pair of wings?"

"Is she as good as that?"

"Better! You can't talk to wings, and you can talk to her. She's a sweetheart, Chet, I wouldn't wish you on no other hoss than her!"

Which was how Fiddle came into the hands of Chester Bent; for his check was written in another moment, and she was taken to the stable by a waiting negro.

Then Bent walked back to the house and up to the room of his guest to watch Destry pack his roll. He pressed him very little to stay.

"I see it in your eye, man," he said. "I almost envy you, Harry. You're free. You have the open country, and ride your own way; I'm tied here to my business like a horse to a post; and I'll take no more of it with me in the end than the horse takes of the post. I feel like a tame duck in the barnyard, when it sees the wild flock driving a wedge across the morning, and letting the music come rattling down. I'm still young enough to understand that music, but after a while I'll get used to clipped wings and not even dream of better things at night. Harry, is there one last thing I can do for you?"

"Lend me a fresh mustang—you keep a string of 'em—and take mine in change. It's a hand picked one, and I haven't ridden the velvet off it, yet!"

Bent went out to give directions for the saddling of the new mount, and Destry, finishing his packing, swung his pack over his shoulder and went down the stairs to the front door. He found the stable boy and note waiting for him beside the new mare, Fiddle:

Dear Harry,
    It's a sad thing to shake hands with a man I may never see again. I couldn't have the heart to stay here and say

good-by. Take Fiddle with you. I saw in your eye what you
thought of her, and I want you to take with you something
that'll remind you that I'm your friend.

Chet.

13

CHESTER BENT did not write one note only, that morning, but as soon as
he had hurried down to his office, he scribbled rapidly:

Dear Clyde,
   This is in haste. Destry has come to see me. He's not
satisfied with Clarence Ogden dead, and Jud Ogden a cripple
for life. It makes no difference that Jerry Wendell has been
disgraced and made a laughing stock. He's determined to
keep on the trail until he's killed or ruined every man of
the twelve of you.
   You know that I'm the friend of Harry. I suppose you
also can guess that I'm yours. I've tried to dissuade him,
but he's adamant. I couldn't budge him a whit.
   He's off now, and on a fast horse. But I'm sending this
message on to you, in the hope that you'll get it in time. I
don't know how to tell you to guard yourself. It may be
your life he's after. It may be only some other scalp that
he'll try to lift, but this thing is sure—that if he has his way
with you, you'll *wish* for death before the end!
   I don't need to point out to you that I run a most frightful
danger in sending you this letter. If it, or any knowledge
of it, should come to the hands of Destry, I suppose he'd
turn on his trail and come back to murder me, friendly
though we are.
   However, I can't resist the chance of warning you that
the sword is hanging directly over your head, old fellow,
and not even a thread to keep it from falling. Take care
of yourself. Remember me to your good wife.

Adios,
CHESTER BENT.

   When he had written this letter, he rang a bell, and when his secretary
came, he said to her: "Send for that scar-faced Mexican who was in here
the other day."

"Do you mean Jose Vedres?" she asked.

"I mean Jose."

She hesitated, looking rather shocked, but she was a discreet woman who had reached the age of forty, guarded against all scandal by a face like a hatchet and a voice like a whining cat. She was attached to Bent by more than a personal devotion, and that was a slight sharing in his secrets. She knew ten per cent inside the margin, and that was more than any other human had mastered of the ways and the wiles of Chester. She knew enough, in fact, to wish to know more, and Bent was aware that she never would leave him so long as the hope of one day having him at her mercy was shining before her eyes. For that very reason he let her look around the corner now and then, just far enough to be able to guess at the direction he was going to take.

She sent for the Mexican at once, and the man came in a few moments, a venomous looking specimen of his race, slinking, yellow-eyed, with nicotine ingrained to his very soul.

Bent gave him the letter.

His directions were short and simple; he merely added at the end:

"If that letter gets to any hands other than those of Clyde Orrin, I'm a dead man, Jose. And if I die——"

He made a slight but significant gesture to conclude, and Jose nodded. He understood very well that his own life was so neatly poised in a balance that it would not take more than the fall of his friend to undo him.

He bowed himself, accordingly, through the door, and, from the window above, Bent watched him as he pitched gracefully up into the saddle, and sent the mustang scurrying down the street.

"Life insurance," said Chester Bent, and striking all of this affair from his mind, he turned back to his business of the day.

Jose, in the meantime, took a short cut from the town, crossed the fields beyond, and soon was headed up the valley.

He did not follow the river road, for, though it was far better graded, it wound too much to suit him. Instead, he chose to take a straighter though more rugged way which skirted along among the trees and through ground that rose and fell gently, like small waves of the sea.

In the first copse he paused, drew off a riding boot with some difficulty—for his boots were the one pride of his life in their fineness and tight fit—and, cutting threads at the top, he divided the outer leather from the lining. In this space he inserted the letter which had been intrusted to him. Afterward, with a fine needle and waxed thread, he closed the seam which he had opened. His precautions did not end here, for he actually threw away the needle and the thread remaining before he remounted and continued his ride.

No animal on dangerous ground could have traveled with a keener and a quicker eye than Jose. It searched every tuft of brush before. It scanned the shadows thrown from the patches of rocks that outcropped. It probed the groups of trees before he was near them. And yet all precaution cannot gain utter safety.

As he shot the mustang down a grade, he heard the easy rhythm of a long striding horse behind him, and, looking back, he saw a long-legged bay swinging down the hill, and in the saddle rode Harrison Destry.

Jose did not spur ahead. One glance at the gait of the horse behind him convinced him that flight was folly. Besides, no one but a fool would present a broad target, such as a back, to Destry. The Mexican drew rein, and was merely jogging as the other came alongside at a similar gait—a soft, smooth gait in the mare, the fetlock joints giving so freely that Destry hardly stirred in the saddle with the shock of the trot.

"Hullo, Jose," said he. "You're makin' good time for a hot day."

"You, too," said Jose, countering.

"Not for this mare," replied Destry. "She don't run; she flies. A flap of the reins sends her thirty mile an hour and she takes a hill from the top to the bottom with one beat of the wings. The buzzards and the eagles have been blowin' behind me in the wind of her gallop. Doggone me if I ain't been pityin' them. Where you bound, Jose?"

"Up the valley," said Jose, with a courteous smile.

He had another manner for most, but Destry was on a special list with him.

"Likely it's the heat comin' on in the flat," suggested Destry. "When the summer comes along, I reckon that you wanta get up to the high pines, Jose. It's a mighty savin' on the complexion, eh?"

This irony apparently missed the head of Jose entirely, for he answered:

"There's nothing to do in Wham. No jobs for Jose! I go up over the range and try to change my luck!"

"I tell you the trouble with your luck," said Destry. "You try too many things. Runnin' up a pack with two crimps in it is a fine art, Jose, and you oughta be satisfied with one. It works on the suckers, and the wise ones will spot your game, anyway. You aimin' at a range-ridin' job?"

"Yes."

"That's why you left your pack behind?"

Jose's eyelids fluttered down, but instantly he looked up again with his smile.

"You know poker is no man's friend, señor. It left me a naked man, this mornin'!"

"What color is your hide, Jose?" asked the other.

"Señor?"

"Stop your hoss, drop your gun-belt, and strip. I wanta look at you!"

"Señor Destry——" began the other.

"Jose, Jose," protested Destry, as one shocked, "you ain't gunna stop and argue, are you, when you see I'm so hurried? And when the sun is so hot? Jus' you climb down off that hoss, and drop your gun, and strip for me! It'll cool you, no end."

Jose made a pause that lasted only a half second. In that half second he had taken count of his chances and figured them accurately as one in five. He was a good gambler, a brave gambler, but he was not a fool. So he dismounted at once and undressed after he had obediently unbuckled his cartridge belt and allowed it to fall, together with the holstered gun which it supported.

Then he stood in the glare of the sunshine, looking sufficiently ridiculous in his nakedness, but with the great Mexican sombrero still on his head.

Destry went over the clothes with care. He found two pair of knives, one long handled, one short, as for throwing. He found a bandana, Bull Durham and papers, a box of matches, a travel stained envelope with the name of Señor Jose Vedres inscribed upon it in feminine writing, childishly clumsy.

This he opened and scanned for a line or two.

"She loves you, Jose," said he. "Then she's like the rest of 'em. Optimists before marriage, and hard thinkers afterwards! Nothin' but a profit in girls, and nothin' but a debit in wives. I guess you ain't ever married, Jose?"

"No, señor. Are you ended?"

"Before I've had a look at the gun, and the boots? Not me, son! Something was blowin' you up the valley away from the town too fast for my good. Everything that runs out of Wham, just now, is likely to have something to do with me, and why shouldn't I take a look?"

He began to thumb and probe the coat, lingering for a time over the shoulder padding; then he picked up the gun, which he took to pieces with lightning speed, and left unassembled again on the fallen coat.

"So's you won't begin target practice at my back till I'm a half mile away, anyway," said Destry.

He took up the boots, next, removed the inner lining, and then with consummate care and attention tapped on the high heels, listening with his ear close to them.

"It's a mighty delicate business," said Destry. "Maybe they's a hollow in here, but I reckon not. Besides, I've wasted enough time. I'm gunna make a short cut, Jose!"

His voice roared suddenly; his Colt leaped from its scabbard and leveled at the Mexican.

"What sent you out of Wham, and who was it that started you on your way?"

"Myself, Señor, and no other!"

"Then get down on your damned wo'thless knees and say your last prayers. I'm gunna have the truth out of you, or stop this trip!"

Jose shrugged his lean, crooked shoulders.

"The saints have stopped their ears to the prayers of poor Jose, señor," said he. "In heaven it is not as on this sad earth of ours; good deeds are better than good words; so I have stopped praying!"

Destry put up his gun in one flashing gesture.

"You're dead game, old son," said he. "You're straight enough to follow a snake's track, I reckon. So long. And don't hurry along too fast, because it might be that I'll meet you where you're goin'."

14

MRS. CLYDE ORRIN agreed with her husband perfectly in the major issue. That is to say, she felt that a "diplomatic" attitude was all the world deserved to see, but whereas Clyde Orrin brought home his official manner to the supper table, Mrs. Orrin felt that there was a time when one should be oneself.

"What great big thought has my boy tonight?" asked Mrs. Orrin at the table, noting a slight vacancy in the eye of her husband.

"Nothing—nothing at all," said Clyde Orrin. "Nothing of any importance."

"Don't come that stuff," said Mrs. Orrin, who had risen from the chorus to be the bride of this rising young politician; she enjoyed letting a little of the old times appear on her tongue when they were alone. "What's eating you, Clyde?"

"Children," said he.

"Children? Oh, rot! There's tons of time for them."

"I don't know. One has to form a habit pretty young."

"I see what you mean," she said. "You think I can run this house, and put up a front with your vote-getting friends, and go gadding to teas and such, picking up alliances for darling Clyde, and then I'm to tear home and stay up all night rocking the cradle of Clyde junior. Is that the idea? It ain't as catching as mumps, honey, if that's what you mean!"

He drummed his pink, soft fingers against the top of the table, and did not answer.

"Look here, sweetheart," said Mrs. Orrin. "Don't be such a great big strong silent man when you come home here to me. Let the office be your Rock of Gibraltar, darling; but when you get in here climb down off yourself."

"Why, dear," he said, "I didn't mean to hurt your feelings."

"I don't mean baby-talk, either," declared Mrs. Orrin. "But if it's a young Clyde that you want squalling around the house, just say so. I'm perfectly willing. There's nothing I'd like so well as to chuck all of this political rot and start a real home. You know it, too! But you have to pasture this girl on the long green, honey, if you expect her to start raising a family. I'm not cook, sweeper, window-washer, bell-ringer, duster, marketer, tea-pourer, handshaker all at the same time even for Darling. D'you follow me, or do I just seem to be saying one of those things?"

Her husband looked down at his plate, and knew that his face was softly, gently thoughtful, though there was almost murder in his heart. Still, he was rather fond of his wife; he knew that she was endlessly useful; twice she had saved his scalp from the tomahawk of a furious political boss, and numberless times she had saved him from time and trouble by being gracious on the street and off it. Moreover, the sharp definition of her character was a relief to him. After the haze of political diplomacy, small and great, in which he lived and breathed all the day, it was a great rest to see the naked truth inside the doors of his house. However, he was convinced that he had married beneath him, and this conviction he knew that his wife secretly shared. Because of that, he guessed shrewdly that his domestic happiness was founded upon sand.

"Suppose that we drop the talk about children, then? I don't want to make you uncomfortable. Only someday——"

"Sure," said she. "Someday is the time, in the Sweet Sometime on Someplace street. It's not children, though, that's occupying your mind tonight. What is it that's eating you, my great big brave, noble boy?"

"Don't you think," he suggested, "that we could at least try to be polite to one another, even when there's no one listening?"

"I *am* polite," said she. "I'm telling you how big and strong and wonderful you are. Pass me the celery, Clyde, and put the official manner in your inside coat pocket, will you?"

Her husband considered her with the gravity of the fabled basilisk, but his wife answered his gaze with the most ironical of sweet smiles. They understood each other so extremely well that it was doubtful if they could ever remain friends very long. Suddenly he put the thought in words.

"No matter what I may be outside; at home, I'm only a tool and a worm!"

"No matter how I may get by away from here," she retorted, "the minute you come home I'm back on the stage and showing my knees. If I lived with you a thousand years, you'd never stop being afraid that I'll some day make a bad break."

"Come, come," said he, "you know that's not true! I know what I owe you!"

"Not love, though?" said she.

He got up from his chair hastily and went around the table to her, but she held out her hand and warded him away.

"I don't want any perfunctory pecks, and I hate reconciliation scenes because they're so sticky," she said. "Being reconciled always makes a girl cry; I suppose because it's better to cry over a husband than to laugh at him. Go back and sit down, Clyde, and I'll try to take you seriously."

He returned to his chair, very pink and haughty, but Mrs. Orrin, who felt that she had gone far enough and who really thought that she might be able to drive even this somewhat flabby carriage to some political height, now softened her eyes and her smile.

He regarded her dubiously.

"You know how to pull in your claws and give the velvet touch," he told her. "Now get ready to put the claws out again. Listen to this! It's a letter from William R. Rock about the T. & O. business."

"Go on," she said. "I knew there was something for mama to hear."

He took the letter from his pocket, unfolded it, looked darkly at his wife, and read slowly, aloud:

> Dear Orrin,
>
> I've just read a copy of your last speech, the one of the seventh. It made me smile, but not on the side of the face you think. You want to get this in your head, young fellow. You're not in there to make the legislature laugh at us but to make it laugh with us. We've retained you for something more than an after-dinner speech. Ten thousand a year is higher than we've gone in this state for some time, and we want returns on our money. You know what we expect. We want a tax reduction and a fat one. You've been fiddling around for a long time and drawing pretty pictures, but now we want to hear from you in headlines. We want you to chuck the funny business and work up a little public sympathy for the T. & O. We want you to make the people feel that we're done for and will have to get out of business unless we're given a helping hand. The state needs us more than we need the state. That's your line, as I laid it down for you months ago.
>
> Now, then, Orrin, come to life and wake up that legislature. We've made enough alliances for you; all you need to do is to start pulling a few of the strings that we've placed in your hands, and the thing will go through. Besides, if you father a really big piece of legislation like that, it'll bring you before your public and double your strength with the voters.
>
> Don't make any mistake. Keep in our saddle and we'll ride you a long way. A governorship, perhaps, or the U.S. Senate. But only if you play our game. The Old Man was down here yesterday and he's not satisfied with you. This is a friendly tip. Get back into harness and help us pull our load and we'll not forget when we get to the top of the hill. You've been paid what you're worth in advance, but if the tax cut goes through, there'll be a bonus, anyway. I don't know just what. Ten thousand more, at least. Put that in your pipe and smoke it, and I think you'll enjoy the flavor of the weed.
>
> Now, boy, this is straight from the shoulder. Personally,

I believe in you! I'm with you and behind you every minute
that you play our game with us. But when you chuck us
and start going for yourself, we're going to plow the ground
from under your feet as sure as God made little apples.

Yours truly,

W. R. ROCK.

He read it out to the signature, slowly, dwelling a little on every offensive
phrase, and as he finished her first remark was: "You poor simpleton,
couldn't you remember the gist of that without bringing it home? Burn it
in the fireplace this minute! That's a bomb that would blow you to pieces
if the newspaper got hold of it! The *News-Democrat* would love to have that!
Can't you see a photographic reprint on the first page?"

"How long would I last with you," he asked curiously, "if things went
bust?"

"I don't know," she said "I'm in here working with a wise man, not with
a sap. Burn that letter, will you?"

"It has to go in the safe," said her husband.

"Suppose that the safe is cracked?"

"What yegg would waste his time on a safe like that?" he asked her. "I'm
not rich. There's not a hundred dollars in cash in it, and as for my papers,
who am I? No, I need this letter to refer to. It may be that they'll try to
double cross me. Here's their definite promise of a ten thousand bonus."

"Would they pay any attention to it?"

"There are certain quarters—not newspapers!—where I could show this
and do them a lot of harm if they were to try to hold out on me. They'd
know that. One reason Rock made this so strong and open was to scare
me into buying it. But I'm made of tougher stuff than that."

She hesitated, glancing at a corner. Then she snapped her fingers.

"I think you're right!" said she. "You *have* a head, Clyde darling, and I
can see it, once in a while. Better go down and put it away now!"

Here the front door bell rang, and they looked at each other with big,
frightened eyes; then Orrin himself went to answer the call.

He let in the yellow eyes and the smoked skin of Jose Vedres, who stood
before him, sourly smiling, a letter in his hand. Orrin, without a word, tore
it open and read.

"Wait here!" he said to the messenger, and hurried back into the dining
room.

He flung the letter down on the table, before his wife, merely muttering:
"Read this, Sylvia!"

Sylvia read, and then, refolding it without a word, she puckered her
smooth brow.

"It's like something in a play," she said at last. "I ought to say: 'Has it
come to this, Clyde Orrin?' "

"It's come to this," said he.

"You look pretty sick," said she. "But what could this man-eater get by clawing you?"

"What did he get by clawing poor Jerry Wendell?"

"Truc," she answered. "You'd better call in the police."

"For what?" he asked.

"For the safe! It has your soul locked up in it. And after all, it's a pretty good idea to keep a soul inside of a steel skin."

"You're not worried, Sylvia?" he asked her grimly.

"Darling," said she, "my heart's in my throat!"

But he knew, as he listened and watched her, that already the woman was preparing herself to see the ruin of her husband.

15

ONE of the strings which lay in the hand of Clyde Orrin connected with the detective branch of the police department and it was for that reason that Detective Hugh McDonald was installed in the little basement room which contained the Orrins' safe. It was a small, bare room, without an electric light, and even after a chair had been installed, and a lamp furnished, the place was not much more inviting. However, Mr. McDonald had sat through longer nights in worse places.

He first looked to the small window and assured himself that the bars which defended it were solidly sunk in the concrete of the sill and window jambs. He shook them with all his might, and still they held. Then he drew down the whitened glass pane, which shut out all sight of the interior to one passing outside. Next, he regarded the door, locked it, shoved home the bolt, and told himself that no agency other than spiritual could effect an entrance to this chamber. After that, he opened his magazine and resumed the narrative which had been interrupted by this call to duty.

To make surety a little more sure, he laid his Colt across his lap; it was a special guaranty against sleepiness, because it would be dangerous to allow that gun to fall to the floor.

Dimly, overhead, he heard the last sound of people going to bed, the creak of a stairs being climbed, and the screech of a chair pushed back from a table. Then silence gathered the house softly in its arms.

It was two o'clock when there came the tap on his window. He looked at his watch, made sure of the hour, and then approached the window carefully, standing to one side, where the lamp could not throw his shadow upon the whitened glass. He was in no humor to throw away chances, for he had not forgotten the strained face of Clyde Orrin when the latter told him that in spite of one or twenty detectives, that room would be entered and the safe opened, if so be that the feared criminal decided to do this thing. Hugh McDonald had smiled a little at this fear; he was used to the tremors of the man of the street.

Now he said: "Who's there?"

"Jack Campbell," said a voice, dim beyond the window. "Open up and let's have a chin, will you? I'm froze out here and wanta thaw out my tongue!"

Mr. McDonald, hesitating, remembered the strength of the bars beyond the window, and his doubts departed.

But first he returned to the lamp and turned down its flame until there was only the faintest glow through the room. After that, he raised the window and peered cautiously out into the darkness. At once a face was pressed close to the bars, a face that wore bristling moustaches which quivered and stood on end as the fellow grinned.

"Who are you?" asked McDonald.

"I'm Campbell. I heard there was another Campbell down here on the job."

"I ain't a Campbell," said the McDonald with reasoned bitterness, "and what's more, I wouldn't be one. I ain't a Campbell and there ain't a drop of blood in me that ever seen Argyleshire, or ever wants to see it. I ain't a Campbell, and I never had a Campbell friend, and what's more, I don't never expect to have one. If that ain't enough for you, I'll try to find another way of sayin' it!"

"Campbell or McDonald," said the stranger at the bars, "there's only one country between us."

"You don't talk like it," said McDonald.

"Don't I? What chance of I gotto talk Scotch when I never was there, but a Scotchman's a Scotchman from London to Yuma, and don't you mistake."

"You talk like a man with a bit of reason in him," admitted the McDonald. "But what are you doin' out there?"

"I'm the outside gent of this job," said the other.

"I didn't know there was goin' to be an outside man," said McDonald.

"There wasn't," replied the Campbell, "but along comes Orrin back to the office and makes another howl, and gets me put on the job to be outside watchdog! What's in there, anyways?"

"Nothin' to eat," said McDonald.

"And me with my stomach cleavin' to my backbone.

"Where'd you come from?"

"Up from Phoenix."

"I never seen you before."

"Because you never been in Phoenix."

"Have they put you on regular?"

"They've put me on for a try, but if they don't give me no better chance than this, what good will a try do me, I ask you?"

"Search me," said McDonald. "What can you do?"

"Ride a hoss and daub a rope."

"Humph!" said the McDonald. "Well, I wish you luck. I'm gunna go back to my chair. You can set on the outside of the window sill, if that's a comfort for you!"

"Thanks," said the other. "But put these moustaches straight, will you?"

"What?"

"Look at 'em," said the other. "I dunno whether they're tryin' to make a fool out of me, or not, but they stuck these on me like a detective in a dime novel. Look at the twist in 'em, already, but I got no mirror to put 'em straight."

"What difference does it make? It's dark. Nobody's worryin' about your style of moustaches."

"It makes me nervous. It don't cost you nothin' to put these right for me, and it keeps me from feelin' like a clown. Look at the way they got me fixed. A wig, too, and the damn wig don't match the moustaches. They're makin' a fool out of me, McDonald."

"Some don't take much makin'," said the McDonald sourly. "Wait a minute, and I'll give those whiskers a yank for you."

He stepped close to the bars as he said this, and when he was near, the hand and arm of the other shot through a gap. In the extended fingers of the Campbell appeared a small rubber-housed bag of shot which flicked across the side of the McDonald's head.

The detective fell in a noiseless heap to the floor!

After this the "outside" man fell to work with a short jimmy which easily ripped the bars from their sockets. He was presently able to pull the whole framework back, and, entering the room through the window, he closed it carefully behind him.

Next, he secured the fallen gun of the man of the law, "fanned" him dexterously but failed to find anything more of interest on his person, and then gave his attention to the safe.

He turned up the flame in the throat of the lamp's chimney, so that he would have ample light, and then fell to work with wonderful rapidity running a mold of yellow laundry soap around the crack of the safe door.

Then, into an aperture at the top of the mold, he let in a trickle of pale, viscous fluid from a small bottle which he carried.

He was engaged in this occupation when the form on the floor stirred and groaned faintly. The other calmly went to him, selected a spot at the base of the skull, and struck with the bag of shot again. The McDonald slumped into a deeper sleep.

A moment later the fuse was connected, lighted, and the intruder stepped back into a corner of the little room and lay down on his face. The next instant the explosion took place, not a loud roar or a great report, but a thick, half stifled sigh that shook the house to its foundations.

The lamp had been put out by the robber before; now he lighted it again and by that flame he viewed the contents inside the open door of steel. In the very first drawer he found what apparently contented him—a letter which began:

"Dear Orrin,

I've just read a copy of your last speech—the one of the seventh——"

He glanced swiftly through its contents and placed the envelope in his pocket. Then he canted his head to listen to the rumble of footfalls coming down the stairs.

He was in no hurry. He even delayed to lean over the unconscious detective and slip a hand under the coat and over the heart of the McDonald. The reassuring though faint pulsation made him nod with satisfaction, and, raising the window, he was gone in a moment more into the outer night.

Still he was not ended for that evening, but hurried to the street, across it to a narrow alley, and down this to a hitching rack where a tall bay mare was tethered. He mounted, and cantered her out of the little suburb village into the adjoining capital city, itself hardly more than a village, conscious of its three paved streets and its gleaming street lamps!

He gained the center of the town, where he tethered the mare again in an alley and shortly afterward was climbing the dingy stairs that led to the rooms of the *News-Democrat*.

The reporters were gone. It was far too late for them, but the editor remained, punching wearily at his typewriter while he held the press for a late item. He was an old man. He had sunk to a country level from a city reputation. His head was gray, his eyes were bleared with the constant perusal of wet print, the glamour and the joy of the press almost had departed from his tired soul, but still a ghost of his old self looked through his glasses at Destry as that robber stood smiling before him, rubbing the crooked moustaches with sensitive finger tips.

"What're you made up to be?" asked the editor, grinning.

"I'm made up to be scandal," said Destry. "You take a look at this and tell me what *you* think?"

The editor glanced at the first few lines, half rose from his chair, and then settled back to finish. At the conclusion, he glanced fixedly at Destry for a few seconds, then ran to a tall filing cabinet from which he produced a handful of specimens of handwriting. With a selection from among these, he compared the signature at the bottom of the page.

After that, he allowed everything except the letter to fall fluttering and skidding through the air to the ink-painted floor while he rushed to a telephone.

Destry started for the door, and heard the editor screaming wildly:

"Stop the press! Stop the press!"

Then, as Destry was about to disappear, the editor's voice shouted after him: "I want your story! Where'd you pick this up?"

"Out of his safe," said Destry.

"Hey? Wait a minute! You mean that you robbed his safe?"

"Out of a feelin' for the public good," said Destry. "So long. Make it big!"

"Make it big! It makes itself! It's the whole front page! It's the T. & O. going up in smoke——"

But Destry waited to hear no more. He hurried down the stairs to the street, only pausing at the first dimly lit landing to take from his pocket a card containing a list of twelve names. Three of these already had been canceled. He now drew a line through the fourth.

16

THE slope was long, dusty, and hot, and Destry jogged up it on foot, with Fiddle following close at his heels, stepping lightly with the burden of his weight removed from the saddle. When they came to the crest, the man paused to roll a cigarette and look over the prospect before him and behind. In front was a steep declivity which ran down to the cream and brown froth of a river in spate, the water so high that it bubbled against the narrow little wooden bridge that spanned the flood. Then, turning, Destry scanned the broader valley behind him.

He could see the cattle here and there, single or in groups, like dim smears of pastel; but only one thing moved to the eye of the fugitive, and that was a puff of dust which advanced gradually across the center of the hollow. He knew that there were six riders under that veil, and the thought of them made him look carefully at his mare.

She had done well, she had done very well indeed to hold off the challenge of relayed pursuers but she showed the effects of the labor, for her eye was not as bright as usual, and though it was as brave as ever, it was the luster that Destry wanted to see back in it. She had grown somewhat gaunt, also, and the ribs showed like faint streaks of shadow under the gloss of her flanks.

She needed rest. She could not endure the continued strain of the race which already had lasted for thirty-six hours since first the handful of riders had spotted him on his way back from the capital and had launched their early sprint to overtake him.

Since her legs were not long and strong enough to distance all pursuit, Destry calmly sat down on a stump and considered the problem gravely, unhurriedly. There was only one salvation, and that was in his own mind.

He could, for instance, nest himself somewhere among the rocks and open fire pointblank on them, when they came struggling up the slope within the range of his rifle, but he knew that he who kills is bound to be killed. Moreover, even if he dropped two or three of them, enough would remain to keep him there under observation; and more men, more horses, were sure to come up from the rear. Aware of this, Destry lighted a second smoke, and with the first whiff of it, he saw the thing that he should do.

He went down the slope at the calmest of walks, therefore, and crossed the little bridge with the mare at his heels. The water had now risen until some of the spray dashed continually upon it and got the surface of the floor boards slippery with wet, yet Fiddle went over with a dainty step and stood at last on the farther side with her fine head raised and turned back toward the ridge of land they had just crossed, as though she knew that danger was coming up behind them.

Destry led her on up the steep way that twisted snakelike among the rocks above. When she was safely upon the shoulder of the table land that appeared here, he put her behind a nest of pines and went back to the edge of the plateau. The bridge was now a hundred feet directly beneath him, and over the ridge which he had just passed tipped the pursuit—six riders, six horses, one rushing behind the other, and their shout of triumph at the view of him went faintly roaring down the wind to Destry's ears.

There were masses of detached boulders lying about, fallen from the upper reaches of the high ground, and one of these monsters he rolled end over end, until its three hundred pounds pitched over the verge, landed not a foot from the bridge, and burst like a shell exploding.

Another great shout went up from the pursuers, but Destry had learned how to find the range and he heaved another boulder to the brink with perfect confidence, regardless of the shots which the six were pumping at him. Bullets fired from the saddle on a galloping horse are rarely more dangerous than a flight of wild sparrows. He carefully deliberated, then heaved the stone over.

This one, falling more sheer, struck a projecting rock-face half way in its descent, and glanced outward. Almost in the center of the bridge it struck, and broke the back of that frail structure as though it were built of straw. The water completed the ruin. The bridge seemed to rise with muddy arms, and in a trice all the timbers had been wrenched from their lodgment and carried swiftly down the water.

So the link was broken between Destry and the six.

He waved his hat to their shaken fists and brandished guns, then returned to the mare and rode her at a walk through the pines, up to the crest, where he appeared again, faintly outlined against the sky, then dipped from view beyond. He was in no slightest hurry.

At the first runlet which crossed his way, he refreshed Fiddle by sluicing water over her stomach and legs, and letting her have a few mouthfuls of grass; then he loosened the cinches and went on, walking in front of her, while she followed grazing here and there, then trotting to catch up with him—sometimes galloping a quarter of a mile ahead, and there pausing to feed greedily, until he came again.

In this manner he walked straight through the heat of the day, and in the early evening, when the sun was beginning to bulge its red cheeks in the west, he came up to Cumber Pass. Through it lay the way to Wham, split cleanly between two lofty mountains, and on the outer lip of the pass was a small hostelry. It had been a shambling little ranch house until the Pass was reopened. Now by the addition of a few shambling lean-tos it had been converted into a hotel, and even a second story had been built, looking like a straw hat on an oversized head on a windy day.

Destry paused here and spoke to a small boy who was seated on the top rail of the corral fence. On his head was a hat brim, without a hat. He wore a shirt with one sleeve off at the elbow and the other off at the shoulder; his father's trousers were upon him, not cut off, but worn off at the knees. But this loose and shapeless attire nevertheless appeared to accent a degree of freedom and grace in the boy. He looked past a liberal crop of freckles and eyed Destry with as firm a blue glance as ever said: "Beware! I am a man!"

"The top of the evenin' to you," said Destry.

"How's yourself?" answered the boy.

"Kind of bogged down with a tired hoss. Is this a hotel?"

"You can see the sign," suggested the boy.

His eyes wrinkled a little as if he would have liked to ask some acrid question, such as whether or not the stranger could read, but he restrained himself.

"You ain't full up?"

"Full up with air. We got nobody yet for tonight," said the boy.

"Then I reckon I'll put my hoss up. Is that the stable?"

"It's the only one."

He slid down from the rail and accompanied Destry.

"She kind of runs to legs, I reckon," he observed.

"Kind of," agreed Destry.

"Them kind don't hold up very good," said the boy, "unless you get the kind that Destry rides."

"What kind has he got?" asked Destry.

"I'll tell you what kind. She cost nineteen hundred dollars, and she was cheap at that. A rich feller down at Wham gives her to Destry. Nineteen hundred dollars!" he repeated slowly. "That's a sight of money."

"It is," agreed Destry.

"Take thirty dollars a month and save it all—how many months——"

The eyes of the boy grew vague with admiration.

"Some people are pretty nigh made of money," he concluded.

"I reckon they are. Who was the rich man? One of them miners?"

"It was that big bug—that Chester Bent. He's one of them that everything they touch turns to money, Pop says. He's got sense enough to want Destry for a friend, you better believe!"

"Why, I wonder?" said Destry. "I thought that Destry was in prison."

"Him? Ain't you heard that he's out?"

"I been up country."

"You been up pretty far!" said the boy, with a touch of suspicion. "You mean to say that you ain't heard?"

"No. About what?"

"Why, Destry's loose!"

"Is he?"

"Sure he is."

"Did he escape?"

"I'll tell you how it happened. He gets tired lyin' around that jail and he sends for the governor."

"Did the governor come?"

"You better believe! Would *you* come, if Destry sent for you? Well, I suppose that nobody'd be fool enough to want Destry to come and *fetch* him! You bet the governor come ahoppin'. Destry says: 'You look here, I'm tired of this here life.'

" 'What's the matter?' says the governor. 'Ain't they treatin' you pretty good?'

" 'They can't make corn bread here fit for a pig,' says Destry, 'it's that soggy.'

" 'I'll have that fixed right away,' says the governor.

" 'Besides,' says Destry, 'they're a pile too early with breakfast, I tell you.'

" 'I'll give 'em word to let you sleep,' says the governor.

" 'They's only one thing you can do for me,' says Destry. 'I've tried your old prison, and it ain't no good. I want a pardon.'

" 'If they ain't anything else I can do to please you,' says the governor, 'here's your pardon. I wrote out a brand new fresh one before I come down. I suspected maybe that was what you'd want!'

"So Destry and him shakes hands, and Destry comes home, and then whacha think that he done?"

"I ain't got an idea."

"Plays scared-cat. Even lets folks slap his face, some says! People begins to laugh. The jury that scattered out of town when they heard he was comin', they drift in back; and then bang! He's got 'em!"

"All of 'em?"

"Three of 'em, quick. He kills one, and he cripples another, and he chases another out of the country, and now he's gone over and showed that another one of 'em was just a low crook, all the time, and the police are lookin' for him. Pretty soon he'll have all twelve of 'em! That's the kind that Destry is! You don't seem to know much about him!"

"No, not much. He always kind of puzzled me a good deal."

"Well, Pop says it's like lookin' down a double-barreled gun to look at

Destry's eyes. That's the kind he is. He could pretty nigh kill you with a look, if he wanted to!"

"Could he?"

"Pop says the same as a bird does with a snake, that's the way of Destry with a man he don't like. Just charms 'em helpless, and then he swallers 'em!"

The boy spoke with great gusto.

"That's a funny thing," said Destry.

"Sure it is, for them that ain't swallered."

"How can he do it?" said Destry.

"Pop says that it's practice. Teach yourself to look straight at things, and pretty soon you bear 'em down. I been tryin' it out at school."

"Have you swallered plenty of the other boys?"

"No, but I've had plenty of fights tryin' it and practicin' it out, and now it begins to work better, if I only had more boys my own size to use it on; but I've licked all of them in the school! Here's the barn. You snake off the saddle, and I'll throw her down a feed of hay."

17

"POP" turned out to be a chinless, weary man, with a little work-starved wife as active as a squirrel. It was she who placed ham and eggs and country-fried potatoes before Destry, while Pop drew up his chair opposite and conversed with the new guest.

"You look plenty tired," said Destry. "Been puttin' in a hard day?"

"Me? I ben tired for years and years," said Pop. "I was took tired all of a sudden, once, and I ain't ben the same man since."

"I could tell you the year and the day," snapped the wife. "It was when we got married and you found out——"

"Ma," said her husband, "I dunno what possesses you that you keep comin' out with that, when it ain't a fact at all. I've argued you out of that twenty times, but you keep right on comin' back.

"Fact is," he said to Destry, "that a woman can make a pile of words, but not much sense. You know how it is! But it takes a man like Destry to come along and make 'em hop into their right place."

"Can Destry do that?"

"Him? Look what everybody says! That rich Dangerfield's girl, her that was gunna wait till Destry got out of prison, when he come back and pretended to be a yaller dog, she turned him down, and what did he do? When he showed himself and kicked the town in the face she was mighty anxious to be noticed agin. Did he do it? He didn't. He wouldn't give her the dust off his boots. Pride is what they like. You take a reasonable man like me, that likes to argue out a point, and they just wipe their boots on him; but when a Destry comes along and slaps their faces, they plumb like it. The snappin' of a black snake is the only kind of music that really makes them step. They's a lot of ways that a woman is like a mule!"

The wife turned back to her stove, merely shrugging her shoulders at this drawling harangue.

"Get me some wood, Pop," she said drily, at the end of it, "or if you won't, let Willie go out and fetch some in."

"Willie, you hear your ma askin' for wood," said Pop irately. "What you standin' around for?"

"Don't you tell nothin' about Destry," said Willie, "till I come back."

And as Willie vanished, with a great slam of the kitchen screen door, Destry asked: "You a friend of Destry?"

"One of the best in the world," said Pop with conviction. "Him and me always took to each other."

"Lazy men and thieves is always matched pretty good," said the wife, without turning around from her stove.

Her husband raised his head and stared at her back with dignified rebuke. Then he went on: "Destry and me, we been like twin brothers, pretty nigh."

"That's mighty interesting. I been hearin' that he didn't have many friends."

"And no more he don't. What would he be doin' with a lot of friends? He wouldn't be bothered. But now and then he goes and picks him out a gent and cottons to him, and that feller's his friend for life, like me. It ain't often that he does it. But when he does, it's for life!"

"That's a strange thing," said Destry.

"I don't think he ever seen Destry in his life," said the woman at the stove.

Her husband laughed with a fierce scorn.

"Listen at her!" he suggested. "You'd think that I sat here and actually *made up* the things that I've heard Destry say, and the things that I've seen Destry do! That's what you'd think! You'd think that I was a liar, you would, to hear her carry on!"

"They is some things," said the wife, "that a body can be sure about, and don't have to stop with thinkin'."

Pop half rose from his chair.

"Woman," said he, "if shame can't shut you up, my hand'll pretty pronto do it!"

"Your hand!" she said. "Your hand!"

And this, or the connotations which the word suggested to her, sent her into a fit of subdued laughter which continued for some time; it was indeed against a background of laughter that Pop continued talking. He first winked at Destry and tapped his forehead, then hooked a thumb over his shoulder as though to indicate that his better half was slightly, but helplessly addled.

"He seems to be makin' a good deal of talk," said Destry. "What sort of a looking man might Destry be?"

"Him? He ain't so big," said the other. "Tallish, sort of. Might be three or four inches taller than you. That's all. Biggish in the shoulders. Run about thirty pound more than you, I'd say. But it ain't the size of him that counts."

"No?"

"I'll tell a man that it ain't! It ain't the size at all, that counts, but just the style of him. You see him settin' still, he don't look like nothin' much, but you see him rise up and walk—then you see something, man!"

"Like what?"

"Well, ever see a cat sleepin' by the fire?"

"Sure. Many a time."

"It don't look much, does it?"

"Nope. It don't. Only sort of slab-sided and all fell in togethers."

"But along late when it opens its eyes and the eyes is green and it goes and sharpens its claws on the leg of the table—it's kind of different, ain't it?"

"Yes. Now you come to put it that way, it *is*!"

"And ornery, and dangerous?"

"Yes, that's true, too."

"And all at once you're kind of glad that it don't weigh twenty pound instead of six?"

"Yeah, I've thought about that, watchin' a cat get ready to go out huntin' at night. I've even dreamed about it afterwards—me bein' the size of a rat, and the cat stretchin' a paw in after me, with the claws stickin' out like big sickles, and every one sharp as a needle!"

"Well, then, I don't need to tell you nothin' about Destry, because he's just that way, and when he comes around, the brave men, and the rough handers, and the gun slingers, and the knife throwers, they curl up small, and get into a corner, and hope that he won't reach out for them. And when he stands up and slips across the floor, slow and silky, you can see what kind of a machine he is!"

"Yeah?" said Destry, entranced.

"You bet! Snap off a man's head quicker'n a wink."

"You don't say!"

"Don't I? I do, though! Tiger, that's all."

"Aw, rot!" said the wife, with a sigh. "You gunna carry on all evenin'?"

The boy, who had brought in the armful of wood and had been standing by listening, agape with interest, now glanced out the window and called out: "Hey! Look see! They's that light winkin' off by the Cumber River! That one we seen a coupla times, lately!"

"What light? Oh, that? That's jest the sun hittin' on a rock face, as the sun goes down," said the father of the family. "I disremember when it was," he resumed his narrative, "when I first seen Destry——"

"It was one night when you was dreamin'," said the wife.

His face contorted into a ball, but gradually the anger relaxed a little.

"Like a pin bein' jabbed into you, the talk of a woman," said he, bitterly.

"But this here Destry, I guess he ain't done much damage to other folks," said Destry, suggestively.

"Ain't he though? Oh, no he ain't!" said Pop in soft derision. "I guess he ain't wors'n Billy the Kid and Wild Bill throwed into one. I guess he ain't!"

"I guess he ain't *twice* as poison as both of them throwed together!" crowed the boy, chiming in with a face brilliant with exultation at so much bloodshed.

"Why," said Destry, "appears like Billy the Kid killed twenty-one men, and Wild Bill done up about fifty, in his time."

"Sure, and what about Destry? He don't do it in front of reporters. He don't advertise none. He just slips up and says to a gent: 'You and me'll take a walk, tonight.' The gent don't think nothin'. Destry goes out with him, and they walk by the river, and Destry comes back alone. Yes, sir! That's the way it happens!"

"Murder?" said Destry, appalled.

"Murder? Why for would he murder? He don't have to. Is there any fun in murder? No, there ain't nothin' but dirty hands. It's the fun that Destry wants, not the killin'. If he kills, it's so they won't talk about him afterwards. But fast as a cat can snap off the heads of mice, that's the way with Destry. I know him like a brother."

"Must be kind of dangerous to have him around, ain't it?"

"Him? Not for me. I know how to handle him. Suppose I sent him word, he'd be up here in a jiffy. The gents around here, they talk pretty careful around me. They wouldn't want Destry to come up and look 'em in the eye. They wouldn't want that, I can tell you."

"No, I reckon that they wouldn't," said the wife. "But if they was only to say boo! at you, you'd start runnin' and never stop! G'wan and gimme a hand with the wipin' of the dishes, will you?"

"Son, you hear you ma talkin', don't you?" asked the father. "G'wan and do what she wants. You can hear me just as good from over there, I reckon?"

"Only," said the wife, "I'd like to know why that light off yonder winks so fast? That ain't like the way that the sun would be off of a rock!"

"What light?" asked Destry, rising suddenly from the table.

He went over to the window and looked out.

"Over yonder," said she, pointing to the range of hills.

"There?"

"Yes."

"I don't see anything just now."

"I reckon maybe it's stopped. Yeah. I guess it's stopped."

"Because the sun's gone down!" said Pop triumphantly. "They ain't no logic in a woman, partner. Logic will always put 'em down, I tell you what! And they got nothin' to do but little things, so's they're always tryin' to rig

up little things into mysteries and they shake their heads and start wonderin'
about nothin'——"

But Destry looked fixedly from the window across the darkening landscape
and toward the blue of the eastern hills on which the light had winked. He
would have given much to have seen the flashing of the light, for there
was such a thing as a heliograph which could send messages jumping a
score of miles as accurately as any telegraph.

The drawling voice of Pop began again, however, and lulled all his senses
into a sleepy security.

18

DESTRY went to bed at once. He was a little particular in his selection of a
chamber, taking a corner one in the second story, where the roof of the
first floor jutted out beneath the window, but, having locked his door, he
threw himself on the bed without undressing and was instantly asleep.

Pop, having heard the key turned in the lock, returned to the kitchen
to his wife.

"Well," said he, "it sort of opened that young feller's eyes, didn't it, when
I talked about Destry? I thought that they'd pop right out of his head."

"They sure did," joined in Willie. "I never seen nothin' like it."

The wife put down a pan she was washing, and with such recklessness
that greasy dishwater spurted from the sink over her apron and far out
on the floor.

Then she turned on her two menfolk. She was one of those excitable
creatures whose emotions appear in their physical actions; now she gripped
her wet hands and shook her head at Pop.

"You know who that there is?"

"Who? The stranger?"

"Yes—stranger!"

"Why, and who might he be, bright eyes?" sneered her husband.

"Destry!"

It had the effect of what is called in the ring a lucky punch. In other
words, it caught Pop when he was walking into danger, not knowing that
it was there. His head jerked back; his hair flopped under the impact; his
knees sagged; his eyes grew glassy. Then he staggered toward his wife
exactly like a half stunned boxer striving to fall into a clinch.

But she slipped away from him, holding him off at a distance while, with
cruel eyes, she struck him again.

"It's him! It's that great friend of yours! It's Destry himself!"

Willie rushed to the rescue.

"Him? You could cut Destry in two," he declared, "and make a coupla men better than him!"

"Oh, of course Willie's right," said Pop. "As if I didn't know Destry when I seen him! This here Destry? You wanta make me laugh, don't you?"

"D'you see his eyes when he watched you? Did you see the smile that he was swallerin' while you puffed and talked like a fool about how mighty well you knew him? Why, I seen they was something on his mind right from the first! And why shouldn't Destry come this way?"

"Why should he, ma?" asked Pop, still staggered and hurt, but fighting to save himself from this new suggestion.

"Wouldn't this be his straightest line between the capital and Wham, if he went back that way?"

"He wouldn't go back that way," said Pop. "He's through with Wham. He'd be driftin' around the country, pickin' off the jurymen. Everybody knows what he'd do!"

"He'd go back to Wham," insisted the wife. "And ain't he ridin' a tall bay mare?"

"A skinny, long-legged thing," interjected Willie. "He said himself that she was so tired that she was plumb bogged down!"

"Gimme that lantern off the wall and we'll go see," said she. "You Willie— you Pop, you never neither of you never had no eye for a hoss! But my old man raised 'em!"

She led the way with rapid steps, which her two men imitated poorly, as they followed stumbling in her rear; and through the darkness, Willie again and again turned his head and stared wistfully, with a sick heart, toward his father. He had been in doubt about this man many a time before, but now he feared that doubt would become crushing certainty.

They entered the barn, passed by a pair of mustangs which were in stalls there, and came to the place of the bay mare. She started as she heard them, and, lifting her fine head, turned it full towards the lantern light which the woman had raised high.

She did not go closer.

"Thoroughbred!" she said. "That's all that mare is."

Pop and Willie did not answer. There was no need, for the truth which they had overlooked now seemed to be stamped in letters a foot high upon the forehead of Fiddle.

"It's Fiddle," said Willie slowly. "And him—he was Destry."

His mother suddenly put an arm around Willie's shoulder and drew him close to her.

"Don't you bother none about this, son," said she. "Men are mostly like this. You hear about 'em and away off in the distance they look as big and blue and grand as mountains. But bring 'em up close and they ain't no more than runts and dwarfs!"

They left the barn, Pop recovering a second wind as soon as they were under the stars again.

"As if I didn't know!" said Pop. "Why, what was I doin' all of the time but praisin' Destry right to his face? What was I doin' but makin' him feel good? You'd think that I was a fool, the way that you carry on. But I know what's what. I know how to handle things. I was just soft-soapin' Destry a little and——"

"Leave off! Leave off!" said the wife. "It ain't that I mind for myself. But Willie—give him a chance to respect you a little, will you?"

Willie, however, had gone rapidly ahead and was now out of sight. It was for him the crashing of a world about his ears. He had not been able to avoid seeing the truth about many phases of his father's idleness and shiftlessness, but, no matter what else he might be, for these years he had loomed in the mind of Willie as a great man, because he was the companion of Destry, the famous. A hundred stories he had told Willie of adventures with that celebrated man, and now the stories had to be relegated to the sphere of the fairy tale!

So Willie ran forward around the corner of the house and up the road with a breaking heart, not knowing or caring where he was bound so long as it was away from the persistent misery of the pain in his heart. He went blindly, and as he hurried up the trail he found himself suddenly caught by both shoulders.

"Who are you, kid?" asked a gruff voice.

Willie looked up to the face of a big man who held him, and behind him appeared eight or nine others, looming more or less vaguely through the dark of the night. It was more mysterious, even, than any of the stories that his father had told him. For every one of these men carried rifles and revolvers, and every one of them was on foot! Here, where men walked two miles in order to catch a horse and ride one, here was a whole troop coming softly down the road with weapons in their hands. The unreality of it made Willie's head spin, as though he were plunged from the actual world into a dream.

"I b'long here," said he.

"He b'longs here, he says," repeated his captor.

"Lemme see him," said another.

They talked very quietly, guarding their voices. The second spokesman now approached him, took him with a jerk from the hands of the first, and shook him so that his head teetered back and forth dizzily.

"You lie!" said the second man. "You been sent up the road with word to somebody. Don't lie to me, or I'll jerk you out of your skin! Who sent you, and where?"

"Nobody sent me no place," said Willie, anger growing greater than his fear. "And you let go your hold on me, will you? I b'long here, I tell you, and I gotta right to walk up the road."

He who was now holding him chuckled a little.

"Listen to the kid chirp up and talk," said he. "He's a game cock, this kid is. You belong back there in that house?"

"Yeah."

"That's the new hotel, ain't it?"

"Yeah."

"Tell me something."

"Yeah."

"Did Destry come by your place last evenin'?"

"Destry?" echoed the boy.

"Don't stop to think up a lie. Did Destry come by your place?"

"Yes," said Willie.

"Did he stop?"

"Yeah. He stopped for chow."

"What did he eat? Answer up quick, now, and don't you try to lie to me."

"He had ham and eggs and cold 'pone, and coffee, and condensed milk in it. He said it was the outbeatin'est coffee that he ever drunk."

"Because it was good or bad?"

"Good, I reckon. He didn't say. Why you askin' me about Destry?"

The other hesitated.

"Because we're friends of his," said he. "There ain't a one of us but has a lot of interest in meetin' up with Destry. We like him a lot, and we sure yearn to find him! That's why we're all here!"

"Well," said Willie, "you're headin' exact the wrong way."

"Which way should we go?"

"Slantin' up the hills, there, to the right side of the pass."

"To the right side of the Cumber Pass?"

"That's it."

"Doggone me," said one, "I wouldn't aim to guess that he would go that far out of his way even if he knowed we was waitin' in the pass for him!"

"The pen has made him careful," said another. "We better turn back and cut through the pass agin and nab him when he comes down the far side. Did he saw where he was gunna go, kid?"

"He didn't say," replied Willie, "but he talked some about Wham."

"He talked about Wham, did he? And what did he say?"

"Why, nothin' much, except that he was needed powerful bad, back there."

They consulted in murmurs.

"He said he was needed powerful bad in Wham. I reckon he ain't needed so powerful as all of that!"

"No," uttered another, "I reckon that Wham could get along tolerable without him!"

He who had first seized Willie said suddenly: "Suppose the kid's lyin'!"

"He wouldn't dare to lie. What would he lie for, besides?"

"Because Destry's always a hero to the kids! They like the idea of the one man agin the many. They always have and they always will—the kids and the women. Maybe Destry's right back there in the house, this minute!"

"We'll go look!"

"It's no good doin' that," said Willie, "because Destry ain't there."

"Ain't he?"

"Besides, ma is down with the scarlet fever, and pa has got a terrible rash——"

"The kid's lyin' like a tickin' clock," said one of the men. "Take him by the neck, and we'll go back and look at all these here fever patients. Take my word—Destry's in that house!"

19

"SAM," asked one of the men, "shall we all go in?"

"I'll go in with a coupla you boys," replied Sam, the leader. "The rest of you scatter around the house. I wish that we had riot guns with us. But whatever you're in doubt about, use a cartridge on it. There won't be any harm in that! If Destry smells trouble, he's gunna be off like a shot. But if we have a fair chance, maybe we'll get him. I'll go in and talk to the folks!"

So he took Willie, still held by the nape of the neck, into the house and found his father and mother in the kitchen, still wrangling, though with voices subdued by the greatness of their guest.

"Hey!" said Pop, "if it ain't Sam Warren!"

"Yes, it's me," said Warren. "I hear that you're all busted out into a rash, and your wife clean down with scarlet fever."

"Is that Willie's talk?" asked Pop, glaring severely toward the boy.

But even in reproof, he was not quite able to meet Willie's eye, and the latter knew, with contempt and disgust, that he had taken the measure of his father forever.

He was more interested in looking up at the man who held him and who led the night party. It was a name which had acquired a sudden fame, along with the rest of that unlucky jury which had condemned Harry Destry to the penitentiary. He had been, only a few months before, a fairly obscure cowpuncher, rather well considered for his speed and accuracy with guns, but now he was celebrated as a marked man.

He was a very tall man, being upwards of six feet, and both his face and his body were unusual. His shoulders and hips were narrow, his body almost emaciated, and the arms and legs very long. Hair grew on the back of his hands, which were long fingered and suggested a strength uncanny in a body so slight. His face was almost handsome, up to the eyes, but these popped out with an expression of continual anger beneath a perpetually frowning brow. The forehead rose high above, swelling out almost grotesquely at the top.

When Willie had marked down the features of this man, he listened again to the conversation.

"Now, Pop," said Sam Warren, "you know why I'm here?"

"Why, I couldn't guess," said Pop.

Sam Warren loosed his hold upon the neck of the boy in order to lay his hand upon the shoulder of Pop.

"You better think it over, Pop," said he. "Mind you, I'm your friend, if you gimme a chance, and so are all of these here boys along with me. But we ain't gunna stand for no foolishness. Is Destry here?"

"Destry?" said Pop blankly.

And suddenly the very heart of Willie turned to water, for he knew that his father would betray the sleeping guest.

He worked, in the meantime, slowly toward the door, and heard Warren saying:

"If we have to search the house for him, he'll hear us and get away; and if we find out, we'll make things hot for you! But if you'll show us where he is—"

"He ain't here at all," declared Pop.

"You lie," said Warren with a calm brutality, and Pop shrank under that verbal stroke.

"Now talk up," said Warren. "I've wasted enough time. Likely he's in the next room, listenin' all of this while."

Here Willie gained the door and stepped back into the shadow. He hardly could believe, for an instant, that these keen manhunters actually had let him go, but expected a long arm to reach out after him.

Yet it was true!

He slid down the narrow hall, pulled the shoes from his feet, and then ran noiselessly to the top of the stairs. He found the door of Destry's room at once, and tapped softly, calling in a whisper through the crack of the door.

There was an answer immediately, the guarded voice of Destry calling: "What's up? And who's there?"

"Sam Warren's downstairs. He's huntin' for you!"

"For me?"

"Yeah. For you. For Harry Destry!"

The door opened.

Willie found himself drawn hastily into the presence of the great man.

"How many are there, Willie?"

"About nine, countin' 'em all. Three downstairs, and the rest circlin' around the house, ready to shoot at anything at all!"

"Warren? You're sure of him?"

"I'm dead sure of him. He's wearin' a pretty nigh snow white sombrero same as he always does; and you can't forget his face, once that you've seen it!"

"Warren," said Destry thoughtfully, "is a mighty rash and pushin' man.

Now, look here, kid. You see if you can get down to the stable and snake out the mare for me, will you?"

"I'll try!"

"Throw the saddle on her. Mind you watch her, because she snaps like a wolf at strangers. Hurry, Willie, and I'll give you something to remember me by——"

He was working busily in the dark of the room, as he spoke, gathering his pack together, and Willie waited for no more, but slipped from the room and hastened in his bare feet down the upper corridor, down the narrow, twisting rear steps, and so to the ground below.

He issued from a window to get to it, and flattened himself out like a snake in the dust. There was need of such caution, for hardly an instant later a form strode through the darkness, and the fall of a foot puffed the watery dust into his face. It filled his eyes, his nostrils, his lungs.

He lay quietly writhing in an ecstasy of strangulation and the overmastering desire to sneeze. It was terrible seconds before that paroxysm ended, and during it, he told himself that he was sure to die, so great was the pressure of blood in his head.

Gradually he could breathe again, and now he made slowly forward. He knew the back yard of the house as intimately as he knew the palm of his own hand, and so he was able to keep up his snake-like progress from one depression to another.

Near the barn, he looked back, and he was just in time to see a dark form slip out from the window of Destry's room. There it hung for an instant, dangling, helpless in this posture, while half a dozen guns began to roar at the same instant.

Never had Willie heard such a bellowing, crashing noise. Men were shouting as the guns were fired, and yet for a long moment that swaying form remained there—surely with the life torn out of it long before— hanging so, merely by the convulsive grip of the hands, no doubt!

Or could it be that the darkness of the night was so great and the excitement of the hunters so intense that they were missing even at this short range?

Willie, his heart cold with anguish, stared dimly at that shadowy and pendulous form, while he heard the excited forms around him, and finally one loud voice that yelled: "I'll get him, damn him, even if he gets me!"

A man rushed foward, rifle at shoulder, shooting, advancing, shooting again.

Then:

"It's a fake! It ain't Destry! It's a dummy he's hung out for us! A fake! A fake! Scatter and look for him somewhere else, or he's sure gone from us! He's snaked himself out the far side of the house, I reckon!"

They did not wait for further consultation, but splitting apart, one to one side and one to the other, they rushed to block any further possible flight of the fugitive.

Willie, however, remained for one moment longer, for he was so overwhelmed with relief at the saving of his hero that he was incapable of movement; so it was he and he alone who saw another form slide out over the sill of Destry's window.

This time it did not hang foolishly by the hands, but flicked like a shadow down the side of the house—a shadow such as a fire casts up and down a wall, sending it flickering from the height to the bottom, all in an instant.

Willie saw no more.

He turned madly and plunged into the barn, tortured by the thought that he had betrayed his own trust by not obeying the orders of Destry long before.

Now he rushed for the stall of the tall mare, and whipped into it—to find himself embraced in long, powerful arms.

"It's the kid, is it?" said the voice of Sam Warren. "It's the scarlet fever kid, is it? And where's the rash breakin' out now? Where's Destry now?"

His hard tipped fingers sank into the flesh of the boy as he spoke. And Willie could not stir.

He could only gasp: "Destry's dead! They've murdered him."

"You lie," said tall Sam Warren. "And here I got you on my hands——"

He found a short way out of that difficulty by rapping the youngster across the head with the barrel of his Colt. It was a crushing blow, but though it felled Willie in a heap, it did not altogether stun him, for through a mist he could see a form leap into the entrance of the barn. Then desperation gave Willie voice to yell: "Look out! Warren's here!"

He heard Warren curse through gritted teeth; he saw the form that had darted through the barn door swerve to the side just as the revolver above him thundered and thrust out a darting tongue of fire.

It was answered swifter than its own echo by a leap of flame from the hand of Destry, and Willie saw the tall man stride over him, picking up his feet in a foolish, sprawling way. As Warren stepped forward, he sent in a steady fire, but Willie knew that the shots were wild. He heard one crashing through the shakes that covered the roof of the shed; he heard another smash a lantern so that there was a jingle of wires and a fall of glass.

Then Destry fired again, and Warren toppled stiffly forward, for all the world like a man tipping off a platform for a high dive. His long body struck the ground with an audible thud, but did not move again. From the dark waters into which Sam Warren had fallen, Willie knew that he never would arise.

But he had no time for reflection. There was work to do, and he sprang up with tigerish eagerness in spite of his reeling head. From the peg he jerked the saddle. He had it over the back of the mare as a pantherlike shadow went by him, flirting the bridle over the head of Fiddle. Quick hands dashed those of the boy aside and jerked the cinches up, as voices bawled from the direction of the house: "What's goin' on back in the barn? Hey—Pat and Bill, come along with me!"

Destry was already out the rear door of the barn, and there he took the head of Willie between his hands—and felt the sticky, hot blood that streamed down one side of his face, for the sight of the revolver had torn his scalp!

20

"DID WARREN do that? He did!" said Destry.

"Go on—doncha wait here!" pleaded Willie. "I'm all right. He had to whang me to keep me quiet, only he didn't whang hard enough. Go on, Destry. They're comin'!"

"You done this for me," said Destry. "May I die tomorrow if I ever forget."

"I only wanta say one thing—Dad was only pretendin'—he knew you all the time—he wouldn't be such a doggone fool——"

"You Pop's all right," said Destry. "He's your father. That's the main thing that's right in him. Willie, so long. I'm comin' back to see you. We're gunna be partners!"

He flashed into the saddle. To the bewildered and admiring eyes of the boy it seemed as though no bird with an airy flirt of the wings ever could have moved more swiftly and lightly. Then the tall mare swept into her long canter that flicked her off around a corner of the barn and instantly out of sight and hearing. At that very moment, there was a jumbled outcry from the men within the barn as they stumbled over the limp body of Warren, and then a yell of fear and of fury as they discovered who it was that lay there.

They would not remain long on the ground after that, the boy guessed, and in fact, there was an instant flight for horse and saddle where they had left their ponies up the road and among the trees.

Still Willie remained, as one entranced, behind the barn, looking in that direction where the darkness had swallowed the great Destry. At last he heard the voices of his mother and father entering the barn; the swinging light of the lantern which one of them carried set the cracks flushing and dimming as it rose and ebbed.

"A fine thing you've done, sicking murderers onto one of your guests!" said the woman.

"I was helpless; they was too many for me!" said he. "Besides, he's a bad one. The law's after him!"

"The law ain't after that fox. A wise hoss that has tasted rope-fire don't never pull agin the lariat again! Neither will Destry. He's got his lesson! They didn't do nothin' in the name of the law, but all in the name of this here Sam Warren that feared for his own hide—and lost his scalp tryin' to save it! Look at him lyin' there! He comes with his eight or nine men, and Destry, he sees him, and finishes him, and then fades out! But if I was——"

Willie heard no more. He had faded off among the brush nearby, for all at once the voices of these people made him sick at heart. He had looked on a hero; he had seen a hero in action; upon his head the hands of the great man had been placed.

So, like a prince anointed for the throne, he turned his back upon the facts of life and wandered off into the woods to commune with his swelling heart, and with the future.

The hands of Sheriff Ding Slater were crammed with news of this affair as he walked down the street to the gate of his garden in Wham. He had telephone messages transcribed among the package of papers in his hand, and he had moreover notes upon verbal reports which had been made to him at his office. And yet the affair of the Cumber Pass and the death of Warren did not occupy a great portion of his thoughts. It was something else that bowed his head as he slammed the gate behind him.

"Hey, Ding!" called his wife from a front window.

He was silent; having closed the gate with much force, he remained there, glaring up and down the street.

"Hey, Ding, what's the matter?"

"Aw, nothin', except that after weedin' the crooks out of Wham, they've come crowdin' all back in on me to bother my old age."

"What's happened?"

"Why, an hour ago a gent with a mask on walked into the Fitzgerald store, stuck up young Fitzgerald, and walked off with the money. Not much. Three hundred. He takes that and says it's enough, and walks out again by the back way. Fitzgerald grabs a gun and tears after him, but there ain't anybody climbing the frame of a hoss in the back yard. Whoever it is must of just gone right on around the corner of the house, takin' off his mask as he went, and walked into the crowd on the corner! Cool as ice! Fitzgerald tears into that crowd, but nobody had seen nothing, because they'd been watchin' down the street! There you are! A package of trouble. Open light of the day. And nobody has no clue. Why, that's enough to start a whole crowd of daylight robberies, ain't it?"

"It's gunna work out all right!" said the wife. "Come on in. Here's somebody to see you!"

"I don't wanta see nobody," said the sheriff. "Send him away."

"It ain't a him," said the wife, "and she's waitin' here and noticin' the things that you say and the way that you carry on!"

"Is she?" said the sheriff.

He came stumping up the steps and flung open the door.

"Hey, Charlie," he called to the visitor. "Where'd you come from?"

"How are you, Uncle Ding?" said she.

"Got the rheumatism and the blues," said he, "and my liver's out of kilter. Otherwise, I'm pretty fit for fifty-five!"

"You oughta have a helper," said the girl. "You can't go on bein' the lead hoss and the wheeler and do the brain work and pull all the load, too!"

The sheriff threw his hat into a corner.

"Who'm I gunna get?" he asked. "I been lookin' all these years for a deputy that was worth his salt, but them that I've tried, they spend their time at home shinin' up their badge, and spend their time away from home showin' the badge off to the boys. It don't take much notice to spoil a man, these days. They're gettin' like girls; they like to be all ornamented. Set down, Charlie. I'm plumb glad to see you. We ain't gunna talk about my affairs no more. What about that Destry of yours, that's gone and got himself another man?"

"He ain't mine no more," said she, with a rather twisted smile. "But I'll tell you what, Uncle Ding. He'd make a deputy for you!"

"He? Him? Destry?" gasped Slater.

"I mean he, him, Destry," she answered.

"Why—honey, you mean it really? Destry's—he's—why, I never heard of such an idee."

"Think it over," she said. "Particular if that rheumatism is bad. He'll pull at the wheel for you, all right."

"What would bein' a deputy mean to him?" asked Slater.

"It would mean that the men who hate him wouldn't be so bold to attack him. It's one thing to go after a common man, but an officer of the law is different."

"I ain't noticed it much," said the sheriff. "However, you're right. But it ain't what he wants. It'd cramp his style, considerable, I reckon, seein' that he's doin' most of the leadin', and the rest of 'em are just playin' on the tricks and followin' suit, most of the time."

"He might of had that idea yesterday, but not today," she replied. "They've hunted him pretty hard, and would of nailed him, too, if it hadn't been for a mite of a boy, people say. Well, that'll make him want to go slower!"

"Sure," agreed Slater. "Fire'll burn you before you boil, and I guess he's been singed a little. But he ain't left his street number with me. I dunno that I could pick the mountain top that he's settin' on now, gettin' ready to pounce like an owl on mice as soon as the evenin' comes."

"He's likely layin' up at Chester Bent's house right now," said the girl.

"What makes you think so?"

"Because Wham's the center, and the folks he's after are scattered all round it. He'll come back here, and he'll likely go to Chet's place."

The sheriff said not a word before he had gathered his hat off the floor, but before he left the room, he took Charlotte Dangerfield by the arm and asked her gravely: "How long'd it take you to work this out?"

"All night," she replied at once, and smiled at him.

"Ay," said the sheriff, "a house you once lived in is always partly home. So long, Charlie. This here may be an idea that I can use."

He went straight up the long street from his house, only pausing at the first corner to look back and see Charlotte saying good-by to Mrs. Slater at the gate. He could guess, by that, that she had made her call for one purpose only.

He continued his way until he came to the fir hedge that surrounded the house of Bent, and opening the gate in the middle of this, he left it swinging, with the latch clicking to and fro across the slot, while he marched up to the front door.

It was opened for him by Destry!

That worthy held out his wrists with a grin.

"I seen you comin'," said he, "and I thought I'd save you the bother of huntin' me up."

Ding Slater had recoiled a little from his unexpected appearance; then he brushed the extended hands aside.

"It ain't for Warren that I'm here," he said. "When a man tries murder, there ain't anything in the law that'll help him when he gets killed. Warren's dead, and Warren's been ripe for dyin' a long time, by my reckoning. I've come here on my own troubles, Harry. Go back in there and set down with me!"

They sat down in the parlor, hushed and dim. Only one shade was raised a few inches to admit the hot light of the middle day. This illumination was only sufficient to reveal them to each other in rough profile.

"Harry," said the sheriff, "sometimes a kid'll play in one back yard just because he don't know what it's like on the far side of the board fence. Maybe you're like that kid?"

"Maybe," said Destry, "I could agree, if I follered the drift."

"You been agin the law or outside of it since you was a kid. Now you're playin' safe, but still you're agin the house. Suppose, Harry, that I offered to give you a pack to deal for me?"

Destry raised his eyebrows in surprise.

"I mean," said the sheriff, "that I need help, and you kind of need a roof over your head to keep the stones from fallin' on you. Suppose, then, that you was to put on a badge and call yourself my man for a while? Hired man, y'understand?"

Destry tapped the tips of his fingers together.

"It's this here Fitzgerald business that bothers you some, I suppose?" he queried.

"I suppose that it does," said the sheriff.

"It'd give me a fine way of fadin' out of the picture for a few days," said Destry, thinking aloud. "It'd make my game easier and their game harder. Why, Ding, I dunno that I can afford to say no to you, no matter how low the wages might be!"

21

THE details of the Fitzgerald robbery were quickly told, and Destry considered them for a moment with the blank eye of a man in deep thought. At last he asked: "What's funny about this job, Ding?"

"What would you of done if you'd robbed a store?" asked Ding.

"Waited for dusk, when the till was fuller of money, and the lights was bad outside."

"What else?"

"Had a hoss handy and flopped onto it and rode of."

"But what did *he* do?"

"All different. He took three hundred. How much more was in that till?"

"Three times that much."

"He took a handful and ran?"

"That's it."

"He ran—" muttered Destry absently.

"Are you day dreamin', son?"

"I'm gunna slide away on Fiddle and try this job."

The sheriff pinned a badge inside his coat, saying: "Mind you, Harry, while you wear this, you don't belong to yourself; you're property of the law!"

"Sure," said Destry. "I follow that, all right. If there ain't anything more, I'll start movin'."

"That's what the cat said when she walked on the stove. Are they makin' it that hot for you?"

"They are," admitted Destry. "When they wake you up at night, nine strong, that's something, ain't it?"

"Ay," said the sheriff. "That'd make me take to an out-trail! I'd never come back, neither! This job is gunna rest your nerves considerable, Harry! Good luck to you. They's one last thing."

"And what's that?"

"It was Charlie Dangerfield that suggested where I'd find you, and that I get you for this job."

"She knew I was here?"

"Yeah. Or guessed it."

"She's mighty thoughtful," said Destry. "She reminds me of the gunmen of the early days, that never let a dead one go without a good funeral. It used to set some of 'em back a lot, buyin' coffins and hirin' hearses. And Charlie's that way. She takes care of you after she's done with you. So long, Ding!"

He departed in haste, heedless of the last anxious words which Slater was calling after him. Out to the barn went Destry, took the mare from her pasture, saddled and bridled her, and then chatted for a moment with Bent's hired man, who eyed him with equal awe and suspicion.

"They've done a lot of improvin' of the roads around here, Mack?" said he. "Since I was away, I mean?"

"They've done considerable," said Mack. "The old roads wouldn't satisfy people none. It wouldn't cost enough just to fix them up. They've even had to build a lot of new ones."

"Where to?"

"Why, up Amaritta way, for instance; and down through the Pike Pass."

"That's down towards the railroad, ain't it?"

"That's the way. They let the old trail go. But right now it's twenty mile shorter. You can see from the upper trail how it would be; you can look right down at it, snakin' along the river bed most of the way, travelin' around shorter curves."

"Why did they ever make a new one?"

"Because to widen the old one for freightin' meant blastin' out a lot of rock. But for hoss and saddle, it's still pretty good, except that it's overgrowed a lot! They was uneasy, though, until they found out this fine new way of spending their money! They had to go and get shut of a pile diggin' out the new road."

Destry departed with no further conversation, for he had learned what he wanted, and, turning up the main street, he jogged Fiddle out the road to Pike Pass. Presently he came to the fork, the new road taking the left, the old trail dipping down on the right, but Destry kept the lefthand way.

As the slope increased against him, he drew the mare down to a walk, but it was faster than a cowpony's gait, the long legs of Fiddle stepping out at a good four mile clip up grade and five down. For she walked as eagerly as she galloped, and kept turning her bright head from side to side to keep note of her master, and of all that lay around her.

As they climbed, the old trail was indeed visible, on the opposite side of the cañon, and far lower down. It was not smoothly graded, but jerked up and down according to the way the action of the water, ten thousand years before, had leveled the rocks.

After a few miles, Destry reached a little shack at the side of the way. Weather ages unpainted wood so rapidly that it was impossible from that clue to determine the age of the house, but the brush and the mesquite still grew up close to the door, and Destry could guess that the place had not been occupied very long. Otherwise this firewood would have been cut back to a far greater distance. A half-breed woman sat in the doorway, patting out tortillas from wet corn meal; she nodded in response to Destry's salutation.

"D'you move up here from the old trail?" he asked her.

"No," she replied. "We ain't been in these parts more'n six months. My man wishes he'd never seen the place, too! But cows is cows, I always say, and them that follers them is bound to live miserable. Too hot in summer, too cold in winter, bogged down in spring, and sold in the fall; that's the life of a cowman, God bring 'em help!"

"I thought that I'd seen you once on the old trail," said Destry.

"Never not me!"

"I reckon some still ride that way," he suggested.

"Some that are powerful hurried out of Wham," she replied. "And some I've seen that fair flew!"

"Not many no more?"

"No, not many. After the new trail was opened, they was still some that kept the old way, 'cause they found out that they might save time; but they used up the legs and feet of their hosses down there, so now pretty nigh everyone comes by my house. I pick up a good deal sellin' meals. You ain't hungry, are you?"

"No," said Destry.

She went on: "One come by there two hours back; not fast, though. Easin' his hoss around through the brush and actin' like he was enjoyin' himself on the ride."

"That so? From Wham?"

"I reckon from nobody else."

"I wonder who. Maybe Jimmy Pemberton. He was ridin' out into the pass today."

"Did he have a pinto?"

"Yeah. He did."

"Then that was Jimmy Pemberton that rode up along the old trail, and you'll never catch up with him on this one!"

"I reckon I won't. I'll just leave him be."

He went on, but no sooner was he around the next hillshoulder than he turned aside, and slid Fiddle down the slope to the bottom of the ravine.

Two hours would have made about the time that the fugitive from the Fitzgerald robbery would have been riding up this cañon if, as Destry suspected, he had been making for the railroad line; and he was willing to wager a fair sum that the rider of the pinto was the man the sheriff wanted. Therefore, in the name of the law and his new office, Destry sent Fiddle scampering up the old trail.

She went as a deer goes, lightly, gracefully, never fighting the steep places as most horses will do, never getting into a sweat of anxiety over sharp drops in the way, but studying out everything in detail and going nimbly about the solution in her own way. She was one of those rare animals that accept the purpose of the rider and then bend themselves intelligently to fulfill it, without starting and plunging at every unexpected obstacle along the way.

He helped her, too, in that perfect partnership. Often the old trail jumped up the almost sheer face of a rock, and then Destry leaped to the ground and worked his own way up, without giving her the pull of that extra burden. Or again, where it plunged sheer down, he was once more running beside her, and leaping into the saddle only where the ground became more favorable.

So they went on swiftly—an amazing speed, considering the nature of the way. But Fiddle could leap little gullies through which most cowponies would have to jog, staggering down one bank and laboring up the other. And she seemed to know, with that extra instinct which seems like eyes in the foot, exactly which stone would bear her weight, and which would roll and make her stumble.

However, no matter what speed they were making, Destry did not push her too hard, for he realized that a stern chase is a long one, and that the pinto had two hours' start on him. He worked rather to come up with the leader by the dusk of the day than to overtake him with one sustained effort.

So he checked Fiddle, rather than urged her forward.

It was bitterly hot in the ravine. Even when the sun made sufficient westing to fill the ravine with shadow, the heat which the rocks had been drinking all the day they now seemed to give up with one incredible out-pouring of locked up energy. No wind could find its way down into the heart of the cañon; the air was close and dead. The mare was cloaked with dripping sweat that rubbed to foam where the reins chafed the sleek of her neck and shoulders. Destry himself was drenched, but he regarded his own comfort less than that of the mare. Four times he stopped to slush water over her, and four times she went on, refreshed, while the pass darkened, and the sky overhead began to grow brilliant with the sunset.

Then Destry called on her for the first time, and she responded with a gallant burst up the long last rise to the summit of the trail. That long mile she put swiftly behind her, and, as he came to the top of the rise, Destry saw before him a sea of broken ground on which the dim trail tossed like the wake of a ship on a choppy sea, swinging this side and that.

But all that he could see of the trail was empty; then something loomed against the skyline—a pinto, surely——

No, it was only a hereford!

But a moment later, as he was digesting this first disappointment, he saw a broad sombrero with a lofty crown grow up against the sky, and a rider beneath it, sitting tall and straight in the saddle, and finally a pinto mustang; all three were only two swales away from him; and, seeing the pinto stumble with weariness, and sag as a tired horse will do, he knew that man, whoever he might be, was within striking distance!

22

A WIND blew across that height and cut against the face of Destry, whipping the dust from his lungs, the weariness from his heart. Across the rise and fall of the hills, he saw the dirty smudge which was the desert atmosphere; behind him the mountains rose up, splitting apart at the pass through which he had just ridden. He gave it one glance, and then made up his mind. The wind came from the left; it was to the right that he sent Fiddle, down into the hollows, so that the wind's own voice might help to stifle the sound of her hoofbeats. Cat claws tore at them as they whipped through, and the mesquite rose up around them like a dusky mist, rolling back on either hand, as he kept Fiddle at full gallop for two miles at least, jockeying her forward with his weight shifted toward the withers.

Then he pulled her up onto the trail, the old trail in the red of the sunset, and, leaping down, threw the reins. She was breathing hard, but cleanly.

He hurried to the crest of the swale before him, and, glancing cautiously over, he saw the pinto and its rider jogging through the hollow beneath, straight into his hands.

He looked back over his shoulder. Fiddle already was cropping grass at the side of the road, and far off he saw a slowly moving cloud of smoke in the lowlands. It might have been dust raised by a whirlwind, but it leaned back too far for that, and he knew it was a train. From this same rise the fugitive—if fugitive he were—would sight his open door to flight.

The thought pleased Destry and all the iron in his heart!

He crouched in a nest of stones and waited. He stayed there until he saw the sombrero grow up on the other side of the rise, then the nodding head of the mustang—and the face of the rider.

It was Lefty Turnbull! It was Lefty, who, during the trial six years before, of all the twelve jurors, alone had sat from first to last with a fixed sneer of hostility on his lips.

It seemed to the startled and vengeful eyes of Destry that the same smile was now on the lips of this man, and it transported Destry back to the courtroom, to the spiderweb in the corner of the ceiling, to the slant shaft of the sunlight that streamed through the window, to the barking voice of the district attorney—and again to this sneering smile of Turnbull!

Or was it merely weariness, the grin of long labor, which will make men seem to smile?

"Hey—!" cried out Lefty softly, and reined in his horse as he saw the mare before him.

"Fill your hand, Lefty," cried Destry, from the side. "Fill your hand." Then, remembering on what commission he rode, he added loudly: "In the name of the law!"

There was an old saying among those who knew that there was enough of the cat in Lefty Turnbull to land him on his feet from any height. Or, hold him by hands and feet a foot from the floor, like a cat he would land on all fours when dropped. Moreover, he was an old and experienced fighter, polished by a trip to the Klondike, and hardened by a few winters in the Canada woods.

To all that was said of him he lived up now.

For at the sound of Destry's voice, instead of drawing a gun and shooting to the side from which the threat came, Lefty flung himself out of the saddle, and, as he dropped past the belly line of the pinto, he was shooting.

The first bullet might well have ended the fight, for it struck a boulder inches from Destry's head and cast a burning spray of rock splinters into his face. Had they volleyed into his eyes, that would have proved the finish! But luck saved him. His own first shot went wide to the right. He knew he had pulled it even as he compressed the trigger.

The second would split the forehead of Turnbull as a knife splits the brittle rind of a squash, yet there was somewhere a hundredth part of a second which Destry could devote to thought, and in that whiplash instant he remembered his word to the sheriff.

He was not his own man, now; he was the servant of the law and, being that, as Harry Destry he did not exist, nor were the quarrels and the feuds of that man of any importance to him. He was not even sure that this was the criminal for whom he had been sent!

So he turned his aim a little to the right, and literally saw the impact of the big slug jerk at the body of Turnbull. The Colt exploded in Lefty's hand; but dropped as it was fired, and rattled down the face of a rock.

Still, disarmed as he was, there was no thought of surrender in the man. He was lying sprawled on the ground, in the perfect position for accurate shooting, when the bullet of Destry plunged through his left shoulder and ruined his shooting hand. Yet he lurched up now to his feet and ran forward to scoop up the weapon with his other hand.

Never was there such fiercely sweet temptation in Destry's soul as when he saw the full target arise before him. The buttons of the coat seemed to glimmer like stars, inviting the attention of the marksman, and the broad forehead seemed unmissable.

Yet he did not fire!

He belonged to the law. He was only a tool in the hands of the sheriff, and bitterly he told himself that Ding Slater well knew the identity of the criminal, and had despatched Destry merely to torment him.

"I ain't doin' murder today," said Destry. "Leave your gun be!"

Lefty Turnbull hesitated, his right hand reaching for the weapon. He was, like most left-handed people, quite hopeless on the other side. He knew that he had no ghost of a chance to manage the Colt successfully under the very nose of Destry's gun, but still the fighting fury ruled him for a breathing space. Then it passed and left him cold, very cold—trembling with the chill of realization that had struck through his mind.

He stood up, his empty hands dangling uselessly at his sides, his gaunt face as fixed as stone.

"It ain't murder," he said with perfect self-control. "It's your right. But tell 'em, when the time comes for the talkin', that I didn't go at you two for one, like the Ogdens, and that I didn't run, like Wendell, nor play the sneak, like Clyde Orrin, nor come at you in the dark, like Sam Warren. Do me right, Harry. Now turn loose and be damned to you!"

"If you was to of been told by me, you wouldn't of said more that I'd like to say myself," declared Destry. "But I ain't playin' my own game, or you'd be lookin' at the sky now, old son, and not seein' the pretty sunset. Stand still. I'm gunna have to tie up that—did it nick you deep?"

"Through the shoulder—that's all," said Lefty.

"Lemme see."

Lefty sat on a rock, while his conqueror, in the ruddy but uncertain light of the sunset, sliced away the sleeve of his coat and examined the wound.

"It went clean through," said he. "Feel as though the bone was smashed, Lefty?"

"There ain't no feelin'."

"Try this!"

He grasped the dangling arm and slowly worked it around, listening closely for the grinding of the broken edges of bone, while Lefty cursed steadily through his teeth, but endured.

"The bone's safe," said Destry. "I'm glad of that. I'll save you whole and sound for——"

He stopped the sentence in its midst.

"For the next time?" completed Lefty. "I'm ready for you any day or time, young feller. I would of got you plenty today, only you had the break of takin' me unexpected from the side. Which I don't mind telling you that I nigh dusted you that time, Harry!"

The familiar sneer of ferocity and contempt was on his face as he spoke.

"You talk fine; you talk like a teacher," said Destry. "Now shut up while I work on you."

With dust he clotted the blood; with strips of his own under and outer shirt, he bound up the wound and fastened the arm tight, from shoulder to elbow, against the side of his victim. All of this, Lefty endured in perfect silence, though the sweat dripped steadily from his chin.

It was utterly dark when the last knot was tied.

"Now," said Destry, "you ornery, low-lifed son of mis'ry, did you rob the Fitzgerald store?"

"Are you doin' errand boy work for the sheriff?"

"Which I ask you a question, which you ask me another. Does that make sense?"

"They's a wallet in my coat," said the prisoner. "You can look in that."

"They is striped skunks and spotted polecats," said Destry, "and you're both if you think that I handle another gent's private wallet."

"The mail—that's different, eh?"

"You fool," said Destry, "if you'd had a right to run me up, d'you think that I'd ever be here on your trail this minute? D'you think I can't take my medicine as well as the next man? I ask you again: Did you grab the coin from Fitzgerald's store?"

"Suppose I did?"

"Then why didn't you clean out the till?"

"That's my business. I needed some change. I didn't want to harm Fitzgerald none. He's white."

"You lie!" persisted Destry. "You wanted a couple hundred so bad that it looked to you like a million. You grabbed what you needed and the rest didn't matter. You wasn't thinkin' about Fitzgerald, but about your own hide!"

"Go on," said the other. "You act like you know!"

"You was sneakin' out of town," said Destry quietly, "because you'd heard about Sam Warren's bad luck, and about me headin' back for Wham. And when you heard that, you figgered on the railroad. You were scared out of Wham, son, and it was me that scared you!"

"That's the grandpa of all lies I ever heard!"

"Lefty, it's the straight! By the look of the case I knew that him that grabbed that money was pretty much on the wing; I figgered that the railroad was where he was headin' for, with enough money to see him out. He only stopped at Fitzgerald's for a ticket, as you might say, and havin' that, he breezed along. Look me in the eye, Lefty, and—"

But though the darkness might have helped Lefty, for some reason he was unable to raise his head, which had fallen on his chest.

"A peer!" said Destry bitterly. "One of the twelve peers! Peer of a gray cat and a yaller hound! I was aimin' to be sorry for you, Lefty, and I was aimin' to figger a way to keep you out of jail, but there's where you b'long, and there's where I'm takin' you! Half of 'em are off the list. But it's still six to one, and I've an idea that the rest of 'em are gunna play their hand together, and close to the chest!"

23

SLOWLY they worked back through the mountains. The way was long, and the wounded man had to have rest and sleep and food. Destry was guard, nurse, and cook for his companion, and silent in all three occupations; and sometimes as Lefty Turnbull lay in the shade, setting his teeth against the pain in his wound, he would feel a slight chill run through him, and then he dared not glance at Destry, for he knew that the latter would be watching him with cold, ominous eyes which it had grown impossible for Lefty to meet.

Savage hate, contempt, bitter disappointment were the iron in the heart of Destry now; and once Lefty strove to banter with him on the subject.

"Now, look here!" he said to his captor. "There's only two dead. There's Wendell scared stiff and driven away from home; there's Jud Ogden cripple, but livin'; there's Clyde Orrin shamed in front of everybody, but livin' too. Why should you pick me out for a killin', Harry? Why should it bust your heart that I'm gunna be sent up to the pen for a dozen years, maybe? Ain't that enough?"

"Why, man," said Destry, "they's some folks that I'd hate to send behind the bars for a dozen days—if I could pick the dozen! But one like you— you'll be at home up yonder. They make trusties out of your kind of a man, and set 'em to spyin' and playin' stool-pidgeon. You might even get promoted to shine the warden's boots, or play catch with his little boy. Prison ain't gunna mean much to you, but the sheriff's tied my hands, and I've had to do his dirty work and leave my own work slip by!"

After that, Lefty did not pursue the subject for most obvious reasons, and so they worked gradually on their way, avoiding all traveled trails, until in the dusk of the next day they came out from the woods upon the shoulder of the mountain overhanging Wham.

There was still light to blink rosily on the windows toward the west, and to show the coiling arms of dust which enwrapped the town; to show also the trailing smoke that traveled up the opposite slopes towards the mines of the Crystal Range.

"You don't look happy," suggested Lefty, staring aside at his companion.

And Destry said gloomily: "They've got together by this time. They scattered when they heard of me comin' back; they joined again when they heard I was tame; they ran again when they seen I wasn't so safe. And now that I've worked down a few of 'em, they'll gather once more!"

"And you're scared, Harry?" asked the other, very curiously, as though he really felt that this was an emotion about which Destry could know nothing.

"Scared to death, pretty near," replied Destry sourly. "Who wouldn't be? What's the old yarn about the six sticks in one bundle, and apart? They're down there plannin' and workin' together. Six rats, cornered, back up agin the wall, poison as rattlesnakes, they're hatin' me so hard! And him—the one that's leadin'—he's the one that I'd like to find!"

"What one?" asked Lefty.

"Him that runs the party for the rest of you!" said Destry fiercely. "Who sent Jose Vedres with the letter to Orrin? That's what I wanta know! Lefty, if you'll tell me that, maybe I'll be able to wangle you away from the sheriff.

I promised to turn you in to him as deputy. What hinders me tearin' the badge off right after and takin' you away agin?"

"For the name of who?" shouted Lefty, irritated by this hope, dangled under his nose. "Who is it?"

"You don't know?" asked Destry, more curious than before. "Does he work in the dark even with you? No wonder that I can't find him out! I tell you, old son, that the thought of him scares me more and more. It wasn't either of the Ogdens, or Orrin, or Wendell, or you, or Warren. Who's left? There's little Clifton. Looks like his forehead is too narrow to hold such ideas. There's Henry Cleeves that knows more about machinery than men. Bud Williams would be fine if it was only fightin' with his hands that he had to do, and Bud Truckman and Bull Hewitt are both too slow to think twice standin' in the same place. They's Phil Barker left of the lot. It might be that they's somethin' more than his jokes about him, but I ain't so sure. Lefty, if I could lean on you for that information, I'd sure pay you back! I'd wipe out the score agin you, and be in your debt for the bullet that snagged you! Who's him that stands behind the show and tells the others what to do? I gotta get him, or I've got nothin'.'"

This speech he delivered in a murmuring voice, for he was thinking aloud, rather than addressing his companion, but when Lefty heard the gist of the words, he was forced to shake his head.

"I dunno who it could be—not nobody!" he said. "You been imaginin' all of this here direction and deep thinkin'!"

"Is rats hard to smell in an old house?" asked Destry.

"I reckon not!"

"I've smelled a rat, and a big one!" said Destry. "Now it's dark enough for us to get down the hill!"

They went down to the rear of the village, and there they moved cautiously, with Destry directing the way, until they came in behind the house of the sheriff.

They could look readily through the lighted kitchen window, and see fat Mrs. Slater washing supper dishes; rounding to the side, they observed Ding Slater himself sitting on the screen porch with his feet in carpet slippers, a newspaper spread out in his hands, and a pipe between his teeth.

"If the crooks hate him, why don't they come and murder him on a night like this?" suggested Destry.

"Because birds don't come nigh to snakes if they can help it," replied Lefty readily. "Harry—whatever I done—the minute you walk me onto that veranda, I'm in hell! I voted with the rest of 'em on that jury——"

"Are you gunna beg like a cur in the wind up?" he asked scornfully.

"No," said the other. "I'm damned if I will. Shall I walk first?"

"Yeah. Go in first."

Destry marched Lefty up the front steps in this fashion, and through the screened door until he was confronting the sheriff. Ding Slater folded the paper in his lap.

"Hello," said the sheriff. "You need a doctor, and not Ding Slater, Lefty. Who's that with you?"

"Me," said Destry.

At his voice, the sheriff leaped to his feet like a boy.

"It ain't Lefty that raked out the till for Fitzgerald!" he exclaimed. "Lefty ain't cut small enough to do that sort of a job!"

Destry threw a wallet on the table beside the sheriff's chair.

"He says the coin is in this. I dunno. I leave it to you to look for it. But here he is. Ding, you knew before I started out that he'd done that job!"

"Confound you, Harry. How should I know?"

"You sent me out to keep me from drillin' him, which is what's comin' to him. Ding, you did that on purpose."

"If I'd knowed who done the job, would I of asked help from any man?" exclaimed the sheriff. "Harry, they's times when you talk like a young fool. But——"

"Take this," said Destry. "I've done enough dirty work for you. I've mopped up your floor once, and that's enough. It'll take me years to wear the stain off of my hands!"

He flung the badge of deputyship on the table and turned on his heel.

"But Harry—Harry!" called the sheriff.

Destry was already gone.

He passed back to the place where he had left the mare tethered and, taking her by the reins, led her slowly past the fence of the rear yards of Wham, until he came to the place of Chester Bent.

Once more he left the mare at a distance, and approaching the house with caution, he slipped around the side of it and came to the lighted front window. He caught the sill, and, drawing himself up, saw Bent himself inside his library, reading, or seeming to read; but every now and then the glance of Bent rose from the book and was fixed in solemn reflection upon the wall.

The front door was not far away, but Destry had several reasons, one better than another, for not going around to it. Instead, he swung himself up on his hands, sat on the sill, and turned into the room. A quick side step removed him from the lighted square of the window and he stood against the wall rolling a cigarette.

All of this had been accomplished so softly that Bent had not lifted his eyes from the big book which was unfolded in his lap, and Destry waited before scratching his match, until he had made sure that his friend was not actually reading, but was immersed in his own thoughts. For though he fingered the edge of the page for some time, he never raised and turned it. At last, Destry struck the match. The explosion of the head sounded wonderfully loud in the room; it sent a shock through Bent like the explosion of a revolver.

But he did not leap up to his feet. Instead, instantly mastering himself, he leaned forward a little in his chair and turned his head toward the intruder.

Then: "Harry!" he said, and laughed with relief.

Destry went to the big library table and sat on the edge of it, swinging one slender foot while he eyed his companion.

"Why the window, Harry?" asked the other.

"A man ain't like a hoss," said Destry. "He gets mighty tired of walkin' through the same gate into the same pasture. So I come in tonight over the bars."

"Into the same old pasture, though. Eh, boy?"

"No," said Destry. "I've found somethin' new to think about. I've found it since I came in here!"

"What is it?"

"A thing I better not talk to you about," said Harry.

The other looked down at the floor, then tapped his fingers lightly on the face of his book. As he looked up once more, Destry said: "Them wrinkles in the back of your neck, and that sleekness all over you, Chet, is it fat or muscle?"

"Muscle? What do I do to get muscle?" asked Bent. "I'm no athlete, Harry. You know that."

"Some men are born strong and stay strong," said Destry. "But that ain't what I was thinkin' about."

"What was it, Harry?"

"I was rememberin' back to a time when a strange boy come to school. He was not very big, but he looked thick and strong and fast. I was scared of him from the first glance. And for a month I dodged him till one day as I went home after school I came up sudden behind him and seen his eyes open big as I went by. By that, I knew he was as scared of me as I was of him; and so we fought it out right pronto!"

"And you won, eh?"

"I disremember, but——"

"Am I afraid of you, Harry?"

The other thought, then shook his head.

"Of the whole bunch," said Destry slowly, "I reckon that you're the only man that ain't afraid of anything above the ground or under it!"

24

IT seemed that this compliment was not altogether pleasing to Bent, for he waved it hurriedly aside and said: "I'm pretty soft. I always was!"

"Some of the soft colts make the hard hosses," observed Destry. "You've growed up, old timer. But I was thinkin' as I stood agin the wall that you ain't everything that I thought you was."

"Maybe not, Harry. You've had pretty high ideas about me."

"Why the book, when you don't read it?" asked Destry.

At this, Bent took his eyes definitely from his own thoughts and stared fixedly at Destry. Then he pointed to the window shade behind his head.

"Fake?" said Destry, his lips compressing after he spoke.

"Fake," said Bent frankly.

"I'm mighty sorry to hear it."

"I knew you would be. But there's the truth. I can't lie to you, Harry." The latter sighed.

"To make 'em think that you're in here studyin'?"

"Mostly that. I'm ambitious. I want the respect of other people. The fact is, Harry, that when I've finished a day at my office, I'm so fagged that I can't use my head for much else. I like to be alone and think things over. That's the way of it! Well, I got into the habit of sitting here; then I heard people talking about my late hours and all that sort of thing, so I rigged up the sham, and there you are!"

Destry nodded.

"I can follow that," he said. "But I'd rather——"

He paused.

"You'd rather that I'd rob a bank than do this?"

"Pretty near, I think!"

"You're right," answered the other. "Any crime's better if it takes courage to do it! You'll never think much of me after this, Harry! "

"I'll like you better, because you told me the straight of it. I suppose I'll like you better for this than if you was to lay down your life for me!"

He went suddenly to Bent and laid a hand on his shoulder.

"Sometimes," he said gravely, "I pretty nigh believe in a God. Things are so balanced! My friends turned out crooks and traitors to me; the woman I loved, she turned me down the first chance; but I've got one friend that balances everything. You, Chet."

He stopped abruptly and snapped his fingers.

"I'm going up to bed. It's my last night here, I reckon."

"Why the last night? Why d'you say that, old timer?"

"I can feel in my bones that they're close to me. Six of 'em are left."

"I thought it was seven?"

"I brought in Lefty, this evenin'. That's where I been, on his trail. Old Ding Slater put me on the job, and I had to bring him back and turn him over."

"Tell me about it! Lefty gone? He's worth two, to have out of the way!"

"I don't wanta talk. You'll hear people spin the yarn tomorrow. Good night, Chet."

"Good night, old man. Only—I should think that you'd feel safe now! In my own house!"

"Of course you'd think that. But you ain't got eyes for every door—or every window!"

He smiled and pointed at the one through which he had entered. Then he left the room.

The instant he was in the comparative dimness of the hallway, his manner changed to that of the hunted animal. Swiftly and lightly he walked, and paused now and again to listen, hearing the stir of voices at the rear of the house, and then the whir of the big clock which stood at the landing, followed by the single chime for the half hour.

Then he went up the stairs, treading close to the wall where the boards were less apt to creak under his weight. So he went up to the attic floor where his room was, but he did not turn in at the door. Instead, he paused there for a moment and listened intently.

There was not a sound from the interior.

Yet still he did not enter, but, turning the knob of the door by infinitesimally small degrees, he pushed it a fraction of an inch past the catch, then allowed the knob to turn back. He drew back, and a moment later a draft caused the freed door to sway open a few inches.

There was no movement within the bedroom. Yet still he lingered, until the current of air had pushed the door wide. Drawn far back into a corner of the corridor, he still waited with an inhuman patience. The dark was thick, yet he could make out the glimmering panel of the door's frame.

Finally, out of this issued a shadow, and another, and two more behind. They stood there for a moment, and then slipped down the hall. Close to Destry, the leader paused and held out his arms to stop the others.

"We're chucking a chance in a lifetime!" said he.

"I've had enough," replied another. "I can't stand it. When the damn door opens itself—that's too ghostly for me!"

"It was only the wind, you fool!"

"I don't care what it was. I've got enough. I'm going to leave. The rest of you do what you want!"

"Bud, will you stay on with me?"

"Where?"

"Back in that room, of course! He's bound to come there. He seen the sheriff, and after that, he'll come here. Likely talkin' with Bent downstairs, right now!"

"I'll tell you," answered Bud, "I wouldn't mind waitin', but not in that room, after the ghost has got into it!"

"Ghost, you jackass!"

"You're tellin' me that the wind opened the door. Sure it did. And it blew the ghost in on us!"

"Bud, I don't believe you mean what you say. I won't believe that! Ghost talk out of you!"

"A wind," said Bud, "that's able to turn the knob of a door, can blow in a ghost, too!"

"You fool, of course the latch wasn't caught!"

"Anyway, I've had enough."

They went down the stairs. Noiselessly as Destry had ascended, so noiselessly did the four go down, and Destry gripped the naked revolver which he held, tempted to fire on them from behind. In spite of the darkness, he could not have missed them!

However, he let them go, still kneeling on the hall carpet and listening.

He thought he heard the opening of a window, but even this was managed so dexterously that he could not be sure. It was only after several moments that he was sure that the house no longer held that danger for him, and he started down to tell Chester Bent about what he had seen and heard.

However, after a moment of reflection he changed his mind. There was nothing that Bent could do except feel alarm and disgust at his inability to protect a guest. The men were gone; Bent could not overtake them in the dark; and since one attempt had been planned for this night, it was not likely that there would be another before morning.

So Destry went into the bedroom, threw himself wearily on the bed, and, without even taking off his clothes or locking the door, went instantly to sleep.

When he wakened, it was not yet dawn. He rose quickly, washed his face and hands, and, sitting down by lamplight at the table, he wrote hastily:

> Dear Chet,
>
> This is to say good-by for a time. I'm going to leave Wham, and even leave you.
>
> I'm traveling light, and leave a good deal of stuff behind me. You might let it stay in this room. It will make other folks, probably, think that I'm coming back here. And the more I can confuse the others, the luckier it will be for me.
>
> They're hot after me, Chet. There were four men waiting for me in my room, last night when I came upstairs. I managed to get them out without trouble, but the next time won't be so easy.
>
> So long, old fellow. You certainly been the top of the world to me.
>
> I'm not thanking you for what you've done. But I'll tell you that you're the man who makes life worth while for me.
>
> HARRY.

This message he thrust under Bent's door, and hurried away into the dark of the morning.

25

THE emotions of Chester Bent were not at all what Destry would have imagined. For when the former rose in the morning and found the note which had been pushed under the edge of his door, his face puckered savagely, and one hand balled into a fist.

He dressed hurriedly and went to the house of James Clifton. It was a little shack that stood almost on the very street, built by the father, and now occupied by his talented son, who was a serious investigator of the mines and therefore, according to the public, a "lucky" investor.

Chester Bent walked swiftly enough to feel his leg muscles stretching, and every step he took restored his confidence, though it did not diminish his irritation. Early as it was, there were already people on the street, and, of the dozen he passed, he knew the face and name of every one. Moreover, each of them had a special smile, a special wave of the hand for him; each looked as though he gladly would pause for conversation. But Bent went quickly by. He knew his own power in that town, however, from the looks he had seen in the faces of the pedestrians, and he was smiling to himself when he came to Clifton's house.

He found the proprietor in his small kitchen, with the smoke from frying ham ascending into his face. Jimmy Clifton turned a face as yellow as a Chinaman's toward his guest. He was like a Chinaman in other ways, for he had a froglike face, with a little awkward body beneath it. Some said that Jimmy Clifton had been through the fire when he was an infant, thereby accounting for the quality and color of his skin, which looked like loosely stretched parchment over the bones.

In spite of his peculiarities, however, Clifton was not really an ugly man so much as a strange one. He had a cordial manner which made him many friends, and he showed it now as he advanced to meet Bent and shook him warmly by the hand, hoping that he would join him at a breakfast which was ample for two.

But Bent refused. His irritation increased and his good humor lessened as he accompanied his host into the next room, which served for dining room, guest room, and living room in the shack. There they sat down, and, as Clifton began to eat, Bent observed:

"Suppose that your father had been tangled up in a row like this? How long would he have hesitated? He would have stayed there in Destry's room until morning. For that matter, he would have stayed there alone, too, and waited until he was in bed!"

He pointed, as if for verification to a long string of grizzly claws which hung across the wall from one side to the other. Old Clifton had killed the animals whose claws were represented there, and Indianlike he had saved the mementoes. There was a tale that he actually had engaged one of the great brutes in a cave and had killed it with a knife thrust. Without imputations upon the courage of little Jimmy Clifton, it was plain that he was a lame descendant of such a hero.

That young man now regarded the sinister decoration on the wall as he tackled his breakfast. The greatest peculiarity of Jimmy Clifton was that he was never perturbed, by words or deeds.

Then he said in answer: "I don't know. The old man was a pretty tough fellow, but I don't know about him staying alone in the same room with Destry. I'll tell you this, though. I tried to get the rest of 'em to stay with me!"

"Bah!" exploded Chester Bent. "Tell me the truth, Jimmy! You were all of you in a blue funk!"

"I was scared, sure," said Clifton readily, "but not in a funk. I would have seen it through, but not alone. I wasn't up to that. You don't know what happened. The infernal latch of the door hadn't caught, and all at once a draft must have hit it, though there was no whistle of wind around the house. But suddenly the door sagged; then it opened, and a whisper of air fanned through the room. A pretty ghostly business!"

"What did you do? When was it that this happened?"

"About ten, I suppose!"

"I'll tell you who the ghost was! It was Destry. He went up to bed at exactly ten, I think!"

"Hello! You mean that he opened the door and stood there waiting for us?"

"Of course he was there in the hall, laughing at four scared heroes as they sneaked off. I was waiting downstairs, and waiting and waiting to hear gunshots. Then I thought that maybe you'd closed in on him and done it with knives. But I decided there wasn't enough blood in you all for that sort of work!"

"Did you?" asked the other blandly.

"I did! And now you've foozled the entire thing, and Destry's gone. He left me a note. Confound it, Jimmy, you've thrown away a golden opportunity!"

The other nodded.

"It was a great chance," he said. "Of course I didn't expect that the boys would get such a chill at the last minute. They were game enough for men, but not for ghosts, Chet. Not for that! They light-footed it out of the room, and they wouldn't come back. That's all there was to it."

"But to think!" groaned Bent. "Four of you—in the dark—and Destry in your hands!"

"Tell me," said Clifton. "What makes you hate Destry so like the devil?"

"I'll tell you, Jimmy, that you'd never understand why I hate him so completely. But let that go. The main point is that I see nothing will ever be done with him, no matter how many opportunities I give him, until I take up the work with my own hands!"

"Is it the girl?" asked Clifton. "Is she still fond of him? With Destry out of the way, d'you think that you could have her?"

"Jimmy," said the other darkly, "that's a confounded impertinence that I can't take even from you!"

The other waved his hand.

"Let it go. I'm sorry. Only, we know each other so well, old fellow, that I thought I could talk out to you!"

Bent shrugged his shoulders, but he added at once: "I'm sorry I lost my temper. You can see this is a blow to me. Now the bird's escaped out of my hand, and God knows how I'll get a string on him again! It's a blow to the rest of you, also! He's snagged six; the six who remain are apt to do a little sweating now!"

"I'm sweating, for one," said Clifton.

"Then we'll have to put our heads together and try again. There's another thing. When you got them into my house, you didn't have to let them guess that I was with you?"

"Not a bit," said Clifton. "The boys thought you'd be almost as dangerous to them as Destry!"

"I'm glad that you've kept me sheltered! A whisper of the truth would bring Destry down on me like seven devils!"

"Of course. No fear of that. I've kept a closed mouth about you. And Destry will never know! People are a little afraid to be too curious about you, anyway, Chet."

"Afraid? Of me? That's a joke!"

"Is it? I don't know," replied Clifton. "There are some who say that there's an iron fist under Bent's soft hand. I'm a little afraid of you myself, old son! Or else I'd have talked before about something that I want to know!"

"What's that?"

"The notes are due today, Chet."

"Hello! Those notes? But not the grace, Jimmy!"

"The grace, too! The time's up today."

"Forgot all about 'em," said Bent, rising. "But I'll have the money for you in a day or two."

"Are you sure?"

"Of course I'm sure!"

"I need it, pretty badly," said Clifton.

"Are you pinched?"

"Yes."

"Drop over to my house this evening, will you, and I'll give you a check?"

"Thanks," said Clifton. "I'll do that!"

And Chester Bent departed with a little haste that was not thrown away on the observant eye of the smaller man.

Back in his office, Mr. Bent sat for a long time at his desk, considering ways and means. His secretary, after one wise and sour look at him, left him strictly alone.

It was not until the mid-morning that he ventured out on the street. Then he went straight to the bank and found the president in, a rosy, plump man of fifty, whose refusals were always so masked and decorated beneath his smile that most of their sting was taken away.

He wanted to know what he could do for Bent, and the latter said instantly: "I have some deals coming up. I need twelve thousand. Can you let me have it?"

The president's eye grew rather blank in spite of his smile. Then he said with the Western frankness which invades even the banking world:

"Bent, this is one of the times that I'm stumped. Look here. You're a rising man in this town. You own property in mines. You own a good deal of real estate—a lot of it, in fact. You're what people consider a rich man. That's the opinion I have of you, myself."

"Thanks," said Bent, "but——?"

"There is another side to it, too. That's this. You're young. You've made a quick success, out of nothing, apparently. You've rolled a big load right up the hill. But one can't be so sure that you're at the top of it!"

"Go," encouraged Bent. "I like to have frankness, of course."

"You'll get that from me. On the one hand, I don't want to antagonize a man whose patronage will probably mean a lot to this bank. Personally I think you're all right. But a banker can't let personalities enter too far into his business dealings."

"I understand that. But even banking has to be a gamble."

"Yes. That's true, but with as narrow a margin of failure and chance as possible. Now, then, Bent, as I say, you seem to have gained almost the top of the hill, rolling up a big ball before you. How you made your start, I don't know. But six years ago you seemed suddenly to come into your own. You extended in all directions. You got your hands on property. Almost like a man who had come into a legacy—"

The glance of Bent strayed a little uneasily out the window.

"You've done wonderfully well, but suppose that several things happened. Most of your property you don't own outright. You have a lot of mortgages. Convenient things—they leave an operator with his hands free for more speculation. At the same time, they're dangerous poison. Here you are, in need of twelve thousand. On the face of it, it's not a large sum. But suppose, Bent, that Wham went bust? It's a quick boom town; it may be a skeleton in another year. There's a new town opening up on the other side of the Crystal Mountains. Seems to me to be better placed than this. Perhaps it'll kill us. That would wipe out your real estate holdings in Wham at a stroke and fill your hands with heavy cash debts—because you haven't bought in at the bottom of the market by any means! As a matter of fact, you've been pretty high in it! I suggest this to you, not because I haven't confidence in Wham, but because I'm trying to explain to you why I don't think it would be good banking to lend you twelve thousand dollars."

"Bad policy?"

"It might be the best policy in the world, Bent. It might secure your faith in us and we'd grow as you grow in the world. But on the other hand there's one chance in ten that you might break, and if you break it would be a serious loss for us. I don't want to take that ten per cent chance. I don't feel justified in doing so!"

"That's business luck," he said. "I don't blame you a bit. And I'll manage this all right. Only a temporary need, old man."

He went out onto the street, and walked down it, still smiling a little, and envious glances followed his contented face. But as he went on he was seeing such a picture as would not have pleased most men, and which did not please Bent himself—a dead man was stretched before him, and the dead man wore the face of Jimmy Clifton.

26

BACK at his office once more, his secretary, Sarah Gann, came in to tell him that a visitor was there for him.

"Send him away," said Bent irritably. "I don't wanta see him, no matter who it is."

"A boy," said Sarah Gann.

"Well, I've told you what to do with him."

"He's come for something about Destry," said she, looking back as she reached the door.

"Destry? Then send him in!"

A faint grimace that might have been triumph appeared on her lips as she went out, and presently at the door appeared as ragged a boy as Bent ever had seen. He had on a coat that reached to his knees, the two side pockets bulging. His feet were without shoes and apparently as hard as sole leather. All his clothing was that of a man, abbreviated and tattered. Yet he gave an impression of a swift, muscular young body beneath those drapings.

"You carrying bombs in those pockets?" asked Bent, leaning a little forward in his chair and resting his elbows on the edge of his desk.

For every man carries within himself a sympathy for free boyhood in which he can plunge and be lost; and Bent had reasons for wishing to be freed from the facts of the moment.

"I got pecan nuts in this pocket," said the youngster.

He was a little frightened, a little awestricken, but a fine straightness of regard was in his eyes.

"You like 'em?"

"They don't weigh much, and they last a long time," said the boy.

He took out a chamois bag and, opening it, revealed a quantity of kernels.

"The other pocket's pretty full, too, eh?"

"Toothbrush," said the boy, and, unconsciously smiling a little, Bent had a glimpse of snowy teeth. "Ma got me plumb in the habit," he apologized. "Then they's a change of socks, and a bandana, and a chunk of soap."

"You're fixed for traveling," declared Bent.

"Yeah. I done a hundred and ten mile."

"In how long?"

"Three days."

"Mountains?"

"Yeah."

"That's good time."

"My feet ain't weighed down with shoes, none."

"I don't see a hat, though."

A battered wisp of straw was produced from behind his back.

"It don't look very much," said the boy, "but it sure sheds rain pretty good, account of it havin' so much hog grease on it."

"Who are you, son?"

"Name of Willie Thornton, sir."

"And what brought you here?"

"Destry."

The man started from his leisurely posture, his leisurely thoughts.

"Destry! What's he to you?"

"He said he wanted to see me agin; so I come to him. Home didn't seem much after he been there. Nobody knows where he is unless you can show me the way. They say you're his best friend."

"I'm his friend, Willie. Tell me. Are you the boy who stood by him when Sam Warren tackled him one night?"

"I was around," said Willie with diffidence.

"Is that where you got the bump on the side of your head?"

"It might of been. I got whacked that night," said Willie.

Bent suddenly realized that something was to be done. He left his chair with a start and held out his hand.

"I'm mighty glad to see you, mighty glad!" he said. "So will Destry be when you show up. He's talked a good deal about you. D'you want to start for him now?"

"I'd like that pretty well, sir."

"You go home to my house, first of all. You need a couple of good meals under your belt and a sleep in an honest bed. Where have you turned in the last few nights?"

"I found a farm once and made a bed of boughs the next night. It was tolerable cold, though."

"I'll bet it was. Ask your way to my house, up at the end of the street. Wait a moment. Take this!"

He scribbled a note on a piece of paper.

"Give that to any one at the house; they'll take care of you till I come home, and if they don't treat you right, you tell me about it, Willie."

Willie shifted from one foot to another.

"If I could find out the trail to Mr. Destry—" he began.

"You'll have that trail told you, Willie. There's no hurry about that. In the meantime, I want to get to know you better. Remember that Destry's my best friend, and I want to know you for his sake. Run along, Willie; I'll be home before very long."

He took Willie to the door, patted his shoulder, and dismissed him; but the last upward flashes of Willie's keen gray eyes unsettled Bent a little. The wolf on the trail is a sleepy thing, and the wildcat is totally unobservant, compared with the eye of a young boy; and Bent knew that he had been searched to the soul and found not altogether such a person as the best friend of the great Destry should be.

Thinking of that, he turned back gloomily into his office. There appeared to be in Destry a force which frightened most people, but which attracted a few with an unexplainable power. Here was this lad, whose eyes grew larger and whose voice changed when he mentioned the great man; and there was Charlie Dangerfield who loved Destry still, as he very well knew. What was there lacking in himself that he failed to inspire such emotion in others? He had ten thousand acquaintances; but no man even called himself a near and dear friend to Chester Bent—no man except him whose death he desired above all things! The irony of this made Bent laugh a little, and the laughter restored his spirits.

So he went on to the end of the day, until the unwelcome time came when he must go home and there face Jimmy Clifton. But he put that time off, ate at a small restaurant across the street wedged in at a lunch counter between a pair of huge shouldered cowpunchers and finally, after dark, went home.

He found Jimmy Clifton in the library, deep in one of the books which he himself pretended to read, and the little man put it aside almost reluctantly, blinking his odd round, flat eyes as he did so.

"You're late, Chet," he observed, "but don't say you're sorry. I've had a good time. I brought the notes over with me. I'll cancel 'em for your check."

The ease with which the visitor got to the heart of the business upset Bent in spite of the fact that he was hardening himself for more or less such a scene. But the matter of fact swiftness of Clifton disturbed him. He looked at the little sheaf of papers in the hand of the smaller man and, with all his heart, hungrily, he wished to have them. Or to touch them with the flame of a match, and let the fire work for one second.

Instead, he had to say: "I want to talk to you a minute about those notes, Jimmy. Of course you can have the money, but as a matter of fact——"

Clifton shook his head.

"Don't start it, old son," he said. "Talk won't help. If you have the money in the bank, I'll take your check now. If you haven't money in the bank,

I'll take it dated ahead. I don't want to be short, but I want to keep us from embarrassing one another."

"Of course," said Bent. "Of course."

But all of his wiles and his prepared persuasiveness shriveled up and became dead leaves in his hand. He could only say slowly: "It looks as if you think I'm not sound, Jimmy."

"Chet," said the other, "in a business way, it's pretty doggone hard, I think, to have to moralize about deals that have been made. When you wanted that money, I gave it to you, because I thought you were a good business man, not because you were my friend. Now the money's due with interest. I want it back, not because you're an enemy, but because the money's due!"

"But speaking only in a business sense——"

Bent paused for a reply and got one straight from the shoulder.

"In a business sense, then, I think that you've been flyin' a hawk with a hen's wings. Or to put it in another way, I think that you're too high up in the air, and that you're going to have a fall. Mind you, there's no reproach to you, Chet. I like you fine. But I think you've extended yourself too much. If Wham stopped booming tomorrow, I don't think you could pay sixty cents on the dollar the next day! That sounds hard, but I want to be straight and open with you. Sorry as the devil if I hurt your feelings. But I want my money now."

Bent hesitated a little longer. All day he had seen the necessity of the thing for which he was now nerving himself, but still he needed a breathing space.

"It hits me hard, Jimmy, as I don't mind letting you see. However, to take a weight off your mind, I can pay you in full at once. But I'm going to take a walk with you—it's too hot in the room here—and see if I can't think up some good business reason for you to change your mind."

"All right," said Clifton. "I've sounded pretty harsh, I know."

"Not a bit, I like to hear business from a business man."

He went to the door, saying that he would be back in a moment, and went up the stairs to Destry's vacant room.

This he entered, lighted the lamp, and closed the door.

A dozen articles that belonged to the other were scattered here and there—an old quirt, for instance, lay on the bureau, a battered hat hung in the closet, in the top bureau drawer there was a hunting knife in a rawhide case, rudely ornamented, in the Indian style of decoration.

This was what he wanted. He took it out, unsheathed it, and tried the edge with his thumb. As he had known beforehand, so it was—sharp as a razor. Of its own weight, well nigh, it would bury itself to the hilt in living flesh.

He put the knife in his pocket and was starting for the door when distinctly he heard something stir. He whirled and ran back into the room, the naked knife instantly in his hand, but as he turned he heard a sound again, of the shutter outside, moved by the wind, and told himself that this was the same.

Yet he was still not at ease as he went down the stairs, and still he felt a weight curiously cold in his heart, as though some human eye had observed him taking the knife of Destry from the drawer.

27

"WE'LL take the short cut home," said Clifton, as they walked out of the house together.

Bent lingered on the steps, as though enjoying the evening; for it was just between the last of the sunset and the total dark of the night when the shadows had blanketed up the glare and the dust of the day, when the ground had yielded up its first radiation of heat, and the night wind began to fan cool through the trees and enter windows that yawned for it. The stars were coming out dimly, twinkling, seeming to advance toward the earth. The very sounds of the day were altered. The wheels and wagon beds of huge freighters no longer rattled and groaned in the streets, with a jingling of chains and hoarse shouts from the teamsters. Hammers that had clanged in the smithies, and thudded in the houses which were building nearby, were now silenced, as was the long, mournful scream of the saws in the lumber yard. Instead, they could hear children playing in the streets, their joyful yells of laughter suddenly blotted out as they turned corners, and coming into ken again, musical with distance; choruses of dogs suddenly began and ended, except for one sullen guardian who barked on the edge of the horizon, a mere pulse of sound.

Now Bent stood on the front steps and seemed to drink in these sights and noises with a smile on his face, while Clifton said quietly, as though ashamed to break in on him:

"Hate to hurry you, old fellow, but I have a meeting with some people at my house, tonight, and I have some things to finish up before they come. If you don't mind, we'd better start on."

"Why the short cut?" asked Bent, stepping down beside the other.

"I don't show myself in the street more than I have to, these days. You can guess why."

"You mean Destry?"

"That's what I mean."

"I don't think he'd murder you, Jimmy. Not off hand like that!"

"Murder's not the worst thing. See what he did to Orrin!"

"Have you been dabbling in politics, too?"

"Not like Orrin, thanks. But as soon as I can wind up some affairs, I'm pulling out of this section of the country until things quiet down a little."

"Meaning by that, Destry?"

"Ay, somebody's sure to get him, just as he's gotten so many others. That's reasonable .to expect. And I'm going to advise the rest of 'em to follow my example when I see them tonight."

"They're all coming—is that the meeting?"

"That's the meeting."

"You'll be giving them a dinner, I suppose?"

"Not me. You know the old saying. A filled belly makes a blunt wit. We'll need our wits tonight."

"You will," agreed the other. "So you all meet there and talk over Destry and what to do with him? I hope he doesn't come and listen in through the window."

Clifton stopped short and raised his hand.

"Let's not talk of that demi-devil any more," said he. "We'll chat about the notes, if you wish."

But the plan which already had been forming in the mind of Bent now took a definite shape; for they were walking along narrow alleys and winding paths where no eye observed them, as it seemed, and the secure shelter of high board fences housed them on either side a great part of the time.

"I don't know about that," said Bent. "Perhaps the best way is just to give you a check and finish the business."

"You can? I'm mighty glad that you're able to, Chet. That's the best way for me, and for you too, in the long run, I daresay. I'm glad that you have the money on hand. Matter of fact, I was afraid that you didn't!"

"Were you?" said Bent. "Were you?"

He laughed, in such odd key that his companion looked quickly up into his face.

"I've got a reserve fund that I don't like to dip into. I'll use it now."

He grew bolder as the sinister irony of the statement came home to him.

"The last time I used it was six years ago! Well, here we are at your back gate, Jimmy!"

The latter raised the wire hoop and pushed the door open, as a dog rushed at them, barking furiously, but immediately began to whine and leap up at his master.

"They see with their noses, eh?" said Ciffton, pushing the dog off, but with affectionate hands.

"Well," said Bent, "I don't know but that it's the better way to see. A lot of things aren't as they seem to the eye!"

"No," said Clifton, "of course they aren't. Come on in."

He pushed open the rear door, and they passed through the kitchen and living room, into Clifton's bedroom, which had a desk in one corner and was evidently his office as well.

He lighted a lamp and hung his hat on a peg in the wall.

"Sit down here, Chet," said he. "Here's a pen and ink, if you want to make out the check at once. It may be a while before the boys come in, but I'll have to hurry you a bit. Make yourself comfortable. I'll go and put the chairs around the table in the other room."

With that, he took a stool and a chair from the bedroom and carried them into the adjoining apartment, where he quickly arranged six chairs around the table.

Bent, in the meantime, took a check book from his pocket and wrote out a check for twelve thousand dollars with the greatest of care, forming the letters with a beautiful precision.

He had finished when his host returned.

The latter scanned the check, blotted it, and nodded.

"That's finished, and a good job," he said. "If I told you what a weight was off my mind, you'd be surprised. At the same time, now that the thing's ended and I know you could pay, I'm sorry that I pressed you so hard."

"Business is business," said Bent, and smiled in an odd way at the other. "You have to have what's coming to you."

"You're a lucky fellow to have a reserve fund out of which you can dip such a bucketful as this!"

Bent bit his lip. The thing for him to do, he understood, was to finish what he had in mind as quickly as possible; and yet all that was evil in him rose up from his heart to his brain and urged him to torture his victim before the stroke. So he lingered, the smile still on his lips.

Clifton smiled in turn, but hesitantly, as one not following the drift of his companion.

"You see how it is," said Bent. "A man needs to have something at his back?"

"Of course," said Jimmy Clifton. "A good reserve—generals plan on one in a battle, but it makes me feel that you're sounder than I thought, old man, when I hear you talk like this!"

"You thought I'm one of these fly by night investors, eh?"

"Not exactly that. I always credited you with insight and brains, but——"

"But what?"

"Caesar was ambitious," said Clifton, smiling at his own small jest.

There was a slight creaking sound, and Bent jerked about.

"What was that?" he asked. "Have they come? Have they come?"

Clifton was amazed at a sort of hard desperation that had crept into the voice of his friend.

"They? The five, you mean? No, they don't show up for a few minutes. But they'll come along. That was the wind handling the kitchen screen door, I suppose. It's in the right quarter for that, just now."

Bent turned back, with a great gasp of relief.

"Thank God!" said he.

"What's the matter, Chet?"

"I thought I was going to be interrupted," said Bent. "But now that I see I won't be, I wanted to ask you if you'd like to know the nature of my reserve?"

"Of course I would. Some good bonds, I suppose? Negotiable securities? Those are the things to have on hand!"

"Yes, but as a matter of fact my reserve is only related second-hand to money."

"What in the world is it, then?"

"A good right hand!" said Bent, still smiling.

Clifton frowned, then started a little as a possible interpretation jumped into his mind, only to be dismissed at once as a total absurdity.

"A good right hand?" he echoed, in a rather worried manner.

"That's it. A good right hand."

"With what in it?"

"Not a pen, Jimmy."

"No."

"No, but a gun, or a knife!"

Clifton looked in the same puzzled manner at Bent, trying to push into his innermost thoughts, but it was impossible now to place any other than one construction upon the fixed and baleful stare of Bent.

The man seemed to grow taller, and stiffer in his attitude. His eyes glittered, and the smile froze on his lips into an archaic grimace, such as that with which the kings of Egypt look at their people in the tombs and on the pyramids.

Jimmy Clifton was not a coward. There was hardly a braver man in all of Wham, but he could not stir in his chair as he heard the other continue:

"For instance, six years ago it looked as though I'd be disgraced and found out as a *petty* thief, and therefore I determined to become a real one, and on a big scale. So I went out and held up the express—the job that poor Destry went to prison for."

Clifton smiled wanly.

"I'm trying to see the point of the joke," he said.

"It's not a joke. That's one reason that I hate Destry, I suppose, because I've wronged him, as the poet says. Oh, no, I'm not here to tell jokes tonight, Jimmy."

"You're not?"

"No."

Clifton stood up from his chair slowly.

His eyes wandered instinctively toward the wall, from which hung weapons enough. And by that glance Bent knew that the man was helpless in his hands.

"Then what in the name of God *have* you come here for, Chet?"

"To cancel the notes, Jimmy, of course, but with a knife instead of a pen!"

28

IT is necessary to return to young Willie Thornton as he approached the big house of Bent earlier in that day and stood at last before it quite overcome with awe. It was the largest and finest dwelling house he ever had seen. It even had little wooden towers at each of the corners that faced on the main street, and those towers, it seemed to Willie, would be marvelous places for princesses to inhabit by day, and ghosts and owls by night. When he had passed the front gate and it had clanked behind him, he made sure that he had taken the first step into a fairyland.

It was hard for him to strike with the knocker at the front door. He had to linger on the front steps and look up and down the street, where a cloud of dust was enveloping a train of burros which were waddling along under great packs. This dust cloud, the burros, and the signs of the shops looked so thoroughly familiar to Willie, and so like any other of a dozen Western towns he had seen, that he recovered somewhat from his awe and was able to use the knocker.

The door was presently opened by a scowling negress, who waved him away and assured him that no dirty little beggars were wanted there. He was so overwhelmed that he barely remembered the note he carried, and then only because he was gripping it in his hand.

This he now presented, and the effect of it was instant! He was not allowed in the front door with his dusty feet, to be sure, but the cook in person issued forth and escorted him around to the rear.

There he was made to visit a pump and wash basin, with soap and a towel, but after that trying ordeal, he found himself in a trice with his legs under a kitchen table and quantities of food appearing before him.

Such food and such quantities he never had known. Ham spiced with cloves, fragrant to the core, and corn bread made with eggs and brittle with shortening, and great glasses of rich milk. This was only the beginning, to be followed by an apple pie from which only one section had been removed.

He took one piece and hesitated.

"He'p yo'se'f," said the cook.

He helped himself. Assisted by another glass of milk, he gradually put himself outside that entire pie. He felt guilty, but he also felt happy; and what is more delicious than a guilty joy?

Immediately afterward, he was sleepy, and straightway his mentor led him up a winding back stair and into a little attic room.

She shocked him into wakefulness for an instant by saying: "Right next, there, is where Mr. Destry lives, honey, if you ever heard tell of that man!"

Destry lived there!

"You lie down," he was commanded.

And the instant that he was stretched upon a bed of marvelous softness, his eyes began to close, as though they were mechanically weighted, like those of a doll. His heart beat fast with excitement and happiness at the thought of having his hero so near to him; but sleep was mightier than his joy.

The last he knew, as his head swam dizzily, was the voice of the cook saying: "Growin' tender-hearted—and to beggar boys! They ain't no tellin' how men'll change. Money to a man is like water to a desert, I declare. They begin to grow kinder!"

But the meaning of this did not enter the mind of the boy, for a great wave of sleep swept over him, and instantly he was unconscious. It was dusk when he wakened.

As he lifted his head, he saw the red rim of the horizon sketched roughly across the window, and by degrees he remembered where he was. His stomach was no longer tight; his head was clear; he was refreshed as a grown man could not have been by sleeping the clock around.

Yet his feet were on the floor and he was stretching himself muscle by muscle before he remembered that the cook had said Destry lived next door. At that, excitement made him instantly wide awake.

He slipped into the dusky corridor and tapped at the door of the adjoining room, tapped three times, with growing force, and with respectful intervals between. But there was no answer.

At last, he tried the knob, found that the door opened readily, and entered.

"Mister Destry!" he called faintly.

He had no answer.

But when he scratched a match and looked around him, the sight of battered boots and a quirt, and a rifle in a corner suddenly re-created Destry, as though the great man was there in the body.

Willie was happy and comforted.

He could have sat among those relics with a swelling heart of pride in his acquaintance with that man of destiny!

Then a qualm struck him, as he wondered whether or not the hero would care to remember him. There is nothing in the living world so proudly sensitive as a boy, but when he recalled the manner of Destry on that night of battle he was reassured. There could be nothing but honesty in such a man as that!

So thought Willie and pursued his investigations, lighting match after match. He even opened the bureau drawers. It was not that he wished to spy on the secrets of Destry, but that every sight of the possessions of that wanderer filled him with pleasure. There in the top drawer, standing tiptoe, he found the hunting knife, and took it out. There were legends about this knife, as well as the gun of Destry. Had not Pop said that Destry could throw a knife accurately a hundred feet?

Pop lied, perhaps. Alas, he had lied in other matters dealing with Destry, and perhaps about this, also. But at least, this was the hero's knife, with a small "D" cut accurately into the base of the handle.

He put it back reverently, in exactly the position he had found it; he had not dared to bare the bright blade.

He had barely pushed the drawer in when he heard a step in the hall and terror mastered him. Suppose that it was Destry, coming to his room, and suppose that a thief or a spy was found therein?

He slid into the closet and hid behind a long slicker, leaving the door a little ajar just as it had been. There he was hidden when Chester Bent entered and lighted the lamp. He saw the investigations of Bent with wonder, and with a growing fear, for there is something in the manner of a vicious man that betrays him as clearly as the manner of a stalking cat. So did that gliding furtiveness of Bent, in spite of himself, cast a light on him.

And the boy, watching, knew by an instinct that all was not well. He saw the knife taken, and, in his excitement, he stirred, and the buckle of his belt scratched against the wall behind him.

The whirl of Bent was like the turning of a tiger, as he ran back into the room, the knife now naked in his hand. For a moment he glared about him, then the shutter moved in the wind and he seemed satisfied that all was well. Still grudgingly he left that room, and the boy remained for a long moment trembling in the closet, surrounded by utter darkness.

However much he was devoted to Destry, his affection for that man was nothing compared with the terror he felt for Chester Bent! When at last he summoned the courage to leave the room, he glided down the stairs intent on only one thing—and that was to escape from this house of guessed-at horrors as quickly as possible.

He left by neither the front door, nor the back, but slid through an open window and dropped from the sill to the ground. The garden mold received the impression of his bare feet up to the ankles, and, stepping back onto the graveled path, he smoothed out the deep imprints which he had made.

He hurried on, now, crouching a little as if to make himself smaller, after the ancient instinct of the hunted, and so he came to the front corner of the house just in time to hear the voice of Bent speaking from the steps of the house.

A moment later, he saw the man he dreaded going down the front path with a smaller companion. And Willie looked after them, breathing deep and thanking God that he did not have to accompany that man of mysterious fear.

Yet it is by the perversity of our emotions that we are governed, as much as by the legitimate warnings which our instincts give us. The horse he fears is the horse the rider mounts. The man she does not understand is married by the girl. The dog who growls at him, the boy tries to pet.

And the instant that Willie told himself he must not remain near Bent, that moment he felt an inescapable longing to lurk near the man. It was something like the horrible fascination of a great height, tempting him to let go his hold and jump. He sweated in the grip of it; but as the gate clanged behind the two, Willie was down the path in pursuit.

The moment he was in action, the fear almost disappeared, and it was sheer delight, merely seasoned with danger, as he followed the two on their way. All the old joy of the hunter was running like quicksilver in the young veins of the boy, and he slipped from shrub to shrub, from tree to tree, from fence to gateway, always keeping his soundless feet on the search for twigs or dry leaves that might be in the path.

He kept step with the two he followed, so that the impact of their heavy heels might drown any sound made by his naked feet, and he could congratulate himself that they suspected nothing as they went in the back way to the house of Clifton.

He had gone far enough in his little scouting expedition, but still he was not content. Success, even in this small way, had mounted to his head, and he was keen as a hound to continue the trail, for he knew that in the pocket of Bent rested Destry's knife, as yet unused!

He determined to go on, but the dog, which had followed the master to the door of the house, bounding and whining with pleasure, now turned back, and made an additional danger. Boldness, he decided, was the better way. So he opened the gate boldly and walked straight up the rear path. His way was blocked instantly by the dog. He was a big yellow and black mongrel with a head like a mastiff's, less squarely made than the model. He came at Willie with a rush, crouching low, but as the bare feet swung steadily forward, the monster slouched guiltily, suspiciously to the side— and the road was open to the spy!

29

THE bravado which had carried the boy past the dog endured until he had reached the kitchen door, with the cold nose of the animal sniffing at his fragile heels; even there it did not desert him, but, hearing voices inside, and seeing the darkness within, he wondered if he could not slip in farther and come closer to the words.

He actually had drawn the door open when he remembered what he was doing—entering a trap quite ready to close on him and hold him for disastrous punishment of which he could not even dream. In that moment, it seemed to the boy that the roar of the river, strongly with melted snow water from the mountains, sang suddenly louder, and in a more personal note warned him away.

He let the door close quickly, not enough to make it slam, but so that the rusted hinges groaned faintly. That sound made him turn to flee, but a sudden weakness unnerved him at the knees. He sank down by the wall of the house, panting. Before him came the dog, growling faintly deep in its throat, the hair lifting along the back of its neck; but a so much greater terror was in the heart of Willie that he did not regard this close danger.

He waited through the eternity of a dozen heartbeats, but no swift step came toward him through the house.

He was spared again!

And, as the heart of a boy will do, now that of Willie leaped up from utter consternation to overbearing presumption. If there was anything worth hearing in that conversation between the knife bearer and the smaller man, he intended to hear it. The opportunity was not far away. Lamplight streamed through another window at the rear of the house, and Willie started up and went toward it.

For the dog he had developed a quick contempt, the fruit of reaction from his greater fear, and he cuffed the brute in the ribs with his bare foot; the cur snapped, but at the empty air, and slunk away mastered.

If anything could have raised the spirits of Willie higher, this was the final touch. He had been the cowering hare the instant before; he was the brave and cunning fox, now.

Through the lighted window came the voices which he sought, but indistinctly at times, so that he could not follow the trend of the conversation; and that made Willie climb up on the base board that encircled the bottom of the cheap little house.

Gripping the corner of the sill, where it jutted out on the side, he was in a difficult position, but one from which it was possible for him to hear every word and, if he dared, look in on the actors. He barely reached that place of vantage when he heard Bent saying in a voice which he hardly could recognize:

"To cancel the notes, Jimmy, of course, but with a knife instead of a pen!"

The voice ended, and there was a breath of silence that stabbed Willie to the heart, like the stroke of a knife. Irresistible instinct made him look, and he saw Clifton just arisen, still partly crouched, from the chair.

He could not watch the face of the victim, but he could see Bent's clearly, and the murder in it.

All that wild action of the night of Warren's death now seemed as nothing compared with the horror of the silence in which Bent looked down at the smaller man.

Willie could not endure it. Choked and faint, he looked away, ready to step down, but fearing to move lest he should fall and the noise attract the attention of the monster in the room, three short steps from him.

He looked away, therefore, trying to steady himself for flight, and he saw the dark, dim rows of the greens in the vegetable garden, the vague outline of the dog not far away, standing remorsefully on guard, with less courage than suspicion. More than that, he heard again the distinct roar of the Cumber River as it hurried through its shallow gorge at Wham; and in some house nearby people were talking—women's voices, rapid, beating one on top of the other, filled with exclamations and laughter that tumbled together like the gamboling of puppies.

Even in that moment, the lip of Willie curled a little, and into his troubled brain flowed other sounds, and above all, that of a mandolin far off. He could hear only the jangle of the strings that kept the tune, and the pulse of a soft singing rather than the actual timbre.

So that moment was filled for the boy, when he heard Clifton saying:

"It's hard to look at you, Chet, you're acting the part so well. I'd almost think, to hear you, that you *would* murder me!"

And he laughed. So rich and so real was his laughter that the boy looked back with a sudden great hope. It was, after all, only a practical jest!

But no! The instant he saw the face of Bent he knew, as he had known before, that murder was in the air!

And Clifton knew it, also. His laughter died away with a break. One hand was behind him, hard gripped, and again the dreadful silence went on, heartbeat by heartbeat.

Then Bent said through his teeth, "You're not a fool, Jimmy. You know that if I let Destry go to prison in my place a thing such as wiping you off the ledger with blood won't stop me for a moment!"

"You know that you'll infallibly hang!" said Clifton, in a shaken tone.

"Don't be a fool," said Bent. "Don't comfort yourself with that, Jimmy! Destry is my professional buffer state. The knife that I stab you with will be found in your body, and there is a clever 'D' cut into the handle of it. I suppose that a hundred people will be able to identify that knife as Destry's. He's been proud of his work with it, you know. He can hit things at twenty paces—sink the knife half the length of its blade into green wood, and that sort of thing. No, no, Jimmy! This will be laid on Destry's shoulders!"

"Then Destry will have you by the throat for it!"

"Have me? He'll never suspect! Destry's one of those clever, cunning people who prefer to keep a blind side for their friends. He has a blind side for me. He knows a dozen of my faults, has seen them, listed them, acknowledged them, but still he can't add up the total and see what I am. Destry's not a fool; he's only a fool about his friend, Chester Bent. The point will be that the cunning assassin of poor Jimmy Clifton stole the knife from Destry's room in my house in order to throw the blame on him! You see? But the rest of the world will have a fine reason for hanging Destry by the neck!"

He, in his turn, laughed a little, and did not finish his mirth in a hurry. Rather he seemed to be tasting and retasting it, and he was still laughing in that almost silent way when Clifton spoke again. His courage was going; with horrible clarity. Willie knew that, and saw a brave man turning into a dog before his eyes.

"D'you hear me—will you hear me, Chet?" he gasped.

"Of course. I want to hear you. I want to see you, too! I want to see you whine, you fool!"

"Chet," said the other, "I've never had anything against you, or you against me!"

"Except the notes, my boy!"

"They're yours! Look! Take and tear 'em up, and tear up your check, besides!"

"Are you a total ass, Jimmy? Tear the things up, but leave in Wham a man who knows all about me—and my reserve fund?"

"I'll forget it, Chet. Good God, man, I'll forget all about it. I tell you what—I'm going to leave Wham. You know that. I'll swear never to come back——"

"You don't have to. A letter to the sheriff would be enough."

"Man, I'll give you my sacred word of honor. The thing's ended with me. I'll say no more. It's finished. Every word you've spoken, and every act I've seen—which isn't much—I'll tear them out of the book of my brain and burn the leaves!"

Bent, listening, smiled with a peculiar gratification, as though the terror of the other were feeding him with a more than physical food.

This smile was accepted by Clifton, rightly as a refusal, and suddenly he slumped to his knees upon the floor.

Bent stepped back, in loathing, and yet in animal-like pleasure at this horror, and Clifton followed on his knees, reaching out his thick, yellow, trembling hands. His head was thrown back. His voice choked in his throat.

"Chet, you and me—for God's sake!—always friends—school together——"

A scream came up in the throat of Willie and stuck there like a bone.

"Stand up, and face it like a man!" commanded Bent.

"Chet, Chet, I've always respected you, liked you, loved you, d'you hear? Old friends! Chet, I'm young, I'm gunna get married——"

"You lie! Get up, or I'll lift you up by the hair of the head, you cur!"

"I swear it's true. Gunna marry Jenny Cleaver. She's to meet me in Denver—young, Chet—life before me—friends——"

Then the monster moved. He did not seem to hurry. It was like the action of the wasp in stinging the spider already paralyzed with horror. So Bent leaned and actually grasped Clifton by the hair of the head and jerked the head far back.

Willie saw the hands of the man stiffen as they clutched at the air, saw his mouth drawn open, and yet he did not scream for help.

Then Bent struck.

Straight through the base of the throat he drove the long knife, and left it sticking in the wound, then stepped back with blood running down his right hand.

Clifton fell on the floor, writhed his legs together, then turned on his back and lay motionless. He was dead! Already the boy had seen a death, but it had seemed to him then the most magnificent thing he ever had witnessed—a strong man rushing into battle against equal odds, and beaten, broken with bullets, snuffed out like a light. It had left glory for the victor, but this was a thing that words could not be used upon!

His long held breath now failed him, and he gasped. It was only a faint sound, but it was enough.

He saw the eyes of Bent roll up and fix steadily upon him, and he knew that the shadows had not screened him. That keen glance had gone out with the lamplight into the dark beyond the window and clearly discerned the face of the witness!

30

THE spell that held Willie Thornton endured until Bent made a move, and then he dropped like a plummet from the windowsill and began to run.

He wanted his best speed to get to the rear gate of the garden and so dodge right or left into the obscurity of the safe night, but his knees were numb, and his breath was gone. He stumbled straightway into a wire erected to support tomato vines and tumbled head over heels. As he came to his feet again, he saw Chester Bent flinging himself through the window with the agility of an athlete, and straightway he knew that the slowness which he had hoped for in that sleek appearing man would never appear.

He reached the gate, snatched off the wire hoop, and whipped through, yet delaying a fraction of a second to jam the loop back in place. Then he headed like the wind straight down the path toward the shrubbery, with the roaring of the river flinging up louder and louder from the very ground on which he trod, as it seemed.

He turned his head and glanced over his shoulder in time to see Chester Bent take the gate in his stride, like a hurdler, with the shadowy form of the dog flying over after him.

Dog and man together against him, Willie felt very much smaller than ever before; but in a sense he was less frightened than he had been when he stood at the window and looked in on the murder.

That had been too horrible for the imagination, but his present case was perfectly clear and exact. If Bent caught him, youth would make no difference. He would be killed!

Once he tipped up his face to scream for help—the thing which he had wondered that poor Clifton did not do—but he knew that as he cried out, his feet would be trailing and stumbling, and he dared not slow up, he dared not lose one breath of wind!

So he went on vigorously, probing at the dark of the winding pathway, making his legs work with all the muscle they had gained from trudging over mountain trails. A sharp stone cut his foot, but it only made his tread the lighter. He fairly flew, leaning aslant at the curves, but he knew that Bent was gaining rapidly!

The river roared nearer before his face, and suddenly he wondered that he could have been such a fool as to run in this direction! For the river was the very place which Bent would have chosen. Its rapid waters would be certain to cover a dead body quickly! Whereas if he had run toward the street, a single shout would have brought people around him!

The sense of his failure and folly made the boy weak. And then the mongrel ran up beside him, snapping and snarling, but not yet with quite the courage to bite; behind came the greater shadow of the man. His footfall sounded like a heavy pulse in the brain of Willie; and the boy could hear his gasping breath.

He swerved from under the very hand of Bent into the brush which rattled and cracked, deafening him. A cat's claw gripped him and spun him around as he lurched away from it, but he darted on, and a moment later, with his lungs bursting and his eyes thrusting from their sockets, he threw himself flat on the ground beneath a bush and waited.

Desperately he strove to control the noise of his breathing; then told himself that the louder voice of the river probably would cover such a small thing as his breathing. So he lay trembling with exertion, hopeful that his hiding place would be overlooked, and at any rate thankful for this moment of rest.

He could hear Bent moving through the bush, cursing the thorns; then he saw the shadow of the man against the stars, moving past him.

He was safe!

Then a growl came at his very ear! It was the mongrel, which had followed the trail with a sense truer than the eyes in this dark of the night. Still the dog remembered the heel which had thumped his ribs, and though he snapped it was only at the air; then he backed up and began to bay the game!

There was no sense in waiting. Willie lurched to his feet, gathering up a broken section of a branch that lay on the ground beside him. With this he struck true and hard between the eyes of the brute. It yowled with pain and fear and fled, but yonder came the silhouette of Bent, rushing straight at his quarry.

There seemed no place to flee, now. The brush had proved a useless screen, and the danger was impending over him. But he sprinted desperately, with renewed wind, straight for the noise of the creek. He could not run as fast as his pursuer, but he had the advantage of being able to dodge more swiftly among the reaching branches of the shrubs.

The trees along the river bank gave him a hope, but when he reached them the hand of Bent was again stretched for him. He dodged, pushing his hands against a tree trunk, and barely escaped into the open.

There that hand gripped the shoulder of his coat!

He was lost, then. But where another boy would have surrendered, Willie Thornton still fought like a cornered rat against fate. The second strong hand of the man gripped him. He whirled, and the loose, over-size coat gave from his shoulders and left him suddenly free!

Bent, lurching back, sprang forward again with wonderful adroitness. There was no chance for the boy to dodge and run again. There was only one verge of the creek bank and the voice of the rushing Cumber beneath.

He did not hesitate. Even a river in flood was preferable to death by the hands of the monster! So he ran straight forward and leaped out into air.

He saw beneath him the glistening face of the water, streaked white by its speed against the rocks—white like a wolf's teeth, he thought, as he leaped into the thin hands of the wind. Then down he went as a rock goes. He smote the water with stunning force, but the cold of it kept his senses alert.

He knew that he was being whirled around and around as he was carried down the stream, and he gripped at the first object that he saw. It looked a soft shadow; it proved to be a sleek rock that sprang up from a root in the bed of the stream.

His grip held, though the current drew him out powerfully, like a banner flapping in a strong wind. He lay on his back, only his nose and lips above the surface, and, looking at the bank, he saw Chester Bent moving along the edge of the water.

Opposite the point where Willie lay shivering with the penetrating cold of the melted snow, Bent paused for a long moment. He crouched upon his heels, the better to study the surface of the stream.

Then the lofty shadow stepped out upon a rock straight toward the place where Willie lay!

He was lost, he told himself, and prepared to loose his hold and try to swim down the stream to safety, well assured that if he did so one of the sharp teeth in that wolf's mouth would spear him to the life.

But Bent remained only an instant on that rock, then he stepped back to the shore. The old coat he tossed into the stream, and climbed back to the upper edge of the bank. There he loitered an instant, and faded away into the trees.

31

FIVE men had gathered, by this time, in the house of Jimmy Clifton, and Henry Cleeves took charge of the assembly. He came first, and had called for little Clifton, their host, who did not appear; then he had glanced into the bedroom and seen the lighted lamp, the bed with no sleeper on it, the chair in front of the desk quite empty.

He didn't examine the room further, but went back to join the others as they gathered. They came in not in pairs, but singly, each stepping with an odd haste through the front door and moving quickly inside of it, so that he would not remain silhouetted against the lamplight to any observer on the street.

Having made this somewhat guilty entrance, each tried to assume a cheerful air, which was promptly discountenanced by their self-appointed chairman, for Cleeves was invincibly grave this evening.

Phil Barker, celebrated for his practical jokes, until that stinging jest of Destry's had altered his habits, was the first to enter, taking off his sombrero and looking cautiously about him as though he feared lest even Cleeves might have something up his sleeve.

Immediately afterward came Bull Hewitt and tall Bud Truckman, so close together that it was plain Bull had dogged Bud down the street, though he would not walk beside the other.

The last to come was Williams, the strong man, who gripped his hat so hard in his powerful hand that he soon reduced it to a ball; at the expense of his hat, he was able to maintain a fair calm of countenance.

Then Cleeves pointed to the chairs and bade them be seated, while he drew down the shades of the windows and closed the front door. He explained that their host apparently had stepped out, but must be back in a short time. They could sit down and open their minds to one another in the meanwhile.

So they sat down around the table and each man looked upon the other as though he never had seen him before and was ashamed to be seen by him, in turn. Only Cleeves kept his mind clear for the business before them.

He said: "We know why we've met here, but I'll say it over again to bring things to a head. Then, if we get any conclusions, we'll tell them to Jimmy when he shows up. He's stepped out for just a moment; there's still a lamp burning in his bedroom. In the first place, Destry is living up to the promise he made to us that day in the courtroom. We've scattered and tried to get away from him; still he hunted us down. Warren and Clarence Ogden are dead. Jud Ogden is worse than dead—crippled forever. Lefty Turnbull's in jail and will soon be in the pen for a long time. Orrin is hiding no man knows where; he'll be tried for graft when found and in the meantime he's looked on as a yellow dog. Jerry Wendell has been hounded out of Wham; his heart's broken. And that leaves six of us. If we can't run away from him, we'll have to bunch together and fight him. We're here to discuss ways and means. As for the money end of it, if that enters, I suppose I can begin by saying that any of us will pay anything up to life to keep life. If I'm wrong, speak up!"

They did not answer. They listened with their eyes on the table, not the speaker.

"I'm right, then," went on Cleeves. "Now, then, we're ready for the ways of disposing of Destry, alive or dead."

"Alive, he'll never stop," said Barker.

"Dead, then. We've got that far. He has to be killed! How?"

No one spoke, until Bull Hewitt lifted his stupid face and said sullenly:

"You gents all know I never was agin Harry so much. I wouldn't of voted him guilty at the trial, if you hadn't crowded me agin the wall, all talkin' together. But now that it comes to the pinch, I say that Destry's gotta die, because I wanta live. There's just a few ways of killin' a man—rope, knife, gun, poison. But hit on one of 'em quick."

After this, there was a bit of a silence, until Phil Barker struck the table with his fist.

"Poison! It works secret, and secret ways are the only ones that'll ever catch Destry. We've tried the other kind and they're no good!"

"Ay, poison. But how?" asked Hewitt.

Cleeves took charge again.

"We've all agreed, then, that we'll use anything from a knife to poison on Destry?"

He took the silence for agreement, and then he went on: "The first great problem is how to get in touch with him. We'll need Jimmy Clifton's good head to help on that. I wonder where he's keeping himself so long?"

They waited, looking at one another.

Cleeves, making a cigarette, scratched a match, and they all saw his big, bony hands trembling as he strove to light the smoke. At last, he snapped the match away, and struck another, looking around the table with a swift, guilty glance.

They avoided meeting it. Then Barker broke out, quickly and softly: "We're all thinkin' of just one thing. Is Destry the reason that Jimmy ain't showed up?"

No one answered, till Cleeves cried: "Ay, and is Destry curled up somewhere, now, and listening to all that we have to say?"

"Or," suggested Bull Hewitt, "is Destry about to slip in with a pair of guns ready to work? He's got us all here in one pen!"

It was at this very crucial moment that they all heard, distinctly, the sound of the kitchen screen moaning on its hinges, and they stood up as though at a command.

The kitchen door yawned slowly open. Cleeves had a gun in his hand.

Barker was reaching for a weapon, when they saw in the dark doorway the smiling face of Chester Bent. It was at least less unwelcome than that of Destry, and there was a faint general sigh of relief. But Bent, standing in the doorway, ran his eyes carefully across their faces.

"Friends," said he, "you're sitting here planning how to kill Harry Destry, and I've come to help you plan!"

Cleeves exclaimed angrily: "Bent, we know that you're his best friend! D'you think that you can come here and listen to us under such a shallow pretext as that?"

"Am I his best friend?" asked Bent.

Then he laughed a little, adding: "Jimmy Clifton can tell you how much of a friend I am to Destry. Where's Jimmy now? I thought that all six of you would be here!"

"You knew about this?"

"Of course. Jimmy told me and asked me to come here; because I have the only scheme that will kill Destry!"

They watched him in suspicion and in amazement. Yet what he had said carried with it a certain portion of self-proof. For if he knew of the meeting, it seemed logical that he must have learned from one of the six, and who would have been mad enough to tell him without good reason?

"Go on, man," said Cleeves. "God knows we *hope* that this is true, because I don't know a stronger hand or head to have us! *You* want Harry Destry's death?"

"More," said Bent fervidly, "than any of you! And more tonight than ever before!"

As he thought of Willie Thornton, and of that lad's knowledge, and of the uncertainty of his death, such a world of sincerity gleamed in the eyes and roughened in the voice of Bent that to see with a single glance was to believe him. There was not only real firmness of will, but a ravening hate which made their own fear-inspired hearts seem bloodless things.

He added quietly:

"You know what was attempted in my house the other night against Destry. Do you think that Clifton would have tried that without my permission and my help?"

It was the final proof and convinced them all. They looked at Bent with wonder, but they also looked at him with a growing hope.

"Where's Clifton now?" asked the new recruit peevishly. "We must have Clifton. He's the one of you who understands my position and can tell you whether or not I'm really with you. Isn't he in his room?"

He pushed the door open as he spoke.

"He's not there," said Cleeves, "I looked a while ago and there was no——"

"Great God!" cried Bent, and rushed into the room as though from the door he had seen something horrible that called him forward.

Cleeves followed him; the others flocked behind; and they gathered about the prostrate body of Clifton, dead, with the knife fixed to the hilt in his throat.

"Dead!" said Bent. "But—how long have you been here? Who was here first? What——"

Cleeves grew pale.

"Are you pointing at me, Bent?" he demanded hotly. "I was here first, if that's what you want to know!"

Williams was leaning above the dead man.

"The knife!" he said. "The knife! Will ya look at it, all of you? Will ya see the 'D' carved into the butt of it? Destry! Destry was here before us! I've seen this here knife in the old days. I've seen him throw it at a mark! I'd swear it was Destry's, even without the letter made onto it!"

Cleeves was drawing down the shade across the window.

He came back to the frightened circle and said firmly: "He's been here. There's his hand on the floor. Now what will we do?"

He turned to Bent.

"You wouldn't be here without an idea, Bent. *He* thinks you're still his friend?"

"Yes."

"Can you draw him back to your house?"

"Not since Clifton made his try there. He won't come back."

"Is there any other way?"

"There's one other way. There's one house that he'd go to, if a message was sent to him."

"Charlie Dangerfield?"

Bull Hewitt cried out in a choked voice: "You mean to use her for bait, to draw Destry into a trap?"

"Look!" said Cleeves, pointing to the floor.

And Hewitt, staring at the dead body and the blank, smiling face of Clifton, turned back abruptly, his argument crushed.

"Can you get a message to him, Chet?"

"I know how to get to him. I'll do it tomorrow afternoon. I'll have to do a bit of arranging, in the first place. I'll have to see Charlie Dangerfield. I'll have to have her written invitation to him. I'll have to get that and bring it out to him. I'll have to do everything, boys. And your only job will be to lie close and get him when he comes. But I'll arrange the details. You'll know everything! Only—what if this thing should happen, and she knew who had led Destry down into the trap?"

They nodded at one another, for they saw the point. If there was one fact in his life which Bent had taken no trouble to hide, it was that he worshiped Charlotte Dangerfield.

"Chet," said Cleeves, "if you can do this for us, you don't have to doubt! The rest of us would kill the man who talked! Great heavens, man, who would be fool enough to say that he took a hand in the killing of Destry?"

"Get Ding Slater, somebody!" said Bent.

He waved to the door.

"Some of you better leave, too, before Slater comes. You stay on, Cleeves. And here's an old friend of Clifton—Barker. You and Barker. The rest of us will start. Move the chairs away from that table. Get the blinds up. And don't touch the dead body. Don't move a thing in this room—not a chair or a rug. Don't touch a thing, so that Ding can use his gigantic intelligence on the spot and try to make out what the 'D' on the knife may mean!"

He sneered as he spoke, and, hurrying to the door, waved his hand at them and was gone.

"I wonder," said Cleeves slowly, as their new confederate disappeared, "who would win the fight if those two were thrown down hand to hand? That wild cat Destry, or this sleek bull terrier, Bent!"

32

THE next morning, Bent rode out to the Dangerfield place dressed like a puncher of the range, not because he wanted to play that part, but because the cowpuncher's costume is the only perfect one for rough riding across the brush-laced country of the Western range. His tall hat turns the heat of the sun or the downpour of the rain. It is hat, parasol, and umbrella all in one. His bandana keeps dust from falling down his neck, keeps off the hot rays of the sun where they are apt to fall with most force—the back of the neck—and in time of need is the sieve through which his breath can be drawn and the dust kept from his lungs. His leather chaps turn the needle points of the thorns. His high heeled, narrow toed boots, foolish for walking, are ideal for a man who is half standing in the stirrups on a long ride and does not wish his foot to be too deeply engaged in case of a fall.

Bent was dressed in this fashion, and he was well accustomed to it. He took a strong, fast horse from his barn and went on a line as straight as a bird's flight from his house to the Dangerfield place. He found "The Colonel" on the front veranda smoking a long cigar.

"Hello," said Dangerfield. "Are you masqueradin' as a workin' man, Chet?"

"I'm a working man every day," said Bent with a smile, as he threw the reins over the post of the hitching rack and came up to the steps. "I have to sit and grind, while you're here in the cool of the wind."

"There ain't any sitting work," declared the Colonel. "The curse of Adam was sweat of the brow, not sweat of the brain."

Bent stood with a hand against one of the narrow wooden pillars of the veranda and smiled down at the rancher.

"What about the worry of the poor devils in the offices?" said he. "Worry and trouble all day long!"

"What do kids do when they sit in the shade?" asked the Colonel.

"Day dream, I suppose."

"A gent that lives on his brain is simply turning day dreams into money."

"He has no pain, then?"

"Not a mite," said the other. "But he knows that he's makin' a living, and that starts him pityin' himself. Most men don't complain of work till they get married, and then it's only to impress the wife. Because he finds out pretty pronto that he's gotta be the comforter if he don't ask to be comforted. But toilin' with your hands, that's different. Seein' the sun stick in one place in the sky for a coupla dozen hours—that's pain, with payday always about a week away."

"I think that I have pain enough," said Bent.

"You got it in your imagination," said Dangerfield. "And there ain't any larger or more tenderer place to have a pain than in the imagination. Women folks used to have that kind; men *always* have 'em, unless they're laborin', and then they don't need any imagination at all. But I've set here on this porch a good many years and never seen much trouble, except thinkin' of the first of the month, now and then. But it wasn't anything serious!"

"Have you lived such a happy life, then?"

"Sure," said Dangerfield. "By not workin' I kept ready for the luck, and when the luck came, I grabbed it and took off its scalp."

He added: "I expect you didn't sashay all the ways out here to talk to me, but if you came to see Charlie, I'll tell you that she ain't good company lately."

"I've never found Charlie dull," said Bent.

"Mostly," said Dangerfield, "young men don't know nothin' about girls. It ain't that girls wanta lie and be deceivin' but they just nacherally can't be themselves when a gent is around. They gotta put the best foot forward. I tell you what, Chet, Sunday's been a mighty miserable day around this place for years and years, with Charlie usin' up a whole week of good spirits on Saturday night. But now she ain't dull; she's just mean."

"Mean?" said Bent. "Charlie mean?"

"A surprisin' thing to you, I reckon. She's so mean that she won't talk to nobody, except a word or two to the niggers. The rest of the time she spends wranglin' mustangs. And the wear that she gives a cayuse in two days is enough to keep him thin the rest of his life. I says to her: 'Charlie, when you break a hoss, aim to save the pieces, will you?' "

"I didn't know that Charlie went in for rough riding."

"Sure you didn't. But she's gotta have some way of lettin' off the steam, I reckon. It ain't the hosses she's mad at."

"What is it, then?"

"Herself. Because she once had that crazy, fast flyin' snipe, Destry, tied to a string, and now she's gone and cut the cord. Where's he now?"

"I wanted to talk to her about that," said Bent.

"Then she'll listen," said Dangerfield, "if you keep close onto that track."

"Where is she now?"

"Anywhere from hell to breakfast—from that broken headed mesa yonder to the corrals."

At the corrals, Bent found her. She had just turned loose a sweating mustang, chafed with white foam and froth about the shoulders; the tired horse merely jogged wearily away. In the meantime, Charlie Dangerfield leaned against the corral fence and criticized the handling of the next candidate for her attention. This was a bald faced chestnut with a Roman nose and the eye of a snake, which was trying to tear the snubbing post out of the ground, and bite, kick, or strike the two men who were working on it. The double purpose kept it from succeeding in either hope.

"Hello, Charlie," said Bent. "That's a pretty picture you're going to fit yourself into, it looks to me."

She waved her hand to him briefly, and hardly gave him a glance.

"Sweet boy, isn't he?" said she. "Look at the iron hook in his nose and the hunch in his back. Up on that back, you'll feel as if you're sitting on Mt. McKinley and looking down at the birds. Hey, Jerry, sink your knee in his ribs and give those cinches another haul, will you? You've got his wind inside that!"

Jerry obeyed, and finally the gelding was prepared for riding. Bent, in the meantime, was looking over the girl quietly, and found her much changed. She was thinner, he thought, and the shadow about her eyes made them look darker. She might have been an older sister of the girl he had known.

"Charlie," he said, "you come away and listen to me. I want to talk to you about Harry Destry."

"Do you?" she replied. "Who's Harry nicked lately?"

The hardness and casual quality of her voice did not deceive Bent.

"Little Jimmy Clifton," he answered gravely.

"Jimmy? What was Jimmy's shameful secret?"

"I don't know. No one ever will know—if there was one— because it died with him, it appears."

Still she would not turn her head, but he well knew that her pretended interest in the mustang had disappeared.

"Died?" she said.

"Yes," answered Bent.

She turned slowly and faced him. He saw she was white.

"What made *that* a fair fight?" she asked. "Did Jimmy have a crowd with him?"

Bent looked down at the ground and seemed to study it before he answered; in reality he was concealing his exultation.

"Of course Jimmy must have had help or Harry never would have tackled him. But—no one knows who was with Clifton. He was found with the knife—er—in his throat, Charlie!"

She threw out her hands as though she were casting away a disgusting thought.

"Not a knife!"

"Yes. It's the worst business of all."

"Stabbed Jimmy Clifton? Jimmy? I don't believe it!"

"I don't either," said Bent hastily. "Only—the knife was there! The 'D' carved on it, and everything!"

"If he'd done such a thing, he wouldn't be fool enough to leave the knife in the wound—not a knife that could be identified. Somebody stole that knife and murdered Clifton!"

Protest, Bent had been prepared for, but not the naked truth so suddenly thrown in his face.

He was saved the necessity of finding words by the girl herself.

"Jerry," she called faintly, "you take that red-eyed devil, will you? I'm afraid of him!"

She put her hand on Bent's arm.

"Start me walking, and keep right on," she said. "I'm mighty dizzy! Stabbed Jimmy? Stabbed him and left the knife in the wound and——"

"Forget that, will you?" asked Bent. "I didn't come to talk about it!"

She stopped short, and her hand gripped his arm fiercely.

"Why should I care a rap about him? Thief, gunman, professional fighter, lazy, shiftless—and now a murderer! Why should I care a rap about him? I'm a fool! I'm a fool!" cried Charlie Dangerfield. "I don't want to talk about him any longer!"

Bent looked hard at her, and then he answered: "If I thought I could believe you, Charlie, I'd lose my heart about saying what I intend to say— what I came here to say. But I don't believe you. Should I?"

"You came out to talk about this killing. You came out to explain it away, I suppose? God knows how Harry can deserve such a friend as you are!"

"What of you, Charlie?"

"Ah, he found me when I was young—I was a baby, only. And he took my heart in his hands with such a grip, Chester, that I've never been able to take it back. What with loving him, pitying him, being shamed for him, fearing him, and then losing him! Why, the thought of Harry's all around me, just as the hills and the mesas are all around this ranch. But what keeps you true to him? That's what I don't understand!"

"Because, Charlie, I don't care to analyze my best friend."

She watched him for a moment, and then he saw her glance melting.

"Dear old Chet!" said she. "One man like you puts all the rest of us in our places! You're true blue! Tell me what I'm to do, and I'll do it!"

"Is there a quiet place, a secluded place near the house, Charlie?"

"What d'you mean?"

"Some shack, say?"

"There's the house by the old well."

"The one that went dry?"

"Yes."

"That would do, perfectly. You're to be there tonight."

"Am I?"

"Yes."

"Night, did you say?"

"Yes. You can't expect him to ride about the country during the day, can you?"

"Harry? Is he to come there?"

Bent set his teeth for an instant—such a joy came up in her eyes, and flushed in her brown face, that bitter envy burned him up. This for Harry Destry, even when she thought that his hands were red with the murder of a helpless man!

"He's to come there, I trust. If I can persuade him, at least."

"And then?"

"And then you're to start persuading where I left off!"

"Persuading him to do what? Am I to reform him? Is that the little thing you expect of me?"

"I expect that you can do anything with him, if you have a chance. If you're not proud with him, I should say! Because there's enough iron in him to resent pride."

"Proud?" said she. "Oh, I'll not be proud! But what would I say?"

"You'd ask him to leave five of the twelve men untouched, and go away with you!"

She considered the idea, trembling.

Then, in a rapid murmur so that he hardly heard the words: "He wouldn't listen, of course. I've failed him when he needed me—when he pretended to need me. I'm dead to him, now!"

"You're not. I don't think so, at least. At any rate, will you make the experiment, Charlie?"

"Ask drowning men if they'll catch at straws!" said she.

33

A HAPPY glow of achievement already possessed the body and the soul of Bent as he returned to Wham. For if he had not actually fulfilled all his purpose, the first part was done, and the remainder seemed easily at hand.

It was not possible that a guilty conscience could move him. Too much is made of guilty consciences. They generally begin to work on criminals after the stern hand of the law has grasped them by the nape of the neck. They prepare for a holy death to make up for a bad life, only after the hangman is assured. So Bent was unencumbered with remorse of any kind.

What fascinated him was the intricacy of his plan, the width of the end which he aimed at, the skill with which his purposes were so dovetailed together that where the one plan ended and the other began would have been hard to tell.

On the whole, everything that he did seemed based upon the putting down of Destry. To the imprisonment of Destry he owed his own safety from prosecution for the train robbery in the beginning of his prosperity. Again, to the cruel fame of Destry he owed it that he had been able to strike down a creditor and cancel that debt. Yet again, the very act which would kill Destry would be interpreted by Charlie Dangerfield as an accident which had taken place through the malice of others, and in spite of the guarding care of the real contriver. She would credit him with having tried to save Destry from any calamity; the very death of Destry he would so arrange that she must feel Bent was least concerned in it.

The death of Clifton had removed the last danger to his fortune. The end of Destry would clear his way to the hand of Charlotte Dangerfield. And as an extra profit, he would receive the undying gratitude of five men whom he had shown a way to rid themselves of a mortal danger.

He knew that his way was not yet clear, but out of the darkness he saw light and was well content. Indeed, as he rode down the street of Wham he was hardly sure that he would have been pleased to gain all his ends by legitimate means; crime, which had been a tool, now was becoming an end, desirable for its excitement.

He drew up at the shop of Cleeves, who came out to him with the soot of the forge on his face, and black streaks of grease on his hairy arms.

"You know the old dry well on the Dangerfield place?" he demanded without prelude.

"I reckon I do."

"Be out there tonight and have the rest of the boys handy. There's plenty of chaparral growing right up to the door where the rest of 'em can hide. But you, Cleeves, you're a shot-gun expert."

"I can handle a shot gun."

"You've got a sawed off gun?"

"I have one."

"You get out there well before dark. Get up into the attic and lie there. Mind you that nobody sees you on the way. You're out to shoot doves, if anybody in the shop asks you when you start. Lie up there in the attic and wait for Destry to come. The girl will be there first. Lie still as a mouse till Destry comes. The fact is, I don't depend on the other four; I depend on you, Cleeves!"

The other nodded. "If I miss that close up," he said, "I'm a fool and I'll never shoot again!"

"If you miss, you'll never shoot again," said Bent. "You're right about that. If you miss, you'll be a dead man, old fellow! But you're not going to miss. What's happened in town today?"

"The merchants have got together and offered a reward for Destry. The coroner has hung the killing of Clifton on him. It's clear sailing in that direction."

"What about old Ding Slater? What's he done?"

"Nothing—as usual. He'll never hold a job in this town when his term's up this time. They're tired of him."

"What happened when Slater got to the house the other night?"

"Nothin' happened. You can't get fresh sense out of a dry brain! He just looked around and clucked like an old hen. After a while, he stood in the doorway and asked if any of the furniture had been moved, and I told him it hadn't. Then Ding says he don't see how Bent could of seen the dead body from the door, or something like that. The old man's pretty far gone!"

This observation made Bent sit a little straighter, but he said nothing. To him, the observation of the sheriff seemed to prove that Slater's was far from a dry brain! However, the news about the reward was far the more important tidings, he judged.

He left Cleeves at once, and riding down the street he straightway encountered the sheriff and dismounted to say to him anxiously: "Ding, it doesn't seem possible that Harry Destry could have stabbed Clifton!"

"He didn't," said the sheriff.

"Didn't he? Then what's all the talk about?"

"I dunno. Some mighty ornery sneak got into the house and stole that knife; or else it's an old knife that Harry give away a long time ago. Anyway, Destry never done the job."

"I knew he didn't have that sort of work in him!"

"You knew right, Chet. They's more knowledge of people in friendship than there is in the law! A mighty lot!"

"But who could have done the job?"

"They're in town—plenty that hate Destry and would be glad to knife Clifton if they could do it so safe!"

With that uncomforting knowledge in his mind, Bent rode on from the town. Yet however keen the old sheriff might be on the trail, it was patent that he did not suspect Chester Bent of the crime, otherwise he would not have spoken so freely. But close trailing of the crime might reveal the real criminal. There was no doubt of that, and, though Bent could not see where he had left incriminating evidence behind him, still he knew that a clever hand and a sharp eye can unravel nearly any crime, no matter how well covered the traces of it may be.

He was reasonably confident, but he knew that his safety was not yet built upon bed rock.

There remained the problem of the boy, as well. If he was alive, then nothing but ruin hung over Bent's head. But there was hardly a chance that the youngster had not been torn to death among the sharp rocks of the Cumber Creek.

With that comfort, with no sureties, but with many excellent high hopes for the future, Bent rode out of Wham and took the old trail toward Pike Pass.

He rode on through the heat of the afternoon, with the rocks burning about him and smoking with heat waves, until the mesquite thinned out, and then the dauntless lodgepole pines, which seem able to live in a furnace or an icebox, began to cluster on the hills.

He had turned a sharp corner of the trail when the voice of Destry called suddenly behind him. He whirled about, his hand instinctively flying to his gun, and there was Destry in the middle of the trail with Fiddle sticking her head out from the trees close by. The man was greatly changed. Continued exposure to wind and sun had browned his face, and as he took off his hat and waved it, Bent saw that the hair of Destry was growing long. The clipped skull had made him seem a criminal by right and profession; now he appeared a typical wild man of the mountains.

"I wanted to see if you'd lost some of the edge of your eye, Chet," he called, "and here you been and let me stalk you like a blind man!"

Bent came back to him, smiling and holding out a hand which was received with a quick grip, like a clutch of iron, a familiar grip to Bent. And every time he felt it, he wondered how his own might of arm would match against that of Destry!

"I was hoping to be stalked," said he, "not dodging it. Harry, I've brought you news. They've put a price on you, for Clifton!"

"For Clifton? What about him?"

"D'you ask me that?" said Bent slowly.

"I do."

"He was found dead last night, and with a knife of yours in his throat!"

"That leaves five," was the first response of Destry. He added: "How come a knife of mine? I wasn't near the town!"

"I'm going to believe you, Harry. Then what scoundrel could have done it?"

"I dunno," said Destry. He asked curiously: "They've put a price on me?"

"Twenty-five hundred, and it'll soon go up."

"How did you know the knife was mine?"

"By a 'D' carved in the butt of it."

"I left a knife like that in your house, Chet. They've stolen it."

"Who would have dared——"

"Why, one of the five, d'you see? To throw the blame on me and bring the law onto their side of this business. When you can't win your own fight, call in a dog to help you! What does Ding say?"

"He's for you. Three people in the world stick to you, Harry. I'm one. And the third is what I've come to talk about. Charlie wants to see you."

"Charlie's kind," said Destry drily.

"Are you going to take it like this?"

"How should I take it?"

"Man, man, she talked to me with tears in her eyes, and she's not a soft headed type, as you ought to know."

"Then what does she want?"

"She wants you."

"Now that I'm a murderer, too?"

"What does she care? She wants you. She's ready to pack up and leave with you. She'll do anything. But she begs you to come down to see her at the old house by the dry well."

"I know the place."

Bent laid a hand on the shoulder of his companion.

"You're arming yourself with indifference, Harry," said he, "but the fact is that you know you love her still!"

"I've taken her out of my mind," said Destry firmly.

"You think you have. She's at the door now. Can you keep her out, Harry?"

Destry drew a great breath.

Then he said thoughtfully: "If they's more than you two that know of the meeting place, I'm no better than a dead man, Chet, when I start down there. You realize that?"

"Who else *could* know?"

"True," said Destry. "They wasn't pity or conscience in what she said, man? She wanted to see me?"

"I give you my word."

Destry threw up his hand. "Look!" said he.

"At what, Harry?"

"My good resolutions. There they go like smoke! And I'll be riding down there this same evenin'; but I reckon that I'll need my guns before that ride is over!"

34

OUT of Cumber River, Willie Thornton had crawled at last like one half drowned; and so exhausted was he that, when he reached the shore, instead of shaking himself like a dog, as most boys would have done, and then taking off and wringing his soaked clothing, he merely sank down on the rocks to rest.

An increasing wretchedness possessed the boy. Not only was he exhausted, but the wind which came down the valley clipped him to the bone with its cold tooth, and his breathing began to send a pain through his chest.

He remained on the rocks in a stupor, for a time, and when he recovered enough to stand up, he knew that he was sick. For his head was heavy, his eyes were dull, and his lips felt numb.

He walked forward without a purpose or a goal, except that he guessed it would be death to remain wet and exposed much longer. When he came to the bank, his legs collapsed, and he had to scramble up slowly, using hands and feet and knees.

At the top, some of the dizziness left him. He kept shaking his head like a stunned prizefighter, to drive that confusion from his brain, but now the dark woods were around him, and with them came the thought of Bent like a prowling panther.

That cleared his brain like a breath of open air after a close room. His very muscles grew stronger, as it seemed, and he went forward cautiously, every now and again pausing to stare about him. And it seemed to the boy that the breathing of the wind was that of Bent, hurrying up behind him, and when a branch caught at him, it was the hand of the murderer on his shoulder once more!

These fancies grew a little less strong as he wandered on through the trees, until at last he came from among them and saw before him the shattered rays of a lamp's light that shone in the distance.

He made straight toward it. Dipping into a sharp sided draw, the light disappeared. The loss of it discouraged him mightily. The old bewilderment returned, but a curious bulldog instinct, such as keeps an army on the go during a forced march, carried him straight ahead, laboring shakily up the opposite bank until he came out in view of the light once more.

It was much nearer, now. He was able to distinguish that it came from a small shack with sage brush growing about it—he knew that by the smell of the bushes when he struck against them in floundering forward. Behind the house there was a stack of hay or straw, and toward this he headed.

Sleep was the panacea which always had cured his ills, and he intended to burrow his way into cover and there close his eyes. He felt guilty over his decision. In his confused mind there was a voice which told him that he must not stop, but must go on and on in the cause of Destry.

What he could accomplish, or what he should try to do, he did not know, but loyal service to a friend seemed to demand an unfailing effort on his part.

However, he surrendered to the necessity for rest and was through the bars of the corral when a voice called loudly behind him: "Who's there? Stop!"

Bent?

The terror of the thought made him suddenly strong to flee. He raced across the corral, vaguely conscious that he was again pursued; but as he strove to slide through the bars on the opposite side of the enclosure, strong hands gathered him up lightly, easily.

He expected that grip to shift to his throat, but his hands lacked strength to struggle.

"A kid, eh?" said the voice of the man. "Come to fetch yourself a coupla chickens, have you? I'm gunna take the hide off you so's you can go back and show the brats in Wham what happens when they come sneakin' out here again!"

He bore Willie back into the path of the lamplight, calling: "I got one of 'em, Jack! I got one sure! We'll make a doggone bright example of this one. Must of fallen into the trough; he's wet as a rat!"

Willie was brought into a region of what seemed to him supernal brightness and before him appeared the face of another man; or did he have two faces?

Curious dimness beset the eyes of Willie; he forgot whatever danger he might stand in and squinted at the face of the second man.

"Hold his hands!" said the captor. "Hold him while I make him dance, the chicken stealin' little son of a gun!"

The hands of Willie were firmly held, but still he squinted up at the face of his jailer, amazed at the manner in which it receded into the distance, and then swept close, as out of a cloud—an unshaven, sun reddened face.

Then a whip lash struck a line of fiery pain across his shoulders. But the pain seemed detached from the brain of the boy. It was as though his body belonged to an impersonal set of nerves. Again it descended——

"Quit it, Pete!" shouted Jack suddenly. "A doggone good plucked one as ever I seen! Clean gritty. He ain't winked an eye. Leave the whip be! Who are you, kid?"

"Willie," said he.

"Willie who?"

"I dunno. Thornton, I guess."

"He ain't very sure of his name!"

"Hold on. The kid talks kind of loony. D'you fall into the trough, Willie?"

"I fell into the river," said the boy. "Destry——"

His mind had snapped back to that controlling thought, but with the name his voice stopped. His throat was oddly dry and hot.

"He's shakin' all over," said Jack. "What's the matter with him?"

A hand was pressed against the forehead of Willie Thornton, and immediately the harsh voice of Pete softened.

"The kid's sick. He's got fever," said he. "And I've put a whip on him! Damn my heart!"

"Look at him shake—he's sick, right enough. How d'you feel, Willie?"

"Kind of like the way a calf looks—wobbly," said Willie.

He heard them laugh. The sound came to him from a distance in booming waves that flooded upon the drums of his ears and ebbed vibrantly away.

"Get him to bed," said Jack. "I'll fix up some quinine and whiskey. There ain't anything better'n quinine and hot whiskey, I reckon."

Then rapid, powerful hands removed Willie's clothes. He tried to help, but his fingers were numbed. He tried to walk, but his knees sagged. He only knew that he was profoundly eager to lie down. The very word "bed" was like a promise of heaven to him.

He was picked up.

"Gimme one of your flannel Shirts, Jack. That'll do him for a nightgown. Gimme a towel first, and I'll dry him off. Skinny little rat, ain't he!"

"Look where you put your marks on his back, Pete."

"I'd rather have 'em laid across my own. I done what I thought was right, though. He run when I called!"

A rough towel burnished Willie dry, almost rubbing away his skin. And his brain spun more and more.

"Destry—" he gasped.

"He's got Destry in his head," said Jack. "Has Destry been after you, son?"

"Yes—no—I mean Destry——"

"He thinks Destry's been after him!" said the other. "Go down to Wham and get some milk for him. He's gunna need milk. Find out who Willie Thornton is. I never heard of no Thorntons around here before!"

Willie was laid between blankets that had a smell of horsesweat about them; but it was fragrance to Willie, so profound was his weariness.

He closed his eyes in an instant torpor, from which he was roused to have a stinging potion of hot whiskey, bitter with quinine, poured down his throat.

It half choked him with pungency and with its horrible taste. But he hardly had lain back, gasping for breath, when sleep rushed over him like a dark flight of crows. He heard the rushing of their wings—or was it the noise of the pulse in his temple?

And then he slept.

When he wakened, he was wet with sweat, he was weak, but his brain was much clearer. He lifted his brown hand from the blanket and wondered at it, for it hardly seemed to belong to him, though he recognized the down-curved nail which had grown to replace the one that was broken off in his fall of the year before.

He turned his head toward the roar of the kitchen stove, freshly crammed with fuel, and smoking and trembling with the force of the fluttering flames.

There stood Jack of the night before, turning a dream into a fact.

He came and stood over the boy.

"You feelin' better, kid?"

"Yeah. A lot, thanks."

"You got scared out of your wits about Destry. And there ain't no wonder. Destry's killed another, and this time it's murder. The worst kind of murder. With a knife!"

"Destry didn't—" began Willie.

"He did, though. Clifton's dead, stuck like a pig for the autumn slaughter. And Clifton was one of the jury. Here, you, lay back and take it easy."

"I gotta get up," said the boy. "I gotta tell——"

"You lay back. You're still pretty woozy; and you lay back and take it easy. You look pretty done up, I guess. Thought Destry was chasin' you into the river, did you?"

He laughed, but added at once: "It's all right, kid. I seen you show your game, and it was first class. You can have my hide whenever you say the word, I'll tell you! That Destry that you're scared of, he's a gone goose now! I always used to think he'd oughta have a better chance, but there ain't a man in Wham that wouldn't take a shot at him now, if he could, excepting Bent. And maybe even Bent has had enough of the murderin' devil by this time!"

"Bent?" said the boy.

And he closed his eyes, bewildered and half sick by the memory of the face of Bent, as the murderer had stood above the dead body of Clifton.

"You're still mighty done up," declared Jack. "Lay still. Don't you trouble yourself, none. Unless you could tell us where you come from, because nobody in town seems to know.

"I'm out of the Cumber Pass. Destry——"

He wanted desperately to explain, but the other broke in before he could speak.

It's all right, son. Destry'll never bother you none. There ain't a man in town that would have a word for that red-handed skunk. Nor no woman, neither, exceptin' Charlotte Dangerfield. But a woman'll always stick to a lost cause like a skipper to a sinkin' ship!"

The name thrust deep in the mind of Willie and gave him a sudden determination. Destry had one friend; therefore, to the girl he must go to carry his tidings about the truth of the Clifton murder. No other person would listen. Had not Jack said so, almost in so many words?

35

WHEN at last Destry saw Bent turn back down the trail, he grew heavy of heart, for this man meant to him more than the rest of the world.

He took from his pockets the last things that Bent had brought. There was a steel backed and rimmed pocket mirror; a good strong knife; a quarter pound of Bull Durham and a supply of wheat-straw papers, some matches; some oiled silk, invaluable to keep small necessaries dry; and above all, there was the last strong grip of the hand, and the straight, steady look of Bent's farewell.

And Destry felt that he himself had failed miserably, for he should have been able to find thanks—not eloquent ones, perhaps, because eloquence was not necessary—but a few words to show something of the gratitude that he felt. But how infinitely he valued not the gifts but the thought behind them, he could not begin to express. He could only trust that something of his feeling might have been conveyed by his own silent hand-shake.

Over three hills he watched the rider appear and disappear, finally dwindling away. Then he turned away with a sigh and mounted Fiddle, who had come out in the trail as though made curious by his movelessness.

He rode her at a walk up the first slope and paused her on a bald headed hill to look over the sun bathed mountains. Naked and grim enough they appeared to the casual eye, but Destry loved them because he knew them. That apparent nakedness did not deceive him. The shadow on the side of Mount Scare Crow was really a wood in which fat deer were grazing; on the flats between he did not need to waste ammunition to make his bag of rabbit, when he cared for that meat—a few simple snares would do instead. Between the Scare Crow and Timber Peak the sage hens were always plump and their flesh more delicately flavored than in any other part of the range, and along the sides of Timber Peak itself the squirrels lived by thousands among the trees. And whose palate grows tired of squirrels, toasted brown above wood coals? Off the side of Chisholm Mountain leaped a brook where the trout were silver flashes in the water; and at its base the elk came down to the salt lick. Bears, too, were everywhere, not to be hunted except with fatigue, but bagged readily enough by those who were content to wait for opportunity to come their way.

So all this rough-headed sea of mountains was really a gigantic preserve for Destry, and the harsh face of it pleased him more than ever did the barbed wire fence of a landowner who wishes to guard his game. Moreover, there was such beauty here as soft green hills, and pleasant meadows, and ploughed fields never could afford; for all about him the giants stood up in glistening armor against the pale blue sky and raised his heart and his thoughts with them.

So Destry felt as he stared about him at the highlands. But yonder in the mist which covered the lower region of Wham and its surrounding valley were many men, danger, deceit, struggle, doubt of one another.

There was also behind that veil Charlie Dangerfield, and the thought of her came home to him with a heady sweetness, like wine. That evening he would leave the mountains and ride down to her, and let tomorrow bring what it might!

The wind had paused with the mare, and stood still. Now it sprang up gently and carried with it a subdued thrumming sound. Destry listened to it with instant curiosity, wondering how the waterfalls on the side of Cringle Peak could send the rhythm of their beat so far as this.

Then he jerked up his canted head with a start, suddenly realizing the thing was impossible. The noise could not blow as far as where he sat the saddle.

The mystery was not a thing to be left uninvestigated. To him, as to a wild animal, every unexplained fact was a possibly potent danger. He turned the mare to the farther side of the crest, and looking down into the shallow valley, he saw the cause of the noise.

Five riders were pushing their horses at a steady trot up the gentle slope.

They saw him at once, apparently, and the trot became a swinging gallop. It was Destry they wanted, evidently. Destry, and the price on his head.

And as he sat in the saddle, with the wind pressing against his face and the sun hot on his back, a fierce resentment surged up in him. If he got into the nest of rocks on the side of the mountain and opened fire with the Winchester, how long would that gallant charge persist?

However, it was not for him to resist with guns. If, in fact, Clifton had fallen at his hand, he knew grimly and certainly that fresh victims would be added on this day to his list; but the very knowledge of his innocence handicapped him in the fight.

He swung the mare about, therefore, and crossed the mountain top to the farther side—and saw struggling through the brush three riders—their faint yells as they spotted him came tingling through the thin air to his ears.

Down the hill, then, to leave them soon far behind!

But as he started down the slope, out of the trees not a quarter of a mile away came a rush of three more mounted men! They fired as they came, trusting to a lucky shot, hardly bringing the rifles to the shoulder. And yet one of the bullets sang perilously close to Destry.

Up the grade he went, therefore, keeping the mare just under full speed, for he could tell that she would need her strength later on.

They had not come with single mounts, these eleven, but behind the last group of riders came two more, each leading a cluster of horses naked of the saddle. They were the relief mounts to be used when the first lot were exhausted. And by their action, Destry guessed the whole troop to be chosen animals.

He was glad of the rough ground. It was through such broken rocks that Fiddle made ordinary horses appear to be tied to the ground, and a mile straight up hill soon worked havoc with the horses behind.

It had taken a great deal from the good mare, also. She had traveled far enough for a day's work already, since sun-up, and that hot mile started her lungs laboring like bellows. However, those behind had their heads bobbing hopelessly, and Destry grunted with complacent understanding of what that meant. At his last look, he saw the posse changing saddles, then he entered high brush that cut off his view.

He had three choices—to keep straight on, or to turn to either side. To keep straight on would be a sheer test of horse power, and he doubted the advisability of that when Fiddle was already so tired. To the left lay comparatively smooth going, where her long stride would tell. To the right was a veritable jungle, in which she would shine because of her deerlike surety and activity of foot. He chose to turn to the right; furthermore, it led him in the distant direction of the Dangerfield place!

He had a good hour of labor without sight of open country. The lodgepole pines stood thick in his path and gave him only the sky overhead, and occasional glimpses of hollow valleys or sheer rocky slopes on either hand.

When he came into the open, he was at the head of O'Mara valley, and there was no sight or sound of the enemy. The sun was dropping already behind a Western peak; far beneath he saw a squatter's shack, and the translucent twist of smoke that curled above it. They were quietly cooking supper in that place, cutting bacon, working up the fire, relaxing with the cool of the evening, and the sweet sense of a night of perfect rest before them. He, too, could relax now, and let the mare rest!

He dismounted at once, slackened the girths, and walked on with the tired Fiddle stepping behind him, lagging more than was her wont. And then, well out from the trees, he heard a roar like the beating of surf, and saw eleven horsemen in close formation charging down upon him along the valley.

He could understand what had happened! Reaching the close covert of the trees, his pursuers had turned the chances over in their minds. They could go straight on, or else gamble that the fugitive would turn to one side or the other; and they had taken the long chance, had swung to the correct side, and here they were! Only by a little had they overshot their mark, but they had the double advantage of second mounts, and horses, moreover, which had been taken straight across open country instead of through the heat and the twisting ways of the woods!

But, though he could understand it, Destry was too stunned by the sense of disaster to move at once. Then, with an oath, he jerked up the cinches, sprang into the saddle, and gave the mare her head.

There was no dodging, now. He was too far out in the valley to venture a cut back on either side, for those behind would be sure to gain ground and fill the mare and her rider with bullets.

No, there was nothing for it except a straight pull down the valley, and a blind trust in the long stride of Fiddle.

He jockeyed her as well as he could. She, with a great heart, sprang out against the bit, ready to win her race or die, but he restrained her with his hand, and with a gently reassuring voice which will give a wise horse confidence up to the very gate of defeat.

Over his shoulder he looked back and watched and waited. They came fast. They came pouring in a rush, with heads straight out, and tails snapping in the wind of their gallop. He had to extend Fiddle more and more. She seemed to be flying now at full speed, but still she did not gain, and in her strong gallop there came a trifling heaviness which only her master could have recognized. Yet he felt a blind faith, a superstitious confidence. All the good that had come his way, in more than six years, had been through Chester Bent. Was not this animal his gift, and could she fail her rider?

Still the long beat of her stride continued. It is marvelous that the pursuers could maintain the pace against her, fresh though they might be.

And now, as he looked back under the red of the sunset, he saw that they actually were failing. Back they fell, raggedly. Yonder a man had pulled up and was now standing beside his mustang, which stood with legs braced far apart, dead beat.

But two riders broke out of the pack, like thoroughbreds from among cold blooded stock. They, unfalteringly, clung to the race. They did not lose ground. Gradually they gained.

Destry called to the good mare. He felt the lurch of her muscles as she responded, but almost instantly she was back in her former gait.

He understood, then. She would maintain that gait until she died, but not even in her great spirit was there the power to do more!

He leaned a little aside.

Her head was stretched out true and straight. But he could see the red stain of exhaustion in her bulging eyes; and her red rimmed nostrils flared in a vain effort to drink in more of the life giving air. Froth dripped from her mouth, flecked her throat and shoulders. She still ran as only a great horse can run; but, with the suddenness of a bullet striking home, Destry knew that she was beaten!

36

IT was not that her stride was shorter or more labored, or less swift, but through her body, through the long rhythm of her gallop, it seemed to him that he could discern the slightest faltering, the slightest wavering from side to side. And he knew that she was gone, beaten, broken, perhaps ruined from that moment, perhaps doomed to die, even if he reined her in now!

Of the posse, there was not a man in sight except the two who rode the fine horses. Durable as iron they seemed, and though they could not gain on Fiddle, at least they were holding her even.

Destry turned down the first short valley on the left, and wound up it to a rough tableland above, in the hope that this might make the two realize that they were hunting dangerous quarry alone. And he even turned and tried his rifle at them, shooting perilously close. But still they kept pounding on! They began to shoot random shots, in return, but the most of their energy was given to driving the horses ahead.

Even looking back from the highlands, Destry could not see the rest of the posse and he guessed that they had been so hopelessly distanced that even the sound of firing probably would not bring them up. No doubt they were telling one another, as they rested far away, that the two lucky fellows who had such horses beneath them might let their nags take them up with the quarry—and then what?

Then what, indeed!

He needed only to pull the mare into the first clump of trees, and, leaping down, open fire with his Winchester. If he could not bag two birds as large as these, and so close, then his hand and eye had lost all skill.

But he knew that he could not shoot them. If only he really had had murder charged against him, then simple, simple to add another two to the list. One cannot be hung more than once, even for a thousand crimes!

But he could not fight them off, and close shooting would never do to frighten these fellows. By something in the swing of their shoulders, by something in the slant of their bodies as they came around curves, he knew that they were young boys, and he knew that they were ready to die for glory. It was no thought of the reward that drove them on, he could swear, but a resistless impulse toward great deeds!

He smiled as he thought of that, but the smile was sour. A bullet sang by his ear; he drew on the reins, called to Fiddle, and pitched himself forward along her neck!

She came rapidly to a halt. As she paused, he felt her trembling, her knees sagging and straightening beneath the pressure of his weight, almost as though the swing of the gallop had been easier for her to endure than to stand still, here, oppressed by her own weight and by that of her rider! Then he heard the pounding of swift hoofs behind him, and a pair of whooping Indian cries of exultation.

"*I* nailed him!" Said one. "I got him clean through and through."

"Ay, it was you, Chip. But go mighty soft and slow, now, because he might be playin' possum."

"I'm gunna sink another slug into him and make sure."

"Doncha do it, Chip. He's never shot no helpless people himself, no matter what else he done."

"You're right," said Chip. "I didn't really mean it, anyway. Is he clean dead? Why don't he drop?"

"Because he happened to fall straight, forkin' the hoss. We'd better go slow, though, because you never can tell. These old timers are mighty foxy."

"Sure they are, but I got this old timer covered so doggone tight that he couldn't be got out of this here fix with a can opener! Step up slow. Doncha go forgettin' that this is Destry himself that we got under our hand!"

"Am I likely to be forgettin' that? Folks are gunna remember us for this day's work, if we never don't do nothin' else afterwards, as long as we live!"

"It was me that shot him. Doncha forget that!"

"I'll remember that, all right, Chip. I ain't gunna steal any of your glory from you—only, it was a kind of a lucky shot, I reckon. Keep him covered, will you, while I dismount?"

From the corner of the eye Destry saw the lad dismount. He was a tall, magnificent youngster, with a fine, brown face, and the clearest and most cheerful of eyes. His companion, Chip, was as brown as his companion, but he was prematurely old, with a sallow look and a sneer already forming on his lips.

He kept his rifle at the ready, but yet not completely at the ready, for the muzzle was turned a trifle away from the target, so that the stock of the weapon turned somewhat broadside on to Destry's eye.

He, watching with the most covert care, wondered if with a snap shot he could strike the stock of that gun and knock the weapon out of the hands of the marksman? If he missed the stock, he was reasonably sure to drive the bullet through the side of the boy; and that would be death for the youngster, a thing which Destry mortally shrank from dealing out.

"Go take that Fiddle by the head," the rider was directing. He appeared to have taken command and direction of the operations from his taller and handsomer companion. "She's sure done run a mighty fine race today. I'm gunna match you to see which one of us had oughta have her!"

"Would she come to one of us?"

"Sure she would! I'll wrastle you for her, Skinny."

"*You'll* wrastle me for her?" said the tall fellow, stopping short in his advance towards the mare. "Why, you sawed off runt, what chance would you have if I laid a hand on you?"

"The bigger they are, the quicker that I cut 'em down to my size," declared Chip.

"You talk like a fool!" declared the other boy. "You happened to get in a lucky shot, and now to hear you a gent would think that you was Kit Carson!"

"You'd think that I was before ever I got through with you, young feller!"

"I'm young, am I? Chip, you oughta listen to yourself and get ashamed. Which I never heard nobody talk so ornery and mean as you're doin'."

"Didn't you?"

"No!"

"Are you aimin' at trouble, Skinny?"

"I told you once that I'd lick you if you didn't stop callin' me Skinny."

"You did. What you say don't make no difference to me. If I can't handle you with hands, 1 can do it with guns!"

"Hey, Chip you don't mean that? You don't mean that you'd shoot me?"

"Like a skunk. Why not?"

"I pretty nigh believe that you would!"

"You believe right! I don't care nothin' about you, Skinny, or what you think, or what you want! I'm gunna have Fiddle, because I oughta have her. You can get half of the money, but I'll take Fiddle——"

"You be damned! You take *all* the money, and I'll have the hoss!"

"So's you can ride up and down through Wham and tell folks that you're the one that really beat Destry, and the proof is that you got his mare between your knees, right that minute?"

Destry had heard enough, and had made all of his preparations. He had been able to steal back his right hand and draw out a revolver; now Chip was turned almost at right angles to him, making the shot he wished to attempt twice as simple as it had been before.

Yet still it was difficult, for he knew that he would have to make the first bullet a snap shot, and a snap shot at any distance at such a thing as the stock of a rifle is a hazardous matter. If he failed in the first shot, the second would have to be for the life of Chip, the third for that of Skinny!

Twice he flexed his fingers on the handles of the Colt, then he flicked it across the hanging neck of Fiddle and fired.

He saw the rifle explode in the hands of Chip as it jerked sidewise and fell to the ground, while Chip, with a yell of pain, caught his right hand in his left.

The revolver bullet, striking the hard wood of the stock, had slithered down it, and thrust a great splinter into the hand of Chip.

Destry sat erect in the saddle, now. The gun in his left hand covered Chip, and the revolver in his right covered young "Skinny," whose own weapon was half drawn.

"We don't oughta have no luck," said Skinny with a wonderful calmness. "We was countin' chickens! Destry, you sure done us fine!"

"I wanted to put a slug through him and make sure of him!" wailed Chip. "Damn me if I ever go even huntin' chipmunks with a fool like you, agin, Skinny!"

"Young feller," cautioned Destry, "if it wasn't that I hadn't wanted to murder the pair of you, I'd of ducked into a grove and picked the two of you out of the saddle. Don't talk killin', Chip. You can shoot pretty straight, but you see you didn't get me today. You didn't even nick me! Killin' talk generally gets them done up that does the talkin', and that's a fact for certain sure! Unbuckle that gun belt and let her drop, if you don't mind. That's it. Now you slide down off'n your hoss—this side, please. You, Skinny, back up the road, and keep on backin' up till you hear from me to stop. That's better. Boys, I gotta borrow your hosses, because my Fiddle is plumb fagged. I've gotta ask you one question, though, before I start. How did you get onto my trail?"

"Why, there ain't any secret about that. Some of the old heads figgered that Bent would be tryin' to see you and let you know how things stood, after the killin' of Clifton. We laid guard watchin', and when Bent left in this here direction, we sure come along his trail on the lookout. That's all that they is to it!"

"That's enough. Boys, keep your hands up, and keep on backin'. That'll do, thanks! Who was leadin' you?"

"It was——" began Chip.

"Shut up, you fool!" barked Skinny. "You wanta get somebody in trouble, do you?"

"Skinny," called Destry, "you're all right, son. I leave your gun belt here for you, hopin' that you sure won't try to snag me while I'm ridin' off.

Chip, you need a little agin' in the wood, but you're sure plumb poisonous just now. Don't you go to eatin' iron till you know that your stomach will up and stand that kind of a diet!"

Of the two horses, he selected a tough appearing buckskin for his mount, and swung into the saddle.

"Good luck to you on my hoss!" called Skinny. "You might of dropped us both, Destry, and I'm sure thankin' you."

Destry waved his hand, and glancing back, he saw that Chip was still scowling with furious hate.

Of such were murderers made, he was sure!

37

THAT morning Willie Thornton slept; they roused him at noon only to have him stare sleepily at them, and turn his head away from the proffered food. They did not try to force him to eat. It was Pete who declared that sleep was better for him than nourishment, and so the boy was allowed to fall into a profound slumber.

He wakened, with a tremor and a shock, late in the afternoon. The blood gushed audibly in his temples, from the force of his frightened heartbeat, and he was oppressed with a cold sense of guilt.

It was Destry. He should have done something long before this to save the great man from danger, and now he sat up suddenly in his bunk. The movement made his head spin. He gritted his teeth and forced down deep breaths until his brain cleared, then took stock of the room which hitherto he had seen only as in a dream: the stove, the rusted pipe, the pans, the homemade broom, the cluttered corners, filled with old clothes, boots, traps, guns, fishing tackle, saddlery, harness. It was a junk shop, odds and ends invading the center of the floor.

Near the head of the bunk, depending from nails, were his ragged clothes. These he pulled down and began to dress. It was not easy. When he leaned, dimness rushed over his eyes, and a pain throbbed at the back of his skull. Weakness was in him a physical thing, like a thin tide of water ebbing and flowing in his veins. Sometimes it washed as low as his knees and made them shake. Sometimes it surged up to his armpits and made his arms shudder. It reached his head, and covered his eyes with a film of darkness.

Yet he persisted until he was dressed, and went to the doorway, feeling his way along the wall. The strong blast of the westering sun struck him like a hot hand in the face, and, piercing his shirt, it scorched his body.

He had to blink his eyes against that brilliance, but yet the force of the sun drove strength into his body, and the air seemed to fill him with more life.

He smiled at the weakness which he left behind him!

An old horse was grazing in the corral, wandering around the edges of the fence and reaching under for the grass that grew outside. It was a lump of a creature with a shapeless head and thick legs, but Willie guessed that there might still be too much life in it for him to handle in his present condition. However, he dragged out a battered range saddle, from which most of the leather had been worn away, or rat-eaten. It was a struggle for him to manage the clumsy weight of it. The effort sent sweat rushing out all over his body; his mouth twitched as though an electric spasm controlled the muscles.

Yet those who have known the pain of labor are schooled in endurance. So the boy endured.

When he got a rope from the shed, he had to follow the old mustang patiently for half an hour. Sometimes it would allow him to put his hand upon the mane, before it whirled away and darted off, throwing its heels into the air. He forced himself to be patient, setting his teeth hard, telling himself that this waste of his strength would not exhaust him too much for the work that lay ahead—if only the devil of a horse could be caught.

Snared at last it was, and then came reluctantly on the rope toward the fence, halting, jerking back, thrusting out its long, stiff upper lip with a foolish expression unmatchable except in the face of a horse.

Willie Thornton endured, snubbed the rope around a post, and so at last worked on the saddle with a mighty heave, then struggled until his head swam to force the bit into the stubborn mouth of the brute. At last that work was ended, but he had to sit down on a bar of the gate to steady himself before he could mount. This he only managed by climbing up on the fence and scrambling into the cup of the saddle from a height.

The mustang went off with a rush, rearing, pitching, while Willie reeled from side to side, his lips grinned back with the agony of effort to keep a grip with his short legs upon the barrel ribs of the horse. The kinks were soon out of the veteran mustang, however, and it developed a rocking lope which surprised Willie with its softness.

Once on the road, he looked back toward the shack with a touch of shame to think of what would fill the minds of Pete and Jack when they considered that their good Samaritanship had been repaid by the theft of a horse. But the future would have to be trusted to put all of that straight!

He came into Wham as wild a little figure as ever appeared in even that town, with his hair on end, clotted with dust, his face pale, his cheeks hollow, his eyes staring with the fever that burned him and froze him in turns.

At the blacksmith shop he asked the way to the Dangerfield place, and the smith came out to stare at him and point out the correct trail.

"You look kind of done up, kid," said he. "Better get down and rest yourself a mite. Ain't that Jack Loughran's hoss that you're on?"

"I'm goin' on an errand for Jack," said Willie, and thumped the big ribs of the horse with his bare heels.

He rode into a queer fairyland, for it was the golden time of the afternoon, and hills and trees to the fevered eyes of the boy were enwrapped with mists of rich fire, shot with rose. The dust that puffed up under the hoofs of the horse rose as a magic vapor; the wind struck it away, or tossed it high and thin in weird shapes. The world was possessed of motion—the hills rolled in waves, the trees swayed, the road itself heaved and fell gently before him.

Willie began to laugh at the strangeness of this universe, and then found himself listening for another voice—so far away and elfishly thin did that laughter sound upon his ear.

Then he discovered that the rolling might not be of the landscape around him, but his own uncertain undulation in the saddle. When he tried to grip with his knees, they gave way from the hips, weakly. He could not control himself; the very reins shook in his hand.

Now it appeared to him, as the mustang seemed pausing between steps, that he was a fool to have come out from the town. The blacksmith, for instance, had had an honest face and might have believed the truth of what he said concerning the murder of Clifton. As it was, he probably would fall from the back of the horse long before it reached the house of the Dangerfields!

All was now so dim before his eyes that it was as though he rode through a storm, and when the sun sank, he was in dread lest he should be lost in the utter dark.

Then a great whirling seized his brain and he felt his senses sinking, as a boat whirls and sinks in the grip of a vortex.

When he recovered, he was sprawled forward across the pommel of the saddle and the neck of the horse, his head hanging down and the blood heavy as lead in it.

The mustang was contentedly grazing at the side of the road!

Pushing himself back into the saddle with both shaking arms, the boy looked desperately around him into thick darkness on every hand, a wall of impenetrable black. He was lost—he would die he knew, if help did not come to him, since he could not find his way to it! But his own death seemed a small thing to Willie. It was the great man, the hero of whom he thought most, Destry!

Now as he concentrated his thought upon that glorious image of Destry, the blackness that had covered his eyes lifted wonderfully. He saw that it was not thick night, but only the time of old gold and tarnished russet, faintly streaked along the horizon. The trees looked as huge as houses; he had to tell himself that the black outline he wanted to find would be marked by a few lights. Then he hammered weakly against the sides of the horse, and it went on, tossing its head until the bridle jingled, stepping out long and free as a horse will do when it feels that the end of the day's work must be near.

He dared not put the animal to a jog or a lope, because he knew that the swift motion would roll him promptly from the saddle, and, once out of it, he doubted his ability to so much as crawl. So greatly had the weakness increased upon him.

Then, with a turn of the road, he saw before him the shining of a lamp through an open window, its rays fanning out in brilliant, trembling clusters. Toward that light he went, when a form seemed to rise before him out of the ground.

It was a man who was saying: "Hullo, kid! Where you from?"

"I'm lookin' for the Dangerfield place."

"Here's the house. Whacha want?"

"I wanta see Miss Dangerfield!"

"Come on in, then. She'll be back, soon."

"I wanta see her real bad," muttered Willie.

"Well, then, you traipse on across the field, yonder, and likely you'll find her. She went out walkin' toward the old shack. You can see the roof of it there between the trees—no, not that way. Look there! Can't you see?"

"I got dust in my eyes," said Willie.

His voice was uncertain.

"Whacha been cryin' about?" asked the gruff voice of the man. "Whacha cryin' about now? You're a mighty lot too big a kid to be cryin'. Y'oughter be ashamed of yourself!"

Willie did not answer.

He knew that the quaver in his voice was weakness, not tears, but the hot shame he felt at the reproof flushed him with a new strength. It cleared his eyes, and enabled him to see the pointed roof of the old shack between the trees, in the dusk before him. Toward it he aimed the horse.

The bushes washed about him; they scratched his bare knees cruelly, but he was glad of the pain, because it helped to rouse him for the words which he must speak when he found the girl.

If he found her!

The thought of failing made the frantic panic leap straight-way into his brain. He fought it back. But another thought now beset him. Friend to Destry though she was, still what could a woman do in such an affair as this? He should have found a man. He should have told his story to Pete and Jack. They were too kind to be dishonest. They would have believed——

So he rode on in a torment, and saw the trees and the bushes divide before him. The old house lay just before him, with the front door open, hanging from one hinge.

Above the door, one deep, empty attic window looked out at him like an eyehole from a skull. There was no life about the place.

"Miss Dangerfield!" he called.

It seemed to Willie that he heard an echo pick up the name and whisper it; or was that a stir in the bushes around him?

"Miss Dangerfield!" he called again.

A quiet voice spoke to him; he saw a woman come around the corner of the building, and slipping out of the saddle, he tried to go to her, only to have his knees buckle beneath the impact of his weight.

38

Now his body was hardly more than a bundle of limp string, but his brain remained clear enough. The girl ran to him, caught him beneath the shoulder, her fingers gripping the flaccid flesh with the strength of a man's hand.

But as for that, he remembered, she was the woman who loved Destry— not to be expected like other women! His faith in what she might accomplish soared suddenly.

"Who are you, son?" she asked. "And what d'you want of me. Why, you're sick! You're hot as fire with fever!"

"I gotta say something!" said Willie Thornton. "Will ya listen?"

"I'll listen! Poor youngster!"

She kneeled on the ground by him, supporting him still beneath the shoulders. Neither she nor the boy was conscious of the form that stepped silently from the shrubbery and loomed beside them, listening.

"You're Charlie Dangerfield?"

"Yes."

"You b'long to Destry?"

She hesitated not an instant.

"I b'long to Harry Destry," she admitted. "Why?"

"You swear you'll b'lieve what I'm gunna tell you?"

"I'll believe!"

"Destry didn't kill Clifton!"

"Ah, ah!" he heard her gasp. "Thank God!"

He raised a hand and gripped weakly on her arm. His head fell back with mortal weakness, but she passed a hand beneath it and held him close to her like a helpless child. He would have resented that support fiercely at any other time, but now he was glad of it, for out of her cool hands strength flowed into him, greater than the strength which pure air gives; and he breathed a delicate scent of lavender, held close against her breast.

"He didn't kill Clifton. I seen. I was in Bent's house. I seen Bent steal the knife from Destry's room."

He could make his lips move, but suddenly his voice failed him; his eyes closed.

"Make your strength hold out one minute," he heard the girl appealing to him.

Her face pressed close to his.

"Try to tell me the rest!"

"I follered Bent and Clifton out of Bent's house. I was scared, but I follered. There was murder'n the air! I come to Clifton's house behind 'em—garden gate—dog——"

His voice trailed off.

"Try, honey, try!" she whispered eagerly.

"I got up to the window. I seen Bent talk to Clifton. I heard him say something about money he owed Clifton. I seen Clifton beg for his life, mighty horrible. I seen him crawl like a dog. I seen—I seen——"

"One more word—then I'll take care of you. I'll make you well again, poor boy!"

"I seen Bent grab him by the hair——"

"Clifton?"

"Ay, I seen him grab Clifton by the hair and yank back his head, and stab him in the hollow of the throat, and I heard Clifton gag, like a stuck pig, and fall, and twist his legs on the floor and——"

The life went out of Willie Thornton suddenly. He hung limp in the arms of the girl, breathing so faintly that she scarcely felt the stir of it against her cheek.

And now, as she looked up from him, ready to call for help to carry him to the house, she saw the silhouette of the second listener beside her.

"Harry?" she gasped.

"It's me," said Destry.

"Did you hear?"

"I heard."

"Is it true, Harry? Could Chet have done such a thing?"

"I'm plumb turned to stone," said Destry. "But the kid wouldn't lie. He's give my life to me once; tonight he's give it to me agin! It's Willie Thornton."

The voice of the boy began again in a fluttering gasp:

"He seen me at the window and hunted me through the dark. Him and the dog. Jumped—the water was mighty cold. But Jack and Pete they caught me—go on, old hoss, because I ain't gunna fall!"

"He's out of his head, poor kid!" said the girl. "He's tremblin' with the fever, Harry. God keep him from no harm out of this!"

"Give him to me," said Destry. "I'll carry him into the house. You go fetch over some blankets and more help, then we'll pack him over there!"

The voice muttered softly, barely audible to them both:

"You b'longin' to Destry, I didn't dare to tell nobody but you. It was a long way, between dyin' and livin'. One side of the road dyin', one side livin'—the old hoss kep' movin'—which I didn't fall——"

Destry stood up, with the youngster in his arms, holding him gently, holding him close.

"He's out of his head," said the girl.

"Quick!" said Destry, and she turned and ran swiftly from the shack, through the brush, and toward the house of her father.

Destry went on into the cabin where he managed to support the boy with one arm while he took out a match with the free hand and prepared to scratch it.

As he did so, something of an incredible lightness touched his face, like a spider's web, but falling toward the floor. He looked up, bewildered, and again there were several light touches against his skin.

"You're mighty strong," said the boy. "You're the one for Destry. You go tell the judge; you swear what I said was true. Them that are dyin' don't lie, which Pop always said in the old days. Me dyin', I'm tellin' the truth. I seen it. I seen him kill Clifton—not Destry—he ain't no murderer——"

"Son," said Destry, "it ain't Charlie that's holdin' you here. It's Destry. I——"

He felt the slim body stiffen.

"Hey! Is it you, Harry?"

"It's me, old timer! You ain't dyin'. Charlie'll get you well."

"Why, I wouldn't care much," said Willie, "me bein' tolerable sleepy, right now. Lemme get down, Destry. I can stand pretty good, I reckon—only bein' a mite sleepy——"

Destry struck a light, and looked down at a face white as the death of which Willie had spoken, and wildly staring eyes, rimmed with black; and pale lips, purple gray, as though they were coated with dust.

Such a horror struck through the man at the sight of this, that he jerked his head up, and saw, as the match flame spurted wide, the thin gleam of a fleck of straw falling from the ceiling above him.

But straw does not sift through cracks in an old ceiling unless it is disturbed. By wind, perhaps. But there was not a mortal touch of wind in the air, this evening! What else was above them in the attic?

He dashed the match to the floor and leaped to the side. That moment, from the trap door, the sawed-off shot gun of Cleeves roared like thunder and lightning.

The flare of the double discharge showed the whole shack lighted, and, behind the leveled barrels of the gun, the contorted face of the marksman.

Destry, springing aside, had snatched his Colt out; now he fired at the point where the pale face had glimmered in the dark of the attic above him, and next stood still.

The boy had fainted. His legs and head dragged down feebly, loosely, but as Destry held the small body close, he felt the uncertain, slow flutter of the heart. Fortune and his own quick foot had enabled him to side step the double charge even at this close range. Too close, perhaps, for the purpose of the sawed-off gun; five feet farther away the charge would have spread out inescapably wide!

What was the marksman above them doing now? Destry poised his gun to shoot a second time, but he feared that the flash of his weapon would illumine him as a target for another shot; furthermore, if he strove to glide back through the doorway, he would similarly be placing himself against a light, no matter how dim a one it seemed. So he stepped back against the wall and waited through a long moment, lifting the head of Willie Thornton until it rested comfortably against his shoulder.

Now he heard, at first too softly to be sure of it, but presently distinctly, a sound which might have been the soft and regular movement of someone crossing the floor, or the creaking of the ladder as someone cautiously descended it, lowering himself softly from rung to rung.

There was this peculiarity about the sound, that it was quite regular, and yet that it seemed to come from different parts of the room, sometimes from the window, or again from the door, or rising out of the very floor, as it were.

The nerves of Destry were firm enough—none firmer in all of the world, perhaps—and yet they began to shudder a bit under this suspense.

He could not stand still. Moreover, there must be something done for the boy, who hung limply in his arms. This might be no fainting spell, but death itself, for he no longer felt the beating of the feeble heart against his breast!

So Destry started moving toward the doorway, and as he did so, a warm drop struck the back of the hand with which he held his Colt ready for a second shot. He stopped with a leap of nerves. Then, passing his hand over the same place, again the warm drop fell upon it.

And then he knew!

His first shot had gone home, and Hank Cleeves lay dead in the attic, whose loosened straw had sifted down and betrayed the presence of something living within the house. Cleeves lay dead. That was the reason there had been no stir of the man as he reloaded his double-barreled weapon. That was the reason that there had been no second shot, and the first spurt of blood, soaking through the crack in the floor, had made that singular tapping sound which had almost frightened Destry forth from the shack.

He shook his head to drive away the concern from his mind. As he did so, he heard a stifled voice just outside the door exclaiming: "Hank! Hank!" There was a pause, and then the voice repeated: "Hank, did you get him?"

And Destry grinned in the darkness and felt the hot blood thrill along his veins. More than Hank had come to make this trap and more than Hank might pay for its catch!

39

SOMEWHERE yonder in the darkness, Fiddle waited for him; somewhere away from him, Charlie Dangerfield was calling together her men who were to carry poor little Willie Thornton to the house. But there was another danger close at hand. He heard voices at the door and a little outside it.

"Hank doesn't answer."

"Call again, then."

"Hey, Hank!"

Louder they called: "Hello, Hank!"

There was no answer from Cleeves. He never again would answer any man. His lips were cold. Until Judgment Day, a thousand trumpets might blow, and Hank never would reply. He whom a hundred thousand eyes had seen now had vanished. He was gone. He was away. Deeper than the seas he was buried, and deeper than the mountains could hide him. The impalpable spirit was gone, and only the living blood remained to tell of him, dripping down into the silence of the old shack, drop by drop, softly spattering, like footsteps wonderfully light and wonderfully clear. Hank Cleeves was ended, and his long fingers and his hairy hands would never again do wonders with hammer and chisel, with saw, and wrench. The boys would no longer stand around and admire the mechanic. They would no longer yearn to grow up to such a man. The chips would no longer fly, nor the nails sink home for Hank Cleeves, nor the rafters ring under his hammer.

He was gone. Yonder lay his body, perhaps with the heavy forty-five calibre slug of lead smashed through the breast and into the vitals. Perhaps the bullet had beaten through brain and brainpan, and so the body lay lifeless. But he was ended; that cunning machine could function no more; that ineffable spark was extinguished.

And Destry stood below in the darkness, still between life and death, with the limp body of the boy in his arms.

He heard from the lips of Willie the faintest of sighs, and it made his breast lift, as the breast of a mother stirs when the infant moves beside her, at night. He felt all of paternity, all of motherhood, also, since both qualities lie mysteriously buried in the heart of man; since he strives to be himself, and also to reproduce physically what cannot physically be born to the world. His ideas, his spirit, his heart and soul he would put into flesh, but they must remain forever unfleshed, ideal, impalpable, here glimpsed at with paint, here staring out of stone, here charmed into words, but always hints, glimpses, and nothing to fill the material arms as a child fills the arms of its mother.

So these mysteries softly thronged down on the sad soul of Destry, and he touched them in their flight as a child might hold up its hands and touch moths flying in the night, without comprehension, with only vague desires and emotions.

But one thing he could know, in the feeble rationalization of all men, with which they strive to reduce the eternal emotions to concrete "yes" and "no," that this boy had once almost died for him, and now actually might be dying for him in very fact. He knew it, and wonder filled him. He became to himself something more than a mere name and a vague thing; he for the first time visualized "Destry" as that man appeared before the eyes of others, striking terror, striking wonder, filling at least the eyes of a child with an ideal!

Knowing this, he felt a sudden scorn for the baser parts that were in him, the idler, the scoffer at others, the disdainful mocker at the labors of life. He wished to be simple, real, quiet, able to command the affection of his peers.

It seemed to Destry that, through the boy, for the first time he could realize the meaning of the word "peer." Equal. For all men are equal. Not as he blindly had taken the word in the courtroom, with wrath and with contempt. Not equal in strength of hand, in talent, in craft, in speed of foot or in leap of mind, but equal in mystery, in the identity of the race which breathes through all men, out of the soil, and out of the heavens.

So it was that hatred for his enemies left him.

In another day, he had derided them, he had contested with them, he had conquered them; for those defeats they had avenged themselves by confining him for six years for an offense of which he was innocent; but, at the same time, of another offense he had preeminently been guilty, for he had looked down upon them, and from a tower of self-content, he had laughed at them.

Why?

Because they were less swift in unsheathing a six-shooter!

Because they stuck less firmly on the back of a horse!

Because there was more weak flesh and less leather in them!

Because they faltered in the climb, weakened under the weight, staggered in the crisis, looked for help where no help could come! So he also had faltered, had weakened, had staggered, had looked about him in the prison.

They were not different. They were made of one flesh and spirit and therefore they were his equals, his "peers." To them the world in which he had been free was to them, in a sense, a prison.

These understandings, rushed suddenly upon him, made him slip back closer against the wall, and hold the limp form of the boy more tenderly in his arms. He, too, had been a child; so were they all, men, and women, children also, needing help, protection, cherishing, but capable now and then and here and there of great deeds inspired by love and high aspiration. It was such a power that had come upon little Willie Thornton. He with his small hand had snatched a life from the shadow of the law and thrown another man in the peril of the gibbet!

So Destry stood close by the door and waited, more stirred with sudden, deep striking thoughts than in all his life before; so that it seemed to him there was a pure, thin light of beauty falling upon the world and upon all of the men in the world, except only Chester Bent. He, like a shadow, lay athwart the life of Destry, and there arose in the latter no boyish and irresponsible hate, no transient hunger for vengeance, but a vast and all possessing disdain and disgust.

With it came a fear, also. For if Bent had deceived him, then he knew that Bent was such a power as he never before had tried his strength of mind and hand against.

He heard the voices continue, close beside him.

"There ain't any answer."

"He's there."

"He couldn't of missed."

"I seen that gun loaded myself with two charges of buckshot. Extra big. It would of blowed the side out of a house."

"I think I heard them shot strike wood, though! They rattled!"

"Sure, but some of them hit Destry."

"I heard him fall!"

"What about the kid?"

"He's scared sick, somewheres in there."

"Maybe the slugs hit him."

"A kid like that ain't much loss."

"Why don't Hank answer?"

"Because he's gloatin'. He ain't a talker, anyways!"

"Go on in, Bud."

"I'm with you, Phil, but I ain't gunna go in first!"

"Come on, all of us!"

"We'll all go in, or Hank'll say we was scared!"

Suddenly four men slid through the doorway, closely packed, one behind the other.

"Hey, Hank!" called one of the voices softly.

There was no answer from Hank Cleeves.

"Hello, Hank, where are you?"

Destry stepped into the doorway, and then outside into the open, pure, safe air of the night, and no eye noted him against the stars beyond the door. Certainly he heard no voice call out after him!

But within the house, he heard a voice insistently repeat: "Hello, there, Cleeves! Where are you?"

And then a faintly groaning throat replied, above them: "Dead, dead, and God forgive me!"

Destry paused, with an odd thrill running through his body, for he remembered Hank Cleeves of old, tall, wiry, pale, thoughtful, an ironic and caustic boy, walking apart from the rest, acclaimed as a genius by boys with lesser talents for the making of sleighs, and toys of all sorts.

Now Hank lay dying in the attic, and his friends were climbing up the ladder toward him, and Destry was filled with a sense of desolation because he was the slayer, and not among the rescuers!

The hot, long school afternoons poured back upon his mind, the races to the swimming pool, and flash of naked bodies from the old log into the water, and Hank Cleeves treading water and throwing back his long hair from his eyes with both hands—a bold, strong, fearless, reckless leader among boys, until Destry adroitly had pushed him to one side. For that very reason, he knew in his heart, Cleeves now lay dying in the attic of the shanty!

But he stepped around the corner of the cabin, hearing the half-suppressed, excited voices behind him in the house, and passed through the thicket to the place where he had left Fiddle tethered. Here he mounted, and leaning from the saddle, he picked up the still senseless body of Willie Thornton, and rode back with him toward the Dangerfield place.

As he went he heard a sudden snorting of horses, a trampling of hoofs, rushing off violently, as if under the thrust of the spur, and a crackling of the brush as the mustangs were forced furiously through it.

The four who remained were in full flight, the four left of the twelve men he had selected as his enemies. Perhaps they feared that he might be rushing on their trail, ready to pick them off, one by one, for he could hear them scattering to either side, and fanning out to make his way behind them yet more difficult.

They were not in his mind, except with pity.

He went on toward the Dangerfield house, and on the way, he met three men and Charlie Dangerfield herself, coming in haste with a litter borne among them, to carry Willie Thornton back to the house.

He gave the child down into their hands. He saw Charlie Dangerfield cherishing his face between her hands, by the starlight.

She paid no more attention to Destry than if he had been a spirit rather than a mounted man. So he turned the fine head of Fiddle toward Wham and rode straight toward it across country, going as the bird flies, regardless of fences and ditches in his way.

40

THE sheriff was not on his veranda, neither was he in his bedroom, but in his small office, adjoining the jail cells, Destry found him bent over a desk which was piled high with papers, photographs, and such encumbrances. Through the window Destry watched him for a moment; then shrank down into the shadows as a noisy group of miners went down the board walk, chattering and shouting in their eagerness to spend a month's pay.

In the dark, Destry considered, but finally he went around to the door of the jail and rapped on it; the jailer opened to him with a growl that turned into a groan of terror when he saw the face of his visitor. He staggered back with his arms high in the air.

"I never was none of 'em!" he gasped. "I never had a hand again you, Harry!"

"I don't want to bother you none," Destry explained. "Turn your back a minute, Tom."

Tom obeyed willingly, and when the click of a door sounded, he looked over his shoulder in fear. But Destry was out of sight!

He stood now before Ding Slater without a gun in his hand.

"You come to give yourself up?" asked Ding quietly.

"I ain't pullin' a gun on you, Slater," said the other. "I reckon that speaks for itself!"

"Of course it does," said the sheriff.

"You'll be pretty set to hang me," suggested Destry.

"For what?" asked Ding Slater.

"For Clifton?"

"I been a long time sheriffing," said Slater, "but I never took no pleasure in the hangin' of a man for a thing he didn't do!"

"Hold on," broke in Destry. "There was my knife in his throat!"

"Sure there was," replied Slater, "but there wasn't your hand hitched on to it."

"Besides," went on Slater, "I never heard of a Destry bein' so plumb careless as to leave a knife stickin' in the throat of a dead man!"

"Who did it, then?"

"Somebody that if I was to tell you who it was, you would almost of rather that you'd done it yourself."

"That's a lot to say, old timer."

"Ay" nodded Slater. "It's a lot to say. What's really brought you in here, son?"

"I wanted to ask you to come along with me and watch me shoot up a gent, Ding."

"Go on. I'm ready for the joke."

"I'm plumb serious."

"What man?"

"I'm going to kill Chester Bent, or be done in by him."

"Bent?" cried Slater, rising to his feet.

"Ay."

"You know about him, then?"

"I know everything!"

"About the old robbery, too?"

Destry hung on the verge of the next prepared sentence which he had been about to speak and looked at the sheriff with amazement. "What robbery?" he managed to gasp.

"The express! The express six years ago!" said Slater impatiently. "The train you were supposed to rob! The robbery that put you in prison—the robbery that's killed or ruined eight of the twelve men who put you there."

"Hold on, Ding," urged Destry. "Don't run away with this here race all by yourself!"

"It was about then that Bent got rich, all at once. Begun to buy and speculate. How? Stolen money, I say! Stolen money, and the man that he was befriendin' so's the ladies cried over him about it, that was the man that had gone to prison in his place. No wonder that he was kind to you, Harry!"

Destry, like a bewildered child, held out one hand and curled up the fingers of it as he counted over the points of the case:

"Chet grabs the money—he plants the package of coin on me—why, I even remember talkin' to him that day on the street, when he gave me the hundred!—he skids me to prison, sittin' by my side in the courtroom—he takes me into his house after I get out, and tries to have my throat cut for me so's he can take in Charlie Dangerfield——"

Truth, at which he had guessed, suddenly was revealed to him with a naked face, and Destry groaned in his anger.

The sheriff finished: "And finally, he murders a man to put the curse of the law on Destry. Harry, I dunno that I got a right to interfere with the right workin' of the law, but I'm gunna go down with you and let you arrest Bent. If you miss him, which ain't likely, I'll pull my own gun on him! Come along. Start movin' to cool off, because you look pretty much on fire!"

They hurried from the jail and down the street, the jailer aghast at the sight of the two men, shoulder to shoulder, and Destry not in irons! In front of the jail they took their horses, and the first fear struck at Destry.

"S'pose that he's guessed something and skinned out of town?"

"It ain't half likely. He's got his whole stake here. There's the light in his library window."

They left the two horses at the corner of the hedge and went on toward the gate; from a house down the street they could hear an old man's voice singing one of the monotonous songs with which a night herder keeps the cows bedded down with comfortable minds. The sticky new sprouts of the fir touched their clothes and hands. Acrid dust they breathed still hanging in the air from the last riders who had galloped down the street.

But all was peace, and the bright mountain stars watching them, as they cautiously drew the gate ajar and slipped through. From the lighted window they looked in on Bent, and the first glance was enough.

He was not busied now with his pretense of study. Instead, he was emptying a saddle bag onto the face of the center table, and out of the bag tumbled packages of green and yellow backs, neatly held together by elastics. There was a little chamois sack, moreover, the mouth of which Bent undid and poured out as a sample of the contents a handful of jewels which he shifted back and forth so that the lamplight sparkled on them before he restored them to the sack.

There was no doubt about it. Bent was about to take wing! He wore not his office clothes but a full cow-puncher's outfit. There was even the cartridge belt about his hips and a holstered Colt low down on his thigh. He was ready to take wing, and with him he was to bear away this nest egg from which he might build up a fortune in another place.

Destry and the sheriff drew back from the window, and inside the coat of the former, Ding Slater pinned the priceless badge.

"The law's made you sweat, son," said Ding. "Now it's time for you to get some advantage out of it. Go in and get him, and bring him out to me! I wouldn't spoil this party for you."

Destry gripped the hand of Slater and without a word glided up the front steps of the house. The door was not locked. It opened silently upon its well-oiled hinges, and Destry passed into the darkness of the hall. The first door to the right was faintly sketched by the light of the lamp, leaking through the crack around it.

He found the knob, turned it softly, and pushed the door wide—then stepped in to find Bent turned toward him with a leveled revolver!

He nodded toward Bent with a smile and closed the door behind him, only noticing for the rest that the money had been swept from the table and restored to the fat saddle bag that lay on a nearby chair.

"You?" said Bent.

And he let the muzzle of his revolver slowly tip down. Not a sudden motion of friendship, but a gradual decline of the gun, while his eyes still glittered coldly at the intruder. Plainly he was asking himself if it would not be worth while to finish off Destry this instant. But his glance flashed toward the window, and he seemed to decide that the noise was more than he cared to risk.

"It's me," said Destry. "Did I scare you, Chet, comin' in like this, soft-foot?"

"You gave me a start," said Bent, and he put up the gun, but still reluctantly.

"I've been out at the ranch," he added, indicating his outfit. "And now, old son, how are things with you? Did you go down to see Charlie?"

Destry had prepared his answer to this question, but he noticed that as Bent asked it, he looked down toward the floor and seemed tensely expectant. Something was known by Bent. How much, he could not say. Therefore Destry changed his mind. He had intended to say that he had not been near the Dangerfield place, but now he said: "Yes, I was there! And half an inch from bein' trapped, Chet."

"How come."

"The skunks had word about what I was gunna do, or else they'd been trailin' me pretty close."

"Trailin' you?"

"When I got there to the old shack, they was outside and inside."

He hesitated.

"What happened?" asked Bent, his voice guarded and husky.

"There was a slip of a kid that came in, Chet. He had something to tell me, he said. I'd barely started talkin' with Charlie when he arrived and the first thing that happened, this kid come sashayin' up. The one that had helped me up in the Cumber Pass. Sick with fever—mighty dizzy—he staggered into the shack——"

"And what did he say?" asked Bent in a snarl.

"Why, I didn't have no good way of findin' out, because the minute that he was startin' to talk, a double-barrel shotgun went off from the attic of the shack, and I seen the face of Cleeves behind the flash of it! I took a snap shot that finished Cleeves, but the buckshot pretty nigh tore the boy in two!"

A glare of the most ferocious joy appeared in the eyes of Bent.

"Killed him, Harry?" he asked, and came toward the other.

"Killed him dead," said Destry, "the poor little devil! And the same minute, the gents outside—for there was the rest of 'em ready—made a rush for the door, but a couple of bullets turned 'em back. And here I am. I come fast to you, Chet, wantin' to ask you what I'd better do next. Because Charlie and me had no chance to talk."

"Go back to her," said Bent. "Go back, and I'll ride along with you, Harry! I'll ride with you out to the place!"

Excess of relief overwhelmed him and he laughed a little, shakily.

41

HE had learned, no doubt, of the appearance of the boy at the house of Jack and Pete, and again of his riding through Wham. That was the death blow to Bent's tower of ambition, for with ten words the youngster could destroy him utterly. He had made his preparations for departure rapidly. Another minute, probably, and Destry would have been too late to catch the fugitive.

But now Bent heard that his small enemy was dead, and life inside the law again became possible for him. For with Willie Thornton out of the way, Destry was the murderer of Clifton!

The relief spread over the face, the eyes of Bent; it appeared in the heartier voice of Bent as he spoke again.

"Harry, you've taken a long chance in coming into Wham. No matter what happened, you should have stayed out there to see Charlie. But I'll take you back. The poor kid was killed, eh?"

"He might have been," said Destry.

"Might?" said Bent.

His voice was almost a shout.

"Mighta been scared to death," said Destry. "But he had a chance to say a few words."

Fierce pleasure filled him as he saw the face of Bent whiten, and the green light of desperation come into his face.

"What did he say?"

"Raved a mite, Chet. Crazy talk. Something about you bein' the one that killed Clifton."

Bent laughed.

But suddenly he was aware that there was no answering smile on the face of his companion, but gravely, keenly, Destry was watching him. His laughter halted abruptly.

"And what about you, Harry?" he asked. "What *d'you* think about the kid's story?"

Destry waved his hand.

"Kid's get a lot of fool ideas," he said. "I ain't so much interested in that, old son, as I am in the yarn that Slater's just been tellin' me about the job that you done on the express six years ago——"

It was a blow so sudden and crushing to Bent, and it came upon him so unexpectedly, that he went back a staggering pace and rested his hand against the wall.

Swiftly he rallied, and Destry covered the moment of confusion by saying: "And I've been admiring the way that you handled everything from that point on, Chet. The way that you passed me into the pen for six years, say, and the way that you pretty nigh cried with joy when I got out again! The way that you been befriendin' me ever since, too, is pretty touching. Traps in my room, guns in the dark, lies and sneakin' treachery!"

His voice did not rise as he talked.

Bent, on the farther side of the room, looked like a half stunned fighter striving to regain full control of his wits.

At last he said: "I'll tell you, Harry, that you've been listening to a poor sick kid and to an old fool. You don't mean to tell me that you believe what either of them have been saying?"

"Not more'n I believe the Bible," said Destry.

"Harry, what's up?" asked Bent, his face shining with sweat.

"This!" said Destry.

He drew aside the flap of his coat, and exposed the badge of office which the sheriff had just pinned there.

"So?" said Bent.

He looked up at the ceiling, but Destry knew that the other's attention in spite of all seeming was constantly fixed upon him.

"Jail or guns, Chester," he suggested. "You can come along with me and be poisoned with the things that everybody's gunna say about you, or else you can take your chance right here and now with old Judge Colt, that don't never make no mistakes!"

Bent drew a quick, long breath and straightened.

"It's better this way," he said. "I've been a fool in leaving you to other hands. I should have known from the first that you're enough of a man to need my special personal attention, which I'm going to give you now, Harry!"

"You'll fight?"

"I'll kill you," said Bent, "With a good deal more pleasure than I ever did any act of my life. Before this, I've been held back by other considerations."

"Charlie, for one?"

The face of Bent wrinkled with malignancy.

"I would have had her," he declared. "Time and a little patience while she forgot the death of the murderer, Destry—and then I would have married her."

"I doubt it," said Destry. "But what made you kill Clifton? Only to chuck the blame on me?"

"I wanted to see you hang," admitted Bent. "I always wanted to see that, from the time when you bested me, when we were boys. Besides, I owed Clifton money, and that was after all the cheapest way of paying him off!"

"Say, I hadn't thought of that! You owed him money? Well, you're a business man, old timer!"

"You stand on top just now, and you gloat a little," said Bent coldly. "But I'll win the game. There are other towns than Wham, other names than that of Bent, other girls than Charlie Dangerfield—though I admit that I've never seen 'em. But better to be a Bent on the wing than a Destry under the ground! Are you ready?"

"You're gettin' tolerable honest, Chet," said the other. "I been wonderin' when you'd try a crooked gun play on me!"

"I don't need to," said the other unexpectedly. "I got you inside the palm of my hand, and I'm gunna keep you there!"

"I reckon that you're in good practice, Chet."

"D'you think that I didn't start preparing for the day you'd get out of prison the day you went into it? Little things are fairly sure to float up to the surface, in time, and there was never a minute when I didn't half expect that I'd have to face you with a gun. The six years that you've missed, I've been working."

A dog yapped shrill and loud across the street; it was silent. And Bent stood at the edge of the table, resting his finger tips lightly upon it.

The very appearance of sleekness seemed to have left him, and the man was hard with muscle as his brain was hard with resolution.

"Knife, or hand, or gun, Destry!" said he. "I'm ready for any one of the three. Which will you take?"

And suddenly fear leaped into the mind of Destry. He who so long had carried the frost of terror to others, now felt it himself. It was not the fear of death, but that much greater dread of being conquered. That which supports the champion is the knowledge that he never has been beaten. Because of pride, he is a superman, until he faces in the ring an equal confidence and feels that stunning impact of the first heavy blow. So it was with Destry. Shaken, chilled, he stared at Bent and saw a faint, cruel smile on the lips of the other. He felt that he could recognize that smile. How often had it appeared on his own lips when he faced lesser men?

"When the dog barks again——" said Bent.

And they waited. There was no attempt on the part of Bent to take an advantage. His finger tips still rested lightly on the edge of the table, his smile persisted, and the cold fire welled and gleamed in his eyes.

Then, shrill and distant as the note of a muted violin, the dog barked again. At one instant the right hands leaped, the guns flashed, and a wrenching impact tore the Colt from the fingers of Destry, flung it back against his body, and toppled him from his feet.

He saw, as he fell, the weapon flashing up to cover him and send home a fatal shot; and he knew that he had met his match at last and had been beaten, fairly and squarely.

All of that rushed through his brain, but as he struck the floor he heard a rapid fire opened from the window. The sheriff, whom he had forgotten!

Straight at the head of Destry, Bent had fired, but the attack from the side sufficiently unsteadied his hand to make his bullet fly wide. It struck the floor and cast dust and splinters into the face of Destry.

Bent, stooping, scooped the crammed saddle bag that carried the cash relics of his fortune from the chair, and ran for the doorway.

He dodged, like a teal in flight, and then the darkness of the hallway received him, while Destry crawled slowly to his knees, to his feet. He could not realize, for a moment, the thing that had happened to him, but stood balancing like a drunkard, uneasy, depressed, fumbling with his mind until the truth drove home.

Beaten, saved only by a masked attack from the side that had routed Bent, he was no longer the man that he had been! He, the conqueror, had been met and conquered! He groaned and struck his fists into his face. Then he sprang for the door.

The world which he knew was now reduced to a great blank in which there lived a single face and a single name—that of Chester Bent. And until they met again and fought to a grim finish, he could not hold up his head and call his soul his own.

Fiercely he ran into the hall, tore open the front door, and crashed against the sheriff, who was lunging in.

"Hey—Harry—are you hurt? Did I hit him?"

"Get out of my way!" gasped Destry.

He hurled Ding Slater roughly from him and leaped down the steps to the gravel of the front path.

When he reached the gate, the violence of his hand upon it wrenched it off the hinges. He left it clattering upon the path before him and turned swiftly down the outside of the hedge toward the horses.

Fiddle, as though she understood, threw up her head and whinnied softly. He whipped the reins up, leaped into the saddle, and started the good mare forward on the run.

From the rear of the house, he guessed, the fugitive conqueror would be riding, by this time, cutting back through the woods and over the rolling highlands beyond.

And so through those woods he drove Fiddle. The trees flicked back on either side. He saw the naked hills, the stars, and against them the shadowy outline of a horseman riding fast before him.

42

MUCH had been taken from Fiddle that day, but she had rested since the strain and now she was willing to run on, straight and swift. And every bound she made lifted the heart of Destry. He felt a cold, hard certainty that unless he overtook his conqueror on this night and fought out the battle with him again, he would never again be the Harry Destry whom other men had learned to fear.

Not that he cared to triumph over them, as he had done before. For now that he had dipped into the valley of humiliation, his heart was softened, and with every pulse of the mare's gallop he swore inwardly that this night would see the last bullet fired from his Colt, whether he won or lost.

It must be a short race, he knew, for Fiddle could not endure another heart-racking effort in this day, but he trusted to her first fierce burst of speed to overhaul the other.

Mercilessly he pressed her on, until her ears flattened, and her head stretched out straight with her labor up the hill, then over it and shooting down a sharp slope at breathless speed. It seemed to Destry like plunging into the dark of a well; and the stars flew back over his head like sparks from a wheel. Then he was riding up the easy floor of a hollow and the trees stood on the ridges at either hand like fenceposts planted regularly.

But all was growing brighter as the moon came up in the east, small and dull behind a rag of clouds. By her light, Destry saw the rider before him far closer than at first and working desperately to drop his pursuer.

It could not be done! With a great upbursting of exultation, Destry knew that the other was surely being overhauled, and Fiddle herself like a hunting dog increased her pace as she saw the race in her grip.

They turned a sharp bend of the valley. The walls of it increased on either hand, and to make surety doubly sure, Destry saw that he had run his prey into a box cañon. Straight before him the way terminated in a low wall over which a stream of water tumbled into spray and showered across the rocks beneath with a continual hushing sound. Beyond the water stood the rim of the moon, so bright that it half dazzled Destry, and made more dim than phantoms the shadowy rocks and trees around him.

But in spite of that dimness he could not but be aware of one form running toward him. It was Chester Bent, who had fled long enough and now turned back to strike at his pursuer.

A bullet clipped the sombrero from Destry's head, the bark of the gun crashed against his ear and the instant echoes repeated it in a harsh jumble. And he fired in turn, half blindly, being desperate with the knowledge that the light was in his eyes, obscuring all things for him as much as it illumined them for his enemy. He was in a thick mist, as it were, while Bent had at least a twilight to strike by. Both weapons spoke again. Pitching down the slip, Bent came, horse and man, like a thrown missile, but the second bullet from Destry at least altered his course.

Up went the mustang on its rear legs. Destry saw the mouth gaped wide under the strain of the reins; the eyes were fiercely bright. It seemed more like a trained fighting beast than a harmless servant of any master.

However, it reared so high and so far that it passed the balance point, and toppled back as Bent, with a yell of anger and surprise, flung himself from the saddle. Horse and man went down, the crashing body of the big animal seeming to land fairly on top of its master. Yet when Destry sprang down from the back of Fiddle, it was to see Bent rolling over and over, then pitching to his feet.

Destry fired. There was no return. Instead, Bent came running in with a peculiarly rapid, dodging gait, so that Destry was amazed. It seemed as though Bent scorned to use a weapon, but preferred to fight out the battle, trusting to his bare hands.

There was no such folly in the mind of Bent, however. The holster on his thigh was empty; his fall from the horse had disarmed him and his only escape from the bullets of Destry was to get at the source of them.

The truth flashed up like fire in the mind of Harry Destry. The hypocrite, the traitor, the false friend he now held helpless under the nose of the Colt. No dodging could avoid the gun at such a distance, but Destry flung it suddenly from him.

For the fear left him. A sort of madness came on him as he saw this enemy rushing in with empty hands. Out of the past a picture poured upon his mind of the twelve men who had gathered to judge him and to rob him of a portion of his life.

All these years it had seemed a frightful mockery, a frightful sham, that verdict delivered by the "twelve peers." Now, in an instant, all bitterness left him. Whatever weakness and sin there had been among them now was nothing contrasted with the overmastering sin of Bent. His evil, as it were, was a fire that burned the others clean.

Here was a peer, indeed, a king among men, towering above Destry in keenness of mind, in craft, in all subtlety. Only in one way could he be matched, and that was in strength of hand. So the pride stood up like flame in Destry. He shouted, as an Indian shouts rushing to battle, there was laughter in his throat as he plunged forward. They looked like two old friends, newly met and throwing out their arms to embrace each other. So it was that they appeared, but when they met, it was with a shock that spun them about. Then they fell into a hard grip.

The hands of Destry slipped and glided on the body of Bent. Now he knew for certain that sleekness was not fat but hardened muscle, from which his fingerhold failed. But Bent, in return, drove home his shoulder against Destry's breast, staggering him; then in the excess of his power, he raised Destry floundering in the air. He was a helpless and clumsy child in the grip of Bent. He who had been so proud of his strength was unnerved and half unmanned by the first onset of his enemy.

Yet not beaten!

He was swung in the air, then hurled down, Bent casting his weight forward to fall upon his victim. But Destry, catlike, turned in the air, struck the earth with feet and hands, and dodged from the hands of Bent. His foot tripped on a rock with a violence that cast him head over heels down the slope. More desperately than ever he fought to regain his balance, came staggering to his feet, and braced himself to meet an onslaught that did not come!

Instead, he heard the beating of a horse's hoofs, and yonder went Chester Bent on the back of Fiddle, rushing up the trail at the head of the cañon.

Vain curses poured from the throat of Destry. He had welcomed this last and greatest battle in a divine frenzy, but even in this he was tricked, eluded, baffled and shamed. He cried out loud, and ran a few stumbling steps in pursuit, until his foot struck the revolver which he had thrown away. He looked blankly down at it for an instant, then scooped it up.

Up the cliff-face on the winding trail went the rider, until at the top he burst out across the face of the moon which now stood just above the rim of the rock. It was an odd and terrible effect, as though Fiddle were snatched into the heart of the sky, racing down the slope of the constellation. Her mane and tail flew out. This was the last instant her former rider would see her, it seemed, and as he rode, Bent waved his hand, laughing.

Loudly, yet as from a distance, that laughter floated down to the ear of Destry, mixed with the ringing beat of the hoofs. It was the laughter that made him recover suddenly from his dream. The gun leaped high in his hand, barked.

And as its nose jerked up with the recoil, Destry saw Chester Bent lurch from the saddle of the flying mare—lurch, so to speak, from the white cradle of the moon. Both his arms were flung out; he dropped at once from view against the rock of the cliff-face.

For an instant, Destry held his breath. In that instant, he told himself that it was impossible. Such a man could not die in such a way, but by a last impossible touch of craft would rescue himself!

Then out of the darkness, Destry heard the impact, horrible, distinct, like huge gloved hands smitten together.

Chester Bent was dead!

Fiddle, in the meantime, had turned back, and coming across the moon once more, she paused there and whinnied anxiously into the dark of the ravine. Only then did Destry raise his head, which had fallen in profound thought. He let the Colt fall from his hand and turned back up the hill, stumbling. Even Fiddle he did not wish near him, for Fiddle had come to him through the dead man's gift!

43

DESTRY went back to Wham, but he did not pause in the town; he went on through it until he came to the Dangerfield house beyond.

He hesitated to approach it. The place seemed dark, until he circled to the farther side and saw the dim glow of a lamp against the drawn shade. Coming up to the front of the old house, he heard voices on the veranda and he paused in the darkness to listen.

It was Docter Whipple and the Colonel. The doctor was saying: "They're like willow. You can beat 'em and bend 'em, but still they're tough and keep their life."

"You mean that he'll come through?" asked the Colonel.

"He's got a tolerable fair chance," said the doctor.

Destry suddenly remembered that there was no call for him to remain sheltered from view in the dark. He was a free man. There was no shadow of legal complaint against him. In all the world no one could give evidence that would place him in danger of the law. A load fell from his shoulders. He came quietly up the veranda steps.

"It's Destry, most likely," said the Colonel. "Is that you, Harry?"

"It's me," said he.

"Set down," said the Colonel. "Ding Slater has just left, and he told us."

"About Bent?"

"He told us everything. You've got him, son, or you wouldn't be back, I reckon?"

"Bent is gone," said Destry soberly. "Did I hear you say that the kid is going to pull through, Doc?"

"If he was ten years older," replied Whipple, "he wouldn't have a chance. But the young ones will bend without breaking. You might go up and see him. He's been talking about you a good deal."

"The fever," said Destry. "How bad is it?"

"Pretty high. He needs sleep and——"

At this, a note of shrill, high laughter came sharply down to them from the upstairs of the house.

Destry listened with a shudder, and started toward the door. The Colonel accompanied him up the stairs to the right door, and there paused with him.

"Charlie is in there with the kid," he remarked, "and before you go in, maybe you'll let me know which turn your trail is gunna take with her, son?"

"Her way is my way," said Destry, "so long as she'll let me go with her."

The Colonel nodded, and Destry tapped at the door. It was opened at once by the girl. She turned pale when she saw the newcomer, but stepped back and waved him in, pointing toward the bed.

Little Willie Thornton lay there, his arms thrown out wide, and looking sun-blackened until they were as dark as a Negro's skin. But his face was pale. He seemed gaunt and old; the skin was drawn tight and looked polished over the cheekbones. And his eyes rolled wildly.

"He's mighty sick," said the girl. "Speak to him, Harry!"

Destry sat on the side of the bed, and took one of the small, clenched fists in his hand.

"D'you know me, Willie?" said he.

"You're Chester Bent," said the boy. "It's you that set me on fire, but Destry'll come and put the fire out. He'll find you, too. There ain't any trail so long——"

His eyes grew vacant.

Destry took the youngster by both shoulders.

"It's me—it's Harry Destry!" said he. "D'you hear me, son?"

Into the eyes of Willie came sudden life and understanding.

"Hey, Harry!" said he. "Hullo! I'm glad to see you. You're safe from 'em, Harry?"

"Account of you, I am," said Destry. "You fixed me up, old son!"

The boy smiled and his eyes closed.

"D'you mean it? And Bent?"

"Bent'll never be seen again."

The boy nodded, his smile increasing.

"I reckoned that you'd tend to him," said he. "Why don't they figger it out with sense? They ain't nobody that ever could give you no trouble, Harry! I reckon that you're the top wrangler everywhere!"

Destry looked back to the swift and desperate fight in the shadow of the narrow ravine and he said nothing, but thought the more. Willie Thornton's closed fist relaxed in the grip of Destry. The haggard tautness relaxed in the face of the boy, and a slight perspiration gleamed on his forehead and moistened his hand. In a moment he was sleeping. Another moment still, and he smiled in his sleep.

"You're the best doctor, Harry!" said the girl.

She had been leaning beside him all this time and now Destry looked up at her through a mist of vast weariness.

"Charlie," said he, "I wonder if this here is the end of the trail?"

She smiled as she looked down at him.

"I mean," he explained, "that I'm plumb tired, Charlie. I'm finished with the game. I'm done up and weary to the bone. But if you still can waste time on a good-for-nothin' gent that never done anything well except the makin' of trouble, I've come back here to ask you to marry me, Charlie."

"You better have a sleep, first," said she. "You're tuckered out and you want to quit now, but tomorrow you'll be on the wing again."

"What makes you think that?" he asked her, too tired to follow her meaning clearly.

"You'll always hunt trouble till you've met a master," said she, firmly. "You gotta ride to a fall, Harry. You gotta fight till you're knocked out."

Destry laughed, and he was so very tired that his head fell loosely back as he laughed.

"I've met my master" said he. "I've met my peer. He beat me to the draw; he beat me with guns, and he beat me hand to hand. I killed him with luck and not with skill. I've throwed the gun away, Charlie. I'm an old man, and finished and done for. A Chinaman could laugh in my face, now, and I'd take it!"

"It was Bent?" she asked.

"Ay, it was Chet."

She drew a great breath.

"I always knew," said she, "that something good would come out of him!"

They were married that month, on the day when Willie Thornton was pronounced able to sit up. Because he expressed a desire to see the affair, it was performed in Willie's room, which was jammed with a crowd that overflowed into the hall and even up and down the stairs.

But, as Ding Slater said, the whole county should have been present, because it meant the end of the old days and the beginning of a new regime in Wham, for Harrison Destry had put away his Colt.

SIX-GUN COUNTRY

1

In all the time I had been hunted by the law, I had had no apprehension quite like that which I experienced when I learned that Andrew Chase had come into the hills to fight it out with me.

I could not get it out of my head that Andrew was invincible, for he had been more than a hero in my eyes ever since that day when he had knocked me flat into the dust after I had fought a fair fight with his brother Harry, and for the second time gained a victory that Harry would have given a great deal to have won.

Now you will remember that I was properly convinced that Andrew Chase was at the bottom of all this mess that I was in. After I had stood up against his brother, Harry, in a gun fight, and come out of the battle unscathed, Andrew had taken the situation into his own hands.

Then there had followed the hiring of Turk Niginski, a gunman, whose services had been bought to put me out of the way, for, reasoned Andrew, it was better that I should die than that his brother should face my weapons again and lose his life.

But Niginski had failed in his undertaking, and you will remember how I had whirled in the saddle and shot him dead, and then ridden straight to the sheriff with my true story of self-defense.

There had followed the trial, and my conviction and sentence to twenty-five years' imprisonment. Not even Father McGuire, with whom I had lived since the age of fourteen, could do anything for me. It remained for Tex Cummins, at that time a perfect stranger to me, to plan my escape and furnish me with a mount with which to make my getaway into the hills.

It was upon that first ride away from pursuit as a fugitive of the law that I met Margaret O'Rourke, "Mike" as I called her, and had fallen promptly in love with her.

So when I had heard that Andrew Chase had come into the hills to get me, and had learned further that he had had the audacity to make friends with Mike, I had promptly warned her to beware of Andrew Chase, that he was not to be trusted. Whereupon we had had a falling out, and I had gotten myself deeper into the entanglements with the law by my headlong rush into more mischief.

Then had come the message that Mike wished to see me, and my heart had swelled within me, only to have my hopes as quickly dashed upon the rocks by her announcement that she loved Andrew Chase and that she had sent for me to exact a promise from me not to fight him for fear that he might lose his life. From that moment I had promptly become a madman, had rushed out into the night, only to meet Andrew and to thrash him to within an inch of his life. Then I had brought him, torn and bleeding, to Mike.

After I heard that Andrew Chase had gained enough strength to leave the bed into which I had put him, and when I heard that, in shame because he could not face the men of the mountains, and because he dared not return to his home in Mendez, he had ridden east; after I heard all this news, I decided to go to see Margaret O'Rourke and ask her, frankly, what chance I had with her.

It was not, really, that I wished to gloat over her because the man she had chosen to love had turned out a rascal—or a rascal to a certain degree, at least. But I knew that Margaret O'Rourke was too brave and too kind and too honest to leave me in doubt as to whether or not I had any hope of winning her in the end. If I had not the shadow of a chance, I frankly wished to tell her that I would never see her face again.

I had had to learn to make decisions and abide by them before. It was now three years since I had lived outside of the law with a price on my head, and the only reason that I had been able to avoid the long arm of the law, I very well knew, was that I had made certain resolutions and stuck grimly to them.

Above all, for instance, I had decided early in my career that I would never associate myself with a partner. For one may be sure of oneself, but never of one's companion, and I had heard of and seen too many keen, alert, intelligent men who could not defy the law because they could not live without companionship. Their companion always proved the weaker link by which their strength was broken.

It was a bitter thing to live like a lone wolf in the mountains through all manner of weather, ever on the alert, and never leaving my secure retreats unless there was an absolute need to go down among other men for the sake of food or of money.

I had clung to that schedule for three years, and the result was that the headhunters had gone without my scalp.

When a man has denied himself human companionship and human liberty, it is possible for him to forswear even the joy of seeing the woman he loves.

With that in mind, I saddled Roanoke and went down to see Margaret O'Rourke.

I rode through the day until I was in the forest at the edge of the big valley. Then, in the dusk, I sent Roanoke down the steep descent to the floor of the valley itself—a dizzy pitch which no horse could have negotiated, but the mule, as a mountain flyer, was to the manner born. He skidded or bounced down the ragged slopes and then bore me across the valley at his swinging trot.

I came up the ravine where O'Rourke lived, in the black heart of the night. It was no longer necessary for me to whistle my signal from beneath the trees opposite the house. All I had to do was to make sure that no one was in the house except the family. They knew me now, and I felt that I knew them well enough to trust them—once in a long while!

For, other than upon exceptional occasions, there were only three people in the world whom I would really trust, and they were Sheriff Dick Lawton, Father McGuire, and Margaret O'Rourke herself. An odd assemblage for an outlaw to know, you may say!

So I left Roanoke under the trees, picking at the grass in the darkness, and I went across to the house to scout around. I looked in the dining room first, to see if Pat O'Rourke had any callers. There were none. He sat in one chair with his boots scarring the cane bottom of another chair, and the newspaper spread in front of him.

But I was fairly certain that Margaret herself was entertaining company, for I could hear her singing and playing the piano in the parlor. Certainly she would not be so gay except for the sake of another person—not when it was a scant fortnight since the man she loved had left the house.

I slipped up onto the porch and peeked in under the bottom of the shade. I could hardly believe my eyes when I saw that she was alone in the room, with her head tilted back, singing like a bird!

So I went to the front door and tapped softly. She opened it a moment later, and when she saw me, she cried out happily and drew me into the room.

"I thought that you were never coming again, Leon," said she.

"I wasn't sure that you'd ever want to see me again," I explained.

"You might take off your hat," said she.

I snatched it off. One can't be three years in the high rocks and remember all the amenities of polite society.

"Confound it, Mike," said I, getting a little red, "you might give me time to get my bearings."

She looked me up and down, surveying my ragged clothes and the two guns strapped at my hips and the Indian brown of my face and hands; and she smiled her crooked smile, which sank a dimple exactly in the center of one cheek.

"There you are," said Mike. "You haven't been here ten seconds—and you begin to fight so soon!"

"That's not fair," said I. "I came—"

"Well, sit down," said she. "Shall I let the family know that you're here?"

"Darn the family," said I. "I want you. I've gone on short rations for a long time so far as seeing you is concerned."

She sat down on the piano bench, still studying me.

"You're bigger than ever, Lee," said she.

"What I've come to say—" I began again.

"And that frown," said she, "is getting to be a habit."

"All right," said I, settling back with a sigh, "when you're through looking me over, I'll try to talk."

"There is to be a pardon granted to you, isn't there?" she asked. "I understand that Sheriff Lawton is doing a great deal to square you with the law."

"I don't know. I don't dare to think about it."

"Everyone else is thinking, though," said she. "We hear that Sheriff Lawton has made a trip to see the governor and talk to him about you."

"Sheriff Lawton is an honest man!" said I.

"Then there's word that Father McGuire has gone from Mendez to back up Lawton with the governor."

"God bless Father McGuire," said I. "I'd rather have his good word than be president of the United States!"

"But all the trouble is going to end, Lee. Oh, how glad I am! It's making an old man of you!"

"What I want to know," said I, "is just exactly how glad you are."

"Nobody in the world could be happier about it," said she.

"Wait a minute," said I, feeling that old, wild hope surge up in me. "Think that over before you say it."

She answered gently: "Unless you've found a girl to marry you, Leon Porfilo."

"I've found the only girl that I can ever marry," said I, very solemn. "That's what I came down here to talk about."

She shook her head.

"Oh," I explained, "I don't mean that I want any promises. I want a chance to hope. That's all."

She said nothing, but looked at me sadly and thoughtfully.

"When I heard you singing so happily," said I, "I thought you might have decided to forget him."

"I can never forget Andrew," said Mike.

"Then that's the end for me," said I, and stood up.

"Lee," said she, "are you really going to run off again with only two words spoken between us?"

"Well, why should I talk?" said I.

"Are we at least friends?" she asked me.

"No," said I. "Either I have a hope to have you someday as my wife, or else I'll never see your face again. I'll go no half measures and torment myself for years. Either I'll have a hope, or I have no hope at all!"

"Am I to tell you just what you mean to me?" she asked.

"Yes, if you will."

"Of course I will. I've always loved you, Lee, since the first day I put eyes on you."

"That's a fair start," said I without enthusiasm. "That's a pretty good opening. You always loved me, so you decided to marry another man?"

"There are all sorts of love," said she. "Andrew Chase took me off my feet. When you came down to kill him—or he you—I suppose that I hated you, for a while. But now he's gone."

"For good?"

"I suppose so."

"Mike, do you really expect that you'll never see him again? Do you care?"

She studied the floor for a moment and spoke with her head still bent down.

"A year ago I would have said that I would despise forever any man who did to Leon Porfilo such a dastardly thing as Andrew did to you in hiring Turk Niginski. Well, since Andrew left, I have thought it over and tried to look at it and at myself frankly. I am ashamed to confess that I do not despise him, Lee. Or, if I despise him, I'm almost fonder of him than ever. Can you understand that?"

"I cannot," said I bluntly.

"I don't suppose you can. You're a man all fire and iron. You want everything or nothing. But women aren't that way, you know. They hardly know what they want in a man, I suppose. But I know this—that I don't want to give you up, Leon! I think of Andrew once a day, and the thought of him makes my heart jump. I think of you every minute, and it always makes me happy—quietly happy. But I know that isn't enough for you."

"It isn't," said I bitterly. "I think of my mule, Roanoke, and it makes me quietly happy. But I want something more than that. I've got to have something more than that! Can you give it to me, Mike?"

"I've told you everything," said she.

"It's not enough," said I, dragging the words up from the roots of my heart. "I'm going to shut out the thought of you, Mike. I've got to do it."

She turned half away from me.

"Mike," said I, holding out my hand, "good-by."

She murmured swiftly: "Will you go quickly—before I start crying like a silly little fool?"

I jammed my hat on my head and strode out of that house, never to see it again, I thought.

2

ONE cannot be forever cautious. Besides, when I left Mike O'Rourke, I was so full of my vow never to see her again, but to shut her firmly from my life, that I did not much care what became of me. I turned Roanoke up the valley and rode straight on at the lights of the town!

It was not such complete madness as you might imagine, because since it was so generally believed that the governor was about to grant me a pardon—what with the good offices of Sheriff Lawton and half a dozen other prominent people on the range—the boys were not so keen to hunt me as they had been before.

They could not be sure, you see, that when they risked their lives to get me, they were not hunting down a man whom a proclamation had cleared of all crime.

I was fairly sure, therefore, that I underwent no real risk in venturing into Sanburn. There was no reason why the people in that town should have a peculiar grudge against me! In fact, I could not recall that I had ever harmed any one of the citizens.

So I let Roanoke drift boldly into the little village, only pulling him aside from the main street and putting him through a side alley. We turned a corner into a huddle of noise and cursing. The Sanburn stagecoach was rolling down the street surrounded by a score of excited horsemen; and from the interior of the coach, now and then, heavy groans reached my ear.

I had only time to hear and see this much when someone shouted:

"He's come back to see what trouble he's raised! Let's get him, boys!"

He who raised the shout fairly led the way by sending a .45-caliber slug through the brim of my sombrero. I could not imagine what the confusion was about, but I did not stay to ask questions. Roanoke turned like a cat, and I drove him through a narrow gap between two houses. There he wove back and forth among boxes and cans, leaped a high back fence, and took me into the open running beyond.

I heard the pursuit crashing and raving among the obstacles in that narrow alley. But the greater part of those hot riders had not tried the narrow pass at all, but spilled out on either side and came combing out after me by more roundabout ways. I gave Roanoke his head, and he streaked away.

He had as much foot as a good cow pony—but no more. When it came to a narrow brush like this one, I was much worried. I could only hope that there were no blood horses in that crew behind me to sprint up to us. There *were* some fast nags, however. Three men began to draw up with me, but they were in no hurry to close. I sent one bullet blindly into the sky above their heads, and they drew back.

By the time they had rallied enough heart to decide to rush down on me again, their fast horses were beginning to be half winded, whereas Roanoke was running as easily as ever. That extraordinary mule could not raise himself above a certain top speed, but he could maintain his top pitch for an uncanny length of time.

So it was now. He held them even for another mile, until we hit the foothills, and after that they were done.

What I wondered at, however, was the venom which had brought these fellows out humming after me. Still I could hear their angry shouts as I galloped Roanoke over the first hill crest. Then we sloped down into the dimness beyond, and I knew that I was safe.

However, I was not content with being safe. I wanted to know what lay at the bottom of this explosion. But I had to keep my impatience with me for a full three days before I learned what I wanted to know. Then I got it from the pages of the Sanburn newspaper.

They had spilled it across their whole front page. News was shy that week, I suppose, for they gave most of the issue to me and my unlucky career.

But they opened up with the following flare:

NEW OUTRAGE BY LEON PORFILO
OUTLAW TURNS STAGE ROBBER
SANBURN STAGE STOPPED
THREE MEN BRUTALLY SHOT DOWN!

That was the opening. What followed was enough to bear out the headlines. The Sanburn stage had been stopped by a tall man riding a mouse-colored mule like Roanoke. He wore a mask and announced that he was Leon Porfilo and that he was tired of waiting for the governor's pardon, and had decided to fill his empty pockets.

Empty pockets, when I had more than four thousand in my wallet at that moment!

It appeared that my ghost had stopped the stage and ordered the passengers out. But these passengers had too much spot cash on them and too many guns and the courage to use them to submit calmly to such a summons. Someone paved the way by dropping to the dust of the road on his belly and blazing away at the sham Porfilo. There were two others who followed suit.

I gathered that if this imitator of mine were a grand liar, he was at least a great fighter, also. For he had dropped those three worthies one after another. Two were badly wounded. One was dangerously shot and might die.

That was the first item of this story. The rest was what might be expected. The governor not only refused to consider my pardon any longer, but he had issued a ringing declaration that he would see that the laws of this State were obeyed and that he would have Leon Porfilo, outlaw, robber, murderer, out of the mountains if he had to call up every man of the militia.

It made me sweat a little, but I could not help grinning when I thought of raw militia boys struggling through the mountains and broiling on the bleak mountains while I was tucked away securely watching the fun. I was not afraid that they would take me.

They had almost as much chance of taking an eagle with their bare hands, for I had been hunted over every inch of that range during the last three years, and I knew the whole country. I could take it to pieces in my mind and put it together again, you might say. Every bird's nest in the region above timberline was pretty familiarly known to me.

Besides, and above all, I had that king of mules, Roanoke, to float me over cliffs like a bird on wings.

So I was not particularly disturbed by the governor's threats. The last governor before him had made threats just as big and announcements just as cocksure. But there were other elements which were not so pleasant. In the first place, I had been robbed of my expected pardon. In the second place, there had been an instant response to this most recent Porfilo "outrage," and the price on my head was a full fifteen thousand dollars!

Now, out West, where a man will work like a dog all of every day and a share of every night for a beggarly fifty a month, fifteen thousand dollars in a lump is like the dream of a gold mine. I knew that I should have to pass through a period like that which had tormented me long before when a price was first put on my head and the mountaineers had not yet learned to have some fear of me.

But what moved me most of all was rage at the scoundrel who had dared to use my name in order to help him in the robbery of the coach.

For my part, I had never attempted a deed so terribly bold as such a holdup. In the second place, I had never dreamed of such a thing as shooting down three inoffensive men who were merely striving to protect their own rights. I thought of the matter in another light, also. When Mike O'Rourke heard the story, she would believe that I had left her determined upon mischief, and she would believe that this bloodthirsty thing was all my work!

What I determined upon was to corner the rascal at once and wring a signed confession from him—or at the least have the satisfaction of filling him full of lead. No, to shoot him down would be no satisfaction at all. It would merely remove my last chance of proving my innocence.

I sat down to figure out the trail of the robber. That may seem odd to you, but as I have said before, I knew those mountains more intimately than any student can know the pages of a book. I closed my eyes and summoned the picture. Then I opened them again and drew out the scene in the sand. I had no sooner done that than one fact jumped into my mind at once—this robber was a fellow who did not know the country at all!

He had selected for the holdup site a spot where the trail dipped, beside the Sanburn River, into a long and narrow valley on either side of which gorges cut away from the river. But the ends of all those gorges were impractical for any animal less adroit of foot than Roanoke, say.

All that an organized pursuit would have had to do would have been to sweep up and down that valley at once and the robber was fairly bottled. The only reason that they had not adopted that measure was that they were fairly certain that if the robber were indeed Leon Porfilo, he would never commit a robbery in such a difficult spot.

If this man had really been aware of the nature of the country, he would have selected a spot on the road where it wound through the badlands of the upper plateau. I could have sworn that this stranger selected the eventual site of the holdup simply because he was sure those side ravines were routes by which he could easily ascend to the upper mountains.

The upper mountains, then, were his goal.

It was a bewildering region, as I knew by many a bitter experience, until I mapped it for myself. Even old mountaineers did not like to cross that section of the hills without a good guide, because the face of the land was knifed across by an intricate crisscrossing of ravines. Men had been known to wander about for half a month before they drew clear of those entangled chasms and blind alleys among the mountains; and in the cold of the winter more than one poor fellow had lost his life in that region.

As for the fellow who had dared to take up my role and play stage robber under my name, I could not help wondering just how he had solved the problem of the ravines! What I felt was that he would probably work grimly and patiently north, guided by the crest of one of the taller mountains. If he was cool enough to shoot three men in one fight, he was cool enough to stick by one landmark.

So, with all these things in mind, I cut across the high country and made straight for Danny Chisholm's camp.

3

CHISHOLM'S was a strictly summer camp. Half the year it was buried in frightful snowdrifts that sagged through the gulch to the north of his place. Six months of the year there were anywhere from five to fifty feet of snow rolled on top of the Chisholm shack. When the first white weather began, Danny Chisholm cached everything in wrappings of oilcloth, put some heavy props under the roofs of his sheds, prayed that they would hold the weight of the snows until the next thaw, and then trekked down for the lowlands.

So the camp slept under sheeted ice and snow during six months of the year, but the remaining six months it was a sort of open-air hotel. It was a queer sort of crossroads that he had chosen for his camp. There were no main trails that passed up and down or across the ridges at this point, but trappers, hunters, botanists, and the bolder spirits among the tourists who loved the high places crossed and recrossed the site of the Chisholm camp.

Besides, there were certain other enforced travelers—as one might call them—who dropped in at Chisholm's. These were men who did not wish to give names, who did not wish to ask questions or answer them. Chisholm was famous for the absence of embarrassing conversation at his camp fire. Altogether, what with one class of traveler and another, Danny made a pretty penny during the warmer seasons of the year.

I came over the south shoulder of Mount Christmas and in the hollow beneath me was the glimmer of the Chisholm fire, made into a single thin ray of red light. I followed it like a star, until I was close to his clearing. Then, at a little distance, I put up Roanoke in an open space where he would find plenty of forage, and went on foot toward the fire. I had slung a pack across my back, so that I could fill the part of a foot traveler.

What I first saw from the shadows of the trees at the edge of the clearing was the active figure of Danny Chisholm. That little man never rested. He was forever cooking or cleaning up, or whirling about like a squirrel on a branch to ask one of his guests if they were comfortable.

Usually, as tonight, his guests slept in the open. In case of need, they could be lodged in very foul weather under one of his damp, tumbledown sheds. Now their blankets were spread in the outer rim of the firelight. In the air was the last tang of coffee which had been made for the latest comer. There was a rumbling of deep, contented voices; and when a puff of wind came, it never failed to raise a sharp tongue of flame that cast a bright wink of light over the clearing and made the nearest pine trees glisten.

I stood there for a moment, enjoying the scene, and the great upper peaks which walked up among the stars in the distance. I felt like a tiny Tom Thumb in the hollow hand of a giant.

Then I noticed the other guests. There were only three of them—one young, and two big-shouldered mountaineers with beards of uncertain date shrouding their faces. As for me, I remained where I was, in the shadow.

For there was never any trace of me, even in a place like Danny Chisholm's, where ordinary strifes were forgotten. This was a court of last resource to which all men resorted when they were hard pressed by wind and weather. The lion and the lamb lay down together in actual fact, and if there were occasional quarrels here, they were the quarrels which originated in the camp itself, and which were not imported from the outside.

But even this atmosphere of truce I could not trust. No unwritten law was strong enough to protect a man with fifteen thousand dollars on his head! For a moment, a great bitterness went through me.

In the old days I was very often set up with a feeling of grandeur because of my very loneliness; but as time went on, that loneliness ate into my spirit, and often a convulsion of something like homesickness made me as weak as a child.

Danny Chisholm came to me at once. When he saw that I preferred the shadows, he did not urge me to come closer to the camp fire. I asked him if he had a cup of coffee left, and he went hastily for it and brought me back a great slab of pone, split open and layered with molasses inside. It tasted better than any cake I have ever touched, and the coffee of another man's making was nectar to me.

I sat with my back to the tree behind me and drank and ate. Danny Chisholm stood near by and talked—about a tenderfoot who had come up to his camp bent on shooting a mountain sheep, about Dad Riley coming in with a load of moonshine, about a new rifle which he had bought, and about the Sanburn holdup.

He chatted on in an easy monotone, never waiting for a reply, only pausing to puff in leisurely fashion at his pipe. But he knew that I was hungry to hear him, as any man who lives like a hermit against his will begins to hunger for the sound of a human voice. To me, that foolish babble was sweeter than wine and honey. It relaxed me, body and soul, and it made me almost sleepy with content. It filled me with an immense good will to fellow men.

Then voices began to be heard beside the camp fire, and Danny hastened back to it.

He stood, ridiculously small in the flare of the fire, gesticulating with both hands. Those three big fellows, each was almost as tall, sitting, as was Danny on his feet.

"I got only one thing to say," said Danny. "If you've come here for a fight, go off somewhere and fight where the loser'll roll into the river where he drops. I disremember what year it was when the Slocum boys come up here and got into a scrap with a couple of old sourdoughs. Two of 'em was killed; two more was laid up. I had to bury them that died—right here in these rocks.

"It was like breaking ground in quartzite. Besides, I had to nurse them two that was down. What did I get out of it? Nothing at all! They was all broke. The pickings in their pockets wasn't enough to feed a layin' hen through the summer season! So I say: If you want to fight, go out where the mountains can see you. I'm too old to be interested in that sort of a show!"

Danny was really what one might call hard-boiled. He never pretended that he had any ultimate interest in his guests beyond getting their money. Everyone liked his frankness.

One of the bearded fellows took up the talk, and at the first word I pricked up my ears.

"Porfilo," said he. "That was what we was talking about. This kid—"

"Porfilo," put in Danny Chisholm, "is a poor thing to talk about day or night, in the valley or up here in the mountains. Because you never know what side folks is gunna take about him."

"Look here," said the bearded man, "there *used* to be two sides. The best side used to be the one that figgered he'd done nothin' that wasn't over-balanced by the good he's done. I was one of them that stood on that side. But along comes this here stage holdup—and that's different!"

"Why different?" put in the youth.

Now he sat up and squared his shoulders and turned his head a little. I saw that he was a whale of a man, boy, rather. For the firelight, streaking down his profile, showed me a fine-looking youngster of not more than eighteen, the sort of eighteen-year-old who has stepped into nearly his full strength.

I had been that sort of a boy. Three long years ago I had been as he was now. One sees such fellows fighting in the prize ring, from time to time, powerful as men but supple as children, recuperating swiftly after hard blows, full of zest and battle.

I, from the altitude of twenty-one, looked with an almost sad wisdom upon this boy. Not three years, but three decades stretched between us.

"There you are," said Chisholm. "You see that you got an argument pronto. Ain't I right about it?"

"This here—kid," said the first speaker, making a little pause of contempt before he named the boy, "is arguin' like a plumb fool. He don't see no difference between what Porfilo has done before and what he's done this time."

"He busted into a house and slammed three men, all on one night," said the boy.

"That was with his fists."

"Well, is guns any worse?"

"Worse by just a mite. Just the mite of difference between livin' and dyin'."

"Who did he kill when he stuck up the stage?"

"By luck he didn't kill none—but he shot three times to kill. One slug just missed the heart of one of the boys. Another plowed through the cheek and tore off the ear of another chap. Them bullets was aimed to kill, which is something that he never done before, except when his back was agin' the wall!"

The boy jerked back his head. "His back was agin' the wall when he held up the stage!"

"How come?"

"They stuck up their hands, and when he lowered his gun, one of 'em made a phony move and started shootin'. They deserved to die, all the three of 'em, for tryin' a double cross!"

"Is that your way of lookin' at it, kid?" said the burly fellow who carried on the brunt of the talk for the other side. "Well, then I got to say that you're gunna make a fine sort of a citizen, one of these days."

"I dunno that I like the way that you say that!" said the boy.

But the other two did not understand. What they heard in his voice was a tremor which was very pronounced and which was exactly like the tremor of fear. But I knew better.

Indeed, there was fear in that youngster, but it was the sort of fear which drives men into the deeds of most frantic heroism. It was the fear which a man feels when he is in doubt about himself. Fear that he will not do all that can be expected of a man.

The instant I heard that tremor in the throat of the boy, I gathered my feet under me and got ready to jump behind a tree out of the path of possible bullets, for I knew that trouble was coming.

Then the bearded rascal brought all to a climax by snorting:

"*You* don't like it? Then what'll you do about it?"

4

THERE was no delay. The boy leaped to his feet.

He was a glorious thing to look at. Opposite him two burly men rolled up and stood braced for action. They were not so tall, not so nimble—but they were as tough and as jagged as the rocks among which they had been moiling all their lives. Under those beards were jaws of iron, broad cheekbones. Under their clothes were muscles like slabs of India rubber. They had great arched breasts, and the strength of their arms made them carry their hands far from their sides.

"I'll do this, to start with," said the youngster, as he dashed his fist into a beard and reached the jawbone beneath and sent one foeman staggering.

I have no doubt, from his fine bearing, that he meant nothing but the best of fair play, for his part. But there was no sense for such matters in the other two. One of them lunged in instantly from the other side and, grappling the boy around the body, carried him to the earth by the shock of his rushing weight.

Neither did these cold-hearted devils mean to let him get to his feet. The first man, shaking the daze out of his head, came striding back.

"Hold him down, Pete!" he snarled. "We'll give him something to think about!"

"You coyotes!" groaned the boy. "Lemme get up, and I'll fight the two of you fair and square!"

He meant it, too. That was enough for me. I had promised myself that no matter how the fight went, I should not show my face. But this was too much for me. I came to my feet and joined that fracas with a rush. I sent a battle cry before me, and the first man wheeled to meet my charge. He put up his hands in good enough posture, but then the firelight struck bright into my eyes, and I heard him shout: "Porfilo!"

It seemed to drain all the strength out of him. It was not a man but a statue of putty that I put my fist into. He went down in a crumbling heap.

His shout released the boy, too. For when the second mountaineer heard my name, he leaped to his feet and sprinted for the woods.

"Porfilo!" said the boy, and sat up with a gasp. "It *is* Porfilo!" he breathed.

"Get back into the shadow," I commanded him, and tugged him to his feet with a jerk. "Get back among the trees, before the pair of them try to pick us off from cover!"

We hurried back into the shadows, but there seemed little doubt about what the two men of the mountains would do. They were rushing off as fast as their legs would carry them; as though they had called on the devil— and raised him quite beyond their expectations! Far away, we heard the crashing of the brush as they sprinted on.

"Porfilo," said the boy, "darned if I ain't sorry that I got you mixed into this mess."

He was not as sorry as I was, however. For, every time I had to step into such a fight, it meant that I made not two enemies, but two hundred. Every new story of violence that was repeated about me went up and down through the mountains and turned the minds of many honest, peace-loving men against me.

"What's your name?" I asked him, very, very heavy with all of these reflections.

"Orton," said he.

"Your first name?" said I.

"Dick."

"Dick, you're a young fool!"

I heard him gasp an indrawn breath. "Porfilo," said he at last, in a voice as thin as the voice of a frightened child, "that's a good deal to take from any man—even from you."

"Is it?" said I, still very angry.

"Too much," said he. "I can't swaller it!"

Then I saw what was in his mind. I had been too sick at heart to understand, before.

"What do you want me to do?" said I.

"Apologize!" said Dick Orton. "Or I'll—"

Yes, there he was ready for it already! His head was back and his body was trembling as much as his voice.

"Oh, the devil!" said I. "I'll apologize, of course. I'm sorry I hurt your feelings, Dick!"

This was a great deal too much for him. There was not much light from the fire in the shadows where we stood, but there was enough for me to see the glassy rolling of Dick Orton's eyes.

"You're joking, Porfilo!" said he.

"Not a bit," said I.

"You're tryin' to make a fool out of me," said he.

"Not at all," said I.

"Porfilo wouldn't apologize to nobody but the devil himself!" said this silly boy.

"Who has been filling your head full of nonsense about me?" I asked him.

He stepped a little closer to me to study me. "You *are* Porfilo," said he, as though there could ever be any doubt as to the identity of my ugly, prizefighter's face.

"I'm Porfilo," I repeated. "I've apologized for hurting your feelings. Is that apology enough?"

"Ah," said Dick Orton, "I didn't mean to ask you to—I mean that I was in the wrong—"

"Of course you were!" said I.

"Then why did you ask my pardon?"

"Because I didn't want to fight."

There was no way of handling that young fool without being in danger. He was worse than a bundle of nettles.

"I'm too small for you, maybe?" says he, lifting his head to his full height.

He was about half an inch taller than I.

"Or maybe," said he, "you figger out that I'm just a kid and that I ought to be home helpin' Ma with the supper dishes. Is that it?"

I had picked up my pack and now I flung it over my shoulders and turned my back on him and strode away as fast as I could. Because he had gone far enough to anger me in spite of all my efforts at self-control. In those days I felt that I was quite a world-weary man, but I can look back at myself and see that I was a good deal of a child. However, that young idiot would have irritated a saint.

I left him behind and made for my Roanoke with a very hearty wish that Chisholm's place and everybody in it were in the hands of the devil. Just as I reached the clearing where I had left Roanoke, there was a crashing behind me, and that young giant blundered out into the open starlight. More than starlight. The moon was somewhere, sifting thin shadows of the trees across the ground and showing me the face of Dick Orton.

"I'm not good enough to get an answer?" said he.

He stood before me with his feet braced and his body bent a little; he was full of that same devil of fear that had made him fight the two at Chisholm's camp a little before.

"Orton," said I at last with a groan, "do you want me to get down on my knees and beg you not to shoot me?"

Because he had come to that point. One hand, shaking with passion, was fluttering at his right hip, touching the butt of his gun and hovering away from it again in little jerky movements.

He was staggered again by what I said. He could not understand. So I added: "Do you want me to breathe flame and eat iron? I'm a peaceable man, Orton, until fellows like you crowd my back to the wall. All I'm saying is: For Lord's sake give me a chance to be friendly!"

Dick Orton gasped. Then his eyes rolled from side to side, as though, under the skin of a dragon, he had found a child.

Then, "There's Roanoke!" he cried softly. "By jiminy, I've been wanting to see Roanoke—and there he is! You *are* Porfilo, no matter how you talk!"

Yes, in spite of what he had seen and heard, he had still been in doubt as to my identity. I was a thousand times too humble to fit in with his preconceived idea of me.

Then he blurted out: "Porfilo, I guess that I've been acting like a fool!"

"I'm afraid to say yes," said I. "Or you'd have a gun out at me!"

"I was scared to death," said he, "but I thought that you were talkin' down to me."

"I'd as soon talk down to a snowslide that was aimed straight at my head," I said.

I mopped away the perspiration from my face. In fact, I had had a rather nerve-racking passage with this young fire-eater.

"Well," he said, "I want to know if you'll forgive me."

"Sure," said I. "Thank heaven that there's no harm done—to either of us!"

"Will you do one thing more for me?"

"Yes," said I, not pausing to think.

"Then let me ride along with you for a day."

"What the devil are you asking for?" I growled at him. "Trouble?"

"You've given me your promise," said he.

"Darn a promise!" said I. "If you ride with an outlawed man—"

"I'd rather ride with you than with a king, Porfilo!" says he.

I saw how the wind lay.

"I have your promise!" he cried, very exultant. "You can't go back on that!"

"Well," said I at last, "go get your horse!"

He was gone in a flash, and I, cursing steadily, put the saddle on Roanoke, because it was not wise to stay near Chisholm's after that evening's scene.

I turned from my work, a moment later, and saw Dick Orton ride into the clearing, and he was on the back of another mule!

I did not have to possess the wits of a detective to put two and two together now. It was perfectly plain to me that Richard Orton, like a dizzy-headed young idiot, had read of the adventures of Leon Porfilo and had started out to parallel them.

But the very first thing he had done was more foolhardy than all of my adventures put together and rolled into one. For it was he who had ridden a mule to hold up the stage, and who had posed as the possessor of my name.

Here was I, who had started out with a hot hatred to find the pretender and destroy him—here was I helpless and buried in gloom. I could not help liking this young idiot. I could not help it. Neither could I say a word to him about the frightful wrong that he had done me for fear he would do some equally insane and romantic act.

If I pointed out to him that this stage robbery had robbed me, at the same time, of my chance to get a State pardon, beyond a doubt he would scurry down to give himself up, confess his crime, and be promptly thrown into prison for the better half of his remaining life!

What was I to do?

I did not know. I wanted to be just to this madman; but I was also hungry to have justice for myself. I decided to go to get advice as quickly as I could.

My companion in the meantime jogged his mule at my side as contented as he could be. We came to a cliff as bare as the palm of my hand.

"Are you going down it?" said Dick, as serious as you please.

I turned and gaped at him. Even a mountain goat would have been dizzy for a month at the mere thought of that precipice.

"Where are my wings, Dick?" said I.

"Why," he muttered in a rather complaining way, "I thought that nothing could stop Roanoke!"

"Roanoke is like me," said I. "Overpraised! A darn sight overpraised!"

But Dick merely shook his head. His idea of me and of that tough-mouthed mule I rode was too deeply fixed in him to be changed by mere words!

I turned up along the edge of that cliff and hit for the higher ground because I had my plan for the night's campaign firmly in mind. On the way, I drew him into talk. Although he seemed to be bubbling over with a desire to hear me chatter about myself, he was young enough to be willing to speak of himself.

"What started you for the high spots, Dick?" said I.

"Hearing about the good times you've been having for the last five or six years," said he.

"Three years!" I corrected him. "Three years, Dick."

"Is that all? Seems to me I can hardly remember when they were not talking about Leon Porfilo."

"As for the good times—" But I could not continue in that strain. How could I tell him about the bitter loneliness of the mountains? How could I tell him of that weak yearning which went like water through my blood a thousand times—the yearning to have other men around me? No, I decided that words could never turn the trick. The more I talked, the more glamour he would feel in what I had to say.

So I changed the theme.

"But there was something more than what you had heard of me that made you go wild," I declared. "What else lies behind it?"

"The old man," said he.

"Explain that."

"The old man," said Dick, "started out selling newspapers in New York. He wound up on a ranch, with plenty of hosses and plenty of coin, but the things that he figgers count the most are the things that he got locked up inside his head while he was stamping his feet to keep the chilblains out of his toes, and shoving papers under the noses of gents on Broadway.

"Back yonder, the big guns are the doctors and the lawyers, and suchlike things. What he has mapped out for me is a lawyer's desk. Me!"

He threw out his arms and laughed. The gesture startled his mule, and the foolish thing began to buck on the edge of the cliff. I was so thoroughly frightened that I could hardly look. But Dick Orton merely laughed and threw spurs and quirt into his nag to make it buck still harder—all of this with perdition six inches away.

Then the mule had enough, and jogged on its way again.

Certainly I had seen enough of this youngster to demonstrate to me that the man who tried to control him was rather thick in the head. I would as soon try to plan the future of an avalanche. I wondered what sort of a brain was lodged above the eyes of Orton, the father.

"Go on," I encouraged him.

"There's nothing to it," said he. "Same old lingo you've heard a thousand times before, I guess. He's packed full of ambition for me. He herded me through high school, and he sure had his hands full doing it!"

I could imagine that. I pitied the school which had existed with a firebrand like this in its midst.

"Four years?" I asked.

"With a couple of breaks," said he. "I busted away a couple of times, but each time the old man came out and nabbed me and got me back. I missed six months each time.

"All the while the old man was talking law at me," went on Dick. "Yep, he never missed a chance. When he was starving back in the big town, he used to go to sleep dreaming about the lawyers that get to be presidents and senators, and the like! So he's got it planned for me. I'm to step right out and get to where he wanted to be. Sure, I waded through the Latin and all that bunk.

"He used to think it was great. He'd sit back and listen to me conjugate a Latin verb like he was hearing soft music; and when I busted out with some French, you would have thought that I'd handed him a shot of redeye—he's that far gone on education!"

"Good for him!" said I, thinking of Father McGuire and all of his patient hours spent to teach me the little that I had learned.

"Hey, Porfilo, are you kidding me?"

"Go on," said I. "I'm listening."

"It's pretty silly. The grand bust came when I was shoved into the debating team because they couldn't find anybody else to take the job in my last year at high school. The boys used to josh me quite a lot about being an orator.

You see? It got my back up. I wrote up a line of lingo. I grabbed a-plenty of it out of books. Then I learned it by heart.

"When I was riding home at night, I used to spout out that stuff big and loud and talk so almighty fiery that I near scared my bronco to death. So when the time come for the debate itself, I wasn't fazed much by the crowd in the assembly room. Back yonder in the rear row was my old man. I took a slant at him, sitting up there looking white and nervous, as if I was on trial for murder.

" 'He thinks that I'm gunna bust down,' says I to myself. 'Here's where he gets one big treat.'

"So, when my turn comes, I sashay out and let the boys and girls have it.

"The others on the teams, they had been talking sort of strained and nervous, as if they was apologizing for being up there pretending to try to talk sense. But I hit 'em from the hip. I pulled my punches right out of the ground and talked like the folks in that room was a measly crowd of mustangs, and I was trying to herd 'em into the only corral where they belonged.

"They liked it. Now and then, while I was roarin' and ragin' up and down the platform, I took a slant at the old man and seen him turn from white to pink, and then he begun to grin, and then he begun to laugh, and then he begun to rub his hands and rock around in his chair and nudge his friends in the ribs and point out to them what a smart and sassy kid his son was!

"I finished up in a blaze of glory and sat down sweating, and pretty near to laughing, because they give me quite a cheer, with the old man the leading voice.

"After that debate there wasn't no doubt left in his head. He figgered it out that his son was one of the smartest men in the country, and was gunna walk right through a governorship to the Senate and out again to the president's chair. All he seen was visions of me deliverin' an inaugural oration. All that he prayed for was to live till the president could have him to lunch in the White House.

"After that, he begun sort of talkin' up to me, like he was a little boy, and I was an old man. He didn't give no more orders to me. He just sat around and suggested things, and when I didn't do what he wanted, he looked sort of sick and sad. He'd come in and sit down and ask my advice about his business. Sure he did. It would of flabbergasted you to see what a difference that debate of mine made to him—a lot of lingo that I'd picked up out of the books and hung together with pins and paste, you might say.

"Well, I hadn't minded it so much in the days when he said that I was to be a lawyer and I said I wasn't, and then he roared out that he'd disinherit me, and give all of his money to charity—me being an only son! That wasn't so bad. It was just a fight.

"But when it got so that I said I wouldn't never be a lawyer, and he only turned white and bit his lip and looked down to his plate and stopped eatin'—why, then it sort of made me nervous. I felt that I was pretty near to doing what he wanted just because I pitied him.

"Finally things got pretty bad, and I seen that I'd have to bust loose.

"So I busted. The first thing that I done was to saddle a mule—because if a mule is good enough for Porfilo, it's good enough for me. I started out to show the old man that I wasn't the timber that they hacked lawyers out of. And here I am, Porfilo!"

5

I RODE along for a while just chewing my lip and thinking not of the kid, but of poor old Orton who was living to see his son president.

"What do you want to do?" said I.

"Anything but be a lawyer."

"Want to be a rancher?"

"That's better."

"Interested in raising cows, eh?"

"Me? Not a bit."

"But you like riding the range, and working with a rope, and tail-ending cows out of tanks where they got bogged down and—"

"The devil, no!" said Dick. "I hate that sort of life! I never wasted the time to learn how to swing rope. It isn't cows that I want to play around with!"

"Just what *do* you want to be?"

"I figger on bein' free, the way that you are! Up here in the mountains—nothing to do but to ride around and have a good time."

"With what, Dick? You're the first man that ever rode two steps beside me in the mountains!"

"Why, if you ain't got men to play around with, you got the winds, ain't you?" he asked almost angrily. "If you got nothin' else, you got the danger of bein' caught, any minute! That's fun enough, by my way of thinking!"

I saw that I could not answer him immediately. But I knew that my heart bled for poor old Orton, somewhere in the hills of the cow-range country.

"How did your father get his start?" I asked.

"He got a little money together. He was sort of wild when he was a kid. That's why he hates wildness in me, maybe. He made some money selling newspapers, although it seems hard to believe that anybody could save money doing that, and then he floats out West. He worked on the range for a couple of years, just drifting around and learning the business, and liking the folks out this way and the way that they live.

"After all of that, he put his money—it was only a few thousand—into cows, and he settled down and got married and began to have luck. He's had luck ever since. He's boomed that little farm into a man-sized ranch, and it keeps growing. He's got a good head to be a rancher, the old man has! But why does everybody have to work?"

I remembered something Father McGuire said to me—that no man could be really happy except through work—but I was not so far gone that I would try salty maxims like that on a young fire-eater like Dick.

But you've no idea how old it made me feel to listen to him. Older than the hills!

We reached a good camping ground, and there I decided to stop for the night. Dick pointed out that it was fairly close to the Chisholm camp, but I felt that I was not apt to be followed quickly—not until they had been able to organize a sizable posse. Perhaps you will think that was vanity on my part, but one has to keep an eye on psychology as well as other facts. People in the mountains were afraid of me. I had come to count on that fear.

I told Dick to go ahead and make camp, because I intended to strike across country to see a man. I would not be back until the morning, I said; but I hoped to return at close to daybreak.

He did not like to have me go, but I persuaded him at last by giving him my word that I would be back and by leaving one of my guns. I pretended that I wanted him to look over the mechanism because it was beginning to be hard on the trigger. As a matter of fact, it worked more easily than I thought!

However, he was flattered to be asked an opinion. He made a little fire, and I left him sitting cross-legged beside it, working away at that gun with all his might.

Then I headed across country, and I made Roanoke work like mad. Because there was a good deal of emotion in me, just then, connected with that crazy youngster. Besides, I was utterly baffled, and I wanted to get to a wiser head than mine was.

I drifted over a bare, flat summit of piled rocks. A dozen big shadows started up before me and pitched over the other side down the side of the mountain—mountain sheep. They were gone, and the noise of their going ended, and the silence was suddenly and strongly upon me again before one could turn around—so to speak!

I peered over the ragged edge. It was a descent so frightful that even Roanoke would not have ventured it even had I the heart for such a risk. But these big creatures had gone down as though on wings. Suddenly I knew what was in the heart of Dick Orton. He wanted to be like those great sheep—wild and free and totally unhampered.

Well, I had read books—mostly poetry—where there is a great deal of talk about untrammeled freedom, but I have to confess that I have always found freedom a pretty painful thing—and the greatest bore in the world! We're made to help one another—or disturb one another. Here and there is a bad man or a worse woman; but on the whole, are not people a pretty reasonable lot?

For my part, I have not much sympathy with the fellows who spend a great part of their time hating others. I can state offhand that I've never come to know anyone without finding a great deal worth liking. That goes for a lot whom I started by hating with all my heart—my bitterest enemies, in fact.

This night, I pushed Roanoke hard, as I said before. The ordinary route would have cost us twenty-five or thirty miles of hard travel. I took the air-line route and landed where I wished to be in just half of that distance and about two hours of time. I left Roanoke grunting and mumbling to himself— a way he had when he felt that he had been worked too hard—and I waded through the forest and the undergrowth until I came to the back wall of a house with just a glinting high light on one window where a star left its image as though in water.

I went up to that window. It was half open, and so low to the ground that I could lean in and smell the warmth of the house and hear the breath of the sleeping man.

"Lawton!" said I.

There was no start or exclamation. Manhunters learn to waken smoothly and noiselessly as they learn to pull their guns. An instant more and he was in front of the window.

"Porfilo," I explained.

At that he grunted very loudly.

"You've come to tell me what a pretty party you've had, I suppose," said the sheriff. "You've come to tell me what the papers left out, I guess. You've come to tell me what fun it was to stand up there and drop three gents one after another—"

"Sheriff—" I tried to break in.

But he was too angry to listen to reason. He went on in full flood: "I want to tell you how much fun it was to have people cracking jokes about me— a sheriff that went up to get a pardon for a man that he wasn't able to catch.

" 'He's swore that he'll put his hands on Porfilo, and this is the only way that he can do it!'

"That's what they said about me!

"Well, Porfilo, it was a lot of fun to go to meet the governor the next morning after you'd held up the stage. Did you know that he was a cow-puncher when he was a kid?"

I said that I did not know it.

"He was a mule skinner, too," said the sheriff, "but the cussing that he done that morning laid over anything that I ever heard tell of from any mule skinner or cowpuncher that I ever seen! The cussing he done was worthy of a governor, I tell you—it was that rare. When he got through cussing, he turned around on me and Father McGuire and told us what he thought of us for having made a fool of him about a gent that had done what you had done."

"Sheriff," I protested, "I didn't stick up that stage."

He only snorted. "The holdup boy rode a mule and admitted to your name, you blockhead!"

"Lawton," said I, "I have four thousand dollars in my pocket which I can prove didn't come from that holdup. You know me. I ask you if I'd hold up a stage when I had that much cash in my wallet?"

It silenced him for a moment, but still he was not convinced. He had been so thoroughly humiliated at the governor's office that he could not swallow his grudge against me all in a moment.

"Who else *could* do it?" he asked.

"A fool kid, eighteen years old, who got tired of a quiet life, had read a lot of bunk about me, and started out to make news."

It struck the sheriff in a heap. It was so unexpected that he saw that I could not have invented it. Then I told him the story as I had heard it—briefly.

"What am I to do?" I asked.

"Shove a gun under his nose and bring him into town and collect the pardon of the governor the next day!" he declared.

"And send one of the best kids I ever met to prison for the best part of his life?"

The sheriff cursed most profanely.

"Well?" said I.

"Damnation!" said the sheriff. "Why d'you bring your soiled life around to me and ask me to launder it for you? Do your own dirty work!"

"I ask you, as a sheriff what would you do?"

He only groaned. Then, "You're right, Leon," said he.

"About what?" said I.

"You might have saved your long ride," said he. "Of course I wouldn't do nothing other than you're gunna do—and that's to give the kid a chance to make good! Now get out of here—I wish that I'd never heard your name, and never seen your face!"

I must add that there was another word from the sheriff as I disappeared—a final greeting which he leaned out the window to call after me as I hurried away through the night. I heard his voice—a little modified for fear lest some other person in the house might gather what he had to say:

"I'm on the warpath after you again, Lee! I'm coming hot-foot. The governor told me that I had to—or quit!"

I was sorry for Lawton. Of all the fine and fearless men who ever drew breath or buckled on guns, there was never a finer or a more fearless one than our sheriff. I loved him as I have rarely loved another man. All my association with him had been a strange one of friendship and of enmity, and I hardly knew what to say of him to myself, except that I had a lasting conviction that if the time ever came when he had me cornered and could put the irons on my wrists, he would wish heartily that it was another man besides himself who was doing it.

Yet it was his duty to hound me to the best of his ability. An ability which no one had dared to question until the long list of his failures to secure me after I had repeatedly broken the law in his own county!

However, I was rather downhearted after my interview with him. That he was right I did not doubt. It was what my own conscience told me. Though, perhaps, some fine quibblers might declare that the sheriff was wrong, and that he would encourage law-breaking by such advice as he had given to me on that night, yet I was sure that he was right. For if Dick Orton were to be sent to the penitentiary, it would surely be the making of a real bad man when he came out.

I knew where the Orton place was, though I had never seen the owner, or heard him described until Dick described him that evening. I calculated that I could get to the Orton ranch by midnight, and that I could round back to the place where I had left Dick by the time that the morning dawned.

So I pressed Roanoke ahead. He had covered a frightful distance and raised and lowered his strong body a prodigious number of yards in the past twenty-four hours, but still there was something in him which responded. I am sure that no horse could have lived with him over half of the journey which he had made. But when he swung into his long trot, he ambled along with as little friction as a wolf.

At that trot I took him down the next ravine which opened over the heads of the rolling hills, and then across the hills to the Orton ranch. It was a typically ugly place. A long, squat building under the brow of a low northern hill. There was not a tree near it. Summer must have burned that house until it was an oven inside, and winter must have frozen it.

I left Roanoke at a little distance, as usual, and took the extra chance of loosening the girths so that he might breathe. Then I went straight to the front door and knocked loudly. There was finally a faint groan and the squeak of a footfall in an upper room. Then a head and white-clad shoulders leaned out.

"Word from Dick," I called softly.

There was an exclamation which did not form any words; the figure disappeared, and presently I saw a light flare behind that upper window. Voices muttered rapidly; then steps descended, and the door was thrown open. I saw a grizzly-headed man I knew must be Orton, and behind him the frightened face of a woman.

"Keep your light back!" I commanded, as he began to raise it above his head. "Send Mrs. Orton back. I'll talk to you alone. Do you understand?"

Mrs. Orton made some sort of an incoherent protest, but her husband, after a moment of thought, waved her back, and she hurried down the hall.

"Will you come in?" he asked me.

He put the lamp down on a hall table and then started violently with a little groan of consternation when the light fell dimly over my face. I have said that it was not a handsome face nor a pleasant one, and my blunt features were too well known through the mountains.

Too many posters had been published showing me and naming the reward upon my head—dead or alive! That was always the frightful part of it, to me. Dead or alive, as though I were already in part a corpse. At least, so far as the law cared for me!

"Porfilo!" breathed old Orton.

But his fear left him instantly. He was too full of a greater emotion than fear to let it control him for more than a moment.

"It's you, eh?" he went on bitterly. "Ah, I might of knowed how it was. It was you that got my boy away at last, Porfilo? Him after talkin' about you and dreamin' about you for three years! Now what more d'you want out of me?"

"A little common sense, and a little patience to hear what I have to say," said I.

He folded his arms and stared grimly at me. He was a big man, like his son, and he had his son's straight eyes, though they were covered with a dense gray brush of bristling hair.

"I'll hear you yap," said he.

"Dick is with me in the hills," said I.

"I guessed it."

"I've come to tell you that I want to get him back to you if I can."

"That's likely—having got him there once!"

"He got *himself* there," said I, growing a little hot.

"How, if you please?"

I was so angry that the words snapped out of their own accord.

"By holding up the Sanburn stage."

The old man blinked at me for a moment, and then in a flush of rage, he lifted his fist as though he would strike me to the floor for blasphemy.

"You blackguard!" cried he. "When you and your mule were seen there— and when you named yourself to 'em?"

"Was it likely that I'd name myself?" said I. "Did you have all of your mules the day after the holdup?"

He had framed an answer to the first question with his lips, but the second question apparently struck a chord in him, for he started and then lowered his hand.

"Porfilo," said he rather weakly, "what does it mean? Will you try to tell me?"

"He played the fool," said I, "because you've talked him almost mad with this law stuff. He wanted to prove that he was fitted for something else— and he's proved it, right enough. With three men in bed on account of the proof!"

Something in the way in which I said this—for truth sometimes is as piercing as the sound of a gong—dropped him weakly into a chair and opened his eyes at me.

"I don't want to hurt you too much," said I, "but I came here tonight to tell you where Dick is, because I know that you must be almost mad."

"Aye," said he in a broken voice. "Almost mad these last days. I thought— he was dead!"

"He's very much alive. As I said before, I'm going to try to get him back here to you. When I send him, I'm going to try to have him in a mood to listen to reason. I'm going to try to have him in a mood to do whatever you want him to do. Even law school, if you can't think of a better thing!"

"Porfilo," said he, "you talk like a white man. Only, my head is sort of spinning. I don't see—"

"He's big and husky, and you've let him have an easy life," said I, "so that he doesn't like the idea of work. That's the whole of it."

"He's had an easy life," admitted Orton.

"He doesn't want work of *any* kind. He thinks that outlawry is a sort of second heaven. He's been envying me for the way in which I've lived in the mountains."

"Aye, I know that."

"Before I'm through with him, I want to teach him that it's pretty far from a rosy dream. You understand? I want to send him back with his wings clipped. But that leaves one thing more."

"The stage robbery!" groaned Orton.

"Which is the one thing that stood between me and the governor's pardon. Now, Orton, if I let your boy know what that freak of his cost me, do you know what he'd do?"

"Ride down and deliver himself up!"

"Exactly."

The rancher gripped his hands together and bowed his head.

"The one way out, Orton, is to fix the people who were in that stagecoach so that they won't testify against him when he *does* give himself up."

"Fix them?"

"You could handle some of the men, I suppose, by simply telling them the truth about who did it and by paying back the money Dick took, and by paying their doctor bills. You could fix some of the cheap ones with a little money. A bit of persuasion of the same kind might smooth things over all around."

"Is there a chance?"

"The only one to keep either Dick or me from jail. I'll give him a fair chance. I'll tell no stories out of school. I'll see that when I send him back to you, he'll have all the holdup money with him. I promise you I'll not let him part with a cent of it. In the meantime, you work on your end of the deal—and remember that they've doubled the price on my head. So make it fast!"

The perspiration was fairly rolling down his face.

"Porfilo," he said, "if I say that—"

"I don't want thanks," said I briskly. "I want results. So long, sir!"

I stepped back into the night and then hurried off to find Roanoke.

6

EVEN that giant of a mule—with a heart as strong as his body—had had enough. There was something uncertain about his gait when he struck the mountains again, and I got down from the saddle and jogged along beside him.

So we struck away as well as we could, but I was falling far behind my established schedule, so that I knew, before long, that I could not possibly reach the camp of Dick at dawn.

Indeed, I was still a good two miles of rough country away when the sun came up in the east. I pressed on with a growing anxiety. I was worried as to what he might do, left to himself in the daylight.

Then, like an answer to my thought, I heard three shots from the exact direction of the camp, which was still a good mile away from me. The distance made the explosions dull and small, and even at that distance I knew that a revolver was speaking, since there is a metal clanging in the sound of a rifle.

Those noises were made by my new friend, Dick Orton. Even that rash head of his would not permit him to shoot a revolver for the mere pleasure of target practice. No, perhaps even that folly would be possible in him, near though we still were to the camp of Chisholm.

At any rate, there was need for me to hurry. Roanoke had recovered something of his strength, due to my long run, and when I swung into the saddle he was able to take me up the slope at his long, swaying trot. We covered the next crest, and then we dipped through a lane of trees down the slope beyond.

We were about halfway down it and a scant half mile from Dick's camp where I had left him when Roanoke braced all four feet and slid to a halt. There he stood with his ugly head thrown high, sniffing danger. I, too, felt something like a shadow of apprehension pass over me. I snatched out a revolver and whirled in the saddle.

There, behind me, half hidden by a tree trunk, was the body of a man with an end of a flung rope in his hand. I saw, but I saw too late, for at the same instant, with a fatal whisper in my ear, the noose dropped over my head and then bit hard around my body and imprisoned both arms at the elbows against my ribs; then came the tug of the rope thrower's full weight, and I was dragged clumsily, helplessly, from the saddle and so, with a stunning thud, fell at full length upon the ground.

It has taken some time to tell of this. But my first glimpse of the thrower was the very instant that the rope dropped over my head and gripped my arms. From that moment I was helpless and lay bewildered, while the very trees around me turned into madmen!

Not two or three men, but a full score leaped out around me, shrieking their triumph at one another and beating backs, thumping shoulders— almost too delighted with themselves to go ahead with the simple task of securing my hands behind me.

They tied me as though my flesh were fire and would burn through ordinary bonds. They swathed me in thirty or forty pounds of rope, and still some of the older men seemed a little anxious. But I had no thought of attempting to escape.

I looked about me on the bedlam with a sort of detached interest. It did not seem possible that I, Leon Porfilo, of Mendez, the son of the town butcher, the pupil of Father McGuire, should have attained such a bad eminence that so many brave and strong men could go half hysterical at the thought of it.

The more serious portions were already making figures on the ground. There were twenty-one of them. How many times did twenty-one go into fifteen thousand?

About seven hundred bucks apiece!

"That ain't bad for a day's work," said someone.

"Something extra for Lefty!" three or four chimed in.

Lefty came blushingly forward, a long-shinned, gray-headed cowpuncher— the same who had caught me in the noose of the rope.

"Aw," said Lefty, "I ain't got a claim to two shares. Anybody could of—"

"Don't believe it," I put in here. "It took an expert to get that rope through the air without a swish that would have scared a whole herd of buffaloes. I congratulate you!"

Here all other voices ceased, and they stared at me. They had treated me before that moment as though I were a beast in ropes, or a demon in a bottle—a thing to be gaped at, but only with horror. They seemed to see something human in me after that.

"How did you manage to make your throw so quickly after Roanoke stopped?" I asked him.

"I seen him begin to slow a mite. So I started swayin' the rope. Just as he got toward a halt, I let her go. About a fifth of a second more, and you'd of drilled me, Porfilo."

He rubbed his chest as though he had a foretaste of where that bullet might have entered.

"I suppose I should," I admitted. "Who's in charge here?"

"Why, nobody," said someone.

I could not believe it, but it was the entire truth. They were simply a random lot of cowpunchers and lumbermen and hunters who, hearing the news of my appearance at Chisholm's camp, had gathered there to hear all that had happened. Then they had blundered up the mountainside the instant the sun rose in a vague hope that they might come on traces of me. Half of them were on foot!

Never was there such a blind and helpless beginning to a manhunt, and never a hunt that turned out more beautifully!

I had been riding in such a blind haste, with my eyes so fixed upon the higher side of the mountain, that I had not seen the telltale prints of the score of men and horses on the ground over which I rode. Well, I have always felt that this was fate.

Although, perhaps, a better explanation may be that long success had made me careless. Just as a man feels that he is invincible—at that very moment the ground is sure to be jerked from under his feet.

I have often been asked just how I felt at the moment of my capture. What terror and horror and despair welled up in me like shadowy waves. But I have to confess that I felt no great amount of any of those three emotions. Neither did my whole life flash before me; neither did I see the yawning gates of the prison.

I was a little frightened and a good deal irritated because I had made such a clumsy end after a rather stirring career; but nothing disturbed me as much as the ache of my bones from my fall.

After that, I think I was rather more amused than anything else, and very busy watching the faces around me and listening to their voices, and getting a cheap pleasure, I confess, out of the joy they felt in capturing me.

On the whole, I don't think that the actual hand of danger is ever so terrible. What breaks the heart and shatters the nerve is the face of danger in the distance. To wait for her approach is a frightful thing. But when she actually strikes, it is not much. I have heard men say that people in the mouth of a lion, gashed and broken by the tremendous jaws, feel no pain whatever. And danger is like a lion. She is most frightful in the distance.

At least, I am certain that when they lifted me to the back of Roanoke and tied my feet beneath his belly, I was not at all enraged with my captors. They were a very good-natured lot, all jovial and smiling, of course, because of that good morning's work which meant a year's pay popped into their pocket for a single half-day's outing.

Lefty was placed beside me, as the post of honor. The rest of them grouped themselves in convenient array to guard against an attempt at escape or a possible rescue. Far before, behind, and to either side they distributed flank, van, and rear guards to take heed of coming danger.

Then there was an inner cordon of five men, including Lefty, who rode around me, each with a gun in his hand, while the remaining nine formed a larger circle beyond these.

In this fashion I was brought down the slopes and back to the Chisholm camp.

Lefty was a very amiable host. He seemed to be rather ashamed of the part which he had played in the affair, and he kept insisting as he rode along at my side that he had no bad feelings toward me—that he wished me well—that he hardly knew why he had ridden out with the posse—and that he earnestly hoped that I would come well out of my trouble.

I could not help smiling at Lefty, but I knew that he meant what he said.

"But," I said to him, "it's too bad that you weren't alone. You would have had the fifteen thousand all for yourself!"

It was too large a sum for Lefty to grasp in one sweep of the eye; another idea startled him.

"Porfilo," said he, "d'you think that I'd of tackled you if I'd been alone? Not in a million years; I ain't such a fool!"

If I had protested, he would have said a good deal more, but I made no answer to him. However, the truth is perfectly patent that, no matter how many there were around Lefty, it was he and he alone who captured me. When I looked at his simple, good-natured face, a great deal of the vanity left me.

So they brought me in to Sanburn, and they brought me in with a veritable army.

For the news had shot like magic across the mountains, and scores of hurrying riders were spurring to reach me; and in the midst of shouting and dust and snorting horses and jingling of bridle chains and spurs and thudding of hoofs, they escorted me into the town.

7

I HAD a sort of triumphal procession into the town, as one might say. That is, everyone came to windows and waved at me and shouted, and I smiled back at them. In fact, I felt no malice. I was only glad that the long fight was over and that I no longer had to freeze and starve on the mountains and live shut away from my fellows.

That is what I felt, I should say, as I passed through the streets of the town, but the moment the doors of the jail closed behind me and sent a long iron clangor through the big empty space within, my pleasure ended. I cast one side glance at Lefty, and Lefty, having met that look, fell suddenly into the background. From that day to this, I have never seen his face!

After that, I was prepared for what they did. First they tried me with questions, to which I refused all answers, except to admit that my name was Leon Porfilo. There was no use dodging that; but for the rest they got nothing from me. Then they dressed me for the cell.

They left me my clothes, but those clothes were wrecked before they were through. They searched every nook and cranny where so much as a needle could be hidden. They probed and reprobed my shoes, and even investigated the sections of which the heels were built, for fear lest I might have something concealed there—some tiny instrument with which I might unlock my bonds and escape.

In the same fashion they went over all my clothes. It took three men a patient hour of searching before they were sure that my clothes did not contain hidden secrets, and even when that search had ended, they did not appear entirely certain that all was well, and they watched me with extremely wistful eyes.

Next they led me to the cell and put on the irons. Heavy irons for the wrists, but with a mercifully long chain connecting the bracelets, and ponderous irons for the feet, hitched to a great ball. It was possible for me to move across the floor at a snail's pace, dragging that impediment behind me, but I made as much noise as a cavalry charge when I *did* move. They were shameful things, those irons, but they were very effective. I have often wondered why that old-fashioned stuff is not more often used. There would be fewer escapes, by far!

There I sat or lay or stood in Sanburn jail for ten mortal days. There I waited, and the crowds filed past the bars every day and pointed and whispered and laughed and gaped at me.

"There is Leon Porfilo!"

They were never weary of filing by. At first I could not endure their glances and my sense of shame, but afterward I schooled myself, and I used to sit back and smoke a cigarette and watch them, and meet every eye in turn. It was very odd.

There is a weight in a steady glance that some people cannot endure. Most of those who went by those bars could not endure my stare. The men, particularly. Their eagerness went out; more than one of them would actually look the other way, with a shudder. I think that they felt I was trying to jot down their faces for future reference, so that I could take revenge upon them for my shame! The women were bolder, strange to say.

Western women do not fear men. These girls and ladies looked at me with horror, sometimes, but more often with pity, and still more often with a sort of smiling good fellowship, for all the world as though they understood exactly what had brought me there, and it was no fault with which they could not sympathize.

But it was a bitter grind—to endure those straining eyes day by day. Yet the days were heaven compared with the frightful, black, hopeless nights.

No, not black, either, for from a far corner of the cell room a single lamp cast a vague glimmer, and there was never a time when I could not make out the faintly gleaming parallel bars which confined me, and beyond them more dim lines of light—a forest of steel.

Sometimes I felt like running at those bars and tearing at them with my hands. I fought that feeling back—always with a horrible thought that someday the temptation might be too great for me. If I slipped into madness once, where would I end?

For I had lived for three years and a half on the mountains as free as a bird, and the cold and the wretchedness which had been driving me back toward other men were now forgotten. All I could remember was that to be free is to be glorious. I yearned for the regions above timberline—and for Roanoke! The ugly head of that mule drifted across my dreams like the symbolic eagle of my country.

It was not always a drifting line of people who paused, and gaped, and went on—men, women, and children who were lifted to gaze at me and learn that bad men came to such an end as this. For now and then the line ended. It was restricted to calling hours, you might say. In between people of importance were allowed to come to visit me. The newspaper reporters were always considered people of importance!

Well, I tried to tell myself that such fellows were beneath my attention. But they weren't. No one is beneath the opinion of any man. What the beggar in the street thinks, troubles the mind of the king. There's no doubt of that. I smile at the rugged people who damn all the world except a few friends. Margaret O'Rourke came to me, too, and I dragged my iron ball across the floor, making a small thunder behind me, and took her small hand through the bars. She did not speak half a dozen words, and those were incoherent. She came in trying to be brisk and cheerful, like her old self. But she began to cry at once, and clung to the bars and buried her face in her arm and wept like a child.

Then I saw, all at once, that I had treated her not as a man should treat the woman he loves, but like a sulky fool. I despised myself. I saw in Mike the truth of her, which was all womanly and gentle.

Her visit and one other were the only ones that did me good.

The other visit was from Father McGuire. I had not seen him for years. But he looked the same. A little older and more tired, but not much. He was full of impatience and could hardly pause to shake my hand.

Then he wagged a lean forefinger at me. "Leon Porfilo," said he, "you did not hold up that stage!"

"Of course not," I said.

"There is not much careless brutality in you. Besides—you would not tell your name—and more than that, if you had been there, really, I don't think that any guns would have been pulled against you! Now I'm going back to see that governor—although I've tantalized him about you until he hates my face. Only this much before I go:

"Keep your head high and your hands clean—as clean as you've kept them up to this time, my boy! I know what you are; and a few others guess what you are. We need you back on our sides. Good-by!"

The world is not large enough to hold two like Father McGuire!

That same day, a little withered man stood in front of the bars and smoked a cigarette and looked me up and down. It was Tex Cummins, who had freed me from the jail in Mendez three years before—freed me because he thought he could use me afterward.

"Well, well, Leon," said he, "I see that you're back to your old tricks again—popping yourself into free lodgings!"

I did not answer him. I knew that I had not sufficient subtlety of tongue to talk with such a man as Cummins.

"But in the meantime," said he, "I wonder if it is not just as well that you are in here instead of out there!" He waved his hand to indicate the outer world. "Because out there, I was coming close on your trail, my lad, and if I ever catch you—you will wish that you had taken a shorter cut to purgatory, Porfilo."

I had to make an answer to that. So I dipped up a little of the bitterness and the scorn that was in me and I said to him: "I've beaten you and your crowd before, Cummins, and I'll beat you again. I'll tell you why: A crook has no real chance against an honest man!"

He laughed in an ugly way.

"Well, honest man," said he, "here's your reward. But if you'd worked with me, you fool, you'd be rich and happy now, Porfilo."

That was the way he left me. But I am glad to say that he did not make me regret.

Now I come to that tenth day of my stay in the prison, which was one of the strange days of my life. I had felt that I was almost at the end of my nerve strength, and I said so to Sheriff Lawton, who came in for the first time.

He told me that the string of visitors who came to gape at me would be shut out from that time forward, and he heartily damned the keepers who had allowed them to come in to me up to that time.

When he questioned me about the stage holdup, I had to admit that I did not care to talk of that affair, and my reluctance angered him a great deal.

"I believe you," he said. "I believe that you didn't do that job. It doesn't ring like Porfilo to me. Stage stick-ups are a little too spectacular for your particular kind of nerve. But, Leon, how the devil am I to base my belief on anything more than a mere hunch? What the devil will a jury say?"

"Juries will give me no sort of a show anyway," said I. "How can they give a show to a man with fifteen thousand on his head?"

Lawton grinned sourly at me. "They've collected their reward," said he. "Well, I'm glad that I didn't have a share in it, boy!"

I thanked him for that, and he talked cheerfully, but about other things, until he left me.

After that, a long, long day followed. From one small, high-placed window on the wall, a spot of sunlight was cast upon the floor. Far slower than the movement of the hour hand of a clock, it seemed to me, that spot of sun crept to my cell. When it reached me, I kneeled and held out my hands to it until my fingers were yellowed and warmed by it. It was more than washing in liquid gold to me, at that moment!

But, after the spot of sun had left the floor of the cell nest, the long evening began. It was an age while the soft light of the end of the day deepened from yellow to rose, and then to violet outside the window. I stared at the window frame as though it were my last hope of life.

Through it there seeped in a faint tang of the alkali dust which was raised by playing children and by passing riders in the street. Never was such a sweet perfume! Through the window, also, came fragments and rhythms of pleasant voices. Oh, who has not noticed that all voices are pleasant so long as they come from human lips and from the distance?

I felt myself growing weaker. I had a queer choking in my throat and a lightness in my head. I knew that my nerve was breaking down. But then the sorrow of the day turned into the black bitterness of the night!

I thought of the pure, cold winds that comb the upper mountains where I had lived so long, and the last bird voices in the wind, and the bell tones of lowing cattle out of the valleys—the deepening dark and the sudden nearness of the stars above my head.

Yes, I was weakening fast. If someone had entered the door of my cell at that moment and exclaimed: "Porfilo, what are the sins and shameful actions of your life?" I should have confessed them all swiftly, almost eagerly!

Western towns fall asleep early, just as they rise early. Now all of Sanburn was lost in silence. Not perfect silence, but that deeper stillness through which occasional noises burst on the ear with a sudden violence—a dog barking, a sharp break of laughter, an oath from a passing man. But even these sounds grew less frequent. Sanburn slept.

But I did not sleep. For two days and nights I had not slept, and I lay on my cot with a thudding heartbeat, telling myself that another night of torture was about to begin, and that when the morning came, if I had not slept, I should be close to hysterical weakness—close to a tearful breakdown. I—Leon Porfilo!

I had always looked upon myself as a creature made out of some stubborn material, as different from the stuff that composes other men as iron and rock are from wood. But now I had a brief inner glance, and what I saw astonished me.

That night wore past its first few ages, and then I heard the guard, who had been rustling a newspaper in the outer office, begin to walk up and down the floor. There was a wooden floor out there—a concrete floor in the cell nest, to embed the lower end of the bars. Every creak of the floor was very audible to me. Once he opened the door and came in to me.

"Hello, Porfilo!"

I did not speak.

"Sulky still!" snarled the guard.

I think he had been drinking a bit. There was a thick, numb articulation in his speech. For that matter, it is no cheerful task to be night guard in a jail.

"Good night," said I.

"It ain't no easier on me than it is on you," he declared. "Why not loosen up a bit and act sort of human? I ain't a wolf, Porfilo. We could help each other waste a little time."

I did not reply. It made me sick at heart to even think of chatting with my prison keeper. So he turned on his heel with an oath, and was off again. The door closed heavily on him; his pacing up and down the office floor began once more.

Then his striding paused. I heard the opening of a door and then, distinctly, a gasping noise, a scuffle—after which the outer door of the jail closed heavily.

Another pause—a muffled voice—and the office door was flung open. I saw the guard come hurrying, the lantern in his hand. Behind him stalked a tall fellow. A sway of the lantern and the upfling of the light struck across a masked face.

"A lynching party!" I thought, and my stomach cleaved to my backbone.

But there was no murmur outside. Lynching parties do not gather so soundlessly. After all, my crimes were not of the variety which induce lynching.

The keeper paused at my door, unlocked it, and stepped in.

"Take your time," said the masked man. "There's no hurry."

It was a deepened, roughened voice, but I knew it—Dick Orton! Suddenly a great spring of joy opened in my heart. A wine of happiness rushed through me. I loved Dick Orton. I loved the whole human race for his sake!

The keeper had seen or heard enough to throw him into a panic. His hands were trembling, but he managed to find the locks and to turn the key in them. The shackles fell from my hands. I clasped my numbed wrists and chafed them. The weights fell from my legs—I stretched myself on tiptoe, turned suddenly lighter and stronger than ever I had been before.

"You," said Orton to the keeper, "stand back in that corner. If you yap, I'll come back and blow your brains out."

He drew me out of the cell and closed the self-locking door on the guard. Then he thrust a pair of guns into my hands. I slipped them in my pockets, however.

"Why?" Dick paused to ask me.

"It's never worth a killing," said I.

He merely grunted, and then he led the way through the cell room. At the office door he paused. Behind us there was a muffled sound—the groan of the guard in shame and in despair!

We stepped into the office.

"There's a rifle," said Dick. "Do you want it?"

I took it from the wall. There is nothing much better than a rifle by way of a club. Then I followed Dick calmly through the front door, first cramming on my head the sheriff's own old sombrero which hung from a nail.

Two horses were tethered at the hitching rack. I saw that they were tall and well made. We untied them and swung into the saddle just as half a dozen punchers came rollicking around the bend in the street and swept by us.

One of them drew rein. The others slowed.

"Where you two been?"

"Trying to see Porfilo. They turned us down!" I laughed.

It was easy to laugh. Now that I was so close to freedom, I felt that a hundred giants could not have recaptured me.

The six laughed, also.

"We tried the same thing today. Lawton has shut down. The tightwad!"

Here a raging voice from the jail cried: "Help!"

"What the devil!" cried I. "What's up in the jail?"

"Help! He's gone!"

"An escape—Porfilo!" I yelled. I pretended to start for the jail door.

All the six were before me. With Indian yells they lunged from their horses and sprinted for the front doors of the jail. Orton and I snapped into our saddles and turned the corner of the street.

Behind us was a confusion of sounds. In the street around us, and staring out from their doors and their verandas were men roused by the shouting from the jail—everyone with a gun. But they did not heed us, jogging slowly along. Oh, it was easy to be calm out of the cursed shadow of the jail!

We turned another corner and now the nerves of Dick Orton could stand the strain no longer. He gave his horse the spurs and we flew out of Sanburn at a raging gallop.

We flew out onto the dark hills beyond, with the wind of our gallop in our teeth and the clear, pure stars above us, reaching down to us, and the great, free mountains looming up into the sky on every side. I threw out my arms to it and thanked heaven for such a man as Dick Orton and for liberty.

Then we rode on. The confusion in Sanburn died behind us. We drew rein of one accord, without any spoken word. I reached for Dick's hand and found and crushed it.

That is the true story of the jail delivery at Sanburn about which the newspapers stormed and fought for so many days. Everyone said "Bribery!" and the jail guard left that section of the country, a disgraced man. But there was no bribery.

The thing had succeeded so simply because everyone expected that the attempt to escape would come from within, not from without. It was believed that I had no friend in the world except a sheriff and a priest. Sheriffs and priests do not break into jails!

8

"AND Roanoke?" said Dick, after we had ridden for some time.

"Ah! If only I were on the back of Roanoke," said I. "Then the ride to freedom would be perfect. But perhaps it is enough that I am free, Dick. Free, free, free! I never knew what was in that word before!"

"It was easy," said Dick Orton rather thoughtfully. "Mighty easy."

"Easy for the man with the right amount of nerve, Orton. But I should have hesitated a good deal, even for my best friend."

"Would you?" said Dick, childishly pleased by that compliment. "But now you're just talkin'. Well, Porfilo, leastways we're on the move, and we're together!"

He said it grimly, as one who has accomplished a great thing. I really believe that to that foolish youngster it was a bit of heaven to be riding with me, simply because the law had proscribed me, and men were hunting me for a great price.

"It'll be twenty thousand after this," chuckled Dick, and I knew that I was reading his thoughts correctly.

He could do nothing but chatter and sing, after that. He told me how he had conceived the idea. After ten days, he felt that they would begin to relax their precautions. Sanburn would be used to the sensation of having such a prisoner in its midst. The guards would be used to him, also.

So, that very evening, Dick had descended to his father's ranch and in the corral he had selected two of the best horses—well-known and tried by him. These he saddled from the harness shed and brought all safely away.

But, before he went, he slipped up to the house in order to play the spy and see what was going on there. He had looked through the window of the living room and seen enough to satisfy him—his mother and father, each screened behind a newspaper.

"The same as ever," said Dick, with a little of childish chagrin. "I thought that they'd do a little grieving about me!"

"You young fathead!" said I. "D'you think that they're going to sit around and hold their hands and cry about you for two whole weeks? Besides, maybe they've found out that they don't need you as much as they thought they did. The doctors cut out meat, and they find that they can still get fat on vegetables!"

He did not take my banter in a very light manner. He mused for some time, heavily, on this subject, and muttered a few words to himself, but I was rather glad to see that he was impressed. He had been an only child and a favored child all his life—and even the most manly fellow is apt to begin to take things for granted after a time.

. I headed toward a house which I knew well. I had stopped there half a dozen times two years before, and I had been able to pay the squatter well for his trouble. He was a dark-faced Spaniard or Frenchman—I don't know which! But he had a foreign accent in his lingo that made me know that he was an outsider. You understand that I'm saying all of these things colloquially.

Well, I suppose that Joe Loveng was what generally went by the name of a "dago." Out West that means some fellow with a bit of Latin blood and black eyes and a swarthy skin and a language which leaves a taint in his English. That was the way with Joe Loveng.

Other punchers had little use for him. He was hard-headed. He ran sheep. His fist was tight. And—he talked queer. That is to say, he did not speak the particular sort of ungrammatical slang which was chattered in that part of the range.

He made his living, as I have said, by running a few sheep on his land. It was not very good land, but he made the best of it. He lost practically no sheep because he tended them as if they were his children, and he always had mutton that weighed twenty or thirty pounds more on the hoof than any other mutton on the range. When other sheep began to get pot-bellied and thin-backed, Joe's flock was as round as butterballs.

Besides, he had a little apple orchard which was in a hollow of rich ground, and he made cider from these and peddled the stuff when it was hard. He had a vineyard, too, rambling over a few hillsides where the soil was gravelly. Those vines gave him grapes enough to make several fine casks of wine every year, and that wine was famous all over the range. Even with these sources of income, Joe was never too prosperous—or at least he never showed his prosperity.

For one thing, whatever he produced, he had eight mouths to maintain. His own, his wife's, and six children, of whom the oldest was a fifteen-year-old girl when I last saw her. Since that time, two years before, I understood that Mary and several of her brothers had grown enough to be worked in the fields, and Joe Loveng was growing prosperous on account of the extra hands which he did not have to hire.

That was the family to which I was taking Dick Orton, and I told him about the place and the people as we went along.

It was a great game for Dick. He had never stayed in the company of an outlaw at such a house.

"But," said I, "there's one danger. If Joe should take it into his head to let it be known that you were seen at his house in my company—"

"He'd be pinched for taking in an outlaw—no matter who was with you!"

"Not a bit," said I. "He'd just explain that he was afraid of being killed if he did not entertain us."

"The coward!" said Dick.

"However," said I, "I think that Joe knows what side his bread is buttered on too well for that. He used to make good money out of me."

"No dago has a thought bigger than a dollar," declared Dick.

I was half inclined to agree with him, which shows that my education in the world was almost as limited as his!

We hove in sight of the twinkling lights of the house of Joe Loveng. It was eleven o'clock or later. We had ridden a full two hours from Sanburn, and I felt that by this time we had gone far enough to avoid pursuit.

Besides, after the first great rapture of freedom and the taste of the night air was out of my throat, I began to ache with weariness. This was the third night in which I had not closed my eyes, and for ten days every nerve in my body had been under a terrible strain.

My plan was to remain at Joe Loveng's and have a fine sleep until just before the break of day. Joe was one who never allowed the sun to see him in his bed, and therefore he would be able to waken us in time. After that, we could have a bite of cold breakfast, and then we would wing away into the gray of the dawn with very little probability that any of the scouts of Sanburn might come in sight of us. Even if we did, as a matter of fact, take a glimpse of them, we and our horses would be fresh and they would be fagged from a night of hard riding.

I confided all of this plan to my companion, and he agreed with it heartily.

Then he burst out into a great tirade of self-denunciation.

"Porfilo," said he, "if it hadn't been for me, you'd be a free man with the governor's pardon in your pocket, able to sass back every sheriff on the range, and as it is, you've got to run like a scared coyote and take to the hills!"

It made me rather gloomy to hear him talk in this manner. I had not realized that he would think the thing over so logically, and come to such a conclusion.

So we hove up to the door of Joe Loveng's house, and I leaned from the saddle and through the window pointed out the scene to Dick. There sat Joe Loveng, with his feet in slippers and his fat legs spread out to the warmth of the stove, and around him sat his flock of seven with their brown faces and their bright, black eyes which were never still. It was a pleasant sight.

But, "Holy smoke!" breathed Dick. "Look at that girl! Is that the reason why you want to come here?"

I looked again. It was Mary, sitting facing us. Between fifteen and seventeen she had turned from a child into a woman, and a lovely woman at that!

9

If I had had doubts as to whether or not Joe Loveng would remember me, they disappeared the instant that I met him at his door. He put out both hands and pulled me by the shoulders into the house. He kept one hand upon my arm; with the other he reached Dick Orton and pulled him in after me. And all the time he kept saying: "Meester Porfilo!"

But I cannot imitate his lingo. His words came up with a bubbling sound in the throat. He talked like a man who has just eaten some oily thing. He sent two of his oldest boys scurrying out to put up our horses. I wondered if it were the kind memory of me that caused this enthusiasm of Joe's, or the kinder memory of the last twenty dollars which I had left with him.

"Food—wine, Mary!" he snapped at his girl.

She was already at the kitchen door and whirled to smile back at us. I saw the flash of her white teeth, and her black eyes go through and through Dick Orton.

We sat down by the fire. Dick was very quiet, thoughtful, and kept observing all in the room with a reflective eye. He looked upon Joe Loveng's younger children, sitting in a bright-eyed, silent semicircle in the corner of the room. Dick Orton smiled upon them.

After that I began to worry.

In the meantime, Joe Loveng was hoping that the reason I was out of jail was because I had the governor's pardon. I could not help telling him that it was because I had something better than a governor's pardon—a friend. At this, Joe nodded and smiled at Dick, and Dick smiled back rather complacently. Then Mary came in with fried eggs and bacon and coffee and a pitcher of wine.

We marched through those provisions like lightning. I was busy eating and talking to Joe Loveng. Dick Orton said not a word, but he used his eyes very busily still, and when I announced that it was bedtime, and we got up from the table, I saw Mary Loveng blushing in the corner of the room.

There were two little attic rooms, and Loveng had his youngsters roll down our blankets there; I said good night to Dick and, drugged and sick with weariness, I blew out my light and turned in. All that I noted, through the window as the darkness flowed in around me, was the white face of a half moon which was riding in the eastern sky. Then I was asleep as suddenly as though I had been struck heavily over the head.

It seemed only an instant later that a hand seized upon my shoulder and the excited voice of Joe Loveng was barking at my ear:

"Meester Porfilo!"

I gathered my senses and both my guns and sat up with a jerk.

"Meester Orton, he has raised the devil!"

I blundered downstairs behind Joe Loveng and in the living room beneath, I found Mary cowering in a corner while Dick Orton marched magnificently up and down before her, like a lion before a lamb.

Loveng told the story with much heat. He had wakened at his usual early hour and struck the door of Mary, expecting her to start down at once to cook breakfast. But there was no answer. He opened her door and looked into her empty room!

Then, bewildered, he had gone to the window, and, looking down, he had seen them seated on a rustic bench beneath an apple tree, and each in the arms of the other. He had rushed down upon them, but when he appeared, Dick Orton had risen and declared that he would step upon Joe Loveng and make him pop with a loud noise—or something to that effect.

Here Dick put in simply that Loveng had drawn a knife on him, and then he had threatened to wring Mr. Loveng's neck if he did not get out of the way. As for the picture upon which Loveng had looked—why, it was very simple. Dick had not been sleepy.

He had lain in his blankets for a time—thinking! Then he had got up and slipped downstairs. When he stepped from the front door of the house, he heard a rustle of a figure disappearing around the corner of the house.

He, Dick, had gone out merely to smoke a cigarette, but now he saw that he might have the pleasure of apprehending thieves about to plunder the house of his host. He turned that corner and in a single bound he had apprehended—Mary Loveng herself!

Dick was very intense and serious about it. He paid no heed to the fury of Joe, but kept his eyes fixed upon me so gravely that I knew that he was telling the truth, and all the truth. Yet it was so foolish that I could hardly keep from smiling—which would have ruined everything.

It seemed that Mary Loveng, like Dick, for some mysterious reason, had not been able to sleep. She, too, had thought of a walk under the stars as a sedative before she tried to close her eyes. Therefore she had gone down—and been terribly frightened at the appearance of a man, suddenly.

However, when they discovered one another, they were rather glad of company. They simply sat down to have a chat. The air of that summer night was warm. It was very pleasant out under the stars to watch the way of the moon, diving through the silver clouds and putting them aside as the bow of a ship puts waves away.

They had remained there—simply in a friendly chat, talking about everything and nothing. Time had suddenly disappeared like a secret thief, and if they had still been sitting and talking when the morning broke—for yonder in the east there was now a thin penciling of gray—they really had no idea how so many hours could have jumped into a pocket. It was quite startling really!

I had not had a great deal of experience in such affairs, but one doesn't need experience. In certain important matters one is born with an instinct which is worth every whit as much as educated brains—no more! These two young idiots—their combined ages would not have added up to the age of good sense—had simply been thrown into a whirl at the sight of one another.

He was spectacular enough to have turned the head of almost any girl, and certainly she was a flashing pretty thing. So they had sat there all night, with never a wrong thought in their heads; and even now they were sick and white with love.

I never could understand why it is that love affects people in that way. Nothing gives folks a more distressed look—unless it is seasickness.

It was perfectly patent to me that Dick had spoken the entire truth. I asked him point-blank with a single stern glance, and his reply was a look as steady as iron. By that I knew, as well as though he had sworn it.

It was far other with Joe Loveng. He had listened to the story with a raging impatience. Half a dozen times I had been forced to put a hand on his shoulder to keep him from breaking in. But, when he had his chance, he broke into a violent explosion of foreign language that rattled out as fast as cobblestones rattle under the iron rim of a cart wheel.

What he said, of course, I had not the slightest idea. But suddenly Mary leaped up with a little cry and ran and clung to Dick. He, like a stalwart young jackass, put his arm around her and threw back his head—a very fine attitude and good enough to be tried in front of any camera. But it almost got him stabbed.

Joe Loveng whipped out a nasty-looking knife, almost long enough to have spitted them both, and I really think that he would have cut the throats of the pair of them if he had had his way. As for Dick, his gun hand was frozen around the girl; I was barely in time to get the wrist of Loveng and put a grip on it that made him drop the knife with a groan. I jammed my heel on the blade and sent it to splinters of flying steel. I was angry, too.

For I hate a knife. I think I like poison more than I like a knife. In the old days in Mendez I had learned to use one. A boy will practice any art of murder because he feels it brings him closer to the possibilities of manhood.

But, since my boyhood, I had come to detest bare steel. The very thought of it, to this day, edges my nerves and runs a sharp bit of ice down my backbone.

I said to Joe: "You're within an ace of getting your neck twisted off, you fool! What d'you mean by pulling a knife?"

Joe cowered for an instant and gave me an ugly side glance. Then his rage and his sorrow came hot in him again.

He declared that Orton had not told the truth—not half the truth. Dick swore that he had.

"Ah!" cried Joe Loveng. "Did you not kees her?"

"Say no!" whispered the white lips of Mary to her lover.

But he had become very grand and stately. "I did kiss her. Besides, she's gunna be my wife. Now, what've you got to say to that?"

What Joe had to say was a great deal. Part of it was in his own tongue, whatever that was, and the small moiety was in broken English. There was no difficulty in understanding, however. All that he had to offer was that if Mary attempted to marry such a man, he, Joe Loveng, would hang her with his own hands to the limb of the apple tree under which she had sat with her American lover.

That was rather rough talk, and I saw Dick Orton grow wild. I tried to catch his eye, but it couldn't be done. He stormed up to Joe Loveng and told him with a good deal of emphasis, helped out by a few curses which came right off the range, that if so much as a tip of her finger were hurt, if her feelings were in the slightest degree injured, he, Dick Orton, would return and take Joe Loveng by the nape of the neck and whittle him to the right size and put him into a frying pan and roast him, slowly.

This, or something to this general effect, was what Dick Orton managed to say through his teeth, fairly trembling with fury. But you cannot control such people as Joe Loveng with threats. I think that if I had been left alone with him, I could have smoothed out everything beautifully, but as it was, there was red blood in the eyes of Loveng before Dick had ended.

He ordered us out of the house, and I told Dick that we had better go hopping as fast as we could.

Nothing would do for Dick, however, but a finish in the grand manner. He had to sweep Mary into his arms and kiss her good-by in the presence of all of us. It was very silly, but it was rather touching, too. I didn't care a rap about Dick and his emotions. I knew that they would change quickly enough, and he would be well over his insanity.

But Mary was another matter. She clung to Dick and kissed him again and again, and vowed that she would die if he did not come back for her.

Well, they would have made a pretty picture if it had not been for the face of Joe in the background. He was a fire-breathing dragon, and no mistake!

I had to pry the lovers apart. Then I took Dick on one arm and with the other hand I gave Joe a twenty-dollar bill. He merely crumpled it in his palm and threw it in my face!

It was a pretty fair indication of how peevish he was. By this time I had worked up enough of a reputation—nine tenths of it totally undeserved— to keep most men from troubling me if they could avoid it, possibly. It was a bit of a shock to have that money thrown back in my face, but I let the matter drop. After all, I felt that we were too deeply in the wrong.

We went out to our horses and saddled them in a silence which lasted until we were well up the trail. Then Dick broke into song.

I am a fairly patient fellow, but that was too much. I drew rein and damned him heartily, from his hair to the tips of his toes, but Dick merely sang on, and raised his voice to drown me out.

"You have raised the devil!" I told him at last.

"It was a lark!" cried Dick Orton.

"May you burn for it!" muttered I. "You will if you dare go back to that girl."

"Dare to go back?" said Dick. "How can I dare to stay away—after I've promised her?"

That was the way with him. A worse thing to make a bad thing better. But after that I didn't attempt to argue with him. I would as soon have tried logic on a range bull.

10

MY chief fear was concerning the wicked tongue of Joe Loveng, which could do Dick irreparable harm by publishing the fact that he was my companion in my flight and probably my rescuer. I had given Joe only one warning as I left, and that concerned silence.

Besides, no matter what Dick had done in the way of indiscretion, he had been guilty of no real crime. I determined that if Joe Loveng peached on Dick, I would make Joe an example never to be forgotten among mountain folks.

That was all for the future, however. For the present, I began as soon as the sun was high and warm to persuade Dick that he must turn back and leave me. He was as obstinate as Roanoke on a cold morning—than which I cannot imagine greater stubbornness. He insisted that he should accompany me—unless I really felt that he hampered me!

Hampered me? After he had dragged me from a prison and while I was half mad for the lack of human company? I told him as much, but I begged him to go back to his home. I gathered together every reason on which I could lay my mind, and there were plenty of them, and all good enough to have convinced even a headstrong child. But Dick was worse than that. He was a headstrong man!

A dozen times I wished with all my heart that he had had my training under Father McGuire. It takes iron to break iron, and Father McGuire was finest steel. He had beaten me into shape of some sort when I was rather unmalleable stuff; he would have changed Dick even at his age.

However, the mischief having been done, there was nothing but to make the best of it, and that I determined to do. First of all, I wanted to drift my wild man away from the vicinity of Loveng's house. I succeeded very well in doing it. It was a full week later, and by keeping to the highlands—most of the time above timberline—I had been able to keep out of touch with trouble.

But then fate stepped into the ring and knocked my plans and my hopes galley west with a single punch.

I had to get word to the father of Dick—though he seemed to have forgotten that there was such a thing as a father and a mother grieving about him. So I decided that I must write a letter and get down to a town to slip it into a mailbox. Dick, of course, went with me. I could not take a step without having him along with me.

We got into a little crossroads town, and I found the box and I mailed my letter which told Mr. Orton that his son was still with me and that I was doing what I could to send him back, but that he was still obstinate. It was not much of a letter, but when I assured Orton that I was trying to keep Dick out of further mischief, I was rather assured that something good might come from it in the way of peace of mind for the old couple.

In the meantime, the pair of us were very keen to get news of the outer world. Seven days of wandering had been nothing to me, but they had made up seven years to Dick. It was he who got the paper—how, I don't know. It was an old paper—too old to suit me! For it was published five days before, and it bore in it in a first-page flare the very tidings which I most dreaded and had most hoped would not arrive.

For, on that page, there was printed a statement by Joe Loveng, which narrated how "the celebrated outlaw," Leon Porfilo, had come to his house and demanded his hospitality and received it—because he was afraid to refuse such a desperate character. Also, in the company of this man was none other than the son of the much respected rancher, Orton!

Dick Orton was furious at such duplicity on the part of Loveng, and I, myself, had a great desire to get at the man. But I needed only a moment of reflection to understand that Loveng had been hard tried by that experience with Dick.

"How far is it from here to Loveng's, do you think?" Dick asked me.

I saw what he was driving at at once.

"You'll not go back there, Dick," said I.

"And let Loveng have the run of me?" said Dick. "Nobody can stop me from going after him!"

I told him that I couldn't let him go, and I begged him to listen to reason. If he returned, it was very probable that the house of Loveng was being watched.

"What of that?" said Dick.

"You've thrown in your luck with me, and the world knows," I told him.

"What have I done, so far as they know? Why can't I go back to see Mary Loveng if I wish?"

"Go back to find her and all you'll see will be the inside of a jail!"

He was furious. He had taken the whole affair in such a casual way that he still could see no reason why the law should be at outs with him.

"This life of mine that you think so wonderful—well, Dick, you're seeing the true face of it now," I told him. "You can't go back to Loveng's place."

"I've got to," said he. "I've given my word."

"To whom?"

"To Mary."

"She'll be the last to want you to run into danger for her sake."

He was entirely bullheaded. Finally he turned his horse back on the trail and asked me if I would go with him or remain where I was.

At that, I rode in front of him and took hold of his bridle rein.

"Dick," said I, "I can't let you go. It's a crazy thing to do."

I should have known better than to take his rein. He was already so excited and so hot that it did not need much to put him quite off balance.

"Drop the rein, will you?" said he.

I did that at once and wished I had not touched it.

"Clear your horse from in front of me!" said Dick savagely.

I begged him to be reasonable.

"I'm not a kid!" thundered Dick. "I have a mind of my own, and I know how to use it! I'm going back to Loveng's. Keep clear of me, Porfilo!"

"You blockhead!" said I, getting a little too heated in my turn. "You shall not stir a foot that way."

"Who'll stop me?" asked Dick.

"I'll stop you if I have to!"

He was so angry that he sat on his horse trembling, for a moment.

"Porfilo," said he, "if you love your life, keep clean back from me!"

He tried to press forward. I kept my horse before him.

"Then, curse you, get your gun!" screamed Dick, and tore out his own Colt.

I was barely in reaching distance, and I was barely in time. I got his wrist just as the weapon came clear of the leather. The bullet went smashing at random against the face of a rock, and I threw my weight in at him.

The very first shock told me that I should have my hands full. He was a shade taller than I, but not quite so heavy. He had confessed that he had never done much work. But he was full of a natural strength.

The shock of our meeting tumbled both of us out of the saddles. We rolled under the bellies of the horses and then twisted apart for fear of their trampling hoofs. The moment I was away from him, I wanted the thing over.

"I've got enough, Dick," I yelled to him. "I don't want to fight!"

But he was entirely blinded with rage by this time. He came at me with a panther spring that I was barely able to dodge.

"Dick," I shouted to him, "I give up! I quit! I don't want to fight!"

I might as well have talked to a whirlwind. He came lunging again and got home a grazing blow on my temple that half dazed me and, worse than that, brought a flush of fighting heat into my own blood. It was a long time since I had had the joy of a personal struggle with another man, hand to hand. I jammed my left under the chin of Dick and hit him away from me.

There was enough force in that blow to make him gasp, but he was game to the core, and started back at me, smashing with both hands. He had some training, and he had a blinding turn of natural speed. But he had not yet stepped into his full power. Perhaps I felt as Andrew Chase felt, six years before, when he struck me to the ground.

"Take it, then!" I said to Dick, and slid my right over his shoulder until the knuckles fitted snugly along his jaw.

It pitched Dick squarely back upon his shoulders, and he did not rise again. It was a wicked blow; the jar of it had sent a tingle to my shoulder, and I was afraid that I might have broken the bone. But when I started to pick him up, he was already grunting and struggling.

He forced himself to his feet and began striking blindly toward me, quite out. There was no more force in his hands than in the hands of a child. I held his arms and begged him to steady up. He waved, and staggered for another instant. Then he shook his head violently, and his eyes were clear.

Through a very long moment we watched one another. I with my heart in my throat, for I was certain that I had lost one of the few friends I had ever made in the world. But, though there was rage in the eye of Dick, there was thought, also.

"You're too strong for me," he said huskily, at last.

"Dick—" I began.

But he broke in on me suddenly: "It was coming to me. It was coming to me, Porfilo. I see that, now. I'm glad that it came from *you*. I couldn't have taken it from any other man!"

"You slipped as you came in at me—" I tried to explain.

But he only grinned at me, a wry, mirthless sort of a grin.

"I understand all about it," said Dick, "I've had my licking. Well, maybe it will do me good!"

There are punishments of all kinds, but none that go much harder on a young man than the necessity of admitting that he has been beaten. When I heard my new friend Orton confess that he had been licked, I suddenly knew that he was twice the man that I had thought him before. I liked him twice as much.

He did not lose a penny's worth of pride, either. Altogether, it was an astonishing thing to me. For, when I had been licked the first and the greatest time in my life, I had blundered on until I was covered with bumps and blood. A priest had done the trick for me!

"Sit down over here, and let's think things over," said Dick.

We let our nags graze, and we sat down in the shade of a scrub oak— for we were in the lowlands at that time. He began to rub the crimson place where my knuckles had ground halfway to the jawbone.

"This is better than ten years of law," said Dick.

I said nothing. I was afraid that whatever I said would be too raw—too *much* to the point. Also, I was so astonished by the way in which he had taken the thing that I was fairly made mute by it. Can you think of striking a lion in the face and then seeing the brute lick your hand? There was a good deal of the lion in Dick.

I was only sure of one thing—that from that moment he was saved. The selfish boy would begin to die in him; he was a man. All in one stroke!

"I didn't think that anyone in the world could do it," he told me. "Not even Leon Porfilo."

"A lucky punch—" I tried to begin.

He merely smiled. "I knew it the minute you got your grip on me. It was like having a ten-tined Jackson fork stuck in my flesh. I couldn't do a thing. I was like a kid in your hands. But now, Porfilo, the main thing is to make out what I should do next. I can't go blundering around trying to clean up the whole range. Somebody else will sap me in the same place—and not let me up when I go down!"

He laughed a little bitterly. "I thought I was a sort of a Hercules!" he said.

I let the poison work in him, because I saw that it was doing him a lot of good; but it was a pretty unpleasant thing to watch the pride and the good sense in him struggle together.

"There's only one right thing," I said at last.

"Tell me what that is?"

"Go back home, and face the music. See your father. Tell him that you've been playing the fool and that you want to do what he thinks is really best for you."

He answered me very indirectly.

"Why didn't you send a slug of lead through me, Porfilo, when I pulled my gun?"

I made no answer.

"Do you know what I would have done if I'd had the chance?" he went on. "I would of shot you down. That was how much temper was in me. I would of shot *you* down, Porfilo! Well, that's what makes me pretty sober now. Not the punch that knocked me out. That was nothing. But the stuff that was in my head just before you hit me. That's what makes me think!"

"Take it easy," I suggested.

"I am. I got only a quarter of what I deserved to get. You should be riding off, and I should be lying in the dirt, there, and looking at the sun, and never seeing it!"

He shuddered.

"Well," he said, "I'm going to do what you want!"

I found his hand and gripped it. "You're a fine kid, Dick," said I with all my heart in my voice.

He shook his head.

"But what about Mary Loveng—" said he.

"Well?" I asked, a little anxious.

"She had my promise to come back."

"She'll forget that."

He shrugged his big shoulders.

"I don't think so," said he. "I don't know. But we were pretty serious."

"Are you serious now?" said I.

"Me? That's not what counts. It's what might be inside of her head. That's what really counts, Porfilo!"

He could not have found a better way to silence me. Certainly this was a very different fellow from the Dick Orton of five minutes before.

"Think it out for yourself, Dick," I told him. "I can't help you now. Because you're not a kid anymore. You've turned into a man."

"I think I have. I want to forget the thing that I've been up to this time."

"Only remember that if you go to Loveng's house, you'll be running your head into a lot of trouble. Remember that Loveng will be waiting for you— and he won't be trusting to his own pair of hands. He'll have help, and plenty of it."

"I ought not to worry about the danger," he decided thoughtfully.

"Not for yourself. You have your father and your mother to think about," I suggested.

He shuddered a little at that. I think that for a moment he was about to give up the entire idea, but it came back on him.

"I agree to that," said Dick Orton. "I've got to think about them, and I shall—from this minute on! But before I go back to them, I have to have clean hands. My hands aren't clean until I've talked to Mary once more."

"Do you think," said I, "that one talk has been enough to fix her for life?"

"I thought so before," said he. "But I'm not quite so fat-headed now. Maybe she's forgotten all about me."

"What do you hope?"

"God knows that I hope she has!"

"I'm glad of that! I thought your head was pretty well turned, for a while."

"It was. But since you knocked some sense into me—well, I've been seeing only one thing when I think of her, and what I've been seeing is not her pretty face."

He paused again and frowned at the ground. It was a sad thing to watch the boy die out of him and the man take its place.

"Only her hands, Porfilo," he murmured. "That's what I'm seeing now. Big, broad, stumpy, calloused hands—like the hands of a man. Confound it, I know that she got those hands by doing good, honest work in the fields, and yet—"

"Good, honest work—and she's a good, honest girl," I reminded him.

"I'm thinking of that," he declared. "Yet—it makes a mighty lot of difference, Porfilo. You understand, don't you?"

"I'm keeping out of it. It's up to you and your conscience, Dick."

At this, he sighed. "Conscience is the devil!" exclaimed he. "Particularly when it's a stranger to you!"

"You've never seen its face before?" I chuckled.

"Never!" grinned Dick Orton. "But, conscience or no conscience, I can't help thinking about her hands, and—"

"Well?"

"Why the devil do people have to eat garlic, Porfilo?"

I couldn't help breaking into a roar of laughter, and he looked at me in a hurt way.

"However," said he, "that won't keep me from going back to face the music. I told her that I loved her and that I wanted to marry her. Well, she said that she loved me and that she wanted to marry me, too. It was the infernal night and the moon, I suppose. I had chills and fevers twisting up and down inside of me, you might say. I hardly knew what I was doing. I've never felt this way about a girl before!"

"I believe that!" said I heartily.

"So I've got to go back and see her once more."

"What can you say to her?"

"I don't know! But I'll manage to find out, after a minute or two of talk, whether she's changed about me as much as I've changed about her!"

I felt that there was nothing that I could say to the point in a case like this. He was his own master, and a better master for himself, at that moment, than I could be to him. If he felt that he had to clear his mind on the subject of that girl, it was best for him to go ahead and do it. That was as far as I could carry my thinking.

So I simply said: "We've gone about eighty miles, air line from the Loveng house. We'll need two days to ride back. We'll be starting right now!"

"*We?*" said he.

"I'm going to see you through this mess," I assured him.

He pondered this for a time.

"I drag *you* back into the mess as well as myself?" he suggested.

"Not a bit! My own conscience is a pretty sleepy thing, but it's beginning to wake up a little about this. I have to go back with you. It was I that brought you to Loveng, and it was I that let him get hold of your name. Come along, Dick!"

He protested no more. We climbed into our saddles and jogged steadily along the back trail.

I think that two or three hours passed before a word was spoken, but at a time like that, one does not need words. I know that the mind of Dick Orton was filled with the same thought that was in *my* mind. What was in my mind was that I had saved a friend and gained a brother. There was a wonderful feeling of closeness. I felt as though my strength had been multiplied by twenty. In fact, I have never lost that feeling!

11

WHEN we reached the house of Loveng, two days later, we paused in a screen of trees two hundred yards away. That delay was partly because we judged that it would be best to pause there until the dusk, at least, and in part because we wished to talk matters over. The chief discussion was as to whether or not we should go to the house together—as I proposed—or Dick should go alone.

The second view was the one which he maintained, and he upheld his idea with such vehemence that I had to give in to him. Because he declared that, if I would not let him go by himself, he would wait there until I changed my mind—if both of us had to starve in the meantime.

There was nothing to be done with such a state of mind in him. I kept struggling with him until after the darkness was complete, however, and even well after that. When I saw that I could do nothing whatever to change his determination, I let him. First I cautioned him to approach that house with care and to keep to cover constantly.

When he was as near to the house as cover would bring him, I advised him to wait until, by sight, or by the sound of voices, he tried to learn whether or not there was only Loveng and his family in the house, or several other men as well. In the latter case, I begged him not to continue.

After that, I had done all that I could. I let him pass on toward the house, but it was with a heavy heart that I saw him go. Loveng meant mischief. There was no doubt of that, or he would never have issued such a direct challenge to me as his statement in the paper had been.

However, I was glad to see that Dick Orton was willing to use caution in his approach to the house, no matter what might happen when the house itself was actually reached. I waited for fifteen or twenty minutes in the place where he had left me. Then I could endure it no longer, and I started out, creeping along as stealthily as I could manage it in the direction of the house and using what small cover lay before me.

I cannot tell you how peaceful and happy that scene was: The yellow flare of two lighted windows of the house of Loveng before me, and the shadowy outline of the house itself, roughened at the edges like an etching by the masses of climbing vines which tumbled over it. Even at that distance, I could smell the rank odor of the vegetable garden which the thrifty Loveng kept in cultivation on a large scale.

Or, when the wind changed a little, there was the fragrance of Mary's rose garden just ahead. Well, there was a real aroma of home about that place. Hard as I felt toward Loveng at that moment, I could not help admitting that he was the sort of stuff out of which good nations and prosperous communities are built.

It was simply that Dick Orton had touched him in the wrong place. Loveng was partly insane on the subject. He felt that he had been wronged, and that his honor demanded that he try for satisfaction. Well, it was a nasty affair to be mixed in.

My chief regard was simply for Dick, however. I had thought of Dick at first as a rather selfish, highstrung, excited, foolish boy; but I felt that he had turned into a man, and I was willing to do a great deal for him.

I pushed on toward the house until I was about sixty or seventy paces away, and directly in front of it. There I flattened myself in the wet dew behind a small shrub, and I loosened my guns in their holsters. There I waited. It seemed a long time.

To him who waits, time always drags slowly. But in the end I was glad that I had come as close as that to the house—I wished that I had come twice as far, indeed!

For, from the left—the orchard—I heard a sudden, challenging shout, followed by a sharp and rattling babel of voices, and after that a shot. Then a dozen guns, or so it seemed, roaring at once. I was on my feet, stooping low, and running as fast as my long legs could carry me over the ground.

I saw a tall form, which I had no doubt was that of Dick Orton, emerge from the shadows of the orchard and plunge across the open toward the next group of trees not thirty paces away. Behind him rushed three men—and then a fourth, all firing, but missing the dodging form of Dick until, in the very shelter of the trees, he seemed to stumble, and plunged to the ground.

I saw that part of it with the tail of my eye, so to speak. Before that I had both guns in my hands, and I was shooting hip high—or between knee and hip to be exact. There's a target almost as big as the body, and a wound there will disable almost as much as a wound through the body itself—unless the other fellow be an absolutely desperate man who fights to the last gasp.

But now I shot with both guns, and I shot at human flesh. At the very instant that Dick was falling, two of those rascals who thought nothing of taking such odds into their favor, dropped to the ground with yells that must have echoed a mile away. Certainly they were echoed from the house of Loveng by the voices of screaming women.

At the same time I shouted: "Loveng! Loveng! If you want action, look this way!"

Loveng was one of the pair I had not hit. But when he heard my voice, I saw the glint of his gun as it dropped to the ground. He threw up his hands and whirled around toward me without the slightest belly for a fight.

"Don't shoot, Meester Porfilo!" he screamed at me. "Do not shoot old man like Joe Loveng!"

There was a frightened yap out of his friend, too. His gun joined that of Joe upon the ground. At that moment, I can tell you that I blessed the storytellers who had given me a false reputation equal to twice what I was really worth. For the ridiculous name which I had been given was what won that fight for me.

Perhaps, too, it was the screaming of the tortured fellows on the ground. That was enough to unnerve most people, and besides, I had come to them from the side, and totally by surprise.

I walked up to Joe and his friend and made them keep their arms stiff above their heads while I searched them. I took away a perfect armory from each of them, and there was no doubt at all that they had been armed for a particular purpose—the dropping of my poor Dick, who lay yonder, terribly still, and terribly silent.

I said calmly to Joe: "If Orton is alive and has a chance to recover, you have a chance, too. But if he's dead—I tell you, Loveng, that you're mortally wounded already!" I meant it, just then.

Joe Loveng and his companion wanted to look at their own wounded friends who were shrieking and begging on the ground—both of them apparently very badly hurt, though I couldn't help despising them for their noise. But I marched Joe and the other toward Dick and made them stand back to back a little distance while I examined Dick as well as I could.

He answered the first touch of my hand and voice with a groan, and then, to my exquisite satisfaction, he heaved himself to his feet.

"Dick!" I shouted at him. "Are you all right?"

"They winged me in the shoulder," he said with beautiful calm. "That knocked me on my face in this rough ground. Stunned a mite. That was all."

"Your shoulder?"

"Nothing broken," said he, as cool as you please. "I can work it a little. Painful, though, and bleeding pretty fast!"

"We'll have you in the house and tie you up in a minute," said I.

"I never want to see the inside of that house again!" said Dick in disgust.

I promised him that this would be our last visit. Then I congratulated Joe Loveng and told him that he was going to be allowed to live—as a special favor. I assure you that there was a groan of relief from Joe when he heard me speak.

In the meantime, we started back to the pair I had winged. Joe and his companion took their heads. I took a pair of knees under each arm, and though they yelled at the pain and begged us to put them down again, we carried them into the house.

Well, there was a pretty mess to look at. One big, hard-faced fellow had a bullet in his leg which had twisted around the thighbone and, entering at the hip, came down by the knee on the opposite side of the limb. When you consider that that wound was made by a .45 caliber slug, and that it was whirling as it tore through the flesh, you have an idea, faintly, of the amount of the damage that had been done to that unlucky chap.

The second of the pair was a handsome boy of about nineteen or twenty who lay grinning with pain at the ceiling and making the sign of the cross over himself from time to time as though he were trying to save his soul from devils. The slug had gone through both his legs just below the hip, and he was bleeding at a frightful rate.

As for Dick, he had a nasty cut, and no more. A bullet had glanced from the shoulder blade and across his shoulder, knocking him down. A little more off the angle, and that bullet would have driven through his heart.

He knew what he had escaped, and he was wonderfully calm about the thing. I left Loveng and his unwounded comrade to tie up the hurt legs. I gave my own attention to the shoulder of Dick, and I sang out to Mary, as she passed by with a bucket of hot water, and asked her if she wished to help.

She did not seem to hear me and went straight on to where the good-looking boy lay on the floor, making a red pool around him. There she dropped on her knees and began to work fast and hard to help her father, who would bark out at her from time to time:

"Devil of a woman! This is your work! She-devil!"

Well, in a way you have to admit that it *was* her work.

"But what does it mean?" I asked Dick. "Has she lost her hearing?"

"She has tonight," said Dick. "She met up with that bird on the floor. I'm glad you winged him! I found the pair of them on the same bench where she and *I* had sat together. But that was nine days ago, and so I suppose that she had a right to forget me.

"It peeved me, though, and I couldn't help introducing myself. That was what started trouble. Bullets began to drop like acorns, and then you jumped down out of the sky and got a little silence. Thanks, old man!"

You see by this that a big change had come over my friend, Dick Orton. He took his punishment—about the girl, which cut his pride a bit deep, I suppose; and about the wound itself—with perfect good nature.

I kept him in that house for five or six long days and nights, lying on his face, while I washed the wound and saw it began to heal after Joe Loveng, who knew something about surgery, it appeared, had sewed up the big cut. He made a good job of it too!

The wound healed with astonishing speed. The perfect quiet, and the perfect health of Dick worked in a wonderful combination. In the meantime, the other pair of wounded men recovered very slowly.

There was not much sign of improvement in either of them, but as they did not develop high temperatures, we knew at the end of that time that neither of the wounds had become infected.

In the meantime, we lived a rather odd life in that house. They looked on the pair of us as two sticks of dynamite, at first, and I think that the entire household was convinced that, as soon as Dick was well enough to move about, I'd murder the lot of them and then leave.

However, I had only one sharp talk with my friend, Joe Loveng. I assured him that if he sent for a sheriff or a deputy, I'd kill everyone in the house before the man of the law got to me. But if I were left alone, all would be well with everyone. He swore, with a gray face, that he would treat me like an angel newly descended from heaven.

I assured him, furthermore, that while I wished him nothing but well, if he did not instantly make a trip to town and retract the statement he had made against Dick Orton, I would guarantee him a short stay on earth. He vowed that he would go in at once and tell them that he had made a mistake in the name and that it was a Dick Norton that had been with me and had assisted me to escape. Since I knew of no Dick Norton on the range, I readily decided that would do very, very well.

Joe went in, as he had promised, and had been soundly cursed by the sheriff for his first report.

After that, we got on increasingly well. Joe gradually discovered that I bore him no grudge. As for Dick, he astonished the entire household by cheerfully stating that he felt he was cheaply out of the mess. It was not very consoling for the girl, but it had a ring of truth about it that delighted Joe Loveng. From that moment he began to take care of us rather as if we had been dear friends than dreadful enemies.

There was nothing but good feeling on all sides when, at last, we left the house.

Dick's shoulder was still too bad to stand much traveling. We simply moved off into the mountains a little distance and then we camped until he was in good shape. Then we started for the Orton ranch and gauged our arrival for the dark of the evening.

It was a warm night, and we found two figures sitting in rocking chairs on the Orton veranda. Somebody in the bunkhouse was tormenting a guitar, and a cow lately robbed of a calf, I suppose, was bawling in the distance. But there is so much space in a Western night that two such sounds as these could not ruin the peace of the evening.

We rode up close to the veranda, and Dick muttered to me: "There they are together. Now, do I get the devil?"

"Not a bit of it," I told him.

"But I deserve it," he said gloomily. "They ought to kick me out for a tramp!"

He swung down from the saddle and began to approach.

"Hello!" sang out old man Orton. "Who's there?"

Dick made no answer, but went on a little more quickly. At this, his father jumped up in apparent alarm.

"Who's that?" he called sharply.

"Dick!"

What a cry from the pair of them! I reined my horse back a bit, but still I could not help remaining to eavesdrop on them for a moment. I saw them standing side by side. I saw them reach out their arms to their big son as he leaped up the steps of the porch. Then they were all tied together in one knot, and I could hear Mrs. Orton weeping hysterically.

That was all I saw as I turned my horse and jogged away.

Then I heard the voice of Dick shouting: "Leon! Oh, Lee!"

I put my horse to a canter, and the noise of the hoofs drowned his voice.

I was afraid that he would be foolish enough to pursue me to bring me into that happy gathering, but he had more sense than that. No horse started after me, and I was allowed to pass over the hills unmolested and journey on into the night alone.

But not as much alone as I had been in the years before. When a man has found a friend, he cannot leave him, really, for it is my conviction that we carry something of the souls of our friends with us around the world.

Well, in a way, Dick had a heavy burden of debt to me, because that matter of the stage robbery was as yet unsolved, but I had an infinite trust in what the influence and money and honesty of old Orton would accomplish in that respect. In the meantime, with the ghosts of Father McGuire and Lawton and Mike O'Rourke, I had the new thought of Dick Orton to keep me company. I felt, as I galloped through the black of the night, that I was more to be envied than to be pitied.

12

I HADN'T seen Mike for three months. You see, it was right after the Sam Dugan murder which some fools hung on me. Of course, Lawton hadn't the least idea in the world that I could have done such a rotten, treacherous thing. But they stirred up such a fuss that I didn't dare to try to slip in to see Mike. Because everyone had known for years that I loved Mike and got down to see her once in a while, and when things were pretty hot, they used to watch her house.

So when I finally went down to see her, Sheriff Lawton crossed my way with three hard-riding man-getters. Every man-jack of them was on a faster nag than my mule, but I kept Roanoke in the rough going, and Dick Lawton was foolish enough to follow right on my heels instead of throwing a fast man out on my course. For he knew what that course was, but it was a sort of unwritten law between us that if I got into the mouth of the little valley where the O'Rourke house stood, I was free.

That may sound specially generous on his side. But it wasn't—altogether. Twice he had pushed his posse up that ravine after me, and it almost cost him his next election. Because that ravine twisted like a snake, back and forth, and it was set out with shrubs and trees as thick as a garden.

I simply laid up in a comfortably shady spot, and when the boys came rushing around the bend, I let them have it. So easy that I didn't have to shoot close to a dangerous spot. I could pick my targets. However, I think that there were half a dozen bad wounds in arms and legs. Also, I pulled too far to the left on one boy and drilled him through the body. So, as I say, the sheriff nearly lost his election after that because it was said that he had ridden his men into a mantrap.

So far as Dick Lawton was concerned, I knew that that valley was forbidden as a hunting ground to him. Of course, I could trust Dick as far as he could trust me—that is to say, to the absolute limit. Because, except when we were shooting at each other, we were the best friends in the world. I know that Dick never shot extra straight at me, and I know that I never shot straight at him. My guns simply wobbled off the mark when I caught him in the sights.

Well, as I was saying, I kept old Roanoke in the rough where he could run four feet to the three of any horse that ever lived—for the simple reason that a mule's feet and skin are a lot tougher than a horse's. By the time I got across the valley, there was a clean furlong between me and Dick Lawton's boys.

So I took off my hat and said good-by to them with a wave that was nearly my last act in life. Because just as I put that hat back on my head a .32-caliber Winchester slug drilled a clean little hole through the brim a quarter of an inch from my forehead.

I've noticed that when a fellow stops to make a grandstand play of that sort, he generally gets into pretty hot trouble. I sent Roanoke into the brush with a dig of the spurs, but the minute I was out of sight, I knew that there was no trouble left.

But I didn't slow up Roanoke. I didn't even stop to roll a cigarette, for I was eager to see Mike. I slithered up the ravine until I got a chance to squint at the ridge, and there I found a little green flag, jerking up and down and in and out in the wind, on top of the O'Rourke house. I knew that was the work of Mike's father. I think that every day of his life the old man went snooping through the woods to see if the land lay quiet. If it was, he tagged the house with that little green flag—green for Ireland, of course!—and then when someone was laying for me near the house, he would hang up a white flag.

When I saw the green I dug into Roanoke and sent that mule hopping straight to the house. As I hit the ground, I heard old man O'Rourke singing out inside the screen door of the porch: "Hey, Chet! Here's Roanoke to put up, and sling a feed of barley into him. Hey, Mother, come and look at that doggone mule! Hey, Mike, there's that Roanoke mule wanderin' around loose in the yard!"

Chet O'Rourke came first, and his old mother at his shoulder, and then the old man came next. I grabbed all their hands. It was like stepping into a shower of happiness, I tell you, to get among people where the feel of their eyes was not like so many knives pointed at you!

But I brushed through them pretty quick. I wanted Mike.

"Hey, Mike!" yelped old O'Rourke. "Ain't you comin' to see Roanoke?"

He laughed. I suppose that he was old enough to enjoy a foolish joke like that. I heard Mike sing out from the stairs beyond the front parlor. I reached the bottom of those stairs the same minute she did and caught her.

She said: "Chester O'Rourke, will you take this man away from me?"

I kicked the door shut in Chet's face and sat Mike on the window sill where the honeysuckle showered down behind her like green water, if you follow my drift. It would have done you good to stand there where I was standing and see her smile until the dimple was drilled into one cheek. She began to smooth her dress and pat her hair.

"My Lord," said I, "I'm glad to see you."

"You've unironed me," said Mike. "Just when I was all crisped up for the afternoon!"

"Have they nailed the right man for the Dugan murder?" said I. Because I was as keen about that as I was about Mike.

"They've got the right man, and he's confessed," said she.

I lowered myself into a chair and took a deep breath.

"That's fixed, then," said I.

"That's fixed," said she.

"Why do you say it that way?" said I.

"How old are you, Leon?" said she.

"I'm twenty-five."

"How old does that make me?" said Mike.

"Twenty-three."

"That's right too. How long have you been asking me to marry you?" said Mike.

"Seven years," said I.

"Well," said she, "the next time you ask me, I'm going to do it!"

"Law or no law?" said I.

"Law or no law," said she.

It made my head spin, of course, when I thought of marrying Mike and trying to make a home for her while a hundred or so cowpunchers and sheriffs and deputies, et cetera, were spending their vacation trying to grab me and the twenty thousand dollars that rested on top of my head as a reward. I moistened my lips and tried to speak. I couldn't make a sound.

"You know that I've done what I could," said I.

"I do," said she. "But now things are different."

"What do you mean?"

"William Purchass Shay is the governor, now," said she.

"What difference does that make?"

"He's a gentleman," said she.

"Well?"

"I think he'd listen to reason," said Mike.

"You want me to go to see him?"

"Just that."

"I see myself handing in my name at his office," said I. "I guess he's not too much of a gentleman to want to make twenty thousand dollars."

"Money has spoiled you, Lee," said Mike.

"Money? How come?"

"You're so used to thinking about how much you'll be worth when somebody drills a rifle ball through you—that it's turned your head."

"Are you talking serious?"

"Dead serious," said she. "Besides, you're not the only one that folks have to talk about now."

"I don't understand."

"Jeffrey Dinsmore is the other one."

Of course, I had heard about Dinsmore. He was the Texas man whose father left him about a million dollars in cattle and real estate, besides a talent for shooting straight and a habit of using that talent. Finally he killed a man where "self-defense" wouldn't work, because it was proved that Dinsmore had been layin' for him. The last heard, Dinsmore was drifting for the mountains.

"Is Dinsmore in these parts?" I asked Mike.

"He showed up in town last week and sat down in the restaurant—"

"Disguised?"

"Yes, disguised with a gun that he put on the table in front of his plate. They didn't ask any questions, but just served him as fast as they could."

"Nobody went to raise a crowd?"

"The dishwasher did, and a crowd gathered at the front door and the back."

"What happened?"

"Dinsmore finished eating and then put on his hat and walked out."

"Good Lord, what nerve! Did he bluff out the whole crowd?"

"He did."

"What's on him?"

"Just the same that's on you. Twenty thousand iron men."

"Twenty thousand dollars!" said I.

"You look sort of sad, Lee."

You'll think me a good deal of a fool, but I confess that I was staggered to find that there was another crook in the mountains worth as much to the law as I was. Between you and me, I *was* proud because I had that little fortune on my head.

"Twenty thousand!" said I.

"Dead or alive," said Mike, with a queer, strained look on her face.

"Why do you say it that way?" said I, in a whisper.

"Don't you understand?" said Mike.

Then I *did* understand, and I stood up, feeling pretty sick. But I saw that she was right. Something had to be done.

"I start for the governor today!" said I.

Mike simply hid her face in her hands, and I didn't wait for her to break out crying.

I saw the rest of the family for an hour or so before Mike came in to us. She was as clear-eyed as ever, when she came, but there was something in her face which was a spur to me. I did not wait for the night. I judged that no pursuers would be lingering for me in the valley at this late day, so I slipped out of the house finding Roanoke refreshed by his rest and a feed of grain. I went away without leaving any farewells behind me.

I cut across country, straight over the ridge of the eastern mountains. Just below timberline I camped that night—a cold, wet night—and I rode on gloomily the next morning until I was over the crest of the ridge and had a good view of the land that lay beneath me.

It was a great, smooth-sweeping valley, most of it, the ground rolling now and then into little hills—but with hardly the shadow of a tree—and so on and on to piles of blue mountains which leaned aganist the farther horizon. They were a good hundred miles away. Between me and that range lay the city that I had to reach.

You will agree with me that it was not a very pleasant undertaking. I had to get myself over seventy miles of open country to the capital of the State. Then I had to get seventy miles back into the mountains once more.

However, there was nothing else for it. That day I went down to the edge of the trees and the foothills, and there I rested until the verge of dusk. When that time came, I sent Roanoke out into the open and headed straight away toward the big town. He could have made the distance before daylight, but there was no point in that.

I sent Roanoke over sixty-five miles that night, however, and he was a tired mule when I dropped off his back on the lee side of a haystack. I could see the lights of the town five miles off. Not a big place, you will think, but there were thirty-five thousand people there, and that made it just about five times as large as any city I had ever seen in my life. It was simply a metropolis to me!

The dawn was only a moment away. So I walked away from the stack to a wreck of a shack in a hollow. There I turned in and slept solidly until afternoon.

I was thirsty and tired and hungry when I wakened. Besides that, I had a jumpy heart, and the strain of the work ahead of me was telling pretty fast! The worst part of the trip was wasting that afternoon and waiting for the night. But as a matter of fact, I didn't wait for the night.

The edge of the sun was barely down before I was streaking across open country, and there was still plenty of daylight when I cut down a bridle path near the edge of the town and met an old fellow coming up. He was riding bareback, and I shall never forget how his white beard was parted by the wind.

He gave me a very cheerful "howd'ye," and I waved back to him.

"Well, stranger," said that old man, "where are you aimin' for, if I might ask?"

"Work," said I.

"Come right along with me."

"What kind?"

He had one tooth in the right-hand corner of his upper gum. He fixed this in a wedge of chewing tobacco and worked a long time at it until he got it loose. All the while he was looking me over with popping, pale-blue eyes. I never before had noticed how close an old man can be to a child.

"Well, partner," said he, "young fellers is picky and choosy; I used to be that way myself. But when I come to get a little age behind me, why, then I seen that it didn't make so much difference what a man done. All kinds of work that ever I see gives you the same sort of an ache in the shoulders and an ache in the calves of your legs and in your brain. Ain't you noticed that?"

I told him that I had.

He said: "Same way about chuck. I used to be mighty finicky about grub. It don't make no difference to me now. Once a mite of grub is swallowed, what difference whether it was a mouthful of dry bread or a mouthful of ice cream? Can you tell me that?"

I could see that he had branched out on his special kind of information. Most old men are that way. They've got a couple of sets of ideas oiled up in their old noodles and whenever they get a chance, they'll blaze away on them. If they're interested in oil wells, you can start talking about lace and they'll get over to oil wells just as easy as if you started with derricks. I saw that this was one of that brand. However, if he would talk, I saw that he might be of some sort of use to me.

So I said: "I've been back country for a long time. I want to have a try working in town!"

He shook his head, very sad at that.

"Son," said he, "I live only two mile out, but I been to town only once this summer. That time I come home with my feet all blistered up and my head aching from the glare of the pavements. I give the town up. If I was you, I'd give it up, too."

I said nothing, but I couldn't help smiling. The old chap began to nod and smile, too. He was a fine fellow, no doubt of that.

"Well," said he, "you can't expect folks to learn by their elders. If they did, people'd get wiser and wiser, instead of the other way. What you want to do in town?"

"Drive an ice wagon, maybe. I don't care. I never seen the town before."

"You don't say!"

"I guess that's the capitol?"

"Yes, sir. There she be. That white dome. I guess you seen it in your schoolbooks when you was a kid? There she be. Look here, ain't you been raised right around near here?"

He had sagged a little closer to me while we were looking at the town, and now I caught him batting his bleary old eyes at me behind his glasses. I knew there was danger ahead.

"No," said I. "I've never been in the big town before."

"Oh, it ain't so big. Me, I've been far as St. Louis. Now, there's a real city for you. It lays over this a mighty lot!"

"I suppose it does. But it hasn't many things finer than the capitol building, I guess!"

"Well, I dunno. It's got a lot of banks and things pretty grand with white stone posts around them. It makes a heap of noise, too. You can hear it for miles. But you can't hear nothin' here."

"Well," said I, "I suppose there are fine big houses there. The governor's house must be mighty fine!"

"Him? No, sir. William P. Shay ain't the man to live big and grand. He's livin' in his ma's old house out on Hooker Avenue—which has got so fashionable, lately, what with the park right opposite with the benches to set on. I passed that way once, and I never forget the smell of the lilacs passin' by Mrs. Shay's house! It was sure a sweet thing."

"I suppose that they're still there?"

"Yes, sir."

"Other folks got 'em, too?"

"Nary a one. Young feller, I can't get out of my head that I've seen you sure, somewheres, sometime!"

I knew very well where he'd seen me. It was in some roadside bulletin board or perhaps just a handbill nailed against a post, showing my face with big letters under it. I knew very well where he had seen me. I decided I had better start along; so I told him that I would go right on into town and get lodgings before it was too dark.

But after I had gone a little way, I leaned down as if to fix a stirrup leather and I had a chance to glance back. Old white beard was already over the hill.

I didn't suspect that he had seen too much of me. But when a man has been a fugitive from the law with a price on his head for seven years, it makes him overlook no bets. I recalled, too, that I was riding a mule, and that in itself was enough to make any man suspicious.

So I snapped back to the top of the hill and through the hollow beneath I could see the old man scooting along. He looked back over his shoulder, just then, and when he saw me, he doubled up like a jockey putting up a fast finish down the stretch and began to burn his whip into that old horse he was riding.

I shouldn't have done it, of course. But I couldn't help wanting to make his fun worthwhile. So I fired a shot straight into the air.

I heard his yell come quavering back to me; and after that the horse seemed to take as much interest in the running as his rider did. He hunched himself like a loafer wolf trying to shove himself between his front legs while he beats for cover.

It was a mighty funny thing to watch. I laughed till I was crying. By that time the old man had disappeared in the night and the distance. Then I turned around and saw that I had a big job to do and to do fast, because as soon as that old fogy got to a house with a telephone in it, he would plaster the news all over town that Leon Porfilo, on his mule, was heading straight for them, ready to make trouble, and lots of it!

How many scores of men and boys would clean up their old guns and start hunting for me, I could only guess.

But right there I made up my mind that I couldn't enter that town on a mule. I put old Roanoke away in a little hollow where there were trees enough to shelter him and a brook in the center to give him water and plenty of long, coarse grass among the trees for provender.

Then I shoved my guns into my clothes and started hiking for the town. It was mighty risky, of course, because if trouble started I was a goner. But I decided that I'd be a lot less looked for on foot. You'll wonder, perhaps, why I didn't wait a few days under cover before I went in. But I knew that the next morning a hundred search parties would be out for me, unless I was already in jail.

13

It was not so bad as I had expected. A city of that size, I thought, would be so filled with people that my only good refuge would be in the very density of the crowd, but when I reached the outskirts, I found only unpaved streets and hardly anyone on the sidewalks saving the few workingmen who were hurrying home late to their suppers. And what a jumble of suppers! One acquires an acute nose in the mountains or on the desert, and I picked out at least fifty different articles of cookery before I had covered the first block.

I started on the second with a confused impression of onions, garlic, frying steak, stew, boiled tomatoes, cabbage, bacon, coffee, tea, and too many other things to mention. Nasally speaking, that first block of the capital town was like the first crash of a symphony orchestra. I went on very much more at ease through block after block with almost no one in sight, until I came to broad paved streets where there was less dust flying in the air—and where the front yards were not simply hard-beaten dirt with a plant or two at the corners of the houses.

For here there were houses set farther back. Some had hedges at the sidewalk—but all had gardens, and most of the way one could look over blocks and blocks of neatly cropped lawns, with flower borders near the houses, and flowering shrubs set out on the lawns. There were scores and scores of watering spouts whirling the spray into the air with a soft, delightful whispering.

They all had a different note. Some of them rattled around slowly and methodically like so many dray wheels, throwing out a spray in which you could distinguish each ray of water all the way round. There were some singing and spinning and making a solid flash like the wheel of a bright-painted buggy when a horse is doing a mile in better than three minutes.

Once in a while a breeze dipped out of the sky and stirred the heavy, hot air of the street, and blew little mists of the sprinklers to me and gave me quick scents of flowers. But always there was that wonderful odor of the ground drinking, and drinking.

I felt very happy, I'll tell you. I felt very expansive and kindly to the whole human race. Now and then I'd see a man run down the steps of his house and go out in his shirt sleeves, and take hold of the hose, and curse softly when the spray hit him, and then give the sprinkler a jerk that moved the little machine to another place. Like as not, he jerked the sprinkler straight toward him.

Then he would duck for the sidewalk and stand there wiping his face and hands with a handkerchief and stamping the water from his shoes and "phewing" and "damning" to himself as though he were ashamed.

But before they went back into the house, each man would stop a minute and look at the grass and the shrubs, each beaded with water and pearled with the light of the nearest street lamps—and then up to the trees—and then up to the stars—and then go slowly into the house, singing, most like, and stepping light. When those men lifted their heads and looked up into the sky like that, I knew that they saw heaven.

When one young fellow ran out from his front door, I saw a girl come to the window and look after him, and hurry him with: "The soup will be stone cold, Archie."

I couldn't help it. I stopped short and leaned a hand against a tree and watched him move the sprinkler. Then, humming under his breath, he ran for the house. There were springs under that boy's toes, I tell you. From what I could see of the girl, I didn't wonder. But at his front door he turned and saw me still standing under the tree, watching and aching and groaning to myself:

"Mike and me—when do we get our chance—when do we get our chance!"

He called out: "Hey, you—what you want?"

A mighty snappy voice—like the home dog growling at a stranger pup. He was being defensive.

"Nothing," said I.

"Then hump yourself—move along!" said he.

Perhaps you'll think that I might have been angered by that. But I wasn't. I was only pretty well sickened and saddened. If ever I were caught—and this night there was a grand chance that the law would take me—the dozen men in the jury box would be no better than this fellow—a clean-living fellow, with his heart in the right place—but snarling when he saw a strange dog near his house! Human nature—I knew it—and I didn't blame him.

"All right. I'll move along," said I.

I only shifted one tree down and stopped again. You see, I wanted to watch that fellow go striding into his house and into that dining room and watch his wife smile at him.

Sentimental bunk? I know that as well as you do, but when a man has lived alone for seven years with mountains, and above timberline most of the time—seven winters, you know—well, it makes him either a murderer or a softy. I hardly know which is worse! But I was not a murderer, no matter what the world might say of me.

The householder had a glimpse of me again as he swung open his front door, and he came flaring back at me with the running stride of an athlete. I saw that he was big, and big in the right places.

He was in front of me in another moment.

"I'm going!" said I, and I turned and started shambling away.

He caught me by the shoulder and whirled me around.

"Look here!" said he. "I don't like the looks of you—and the way you hang around—who are you?"

I shrank back from him against a tree. "A poor bum, mister," said I. "I don't want no trouble. But I was lookin' through the window. It looked sort of homelike in there."

"You're lying!" said he. "By heaven, I'll wager you're some second-story crook. I've a mind—"

He put his hand on me again.

You'll admit that I'd taken a good deal from him. But it's easy for a big man to take things from other people. I don't know why that is. Little fellows always have a chip on their shoulders.

But big fellows learn when they're young that they're not to fight—because they're always too big for the other boys! But still, I was a bit angry when this young husband began to force his case at my expense. There were two hundred and twenty pounds of me, but down to the very last pound of me, I was hot.

Just then the girl's voice sang out: "Archie! Archie! What are you doing—oh!"

There was a little squeal at the end as she sighted me.

"You see?" said I. "Let me go. I won't trouble you any. You're scaring your wife to death, you fool!"

"What? You impudent rat—"

He started a first-rate punch from the hip, but I caught his wrist and doubled his arm around behind him in a way which must have been new to him. He was a strong chap. But he hadn't my incentive, and he hadn't my training.

We stood with our faces inches apart. Suddenly he wilted.

"Porfilo!" said he through his teeth.

"Do you think I'm going to sink a slug in you?" I asked.

I saw by the look of his eyes that he did, and it made me a pretty sick man, I can tell you! I dropped his arm, and I went off down that street not caring a great deal whether I lived or died.

I went down that street until it carried me bang up against the capitol building in the middle of the great big square. Off to the right was the beginning of the park. I went off down the street that faced on it.

I think I must have passed five hundred people in that square, but I'm certain that not one of them guessed me. It would have been too queer to find Leon Porfilo *walking* through a street. They passed me by one after another—which shows that we see only what we expect to see.

In the street opposite the park it was easy going again. It was a fairly dark street, because there were no lamps except at the corner, and the blocks were long. Lamps on only one side of the street, too—because the park was on the other side and that was a thrifty town!

I walked about half a mile, I suppose, from the central square and then I found the house without looking for it. It was simply a great outwelling fragrance of the lilacs, just as the old man had told me. There was the yard filled with big shrubs—almost trees of 'em, and in the pool of darkness around the trees were rows and spottings of milk-white lilies.

It was a good thing to see, that yard. It was so filled with beauty—I don't know exactly how to say it. It was filled with hominess, too. I felt as though I had opened that squeaking gate a hundred times before and stepped down onto the brick path where the grass that grew between the bricks crunched under my heels.

Then I sidestepped from the path and among the trees. I went to the side of the house. I climbed up to the window in time to see the ceremony begin. About a dozen people piled into the room—and when the seating was over, a grim-faced, middle-aged man sat at the head of the table and a pretty-faced girl of twenty-one or so at the other.

Then I remembered that the governor's wife was not half his age.

I thought I understood one reason for the tired look in his face! In the meantime, there was nothing for me to do for a time. So I found a bench among the trees and lay down on it to watch the stars.

I waited until the smell of food went through me, and I tugged up my belt two notches. I waited until the humming voices and the laughter that always begin a meal—even a mountain dinner—died off into a broken talking—noise of dishes. Then music, somewhere. Well, I was never educated up to appreciating the squeaking of a violin!

A long time after that, somebody was making a speech. I could hear the steady voice. I could almost hear the yawns.

Somehow, I pitied the pretty girl at the far end of the table!

14

I WAITED a full hour after that. Then people began to leave the house, and finally, when the front door opened and closed no more, I began my rounds of the house. I found what I wanted soon enough. It was not in the second story, but a lighted window in the first, and I had a step up, only, to get a view of the inside of the room, and a broad-gauge window sill to hang to while I watched.

The window was open, which made everything easier. There was not much chance for me to be betrayed by the noise I might make in stirring about, for the wind was dipping and rustling among the trees.

I was looking into a high, narrow room with walls covered with books, and queer, old-looking framed photographs above the bookcases. There was a desk that looked as solid as rock. In front of the desk was the governor. I could have told that it was the governor even if I'd never seen him before, because he had that gone look about the eyes and those wrinkles of too much smiling that come to men who have offices of state. A man like that, when his face is at rest, is simply giving up thanks that he's not offending anyone.

The governor had a man sitting beside his desk—a man who looked only less tired than the governor himself. He was scribbling shorthand while the governor turned over and fiddled at a pile of papers on his desk and kept talking softly and steadily. All sorts of letters.

Well, he had to dictate so many letters, and make them all so different, that I wondered what fellow's brain could be big enough to hold so much stuff, and so many different kinds. I suppose that in that hour he dictated more letters than I'd ever written in my life. I could see new reasons every minute for that tired look. I began to think that he must know everyone in the State.

I heard the secretary ask him if he needed him any longer. I saw the governor look up quickly at him and then stand up and clap him on the shoulder and say:

"Go home to sleep! I've not been paying enough attention to you, but forgive me!"

I saw the secretary fairly stagger out of the room. Then there was the governor sitting over the typewriter and reading his correspondence on the one hand and picking at the machine with one finger on the other, and swearing in between in a style that would have tickled the ears of any cowpuncher on the hardiest bit of the range.

I didn't hear anyone tap at the door. But pretty soon he jumped up with the look of a man about to accept ten million dollars. He opened the door and the pretty, young wife stood there wrapped up to the chin in a dressing gown. She looked him up and down in a way that smeared the smile off his face and left a sick look that I had seen there before.

It was an old-fashioned house, and there was a transom over the door. She pointed at the open transom and said half a dozen words out of stiff lips. She didn't say much. Just enough. A bullet isn't very big, either, but if it's planted in the right place it will tear the heart out of a man.

She jerked about on her heel and flounced away, and the governor leaned against the wall for a minute with all the sap run out of him. Then he closed the door and the transom and went back to the typewriter.

He was pretty badly jarred, though, and he sat there for a moment all loose, like a fellow with the strength run out of him. Then he shook his head and set his jaw and began to batter that typewriter again. I could see that he was a game sort of a man. Mighty game and proud and clean; I liked him all the way through; and yet I felt a mite sorry for the girl wife, too, when I thought of the way the governor's language must have been sliding out through that transom and percolating through the house. I suppose that a real respectable house would take a couple of generations to work language like that out of the grain of it!

I slid a leg inside the window, and made just enough noise for the governor to stop work and sit with his head up; and his right hand went back to his hip pocket—and came away again.

I stepped inside the room and was standing there pretty easy when he turned around.

He didn't jump up or start yapping for help or doing anything else that was foolish. He just sat and looked me over.

"Well, Porfilo," said he at last, "I suppose that you've tried to work out the most popular spectacular job in the State and decided that the governor's house was the best place for it. Is that it?"

I merely grinned. I knew that he would take it something like that, but it was mighty good to hear him talk up. It sent a tingle through all the right places in me. I just took off my hat and made myself easy.

"What do you want?" said he, frowning as I smiled. "My wallet?"

He tossed it to me. I caught it and threw it back. I had both my hands. Somehow, I hated to show a gun to that man.

"Something bigger than that?" said he, sneering. "I suppose that you'll want the papers to know how you held up the governor without even showing a gun?"

I got hot at that; in the face, I mean.

"No, sir," said I. "I'm not a rat."

"Tell me what you want," said he through his teeth. "There was a time when I served as a sheriff in this State, young man. There was a time when I carried guns. Now the fewer moments I spend with you, the better."

"Governor," said I, "do you think I'm a plain skunk?"

"No," said he, very brisk, and with his eyes snapping. "I should call you whatever you please—a purple, spotted, striped, or garden variety of skunk. Never the common sort! Now what do you want with me, young man, if you don't want money? Is it a pardon?"

There was so much honest scorn in the governor's face, to say nothing of his voice, that all the starch went out of me. I could only mumble, "Yes, sir, that's what I want."

He threw up both his hands—such a quick gesture that it made a gun jump out of my pocket as quick as a snake's head out of a hole. I couldn't help it! But he saw the movement and he sneered again.

"Porfilo," said he, "I suppose you are going to threaten to shoot me unless I turn over a signed pardon to you?"

I shoved that gun away in my clothes. I was beginning to get angry in turn.

"I've come to talk, not to shoot," said I. "I've come to play your own dirty game with you!"

"Is my game dirty?" said he through his teeth.

Oh, yes, he was a fighting man, that governor! I wished that his young wife could have seen him then.

"Isn't it," said I, "a lot dirtier than mine? You beg people for their votes."

"Entirely false," said he. "But I enjoy a moral lecture from a murderer."

"I never murdered a man in my life," said I.

It made him blink a little.

"But you," said I, and I jabbed a finger into the air at him, "you get up and talk pretty sweet to a lot of swine that you hate."

He parted his lips to answer me, but then he changed his mind and sat back in his chair and watched me.

"About the murders," I went on. "I never shot a man unless he tackled me to kill me."

He parted his lips again to speak, but again he changed his mind and smiled.

"You are an extraordinarily simple liar," said he.

It's a good deal to be called a liar and swallow it. I didn't swallow this very well.

I snapped back at him: "Governor, I came here to see you because I was told that you're a gentleman."

"Well, well, Porfilo," said he, a little red. "Who told you that?"

"A girl," said I.

"*The* girl?" said he.

"Yes," said I.

"Good heavens, Porfilo," said he, "are you going to try to hide behind a woman who loves you?"

"I don't hide," said I. "What I ask you to do, is to go down the record against me and figure out where I've sunk lead into anybody that wasn't gunning for me. Was there ever a man I sank that wasn't a gun fighter and a crook before he ever started after me? There never was!

"I've ridden a hundred miles to get out of the way of trouble, when trouble was showing up in the shape of a clean, decent man. But when a thug came after me, I didn't budge. Why should I?"

"Well," said he, "I'll tell you what you've done. You've made me listen to you. But just the other day Sheriff Lawton had two fine citizens shot by you."

"Leg and arm," said I.

"Yes, they were lucky."

"Lucky?" said I. "Do you think it was lucky, governor? If I've practiced hard at shooting every day of my life for the last ten years, at least, do you think that I'm so bad that I miss at forty yards? No, governor, you don't think that. Nor do you think that I've stood up to so few men that I get buck fever when I have a sight of 'em. No, sir, you don't think that, either!"

The governor scratched his chin and blinked at me. But I was pretty pleased, because I could see that he was getting more reasonable every minute.

"I don't mind admitting," said he, "that I'm inclined to believe the nonsense that you're talking." He grinned very frankly at me. However, I saw that I still had a long way to go.

"Are you armed?" said I.

"No," said he, "because very often in my official life I have a desire to use a gun. And I'm past the age when pleasures like that are becoming."

"Are you taking me serious?" said I.

"More than any judge would," said he.

"I believe you!" said I, and I couldn't help a quaver in my voice.

I saw that that put back my cause several lengths and would make the rest of the running pretty hard for me.

He said in that stiff way of his: "Have no sentimental nonsense, Porfilo!"

"I'm sorry," said I. Then I burst out with the truth at him, because I could see that there was no use trying to bamboozle him.

"A man can't help feeling sorry for himself when he gets a chance," said I.

The governor twisted up his mouth, and then he laughed. It did me a lot of good to hear him laugh, just then.

"As a matter of fact," said he, "not so long ago I was pitying myself! Now, young man, I think I can say that I like you. But that won't keep me for an instant from trying to have you hanged by the neck until you're dead."

"Do you mean that?" said I.

"I'm too tired to talk foolishness that I don't mean," said he. "I'll tell you what, Porfilo. If a petition for your pardon were signed by a thousand of the finest citizens in this State, that petition would have no more chance than a snowball in hell!"

He meant it, well enough, and I could see that he did. It made me within a shade of as sick as I'd ever been in my life.

"Well?" said he.

"I'm studying," said I, "because I know that I've got something more to say, but I can't figure out what it is!"

The governor laughed. He said: "I come closer to liking you every minute. But why is it that you think that you have something more to say?"

"Because," said I, "I know that I'm an honest man and a peaceable man!"

He laughed again, and I didn't like his laughter so well, this time.

"Well," said he, "I won't interrupt you!"

"You *know* that I'm a crook?" I asked him.

"About as well as any man could know anything."

"Have you looked up my whole life?"

"A few chunks of it have been served up to me—such as the Sam Dugan murder."

"The rest of your information is about as sound as that!" I snapped back at him, thanking heaven for the chance. "The murderer of Dugan has confessed and is in jail now!"

The governor blinked at me. "I didn't know that," muttered he.

"Of course you didn't," I cried to him. "Every time they have a chance to hang a crime on the corner of my head, that makes first-page news. Every time they don't know who fired the shot that killed, they say: 'Porfilo!' But when they find out the facts a couple of days later, it makes poor reading. So they stick the notice back among the advertisements—"

The governor nodded. I could see him accepting my idea and confessing that there was something in it.

"Well," said I, "I ask you to start in and look up my life. It won't be hard to do. One of your secretaries can unload the whole yarn for you in about half a day's work. Then sift out the proved things from the unproved. Give me the benefit of a doubt!"

"That sort of benefit will never win you a pardon from me," said he.

"I don't want a charity pardon," said I.

"What kind do you expect?"

"An earned one!"

"Confound it," said the governor, rubbing his hands together, "I like your style. Now tell me how under heaven you are going to win a pardon from *me*."

"You've heard of Jeffrey Dinsmore," said I.

"I have," said he.

"Is he as bad as I am—according to reputation?"

"Dinsmore is a—" he began. Then he shut his teeth carefully, and breathed a couple of times. "I should say that he's as bad as you are," said he between his teeth.

"All right," said I. "Here's my grand idea that brought me as close to the rope as the capital city, here!"

"Blaze away," said he.

"Dinsmore has twenty thousand dollars on his head, same as me."

"I understand that."

"We're an even bet, then?"

"I suppose so, if you want to make a sporting thing out of it."

"All right," said I. "What's better than two bad men—"

"One, I suppose," said the governor. "But I wish you wouldn't be so darned Socratic."

I didn't quite understand what he meant, so I drilled away.

"The catching of me has been a pretty hard job," said I. "It's cost the State seven years—and they haven't got me yet. But it's cost them a lot for the amount of money that they've spent hunting me."

"Besides your living expenses," said the governor with a twisted grin that hadn't much fun in it.

I caught him up on that.

"My living expenses have come out of the pockets of other crooks. I've never taken a penny from an honest man. Look up my record!" said I.

At this, he seemed really interested, and sat up and rubbed his fine square chin and scowled at me—not in anger, but as if he were trying to search my character.

"Well," said he, "you are the darndest crook I've ever heard of—with twenty thousand on your head and pretending to live like an honest man!"

"For seven years!" I said, rubbing the facts in on him.

"Aye," said he, "but will you insist that you've been honest all the time?"

"I helped in one robbery, and then I returned the money to the bank. You can get the facts on that, pretty easy. I had about a quarter of a million in my hands."

"If you have a record like that, why hasn't something been done for you?"

"I was waiting," said I, "for a governor that was a gentleman; and here I am."

"Ah, well," said he, "of course I'll have to look into this. It can't be right. Yet I can't help believing you. But what is this about earning your pardon?"

"I was saying that the State had spent a good many tens of thousands on me, and there doesn't seem to be much chance of it letting up on the expenses right away!"

He nodded.

"This Jeffrey Dinsmore is a fellow with lots of friends and with a family with money behind him. It will surely cost a lot to get at him!"

"It will!" said the governor with a blacker face than ever.

"I want to show you the shortest way out."

"I'm ready to listen, now. What's in your head, young man?"

"Let Dinsmore know the proposition. I say, let it be a secret agreement between you and me—and Dinsmore—that if he brings me in—dead or alive—you'll see that he gets a pardon, and the reverse goes for me."

The governor stared at me with his eyes enlarged. He began by shaking his head.

I cut in very softly—hardly loud enough to interrupt his thoughts.

"I can promise you that there'll be no living man brought in. One of us will have to die. There's no doubt about that!"

"I know that," said William Purchass Shay. "I believe you, Porfilo. By the way, are you Mexican?"

"My mother was Irish," said I. "Away back yonder, there was a dash of Mexican Indian in my father's blood."

It seemed to me that his smile was a lot easier when he heard that! Then he got up and took my hand.

"After all," he said, "one gets good laws in operation by hard common sense." He paused. "Is there anything that you need, Porfilo?"

"Wings to get out of this town!" said I.

He nodded very gravely. "I don't see how the devil you got into it."

"Walked," said I.

"While they were looking for a man on a mule! That was the alarm that came in—from the old man you shot at! Did you shoot at him, Porfilo?"

"The old scamp was burning up the country to get to a telephone and blow the news about me. So I thought I'd give him a real thrill and I fired into the air. That's all there was to it!"

"There's seventy miles between you and the mountains where you are so safe," said he.

"Open country!" I nodded. "Seventy miles to Mr. Dinsmore, too!"

"Are you sure of that?" asked the governor, with a start.

"Why, that's where the report located him."

"The report lied, then! It lied like the devil!"

He said it in such a way that I could not answer him. I held my tongue until he reached out a sudden hand and wrung mine, and his eyes were fixed on the floor.

"Good luck to you—the best of luck to you, Porfilo!" said he.

I slid through the window, and when I looked back, I saw him standing just as I had left him, with his eyes fixed upon the floor.

Well, I couldn't make it out at the time, but I figured pretty close, and I was reasonably sure that something I had brought into his mind connected with the idea of his wife, and that was what had taken the starch out of him.

However, I was not thinking about the governor ten seconds later. For, as I dropped from the window for the ground beneath, I saw a glint like that of a star through thin clouds. But this glimmer was among the leaves of some shrubbery, and I knew that it was a touch of starlight on the polished barrel of a gun!

15

WELL, when you hear people speak of lightning thinking, I suppose that you smile and call it "talk"—but between the time I saw that glimmer of a gun in the brush and the instant my heels hit the ground beneath, I can give you my word that I had figured everything out.

If I were caught, people would want to know what Leon Porfilo had been doing in the governor's office. Even if I were not caught, it would be bad enough. Because there would be no end of chatter all over the State. But, as a matter of fact, if I wanted to help the reputation of a man who had given me a mighty square deal, the best way for it was to cut out of those premises without using a gun or even drawing one.

I say that I thought of these things while I was dropping from the window to the ground, and I hadn't much time besides that, for as I hit the ground and flopped over on my hands to ease the shock, I saw a big fellow with two more behind him step out of the brush and the lilacs about five paces away. Five paces—fifteen feet!

Well, you look across the room you are in and it seems quite a distance, at that. Besides, I had the night in my favor. But I give you my word that when I looked at those three silhouettes cut out against the starlit lilac bloom behind them, and when I saw the big pair of gats in the hands of the leader—and the gun apiece in the hands of the men behind—well, I knew in the first place that if I tried to run either side, they'd have me against the white background of the house and fill me with lead before I had taken two steps. I turned that idea over in the fifth part of a second while the leader was growling in a professionally ugly way—if you've ever heard a detective make an arrest, you'll know what I mean.

"You—straighten up and tuck your hands over your head pronto!"

"All right!" muttered I.

He could not have distinguished the first part of my movement from an honest surrender. For I simply began to straighten as he had told me to do. The difference was in my right hand—a five-pound stone. As my hands flew up, that stone jumped straight into the stomach of the leader.

Both his guns went off, and there was a silvery clashing of broken window glass behind me. One of those bullets was in a big scrub oak. The other had broken the window of the governor's office and broken the nose of the photograph of Shay's grand-dad—and drilled through the wall itself.

But the holder of the two guns threw out his hands to keep from falling, and in doing that he backhanded his two assistants. One of them started shooting blindly. The other dropped his gun, but he had enough sand and wit to make a dive for me. I clubbed him over the head with my fist, as though it were a hammer, and very much as though a hammer had struck him, he curled up. I almost tripped over him. By the time I had disentangled my feet, the chief was shooting from the ground.

But he was a long distance from doing me any real harm. The nerves of those three were a good deal upset. I suppose, in fact, that they had not had much experience in trying to arrest men who can't afford to go behind the bars and be tried for their lives.

At any rate, I was lost among those lilacs in a twinkling. At the same time, a considerable ruckus broke out in the house. Windows began to be thrown up, and voices were shouting, and the three detectives themselves were making enough noise to satisfy fifty.

Under cover of that racket, I didn't bolt out onto the street in the direction for which I was headed. Instead, I whirled around and under the shelter of those God-blessed lilacs, I tore back down the length of the yard.

I cleared the house—and still all the noise was in the rear and out toward the street. When I got into the back yard, I saw one discouraging thing— a tall fence about nine feet high and a man just in the act of climbing over. He had jumped up on a box; and the box had crumpled to nothing under him as he leaped. However, he had made the top of the fence.

I had to make the same height, without a box to jump from.

In the meantime, who was the man who was trying to make his getaway even before me?

I didn't stop to ask. I went at that fence with a flying leap and got my hands fixed on the top of it. With the same movement, I let my body swing like a pendulum. So I shot myself over the top a good deal like a pole vaulter.

When I let go with my hands, and while I was pendent in the air, falling, I saw that the man who had gone over ahead had stumbled just beneath me, and, like a snarling dog, he was growling at me. He fired while I was still hanging in the air, and the bullet clipped my upper lip and let me taste my own blood.

It's very bad to let an Irishman taste his own blood. It's bad enough to let one who's half Irish do the thing. At any rate, I went half mad with anger. Then I landed on him.

He wasn't big, and my weight seemed to flatten him out.

It was an alley cutting through behind the grounds of the governor's house, and there was a dull street lamp in a corner of the alley. It shed not very much light, but enough to show me a handsome-faced young fellow—not made big, but delicately like a watch, you know. A sensitive face, I called it.

He was too small for hitting. I just picked him up while he was winded, and then I dropped him on the pavement, which I thought might be pretty bad for that pretty face of his.

Then I started on. One thing I was glad of, and that was that there was a neat-looking horse tethered at the end of the alley, and from the length of the stirrups—as I made the saddle in a flying leap—I sort of thought that it might have belonged to the fellow I had just left behind me.

I cut the tethering rope from the saddle with my sheath knife, and then I scooted that horse across the street and down another alley.

I pulled him up walking into the next street beyond and jogged along as though nothing particularly concerning me were happening that night. A very good way to get through with trouble. But the trouble was that there was still hell popping at the governor's house. I could hear their voices—and more than that, I could hear their guns, and so could half of the rest of the town.

People were piling out of every house, and more than one man who was legging in the danger direction yelped at me as I went past and asked where I was going. But that was not so bad. I didn't mind questions. What I wanted to avoid was personal contact!

Here half a dozen fellows on fine horses took the corner ahead of me on one wheel, so to speak, spilling out all across the street as they raced the turn. When they saw me, one of them shouted: "What are you riding *that* way for?"

I knew that they would be halfway down the block before they could stop, and besides, I hoped that they wouldn't be too curious if I didn't answer.

So I just trotted the horse around the same corner by which they had come. But one question unanswered wasn't enough for them. They were like hungry dogs, ready to follow any trail.

"Hello?" yelled the sharp, biting voice of that same leader, to whom I began to wish bad luck. "No answer from that gent. Let's have a look at his face!"

I could hear the scraping and the scratching of the hoofs of the horses as the riders turned them in the middle of the block with cowpuncher yells that took down my temperature at least a dozen degrees.

In the meantime, I was not marking time. I scooted my mount down the next block. The minute he took his first stride I knew that the race would be a hot one, no matter how well they were fixed with horses. Because that little horse was a wonder! I never put eyes on him after that night, but he ran with me like a jack rabbit—a long-winded jack rabbit, at that!

My weight was such a puzzler for him, that he grunted with every stride, but he whipped me down that street so fast that I had nearly turned west on the next corner before the pursuit sighted me. But I failed by the stretched-out tail of that little Trojan; and by the yell behind me I knew that they were riding hard and riding for blood.

I turned again at the next corner, and as I turned, I saw that two men were riding even with me. They had even gained half a length in the running of that block!

I made up my mind right away. If they had speed, they could show it in a straightway run, because it kills a little horse to dodge corners with a heavy man on his back. So I put my pony straight west up that street, running him on the gutter of the street where dust and leaves had gathered and made easier padding for his hoofbeats.

In a mile we were out of the town, but those six scoundrels were still hanging on my rear, and raising the country with their yells and their whoops.

I could hear others falling in behind me. There were twenty now, shoving their horses along my path. Every moment they were increasing in numbers. Besides, after the first half mile, my weight began to kill that game little horse. He ran just as fast, nearly, as he had before. But the spring was going out of his gallop. Then I was saying to him—just hold out over the hill and into the hollow—just over the hill and into the hollow.

Well, they were snapshooting at me as I went up that hill, and the hill and my weight together slowed my little horse frightfully. However, he got to the top of it at last, and my whistle was a blast between my fingers. Fifty yards of running down that hillside—with my poor little horse staggering and almost dying under me. My heart stood in my mouth, for if Roanoke were gone, I was a lost man with a halter around my neck.

But no—there he was, sloping out of the brush and heading full tilt toward me. As I came closer, he wheeled around and began to shamble away at his wonderful trot in the same direction I was riding. So I made a flying jump from the saddle of the little horse and onto the rocklike strength of the back of Roanoke.

16

THERE was not a great deal to the race after that. I suppose that there were a half a dozen horses in the lot that could have nabbed Roanoke in an early sprint. But the little gamester I rode out of town had taken the sap out of the running legs of the entire outfit.

When I left him for Roanoke, that old mule carried me up the course of the hollow—where water must have stood half the year, by the tree growth—and after he had run full speed for a few minutes, they began to drop back behind me into the night.

The moment I noticed that, I dropped Roanoke back to his trot. Galloping was not to his taste, but he could swing on at close to full speed with that shambling trot of his and keep it up forever. It did not take long. The hunt faded behind me. The yelling began to grow musical with the distance; and finally it died away—first to an occasional obscure murmur in the wind, and then to nothing.

I think we did thirty miles before the morning was on us. Then I put up and spent another hungry day in a clump of trees. But food for Roanoke, not for me, was the main thing at that time. When the day ended, I sent that old veteran out to travel again, and we were soon in the mountains, soon climbing slowly, soon winding and weaving ourselves up to cloud level.

Until I got to that height, back in my own country, I did not realize how frightened I had been. But now that the mischief was behind me, I felt fairly groggy. I sent one bullet through a pair of fool jack rabbits sitting side by side, the next morning, behind a rock. They barely made a meal for me. I could have eaten a hindquarter of an ox, I was so hungry. I kept poor Roanoke drudging away until about noon. Then I made camp and spent thirty-six hours without moving.

I always do that after a hard march, if I can. It is always best to work hard while there's the least hint of trouble in the offing, but when the wind lets up, I don't know of a better way to insure long life and happiness than by resting a lot. I was like a sponge. I could work for a hundred hours without closing my eyes; but at the end of that time, I could sleep two days, solid, with just enough waking time to cook and eat one meal on each of those days.

Roanoke was a good deal the same way. We spent a day and a half in a sort of stupor, but the result was that when we *did* start on, I had under me an animal that wasn't half fagged and ready to be beaten, but a mule with his ears up and quivering; and my own head was rested and prepared for trouble.

I hit for my old camping ground—not any particular section, though I knew every inch of the high range, by this time—the whole wide region above timberline—a bitter, naked, cheerless country, in lots of ways, but a safe one. For seven years, safety had to take the place of home and friends for me.

An infernal north wind began to shriek among the peaks as soon as I got up there among them. But I didn't budge for ten wretched days or more. I spent a shuddering, miserable existence. There is nothing on earth that comes so close to above timberline for real hell!

I've heard naturalists talk about the beauties of insects and birds and whatnot above the place where the trees stop growing. Well, I can't agree with them. Perhaps I haven't a soul. But those high places make me pretty sick! When I see the long, dark line of trees end, that cuts in and out among the mountains like the mark of high water, it sends a chill through me.

But for seven years I had spent the bulk of my life in that horrible part of the world. Seven years—eighteen to twenty-five! Every year before twenty-five is twice as long as every year after that time.

Well, I stayed in the old safe level, as I have said, about ten days. Then I dropped Roanoke five thousand feet nearer to civilization and stopped, one day, on the edge of a little town—right out between two hills where there was a little shack of a cabin standing. I knew that cabin, and I knew that the man inside it ought to know me.

I had stayed over with him half a dozen nights, and every time I used his house as a hotel, he got ten or twenty dollars out of me. Because that was one of the rules of the game. If a long rider struck up an acquaintanceship with one of the mountaineers, he always had to pay for it through the nose in the end.

However, I couldn't be sure that the old man Sargent hadn't changed his mind about me. I left Roanoke fidgeting among the trees on the hillside, for he could smell the sweet hay from the barn at that distance, and his mouth was watering. Then I slid down the hill and peeked through the windows. Everything seemed as cheerful and dirty and careless as ever.

Sargent had two grown-up sons. The three of them put in their time on a place where there wasn't work enough to keep one respectable two-handed man busy. There wasn't more than enough money for one man, if he wanted to be civilized. But civilization didn't harmonize with the Sargents. They wanted to live easy, even if they had to live low.

When I saw that there wasn't any change in them, I took Roanoke to the barn and put him up where he could eat all the hay he wanted. Because you can trust a mule to stop before the danger mark—which is a trust that you can't put in a horse.

Then I went to the house, and the three of them gave me a pretty snug welcome. Old man Sargent insisted that I take the best chair—his own chair. He insisted, too, that I have something to eat. I had had enough for breakfast to last a couple of days, but I let out a link and laid into some mighty good corn bread and molasses that he dished up to me along with some coffee so strong that it would of taken the bristles off of pigskin.

I said: "How long ago did you make this coffee, Sargent?"

"I dunno," said he.

"He swabs out the pot once a month," said one of the boys, grinning, "and the rest of the time, he just keeps changing the brew a little! A little more water—a little more coffee!"

Well, it tasted like that, sort of generally bad and strong—mighty strong. I put away half a cup, just enough to moisten the corn bread that I swallowed.

"Have you come down to get Dinsmore?" said Bert Sargent.

The name hit the button, of course, and I turned around and stared at him.

"Why, Dinsmore has been setting waiting down in Elmira for three days!" said old man Sargent.

"Waiting for what?" said I. "I've been up in the mountains, and I haven't heard."

Of course, they were glad enough to tell. Bad news for anyone else was good news for those rascals. It seems that Dinsmore had appeared, suddenly, in the streets of Elmira. At noonday. That was his way of doing things—with a high hand—acting as though there were no reason in the world why he should expect trouble from anyone. He went to the bulletin board beside the post office and there he posted up a big notice. He had the roll of paper under his arm, and he tacked it up with plenty of nails, not caring what other signs he covered.

Well, sir, the reading of that sign was something like this:

"Attention, Leon Porfilo! I want you, not the twenty thousand. If you want *me,* you can expect that I'll be ready for you any day between three and four if you'll ride through Main Street. I'll let you know which way to shoot!

Jeffrey Dinsmore

I don't mean to say that the Sargent family told me this story with so little detail. What they did do, however, was to give me all the facts, among the three of them. When I had sifted those facts over in my mind, I stood up. I was so worried that I didn't care if they saw the trouble in my face.

"You don't like this news so well as you might, partner?" says old Sargent very smooth and swallowing a grin.

I looked down at that wicked old loafer and hated him with all my heart.

"I don't like that news at all," I admitted.

The three of them exclaimed all in a breath with delight. They couldn't help it. Then I told them that I was tired, and they showed me to a mattress on the floor of the next room. I lay there for a time trying to think out what I should do, and all the time I could hear the malicious whispers of the three in the kitchen. They were discussing with vile pleasure the shock that had appeared in my face when I had been told the news. They were like vultures, that trio.

Well, I was tired enough to go to sleep anyway, after a time. Then I wakened with a start and found that it was daylight. That was what you might call a real hundred-per-cent sleep. I felt better, of course, when I got up in the morning, and in the kitchen I found old man Sargent with his greasy hair tumbling down over his face and his face as lined and shadowed as though he had been drinking whisky all the night. I suppose that really low thoughts tear up a man's body as much as the booze.

He gave a side look as sharp as a bird's to see if there was still any trouble in my eyes, but I put on a mask for him and came out into the kitchen singing. All at once, a sort of horror at that old man and at the life I had been leading came over me.

I hurried out of the house and down to the creek. Of course it was ice cold, but I needed a bath, inside and out, I felt. I stripped and dived and climbed back onto the creek bank with enough shivers running up and down my spine to have done for a whole school of minnows.

But I felt better. A lot better.

When I went back to the house for breakfast, I saw that one of the two boys was not on hand, and I asked where he was. His father said that he had gone off to try to get a deer, but that sounded like a queer excuse to me. I couldn't imagine a Sargent doing such a thing as this, at this hour in the morning! I began to grow a little uneasy—I didn't exactly know why!

After breakfast, as I left, I offered the old rat a twenty-dollar bill, and he took it and spread it out with a real gulp of joy. Cash came very seldom into his life.

"But," said he at last, peering at me hopefully and making his voice a wheedling drawl, "ain't I give you extra important news, this trip? Ain't it worth a mite more?"

I was too disgusted to answer. I turned on my heel and left, and as I went out, I could hear him snarling covertly behind me.

17

HOWEVER, I didn't like to fall out with the Sargents. I knew that they were swine, but, after all, I might need their help pretty early and pretty often in the next few years of my life.

I went out to Roanoke and sat in the manger in front of him, thinking, or trying to think, while the old rascal started biting at me as though he were going to make breakfast off me. I decided, finally, that the only thing for me was to head straight for Elmira and take my chances there, because if I didn't meet Dinsmore right away, my name would be pretty worthless through the mountains. Besides, it was the very thing I had wanted.

But I had never dreamed of a fight in a town—and a big town like Elmira, that had a four-story hotel, and a regular business section, and four streets going north and south and four streets going east and west. There were as many as fifteen hundred people in Elmira, I suppose.

It was a regular city, and it seemed a good deal like craziness to try to stage a fight in such a place. As well start a chicken fight in the midst of a gang of rattlesnakes. No matter which of us won, he was sure to be nabbed by the local police right after the fight.

I wondered what could be in the head of Dinsmore, unless he had an arrangement with the sheriff of that county to turn him loose, in case he were the man who won the fight. I decided that this must be the fact, and that worried me more than ever. However, there wasn't much that I could do except to ride in and take my chance with Dinsmore. But one of the bad features was that I had never seen Dinsmore, whereas everyone had

had a thousand looks at me in the posters which offered a reward for my capture.

Well, I saddled Roanoke and started down the Elmira trail. The first cross trail I came to, there I saw a board nailed on the side of a fence post and on the board there was all spread out a pretty good poster which said:

DINSMORE—TWENTY THOUSAND DOLLARS'
REWARD

I made Roanoke jump for the sign to see the face in detail. It was rather a small photograph, but it was a very clear one, and I was fairly staggered when I leaned over and found myself looking into the eyes of the very same fellow who had climbed the back fence of the governor's house a second before me on that rousing night in the capital city.

So that was Dinsmore!

It wasn't a very hot day, but I jumped out of the saddle and sat down under a tree and smoked a cigarette and fanned myself and did some very tall damning.

It was all a confusing and nasty mess, of course. A *mighty* nasty mess! I hardly dared to think out all of the ideas that jumped into my mind. There had been the anger of the governor when I mentioned the name of Dinsmore. There had been a sort of savage satisfaction when I suggested that the other outlaw and I shoot it out for the pardon. That, together with the unknown presence of Dinsmore at the house—and the pretty face of the governor's wife—well, I was fairly done up at the thought, you may be sure.

I could remember, too, that Dinsmore, though he had always been a fighting man, had never been a complete devil until about a year before— which was about the date of the governor's marriage.

I don't mean to say that I immediately jumped to a lot of nasty conclusions. But a great many doubts and suspicions were floating through the back of my brain. I didn't want to believe a single one of them. But what could I do?

The first thing was to throw myself on the back of Roanoke and go down that hillside like a snowslide well underway. Blindly as a slide, too, and the result was that as I dipped out of the trees and came into the sunny little open valley below, I got two rifle shots squarely at my face. I didn't try to turn Roanoke aside. I just jammed him across that clearing with the spurs hanging in his flanks, and I opened fire with both revolvers as I went, firing as fast as I could and just in a general direction, of course!

Well, I got results. Snapshooting is always a good deal of a chance. This snapshooting into the blind brush got me a yelp of pain that meant a hit and was followed by a groan that meant a *bad* hit.

After that, there was a considerable crashing through the brush, and I made out at least three horses smearing their way off through the underbrush.

But what mostly interested me was that the groaning remained just as near and just as heavy as before. So I went in search of it, and when I came to the place, I found a long fellow in ragged clothes lying on his face behind a shrub. I turned him over and with one look at his yellow face I knew that he was dying.

It was young Marcus Sargent.

Of course I knew at once why he had been missing at the breakfast table. They guessed that I would head straight for Elmira now that I had the news. So young Marcus thought of the twenty thousand dollars and decided that there was no reason why he should not dip his hands into the reward!

He wasn't a coward. He was in such pain that it changed his color, but it didn't keep him from sneering at me in hate. When you wrong a man, hate always comes out of it—on your side.

But I didn't hate him, in turn. I merely thanked heaven that he had missed; and I didn't see how he had, because I'd watched him ring down a squirrel out of a treetop many a time.

"How did you happen to miss?" I asked him. "Hand shake, Mark?"

The first thing he answered was: "Am I done for?"

I answered him brutally enough: "You're done for. You can't live two minutes, I suppose; that slug went through you in the spot where it would do me the most good!"

"You're a lucky swine!" said Marcus. "Well, anyway, I dunno that life is so sweet that I hate the leavin' of it. But over in Elmira—if you should happen to run across Sue Hunter, hand her my watch, will you? Tell her it's from me. You'll know her by her picture inside the cover."

I hated nothing in the world more than touching that watch. But I did it, at last, and dropped it into my pocket.

He didn't want to die before he had done as much harm as he could. He turned on his own family, saying: "It wasn't me alone. The whole three of us talked it over last night!"

"Look here, Mark," said I, getting a little sick as I watched his color change, "is there anything I can do to make you more comfortable?"

"Sure," said he. "Lend me a chaw, will you?"

I didn't chew tobacco, and I told him that I had none for him.

"Well," said he, "then fetch me my own plug out of my hip pocket, will you?"

But before I could get it for him, he was dead.

I didn't like this affair for a lot of reasons. In the first place, I've never sunk lead in a man without hating the job. Though I've had the necessity or the bad luck of having to kill ten times my share of men, there was never a time when I didn't loathe it, and loathe the thought of it afterward.

But that was only half of the reason that I disliked this ugly little adventure in the hollow. I had a fair idea that the two or three curs who had ambushed me with young Sargent would now ride for Elmira full tilt and tell the sheriff of what they had tried to do and of where they had last seen me.

So, in two or three hours, the sheriff might be setting a fine trap for me in the town.

Of course, I only needed a moment of thought to see that that was a foolish idea. No matter how little the people esteemed me, they would not think me such a perfect idiot as to ride on toward the town after I knew that a warning was speeding toward it in the form of three messengers.

No, the sheriff was really not very apt to lay a plot for me in the town. Rather, he was pretty sure to come foaming down to the place I had been seen and try to follow my trail from that point.

Well, I decided that if that were the case, he could pick up my trail if he cared to and follow it right back to his own home town.

In short, my idea was that when people heard I had appeared so close to Elmira, every gun-wearing citizen would take a turn on his fastest horse and treat himself to a holiday hunting down twenty thousand dollars' worth of "critter."

I believed that that town would be well cleaned out and that the best thing I could do was to drive straight for Elmira itself, simply swinging a little wide off the main trail. Perhaps nine tenths of the fighting men would be out hunting me when I reached Elmira, hunting Jeffrey Dinsmore!

Jeffrey Dinsmore, slender and delicately made, and as handsome for a man as the governor's wife was lovely for a girl! Thinking of her and of Dinsmore, I could understand why it was that Mike O'Rourke was only pretty and not truly beautiful. Molly might grow plain enough in the face in another ten years, but the governor's wife was another matter. She would simply become charming in new ways as time passed over her head.

There was something magnificent and removed and different about her. She was the sort of a person I wondered any man could ever have the courage to love—she seemed so mighty superior to me! Well, you can guess from all of this that I wasn't in the most cheerful frame of mind in the world until, about two hours afterward, I looked through a gap in the trees and the brush, and I saw about a hundred men piling down the hillside in just the opposite direction and knew that I had guessed right!

18

ELMIRA had turned out its best and bravest to swarm out to the place where my trail had been found and lost by those three heroes who accompanied young Mark Sargent. They had a long ride before them, and no matter how fast they spurred back toward Elmira, they were not apt to arrive there until many hours after I had passed through. My chief concern now was simply lest there still remained too many fighting men in the town. But I was not greatly worried about that.

I felt that I had reduced the dangers of Elmira to a very small point. The danger which remained was from Dinsmore alone.

How great that danger was I could not really guess. It was true that he established a great reputation for himself in Texas, but before this I had met with men of a great repute in distant sections of the country, and they had proved not so deadly on a closer knowing.

Furthermore, when one has picked up another man and dropped him on the pavement, one is not apt to respect his prowess greatly. Which may explain fairly thoroughly why I thought that I could handle Mr. Dinsmore with ease.

I did not think, however, that he would be prepared for me in Elmira. I thought that I probably would be permitted to canter down the street unobserved by Mr. Dinsmore; because if the entire town was so busy hunting me, it seemed illogical that I should drop into Elmira.

I expected to canter easily through the town, with only the danger of some belated storekeeper or some old man seeing and knowing me, for the rest of the town seemed to be out in the saddle.

Of course, I hoped that Dinsmore would not be on hand, because after I had answered his first invitation and he failed to appear, it would be my turn to lead, and I could request him to appear at a place of my own selection. The advantage would then be all on my side.

Outside of the town I stopped for a time. I let the mule rest, and I took it easy myself. I had a few hours on my hands before the appointed time to show myself to little Dinsmore in the town.

However, though Roanoke rested well enough, I cannot say that my nerves were very easy. The time was coming closer, faster than any express train I ever watched in my life. The waiting was the strain. Whereas Dinsmore, knowing that the fight might come any day, paid no heed, but could maintain a leisurely lookout—or none at all!

A pair of eternities went by at last, however. Then I swung onto Roanoke and started him into the town. Everything went on about as I had expected it. The town was emptied of men. The first I saw was an old octogenarian with his trousers patched with a piece of old sack.

The poor old man looked more than half dead, and probably was. He didn't lift his head from his hobble as I rattled by. The first bit of danger that came into my way was signaled by the screaming voice of a woman.

"There goes Leon Porfilo! There'll be a murder in this town today!"

It wasn't a very cheerful reception, take it all in all. But I pulled Roanoke back to an easy trot, and then I took him down to a walk, because I saw that I was coming pretty close to the place of the rendezvous. When I passed that place—though I wanted most terribly to pass it fast!—still I had to be at a gait from which a man can shoot straight—and I've never yet seen anyone but a liar that could come near to accuracy from a trot or a gallop. Try it yourself—especially with a revolver—and see what happens. Even a walking horse is bad enough. It's hard when the target is moving; it's a lot harder when the shooter is in motion.

So I steeled myself as well as I could and reached a sort of mental bucket down into the innards of myself and drew up all the champagne that there was in me. I mustered a smile. Smiling helps a fellow, somehow. I don't mean in any fool way like they have it in ragtime songs and old proverbs. But smiling makes your gun hand steady.

Pretty soon I was right in the midst of the place where danger was to come at me, according to the warning that Dinsmore had sent out. I began to think that the whole thing was just a great bluff and that nothing would come out of it! It was a big play on the part of Dinsmore, and he hadn't the least idea of living up to his promise.

Just as this thought struck me, I heard a calm, smooth voice call out behind me: "Well, Porfilo?"

It was the sort of a voice that comes from a man who doesn't want to call any public attention to himself. He aims to reach just the ear of the man to whom he is speaking. But, at the same time, I knew that that was the voice of Dinsmore, and I knew that Dinsmore was mighty bad medicine; and I knew that the fight of my life was on my hands.

I spun about in the saddle with the gun in my hand—and I saw that he had not even drawn his weapon!

The shock of it sickened me. I couldn't keep from shooting—I was so thoroughly set for that pull of the trigger—but I did manage to shoot wide of the mark. Just as the gun exploded, I saw my new friend Dinsmore make as pretty a draw as I have ever had the pleasure of witnessing. One of those snap movements that jump a gun out of the leather and shoot it from the hip.

In the meantime, I jerked my own gun back and fired again, but my hand was mighty uncertain. The whole affair was so infernally unnerving that I was not myself. The idea that any man in the world would dare to stand up to me and give me the first chance at a draw was too much for me!

I got in my second shot before he fired his first, but all I did with that second bullet was to break a grocery-store window! Then a thunderbolt clipped me along the head and knocked me back in the saddle.

I was completely out—as perfectly out as though a hammer had landed on me—but it happened that in falling, my weight was thrown squarely forward, and my arms dangled around the neck of Roanoke. He started the same instant, I suppose, with that shambling, ridiculously smooth trot of his; so that I was able to stick to his back.

I think that the wild yelling of old men, and women, and children was what brought me back to my senses. Or partially back to them, for my head was spinning and crimson was running over my eyes. However, I was able to sit straighter in the saddle and put Roanoke into a gallop.

I was a dead man, of course. I learned afterward about the miracle that saved me. For the gun of that great expert, that famous Dinsmore, failed to work. The cylinder stuck on the next shot, and before he could get the other gun out to blow me out of this life and into limbo, that wise-headed mule of mine had put a buckboard at the side of the street between himself and that gunman.

Dinsmore had to run out into the middle of the street to get the next shot. But when he saw me again, I suppose that the distance was getting too great for accurate work even for him, and besides, Roanoke was shooting me along under the shadow of the trees.

At any rate, there he stood in a raging passion and emptied that second gun of his without putting a mark upon either the mule or the mule's rider. I suppose there is no doubt that the fury of that little man was what saved me more than anything else.

But presently I was blinking at the sun like a person wakened out of a dream, and behind me lay Elmira in a hollow; and up and down my head ran a pain like the agony of a cutting knife through tender flesh; and down in Elmira was a man who was telling the world that the "coward had run away from him!"

I should like to be able to say that, halting only to tie a sleeve of my shirt around my head, I turned and whirled back into Elmira to find him again. But I have to confess that nothing could have induced me to face that calm little devil of a mankiller on that day. For the moment, I felt that I could *never* have the courage to fight or face him again! I felt that I would take water sooner.

First of all, I found a little hollow about ten miles back among the hills, and there I made myself comfortable, heated some water, washed out my wound, and bound it up. Then I rode straight on to the next little village. On the way, I had to duck three or four parties of manhunters. I didn't have to ask who they were hunting for. I simply wanted to dodge them and get on, for I knew that they wanted either Dinsmore or me.

The next town had not much more than an ugly look, a hotel, and half a dozen shacks. But in one of these shacks was an old doctor, and that was what I wanted. The new-fangled ideas had taken his trade away from him. But he was good enough for me, on that day.

I left Roanoke behind his house and went to the back window and saw the poor old man sitting there in a kitchen that was blackened with the shadows of the trees that hung over the place—blackened with time, too, if you can understand what I mean by that. I pitied him, suddenly, so much that I almost forgot the pain in my head. Young men are like that.

They pity almost everyone except themselves. I never ride through a village without wondering how people can live in it. Yet I suppose that every one of them is prettier than my home town of Mendez.

I went in, and the doctor looked sidewise from his whittling of a stick and then back to it.

"Well, Porfilo," said he, "I been hearin' that you got licked, at last! And a little feller did it! Well, for some things bigness ain't needed."

He stood up—about five feet in his total height. I hung above him, ducking my head to keep from scraping the cobwebs off the rafters.

"I've got my head sliced open. Sew me up, pop," said I.

"Set down and rest yourself, son," said he. "I see you got sense enough to let little men fix you *up*, anyway!"

19

I LISTENED to him mumbling and muttering to himself, while I set my teeth and snarled at the pain, until the job was done and my head washed and bandage arranged around it. He gave me a lot of extra bandage, and a salve, and he asked me if I had a good mirror so that I could watch the wound every day. I told him that I had, and asked him what the price would be.

"If you're flat busted, the way most of your kind always are," said he, "there ain't no charge, except for your good will. Besides, any young feller has got a reward comin' to him when he listens to an old goat like me chatterin' for a while. But if you're flush, well, for bandagin' the head of an outlaw and a mankiller like you—well, it's worth about—thirty dollars, I reckon!"

I sifted a hundred dollars out of my wallet and put it in his hand.

I was out of the door before he had counted it over and he shouted: "Hey, you—"

I was on Roanoke, with that fine old fellow standing in the doorway and shouting: "Come back here! You give me too much."

I sent Roanoke on his way, and the last I saw of him, that poor old man was running and stumbling and staggering after me, waving his glasses in one hand and his money in the other hand and telling me to come back. But I only saw him for a moment. Then I was away among the trees, with Roanoke climbing steadily.

I kept him south through the highlands. When I was far enough away from the last trouble, I made small marches every day, because I knew that a wound won't heal quickly so long as a man is running about too much. While I was lazying around, I worked until both wrists ached over my guns. Because there was fear in me—real fear in me! I had gone for seven years from one fight to another, never beaten, always the conqueror. Now a little fellow had blown me off my pedestal!

I had to get ready to fight him again. I knew that, and I can't tell you that I didn't relish the knowing. In the meantime I had to get in touch with Mike. For she would think, as probably everyone in the mountains thought, that I had either been killed by the aftereffects of that wound in the head received from Jeffrey Dinsmore, or else that I had been so thoroughly broken in spirit as a result of that first defeat that I had shrunk away to a new land and dared not show myself in my old haunts.

Well, I thought of a letter, first of all; but then I decided that it would be better to see her, because it might be the very last time that I should ever see her in this world. For, having once witnessed the gun play of Jeffrey Dinsmore, I knew that at the best I would need a touch of good fortune in order to beat him in a fair gunfight. What with my bulk and my experience, how could I challenge him with any other weapon?

So I drifted farther south through the mountains until I came one midnight to the O'Rourke house and stood underneath the black front of the house— all black, except for a single light in the window of Mike.

I called her with a whistle which was a seven-year-old signal between us. She did not open the door and first look down at me, but she came flying down the stairs and then out the front door and down the steps and into my arms. But, when she had made sure that it was I, she stood back from me and laughed and nodded with her happiness. She told me that she had been sure that I was dead, in spite of other rumors.

"What sort of talk has been going around about me, then?" I asked her.

She shook her head. But I told her that I would have to have it.

"They are fools," said she, but there was a strain in her voice. "They say that you are afraid to go back and face Dinsmore!"

Well, I *was* afraid. So I blurted out: "I *am* afraid, Mike."

I saw it take her breath, and I saw her flinch from me. Then she answered very calmly: "However, you'll go back and fight him again!"

I was mighty proud of her. You don't find women who will talk like that very often. But Mike was the truest mountain-bred kind—thoroughbred, in her own way. I spent a single hour with her there in the garden. Then I told her that I was starting back.

"North?" asked Mike.

"North, of course," said I. "You don't think that I'll try to dodge a second meeting?"

"Of *course* I didn't think so!" said she. However, I could feel the relief in her voice. She began to pat the neck of old Roanoke.

"Roanoke," said she, "bring him back safe to me!"

So I left Mike and rode north again.

It was a hard journey. I had gone for seven years more or less paying no attention to decent precautions, because they had not been so necessary to me. In fact, I had not appreciated the change in my affairs until I started that northward journey again.

It began in the first house where I put up for a night. Old Marshall's house was a pretty frequent stopping place for me. His family had taken a good deal of money out of my hand, and more than that, his nephew,

who ran the little bit of cattle land the old man owned, seemed to respect
me and to like me, because he was always trying to find a better chance to
talk to me.

But when I came to the house this night, everyone merely stared at me,
at first, and then I could hear them whispering and even chuckling behind
their hands. People had not done that to me since I was a little boy in
school. It made my heart cold, and then it made my heart hot.

But I waited until something came out. With people like that, nothing
could be left to silence very long. They had to bring out what they thought
and put it into words.

So big Dick Marshall, the nephew, came and lounged against the wall
near my chair.

"We hear that you been having your own sorts of trouble?" said he.

I lifted the bandage which I still wore, and showed him the scar.

"I was nipped," said I.

He laughed in my face. "You didn't go back for any more of *that* medicine,
I guess?" said he.

I wanted to knock him down. But after a moment I decided that there
was no use in doing that. Because he was not a bad fellow. Just a clod. No
more cruel than a bull in a herd—and no less.

That, and the mischievous, contemptuous smile with which he watched
me out of sight the next morning, as I rode away, should have convinced
me, I suppose, that there was worse trouble ahead. But when I really found
it out, it was merely because four young fellows came bang—over a hilltop
behind me and tried to ride me down in the next hollow. When they saw
that I was making time away from them to the tree line, they opened fire
at me.

When I got to the trees, I told myself that I was all right, but to my real
astonishment, just as I drew up on the rein and brought Roanoke back to
a walk, I heard the whole four of them crashing through the underbrush!

I sent Roanoke ahead again, full steam. He was as smooth a worker as
a snake through the shrubbery, and the four began to fall behind. I could
hear them yelling with rage as they judged, by the noise, that they were
losing ground behind me. But all the time I was thinking hard and fast.
It wasn't right. Four youngsters like these, not one of whom had probably
ever pulled a gun on another man, should not be riding behind Leon
Porfilo. By no means!

Well, I decided to find out what the reason was. So I cut back through
the forest. The trees were pretty dense, and so I was able to get right in
behind the party. I sighted them and found them just as I wanted to find
them. They were strung out by the heat of the work, and one fellow was
lagging far behind with a lame horse.

He had no eyes for the back trail, and he could hear no sound behind
him, he was so eager to get ahead. It was easy enough to slip along in a
dark hollow and stick a gun in the small of his back. I clapped my hand

over his mouth so that I stifled his yell. Then I turned him around and looked him over. He was just a baby. About eighteen or nineteen, with big, pale-blue eyes, and a foolish sort of a smile trembling on his mouth.

He was afraid. But he was not afraid as much as he should have been at meeting Leon Porfilo. This may sound pretty fat-headed, but you have to understand that I had been the pet dragon around those parts for the past seven years, and I wasn't in the habit of having infants like this boy on my trail!

I said to him: "Son, do you know who I am?"

"You're Porfilo!" said he.

"Then what in the devil do you mean by riding so hard down my trail?"

He looked straight back at me. "There's twenty thousand dollars' worth of reasons," said he, as bold as you please.

"Is it a very safe business?" said I.

He wouldn't answer, but those big pale eyes of his didn't waver.

"You can do what you want," said he. "I didn't have no fair chance— with you sneakin' up behind like that. No matter what happens, my brother'll get you after I'm dead!"

"Am I to murder you?" said I.

"You don't dare to leave me on your trail!" said he.

Well, it sickened me, and that was all there was to it! He actually wanted to fight the thing out with me, I think.

"You're loose!" said I, and dropped my gun back in the holster.

He jerked his horse back and grabbed for his own gun. Then he saw that I was making no move toward mine, and so he began to gape at me as though he were seeing double. Finally he disappeared in the trees. But it's a fact that I couldn't have fired a shot at that little fool.

This thing, and the talk of young Marshall, showed me how far I had dropped in the estimation of the mountain men since they had heard that little Dinsmore beat me in a fair fight. I knew that I would be in frightful danger from that moment on.

20

I KNEW that there was danger because my cloak of invincibility was quite thrown away. For seven years I had paraded up and down through the mountains, and men had not dared to go out to hunt me except when they had celebrated leaders to show them the way, and when they had prepared carefully organized bands of hard fighters and straight shooters.

It had been easy enough to get out of the reach of these large parties. But when the hills were beginning to buzz with the doings of little groups

of from three to five manhunters—well, then my danger was multiplied
by a thousand. Multiplied most of all, however, by the mental attitude of
the people who rode out against me.

For there's only one reason that so many straight-shooting frontiersmen
fail when they come to take a shot at a so-called desperado. That reason
is that their nerve fails them. They are not sure of themselves. So their
rifles miss, and the desperado who has all the confidence that they lack
does prodigious things. One hears, here and there, of terrible warriors
who have dropped half a dozen men, and gotten off unhurt!

Of course, I was never on a par with these. In fact, my principle was not
to shoot to kill unless I had a known scoundrel up against me. But now I
felt that my back was against the wall.

There was only one solution for me, and that was to get at Dinsmore as
soon as possible and fight it out with him, and by his death put an end to
the carelessness of the fools who were hounding me through the hills. But
in the meantime, how was I to get at Dinsmore himself?

I decided that I must try the very scheme which he had tried on me. I
must send him a message and a challenge in the message to meet me at a
place and a time of my own choosing. Two days later chance threw a
messenger into my path.

I was in a tangle of shrubs on the shoulder of a mountain with Roanoke
on the other side, his saddle off, rolling to freshen himself, and playing
like a colt, as only a mule, among grown animals, likes to play. While I sat
on a rock at the edge of the brush, I saw a pair of horsemen and then a
third working up the trail straight toward me.

I was in no hurry. This was rough country of my own choosing, and
Roanoke could step away from any horse in the world, in that sort of going,
like a mountain sheep! I simply got out my glasses and studied the three.
As they came closer, rising deeper into the field of the glass, I thought that
I could guess what they were—three headhunters, and mine was the head
that they wanted.

For they were too well mounted to be just casual cowpunchers. Every
man was literally armed to the teeth. I saw sheathed rifles under their right
knees. I saw a pair of revolvers at their hips. One fellow had another pair
of six-shooters in his saddle holsters. They looked as though they were a
detail from an army!

I went across the knob of the shoulder of that mountain and I saddled
Roanoke. But I didn't like to leave that place. I was irritated again. Four
youngsters had been out hunting me the last time. Now it was three grown
men! Three!

You might say that my pride was offended, because that was exactly the
case!

I ended by dropping the reins of Roanoke, and the wise old mule stood
as still as death in the shadow of the trees, flopping his ears back and forth
at me, but not so much as switching his tail to knock away the flies that

were settling on his flanks and biting deep as only mountain flies know how to bite!

I have always thought that Roanoke knew when there was trouble coming, and that he enjoyed the prospect of it with all his heart. There was faith and strength and courage in the nature of that brute, but I am sure that there was a good deal of the devil in him, too!

I left him behind and started down among the rocks until I found exactly the sort of a place that I wanted, a regular nest, with plenty of chances to look out from it with a rifle. I had a fine rifle with me, and ready for action. As for my humor, it was nearer to killing than it had ever been in my life.

The three came up with surprising speed, and I knew by that that they were well mounted. As they came, I could hear their voices rising up to me like echoes up a well shaft. These voices, and that laughter, was sometimes dim, sometimes loud and crackling in my ear. Because in the mountains, where the air is very thin, sound travels not so freshly and easily. The least blow of wind may turn a shout into a whisper.

Have you never noticed that mountaineers, when they come down toward sea level, are a noisy lot?

I could hear all the talk of the three, and by their very talk I could judge that they were in the best of spirits.

Then: "Will you keep that darn bay from joggin' around and tryin' to turn around in the trail, Baldy?"

"It ain't me. It's the hoss. It wants to get back to that stable—"

"A hired hoss," said a third voice, "is something that I ain't never rode."

They came suddenly around the next bend of the trail, and I barely had the time to duck down in my nest of rocks. I had thought them at least fifty yards farther away from that bend!

I was not quite in time, at that.

"Hey!" yelled the first man—he of the bay horse.

"Well?" growled one of the others.

"Something in those rocks—"

"Maybe it's Porfilo!" laughed another.

"That's the gent you want!"

"Just run up to them rocks and ask him to step out and have it out with you, Baldy!"

Baldy said apologetically: "Well, I can't keep you from laughing. But I would of said that the brim of a sombrero—"

I took off my hat and prepared my rifle. As I freshened my grip on it and tickled the trigger with my forefinger, I have to admit that I was ready to kill. I was hot and sore to the very bone. They came laughing and joking on my trail. It was a vacation, a regular party to them!

As they came closer, as the nodding shadow of the bay appeared on the white trail just before my nest, I stood up with the rifle at my shoulder.

There's something discouraging about a rifle. About ten times as much can be said with a rifle as can be said with even a pair of revolvers. The revolvers may have a lot of speed and lead in 'em. But they *might* miss—they're pretty *apt* to miss. Even a coward will take a gambling chance now and then. But when a rifle in a steady hand is looking in your direction, you feel sure that something is bound to drop. Somehow, there is an instinct in men which makes everyone think that the muzzle is pointed directly at him.

Only one of the three made a pass at a gun. The two boys behind shoved their hands in the air right pronto. But Baldy, up in the lead, passed a hand toward his off Colt. He was within the tenth part of a second of his long sleep when he did that. I think that there must be something in mental telepathy, because the moment that thought to kill came into my mind, he stuck both of his paws into the air and kept his arms stiff.

His bay turned around as if it were on a pivot and started moving back down the trail.

"Take your left hand, Baldy," said I, "and stop that horse pronto!"

He did exactly as I told him to do.

"Now, boys," said I, stepping out from the rocks with that rifle only at the ready, "I suppose that you recognize me. I'm Leon Porfilo. If you want to know me any better, make a pass at a holster. You, Baldy, were about half a step from purgatory a minute ago. The rest of you, turn your horses around with your knees. If you're not riding hired horses, they ought to do that much without feeling the bit. Turn your horses around. I like the looks of your backs better than your faces."

There was not a word of answer. They turned their nags obediently around. There they sat with five arms sticking into the air.

I made them dismount—the rear pair. Then I made them back up until they were near me. After that, I took their hands behind them and tied cords over them—tied them until they groaned.

"You pair of sapheads!" said I. "Sit down over there by that rock, will you—and don't make any noise—because I feel restless today. I feel mighty restless. Baldy, you're next!"

I tied Baldy with his own lariat, and I tied him well. I tied his hands tight behind him, and I tied his feet together under the belly of the bay.

Then I took an old envelope and wrote big on it:

> To everybody in general, and Dinsmore in particular:
> Dinsmore got the drop on me in Elmira. I want to find
> him. I ask him to come and find me, now. I'll meet him
> any afternoon between three and four in the Elmira Pass.
> This holds good for the next month.
>
> Leon Porfilo

I pinned that on the back of Baldy. Then I turned him loose. All that I wanted was to have the world see my message back to Dinsmore to let them know that I was waiting for him.

How that bay did sprint down the hill! There was a puff of trail dust, you might say, and then the bay and Baldy landed in the hollow of the valley below the mountain, and after that, they skimmed up the mountain on the other side. The bay was certainly signaling that he intended to get to that stable!

Then I went back to the other two. I didn't say a great deal, but they seemed to think that it was worth listening to. I told them that I had gone for seven years, letting people hound me through the mountains and not shooting back.

I told them that my next job was to find Dinsmore and kill him, but that in the meantime I intended to shoot, and to shoot to kill! If I met the pair of them again, they were dead men—on the street or in the mountains—it made no difference to me!

I think those fellows took it to heart. Then, because I hadn't the slightest fear that they would overtake the bay, I untied their hands and let them mount and ride back the way that they came.

21

ALL in all, I thought that this move of mine was a clever one and that it would reestablish me a great deal through the mountains; but the answer of Jeffrey Dinsmore was a crushing blow, because that rascal went into the office of the biggest newspaper in the capital city ten days later and called on the editor and introduced himself, and allowed the editor to photograph him, and dictated to the editor a long statement about various things.

It was a grand thing in the way of a scoop for that paper. I saw a copy of it and there were headlines across the front page three inches deep. Most of the rest of the front page was covered with pictures of the editor, and the editor's office where the terrible Dinsmore had appeared; and, in the center, surrounded with little pen sketches of Dinsmore in the act of shooting down a dozen men in various scenes, was a picture of Jeffrey— the picture which the editor had snapped of him.

It showed him, dapper and easy and smiling, smoking a cigar, and holding it up so that the camera could catch the name on it. That was a cigar which the editor, mentioning the fact proudly in his article, declared that he had given to the desperado.

Altogether, it was a great spread for Dinsmore, and the editor, and the newspaper, and a great fall for me. I understood afterward that the editor got three offers from other newspapers immediately afterward, and that his salary was doubled to keep him where he was.

He couldn't say too much about the affair.

Dinsmore had appeared through the window of his office, four stories above the street, at nine o'clock in the evening when most of the reporters were out at work on their stories and their copy. The editor of *The Eagle*, being busy at his desk, looked up just in time to see a dapper young man sliding through the window with a revolver pointed at the editorial head and the smiling face of Mr. Dinsmore behind the revolver.

So the editor, taking great pride in the fact that he did not put his hands into the air, turned around and from his tilted swivel chair asked Dinsmore what he would have.

"A good reputation!" said Dinsmore.

"From that point on," declared the editor in his article, "we got on very well together, because there is nothing like a good laugh to start an interview smoothly!"

They talked of a great many things. That editor's account of Dinsmore, his polished manners, his amiable smile, was so pleasant that it was a certainty no unprejudiced jury could ever be gathered in that county. If Dinsmore had murdered ten men the same night, he would have secured a hung jury on the whole butchery.

That editor was a pretty slick writer, when you come right down to it. He made Dinsmore out the most dashing young hero that ever galloped out of the pages of a book. It was almost a book that he wrote about him!

He declared that if Dinsmore were anything worse than an impulsive youngster who didn't know better, he, the editor, would confess that his editorial brain was not worth a damn, and that he had never been able to judge a man.

Of course, the chief point in the interview was Dinsmore's own account of his fight with me. That was the main matter, all the way through. Because Dinsmore had called at the editor's office in order to explain to the world why he did not ride back into the mountains in order to answer my challenge.

I won't put in any of the bunk with which that article was filled, where the editor kept exclaiming at Dinsmore and asking him how he dared to venture through the streets unmasked—and how he had been able to scale the sheer side of the building.

I leave out all of that stuff. I leave out, too, all that the editor had to say about Dinsmore's family—how old that family was—how rich the estate was—how good and grand and gentle and refined and soldierly and judgelike the father of Dinsmore had been. How beautiful, womanly, gentle, and Southern his mother had been. How Dinsmore himself seemed to combine in himself all of the good qualities of both of his parents.

"So that," said the editor, "I could not help feeling that what this young man was suffering from was an overplus of talents, of wealth, of social background. His hands had been filled so completely full since his childhood with all that other men hunger for, that it was no wonder he had turned aside from the ordinary courses of ordinary men. Alas, that he did not live in some more violent, more chivalric age! Then his sword and his shield would have won a name."

The editor rambled on like this for quite a spell. Not very good stuff, but good enough to do for a newspaper. Newsprint stuff has to be a bit raw and edgy in order to cut through the skin of the man who reads as he runs.

The whole sum of it was that Jeffrey Dinsmore was a hero, and that he was a little too good for this world of ours to appreciate.

Finally, Dinsmore told about me.

He had gone up into the mountains, to Elmira, he said, because he wanted to find me where I would be at home among my own friends—because he didn't want to take me at a disadvantage.

"But why did you go in the first place?" asked the editor.

"I'm rather ashamed to confess it," said Dinsmore, with an apologetic smile, "but when I heard of all of the atrocities of this fellow Porfilo, and how he had butchered men—not in fair fight but rather because he loved butchery—and how helpless the law had proved against him—well, sir, I decided that I couldn't stand it, and so I decided that I should have to get up into those mountains, and there I'd meet Mr. Porfilo hand to hand and kill him if I could!"

The editor couldn't let Dinsmore say any more than this without breaking in to comment and praise Dinsmore and show that he was like some knight out of the Middle Ages riding through the dark and unknown mountains to find the dragon.

Well, as I said before, that editor was a good editor, but what he had to say began to get under my skin. I looked again at his picture. He had a thin face and he wore glasses.

I wonder why it is that spectacles always make me pity a man?

Dinsmore went on to tell how he had met me, and how I had whirled on him and fired the first shot, while he was waiting to talk. Well, that was all very true. Twenty people could swear to the truth of that, but not one of them had the sense to know that I had fired wide.

Then he said that the firing of that first shot showed him that I was a coward and a bully—a coward because I was a bully, and a bully because I was so very willing to take advantage of another man who only wanted to stand up and fight fair and square.

I couldn't read farther in the paper at that time. I had to walk up and down for a time to cool off. Then I looked hurriedly through the paper to try to find a statement by Dick Lawton, or somebody like that, defending me. But there wasn't any such statement. Only, on the fourth and fifth pages of the paper there were opposite accounts of the pair of us.

On one page there was the story of Dinsmore, with little illustrations inset, showing the great big house that he had been born and raised in; and how Dinsmore looked in his rowing squad at college in the East, and how Dinsmore looked in his year of captaincy of the football team, when his quarterback run had smashed the Orange to smithereens in the last two seconds of the game.

It showed how he looked on a polo pony—and what the five girls looked like that he had been engaged to at various times in his life—and how he looked standing beside his father, Senator Dinsmore—and how he looked arm in arm with his dear old mother—and how he looked when he rode the famous hunter, Tippety Splatchet, to victory in the Yarrum Cup.

Well, there was a lot of stuff like that, with the history of his life written alongside of it.

On the opposite page it showed the house I was born in in Mendez, and there was a picture of the butcher shop that my father had owned. There was a picture of myself, too, showing my broad face and heavy jaw and cheekbones.

"Like a prizefighter of the more brutal kind!" Dinsmore had said.

But there was only a dull account of my affairs—"butcheries," the editor called them. I was made out pretty black, and there was not a word of truth said to defend me. When I got through, I wanted to kill that editor!

I went back to Dinsmore's account. He told how he had decided that I was a swine, and then he had fired after my second shot, and the bullet had wounded me in the head—after which I spurred the mule away down the street as fast as I could!

There were plenty of witnesses who could prove that the bullet stunned me and that I did not begin to flee of my own free will. But of course none of their statements was wanted. Nothing but the word of the hero!

As for coming back into the mountains, Mr. Dinsmore said that after standing in the street of Elmira and firing shot after shot "into the air" and watching me ride "like mad" to get away from danger, he had no wish to come back to find me again.

He said that he felt he had fairly well demonstrated that the bully Porfilo was a coward at heart. He, Dinsmore, feared a coward more than he did any brave man. For a coward was capable of sinking to the lowest devices! He knew quite well that if he accepted the invitation to face the challenge of Leon Porfilo, he would be waylaid and murdered!

So much for his opinion of Leon Porfilo.

Now, as I read this letter, such a madness came over me that I trembled like a frightened girl. Then I steadied myself and sat with my head in my hands for a long time, thinking, wondering.

But what I made out at last was rather startling.

For it was declared in the paper that Mr. Dinsmore had said that he was in the capital city because he was then engaged in the task of drifting himself rapidly East and that the West perhaps would see him never again.

But, as I read this statement, I could not help remembering that I had seen him once before in the capital city, and I remembered, also, all of the nasty thoughts that had gone through my mind at that time.

22

PERHAPS I should hardly call them "thoughts," when they were really no more than premonitions, based upon the prettiness of the governor's wife and the thoughtfulness of the governor—and Jeffrey Dinsmore, gentleman and gunman, climbing the back fence of the governor's house at full speed.

I considered all of those things, and the more that I thought of them, the more convinced was I that the celebrated Dinsmore was *not* passing through the capital city—certainly not until he had seen beautiful young Mrs. Shay.

So I turned the matter back and forth in my mind for three whole days, because I am not one of those who can make hair-trigger decisions and follow them. The result of all of my debating was that I saddled Roanoke and began to work some of his fat off by shooting him eastward.

We came through the upper mountains, and I had my second view of the lowlands beneath me, silvered and beautified in evening mist. Once more I reached the lowest fringing of trees in the foothills and slept through a day. Once more I started with the dusk and drove away toward the city. Not the city, now! But in my mind there were in it only three people: William P. Shay, his wife, and Jeffrey Dinsmore.

Naturally I passed that last name over my tongue more frequently than I did the other two. Every time it left the acid taste of hate. I was hungry— hungry to get at him. Not that I feared him less than I had been fearing him. Simply that my hatred was too intense a driving force to let me stay away from him.

On the second night I was on the edge of the town, as before, and in the very same hollow where I had left Roanoke before, I left him this time. Only that I did not keep a saddle on him because I was hardly capable of doing all of my work in a single evening in the town.

I hid the saddle in the crotch of a lofty tree, and with the saddle I left my rifle and all my trappings except a little stale pone, hard almost as iron, but the easiest and most compact form, almost, in which a person can transport nutriment. I tucked that stony bread into my pockets. I had two heavy Colts and a sheath knife stowed handy in my clothes. Then I was ready to take my chances in the city again.

I walked in by the same route, too, except that when I came through the deserted outskirts of the city I began to bear away to the right, because I had a fairly accurate idea of where the governor's house was located. As a matter of fact, I brought up only two blocks away from it, and presently I came in behind that house.

I had made up my mind before, and I put my determination into action at once. The house was fenced, behind, with nine feet of boards as I have said before. But I managed to grip my hands on the upper edge and swing my body well over them by the first effort. I dropped close to the ground and squatted bunched there to look over the lay of the land and see what might be stirring near me.

There was not a soul. The screen door of the back porch slammed and I heard someone run down the steps. However, whoever it was kept on around the house by the narrow cement walk. I heard the heels of that man click away to dimness; I heard the rattle of the old front gate, and then I started for the corner stables.

Once that barn had been much bigger. One could tell by the chopped-off shoulders of the barn that it had once extended wide, but now perhaps it was the carriage shed which was trimmed away, and the barn that remained stood stiff and tall and prim as a village church.

I didn't care for that. I slipped through the open door of it and stood in the dark, smelling and listening—smelling for hay and finding the sweetness of it—and listening for the breathing of horse or cow—and not hearing a whisper!

So I went a little farther in and lighted a match. It was exactly as I had prayed. There was a heap of very old hay in one end of the mow—perhaps it had been there for years, untouched. The dry, dusty floor of the horse stalls showed me that they had not been occupied for an equally long time. This was what I wanted. I decided that people would not readily look for Leon Porfilo in the governor's barn—no matter how imaginative they might be!

I was a little tired, so I curled up in that haymow and slept until a frightened mouse squeaked, half an inch from my ear. Then I sat up and snorted the dust out of my nose and nearly choked myself to keep from sneezing. When I passed out into the night, I found that the lights were still burning in the Shay house.

There was an inquisitive spirit stirring in my bones that evening. The first thing I did was to remove my boots and my socks. I figured that my calloused feet would stand about all the wear that I would give them that night.

I left boots and socks in the barn. I left my coat with them. I took all the hard pone and the sheath knife and one revolver out of my clothes. Then I rolled up my trousers to the knees. By that time I was about as free as a man could wish, except he were absolutely naked. I felt free and easy and *right*. I could fight, now, or I could run. Also, I could investigate that tall old house. I guessed that there was enough in it to be worth investigation.

First I took a slant down to the window of the governor's little private room. I skirted around through the lilac bushes, first of all. When I had made sure that none of those infernal detectives were hanging about to make a background for me, I drew myself up on the window sill and surveyed the scene inside.

It was what I suspected. That was the governor's after-hours workshop—

and I suppose that he spent more hours there than in his office. Here he was, with a secretary on one side taking shorthand notes, and beyond the door there was the purring of a typewriter where another secretary was pouring out copy of some sort. Governor Shay was just the same man in worried looks that I had known before.

I spent no time there. He was not the man I wanted. First I skirted around the house and peered into other rooms until I made out that Mrs. Shay was not in any of them. Then I climbed up to a lighted window in the second story. It was easy to get to it, because there was a little side porch holding up a roof just beneath it.

I curled up on that roof and looked inside. There I found what I wanted!

Yes, it was more than I could have asked for! There were all of my suspicions turned into a lightning flash before my eyes! There was Mrs. Shay, and, standing before her was that celebrated young man of good breeding, Jeffrey Dinsmore, doing his very best to kiss her.

But if he were masterful with men, he was not able to handle this slender girl. She did not speak loudly, of course. Her words hardly carried to me at the window. But what she said was:

"None of this, Jeffrey! Not a bit of it!"

He stepped back from her. I've seen a man step back like that when a hard punch has been planted under his heart. That was the way Jeffrey Dinsmore stepped away. The pain in his face went along with the rest of the picture. He was a badly confused young man, I should say. That was not what he had expected.

Mrs. Shay was angry, too. She didn't tremble; she didn't change color; she didn't change her voice, either. She wasn't like any girl I had ever seen before in that way. But one could feel the anger just oozing out of her, so to speak. Jeffrey began to bite his lip.

"I didn't think that you would use me quite so lightly," said she. "I didn't expect that!"

He said: "I am a perfect fool. But seeing you only once in weeks and long weeks—and thinking of you, and breathing of you like sweet fire all the time I am away—why, it went like flame into my brain, just now. I won't ask you to forgive me, though, until you've had a chance to try to understand."

He said it quietly, with his eyes fixed at her feet. While he stood like that, I saw a flash of light in her eyes, and I saw a ghost of a smile look in and out at the corner of her mouth. I knew that she really loved him—or thought she did.

"I ought to have time to think, then," said she. "I'm afraid that I'll have to use it. I am just a little angry, Jeffrey. I don't want to spoil our few meetings with anger. It's a dusty thing and an unclean thing, don't you think so?"

He kept his head bowed, frowning, and saying nothing. This wasn't like my mental picture of him. I thought he would be all fire and passion and lots of eloquence—buckets full of it! Then I saw. He was taking another role. He was being terse and very plain—that being the way to impress her, he thought.

"So you'd better go," said she.

He answered: "I'll go outside—but I'll wait—in the hope that you'll change your mind."

"Good-by," said she.

I expected him to come for the window. Instead, he opened the door behind him and quickly stepped out into a hall!

I was down from the roof in a moment, and I began to rove around the house, waiting for him to appear. For five or ten minutes I waited. Then I realized that there must be more ways of getting in and out of that house than I had imagined. There might be half a dozen cellar exits and ways of getting from the second story to the cellar.

It was a time for fast thinking, and this time I was able to think fast, heaven be praised!

What I did was to swing up to the roof of the porch and get back to the window where I had witnessed this little drama. Mrs. Shay was lying on a couch on the farther side of the room, and her face was buried in a cushion. Her shoulders were quivering a little. However, I had no pity for her, because I was remembering the face of the governor.

I simply slid through the window and stood up against the wall. The floor creaked a couple of times under my weight.

"Yes?" said she.

I suppose she thought that it was someone at the door, tapping.

"There is no one there," said I.

23

OH, she was game! She didn't jump and squeal, but she looked around slowly at me, fighting herself so hard, that when I saw her eyes they were as cool as could be. But when she managed to recognize me, she went white in a sickening way, and stood up from the couch and crowded back into the corner of the room. She said nothing, but she couldn't keep her eyes from flashing to the door.

I said: "I have that door covered, and I'll *keep* it covered. No help is coming to you. You're in here helpless, and you'll do what I tell you to do."

Still she was silent, setting her teeth hard.

I went on: "First of all, I'm going to wait here to make out whether or not Mr. Dinsmore was outside and saw me come through the window. If he saw me, I think that he's man enough to come after me."

There was a flash of something in her eyes. A sort of assurance, I think, that it would be a bad moment for me when her hero showed up.

But still she wouldn't talk. Oh, she was loaded to the brim with courage. She was meeting me with her eyes all the time. I liked her for that. But that was not enough. There was something else for which I hated her. It was boiling in me.

I went on to explain: "When I saw him leave the room, I went down to the yard and tried to find him as he came out of the house. But he must have vanished into a mist."

At that the words came out quickly from her: "Were you watching when he left the room?"

"Yes," said I, and I looked down to the floor, because I didn't care to watch her embarrassment. But, for a moment, I could hear her breathing. It was not a comfortable moment, but sooner or later, I had to let her understand what I knew.

"If Mr. Dinsmore—" said she, and stopped there.

"If he doesn't come back," said I, "I don't know what I'll do—yes, I have an idea that might pass pretty well!"

So we waited there. That silence began to tell on her and it told on me, too, partly because I was waiting for Dinsmore's step or voice and partly that just being with that girl in that room was a strain.

It was not that she awed me because of the fact that she was the governor's wife, but just because she was a lady, and this was her room, and I had not a right in it! It was full of femininity, that room. It fairly breathed it. From the Japanese screen in the corner to a queer sort of a vase of blue stuck in front of a bit of gold sort of tapestry—if you know what I mean.

Well, I stood in the corner of that room, with the ceiling about an inch above my head, and as I stood there, I was conscious, I'll tell a man, that my feet and legs were bare to the knees from my rolled-up trousers—and I knew that my shirt was rolled up, too, to the elbows—and that my hat was off and that the wind had blown my hair to a heap—and that I was sun-blackened almost to the tint of an Indian.

I was a ruffian. I had a ruffian's reputation, and yonder was the governor's wife looking like the sort of a girl that painters have in their minds when they want to do something extra and knock your eye out.

No, I wasn't extra happy as I stood there, and neither was she. The pair of us were waiting for the sound of his feet.

Then she said: "Do you think that I'll keep silent when I hear him—if he comes?"

"You may do what you want," said I. "But if you make a sound, he won't be the only one that hears!"

No doubt about it, a gentleman couldn't have said such a thing. Well, a gentleman I cannot pretend to be!

I said: "You'll make no noise. You'll sit tight where you are."

So she looked quietly up to me and studied me with grave eyes. How cool she was! Yet I suppose that this situation was more terrible to her than a frowning battery of guns pointed in her direction.

"Do you imagine," said she at last, "that I shall permit you to murder him?"

I answered her quickly: "Do you imagine that I wish to murder him?"

Her eyes widened at me.

"I understand," said I. "Dinsmore has filled your mind with the same lies which he has published in other places. It is going to be my pleasure to show you that I am not a sneak and a coward, even if I have to bully you now—for a moment!"

Then she said: "I almost believe you!"

She looked me up and down, from my tousled head of hair and my broad, ugly, half-Indian features, to my naked toes gripping at the floor.

"Yes," said she, "I do believe you!"

It was a great deal to me. It almost filled my heart as much as that first moment when Mike O'Rourke said that she loved me.

"But if he has not seen you? If he is not coming?" said Mrs. Shay.

"Then you will make a signal and bring him here to me!"

She shook her head. "What would happen then?"

"You guess what will happen," said I. "I have no mercy for you. I have seen the governor. I think he is a good man and a kind man."

"He is," said she, and dropped her face suddenly into her hands.

"If you will not call Dinsmore back, I shall go to the governor."

"You will not!" gasped she, not looking up.

"I shall!"

Then she shook her head. "I have no right for the sake of my own reputation—or what—"

"Listen to me," said I, standing suddenly over her so that my shadow swallowed her, "if you speak of rights, have you a right to touch Governor Shay? This thing would kill him, I suppose."

She threw back her head and struck her hands together. Just that, and not a sound from her. But, I knew, that was her surrender.

Then she stood up and went to the window, and I saw her raise and lower the shade of the window twice. Then she returned to her place, very white, very sick, and leaned against the wall.

"I am sorry," said I.

But she made a movement of the hand, disclaiming all my apology.

"There will be a death," said she huskily. "No matter what else happens, I shall have caused a death."

"You will not," said I. "Because after two men such as Dinsmore and I have met, we could not exist without another meeting. Will you believe that, and that our second meeting must come and bring a death?"

She cast only one glance at me, and then I suppose that there was enough of the sinister in my appearance to give her the assurance that I meant what I said.

"Because," I went on, "one of us is a cur and a liar. I hope that heaven knows which one by the fight! You are going to be standing by!"

"I!"

"You are going to be standing by," I insisted.

She dropped her head once more with a little gasp, and so the heavy silence returned over us again. It held on through moment after moment. I thought that it would never end.

Perspiration began to roll down my forehead. When I looked to the girl, I could see that her whole body was trembling. So was mine, for that matter.

But, at last, no louder than the padding of a cat's foot, we heard something in the hall, and we did not have to ask. It was Dinsmore! As if he had been a great cat, I could not avoid dreading him. I wished myself suddenly a thousand miles from that place.

His tap was barely audible; and the voice of Mrs. Shay was not more than a whisper. The door opened quickly, and lightly. There was Dinsmore standing in the doorway with a face flushed and his eyes making lightnings of happiness until his glance slipped over the bowed figure of the girl and across to me in the corner, dressed like a sailor in a tropical storm.

Then he shut the door behind him as softly as he had opened it.

He stood looking from one of us to the other, and there was a fighting set to his handsome face, although the gaiety and the good humor did not go out of it for a moment. I felt, then, that he was invincible. Because I saw that he was a man unlike the rest of the world. He was a man who *loved* danger. It was the food which he ate, and the breath in his nostrils.

He only said: "I thought it was only a social call; I didn't know that there was work to be done. But I am very happy, either way!"

24

EVEN the sang-froid of this demidevil, however, could not last very long; for when his lady lifted her face, he saw enough in it to make him grave, and he said to me:

"You could not stand and fight, but you could stay to talk, Porfilo!"

Then I smiled on this man, for somehow that touch of malice and that lie before the girl gave me a power over him, I felt.

So I said to him: "We are going down to the garden, the three of us. The moon is up, now, and there will be plenty of light."

For the electricity in the room was not strong enough to turn the night black. It was all silvered over with moonshine.

"What's the trick, Porfilo?" said Jeffrey Dinsmore. "Are you going to take me down where you have confederates waiting? Am I to be shot in the back while I face you?"

"Jeffrey!" said his lady under her breath.

It made him jerk up his head.

"Do *you* believe this scoundrel?"

Her curiosity seemed even stronger than her fear; for she sat up on the couch and looked from me to Dinsmore and back again to me, weighing us, judging us as well as she was able.

"Every moment," said she, "I believe him more and more!"

"Will you go down to the garden with us?" said he. "Will you go down to watch the fight?"

"Leon Porfilo will make me go," said she.

"He and you," said Dinsmore, "seem to have reached a very perfect understanding of one another!"

"You will lead the way," said I.

"Are you commanding?" said he with a sudden snarl, and the devil jumped visibly into his face. So that there was a gasp from the girl.

"As for me," said I, "I had as soon kill you here as in the garden. I am only thinking of the governor's wife!"

He bit his lip, turned on his heel, and led the way out of the room. I saw at once what the secret of his goings and comings was. This was a dusty little private hallway—and it connected with what was, apparently, an unused stairway. Perhaps, at one time, this had been the servants' stairs and then had been blocked off in some alteration of the building.

At any rate, it led us winding down to the black heart of the cellar, where I laid a hand on the shoulder of Dinsmore and held him close in front of me with a revolver pressed into the small of his back.

"This is fair play, you murderer!" said he.

"Listen to me," said I. "I know you, Dinsmore. Do you think that your lies about me have *convinced* me?"

This was only a whisper from either of us, not loud enough to meet the ear of the girl.

We wound out of the cellar and stood suddenly behind the house. There was a very bright moon with a broad face, though not so keen as her light in the high mountains. Enough to see by, however. Enough to kill by.

"Now," said Dinsmore, turning quickly on me, "how is this thing to be done?"

I could see that his hand was trembling to get at his gun. He was killing me with his thoughts every instant.

He added: "How is this to be done, with a poor woman dragged in to watch me kill you!"

"I needed her," said I, "to make sure that you would fight like a gentleman. Also, I needed her to see that, when I kill you, I shall kill you in a fair fight. Otherwise she might have some illusion about it. She might think that her hero had died by treachery and trickery. Besides, I wanted her here because, as the time comes closer, she will have a better chance of seeing that you are a cur or a rat! The devil keeps boiling up in you continually. She has never seen that before."

"Will you step back among the shrubbery?" said he to her.

"If I go," said she, "I shall only be turning my back on something that I ought to see."

"You will see me dispose of a murderer, and that is all."

"If he were a murderer, he could have shot you in the back—and the people who heard the sound of the shot would have found you lying dead— in my room—at night. The governor's wife!"

"You remember *him*, now!" said Dinsmore, his voice shaken.

"I remember him, now," said she, "and I hope that I shall always remember him a little—if not enough!"

He clapped his hand across his breast and bowed to her. "Madame," said he, "I see that you are cold."

"Are you spiteful, Jeffrey?"

"Spiteful?"

He stepped backward, after that, and he faced me with a convulsed face. I could see, now, why she had been shrinking farther and farther away from him. She was having deep glimpses of the truth about this gentleman of good breeding, and of an old family.

"Are you ready, Porfilo?" said he quietly.

"Ah, God have mercy—" I heard the girl whisper.

But I saw that she did not turn her head away. No, not even then.

"Do you know the time?" said I.

"I do not," answered Dinsmore.

"Do you, Mrs. Shay?"

"It is nearly ten—it is almost the hour."

"I have heard the big town clock," said I. "At the first stroke, then, Dinsmore!"

"Good!" said he. "This ought to be in a play. At what distance, my friend?"

"Two steps—or twenty," said I. "You can measure the distance yourself."

"Jeffrey!" cried the poor lady. "It is not going to happen—you—"

"It means something one way or the other," said I. "It has to be decided. There is a witness needed."

Now, as I said this, I looked aside, and I saw, through the shadows of the trees and dimly outlined at the edge of the moonlight, the tall, strong figure of a man. I hardly know how I knew him; but suddenly I saw that it was the governor's self who stood there.

It made my heart jump, at first, but instantly I knew that he had not come on the moment. He had been there from the first—or at least for a space of time great enough to have heard enough to explain the entire scene to him. Yet that did not make my nerves the weaker.

After all, it was his right to know. I really thanked heaven for it, and that he should realize, if I died in this fight, it was partly for his sake as well as for my own. Or, if the other fell, it was also for his sake as well as for my own!

Then, crashing across my mind, came the clang of the town bell, and I snatched at the revolver.

It caught in my clothes and only came out with a great ripping noise. I saw the gun flash in the hand of Dinsmore and heard its explosion half drown the scream of Mrs. Shay.

But he missed! Almost for the first time in his life, he missed. I saw the horror and the fear dart into his face even before I fired.

He was shot fairly between the eyes, turned on his heel as though to walk away, and fell dead upon his face.

The shadow among the shrubs reached him and jerked him upon his back. It was the governor. He did not need to tell me what to do, for I had already scooped up the fainting body of Mrs. Shay and carried it toward the house.

There, close to the wall, he took her from my arms.

"Ride, Porfilo!" he said. "I shall keep my promise. God be with you!"

But I did not ride. I went back and stood beside the body of the fallen man until the servants came tumbling out of the house and swarmed about me. I tried to get one of them to come to me and take me a prisoner and accept my gun. But they were too afraid. One of them had recognized my face and shouted my name, and that kept the rest away.

At length, one of the secret-service men who were presumed to keep a constant guard about the house of the governor, came to me and took my gun.

Then he marched me down the main street of the town to the jail. A crowd gathered. Perhaps it would have mobbed me, but it heard the great news that the brilliant Dinsmore, the great gunfighter, was dead, and that numbed them.

25

WELL, when the doors of the jail closed behind me and when I was hitched to irons in my cell, I decided that I had been a fool and that the wild life in the mountains had been better than such an end to it. But when Mike O'Rourke came up from the southland and looked at me through those bars, I changed my mind. After all, it was better to live or to die with clean hands.

I began to discover that I had friends, too. I discovered it partly by the number of the letters that poured in to me. I discovered it partly by the amount of money which was suddenly subscribed to my defense.

But I did not want a talented lawyer at a high price. What I felt was that the facts of my life, honestly and plainly written down, would be enough to save me and to free me. I wanted to trust to that. So I had Father McGuire, who had been my guardian up to the time that I broke jail and became an outlaw, and who was one of the first to appear, select a plain, middle-aged man.

He was staggered at the fine fee offered him. He was staggered also by the importance of this case which was being thrust into his hands. So he came to me and sat down in the cell with me and looked at me with mild, frightened eyes, like a good man at a devil.

He wanted to assure me that he knew this case would make him a fortune by the notoriety which it would give him. He wanted to assure me that his wife begged him with tears to accept the task. But he had come in person to assure me that he was afraid his conscience would not let him take a case which, he was afraid—

I interrupted him there by asking him to hear my story. It took four hours for the telling, what with his notes, and his questions. Before the story was five minutes old, he said that he needed a shorthand reporter. There was no question about him wanting the case after that!

He took down that entire report of my life, from my own lips. A very detailed report. I talked for those four hours as fast as I could and turned out words by the thousand. When it was all ended, he said: "I only wish to heaven that I could make people see the truth of this, as you have told it to me! But seven years have built up a frightful prejudice!"

"Give it to the newspapers," I told him.

He was staggered by that, at first. To give away his case into the hands of the prosecution? But I told him that I would swear to every separate fact in that statement. So, finally, he did what I wanted, and against his will.

I suppose you have seen that statement, or at least heard of it. The editor of the local paper came to see me and begged me for a little intimate personal story to lead off with—an interview. I asked him if he were the man who wrote up the statement of Dinsmore.

He said that he was and apologized and told me that he realized since I had beaten and killed Dinsmore in a fair fight, that there was nothing in what Dinsmore had said. He begged me to give him a chance at writing a refutation. Well, I simply told him at once that he did not need to ask twice. He was the right man in the right place, and I told him to do his editorial best, to give me journalistic justice.

He did! He began with the beginning and he finished with the end. He made me into a hero, a giant, almost a saint. I laughed until there were tears in my eyes when I read that story. Mike O'Rourke came and cried over it in real earnest and vowed that it was only the truth about me.

However, that editor was a great man, in his own way. He didn't really lie. He simply put little margins of embroidery around the truth. Although sometimes the margins were so deep that no one could see the whole cloth in the center!

That great write-up he gave me saved my skin, at the trial.

But while the trial was half finished, another bolt fell from the blue when the governor announced that, no matter what the jury did, he intended to give me a pardon after the trial was over.

From that point I had the governor's weight of authority so heavily telling in my favor that the trial became a sort of triumphal procession for me. There was no real struggle, for public opinion had begun to heroize me in the most foolish way in the world. I was still a prisoner when people began to ask for autographs.

You know how it goes when the newspapers once decide to let a man live. The jury itself would probably have been lynched if it had so much as decided to divide on my case. They were only out for five minutes.

When they brought in a verdict of acquittal, the real joke about that matter was that they were right and not simply sentimental, because as I think you people will agree who have followed my history down to this point, I had not as yet committed a real crime. The cards had simply been stacked against me.

Three great factors fought in my behalf—the governor's word first—the honesty of my stupid lawyer—and the genius of that crooked editor! I don't know which was the more important. But what affected me more than the acquittal, was the face of Mike O'Rourke in the crowd which cheered the verdict.

TROUBLE TRAIL

1

"CHERRY," said I, "you are a nice girl, and all that; but, curse it, I wish that you would talk."

That was what I said as we came over the rim of the hills, and a blast of sand came up on the wind and cut into our eyes. I blinked out some of it, and wiped out some, and seen that Cherry had just shook her head a little and smiled a bit. That was her way, uncomplaining and cheerful, no matter hardly what happened. But when the sand was blinked out, and a tear or two was running down my face because of the grit that had cut into my eyeballs, I looked across the desert, and there was nothing between me and the edge of the sky.

That was when I spoke up rough and sudden and mean to Cherry, poor girl. Now, after her and me had marched so many miles with the sheriff ding-dong-ing at our heels, and after he had give up in despair, or because he knew that the desert would kill us even if his bullets couldn't, after all that had passed behind us, you would say that a gent would speak more kind to a lady.

But I tell you that the desert will eat right into the heart of a man and give him no decency, sometimes. And other times it will expand you, sort of, so that your heart gets as big as this side of heaven and the other side, too.

That day was one of the bad ones. There was only one quart of blood-warm water left in the big canteen, and I knew that that would have to do for her and me. But when we topped the ridge, I had a hope that there might be a blueness of mountains somewhere off in front of us; and where there is mountains, there is sure to be water, somewhere, too.

Well, there we were on the top of the ridge, and all that I had seen before me in the way of hope was the blind face of that desert, mostly gray, with a streak of smoke, where the greasewood growed in the hollows, here and there, and a black patch now and again, but mostly only grayness, between us and the edge of the sky.

No water out there!

I turned around and looked behind me. Somewhere in the rear of me the sheriff and his boys were sweating and damning and wishing for the hide of Larry Dickon. But it wasn't the sheriff and all his guns that kept me from turning back. It was only because, having got across that stretch of misery, it was terrible hard to go back into the heart of it again. This stuff that lay ahead looked worse—maybe it *was* worse. But anyway, it was new. And I like newness, even in a desert. There was no hope behind me. No hope of water, I mean. And I would of bet my money that there was no hope ahead of me. But still, there was a chance. A hundred to one shot.

Well, that is better than nothing.

Only, when I faced forward, I couldn't help pouring out my meanness, and there was nothing but Cherry near me to listen, so I give it to her.

"Yes," said I, as we started down the long slope, "you got your points, and I ain't the man to deny them. You're pretty, Cherry. I admit that. You're mighty pretty."

She just went on, with her eyes fixed off toward the skyline. Oh, I might be downhearted, but there was no beating Cherry. She would always have hope. She never was done! That light was never out of her eyes.

And seeing her courage, it sort of made me meaner and madder.

"You're pretty," I went on at her, "and, on the other hand, you're proud, Cherry. You're too damn proud, and I'm here to tell you about it. Yes, you're too damn proud. You're set up, you are. And maybe the thing that has turned your head is the way that folks have always set their caps for you. It's the number of gents that have broke their hearts for you. It's the way that they've fell in love at first sight. Is that what's made you so damn high-headed?"

That, you would think, would be enough for a gent to say. But it didn't hold me. I looked at her, and I looked at the desert; and the wave of heat that came up from it, it seared into my face and burned the tears dry in one second.

Oh, it was bitter hot! The leather band of my sombrero was all fire. And there was fire showering down in little flakes and burning through my shirt at the shoulders, where the shadow of the brim of my back didn't spread. And the sweat kept leaking out of me, and turning to salt the minute that it appeared, with no halfway chance to cool me off. And the backs of my hands, they blistered with the heat.

What shape was Cherry in?

Why, she was worse than me. She went along with her dainty steps; and her gay way, but I could see that her knees were sagging; and she stumbled, when a little hummock come into her way.

"Or is it your good looks that have set you up so much, and your little feet that you're always looking down at them?" says I to her. "Will you answer me that?"

No, she wouldn't answer. Not her.

There was times, in the past, when she got rambunctious and showed bad temper and foolishness; but that was always when things had been going too easy with us, and when we had stayed over for a long time in one place, and then, when it come to take the trail again, Cherry could be as mean as any girl in the world.

But when the pinch come, and the long grind of the miles had to be got over, she never faltered.

I suppose that it was thinking of the beauty of Cherry, and wondering how it was that God ever should of trusted anything so good, so beautiful, and so wonderful to an ordinary, good-for-nothing, low-down gent like me—it was thinking of that, I suppose, that made me all of the worse. And I begun to hate myself pretty hard, and love Cherry more than ever, if that was possible. But the more that I loved her, the meaner I had to talk, somehow.

Maybe you have been the same way yourself, sometimes?

Never with a lady, you say!

Ah, well, son, that's because you ain't married to one of them.

But when you have took one and give up all the rest, till death do us part, and all that, why, it gets different.

We went on into that desert until I felt that the ground was wavering and staggering in front of us, and poor Cherry could hardly breathe, so that I knew that the time had come for us to finish off the water.

One quart between the two of us!

Why, that sounds like a good deal to you, sitting cool and easy in your chair, with the window open beside you, reading this here history of misery. But I can tell you, man, that it's different in the places where a quarter of a inch of rain falls every other year, and even the cactus gets yellow and sick to look at, and the sand draws the moisture out of the soles of your shoes, until they begin to buckle and warp.

A mighty *lot* different, and believe you me!

Well, as I was saying, I seen that the time had come to use up the last of the water, because my tongue was swelling so much and getting so painful that it was hard for me even to talk mean to Cherry.

She seen me pull out the canteen, and she stopped short, and looked at me with a bloodshot, wistful eye. Well, I treated myself to one little swig at that canteen. Then I got down and first of all I eased up the cinches of the saddle so that Cherry could breathe a mite easier, and I moistened my hand with a few drops of the water and I used it to wipe the sand out of her flaring, red nostrils. And her ears went forward to thank me for that bit of moisture—that God blessed mare!

And you could see that she was hankering after the water bad enough to eat the metal of the canteen! But she wouldn't show no sign of it.

No, sir, she would act contented, and as if she didn't wish or ask for anything more in the line of drinkables. But she shook her head and raised it, and looked out at the horizon as brave as you please, as much as to say: "You hop into the saddle again, Larry, and I'll sure fetch you to good water,

clean water, running oceans of it, and there we'll drink till we can't hold
no more, and then we'll lie down and we'll roll in it, and we'll laugh in it,
and wash in it, and wish for nothing else in the world!"

That was what she seemed to say.

I put my arm around her neck.

"Cherry, darling," said I, "you get the rest of the water that's in this here
canteen. It's all to you, and you're mighty welcome. And if there was a
gallon of it, it would do me a lot of good to see you have it all."

I opened up the canteen, and when she seen what was coming she raised
her head, and I let her hold the neck of the bottle in her teeth, which was
a trick that she and me had between us, and she drank down that water,
every drop, and I heard it gurgle.

Yes, sir, it done me as much good as if I'd poured it all down my own
throat; and when I got back onto her back, right away, to show me how
grateful she was, she wanted to start off at a gallop, but I slowed her down
to a walk, because there is only one way to go across the desert, and that
is the slow way, you can be sure!

So, on at a walk we went, and always that horizon stayed at just the same
distance, and there was no change in it until, along late the afternoon,
some blueness began to roll up in it.

Yes, I knew that they was hills. But a long way off! No man could guess
how far they were away.

I seen that there was only one thing to pray for, and that was that the
night would come soon and bring us freshness and coolness.

We would have to keep plodding along.

I got down out of the saddle. I loosened the cinches until they sagged
an inch beneath Cherry's belly. Then I started walking along beside her.
I was pretty far gone, but she was wobbly, too. And so we staggered across
the burning sand and wished and wished for the night.

2

NIGHT came by steps, very slow. And when the darkness arrived it wasn't
any help. The ground was still hot as the top of a stove, and a burning
wind cut right into our faces. It swelled my tongue up immediate and made
me open my mouth a little to breathe, and the minute that I had to open
my mouth it was as though ashes and lye was poured down my nostrils
and my throat.

Only the darkness was good and easy on the eyes, and after a while I
went along with my right elbow hooked over the horn of the saddle, and

Cherry Pie taking most of my weight and all of the responsibility of getting us to water.

She was too weak, now, to carry me. But she could sort of drag me along as long as I could keep my legs swinging. Now and then she would hit a hummock and sag right down almost to the ground, her legs had turned off so weak. And once I stumbled on rocks and knocked myself out with a whack on the back of my head. And when I came to, there was the hot breath of Cherry Pie in my face, and I seen her standing with her legs braced out wide, right over me.

If that had been the death of me, she would never of left to go on and find water. She would of stuck by me until the thirst killed her in terrible torments.

Hunger, you get used to that, after a time. But thirst—well, it never lets up on you till you get delirious. It's like a combination of being choked together with burning up.

Maybe you understand what I mean?

I got hold of the stirrup leather and finally I pulled myself up and hooked my arm over the pommel of the saddle and Cherry Pie and me went along, wabbling and weaving through the dark.

Not that I had any hope, but because, with my tongue bleeding and paining so much, and my lungs filled with cinders, all that I wished for was to die good and quick, or get delirious, so that I would have no wits to know how much I was being tortured.

Sometimes I wondered why Cherry didn't kick me away from her and go on to water, if there was any near to us. Any mustang would of served you that way. But not Cherry Pie. And when my senses brightened, now and then, I would always see her nodding and plugging away. And when I spoke, her ears would always prick up. And finally, I couldn't speak any more, but just groaned, and still that was enough to make her prick up her ears.

Now, after a million years of hell fire, I felt her tugging along as though she was trying to get away from me. And I opened my eyes and looked ahead of me and seen something that made me think that I was sure turned crazy—because there was the moon sailing along *right under my feet!* I closed my eyes again and waited for the wits to steady and clear, but when I looked again, there I seen that it was just the same thing.

And finally it hit me like a hammer blow.

It was a broad-faced pool of water with the clouds and the moon blowing across it!

Then my feet went plump, plump! into muck, and reeds rattled, waist high, and then there was a little strip of clean white sand laid down like silver by the edge of that water, and I fell on it with my face in the ripples.

We drank, and we rested, and we drank again.

We rolled and we swam in it.

We danced and we played in it.

And I threw water into the face of Cherry Pie, and she loved it and come wagging her head at me.

And—oh, well, it was a grand night.

After a time, the pain went out of my tongue, but when I talked to Cherry there was still a good deal of discomfort, and I sounded like a gent that had lost his palate.

But finally I got together wood and made me a fire, good and plenty big, because I knew that there was no danger of the sheriff ever cutting across that desert. No, that was the reason that he had turned back, because he knew this country a lot better than I did. And now the best that he could manage was to just wire around to the other side and warn the folks around there that they was to look out and try to grab me when I come through that direction.

Ah, but then I would have Cherry and myself in good good shape, and they could step high and lively, I can tell you, if they was to try to stop us.

I made myself some flapjacks, and when Cherry smelled them, even the taste of the sweet green grass that she was eating couldn't keep her from coming over and begging.

A terrible nuisance was Cherry, when she begun to beg, and many's the time that I wished that I hadn't taught that trick to her. Because, when she sat down like a dog and pawed with one fore-hoof, she looked so mighty pretty and ridiculous, at the same time, that I never could help giving her whatever I had.

I seen her coming, and I wolfed down most of those hot cakes as fast as I could, but before I was through with them, there she was sitting under the moon and pawing a bit, and nickering at me to let me know that she was there and what she wanted.

I smeared a mite of syrup over a part of a flapjack and throwed it to her.

Why, it was a wonderful thing, the way that Cherry could catch a flapjack out of the air! She made a tremendous lot of noise eating it, too, and raised a pother and frothing you wouldn't believe.

I couldn't help laughing at her, the way that she would sit there most like a dog, with her head on one side, watching.

However, she finished up the rest of those flapjacks for me. I never seen such a greedy horse. A regular pig, was Cherry. You would of been surprised—and her one of the finest ladies in the land!

And after that I stretched out in my blankets and went to sleep, watching the sky, and the stars, and the moon that was dying into the west, and wondering how the same God ever could of put so much misery and pleasantness onto the same old earth at the same old minute.

Then how I did snooze!

It was about three weeks since Sheriff Wally Ops and me started playing tag with each other, and I can tell you that during that time I had never slept more than three hours at a stretch, because, when Wally Ops came after you, he didn't have no manners. Any time of the day or the night was a good time for Wally to catch himself a fresh horse and start whanging away on your trail. Any old time was good enough for him to rout out folks from their beds and send them riding and damning away after a poor gent that was skulking off through the hills, just hoping that he could get shut of Wally Ops and all like him, forever.

But now I knew that I was safe from Wally.

Smart as Wally was, he was too doggone smart to risk himself and his men crossing that there desert. And so, the thing that he done was to turn back and make himself comfortable and turn to the telephones! Just the way that I figured out that he would do.

So, feeling that I was safe, I let go all holds and I dropped into a good, sound sleep.

Ah, when you speak of "dropping" to sleep, I wonder if you've ever slid about a thousand miles down hill, the way that I done that night. Because I was dead and gone. You could of took me by the shoulder and shook me, and you would never of waked me up.

Once it seemed to me that I heard the calling of Cherry Pie, but I waked up just enough to tell myself that could only be a bad dream, and then I turned over and went to sleep again.

When I woke up finally, there was the old sun showing his face over the edge of the sky and warming himself up right quick, and gathering all of his strength, and telling himself that he would sure burn up the world for fair, that day!

I got up and stretched myself, and then the sight of that pond made me laugh right out loud for the pleasure of looking at it, and remembering what I had been yesterday afternoon, and what I wasn't no more.

And then all at once it struck me that I was sort of lonesome. I flashed a look all around me.

I hollered: "Cherry! Hey, Cherry! Cherry Pie! Damn it, where might you be?"

Well, there was no sign of a nicker from Cherry to let me know where that she was. There was no sign and there was no sound of her. And I started running around like a mad man, hunting for the traces of her going.

I found them easy enough.

Why, there must have been half a dozen gents that rode through past the lake, that night, and watered their horses. I could see where they had come by right close to me—near enough to of waked me up a thousand times over, ordinarily, but that night I was all stretched out and sure of myself, and so nothing but a knife stuck into me could of waked me.

So they must of said to themselves: "We might rap this poor tramp over the head, and go along with his horse, but a gent that sleeps as steady and as sound as that, he ain't likely to make us any trouble! He'll have his own little job cut out for him in trying to get away from this here desert!"

Now, I could see that they had me beat.

It would be bad enough to try to trail them right across the desert, but once that I had got across, how could I dodge Wally Ops on the one hand, and chase that gang of crooks on the other hand?

Anyway, they had beat me. They had gone, and taken Cherry Pie.

But I held up both my hands to the sky and I swore to God that I would never leave off trailing them until I had made them pay for it, every one.

And that oath I kept, right down to the last syllable.

3

To make sure of the desert catching me, they had cleaned me out. They had even found the revolver which was tucked under my blanket near to my head, because the last few years I had had to get into the habit of sleeping like that.

My guns and my ammunition was gone, and all my pack of chuck.

What I had left was the blanket that I was sleeping in and my knife.

So I sat down and looked at the lonely water of that little pool. And it didn't seem half so fine, just now. If I stayed there, I'd starve quick. If I left it, I didn't have even a canteen for the carrying of water.

So I looked away to the south where those mountains had been showing up blue and fine the evening before.

They was close enough to be brown, now, and that meant that they couldn't be such a terrible long way off. But they must be far enough, and I knew that there was nobody able to lay down the distances by just looking at mountains in the distance. The air was clear as a glass, this day, and maybe there was fifty miles between me and the foothills.

Besides, maybe the mountains was not the way that the six of them had started off with my Cherry.

I went down to the lake and took a long drink. Then I took a squint at the sun and damned it for its brightness. And after that, I settled down and trudged out along the sign of the thieves.

I could tell, now, why it was that horse stealing had been a surer way than murder of getting the thief lynched in that part of God's country. Because when a horse is stole from you in the desert, it's the same as murder—of the worst and slowest kind!

Ordinarily, I would of been so scared and sick that I would of just folded up and sat down to die, maybe; but I'd been through so much, since the sheriff took up my trail, that I was used to bad luck and hardship, so I just buckled down to that trail.

It was clear enough reading, and pretty soon I had something to be grateful for, because the wind fetched around into the north and blew a few jags of clouds across the sun and then filmed the sky across with thin gray—just enough of it to take all the fire out of the air.

Otherwise, I wouldn't be alive to tell this, because that day I walked fifty miles without another drink of water—fifty miles across the sand to the bottom of those hills, and into them until I found a dirty little muddy stream.

There I rested for a good long hour. And then I started up the slopes puzzling out the trail that grew a bit hard to manage, now and then, because it often passed across hard granite where a shod hoof left hardly a scratch. And besides, that long march had left me dizzy and sick, and I was only gradually getting my strength and my senses back.

They had gone brisking across the desert and piled up a pretty big lead on me, during the first part of the day, but now as it come along to the late afternoon and the evening, they slowed up to nothing. They had done a good hard day's march, and now the signs grew fresher and fresher, and I could feel reasonable sure that I would catch up with them before the next morning.

The dusk began to gather. And just then, not a mile ahead of me, I seen the pale glow of a campfire, just a couple of strokes brighter than the last of the daylight.

I knew that I had them, then.

I headed straight on, making pretty good time, and after a while I cut around to the lee of their camp and sneaked up from rock to rock and from bush to bush until I was stretched out and could peer down at them from behind a little thicket.

The first thing that I seen was Cherry Pie, hobbled close and pegged out, too, and standing with her head down, pretty sick looking. And she wasn't touching that fine grass.

You'll say that horses ain't made that way, that they can't miss a man enough to go hungry for his sake. Well, I don't argue. I don't say that they will or that they won't. Maybe Cherry Pie was sick that evening, though she didn't show no signs of it a little later. But all I know is what I state—that there she stood not touching the grass.

One of the gents by the fire sings out: "Try her with a handful of that crushed barley, Sandy!"

"I've tried her," says Sandy. "She won't touch it. Except that she tried to take my hand off! She snaps like a tiger!"

It pleased me a good deal, that.

I turned away my eyes from my gold and silver beauty and begun to size up the men.

I had followed six horses, and there was a man for each horse. I learned their names, while I was lying there, drinking in the information, and printing their faces into my mind.

Sandy Larson was a big Swede or Scandanoovian of some kind.

There was a Mexican they called Dago Mendez. I suppose that Dago come from "Diego."

There was a big Negro that went by the name of Little Joe.

There was a long, lean, shambly looking tramp—Missouri Slim.

There was a brisk-looking gent with nervous, snappy ways—a stocky-made man, called Lew Candy.

But the only name that I had ever heard before was that of the chief of the gang, Doctor Grace.

Of course everybody else had heard of the doctor. And a lot of sheriffs in one place or another would of been pretty glad to set their eyes on him— if they had enough numbers on their side to give them a show at capturing him! Because it meant money to get Grace, dead or alive. I know what it amounted to, later on. But even then, I think that it was something like twelve or fifteen thousand in hard cash that would be got by him that downed Doctor Grace.

Still, here he was at liberty.

It done me a lot of good to have this chance to watch him, because I figured then, as I lay on the rock, and squinted through the brush at the circle of them, that my hardest job would be in the handling of that same Grace. And I wasn't mistaken.

He was a picture-man, was the doctor. I mean to say, that he looked like a drawing out of a book.

In those days, mustaches was still fashionable, and the doctor had a black, silky beauty, so mighty well trained that it never fluffed out and got rough looking or fell in his way. You could tell, just to look at him, that that mustache would never get tangled with the cream on his cup of coffee.

He had a black eye to match the mustache, and he had, besides, the finest kind of long, half-curling black hair—because the style was for a gent to wear his hair pretty long. It was sort of poetic, folks thought in those days, just the way that they think now it's very neat to show the white of your scalp all the way up to the crown of your head, so's the back view of a gent is like the back view of a porcupine.

What set off the blackness of the doctor's mustache and eyes was the whiteness of his skin. You would think, by the look of his hands and his face, that he had never spent a single day riding out under the hot sun. And the same was true about his clothes. I mean, he took care of his clothes just as though they was a part of his skin—something that he felt. To have anything wrong with his clothes, you could see, would upset him, and a hole in his coat would be almost like a bullet through his hide.

So he looked as neat and as dapper as you please, sitting there by the fire.

"You need not worry about the mare," he said. "She will come to time in a very few days. I think that she misses her master."

By the way that they gaped at him, it was easy to tell that they would of broke out laughing, if it had been anybody else.

But Missouri Slim said:

"Do you mean, Doctor, that she's grieving for her boss, and that's why she won't eat?"

"That's exactly it," said Doctor Grace.

"Humph!" said Slim. "I used to think that I knew a good deal about horseflesh."

"You do, Missouri," said the doctor in his gentle voice. "You know a very great deal about them, but there are a few things which have never come to your attention. You really must not forget that a horse cannot be studied pound for pound and known."

"And why not?" asked Missouri.

"Because a horse has a soul," said Doctor Grace, as solemn as you please.

"Gunna go up to heaven with their souls, then?" grinned Little Joe.

"And why not?" said Doctor Grace. "When I remember some of the horses who have lived with me and died for me, I feel certain that they could not be snapped out like a candlelight. No, we shall find them hereafter, I think."

He said this serious, not smiling. And the gents around the campfire frowned and hung their heads and looked on down to the fire, like folks that want to talk back but partly don't know how to do it, and partly they're afraid of making a fuss.

It was wonderful to see how Doctor Grace had that lot in hand, and yet they was as rough a bunch as I ever saw collected in one herd.

Pretty soon he said: "When you've finished that cup of coffee, you might take a walk around and look over things, Sandy. Not that anyone has followed us, but we may as well make sure."

So Sandy walked out of the camp, and into my hands.

4

MIND you, when I say that Sandy Larson walked out of the camp and into my hands, it was not as simple as all of that; but, as he strolled along, I fetched myself along after him. And a cat that could of heard a snake walking, could never have heard me, because I intended to finish Sandy, and I intended to finish him complete and final; and when you've had a few years of chasing and being chased through the mountains, you don't make a lot of noise when you're going on the death trail.

He went straight ahead, leaning a bit back against the wind, which was rising fast, and sloshing along the slopes of the mountains out of the south. And when he got to a little distance, he paused, but from the hill where he was standing, there was a rise of woods that shut in part of his view of the lowlands.

You could see that Doctor Grace had taught his men to be thorough. This Sandy Larson seen a sizable jag of rock rising up a couple of hundred feet higher, and he started for it as a sort of a lookout tower.

I started, too, but in a different direction. I circled around. I kicked off my shoes and went up those rocks by moonlight as easy as you please, and when Sandy came to the top of that rock pile, he found me waiting for him, with a knife at his head.

He was a very cool one, I got to say, and all that he did when he arrived there and seen the knife, was to nod his head.

"I told the boys that they had better cut your throat than to leave you loose to follow us," said Sandy.

I looked him in the eye, and the moon was full in his face and I sort of pitied him.

"Sandy," said I, "you keep your hands up over your head."

Then I took out his guns. Three of them the scoundrel had, tucked away, one of them hanging from his neck, beneath his shirt, and he seemed a bit green when he saw me take that. But it was a fine thing to have three guns instead of none. It made me breathe easier.

I stepped back a mite and shied the guns onto the ground.

"Now, Sandy," said I, "you got a good big knife in your belt. Do you know how to use it?"

"I been eleven years in Mexico," said Sandy by way of answer.

And it was answer enough!

"Pull out that knife, then," said I. "Because by rights I should give you no chance, but shoot you down like a dog, the same way that you left me helpless when you met me, the other day."

"True," says Sandy. "We gave you a bad chance at living. And I'll tell you, Dickon—"

"You know me?" said I.

"We knew you, Dickon," said he.

"Then you *were* fools," said I, "to think that I was ever born to choke to death in any damned desert!"

"Ay," said he, "we were fools to think that. We should of guessed that you were intended to die with a knife stuck into your gizzard!"

It done me good to hear him talk, and see the mean light that glittered in his eyes. Why, that man loved a knife, and he loved it so much that he wouldn't wait any longer to talk. He just came at me on the jump, with his lips grinned back from his great gash of a mouth. An ugly man was that Sandy Larson, with a good length of leg, arm, and a supple wrist, which counts in knife work.

But I doubt if he'd ever spent much time when he was a boy standing against a wall and dodging the knives which gents chucked at him by way of practicing their hands. Because to be on the receiving end of a knife play teaches you about as much as to be on the giving end.

He made a feint at my body and then flicked across a neat cut aimed to cross my eyes. But I dipped just under it, and felt the sharp edge pull and tear at my hair as it whished through.

And at the same minute, I came up under that big, flying arm of his and pushed my knife home between his ribs. It was a smallish, thin-bladed knife, but very useful.

Then I turned Sandy on his back, because it seemed to me that even a murdering hound like him had ought to be looking at the stars, when he lay dead.

After that, I went through him very careful. He had eleven hundred and fourteen dollars on him, and he had nothing else worth talking about, outside of a picture of a wide-faced Swedish girl with a foolish-looking smile. Most likely he had intended marrying her, so I had done her a good turn without ever having seen her.

Then I sized up his guns. The neckpiece was a neat little trick, but no good for me. I let that stay, but I took the Colts, which was new, clean, and all loaded. Besides, I took enough cartridges from Sandy to load up my belt.

After that, I climbed down, got my shoes, and went back toward the camp.

Lying watching them with no weapons was one thing. Lying with two good gats handy was quite another. I had a blind, black wish to turn loose and spray the whole lot of them with lead. There was only five of them. And God give me the wits in each hand to keep a pair of guns chattering and every bullet aimed. I thought that I could kill or down them all. But still I couldn't bring myself to it. I knew that they needed killing, all of them. I knew that Doctor Grace never took with him anything but the worst kind of killers. But still, I couldn't do it, and that was flat. Because I had my record and it was long enough, but I never yet killed a man except in fair fight, standing up, with equal chances on each side.

But what could I do? I couldn't call them out one by one and ask them to fight fair. I might be willing, but would they be?

No, they knew me too well for that. Doctor Grace would be a match for me, but never one of the rest of them.

However, the next best thing to do, it seem to me, was to go to Cherry Pie and get her free and a saddle on her back, if possible.

And getting to her was a bit of a trick, because she was standing right out in the open, down-headed still, with the firelight flickering straight out to her and falling about her feet.

But I wormed my way down through the rocks and across the ground toward her, stopping the minute anything or anyone moved around the fire.

Once Little Joe stood up and looked toward me. And once Dago Mendez got up and walked in a circle around the fire, but neither of them saw me, because their nearness to the fire blinded them, and the moon was still low in the sky and not giving a very bright light.

When Cherry Pie got the wind of me, I thought sure that she would give us both away, because her head went up and she stood like a picture, with her ears pricking.

And what a picture Cherry made, when she was showing herself off!

Well, she seemed too surprised to move, and I wormed in close and knifed those ropes in two with a couple of touches. After that, I wormed right back again behind the rocks and to a place where a growth of shrubs went up, big enough to shelter me, standing upright.

Cherry Pie followed me, and just as she was coming to me behind the brush, I heard Lew Candy say: "There goes the mare. She's begun to feed, and now she'll be all right!"

She'd be all right. Yes, I could answer for that!

I stood beside her for a minute, until she got through biting my shoulder to show how glad she was to see me. The pile of saddles lay right ready to my hand and Grace was a fool not to have stacked them in the firelight. I could pick out my own just as I pleased, and I did, and cinched it quietly on the back of Cherry.

After that, I went through a few of the saddlebags and took out a few things that I needed. Why, I could of taken hundreds of pounds of stuff, if I'd wanted to load myself down, but I never believe in traveling with weight when you're on the mountain-desert. It ain't handy or comfortable, to travel light, but it's safe—oh, it's very safe!

"Where's Sandy?" sang out Missouri Slim, about this time.

"He's seen lights on the desert," said Candy, "and he's studying them before he comes back. He's a careful gent, old Sandy is!"

I didn't smile. No, you don't smile about dead men, if you happened to do the killing. I always kind of noticed that.

But I figured that I had done about all that I could do, safely. I had got my horse back, and I had a set of guns, finished off with a fine new fifteen-shot Winchester that I took out of one of the saddle holsters.

If I hung around there, the whole gang would jump me pretty soon. So I just sat down and with the point of my knife I wrote on one of the saddle flaps:

DEAR GRACE,
    Most usual, you should keep a lookout on the saddles.
    And on the lookouts, too!

I didn't sign it, because I didn't think it would need signing. He would be able to make out for himself what had happened.

I sneaked back, with Cherry following me. We got into the first draw, and we traveled up it until I seen an inviting looking ravine that opened off it, and I went up into it, seen that it wasn't blind, and found a place of a sort for a camp. There was good water and grass for the mare. And as for me, it didn't make no difference. I had to chew hardtack, because I didn't dare to risk going along with the cooking of a meal, even over the tiniest sort of a fire.

However, even hardtack was licking good, washed down with spring water, after my march across the desert the last two days. Then I turned in and went to sleep. But you can lay to it that I didn't really close more than one eye. And never would again, as long as I lived!

5

YOU would say that I had had about enough trouble, in the last couple of days, without running into anything extra to fill up the cup.

But what I bit the next morning was so tough that nothing but Cherry Pie could have saved me from it.

I was just drifting down the pass, after a hardtack breakfast, wondering whether it would be better for me to tackle Doctor Grace and his thugs or to wait till the sheriff got off my trail before heading for him, when something blinked in the sun straight ahead of me, and I didn't need a schoolteacher to tell me that that was the wink of sunshine on steel.

I ducked as a bullet stung the air where my breast had been. At the same time I jumped Cherry Pie sideways, and then whirled her around and ducked down the pass.

All five of them was behind me, pumping lead as fast as repeating rifles could chuck it at me.

But did you ever watch a teal flying down the wind? That's the way that Cherry Pie could run, dodging this way and that. I used to train her, running her full speed through lodgepole pine woods. And she learned to dodge or else to break her neck. So all that I had to do when I wanted her to perform like that was to take a short to the side of the cañon wall, yet she was going at full speed by the time that she got there.

And it was a rare caution to see her handle herself. She knew that there was horses coming behind. She could see them tearing at us from in front, and she knew that old game of tag as well as any man could of known it. So Cherry jumped at that mountain side as though it was no more than a hedge.

She landed high up on the side of the sheer bank. I was out of the saddle at the same instant, and running beside her. She had no right to get up it, but her hoofs turned into claws, for the minute, and that hoss heaved herself right up among the boulders; and the next minute I was in the saddle and driving her along at full tilt, cutting in and out among the rocks, and working higher and higher up, all of the time.

And below me I heard a roar, and there was a few bullets that splashed on the stone-faces around me, but that was all.

After that, I was out of the picture, and the fun went on between the other two sets. Because, just at the same minute that Cherry and me faded out among the rocks, the sheriff and his gang rushed right up into sight of Doctor Grace and his boys.

Well, I heard a chorusing of yells, and a rattling of guns that went booming in echoes up the mountains and fair making the leaves tremble all around me, while I reined up Cherry Pie, and looked back to enjoy the fun.

It *was* fun, too. Because there was Grace and his lot hoofing it down the valley as fast as their nags would run, and there was Wally Ops and his lot rushing behind them like a river, with the dirt spitting up in chunks from the hoofs of their horses.

With half a chance, the sheriff would have rubbed out the famous Grace, then and there. I have heard a lot of talk about that thing. And I have heard how Grace rode in the rear and held back the sheriff and his men with two revolvers, and how Wally Ops was scared to close in on him too fast—and so gave him a chance to get away; but the real honest truth about it is that Grace rode as hard and as furious as the rest of them to get clear. And all the shooting that was done was by the gents that happened to be the hindmost and the most scared of the gang of Grace.

But the chief reason of all that he got away was that Grace and his boys had fresh, fine horses, and the sheriff and his men were pretty fagged with their work on my trail. Besides, the same snaky windings of the valley that had saved me from Grace saved him now from the sheriff.

The last that I seen of them, the hunters were losing every second, and the thugs were drawing clear.

Then I rode Cherry quietly back down into the valley and I took the same backtrail over which the sheriff had just rode.

Well, you will say, sure a man would never go back through the same desert that had given him hell such a short little time before! But the fact was that I was burning up with meanness. Wally Ops had done a lot of hunting of me before, but somehow the way he had played a hand with Grace was too much for me. And I swore that I'd make Wally find out for himself why there was a price on my head.

I rode my Cherry straight back for that desert, and I melted into it, and I lined away for the lake that had saved the lives of the blessed pair of us not so long before.

Besides, I figured in a way that I couldn't do anything much better to throw him off my trail. Even suppose that he was to give up Grace and turn back to my single track, it was most likely that he would comb around through the rocks of those mountains, breaking his heart to find out my trail, but he would never dream of hunting for me back there toward the desert.

I got to the lake, and the ride wasn't so bad, considering. Because it wasn't an unknown land that I was diving into, now, and I could look at the far horizon without bothering to wonder what lay between me and it.

I got to the lake in the middle of the afternoon, after a march that wasn't bad at all. There I laid up and made myself comfortable and let the mare graze and eat, and lie down and roll and rest a while. I stayed on there for about seven hours, and before midnight, after a few hours' nap myself, I headed back across the desert again, waltzing along just on the line that I had followed out.

Why, there was nothing so terrible about that desert, if you knew what to expect, and if you knew how to take it. We went right along through it, and though the last few hours was pretty bad, still, we only went the last hour of the next afternoon without water. And what was a little thing like that?

I laid up in the hills, safe and snug, for three days, letting Cherry strengthen up a mite after the big marches. Then I headed along again, driving straight for the place where I intended to hit the sheriff and to hurt him bad. It took me seven days of steady riding, but at last I came out where I could look down on the things that meant the most to the sheriff.

I had been by that way about eight years before, and seen the valley, and the house, and everything. But I never was prepared to see what a change there was, since Wally took over the place from old man Griswold, nor the way that he had fixed everything up, nor the way that he had improved it all, so wonderful!

6

IN the old days, when Griswold was the boss in the valley, it was pretty uncomfortable to look down there and see the runty mules and scraggy mustangs, and the no-account longhorns, that could live on thistle, but that couldn't get fat even on cottonseed cakes and good oat hay. The fences leaned all together to the south, which way the wind mostly blowed in winter, when the ground was wet; and the house was a knock-kneed, broken-backed sort of a shack with sheds around it that you could see right through. Take it by and large, the old Griswold place had always looked as though an army had bombarded it, and then sacked it, and then marched on along just leaving behind the cripples out of its livestock.

That was all very different, now.

You take that Wally Ops, he *was* different from most.

Up to this time, I had loafed it around taking things easy and doing what I wanted to do, and when I wanted it. But along comes Wally, and then I got thin and Cherry lost some of her figure, too. You would say that Wally Ops just nacherally *hated* to stay still.

You would say that to be on the jump, wearing out horseflesh and manflesh, was his idea of a good game.

The same way down there in the valley. Looked like he had been working night and day these past eight years, whacking the valley into shape.

I never seen so much prosperity. There was big fat-bellied haystacks, and black-topped straw stacks from last harvest time, and there was a stretch of ground all checked off with regular corrals and feed sheds, where he could put up the section of the cows that got run down during the bad weather. Besides all of that, the sheds were fixed up, and a lot of new ones built, and I couldn't make out the Griswold house at all, until I seen that what it used to be was now just used as the kitchen part of the new place.

Trees, too! They changed the face of everything. Of course old man Griswold had just gone out and chopped down everything near the house for firewood, and it amazed me to think that trees could of growed up to look so real and so nacheral and so big in eight short years. Which they couldn't, either, and I knew that all of that grove by the house must of been dug up as good big standing saplings by Wally Ops and brought down to plant around the house. Why, man, it would stagger you to think how much work that meant! Any sort of a sizeable sapling, with its roots dug out far enough to make sure of it living, and all the mold and the moss and the dirt sticking to it, why, one sapling would make a whole wagon load. But anyway, there was the trees, and not just one or two of them, but a whole little wood of them standing around the house and covering it right up to the red edge of the roof.

It made the sun seem hotter, to look down into that pool of coolness and greenness and shadow. Cherry had noticed it right away, of course, and she had her head cocked up high.

But of course I couldn't go prowling around there in the daytime.

How I was to soak the sheriff, and soak him most hardest, I couldn't make out; but I knew that, with him having a place as big and as flossy as this, it wouldn't be hard for me to work some way out.

I took Cherry back into cover in a nest of rocks and smoked cigarettes in the shade for the rest of the afternoon while I worked out ways of making Wally Ops damn the day when I was ever born and he took up my trail.

Because I decided that I had stood enough and that the time had come for me to make an end of this thing and to set Wally Ops up as an example, so that the next sheriff that come onto my trail would have Wally to remember by, and not wear himself out chasing me any more than his reputation required.

After I had fixed Wally good and proper, then I would go back and take up with Doctor Grace and his yeggs, right where I had left off.

This idea seemed sensible and sound all over. I allowed that I couldn't improve on it, so I took a last look at the blue of the sky and the gray of the rock that leaned out over me, and I closed my eyes for a little snooze.

It was dusk when I woke up. I was hungry, but I was ashamed to do my own cooking when the smell of woodsmoke sloping out of the valley told me that there was women folks at their cookery down there below me. So I smoked another cigarette, and listened to a bird singing his head off somewhere over my head, and when the bird stopped singing, and the dark come, I went down to have a closer look at things.

Coming across a field, a bunch of shorthorns heaved themselves up out of the shadows and went away grunting, with their round sides flobbing up and down and the water sloshing and jostling and gurgling in their stomachs as they trotted.

There was a bull with that set. He took no kind liking to me and aimed to slide his horns into Cherry, but she flicked across the first fence, and we heard that bull go crash! into it.

The fence posts held, though they groaned under the shock. I looked back at Mr. Bull standing in the field shaking his head after us, and snuffing at the ground, and blowing up clouds of dust, and pawing back great chunks of sod. There ain't anything more foolish than a bull.

Down in the floor of the valley everything was easy. I just left Cherry Pie standing on the outer edge of the trees, and I sneaked up and walked around the house.

It was very slick. There was a couple of sprinklers spinning on the front lawn and whirring out spray that flew so high the wind caught it up, every now and then, and blew a breath of it across to me, under the trees. There was a good smell, too, of rich, wet muck in the garden beds, with roses flowering on top of it, and other blossoms, too, that I could only guess at. Because I'm not much of a hand at flowers. Except that roses you can tell them by the peppery something in the smell of them.

There was a veranda running on two sides of the house. That veranda was built deep and low, and floored with narrow boards just like the slickest kind of an inside room. You could of danced on that veranda, I tell you, because the lamplight that spilled out of a window across it was as bright as the moonpath over a muddy pool.

The whole house was set down low and comfortable toward the ground. You could look into the rooms as you walked around, because every window was wide open and the curtains drawn back, and wherever there was light enough you could see everything that was there.

I had aimed to go into that house and snoop around through it, but somehow I couldn't do it, now that I was there. You can't steal from a gent that offers you his purse. And it was sort of like that, finding this house so foolish and so open. I was main surprised that the sheriff was fool enough to leave his place without no better instruction than that. But when I come to think about it, I seen that it was safe enough, because most of the boys, even the tough ones, would of stopped a bit at the idea of robbing the sheriff's own house.

However, as I was saying, I couldn't go inside. I just went around, admiring to see how fine all the rooms was, with lots of red carpets, and such cheerful things, and more pictures on the walls than you could look at in a year of Sundays. A good summer house, and a good winter house, too. There was about all that you could ask for!

When I got to the kitchen, I seen that it was fixed real fine, with a new big wood range built into one end of the room, and great sinks and such, of stone, standing handy by, and a neat little oil range for breakfasts, and such.

Everything was clean, too. And the litter was of pots lying on their sides, with the creamy streaks of mashed potatoes showing on the bottoms, and baking pans with their black iron lids lying a bit off center and breathing out a slow, rich, lazy steam; and there was a half dozen of flat layer-cake pans with the leavings of the cake crusted on them, and the smell of butter, and spices, and baking, and such, all about.

I leaned beside the window, looking this all over, and while I was looking, I fetched from the window sill a loganberry pie that was sort of standing there and cooling off, d'you see?

It was the sort of a pie that you would expect from that kitchen. There is pies and pies. I would say that apple pie is as good as most, and I can eat my half of a good cream pie, and I ain't backing up when a lemon pie walks up and looks me in the face, and blackberries can be prime; but, you take them by and large, when the loganberries is ripe enough but not soggy, and when the crust is made thick, and there is just the right amount of sugar worked in, and when there is a little jerk of something else put in to polish it off, there ain't anything in the way of eating that comes over a loganberry pie.

This pie that I'm speaking about, it was right. I couldn't say no more. By the time that I had finished looking, that pie was gone, and if there had been a brother of it standing lonely like behind, I wouldn't of left it stay.

I crossed around from the kitchen, though, with just a look into the creamery.

Most creameries ain't so pleasant to see, or even to think about. But the first thing that you could smell in this one was the good yellow soap that had been used for the scrubbing down of the floors and the tables and the walls. I went inside, and I listened to the sound of the water, dripping down along the sacking of the coolers. I pulled open a couple of the doors and seen the glimmer of the milk pans standing one above the other, and I went out almost as contented and rich feeling as though that place had belonged to me!

By my left there was the smell of a shed of cords and cords of good, sweet, dry wood stacked up, as I went along, and then I stopped to look in at the dining room.

There was where I seen the family for the first time.

7

YOU would of known that a little, dried-up, waspish sort of a man like the sheriff would have a wife laid out on the general lines of a Percheron. I should of expected it, but it took me so by surprise that I nearly laughed out loud at the window.

She was all billowy. Do you know what I mean? God had been making New England Yankees, and he was tired of straight lines when he come to her. A lump of ice on the forehead was what she looked like needing, all of the time.

But she was jolly, and she was always saying something that wasn't worth even a smile, and then laughing at it herself with her elbows working up and down like two pump handles. She shook all over, when she laughed, and so did the whole room. The tablecloth trembled where it hung down in folds, and the forks shivered against the spoons, and the water quavered into little waves in the glasses. You could see that she had cooked this meal, and you could see that nobody was going to enjoy it any more than she did. Now, music is fine for some, and theaters for others, and pictures for the smart people, but for me, I would stop for dinner, y'understand? Mrs. Ops, she sounded to me!

More I looked at her, the more I could see to her. First look, I wondered how come the sheriff had ever married such a tubby woman, but if you could blow away the bubbles and the froth and look at the real drink— which I mean to say, if you could look through the fat to what she once was, she was mighty pretty. She had ten pounds of blond hair piled onto the top of her head, with the fag ends of the lower part curling around little pink ears that she wasn't ashamed to show, and no wonder. And the nacheral smallness of her hands throwed the fat of her fingers into dents and dimples ever whichway.

Not that she was the only one at the table, but, being the chief engineer of that meal, I had to begin with her. But the sheriff's son, Lew, was there, too. He was about twelve with blond hair like his ma and freckles and a black eye that had reached the purple-green stage. And opposite from Lew there was the girl, whose name I gathered was Julie. It was a real rest to look at her. She had her dad's black hair and her mother's blue eyes and she looked like she was too full of life to do any sleeping. She was very good-natured, you could see, but smiling was her best bet, than which nobody ever done it better or more dimpled on one side of her face.

"Why don't you put another beefsteak on your eye, Lew?" says the girl to her brother.

He was admiring himself in the mirror when she spoke, and he gave her a scowl.

"It ain't *your* eye," says he, "and you didn't fight two boys to get it."

"They were both smaller than you," says she.

"Will you listen to Julie talk?" says Lew. "Anybody knows that Sam Marvin is half an inch bigger than me. And Chuck ain't much smaller."

"Stuff!" says Julie. "I could hold them both with one hand and spank them with the other!"

The kid, he started to answer, and then he changed his mind and he scowled at her very dark.

"Jiminy!" says he. "Wouldn't I want to be by when you was trying it? Ma, will you pass the carrots?"

"There's pie and cake coming," says Ma. "You better keep a corner. Julie, we'll clear off."

They snaked the dishes off of the table.

"Sammy is a skinny little runt," says Julie, taking out a load.

"He's got a terrible reach," said Lew. "And that's what counts. I never seen such a girl. If Danny Murphy could hear you talk, he wouldn't be so hot to take you to the dance tonight and—"

He laid off talking, as she went through the kitchen door. But when she come back on the next trip he says good and loud:

"You like that Murphy, don't you?"

"Who said I did?" says Julie. "And why shouldn't I, Lew?"

"Well, you know what the other gents call him?"

"What do they call him?"

"Dummy!" says Lew. "Dummy Murphy, they call him, he's so thick!"

He had his laugh, then, and his mother, she laughed, too. She would always laugh at anything, but Julie, she turned up her nose and sailed out with another pile of vegetable dishes and things, not seeming to notice.

A minute later there was a whoop.

"Lew!" yells his mother.

He gave a jump and his chair rattled. You could tell that he was pretty familiar with that kind of a call.

"Yes, Mother," says Lew, very sweet but a little shaky.

" 'Yes, Mother!' " says Mrs. Ops, coming humming back, and crowding herself through the doorway. "Where's that pie?"

Lew walled his eyes a little.

"What pie?" says he.

"The pie I left cooling on the window sill?" says Mrs. Ops.

"Oh," says Lew, sort of relieved. "I dunno. What about it?"

"What about it?" says Mrs. Ops. "What about it? I'll let you know what about it in a minute, unless you confess right up that you snaked it off and ate it—"

"Why, Ma, I didn't touch it. I didn't even know where it was!"

"A loganberry pie—you didn't know where it was! I suppose that it had legs, then, and it walked off?"

"I dunno," said Lew. "Don't ask me. I don't read the minds of pies!"

"D'you dare to lie right to my face?" says Mrs. Ops. "Who *would* steal it?"

"You can search me!"

"You little good-for-nothing! You come with me!"

She fetched a hold of him by one ear, with a good twist, and brought him out of the chair and dragged him into the kitchen, him hollering: "Hey, Mom, you're tearing my ear off—"

I shifted around to the kitchen window. I was sorry for the kid, but I was curious, too. I seen Mrs. Ops snatch a whip from a nail on the wall and swing it, and I seen the kid trembling, but standing for the licking, even if he didn't deserve it.

"Don't!" says Julie, all at once, and she stood in between them.

"Julie," says her mother, "will you stand away? Or do I have to—"

"Don't whip him!" says Julie. "He's too big—and it shames him too much, Mother. Please don't—"

"Am I gunna waste my time and strength on *you?*" says Mrs. Ops. "Stand away from him, Julie!"

"Mother," says Julie, "I was hungry, and *I* took the silly pie! I didn't know—"

"Julie!" says Mrs. Ops, and she dropped the whip.

"It was a silly thing to do," says Julie.

"And *that's* where your appetite went to," says Mrs. Ops. "And you *nineteen!* When your pa comes home, he's gunna hear about this!"

"Yes, Mother," says Julie, but she winced a little, and you could see that it wasn't only the crooks in the mountain desert that was afraid of Wally Ops.

"Go back and sit down!" says Mrs. Ops.

"I would like to help!" says Julie, very scared and small.

"You would like to help!" says Mrs. Ops in a terrible voice. "You go back and sit down!"

Back went Julie and Lew and sat down like two frightened mice, making big eyes at each other across the table.

"My God, Julie," says Lew, "you are most terrible white. I swear I didn't steal the pie."

"I know you didn't, dear," says Julie. "I can tell when you fib. But who *did* take it, then?"

Mrs. Ops come back carrying the cake and she put it down, looking very dark and stern; but when she knifed into it, and the frosting crumbled down even and smooth in front of the knife edge, and the slice lifted off as neat as you please, her frown disappeared.

"There's no dance for you tonight, young lady."

"No, Mother," says the girl, very submissive.

"Hey, Mom," says Lew, "you don't mean it! With Danny Murphy coming all this here way to fetch her and—"

She pointed the cake knife at Lew.

"You've said enough!" says Mrs. Ops. "Your sister is sick, that's what she is. She's in bed with a terrible, raging headache, that's what she's got. Like the same kind that she has when that fine, clean, respectable Charlie Goodrich comes over to call on her. A whole loganberry pie! What on earth possessed you?"

"It looked so good, Mother," says the girl, pulling down the corners of her mouth.

"Stuff!" says Mrs. Ops, and passed over a slice of cake. "Ain't you eating that?"

"I—I—" says Julie, and then she drops her head into her hands and a shiver runs over her back.

Mrs. Ops straightened in her chair.

"Julie!" says she.

"Yes, Mom-mom-mom-mother!" says Julie. And here she begun to sob hard and heavy.

And why not, I ask you, having got her heart fixed on a dance, and all flounced and fluffed up in white frills so dainty you never seen anything like it, and then got herself into trouble for the sake of her brother? It made me feel like stepping in there and telling them the truth. It made all the punching muscles turn hard along my arms. It pretty near brought the tears into my eyes.

And then she turned her head a little. And what do you think that I seen?

Why, man, she wasn't crying at all. She was just laughing till the tears ran down the face of her, except that she was smart enough to make the laughing sound like sobs!

Would you believe it? No, you wouldn't, nor wouldn't I, neither. But that was the fact.

8

IT scared me, in a way, to see a girl act as smart as that. What would even a man do, if he hadn't been able to get a side look at her face, that way that I had?

Mrs. Ops stood it with her lips set for a moment, but Lew was busted up and he said: "Aw, Julie, aw, what's the matter?"

"You be quiet an' leave the room!" snaps Mrs. Ops, who had to be mad at somebody.

Lew got as far as the door, and there he stuck, looking back at his sister, while Mom Ops run around the table and laid her fat hand on the back of Julie.

"Now, Julie," said she, "now don't you go carrying on like a silly!"

The sobbing of Julie—I mean the laughing—it got worse than ever.

"If it's the dance, I don't suppose that I'd stand in the way of your going," says Mrs. Ops.

She stood back and took a side squint at Julie, and that girl, she settled forward and laid her head on her arms.

"What would your pa say was he to see the state that you're in?" says Mrs. Ops.

"Poor father!" says Julie.

"Is it him that's worrying you, honey?" says Mrs. Ops. "He's g-g-g-gone to fight that m-m-murdering Larry Dickon!" sobs Julie.

"Yes," says her mother, "and he'll bring him back in irons."

She settled down to do some more comforting.

"It's been preying on you, child," says she. "It's worn your nerves thin, thinking about my Wally. But don't you worry. Wally ain't the kind to be beat by any one man. I looked over a lot of men before I picked him out, and I've never regretted it. If he'd only get some flesh on his bones! Julie, will you please stop crying, honey? Because what will Danny Murphy think when he comes and finds you—"

"I don't care!" says Julie. "I won't go with Danny!"

"Julie!" gasps Mom Ops. "And Danny with his fine new rubber-tired rig and his new span of sorrels coming all shined up to take you—"

Now, I slid away from the window, at that. There wasn't a great deal of brightness on this night, but I aimed to believe that I could tell a span of sorrels taking a new rubber-tired rig down the road.

I went back to Cherry and took her out from the trees and jumped the fence into the road. She was very neat at fences, my Cherry! I cantered straight up the road for a quarter of a mile to the first forking, and then I waited in the shadow of the trees.

I hadn't been there for a half hour when I heard the clicking of trotting horses coming down the road with no rattle of steel tires behind them, but only a whirring sound, which made me guess that it was Danny. Then, squinting ahead, I saw a pair of high-headed roadsters coming with the checkreins snapping above their necks, and behind them the starlight glistened on the wheels of a new-painted rig and streaked a highlight along its body.

That ought to be Danny Murphy's layout, I thought. But there wasn't enough light to tell them bay or sorrel, as they went by. But they was no sooner past than I leaped Cherry after them.

"Steady up, Danny!" said I.

He hadn't heard Cherry come, because her gallop was as light as blowing dust. But at my voice, he jerked his head around and gave a good look at the muzzle of my Colt.

Then he pulled up.

He was a cool kid. You could tell by the acting of him that Julie must have picked about the best young gent in the countryside to take her to that dance.

He says: "All right, partner. You have me dead to rights. But just tell me how I'm to get my hands up over my head without having these high-headed fools run away with me?"

"You don't need to have your hands up, Danny," said I. "Just you keep your hands on the reins for a minute. Keep a hold on them still, get down from the rig, and walk up to their heads. And all the time, I'll ask you to remember that there is plenty of light for me to see by."

He turned his head and looked at me, once more. I could see that it was poison for him to give in without a fight, but when he turned his head this time he started a bit and said: "Larry Dickon!" under his breath.

For even at midnight, under a clouded sky, you couldn't help recognizing Cherry by the silver of her mane and tail. It was embarrassing, in a way, to get myself known, but I was glad of it, in a way, because it was most likely that even a hot-head like Danny Murphy wouldn't take a chance against me.

He did just as I told him. And when he arrived at the head of the span, I had him lead them to the side of the road. I watched him tie them to a post, and then I tied Danny.

He put up a stiff fight—talking. He explained that he had seventy-two dollars on him, and that he was glad enough to let me have all of it, and that if I would turn him loose, after taking that money, he would swear not to inform against me, but that he was going to a dance that night with a girl that meant a lot to him—

I listened to this talk, holding the rope in my hand, and as I shook my head for the last time and told him to hold out his wrists to have them tied, he set his teeth and let drive straight at my head.

By instinct I pretty nearly pulled the trigger of my Colt and sent him out where the lights don't shine no more, but I managed not to do that. I just sidestepped that smashing punch and, as he came lurching on in, I let him have a right hook that started from my hip and nearly jerked my own shoulder out of place as it slammed home on the point of Danny's jaw.

He folded his arms across his face and spilled on the ground, so there I tied him and gagged him—not a mean gag, but one that had ought to of kept him working for a couple of hours before he could do much noise making.

After that I went to the team, unhooked them from the traces, brought them into the woods, drew the buggy in after them, and when I seen that all was clear out of sight from the road, I took Cherry back to her place near the sheriff's house.

It was a neat little job, and I was pleased. Because though knives and guns have their places, there ain't anything so satisfying as to land one solid, honest punch and see the other gent turn into a sandman and crumble away into the dirt. If trouble hadn't started so early with me, I always had intentioned going into the ring and trying my whirl with the best of them. Even Choctaw, that never agreed with me about anything else, always said that it was a shame that I couldn't make an *honest* living out of fighting.

Well, I spruced myself up a bit, and parted my hair with my hands, and dusted the outside inch of sand off my coat and my face, and I sashayed up to the front door of the sheriff's house.

I didn't know exactly what I aimed to do, except that I was pretty glad that I was standing there. Lew come in answer to my knock.

"Hello, Lew," says I, "is your sister here?"

"Hello," says Lew. "Who might you be? Sure she's here. Come on in!"

Free and easy, that boy always was. He was always at home himself and he wanted everybody else to be at home.

I said that I was all over dust from such a long ride, and that would he just call his sister to the door? He said that he would, and along come the sheriff's daughter.

She didn't stop inside the door, or the screen door, either. She just walked right out onto the porch and stood looking up to me. It was a considerable comfort to me to see that she didn't come no higher than my chin, or not much. Because I was made more broad than long.

I told her that I had come along with a message from Danny Murphy that he was held up and that he wouldn't be able to get along to see her for about an hour later than he had expected.

"An hour!" says Julie. "Now, what in the world has happened? Come inside and tell me about it?"

"Matter of fact," says I, "I'm too dusty and I ain't cleaned up fit for lamplight."

"That makes no difference," says Julie. But she didn't insist. "What's happened to Danny? Has he had another fight?"

"He's a great one for that, ain't he?" says I.

"He is," said Julie, "but he promised me—oh, well!"

She stopped on that.

"Who was it this time? And has Danny a black eye to take to the dance with me tonight?"

"Nothing," says I, "except a lump on the side of his chin that don't look bad at all. Just as if it was a mosquito bite, and no more than that."

"Humph!" says Julie. "I didn't hear you say who you were, though?"

"Name is Ripley, called Hank."

"Are you an old friend of Danny's?"

"Not special, but I was riding along past his place, down the road, and he spotted me."

"Oh," says she, "you were coming down from the hills, then?"

I thought I might as well say yes, and so I did.

"Isn't it odd, though," said Julie, "that Danny never has mentioned your name to me? And—you must be an assistant sheriff, or something. Because here you are, wearing two guns! Are they real?" she asked me, laughing a little.

"Oh yes," says I.

She reached right into the nearest holster and pulled the Colt out. "It feels *heavy* enough to be real," says she. "And I think it *is* real. So hold up your hands, Mr. Ripley!"

9

I DIDN'T have to look down at that gun which she had just taken from me, because I could feel the nose of it jabbed good and deep into my floating ribs and there was no quiver running down that gun, by which I knew that she had a steady hand.

All that I looked at was her eyes, and *they* was steady, too.

"Please don't do that, Miss Ops," says I. "Because even a sheriff's daughter might make mistakes while she was joking."

"Is this a joke?" says she.

"Why," I began—

But she jumped in with: "Keep your hands away, Mr. Ripley, and raise them up level with your head. And don't do anything jumpy, because I think that there's either a heart or a liver or something between the muzzle of this gun and your back."

Yes, she was as cool about it as that. She didn't raise her voice a mite.

"This makes me look a good deal like a fool," says I, getting dignified. "Even if it's a joke."

"I hope that it turns out a joke," said she, "but I've got my doubts. Will you put those hands up?"

"All right," said I. "You can have your own way!"

It was pretty bitter. I don't suppose that I ever done anything in my life that was harder than lifting my hands up and getting them past the place where I could grab that gun. But something told me that she was not bluffing, and that she had a good, tight grip on that Colt, and I knew how terrible light and easy the trigger pulled.

Anyway, I got my hands up level with my head at last.

"I'd like to know why all of this is done to me," I asked her.

"I don't mind telling you," said Julie. "Because there's no road that runs past the Murphy place. The road just ends there!"

She added: "Besides, it doesn't come down from the hills. You ought to fix up the geography of the next story that you tell!"

Can you imagine anything neater or easier than the way that she had caught me? What beat me was her being just a girl and working the game so smooth, because she had listened to me making my blunder without wincing a mite, and the next instant she had that gun out of the holster and slipped into my ribs. I could see that she was her mother's daughter, and her father's daughter, too!

"It's a queer thing—" I began.

"It's just that," said she. "But now you begin to walk forward not more than an inch or two at a time, while I back up until we get to that window, where there'll be a bit of light on your face."

I obeyed. There was nothing else to do. It was to me just as though the sheriff himself had been on the delivering end of that gun. He couldn't have been cooler or easier.

All the time you can lay to it that I was thinking, but thinking doesn't seem to do any good. I didn't see any way out. I kept hoping, first of all, that when I edged into the light and she seen my face, she wouldn't recognize me, but then I remembered how her father had scattered pictures of me all over the mountains, as soon as he got into office, and I knew that there was no hope on that trail. She wasn't blind any more than she was a fool.

"Thank you," said Julie, "for not making any noise. But it's to your own interest, also. Because I don't want you to appear a fool if my brother runs out here. And I won't send for him until I make sure that I don't know your face—"

You can see that she was aiming to be square, even in a time like this, and not just tickled with her own smartness. But I almost laughed at what she said, because it was a sure thing that she *would* know my face, but that I wouldn't be saved by that!

Then I knew that there was only one way for me to get clear of this mess, and that was to take about the worst chance that I ever went through in my life. Worse than even when Cherry and me rode through Tally Seven with guns talking to us, either side of the way.

She had her eyes raised to me, and as we got to the edge of the window's square of light I leaned right out into it, so that she could see me fair and clear.

Not meaning either that I'm fair or clear!

But when she seen me, even the nerves of the sheriff's daughter jumped a little at the look of me and my scars and my hollowed-out face, and my mean look. The look that you get from squinting across the desert to see what cuts up into the desert, or from wondering what's coming around the next corner—

Anyway, as she seen me, she gasped: "Larry Dickon!" and the pressure of the Colt into my ribs weakened just a mite.

That gave me my tenth part of a chance. I brought down my left hand like a shot and grabbed the gun and her hand that held it and knocked them away from me—and thank God that the gun didn't explode, because I would have been a dead man, sure.

And with the other hand I caught her and held her so she couldn't see. Of the whole thing, what worries me most of this day is what I said as I got the gun and her safe, which was:

"You young she-devil!"

I would give a lot to take that back. But when a word is spoke, it is spoke. That's all that there is to it, as I think somebody may have said before me.

You would like to know what she done, when I had her so quick?

Why, jammed as she was up against me, she said so quiet that nobody but me could have heard: "Larry Dickon, you have killed Danny!"

Cool? Tool-proof steel. That was her!

"No," I says, "I ain't killed Danny. He's safe and he's sound, and he won't come through any worse than he started."

"Except for that lump along his jaw?" said she.

"Exactly."

"Well, then," said she, "do you know that you are smashing my hand against the revolver?"

So I was. As I let go, I could realize that I must of been nearly smashing her hand to pieces.

"Thanks," said Julie, "and besides, do you mind hugging me not quite so tight? I can't breathe, you know, very well."

Why, it made my face burn, I can tell you!

I loosened up right quick.

"I sure beg your pardon," I told her. "If you would please mind not raising a holler?"

"That's only fair," says she.

"You wouldn't mind passing your word?" says I.

She held out her hand.

Yes, sir, when she shook with me, there wasn't the least trembling to her fingers. She was steady as a rock!

"The fact is, ma'am," says I, getting more at sea every minute, "that I didn't aim to er—I mean—that is—I wouldn't of seemed to—"

"To hug me?" said Julie Ops. "Oh, that's all right. No bones broken, I *think*. Were you telling me true about Danny?"

"Does he mean such a pile to you?" says I.

"Ah," says the girl, "you *were* lying, and the fact is that you've simply—"

"No," said I, "he's safe and sound. I give you my word."

She gave a big sigh of relief.

"Tell me," she says, "did Danny put up a good fight?"

No, she never said the thing that you would expect her to say!

"It was rather brief," I admitted, "but Danny is game. He's dead game. He had an idea that his fist could travel faster than a bullet."

"You *did* shoot him!"

It made me mad.

"Look here, girl," said I, "I don't take that sort of talk from nobody. I've told you a fact. And I don't lie. I don't *have* to!"

That was talking a bit rougher and meaner than necessary, but she was extremely irritating, in her own way, I can tell you!

"I beg your pardon," said she. "You knocked Danny down with your gun, then, but you didn't shoot?"

"I used the knuckles of my fist," said I, still pretty heated.

"And what in the world is all this driving at?" said she. "Am I to be kidnapped to get even with Dad for hunting you?"

"I would even say," said I, "that you have come pretty near to it. But there was one thing that stood in between."

"Well?" said this girl.

"It was a pie," says I.

"What?"

"A loganberry pie," says I.

"What on earth—" says Julie.

"I mean, that I ate the pie, and that I thought I had better come around and explain—"

"*You* ate the pie?" said she.

"Yes," said I, "and afterward, I thought that I had better come around to explain that I done it, and I thought that the explaining would take a good deal of time, and so I arranged for Danny to stop up the road until I was all through—and I seem to of made a mess of things!"

"You do, sort of," she answered.

"Which I would put right, if I could," said I, "for the sake of the way that you stood by Lew, if you would tell me what I could do to make up."

Did she stand there thinking of what she would want? No, she didn't. She had her answer right ready on the tip of her tongue, but you never would guess what it was.

10

Suppose that you stop for a minute and think it over. Here is a young girl raised as fine as could be, and mighty delicate, and all that, and right in front of her is an outlaw, a bad actor, with eight thousand dollars on his head, him that she herself had called "murdering Larry Dickon" not so long before. Now the outlaw up and says that he wants to know what he can do for her, and what does she say? Does she tell him to just vamoose and raise a dust up the road as fast as he can go?

No, but she looked me right in the eye and she said: "If you're here, Cherry Pie isn't far off. I'd like to see Cherry!"

I reached for the nearest wooden pillar of that veranda and steadied myself a little, because I'm free to say that I'm not used to being taken so free and easy. I have known hardy gents to turn white at the sight of me, you understand, not because of what I am, but because of what folks have said about me, and what the fool newspapers have printed.

But this girl walked along beside "murdering Larry Dickon," and: "Mind the ditch," she says. "I nearly sprained my ankle there, last week." And then: "This way, please. Because that ground is all planted with sweet peas. There's the moon to let me see Cherry. What luck!"

. Because a big, fat-cheeked, golden moon had come up through the eastern trees and set the woods drifting with shadows, like images in water.

I whistled, and Cherry came out to us.

She stopped at the sight of the girl and pricked her ears.

"What a darling!" says the girl.

"Now go steady," says I, "because Cherry ain't fond of strangers—"

She didn't seem to hear me. She walked right up and rubbed Cherry Pie's nose, and by the look of Cherry, you would have said that she was getting sugar, she was so happy.

Julie was no baby about horses, either. She stepped back and looked over the lines of my mare.

"No wonder that Dad has such a time corralling you," says Julie. "Why, if I had a horse like this, *I* could be a bandit."

"Julie!" sings out a voice from the house, and just at the same minute, I heard a horse galloping down the road, and by the moon it was easy to see Danny Murphy, that had worked himself loose five times quicker than I thought he could and was coming bareback on one of his nags to see what was what.

"Thanks for telling me about the pie," says Julie Ops. "It saves me from thinking that Lew might have told a lie to me. So long—I hope you have all the luck that's coming to you!"

And as I ducked into the saddle, that girl stood there and waved to me, and a minute later she was screeching: "This way. He's here, Danny!"

It didn't make me mad. She was simply playing the cards the way that they had been dealt to her. And since she had been half an inch from collecting eight thousand dollars and a lot of headlines for being a "heroine," you couldn't blame her for wanting to see me done for.

Danny Murphy came on as fast as his horse would let him, and it was a good horse, too. But I jumped Cherry over the hedge back into the grove, and when I cut out on the other side, all that Danny could do was to empty his revolver at me from a distance, as Cherry bobbed away through the moonshine.

Altogether, I felt pretty good over this thing. But if I sat down and tried to figure out why, I was puzzled. Because I had come down here to raid the sheriff's house and raise Ned, and all I had done was to steal a loganberry pie!

However, there ain't any accounting for the things that make you happy, any more than there is for the things that make you sad.

I streaked Cherry right across the country for eight miles and got down at the shack of the only man in the world that valued me more than the price on my head. I mean, that was old Choctaw's place.

Why he was called Choctaw, you know as well as I do, except that when he was a youngster he had been as wild as any Indian. He was smoking his pipe in front of his house when I drifted up through the woods.

Even before I brought Cherry to a walk, he sang out: "It's all right, son. The coast is clear, except for me. Put up Cherry and give her a feed of barley. The bin is full up."

I did as he said, and left Cherry having a go at that good fodder while I went back and sat down beside Choctaw.

I got out my own pipe, and it was real restful to sit there and watch the tree tops stirring across the stars.

"Grace made it too hot for you, I see," says Choctaw.

"What do you know about Grace?" I asked him.

"Doctor Grace," says Choctaw, "is a real wicked man that salts mines and sells them to tenderfeet when he ain't got a fine murder job on his hands. I would like to know, how come you had to try your hand on Grace? Wasn't Wally Ops enough for you?"

It was no good asking him where he had got his information so sudden. Matter of fact, telephones and telegraph wires had been laid so free and far, lately, that the whole country was getting uncomfortable, and everybody was apt to know more about you than you did yourself. But even before telephones and such, old Choctaw seemed to have underground ways of knowing. He was a wise old devil, for fair.

"Grace stole my mare," I told him, "and I followed along and snagged one of his gang."

"I know. But Sandy was the foolishest of the bunch. You won't handle the rest as easy as all of that! Not when they get onto your trail again!"

"Listen, Choctaw," I said, "it ain't a question of them trailing me. It's a question of me trailing them. Didn't I tell you that they stole my mare and left me stranded without even one gun in the middle of the desert?"

"Sure," said Choctaw. "I hear you talk."

He was busy filling his pipe, and I lay back in my chair and sang a song.

"There is only one thing," said Choctaw, "that you ain't instructed me about. I've got your money all invested as safe as can be. But you ain't told me what am I to do with it when you get snagged?"

"Keep it and spend it," said I.

"No," said he. "I wouldn't take the coin of a partner. You got to give it to somebody else. But tell me, old son, what that somebody or something could be. Churches is good on the receiving end of gifts!"

"Churches may be damned," says I. "How come you to talk so much about me dying, Choctaw?"

"Because the time ain't far off," says he.

I sat up. When you heard Choctaw yap, it meant something.

"The time ain't far off? Well?"

"That's what I said."

"What do you know?"

"Oh, I know enough!"

"I mean, what's the deal that I got against me?"

Choctaw made one of his long pauses. A damn mean man about slow talking, that Choctaw was.

He said: "You having that Wally Ops after you don't count, and getting mixed up at the same time with Doctor Grace—that's nothing worth talking about, I suppose?"

"I'll handle them," I told him. "What else?"

"Stop singing, then."

"Go ahead."

"I was saying that Ops and Grace ain't enough to bother you very much. It's something else that makes me know that you're about at the end, my lad."

"I'm listening."

"When a gent plays a lone hand," says Choctaw, "he gets by pretty well. But when he ties himself up to partners, then he's in for trouble. How many times have they laid for you, because they knew that you was my friend, and that you would come this way if you was in my part of the country?"

"They've tried to tag me three times here," I admitted.

"Which is bad, Larry. But there is something a lot worse than a man for a partner. I mean, a woman."

I jumped up.

"Hey, Choctaw," said I, "what are you talkin' about?"

"I say that you got a woman back in your head, lad, and you ain't gunna sleep so sound on account of her, and you ain't gunna shoot so straight!"

It upset me a good deal.

"Choctaw," I told him, "you listen to God honest facts, will you?"

"Sure," said he.

"Now I tell you that there ain't a woman in the world that I'm dizzy about."

"You do some thinking and unsay that," said Choctaw.

I thought back. I had hardly laid eyes on women folks half a dozen times in the last year.

"No," said I, "there ain't hardly a one that I've so much as looked at!"

"Hardly?" says he.

"Oh," I told him, "that's the sheriff's daughter, that stuck one of my own guns into my floating ribs tonight and tried to get herself famous. She's a nervy little runt, Choctaw!"

"Ha!" says Choctaw, breathing out a big chunk of smoke. "That's Julie, eh?"

"That's her name."

"Well," says Choctaw, "she would make a good wife for a hard-handed gent. Maybe you are him. But she means trouble, old son. Couldn't you pick out something easier than a sheriff's daughter?"

"Listen, Choctaw," I tried to explain. "I ain't picked her out. The reason that I come up here was to raid the sheriff's house and—"

"But you seen Julie and forgot?" said Choctaw.

It made me mad. But what could I say? I just damned and sat back and lighted my pipe.

"What's filled your head full of this kind of an idea?" I couldn't help saying.

"Why," says Choctaw, "when I was young, I was in love, too."

"Was you?" said I, sort of interested. "But never married?"

"Only three times," says Choctaw.

"Three times married!" I shouted. "And nobody ever knowed about it?"

"One died of whooping cough, which is a fool thing for a growed up person to die of, but she had got her throat real tender by sitting up late, lecturing me about what I was and wasn't. One of them ran off with another gent while I was on the trail of a gold mine that never turned up, And one of them turned out to have another husband cached away some place before me. So out of the three I drawed this shack, and a billion dollars' worth of peace, son. But each of them three made some kind of a fool out of me. But never the kind that *you* been turned into by your woman."

"Tell me what kind that is, Choctaw."

"A singing fool, Larry," said he. "No woman ever made me a singing fool, and Julie Ops has done that for you. That was how I knowed that you was gone."

I started to answer him, pretty severe. But then I got to thinking. How long had it been before tonight since I had done any singing?

I couldn't even remember!

11

IT was a queer thing.

It reminded me of once I had been out in a little party with some gents and one of them had got nipped through the body with an old-fashioned, sharp-nosed forty-four caliber slug. But he seemed all right, and he was laughing and joking and singing a little, and always asking for the brandy flask, and saying when he got fixed up how he would ride right after Sam Butler, that done the shooting of him, and finish the fight.

This while the doctor was examining of him.

"Hurry up, doc," says my friend. "Pull a bandage around me. I got a little riding to do before the morning comes."

The doctor was a gent that never wasted many words.

He looked up and he said: "Bandages will do you no good, Lorrimer. You are going to die."

Just like that, he said it. And I still can see poor Lorrimer's jaw sag as the idea hit home in him. I can still see his eyes turn glassy and his face turn white. And when he died, five minutes later, it was more as though what the doctor said had killed him than as though the bullet was responsible.

Now it was a good deal the same way with me.

When I heard old Choctaw say that I was in love, it made me mad, at first, and then I wanted to laugh at the idea and I did. But that laugh ended up squeaky and high and weak and stopped short like a horse that has broke down.

Because what Choctaw had said had struck home in me and made me sick.

I said: "Well, you're wrong."

"All right," said he, "I'm wrong, then. But just the same, before you ride on, I wish that you would make out your last will and testament, as the papers say."

"Damn it, Choctaw," said I, "you act like I was already stretched out with the coroner talking over my dead body!"

"You are, practically," said he.

"Damn the money," said I. "You can keep it yourself or give it away, just as you please."

"I'll pick out a first rate charity," said Choctaw. "I always been hankering after giving some money to one of those missionaries that gets et up by cannibals in the South Seas, or something."

"I sure hope that you get pleasure out of it," said I, "but you try to remember that I ain't a corpse yet, Choctaw."

"No," said he, "but if I was your wife, I'd order mourning in, just the same. Because, if you fell in love with Julie Ops, you're as good as done for. You'll hang around this part of the country until the sheriff, or Grace, or somebody else has snagged you—and that's the end of it! The only way for you to live, son, with ten thousand on your head, is to keep right on moving!"

I was sort of desperate, in a way. I jumped up and started to answer him. But I tell you that the weakness was spreading through me. It was one thing that most done for me. It was thinking of her lying over the table with her head in her arms, laughing, and making it sound like sobs.

And every time I thought of that, my whole soul opened up, like a cash register with the ringing of a bell.

Well, you can lay to it that I wouldn't give up as easy as that.

I hollered at old man Choctaw: "I'll show you, Choc, that you're all wrong. I'm gunna blow out of here, and I'm not coming back inside of a year, and if I do, may I be—"

"Steady!" said Choctaw. "You better save that promise. Because I hate a gent that tells lies to himself!"

Mean, that was; real mean of Choctaw to talk like that. But I got too mad to talk to him any more. I give him a good damning, that didn't seem to bother him none, for he just went on smoking of his pipe, and so I stamped back and called Cherry and marched away across the hills, only aching for trouble—longing for trouble—sick for it, I can tell you!

And I found it!

I forgot Doctor Grace. I forgot Wally Ops. I forgot about everything except putting so much action between my mind and the memory of Julie that there wouldn't be a single chance for her to get my attention.

I headed away like a bird and dove through Arizona, making all the stops, like a local train; and everywhere I stopped, I had my fun, and pretty soon they knew what direction I was coming in, and they would be waiting for me, but I always managed to slip through the lines, as you might say, and I had my little party, and I went on.

I went clean on to the border, and dipped across it and had a hard fight with some mescal, and then I turned around and I winged back through Arizona and I headed through New Mexico; and all the way, my trail was one that you could follow by the smoke, you might almost say!

It took me close onto five months, altogether.

Those five months, there was something happening every day, or else about to happen, or else it had just happened. Which I am proud to say that there was no dead men that they could lay up to my charges during that trip except a couple of Mexicans that jumped me on the border of the old country; the only reason that I mention the Mexicans at all is to show you that I am telling you the whole truth and not leaving out nothing.

And at the end of the five months, I looked back and I told myself what a rip-roaring good time I had had, and how fine it was that two state governors had sent reprimands to county sheriffs because I was still roving around abroad, and because the price on my head had been boosted to twelve thousand dollars.

Not that I had done anything, except that I had made a noise and let myself be talked about.

Anyway, at the end of that time I had come along to a little joint where I knew from a long time before that I would be pretty safe and welcome, because I had salted down the gent that owned the shack with such a fat lot of money, several times.

And finally, as I was stretched out in a corner room of that shack, I heard the little girl of the house say to her mother: "Ma, what's that man sick of?"

"Sick?" says the woman. "Sick? He ain't sick."

"Yes," says the girl, "he looks just like he'd got the stomach ache—"

Well, I got up and had a squint at myself in the mirror. I got to say that I didn't think it was as bad as all of that, but just the same, I was changed a good bit. And it did look as though I might be in a good deal of pain.

What could have made that, and me after five months of real vacation, never worrying about how much trouble I made, never bothering to cover up my trail, but just blazing away and enjoying life in earnest?

I thought it all over.

And while I was thinking, the picture of Julie laughing at the table come whang into my mind, always like the ringing of a bell.

And I seen in that mirror how the sweat started out and rolled down from all over my face.

So I knew, right then, that it was no good. That girl had got me. And old Choctaw was right. Though I still sort of blamed him for my trouble, just the way that my friend had blamed the doctor for telling him that he was going to die.

I saw the end as clear as a whistle.

I loved her too much to stay away from her. I was weak in the stomach and I was dizzy in the head and I was wobbly in the knees, because that is what love does to you.

And since I couldn't stay away from her, I had best go back and face the music. Though I wouldn't last long in that neck of the woods before the sheriff or Grace or the both of them had cornered me and had got me.

It was sort of sad. But the minute that I had made up my mind to go straight to the girl, I can tell you that I was ready to sing, I was so happy. And if I had seen a gun leveled straight at my head, would it of made any difference? No, it would not!

12

ACROSS my sleep that night, the whinny of my mare ripped like a snatch of lightning through the sky. I got up quick, shoved my feet into my shoes, and dragged a hat onto my head. That took me half a second. The next half I was gathering in my rifle and getting to the window, and the whole of the next second after that, I was getting through that window and dropping toward the ground.

I knew that there was trouble, because, ever since that Cherry had let

Grace and his hounds run away with her, I had been pretty well set on teaching her that she was to let nobody but me handle her, and she was to sound up the minute that anybody else got at her.

It was a terrible nuisance, teaching, because Cherry was a good-natured sort, very cheerful and friendly, and she would stop and take sugar from anybody's hand. You could tell from one look at her fine, wise head, that she had too much sense to make mischief, and little children was always free with her. She wouldn't have hurt a mouse, except for her friskiness.

But after my trouble about losing her in the middle of the night, I was scared, of course, and I had been working steady to get her into acting as a sort of an alarm clock. All these months, I never let up, and that was why I knew that her whinny from the corral on this night meant something.

I said that I went through the window fast, but I don't mean by that that I made any extra noise, and so, as I slipped around the corner of the house, I almost run straight into Ham Turner talking with two gents.

Ham was the owner of the shack. I had spent plenty of money on him, but not enough to keep him straight. He was one of those low-life hounds that never done anything worse in their lives than shoving a bit of the queer, now and then, but it was only being scared to take bigger chances that kept him from doing worse things.

He was doing something worse, now, but he was making a great pother about it. He was saying:

"But look at the chance that I take!"

And one of the other men up and said: "Look here, you know me, or don't you know me?"

"I don't know you," said Turner.

"Then do you know Lew Candy, here?"

"No," said Ham Turner, "I don't know Lew Candy."

"Maybe you don't know Doctor Grace, either?"

"I know Doctor Grace, sure."

"Well, old son, that same Doctor Grace is out yonder corralling that smart mare, Cherry, and as soon as he's got her, he'll be kicking along here to ask you if you'll give him a chance to get a try at this Dickon. What d'you say?"

"A try at Dickon? Hey, young man, Larry Dickon has always been a good friend to me! Does Grace mean for me to betray a gent that has—"

The voice of Missouri Slim came snarling in.

"Grace don't beg for nothing, but he just offers to buy. Now what do you say. Will you sell, Ham?"

Ham snorted, and Lew Candy put in: "Shut up and pipe down, Turner! Are you trying to warn that Dickon that we're out here? Because I'll bash your face in if I think that!"

Rough and mean, was Lew Candy. Terrible mean!

But Ham buckled right down. "Look here, boys," he said. "I want to be reasonable. I only want to be reasonable, and it ain't reasonable to suppose that I wouldn't a lot rather have Doctor Grace for a friend than for an enemy—but a man has got to get his living in his own way, and taking in paying guests, once in a while, of them that *needs* places to stop at—"

"You poor damn fool!" said Missouri Slim. "Do you think that Grace is any piker? What do you want?"

"Not money—that ain't what I'm talking about," begins Ham Turner.

What a low skunk and hound he was!

"All right," said Candy. "Here is ten bills. You can light a match and look at them. Each of them is for twenty dollars. Each of them means twenty iron men, old sport. You collect that much if you let us through the door, as soon as Doctor Grace comes along!"

Ham Turner hung fire for a minute, and as I stood there, flattened out against the wall of the house, I hoped that maybe he wouldn't sell. Because, for one minute, he hesitated.

Why, I was all the more of a fool. It wasn't decency or his word to me that he was thinking about, but only that price that he was getting.

He said: "Now, let's talk sense."

"Yes," says Candy, "that's just what I want to do!"

"All right. Then you begin by taking a look at what this here Larry Dickon is. He ain't a lapdog, exactly?"

"No, we're admitting that he ain't."

"And if you was to slip up and not nail him now, why, what would that Larry Dickon do to me? He'd murder me and all my family!"

"We won't slip up, Ham, if that's what's worrying you. Does Doctor Grace slip very often? And ain't he got enough helpers now to handle three like that Dickon?"

"I hear you talk," said Ham Turner. "That's all right. But the fact is, you know, that he got through you once before."

"Because we took pity on him and didn't finish him off the same time that we took his mare away from him."

"You got his mare while he was asleep, and then he follered you right along and he found you camped, and he killed one of the best of you, and he took back his mare, and everything else that he needed, and if he hadn't been a fool, he would of turned loose a rifle at you while you was sprawling around your camp!"

That brought an oath from Candy.

"Does this Dickon say this?" he asked.

"Dickon don't talk," said Ham. "But everybody knows about that."

"It's that nigger," said Lew Candy. "That damn Little Joe has been shooting off his mouth and telling everything that he knows. I wish that Grace would junk him! Well, Ham, I give you my word that Grace means business, this time, and when he gets through with Larry Dickon, there won't be nothing for you to worry about. Understand?"

"I hear what you got to say," replied Ham, "but this sounds to me like a job that's worth three hundred dollars, anyway."

"Well," said Candy, "take the money, then, and do your part of the job.

What the devil does Grace mean by making so much noise out there in the corral?"

For there was a regular ruction going on in the corral.

"Y'understand," said Ham Turner, "that the only reason that I'm doing this ain't because of the money, but because of the way that this here Dickon has acted. Kind of too damn familiar with my old girl—"

Well, when I heard that, I couldn't help tipping up the muzzle of a gun. It was a close shot, and I had the stars outlining the body of Ham. I couldn't have missed him, but still I couldn't shoot for the same fool reason that I wasn't able to shoot into the gang of Grace when they was sitting around their fire. A kind of weakness of the nerves comes over me, and I ain't able to do the sensible thing.

"We know what you're afraid of," sneered Lew Candy, and his voice was fairly oozing with contempt, "but the matter of fact is, Ham, that we want to get on with this job right away, and so if you'll just—"

Well, it was heart-breaking. Here was the lowest-down sneak of a trick in the world being played on me, and here I had three of them right under my guns, and yet I couldn't go for them without a fair warning given. You would think that God had made me like a rattlesnake, that couldn't bite without sounding off a warning first hand!

And if I tackled this gang, there was my mare out yonder in the corral, and a rope would sneak around her neck, the next minute, and then I would *sure* be done for, so far as making an escape was concerned.

I decided that I would show Cherry the way to me and give these three sneak-knives a warning at the same instant. So I raised the old signal whistle, short and sharp and stabbing through the night like steel.

Ham Turner and Slim and Lew Candy nearly jumped out of their skins. Missouri and Lew jumped for the shrubs that grew handy, but that Ham Turner, the mean low sneak, he done a still wiser thing, because he just dropped for the ground and, when he hit it, he must of lay face down, and not even breathed, because I didn't see no sign or no sound of him.

I didn't have time to stop and look. I made for the brush and took the gent that turned to the left. I dived right through the brush at him and a gun spat fire into my face. By the flash of it, I saw Missouri Slim crouched close to the ground, with a pair of guns out and his long, narrow face all drawed and twisted out of shape with fear, and his eyes fairly popping out.

"Help, Lew! He's here!" screeched Missouri, and that was the last word that he spoke, because as his gun spatted at me and he yelled, I sent a bullet through his head and then turned and went hunting for Lew Candy.

He was different stuff. He was turning loose a steady fire from behind the next shrub, and he was cutting the dust around me with such neatly placed slugs that I knew that he wasn't helpless with fear, not by a long sight!

In the meantime, there was the frisking of hoofs coming rapidly toward me and I sneaked back to meet it as fast as I could jump.

Cherry Pie came at me with her ears pricking and a nicker to show me that I was welcome, and I jumped onto her bare back and with a pat of my hand and a pressure of my knee I showed her which way to steer.

13

CAN you imagine running out of a wasps' nest?

That was the way it was, getting clear of the tangle of fences around the Turner shack. I could hear a voice ringing and clanging behind me in the night, giving orders, and tearing straight after me, itself, and I knew that that was Doctor Grace, coming for blood. And he and his boys was all the finest riders that you would ever want to see, and I knew that Grace rode thoroughbred stock and kept the same kind for his boys, whenever the luck was with him. They foamed across the country after me fast as lightning streaking, for a mile or so, but after that, they dropped back very fast.

It was always that way. There was plenty that could stay with my Cherry Pie for a mile or so, but when loose or hard going began to bog them down or to hurt their hoofs, or when the distance and the pace began to tell, then you would see Cherry flaunting off by herself and leaving the rest dying behind her. There was nothing else like her, not at all!

And the damning and the shooting of Grace and his lot fell off and left me alone, with the night rolling into my face and all hell boiling in my heart.

Because, you see, I fair hated myself for not having turned loose with both guns on Ham Turner and those two men of Grace. Not that I wanted Slim and Lew so much, but it would of eased me a lot to of sunk a slug through that narrow sconce of his.

However, there was one less of them, and that pleased me a lot. Because I knew what a big effort Doctor Grace had made to snag me, and how he had sent out the word everywhere that he would let everything rest and hang until he had finished off the gent that had murdered Sandy Larson.

That was the way that he put it, of course. But you can see why this was important to him. Grace had gone along all of these years so terrible successful that when one of his gang was snatched right out of his very hand, as you might say, and then a horse grabbed away from him—why, it was too much, and if he wanted folks to respect him and fear him as much as they had always done before, he would have to get out and run down the gent that done the shooting.

He had let folks all know what he intended to do, and that was why a lot of people thought that when I went tincanning south for the border, I was simply running away from Grace as fast as I could, not just out to have a little party all by myself; and now Grace had laid his trap for me and got all set to eat me alive—

But he wasn't enjoying the meal none too much.

Here I was, safe and free as the finest horse in the mountains could make me, and there was Doctor Grace and his three men with a dead hand to bury.

Why, it was pretty sweet, and this night's job would put a spike in the Doctor's reputation. People wouldn't be so ready, after this, to believe that he could do anything in the world that he wanted to try, and people would have a mite more respect for Larry Dickon, or I missed my guess.

Yes, I was terribly interested in the way that my reputation grew. Which I should be ashamed to say so, I suppose, but always the knowledge that folks was having a chance to hear about me and about the things that I had done, and that maybe here and there a gent would say: "That was neat!" or "That was nervy!" or "I wish that I had done that!"—why, the thinking about such things was a tremendous big comfort to me. Though most likely it's childish to say so.

We come up from the draw where the Ham Turner shack stood, and then we floated along through some hills with me very contented, and wondering was it worth while for me to ride on, or had I better turn right back and try to shoot up the rest of the gang while they was more thinking about how they was to hunt me than about how I was to hunt them.

But I guessed that that wouldn't do, because the Doctor was too smart to be caught by any little tricks. It would take something mighty big and bold and strong to down him and his lot twice in one night.

So I gave up the thought of that.

I admired the Doctor about as much as I hated him, to tell the truth. Because you can see for yourself that to try to locate me while I was flying around for six months across different states, and hardly sleeping twice within twenty-five miles of the same spot—why, to reach out and touch me while I was flying around like that was a good deal of a job even to imagine. But Doctor Grace had managed it, and if it hadn't been for the warning that I got from my mare, why, who could tell what would of happened?

In the meantime, I didn't have a saddle, and if you never rode a distance bareback, you can't guess how tiring it is. It was a mean, sweaty job before I came in the gray of the morning to the sight of a ranch.

Nobody was stirring that early. I went down to the barns and I found the saddle room quick enough and picked out something that would do for the mare. I didn't take any of the fancy saddles that looked as though the punchers had set their hearts on them. I just took a plain old one with the leather scruffed up a good deal, and a bridle and a couple of blankets to match.

Then I wrote out a little note and I hung it on a splinter on the wall:

> Sorry that I had to borrow these things. I am leaving the
> money for them on the top of the barley box.
> LARRY DICKON.

So I put down there the full price for all of those things as they would of cost when new. Because that is the only way that you can keep everybody contented—to over-pay. And in spite of the bad things that I have done, here and there, nobody can ever say that I've short-changed anybody, or that I've bore down on any poor sheepherder or squatter and taken more than I paid for twice over, or that I've ever borrowed anything, from a fishing rod to a horse, without leaving the value in hard cash behind me, and something more than the value.

Now, you would say that when this gent found a mangy old saddle and bridle gone, and such a fat price for it left behind, he would of shut up and done no talking. But that ain't human nature. He had to go right around and circulate the news that Larry Dickon, the robber, had been there and had raided his ranch. And the reason that I know he did that talking, I'll explain later.

Which will make you say: Why did I leave a note and my name to it?

For the simple reason that, when you go alone and pay for what you take, this way, about every third time you run across a gent that appreciates being treated like a man instead of a dog, and when that happens, for all you know, you may have picked up a friend, and every friend that you can get, while the law is chasing you up and down, is worth more than his weight in gold. Here and there, spotted around on the desert and through the mountains, I have my partners that would do a good deal for me, and a surprising lot of them was made just by fair and square dealings, such as I've been talking about.

Now that I had some sort of an outfit, I took Cherry into the hills and laid up for three whole days, because if Grace or a sheriff or anybody else had been trailing me close enough to get an idea that I was heading in any particular direction, I wanted to let them think that they was wrong.

After I had rested up myself and Cherry, I drove straight north for two full day and night marches and come down into a little town where a couple of roads crossed and there was a river with a bridge across it right at hand. I forget the name of the town, but I think that the river was called Grundy's Creek.

When I hit that town, I saw that there was telegraph wires running into it, so that it would be sure to spread news as fast as any big city. I also found out, pretty soon, that there wasn't more than eight growed up men in that whole place, and four of them was playing poker in the back room of the General Merchandise Store.

When I walked in and took the fifth hand, they all seemed glad enough to see me. I was new money in that game, and since I didn't mind losing enough dollars to keep them happy, they loosened up quite a lot and everybody got cheerful until an old sand-faced gent with a patch over one eye come in and fixed his other bleary lamp on me and turned pale.

I knew that he had recognized me, but since I *wanted* to be recognized, I didn't much mind.

A little after that, I said that I had lost as much money as I could afford to lose, and I got up and left the room, and as I went down the hall, with the door open behind me, what do you think?

That old gent with the patch over one eye had the nerve to pull out his gat and try a shot at me!

And him closer to seventy than to sixty!

Anyway, that bullet plowed out a chunk of plaster and sprayed me with white powder. So I ducked around the next corner into the front of the building and sprinted for Cherry Pie where I had left her on the edge of the town in some poplar saplings.

Me running away like that put no end of courage into those gents. They followed me, and I let them hunt me north for about twelve miles before I opened up a notch with Cherry and let them drift out of sight behind me.

Now, by this time I figured that I had let the whole world know that I was heading straight for the north, and if telegraph lines was any good at all, they should certainly pull out a couple sheriffs and posses to bag me.

So, that same night, I turned Cherry south and east through a granite pass and I was heading straight back for Julie Ops.

14

I GOT to break off here and tell you some things which are important, though I wasn't on hand to see them with my own eyes or to hear them with my own ears, but I gathered in the drift of them, afterward. So I write them down here, because they are things that you need to know, to understand what comes afterward.

You'll see that I had wrote down Choctaw as a great friend of mine, though the only thing that I've showed him doing, so far, was growling and grumbling at me. But just the same, he thought a lot of me, and the one man in the world that I could depend upon doing his best for me, always, was that same old grouch.

Now, one day he drawed a map on the sand in front of his doorstep, when he was setting down, cooling off after chopping a lot of wood, because he wasn't as spry as he'd once been. And so he put down that map. You got to understand that that whole section of the country, for hundreds and hundreds of miles, was wrote down in the mind of old Choctaw, as clear as if he had been a real Indian; and as he sketched in the main features, of rivers and mountains and forests and such, he begun to stab down all the places where he had heard that I had been and as I said before, he always got the best information and got a little more of it and got it a little sooner than anybody else.

By the time that he had noticed all of the dots that he had put into his map, he saw that he was marking out a sort of a loop of the line of my traveling.

If you was just to hear about where I had been and what I had done in those six months, perhaps it would just seem that I was roaming sort of foolish and headless, but when old Choctaw had finished making the dots that marked the places where I had been, he saw that I had begun, for several months, by riding right straight away from the valley where the sheriff lived. But after that, I turned and come looping back.

Last report of all, I had broke away toward the north and the mountains was boiling to catch me. But that didn't fool old Choctaw. He made out to his own satisfaction that I was heading back for the place from which I had started. Besides, that agreed with his first idea, that I was out of my head because of that girl, and of course a man likes to think that he's right.

Anyway, when he had made up his mind, Choctaw put a saddle on his mule—he never kept horses any more—and he jogged that mule straight along over the hills and through the hollows and winding along among the woods, until he came to the house of the sheriff, and there he seen Julie in the tennis court, playing a game with a schoolgirl friend of hers that had come down to visit her.

Choctaw watched that ball flashing back and forth, and he says that to see the way that Julie handled that girl was a shame, because she always let herself get just a little beaten, so that her visitor would be happy, but all of the time, Julie was playing like a cat with a mouse. And when she set herself out to really make a point, she would whang that ball down the court and over the net like fury, and the other girl didn't have a chance to use her racket at all. And when Julie wanted to lose some points, she would back not six inches beyond the base line, or three inches past the sides. She was practicing up her game and having a good time in her own way, and her visitor all the while was tickled to death, nearly, because she was making the most points.

After Choctaw had watched this game for a time, he had an idea that this girl Julie was a bit out of the way of most ordinary women folks.

He waited until the game was clear over and Julie saw him and she called out: "Hello, Uncle Choctaw!"

She came over and leaned her racket against the ribs of the mule and stood there sweating in the sun, and laughing, and panting, and happy as a lark, while the other girl stretched out in the shadows beneath the trees, clean spent.

"Look here, Uncle Choctaw," said Julie, "how come you don't ever ride a horse no more?"

"Hey, Julie!" snapped Choctaw. "Is that grammar, I ask you? Ain't you learned no better than that how to speak up for yourself? How come you to talk like that, girl?"

She only laughed at him.

"You tell me about the mule, Uncle," says she. "And then I'll explain about the grammar."

"Horses," says old Choctaw, "is just a nuisance, always stumbling around and landing you on your head and falling down and tiring out."

"Oh, I can remember you," said Julie. "When I was little, I've seen you streaking around the country as fast as anybody, and nothing but blood horses would really do for you then!"

"I'll tell you the truth, honey," says that old rascal; "I been tired out. Tired out of fast ways and ready for slow ones. And besides, horses is a temptation, Julie."

"A temptation to what?" says she.

"A temptation, honey, that makes you want to see if anybody can catch you. Y'understand? And I'm tired of being chased, and I'm tired of chasing."

"Humph!" says Julie. "You were always honest, Uncle Choctaw. You can't talk balderdash to me!"

"I was always a mite scary—not honest," says he.

"Why don't you get down and rest your feet?" says Julie. "We have some Old Crow in a jug in the house and I know where it is."

Choctaw licked his lips and closed his eyes and sighed.

"I don't get off this mule," says he, "until I've said what I come to say."

"Fire away," she told him, and she stood back and nodded a little at him, and smiled at him, and admired him, and mocked him a little. If you can understand how one person could do all of them things at the same minute.

He dropped a forefinger like a gun at her.

"I've come here to talk to you about your sins, Julie!"

"What kind of sins?" says Julie.

"You admit that you got 'em?"

"Millions, Uncle Choctaw. Just tell me which?"

"The sin of rarin' and tarin' around with the hearts of young gents!"

"Who's been talking to you now?" says she. "And who do you want me to marry?"

"I ain't gunna ask you to marry no friend of mine," says Choctaw.

"Danny Murphy is a friend of yours?" she asks.

"Bah!" says Choctaw. "For why should I be bothering myself about the gents here in this valley? I've seen them all. And they ain't worth troubling over. But what I want to do is to talk to you about yourself and a real hundred per cent man that you been raising the devil with."

"I don't know who you mean," says she.

"How many gents he has killed since you sent him off on the warpath," says Uncle Choctaw, "you probably know a lot better than I do."

"What in the world are you talking about?"

"You couldn't guess?" says he, very sarcastic.

"No, and I couldn't. I don't know anybody as important as all of that."

"Murdering and hell-raising is important to you, then?"

"I'd rather talk five minutes to a gunfighter," says she, "than to some pink-and-white mama's boy!"

"Well," said he, "you're gunna have your wish before long. Inside of about five days, I should say."

"Ah?" said she.

"Yes, because he's coming for you, and he's coming fast!"

"Uncle Choctaw, Uncle Choctaw," she called at him, "will you tell me what on earth is in your wits?"

"Dust and cactus thorns and rattling bones is in my wits," says he, "because I see the death of a fine man coming along very pronto."

"Stuff!" said she, but she was terrible interested. She spun the racket around in her hands and watched his face as though it was a book.

"He's gunna come along here," said Choctaw, "and he's gunna see you, and your silly head is gunna spin right off of your shoulders, if it ain't spun off already, at the way you've talked to him—"

"I promise you," said she, "that I don't know who you're talking about."

"Tell me," says Choctaw, "will you cross your heart to die if you ain't had oceans of letters from him all the months that he's been away from you?"

"Who? Who? Who?" she yipped, dancing up and down like a terrier.

"Who? Who? Who?" he mocked her. "As if you didn't know perfect?"

"I don't, I tell you!"

"You don't know," drawled Choctaw, "that you sent him spinning away to raise the devil?"

"I don't know anything. But I'll go mad if you don't tell me what you're talking about!"

"And you don't know," said Choctaw, "that he's started back to get to you, now, and that he's murderin', and smashin' and crashin', and hashin' things up as he comes?"

You can see that Choctaw had a large and liberal supply of talk when he cared to use it.

"Choctaw," said the girl, "don't you see that you are burning me alive with curiosity, talking like this? Please, please, please tell me who it is that you mean, because you're all wrong!"

"You don't know him, you ain't ever seen him, nor his mare either, I suppose?" says Choctaw, dry as dust.

"Heavens!" says she. "By any wild chance can you possibly mean Larry Dickon?"

"By any wild chance," says he, "could I possibly mean anyone else?"

15

You can see by this, maybe, just how the mind of old Choctaw had been working.

And there was the girl gaping at him. And it seems that she turned a little red—with surprise, no doubt, and sort of excitement. And when she changed color, of course it seemed to Choctaw like a confession that everything that he suspected was right, and he sat in his saddle nodding down at her and grunting.

"Larry Dickon! Larry Dickon!" she said, over and over. "Uncle Choctaw, I forgot. Dickon is your best friend!"

"I thank God," says Choctaw, "that I can call him a friend!"

Which was a fine thing for Choctaw to say about me, and I thank him for it, here and now.

"And did Larry Dickon talk to you about me?" says she.

"Humph!" said Choctaw, "is that what I'm asking about?"

"It's what *I'm* asking," said she, "because the only time that I ever *saw* that man, I tried to hold him up with his own revolver, and then I tried to send Danny Murphy ahead to capture him; and that's the honest truth, Uncle, so how could he do anything but hate me?"

"You tried to hold up Larry," nodded Choctaw—the old duffer!—"and you tried to do it with his own gun. And being what he is, I suppose that that must of scared him a good deal."

"Scared him?" said she. "He had his hands above his head and he was doing everything that I told him to do, mighty serious and sober, until the shock of surprise—seeing his ugly face and recognizing it—gave him a chance to master his gun, again!"

"Humph!" said Choctaw. "Gave him his chance? He wasn't just playing with you, maybe, the same way that you been playing with that other girl, over yonder?"

She got a little redder still, at that.

"You're entirely wrong," said she.

"I guess I'm too old to be right any more," says Choctaw, dryer than ever. "And then you sent Danny Murphy after him—did I hear you say that you sent Danny Murphy along to capture *him?*"

"Why not?" says the girl. "Danny is—"

"All right, all right," says Choctaw. "I come over here to talk sense and reason, and if that don't please you, I'm through, and that's all that there is to it. So long!"

And he swung his mule around.

She got to the head of that mule in a flash and held it by the bridle.

"Look here, Uncle Choctaw," she said, "you can't run away like this and leave my head in a complete whirl."

"Your head in a whirl? Honey," he told her, "you needn't laugh at me. You're safe enough. It ain't *you* that I bother about. Because making fools out of young men is sort of a business with you. Only I wanted you to lay your hands off'n Larry, because fooling with him is dangerous. Y'understand?"

"And *what* have I done to him?"

"Nothing," growled Choctaw. "By your way of thinking, you ain't done nothing to him. But by my way of thinking, you've nearly wrecked him. You've sent him away a thousand miles, whaling and sailing through troubles, and whacking and cracking away at—"

"Are you going to blame *that* on me?" she said. "If a man sees me, is that an excuse for him to go murdering?"

"To try to forget you," said Choctaw. "To try to rub you out of his mind! That's what!"

"Heavens!" said Julie.

"There ain't any heaven in this. There's nothing but hell, and a lot of that!" said Choctaw. "And maybe you'll begin to see, before very long!"

She shook her head, by way of saying that she still didn't understand at all, but Choctaw took it for meaning that she didn't see how having bagged me made any difference more than usual, and that made him real mad, and he said:

"Looks simple and fine and easy to you, of course, but lemme tell you that while Dickon is hanging around you here, ain't the chance better than four out of five that he's gunna see your old man?"

"If he comes here—and if he sees Dad—"

"If he sees your dad, your dad is a dead man, and that's all there is to it," said Choctaw. "I happen to know that he come back here because he was tired of having your pa chase him, and he intended to raise so much hell at the sheriff's house that Wally Ops would come hopping back here—and then they would meet and have it out together. But when he arrived—he seen you and he made you out to be more dangerous than your old man by a long shot!"

Starting in to begin with, Julie had felt that Choctaw was just sort of crazy, but now she began to see that he was telling the truth, or a part of the truth, and she couldn't make out how much. But at least, she could see that this was a serious deal. She kept her grip on the bridle of that mule while she said:

"Choctaw, you talk to me!"

"What have I been trying to do?"

"Tell me, honest Injun, how could that man ever have given me more than a single thought—seeing me only an instant—"

"Honey," said old Choctaw, shaking his head, "here you been flirting with gents all these years, and now I have to tell you that love ain't no different from a gun, and that it hits just as quick, and that the hurt of it can be just as bad. Are you gunna ask me what he seen in you? I dunno. He's never been bothered about girls before, but I suppose that a snipe of a girl that dared to stand up to him with his own gun—I suppose that that knocked him off balance. But I know that when I seen him, just afterward, he was as moony as an owl. He was gone, complete. I told him to keep away. He said that he was going to. And ever since then he's been riding around and raising more devil than you could shake a stick at! Which ain't his way. Because he's a quiet gent!"

"Outside of a few robberies, and such things, now and then, just for fun?" put in Julie, by way of being a bit sarcastic herself.

"Julie," said Choctaw, "don't you start making me mad. I know that boy better than I know myself or you, and I know what sent him adrift, which was one of the worst and the rawest deals that any gent ever got in this here world!"

"Tell me about it," says Julie.

"For why?" asked Choctaw. "All I've come to say to you is that he's heading back here at last. He's tried to rub you out of his mind, and he can't do it. He's been fighting Doctor Grace, and running through all kinds of wild action, but it wasn't enough to keep him from thinking about you; and now he's coming back here, and I've rode over here to ask you, what are you gunna do with him?"

"What am *I* going to do with him?" echoed the girl.

"That's what I said to you, Julie."

"Will you please tell me what I *can* do?"

"Nothing but kill him or save him," said Choctaw. "You can be sweet to him, and smile at him, and be nice and kind and hold his hand, and—"

"Uncle Choctaw!" she snaps at him.

"Well," says he, "how do I know how you carry on? But that's the way that girls used to do when they wanted to turn *me* around their fingers, and I tell you that they never found any very hard job of it! But I say that if you talk mealy-mouthed to Larry Dickon, you'll have him inside of the trap, well enough, but it'll be the murdering of your father, and the death of other gents, too, and the killing of poor Larry himself before the end, and all because you would like to have a great gunfighter and outlaw hanging around and looking foolish about you, and telling you how much he loves you and—"

"Uncle Choctaw!" she cried at him. "*If* it's true that I mean anything to Larry Dickon—I'll—I'll—I'll never look at him again, if I can keep everybody from such trouble!"

"Ah, honey," says Choctaw, sliding down from the saddle and going and taking her hands, "do you mean it?"

"Don't I, just?" said she. "But what am I to do?"

"Will you lemme tell you?"

"Yes, yes, yes!"

"Then, when he shows up here in a couple of days—"

"In a couple of days!"

"Yes."

"But the last news is that he's breaking for the north—"

"All a fake and a bluff," said Choctaw, "because poor Larry is being drawed back to you, here, in spite of himself!"

"*Can* it be true?" says she.

"Can it be anything else *but* true?" says Choctaw. "Ain't I telling you, and don't I know him like a father, or better?"

"Then tell me what to do. Because I feel just helpless and hopeless, Choctaw. *What* can I do?"

"I'll tell you. This Larry Dickon that I know so well has got one very bad fault. He's proud. He's very proud, and when he comes along here, all that you got to do is to meet him and say to him—"

"It would be better for me not to see him at all!"

"Could you keep him from getting to you? No, you couldn't. He'll come, and when he does, I'll tell you what—you see him and you act as cold as you can, and you tell him it is a terrible tiresome and a disgusting thing, him to be hanging around you like this, and would he please take himself away and never come back, because you are aiming to quietly marry a good decent man, pretty soon, and that you don't want your front yard all littered up with outlaws, and such!"

"Heavens!" says Julie. "How can I talk to a man like that?"

"No," sneered Choctaw. "Don't you do it. You just be nice to him, and then in a couple more days you can be congratulating him on how fine and straight he shot when he killed Wally Ops—"

She stopped him with a little screech, and there was tears in her eyes.

"I'll do exactly as you say!" she said. "Oh, Uncle Choctaw, what have I ever done to deserve so much trouble ?"

"Busted hearts since you was out of short skirts," says Choctaw. "And all the trouble you get is only what you deserve!"

16

WHEN I come down out of the north, at last, I was pretty sure that I had beat the guessing of everybody that was interested in where I might go or what I might do. I thought that I would have a clear stretch before me to the house of Wally Ops. Somewhere behind me was Doctor Grace, raving on my trail and, I thought, pretty sure to miss it. Because he would think that when I went north I was trying to run away from him. And to the north, too, there would be the folks getting ready to hunt me through the mountains as I come along. The sheriff, I figured, would be clean away from my track, and so I didn't have much worry on me. You can judge for yourself, then, that I was tolerable mad when I got through the Windover Pass and, stopping Cherry for a breath of air and a rest, heard the clinking of hoofs come up the gorge behind me.

I left Cherry with her cinches loosened, breathing a bit, and snatching at a few mouthfuls of grass, while I ran back to the next turn and looked down the trail; and there, by confounded luck, I seen fifteen riders with their horses polished by sweat until they looked like iron statues in action, with the sun flashing on them and the dust going up like steam from around them.

You will say that fifteen mean more than one. But not when the one is the sort of a gent that was riding at the head of that gang. He was made low and broad, with long legs, so that he fitted onto the back of a horse as neat and as strong as a clothespin onto a small rope, and he had a sombrero with a limp brim that flapped up and down across his eyes. He looked like any old desert rat, at a mite of distance, but he was riding a whacking good horse and the way of his riding was familiar to me. Most punchers let a horse ramble on a loose rein, but this gent kept a tight hand, and he always seemed to be sort of lifting his horse along over the road, and picking out the best spots, and studying every inch of the way.

So I knew by the first glance that this was Wally Ops. And of all the men that ever rode down my trail, there was none that I feared so much as him. Because he was like a cross-breed between bulldog and greyhound.

I went back to Cherry and cinched her up again, while she turned her head and watched me in a hurt sort of a way, as if she knew that she had done enough work for that day, and so it was time to rest. But that was always the way. When others came at me, I had Cherry Pie fresh and ready, and we frisked away from them like nothing at all, but when Ops showed up, there was sure to be a tired mare under me.

However, we had the whole length of Windover Valley ahead of us, and I made sure than even a tired Cherry would be better than the best that the sheriff could have with him.

And she was!

She went floating down the valley, and behind me, pretty soon, I seen the sheriff and his men streaming out like a flag blown ragged by the wind of their own galloping. They fought hard to get at me, but the nearest that they could come was long rifle range, and if that's dangerous, then there ain't anything in a road agent's life that can be called safe.

It was the bright time of the early morning when we started that ride. It was noon when I pulled out from Windover Valley with the sheriff and his gang dead beat behind me; but over to the left, I seen riders come crashing through a dust cloud into the foot of the valley, and through the dust cloud, I could see that there was more horses than men!

Something told me, then, that the sheriff had managed to get word ahead of him, in some manner, and that these was gents coming down with fresh mounts for the posse.

Damn the telephone, I say. Electricity, it sure has made life hard!

Well, what was I to do?

Press straight ahead and get as much of a start as I could, and hope for some way of blinding my trail for them?

Well, in those smooth, rounding hills, with plenty of soft surface dirt, you couldn't hide a trail from microscope eyes like those of the sheriff. No, there was no hope of that.

In the next hollow there was a muddy stream running along. I dismounted and stripped the saddle from the back of Cherry, and I began to slosh the water over her. She was so hot that she turned to steam, with the sun on the outside and her boiling blood on the inside; but pretty soon she cooled down a good deal, and the pain went out of her eyes, and she began to reach for the green fringe of grasses that growed along the bank of the stream.

When she done that, I started right along, because I knew that she had had enough cooling.

There was three miles of steep climbing and soft dirt for a trail ahead of me. And my hope was that even Wally Ops, when he got his men to this place, wouldn't be able to keep them from rushing the rise of ground, because on their fresh horses, they would feel as though they could eat me right up! Well, if they charged that slope, and tried to gallop uphill through that soft dirt, they was about done for, by my way of figuring!

In the meantime, I had to save Cherry.

Well, God gave me strength all over my body, and he gave me too much in the hands. But hands and feet and legs and back all had to work, now. I made up my mind that I would carry that heavy range saddle and the guns and the pack, and all, to the top of that rise. And I hit it at a dog-trot, the same way that Indians do—and, like an Indian, I put the saddle on the top of my head.

Did you ever try to handle a range saddle like a pack? It's heavy to begin with, but, worse than that, it's made awkward. It always wants to slide the wrong way, and I was tripping and stumbling all the time, with first one stirrup and then the next getting between my legs.

Cherry, you would of laughed to of seen her! She thought that I was crazy. She ran after me and sniffed at me, to make sure that I was her boss, just the same as usual.

And then she nipped at my shoulder until I damned her. And then she went and stood in my path until I beat her out of it.

But finally she just walked along beside me, nickering now and then, and trying to get used to me.

Poor Cherry! There was always something new for her to try to understand about her boss!

Well, that was as killing work as I ever did, with my feet slipping back one foot for every two that I went ahead, and my shoes driving ankle deep in the soft sand, and the dust even of my own going chugging up into my face and filling my throat and drifting like grit down my back and mixing with the sweat on my forehead and running down into my eyes—and then the dangling stirrup leathers getting between my legs and always tripping me up, and something always falling from the pack, and the heat of the sun baking me, and a damned side wind smashing at me now and again—

I should say that that was three miles of hell, but all that time I was resting my mare, and Cherry was coming back to herself with every step that she made.

I got over two miles of that grade, and I was sick and blind when I turned around and seen the posse stream across the valley floor and hit the work behind me.

Yes, they come at a gallop, waving their hands, eager to eat me up.

No matter how eager, they *couldn't* gallop all the way after me.

Cherry heard them and saw them, and she flattened her ears along her neck. She was used to being chased, and she loved nothing better, and it always made her a little mad when any other horse dared to think that it could catch up with her.

I will tell you how bad and how mean and how slippery and sandy that slope was, when I say that, though they was spurring and beating their horses along behind me, and getting in each other's ways, and raving and yelling like buzzards, still I had time to cover the next mile before they got within striking distance.

I had done what I set out to do. I had climbed up the whole three miles of that slope carrying the saddle and the pack, and letting my mare get back her strength, but it near killed me. And when I tried to swing the saddle onto the back of Cherry, it just slipped out of my hands, and I would of fallen and not been able to get up if I hadn't blundered blind against Cherry. I held my arms around her neck until my head cleared a little.

Then I saddled her, my hands trembling terrible and the blood rushing in waves behind my eyes and trying to press them out of my head, and blackness circling and swinging around in front of me.

I saddled her, with the sheriff's men coming lunging for me up the slope.

There was a couple of shots fired, but then I heard somebody's voice squeaking from the rear:

"Don't shoot! We'll take him alive, damn him!"

That was Wally Ops!

It made me so mad that my head cleared up right away. I jerked the cinches home and snapped into the saddle. And as I went over the crest, I looked back to the posse.

They was all riding hard and fast. They was all pressing their horses for a gallop, and getting not much more than a walk, and I seen the horses shaking their heads and the foam flying from their bridles, and I seen them lowering their heads, in spite of the sand and the dust that they snuffed in. And I knew somehow, by the steaming and the reeking, and the staggering of that whole outfit, that they was beat—that they was entire beat, and when they got to the down slope they would see what the mare could do with them!

There was only one exception. Away off to the rear come Wally Ops, and the little devil was walking, the same as I had done, except that he wasn't carrying the saddle, of course, and he was leading a whacking fine looking big gray horse, and right then and there I smelled trouble!

17

WHY, what happened when we went down the slope was just what I expected. Those boys had rode most half the day to get me, and they had used up one set of horses, and they knew that my mare hadn't been freshed when they begun running me in the morning. So it didn't seem less than right that with their new mounts they should gallop right over me. They forgot that you can kill a horse with a three-mile sprint just as well as you can by a fifty-mile gallop.

I went down the slope with Cherry running like a sailing hawk, and when I looked back, I seen the posse come over the crest, and when they hit the down slope and used their spurs, those horses staggered like they was drunk, and one went down, and throwed its rider about a mile into the air.

I laughed and called Cherry Pie back a notch. Because I didn't think that there was any use in her killing herself off for the sake of that bunch. And I couldn't help leaning back and brushing the sand off of her hips and quarters and then off of her all over, so that they would be able to see her shining like gold and silver as she walked away from them across that desert.

And I knew that before the night come there would be gents that would swear my mare wasn't nacheral flesh and blood, and there would be a lot more of them that would be willing to pay down her weight in gold and diamonds for the sake of owning her.

However, that posse was a ruined lot of fools before they got to the bottom of that slope, and as they come down, stopping every step, and their poor tired nags going up and down like rocking horses, without getting ahead, I seen Wally Ops come striding through them on the gray.

He looked fine, and his hoss looked fine and fresh, and beside him out of the rear there rode three other gents that had saved their mounts a little on that killing slope.

Well, four was better to handle than fifteen. But when I seen the look of that gang, I couldn't help reaching for my rifle, because they looked extreme like business, I can tell you!

I steadied my Cherry Pie to her work and I started riding her to save inches and ounces.

There was no use waiting until she was beat before I started to lighten her. I chucked away my whole pack, I cut away my saddlebags. I throwed off my cartridge belt. I stripped away all that I had except the saddle and the rifle and one revolver, with the bullets that was in those guns.

I couldn't tell any difference in the striding of the mare, after she was lightened by those pounds. I looked back and hoped that the boys in the rear would stop to scoop in the plunder, but they didn't.

They rode right on past it—past my slicker, and all my pack, and those fine, shiny new guns, lying one after another in the dirt, so that even while I was riding away from them for my life, I couldn't help admiring in my heart of hearts the way that the sheriff was able to get together such first-rate men, and how he could teach them the rules of the game. Because I had had enough experience with posses to know what fools they can be.

For these four come on, not riding in a huddle, where the dust of one would bother the other, but spread out, maybe a dozen yards or more between each one, and, for that reason, looking more fine and formidable by a lot. They was four picked men. Each one of them a handful, and each of them riding on a picked blood horse that had stood up under the grind that had killed off the other mounts.

They worked those horses for a solid hour, and for an hour I jockeyed my Cherry along, waiting for the time when her head would begin to come up a little, and waiting for the time when her hoofs would begin to pound—

No, she didn't pound! Her gallop was as light as a bird skimming along, but, by the stretch and the strain of her neck and by something that come quivering up to me along the reins, I knew that Cherry was running with her heart and her nerves more than with her strength.

And it turned me sort of wild, to think that she was killing herself for my sake. And I turned in the saddle and I yelled at those gents behind me, and damned and raged at them. And then I turned back and rode Cherry with all the wits that I had in me, studying the trail, when there was a trail, looking for the easiest grades, when we come to the hills again, and always fighting and working.

And—though God knows how she managed to do it—she kept them off, and when I looked back again, I could see them doing what I had done before—cutting away everything, and stripping their hosses to the quick, except for a gun or two apiece.

Ay, and if they had done that when *I* did it, there would of been an end to me five miles back, but now I sort of hoped that it would be too late.

Too late for three of them.

Besides the sheriff, there was a brown, a blue roan, and a fine young bay. The brown went first, jerked back bit by bit as though somebody had a line hitched onto him and was pulling him back.

And then we hit a rise in the ground and the bay crumpled and lay dying on the ground, and the roan curled up, too, and stood with braced legs, and with hanging head.

But still Wally Ops came on after me!

I couldn't believe it, really. I looked back, and I looked again. Because it wasn't, you might say, in the rules of the game for Wally Ops to ride along after me, like this, when he had no more men with him. At least, there wasn't much sense in it.

What could he gain? He wasn't as young as he might be, but young or old there was never a day when he could of stood to me, and he should of knowed it. And he *did* know it, I suppose, except that he was wild and raging to get at me.

The three were stopped. And as we got into a nest of rocks, I seen that Cherry was spent and done for.

The gray had her beat complete. There was nothing for it except to take Wally Ops, or let him take me. And I made up my mind that I would let the world have a dead sheriff in another five minutes.

I swung Cherry in behind a stone as big as a cottage, and, fagged as she was, she answered the bridle as light and as quick and as true as though I had just rode her out from the barn on that morning.

As I jumped out of the saddle, I gave her one look.

Would she live, or would she die?

Well, I didn't know. There was that in her eye told me that she was gunna die, and there was that in her eye that told me, maybe she would live. But I can tell you that, when I seen the deadness in those eyes of hers, I wanted to tear the sheriff and all of his gang to pieces and to feed them to the dogs, bit by bit, and I run and got into a niche of the rocks from which I could fill Wally Ops full of lead.

I heard the gallop of his gray coming, and I knew that I had stopped just in time, for that gallop was pounding, but still there was lots of strength into it. It would of been a finish for Cherry, if we had kept on, and somehow it was better for her to stop while she was still ahead, and to feel that she was a winner, even if she had to die for it.

Yet, as the gray swung along closer, I wondered about the sheriff, what he could be thinking about. To ride right at a bunch of rocks, like that, where a hundred gents might be hiding from him, and to ride on, too, when he must have seen that the noise of Cherry's hoofs had stopped away in front of him.

But then I seen the sheriff coming, and I knew how it was.

That ride had been a hard one on me, with only myself and my horse to think about, but the sheriff had had in hand, all of that day, himself and fifteen men besides, and he had had to think and talk for them and to them, and damn them, and praise them and keep them working together, until finally he had seen four of them riding me down—and still I had got away, and here he was alone—

Why, it had drove him sort of mad, and he come busting down the trail with his mouth a little open, and the lips grinned back, and the wobbly brim of his sombrero going up and down and his pale-blue eyes all bloodshot and staring—

Why, I don't seem to get a hold on the words that can tell you what Wally Ops was like when he come rushing along up that trail, but he looked like a gent that is chasing a ghost.

And somehow, shooting from behind a rock wouldn't do. There was only one to fight, and I never used no advantages against one man.

So I sidestepped into the open and covered him with my revolver and hollered to him to pull up!

Pull up?

That damn little fool, he gave a screech like a wild beast and he swung his gray hoss around and he whanged out two long Colts.

I say, he made a double draw, and me standing there with a bead drawed on him!

I hated to do it. It was a good hoss, that gray, tall, and made for carrying weight, and fast, and clean-winded, as I had seen proved that day, a plenty. He would of been just the thing to take along and pair with Cherry, him carrying the packs and her carrying me, or spelling each other.

But it was either the horse or the man—and, though I was filled with a terrible wish to kill Wally Ops, somehow it cut deep to kill the father of Julie.

I shot the gray horse straight through the brains, and Wally went down with a crash into the dust, both of his guns roaring.

18

I PICKED Wally out of the dust and yanked the guns out of his hands. Why, the damn little fool drawed a knife and tackled me with that, and I barely dodged the cut of it.

"Now, I'll tear you in two, Wally," I told him. "Are you crazy, man?"

He seemed to come to himself, little by little, looking at me and at my gun.

He threw his knife away and wiped the dirt and the sweat from his forehead.

"I've lost!" said Wally. "I've lost again!"

And he seemed to sag all over until he seen the mare and he said: "My God, Dickon, Cherry Pie is dying!"

She looked it. She sure looked as though she was dying, standing there with her head dropped and her eyes glassy, and the sweat dropping off of her.

"Stand here, Ops," I told the sheriff, feeling blacker and meaner than I ever felt in my life before. "Because if Cherry dies, you and me are gunna fight it out, and I'm gunna kill you, damn you, for the sake of this day's work!"

He was a queer one, that Wally Ops.

He just said: "You talk like a fool! Are you gunna stand here and let Cherry die?"

And he run to her and begun to rub her down.

There was sense in that. He took one side of her and I took the other, and we whipped the sweat off of her, and then I dug into her muscles and stripped them down, and I felt how flabby and weak they felt under the tips of my fingers.

We worked for a whole hour, until Wally was groaning with agony, every stroke he give, he had worked so hard.

"Now lead her up and down!" says Wally. "She's getting cold!"

She was, too, and trembling, and still her head was down. But when I pulled at the reins, she didn't budge.

I jerked the bridle off, so as she stood free from bit and saddle, the same as she was the first day that I seen her on the desert, which was the beginning of the ten months that I hunted her. It seemed right that she should die free.

"You damn fool," sings out Wally Ops, "are you gunna stand there blubbering while she dies? Can't you talk to her? Can't you persuade her into walking?"

I stood off and called her, and she tried to come to me, and come staggering, with her knees bending, but her ears pricking.

And Wally stood by crying like a baby and saying: "D-d-d-damn it, how she l-l-loves you, Larry!"

But I walked up and down, calling to her, and she following me, and reeling every step, and dying on her feet, but still trying to come to me. And it was the dusk of the day, with the stars coming out to watch us, in twos and threes, and I looked up to them, and I sort of said in my heart: "God, if you let Cherry live, I'll be a better man by a lot, from this time onward!"

Not that I would be called a praying man, or superstitious, but who can tell what happened? All I know is that Cherry begun to pull together a little, and pretty soon her head was right at my shoulder, as I walked her up and down.

Wally took the saddle blankets, and our coats, and we blanketed her up. So we went on for another hour, rubbing her down and walking her, and rubbing her down again. And finally her head come up a little, and she breathed more free and steady, and her knees seemed to gather under her, and her muscles was firmer under the touch.

We bedded her down with soft brush, and I made her lie down. Then we went off to get water, and while we was finding it, I could hear Cherry Pie nickering for me, but not strong enough to get up and follow.

But we found water, I thank God, and we brung back two canteens of it and two hatfuls, and we poured it down her throat with Wally Ops laughing to see how she could drink out of a bottle just the same as any other man.

The water done her a tremendous lot of good.

She should of died, as Wally and me both agreed, but she didn't; and along about midnight, while we sat watching, she made an effort and then she got up, and pretty soon she was picking at the grass. And so I knew that by the morning time she would be almost as good as well again.

I stretched out my hand and found Wally's and I pressed it, because there was no words that I could find handy, at the minute, and no words that was needed, him being an understanding man.

After a while, I said: "You better go back and find your boys, Wally. They'll be messing around and looking for you, and you better go back to them. But if you was to take so much time that you didn't locate them until about noon tomorrow, I would appreciate it a lot."

"By rights," said Wally, "I should be a dead man, Larry."

"By rights," said I, "Cherry Pie should be a dead mare, but she ain't, and that's owing to your help, because I never could of brought her through alone. All accounts is squared and wrote off between us. You go back and start the chase again, whenever you want. Except that the next time you come, I'm gunna start shooting, Ops, and I'm gunna shoot to kill!"

"Bah!" says Wally Ops. "Maybe you would think to scare me away from your trail, Dickon?"

A mean little man was that same sheriff, standing there in the starshine, with his hands gripped at his sides. But I couldn't help admiring him and wondering at him, because fear was a thing that he knowed nothing about, whatever!

Well, I watched Wally walking off into the night, with a sort of a feeling that of all the gents in the world the only two that was honest enough for me to want them as partners was Choctaw, which was a lot too old for the work, and the sheriff, whose business was to find me and land me in jail, or in a grave.

However, I knew that there wouldn't be any need of worrying until the middle of the next day, because the sheriff would never let the boys come onto my trail again until the time that I had mentioned. So I used all of those hours letting Cherry rest.

She was made of whalebone and fire, and so even by the morning, her eyes seemed bright again, and there was no sign of the terrible work she had done the day before except for her being gaunted up a little. But she wasn't stiff. No, she was as supple as ever!

About this here run of Cherry's, I dunno that the distances was all charted down exact. There is some that say that she done a hundred and thirty-five miles. And there was others that rounded off the figures, so that to this day you will run across folks that will swear that Cherry Pie did a hundred and fifty miles.

Altogether, I know that they're wrong. I have rode over that ground myself other times, and by the distances that are generally took, I should say that, between the time she started traveling in the dawn of the day to the time when she finished off among the rocks, she done about a hundred and twenty-five miles. Other horses have done more distance, I know, but the thing that made Cherry's run so great was that she was taken up by two fresh sets of horses and run across rough country, and that she beat them all off except one, and that one was one of the finest animals in the mountains, as I heard afterward, and was a cross between a half bred blood horse and a pure thoroughbred. Besides which, he had been hardened to mountain running all of his life. But even so, if the sheriff hadn't been a lot lighter man than me, Cherry would of killed them all off.

Of the horses that followed us, on those two runs, down Windover Valley, and then out of the valley, and up the sand slide, and across the desert beyond, there was used altogether thirty-four animals, mostly of a mighty good quality.

Of those thirty-four, five was rode to death and dropped dead under their riders, or right afterward, and three more was staved up so bad that they was of no account ever afterward.

As for Cherry, I have told you how close she come to dying. But the very next day I could of rode her. Which is something that most folks won't believe.

But I put the saddle on her back, and I made a ten mile march leading her into the mountains for a good place to rest up. She finished up that ten mile march as free and as frisky as you please.

There was a little stretch of maybe ten acres among the hills, and there I kept Cherry Pie and let her get strong, with sun-cured bunch grass to eat, than which nothing is so good for a hoss, and there was plenty of the finest soft water for her to drink, and good shade and no flies for the middle of the day.

Two days I kept her there, until her stomach had rounded out again.

All that time, I was on the lookout for trouble, but I wasn't bothered, and the reason was that when the sheriff went back to the posse he found that they was tired of chasing me and they said that the damned mare had wings and until they had the same sort of fliers to ride, they would never take my trail again.

However, Wally Ops was as set as ever on getting me, or *more* set. And he went back to town, had the state and the county pay the price of the dead horses, and the cost of the posse, and then he got together another little bunch of picked men, and he started cruising once more for me.

Sometimes I wondered why folks would let him spend so much time and money on the catching of just one man, but the explaining of it is that he made such a reputation by those hunts and rides after me that other crooks shied clear of his county, saying that unless they had a horse like Cherry Pie it was no use trying to match themselves against that wild devil of a sheriff. And perhaps they was right!

19

WELL, everything looked lucky for me, with Grace out of the way for a minute, as I thought, and the guns of the sheriff spiked once more. So when I seen Cherry tossing her head in the dew of the morning and laughing at me out of her eyes, I decided that it was time to drift on back toward the valley and the girl. And we went down on the run, taking things easy, but covering miles, because Cherry didn't know what slow paces meant. Her walk put the ground behind her brisk as the jog-trot of most mustangs, and her trot slid her along as smooth as silk, so that you sat like in a boat going down a stream, but oh, how that trot snaked you along. Her canter wasn't like the lope of a cowpony, because a cowpony lopes by nacher and lazies along not getting anywhere in particular, but the canter of Cherry was an easy stretch that didn't seem to tire her none, and that would float us along as brisk as you please. As for her gallop, why, I've given you some idea of what that was like, except that words don't do it justice. But when you called on her for a gallop, it was like hitching yourself to a kite and turning a wind loose.

So, as I was saying, we blew down to see Julie; and when we got near, I seen in front of the house that span of sorrels that Danny Murphy drove, and it made me feel a bit edgy, as you may imagine.

I put Cherry in the woods and there I waited snug enough and listened to a fool squirrel chattering his head off on a branch above my head until Danny Murphy came out of the house, and the girl along with him. They went out and fetched a neat little black gelding which they hitched on behind the rig, and then up the road they went as gay as you please, toward the west, with the sky turning red in front of them and everything in the valley quiet, except the birds that was settling down to a happy time of it for the night in their nests.

I waited until there was a bit more dusk, and then I pelted Cherry Pie along after them, taking a detour across country that kept me out of sight of the road. Because I expected that Julie was just going for a spin with

Murphy, and that she would be coming back, before long, with the black horse.

According to that idea, in the dusk I pulled over and jumped Cherry into the road across a mean looking barbed wire fence, and then waited in the shadow of some trees.

A whole hour I waited there, while the earth turned black and the sky was peppered with stars. But I had taken on a lot of friendly feeling for the stars since the night that I asked help of them for Cherry, and she was pulled through. They seemed sort of companionable and lucky to me, as I waited there by the trees. And after a time, that hour ended, and I heard the pelting of a horse coming at a full gallop down the road.

Well, how would you expect Julie to come?

With both spurs dug into the ribs of that poor nag, and swinging her hat in her hand to make him go faster, and her hair with all the pins out of it blowed straight back behind her, and her face up to the stars, and while that black mustang stretched out straight as a string with his full speed, she was singing at the top of her voice.

It was a good strong voice, too, and she knew how to use it, so that it came to me as clear as you please, and as happy as a hawk dropping out of the sky at a hen in the yard—

Me being the hen, maybe!

Well, I felt like that, as I listened to her coming, and then saw the shadow streaking down the road. I mean, I felt rather weak and helpless, and kept rubbing the neck of Cherry hoping to get courage out of her. She begun to fidget, because whenever she saw a horse running fast, she thought that it was a call for her to do the same thing.

I let the streak go by me. And I had a pale glimpse of the face of Julie against the stars, laughing into the wind with her song.

Then I loosed up the reins and said one word to Cherry Pie.

She nearly jumped out from under the saddle. In six jumps she was skimming at the side of that black mustang, and I had to take a strong pull, until her chin was almost touching her chest, before I could bring her back to the speed of the other nag. I looked to Julie, for a sign.

Why, man, I tell you that she just rode right on down the way, with her head still back, and her eyes, closed, and the song bubbling and ringing out of her throat, and hanging in the air behind us.

Did she know I was there, while she was riding on so blind?

There wasn't any doubt in me. She knew that I was there, and she was showing me that my coming didn't make any such great difference.

Well, I said a word to Cherry, and she began to slow up, but shaking her head, like she hated to do it, and wanted to go on and show that girl and that horse what the shape of a clean pair of heels looked like.

The minute that Cherry began to drop back, Julie come to life and pulled up the black. And when we stopped, we stopped side by side.

What would she say by way of a greeting, I ask you? I mean, to me, the outlaw, and all such, and the gent that she had tried to hold up, not so very many months before?

Well, she said: "Cherry Pie doesn't seem to be able to stand the pace, Larry!"

Yes, that was what she said. As though her and me had spent the day together. No more surprised than that. She should of been a gambler, she was that cool and easy.

"Maybe Cherry is tired out," said I.

"Tired of what?" says she.

"Why, tired of laughing at things in general."

"At men who try to catch her, say?" suggested Julie.

"Perhaps."

"And sheriffs?" says she.

"Why," I had to confess, "sometimes sheriffs ain't laughing matters."

"Hum!" says Julie.

And she waited a minute.

Then I wondered what she had heard about the chase which her father had given me.

"Where are you bound?" says Julie.

"Somewhere on the edge of the sky," I told her. "I ain't just picked out the place. I just happened along—"

I wouldn't of said that, of course, if I had known the way that old Choctaw, damn him, had given me away to her. I wouldn't of said that, knowing how foolish it would seem and sound.

"I thought," says Julie, "that maybe you had come down for the wedding."

"Wedding?" I asked her.

"Danny is to marry me tomorrow," said Julie. "Are you riding along this way?"

And she started her mustang down the road.

I didn't hear the last part of what she said. I was in a trance, pretty nearly, from the first part of it. And so I let her go away and sat like a dummy in the saddle.

Why, of course she was doing what she had promised to Choctaw that she would do. But how was I to know that? No, it looked to me like a clean swipe and no place for Larry Dickon. It was a considerable time before I collected the pieces of myself, and it was a queer thing that the world that had seemed so busting full of fine things only a minute before was a total vacuum now!

I'm mighty ashamed to say that my first idea was to up and find Murphy and sink a slug of lead through his heart.

But I cooled down, and I begun to think steady and clear, after that. I knew nothing but good things about Danny. He was the sort of a boy that ought to make her a good husband. And of course, that was what I should hope for her, if I wasn't a complete pig.

However, trying to reconcile myself to that was no easy job. It was the

best part of an hour before I saw the way that I had to back myself out of
this job and leave this part of the country and never think of it again, and
never see it again.

Ay, and how I wished that I never *had* seen it!

I couldn't pull out in cold blood. I had to do something. So what I did
was to blow for Danny Murphy's house.

If he was to marry this girl tomorrow, he wouldn't be staying very quiet
this evening. And when I come up to his place—it was a small shack of a
house—I could hear Danny whistling as gay as a lark, and every note of
that whistling made me want to do a murder.

However, I had to go through with what I had staked out for myself. I
left Cherry Pie in the field behind the house and I sneaked along up the
far side of the hedge and so I come into view of the shack itself. I had
passed it before and give it a glimpse. But now it seemed to me a miserable
small sort of a place for a girl like Julie to be housed. I could set back and
see her drudging around that house, and getting raw-handed from dishwater,
and down-shouldered from leaning over the laundry tub, and I could
almost hear the squawling of the baby in the front yard because the chickens
had come and pecked at its pink fingers—

Well, I was sort of sickened and saddened.

Still, I had to admit that it was fine of her to pick out a gent like Danny
for a husband. He had a growing farm. He was making good money. And
when he decided to spend, he could build them a bigger and better house,
maybe—

But still, I couldn't help damning a gent that will spend his money on a
fancy span of nags and a rig to take his girl driving, while he keeps a mean
shack for her to make a home out of when he has once persuaded her into
marrying him.

It was a low moment for me. I was sick. I was *very* sick. But I marched
on for the house and the whistle of Danny.

20

I WOULD ask to be please excused for dodging about now, and putting
things in order exactly as they happened, instead of the order in which *I*
first knowed about them. I mean to say that it would maybe be better for
me to go right ahead and tell what happened at the shack of Danny Murphy,
but as a matter of fact, it seems clearer to explain other things first, according
to what I learned of them a long while later.

I was saying that Julie went on back to the house of the sheriff on her black mustang, but when she got close to it, she seen some shadows trooping down the road toward her, and then the black give a whinny and kicked up his heels, so that she guessed those were horses that her pony knew. She rode down to see—and she found Wally Ops coming straight along through the night.

There was a good deal of kindness, it seems, between Wally and his girl. Perhaps him being so saw-off and ugly and her being so slim and so pretty had brought them together, as you might say. Because folks that are different can understand each other a lot better than those that are the same kind.

When she gave Wally a hug she says: "Dear old Dad! I hope the next time there'll be better luck!"

And Wally Ops says: "There ain't gunna be no next time!"

No next time riding out and hunting for crooks like Grace and me, was what he meant by that. And of course she understood, but she didn't say a word, and she turned around and begun talking to Choctaw, who happened to of met up with the sheriff and was riding in with him. Because they was great friends, Choctaw having taught Wally how to ride and shoot when Wally Ops was a boy.

A funny sort of a boy he must of looked!

Well, the three of them got to the house and of course Mom Ops come running out and grabbed Wally and sort of swallered him in her fat arms and dragged him into the house and sat him down and wiped the grit off of his face and kissed him on the end of the nose and called him her old duck, or something ridiculouser, which I aim to forget, though Choctaw, he reported everything to me, word for word.

Anyway, there was a fuss about the sheriff, but he was so tired that nobody dared to ask too many questions until that Lew come in, and when he seen his dad he let out a yip.

"Is it true that you chased Cherry Pie and Dickon for a hundred and fifty miles, Dad?" he sings out.

The sheriff closes his eyes and puts back his head a little and he says with a groan: "Chased? God knows how many miles it was. I can tell you in horses, but not in miles, Lew! Do you all know that Sammy horse of mine?"

They all did.

"When we started, I was riding Sammy. I rode him into the ground by noon. There was only a wreck of him left, and it's going to be a month before I can get him home. He's only a hollow horse, now! Then I had Dingwall's gray, which of course you all of heard about—"

He stopped talking.

They waited till he was ready to talk again. All that they had heard about the chase had been just dribbles of news that had come in over the wire and that had been changed around and twisted a good deal, being passed from mouth to mouth.

"I rode the gray till he could just manage to raise a stagger," said the sheriff. "And I had the pleasure of seeing Cherry Pie wobbling ahead of me, looking as though she would go down, every next stride!"

That brought a gasp out of them. The sheriff closed his eyes and opened them again, and when he opened them he said:

"Dickon got into a nest of rocks. I lost sight of him. There was a roaring in my ears. It seemed to me that I could still hear a horse galloping just ahead of me. Maybe it was only the echoing of the hoofs of the gray—but I turned a corner and rode straight onto Dickon, with a gun in his hand—"

He made another stop, closing his eyes. And you can believe that nobody hurried him none, they was too scared.

"And then," says the sheriff, "I was fool enough to try a gun play, while Larry Dickon had the drop on me!"

He laughed, sort of sick.

Then he said: "Dickon had the choice. Me or my horse. So he killed the horse, instead of me, and picked me up out of the dirt like a damned, good-for-nothing rat!"

He was feeling low, the sheriff, was, as you can see for yourself. However, he gathered more strength, after a minute, and Choctaw says that his eyes begun to shine a little.

"We seen that Cherry was nearly dying," says the sheriff, "and we had a hard job over her, hour after hour, rubbing her down. Why, Choctaw, you would of laughed to see that Dickon walking up and down with the tears streaking along his face, calling to Cherry, and her just able to manage to wobble along after him!"

The sheriff, he did the laughing. The others didn't, says Choctaw.

All at once, the girl busts out: "Dear old Dad, I'm mighty glad that you'll never have to bother about him any more! About Larry Dickon, I mean!"

"Never bother about him?" says the sheriff. "What d'you mean?"

"Nothing," says the girl.

"Nothing? Julie, what's in your head?"

"I mean, he's going away, I think," says Julie, "and I don't believe that he'll ever come back."

"*You* believe that he's going away?" says her father, standing up. "What the devil do *you* know about him?"

Why, she was cornered, and she had to say what had happened.

So she came out with it, a little halting, how Choctaw had told her about me, that I was hard hit, and that I was sure coming back that way, and that I *had* come back.

The sheriff could hardly hold himself.

"What's this, Choctaw?" says he. "What's the meaning of this? Does a low-down hound, a man-killing, gunfighting road agent dare to look at my Julie? *My* Julie?"

Well, Choctaw was a little flabbergasted, but he got help where he least expected it. Because Julie up and says: "Is that any way to talk about a man who could have taken your own life, Father, and who let you go free?"

"Damn my life!" says the sheriff. "Go on and tell me! What happened? You seen this sneaking Dickon?"

"I did," says the girl, "and I'm afraid that Choctaw was right, from the way that he acted. But I did what Choctaw told me to do. I sent him away."

"*You* sent him away?" shouted the sheriff, getting hotter and hotter. "You told him to run away, little boy. And he run, I suppose? Am I crazy, Julie?"

"No," said Julie, "I told him that I was to be married tomorrow!"

"The girl's out of her wits," said the sheriff. "What a fool thing to say—and what's the meaning of it?"

"He sat in the saddle without speaking, as though I had shot him," said Julie. "And I'll swear that he's leaving this part of the country—because Choctaw was right! Choctaw, say something!"

"Me?" says Choctaw. "I say that you're right. When Larry hears that, he'll cut loose and drift for some other place."

"But what if he hears that it ain't the truth?" barked the sheriff.

"He'll never have a chance to hear that," said Julie. "Is he likely to go *ask* the man that I said I was to marry?"

"Wait a minute," cut in Choctaw. "You didn't give him any *name* of a man, did you?"

"What's wrong with that?" asked Julie.

"Wrong?" growled the sheriff. "Everything's wrong. Who did you name?"

"Why, he saw me drive up the road this evening with Danny Murphy."

"God A'mighty!" groaned the sheriff. "Was that Dickon near my house this same evening? Danny Murphy—was it Danny you said that you was to marry?"

"Yes."

The sheriff hollered: "Lew, saddle the blue roan for me. Choctaw, will you lend a hand? No, I'll ride by myself and find him, even if he *is* a devil!"

Lew had scooted for the door. The sheriff started after him, but he had a heavy anchor to drag along with him, because Mom Ops had fetched a hold on him and she was saying: "Wally, what does it all mean? What has happened? What has Julie done?"

"What has Julie done?" yelled the sheriff. "Nothing except to get Danny Murphy murdered! That's all that she's done! My God, it's the worst thing that ever happened in my life—my own daughter—Dickon—poor Danny—lemme go—"

And he fought himself clear of Mom and dived through the doorway.

Julie would of followed, but Choctaw caught her by the shoulders and held her back.

"There ain't anything to do," says he. "I'm too old, and you're a girl, and when hell begins to bust loose, what can you and me do?"

"Uncle Choctaw," says Julie, crying with excitement, "what does Dad mean? Is he wild enough to think that Larry Dickon would try to—"

"Hush up!" said Choctaw. "It ain't any use crying. Set still and keep your head high."

"But tell me the truth, because you know Larry Dickon as nobody else knows him!"

"Why," says Choctaw, "you had better get yourself braced right now and ready for the truth, because otherwise it would be a terrible shock to you. But I tell you, Julie, that poor Danny Murphy is dead as sure as though you had took him and throwed him off the top of Cumberland Rock!"

And he pointed out the window, as though she could see through the black of the night to Cumberland Rock, big, and dark, and scarred, and mean-looking, and so high that it scared you just to look up at its face.

21

PERHAPS, because you have been following me around so steady, it may seem queer to you that so many folks that knew me might of thought that I would murder the gent that was to marry the girl that I loved. But that, maybe, is because I have showed myself a little better than the fact, seeing as how you can't talk about yourself very well without putting your best foot forward. Or, even if you put down all the facts, you arrange them in such a way that everything looks right and nacheral that you did. If that wasn't the case, then there wouldn't be any very great need for twelve men on a jury and law and judges, and what not. Because nobody is going to make himself out very wicked.

Well, the fact is that while these things went on at the house of the sheriff, I sneaked up behind the little shack of Danny Murphy, and when I looked in through the back window, I could see that it wasn't so bad at all. As a matter of fact, it was laid out good, so far as the furniture went. The kitchen had everything that a body was to want, and the kitchen would be almost the first thing that would appeal to the heart of a girl that was to marry a small farmer. Still, somehow, I wondered at that girl picking out this sort of a life instead of tying up with a rich rancher, such as I knew that she could of picked and chose among.

However, marrying ain't the sort of a thing that a good girl will use much logic on. I had to remember that. Because if there was any logic in it, how had I ever dared to let myself fall in love with her? It would of been a hopeless job for me!

Thinking of these things, I followed around to the front of the house, where the whistling was going on, and there I saw young Danny walking back and forth with his hands in his pockets and the whiff of a good Havana coming back to me.

An old black woman went out to him and asked, just then, could she have the next afternoon to go to town, because her niece was going to get married pretty soon, and she wanted to buy a present.

"Is it marrying, Dinah?" says Danny Murphy. "Of course you can go! Only, don't you get into the marrying habit yourself, because what would I do without you, Aunt Dinah?"

The woman laughed and went back into the house, and the front screen banged and jingled, and her steps went slugging and shuffling off through the house.

At the next turn, I stepped out and laid a gun in the small of the back of Danny.

"Take this easy, Murphy," I said.

He had a good memory for voices, that boy did. He stopped right still and he said under his breath:

"It's Dickon, by God."

"It's Dickon, right enough," I admitted. "The first thing for you to know is that I ain't come here to do you any harm."

He was steady enough, I got to say, though I wasn't very anxious to find out good things about him.

He said: "What is that you want, Dickon? A layout of chuck for yourself, and some oats for Cherry Pie? Is that it? Or are you hard up for cash?"

It was so mighty reasonable, to hear him talk like this, that I softened a good deal toward him.

"I ain't come for your chuck or for your money, Danny," I told him. "All that I've come to do it to talk to you a little mite about your marriage."

"About my which?" says he.

"Your marriage," says I. "Does it seem queer that I should know about it?"

He laughed a little.

"Why," says he, "as a matter of fact, it *does* seem a little queer."

"She told me her own self," I said to him. "So the first thing that I want to do is to congratulate you, Danny, on getting a girl like Julie Ops for a wife—"

"Julie!" he gasps. "By gad!"

"Well?" I said.

"Nothing," says he. "But would you mind telling me when she told you this?"

"Right now, as I met her on the road," I said.

"It's queer—but—well, let it go! What's in your mind, Dickon?"

"I wanted to know, Danny, if you got the things that you need for starting in on a married life. Will you tell me that?"

"Like what?" he asked me.

"Like enough horses to work your fields, and rakes and mowing machines, and such."

"I suppose not," says he, chuckling a little, "but then a girl wouldn't be marrying a set of farm tools, would she?"

"I ain't joking," I warned him.

"Ask your pardon, then," says young Murphy.

"I've come to offer help," I told him.

"Help? The devil you have!"

"I mean it."

"How would you help?"

"I have some money here," says I. "I want you to take it, Danny, and use it to fix things up so as you can give that girl an easier life. You understand me?"

He understood me right enough, and he fired back at me: "Look here, old-timer, are you aiming to make me a cash loan?"

"Loan be damned," said I. "I would be an honest rancher right this minute, if it wasn't for a loan that a friend made to me, once. That loan kicked me out of my house, took my horse from under my saddle, swiped the tools on the place, ate up my land little by little, and carted the hay and the straw right out of my fields. A loan is a sort of a dragon for a farmer, specially for a young one. No, Danny, I don't mean that."

"What the devil do you mean, then?"

"I mean, it's a free gift."

"What? Wait a minute, Dickon, because—"

"I'm free to say that this ain't money that was took from any honest man, so you don't need to think that you're using stuff that you shouldn't. If it stayed with me, it would pretty soon be spent on Old Lady Roulette, or Miss Fan-tan, or some such girl as that. Y'understand? It ain't enough to make such a lot of talk. But what there is of it, is yours. It ain't much. But if you pick out the spot where you need money the most—like a couple of spans of horses and harness, say, or some mowing machines, or maybe a new barn, or something like that, and invest it all on that one spot, then you'll have something to show for it. I mean, it's a thousand, Danny. And here you are."

I slipped it into his pocket and backed away.

"Hey, Dickon!" he called, and whirled around at me.

I whistled the call for my Cherry, and I heard her hoofs swinging toward me quick as a flash out of the field behind the house.

"Don't argue, Danny," I told him. "The fact is that I'm interested in how you and her get along, and if you land up in a pinch, after a while, why, maybe I can get hold of something that will pull you out of the hole. It'll give me something to live for, outside of myself and my horse. And—"

"Dickon," says he, "tell me straight. You wanted that girl for yourself!"

"Let that slide," says I, "but what—"

"Man, man," says he, "take back this money and take it quick. By God, Larry, this is wonderful white of you! It's the sort of thing that might be read of in a book but that wouldn't be believed—only, you see—"

"Never mind the talk," said I, "because this here job is done; and now that I've seen you and had a few words with you, I can say that, as long as she had to marry some other gent, I'm glad that you're the one that had to be—"

Cherry came swooping for me like a hawk out of the sky.

And Danny came at me, calling:

"It's a mistake, old-timer! It's all a mistake, Larry. God bless you for it, man, but it's just a joke that—"

I didn't wait to hear the rest. I could see that he needed the money, And of course any young gent with pride wouldn't of wanted to take money like that from a stranger. But, now that I had given him the coin, I wanted to back out as fast as I could. So I hooked onto Cherry as she come up to me, and I went into the saddle and away with her, without her ever breaking out of her gallop—which was a trick that her and me had practiced by the hour. Real circus stuff that looks pretty good when it works, and looks pretty foolish when it only lands you on your head in the dust.

Anyway, there I was, all in the saddle, and waving back to Danny Murphy as he ran after me, screeching something that the wind of my gallop made dim in my ears, but he was still holding out that money in the starlight and talking about a mistake, as near as I could make out.

However, I was glad to have Cherry over the fence and into the roadway I was glad to have my duty done behind me, and for a time I swore to myself that I would never want to see the face of him or of his wife, so long as I lived; but that only lasted for a minute. And then I begun to figure that this wasn't so bad. There wasn't so much bitterness in me as I thought that there would be, because, having started out like that, now I was sort of interested. And I thought that maybe there would be sort of fun in giving a hand to Danny, now and then, and putting him straight when he got in crooked.

A miserable sort of happiness that was, though. And just then I had something else to think about, because I heard a roar of galloping horses ahead of me.

I guessed that it might be intended for me, and so I hopped Cherry into the woods and waited. And pretty soon four riders come whishing by, and against the stars I could of swore that that was little Wally Ops, riding slanting, with the brim of his sombrero furled up away from his ugly face.

So I knew that he was after me again, and I went all sick, because I was sure that the girl had give me away!

22

NOT reasonable to think that she would want to protect me. No, but a gent doesn't go by good hard logic and thinking, most of the time, and, liking her so much, I couldn't help expecting that she would like *me* a little. Same as when you hold a mirror up before a light, you expect that some of the brightness will be returned to you.

However, I was forgetting that I was the gent that had made her father miserable for years. I was the gent that had made things unhappy and dangerous in his life, and so of course she would want to see me bagged, if she could!

Well, I want to say that those were a few miserable minutes, while I was driving down that road again.

A steeple came into my sight, stabbing up above the trees and into the stars. I pulled up Cherry and rode right over to half a dozen gents that was coming out of the church along with their women folks.

"Is this the church where the wedding's to take place?" I asked them.

"What wedding?" they asked me.

"Why, the wedding tomorrow," I said.

"What wedding?" says one of them. "What wedding tomorrow that we ain't heard about?"

It made me mad, somehow.

"Do you know Julie Ops?" I asked them.

"Do we know ourselves from horses?" they laughed.

It was plain that Julie was somebody in that valley.

"Why, then," says I, "ain't she the one that's to be married tomorrow?"

"Stranger," says one of them, "I dunno, but if this is news, it is *real* news. Who's the lucky gent and—where did you get that hoss!"

Because, just then, he happened to take a good look at Cherry, and there was enough starshine to show the silver curving of her tail and the white blowing of her mane in the wind.

He backed up, gasping: "Dickon!" and the others gave me plenty of room, too. And so I saw that I was a fool to risk myself any more and I took the mare sidling away, with my eyes still fixed on them.

Not one of them made a move at me, but I seen one tallish gent with a square-cut, old-fashioned beard, and a long, scrawny neck, and a pair of little twinkling eyes like a bird's, and somehow that glance of his, it ate into me like acid.

Well, I left them and twitched Cherry away into the shadows and then sneaked across country for the house of Choctaw.

I went up to it slow and soft. Because folks, by this time, seemed to know plenty of them that I was around, and the very first place that they would be sure to lay for me would be Choctaw's house. I sneaked around that shack like a snake through green grass, but there seemed to be nothing around.

Then I went inside and found that Choctaw wasn't there. I lit a match and found the chuck. Every day, winter and summer, unless he *knew* that I was more than two hundred miles away, old Choctaw was sure to leave a snack out for me, no matter what time of the day, when he was away from his place. How much time and trouble he put into it, and how much it cost him, I would sure be ashamed to say, but the old codger, he always done it.

There was some cold pone in the cupboard for me, and there was some cold, crisp fried bacon, and some plum jam, about which I have always been extra partial. Which old man Choctaw knew, and though he hated sweet things himself, he was always sure to have some of that jam spread out on the stuff that was left for me. Even though it spoiled it for him, when I didn't show up.

Ay, he was a grand old man, was that Choctaw. Patient, I mean, and like an Indian, he never stopped loving a friend, and he never stopped hating an enemy.

I had my eats, and then I got back into the saddle on Cherry, and I started away through the woods, headed I didn't know where, but I aimed to stay up somewhere in the woods not too far from Choctaw's place and then to scout down in the morning and try to have a talk to him, and find out what all this tangle about the marriage might be—the marriage that nobody except Julie seemed to know much about.

Well, then, I went on up into the woods and I found me a nook by the side of a little stream that ebbed out of a spring—a trickle of water no bigger than your wrist, but it flowed down into a nacheral rock bowl, and there it was all fine for me.

I made me down a little bed of cedar boughs, and there I laid down and had the hardest and the soundest sleep that I had ever had in my life, except for the time when that Doctor Grace and his gang of hounds come by and lifted my Cherry.

There I slept like a dead man, because I had been through such a pounding, the last ten days, that it would of made any man feel pretty sick. I mean, not only long rides, but the tearing up that I had got when I thought that I was riding Cherry Pie to death, and then when I thought that I was seeing her pegging out while she stood watching me, and after that—there was the smash when I run into the news about Julie—

I mean, you can understand how it is that a gent would be laid out by such things as these, and so I slept about three times deeper than usual, and that was the second night in my life when I had a need to sleep no sounder than a wolf away from its own cave.

I didn't wake up until the dawn light was sneaking through the trees, and then I sat up and yawned and stretched myself and give a shudder, because the dew had soaked down into my hair and my face and my shirt around the shoulders.

"Ay," says a gent's voice. "It's a pretty cold morning."

I looked across, and there sat a gent that I had seen before.

I had to give my memory a shake and a wriggle, and then I remembered where—it was only the night before that I had watched that square-cut beard and those little glittering eyes, and that scrawny neck.

There they were again, and there was the same starved look about him. Except that the night before he looked like a gent that needed food bad, but had none in sight, and now he looked like starvation sitting down to turkeys and mince pies, and such. Me being the turkeys and trimmings, if you got to have it explained to you!

I didn't pay all my attention to his face, neither. His hands come in for a share of my regards. I seen that they was big enough to make two, and that they had brown-black covering, that looked more like gloves than like skin.

Now, when I took in all of these here details, I made pretty sure that this man was a bulldog whose grip I wouldn't be able to shake off very easy.

Next, I noticed that he had in his hands a big shotgun, with double barrels, all sawed-off and ready for action; and, somehow, looking at the mouths of those barrels was like looking through the eyes of a dumb man, and seeing all that was in his mind. I didn't have to be told how those guns was loaded. I could tell, almost as though I had charged them myself, that they was filled up with ragged bits of steel and iron junk, and pellets of lead—and the big fingers of that farmer was hooked around both of the triggers.

He didn't mean to take no chances. The discharge of both of those barrels at the same time would knock him right back off of that stump that he was sitting on. But, at the same time, what would happen in the front of that gun?

Over a space about five feet wide—considering the distance that I was from him—there would be a regular hail of misery flying. If there had been ten men sitting there beside me, all ten of us would have been showed through the door and into the long, dark hall outside.

Now, after that, I knew that the jig was up, unless I could work him into a bad position. I was willing to risk almost anything up to death, to get away. Because if they ever got me into jail, it would be life for me. They could rake up enough charges to fill a book. A book of pretty mean reading, too!

Well, I didn't have any particular long time to think these things over.

I says to him: "How long have you been sitting there, partner?"

"Not long," says he. "Not more'n about three hours."

Not more than about three hours—and in the cold of the night! I could see that he was turned all a sort of a blue. But I wouldn't take chances on him being numb. All of him might be nearly ice. It was only his forefingers that had to be active.

"Sorry," said I, "that I wasn't up when you arrived."

"Thanks," says he, "but I didn't mind waiting."

No, he could take a joke. There was just a flash in his eyes. But that was all.

"Besides," he said, "I wanted to think it all out."

"Think what out?"

"How I was to handle you."

"Yes?"

"Because," says he, "it seems that you mean just as much dead as alive."

"Sure," says I, "that seems to be the way of it, and a good many wouldn't of wasted any time in putting the gun alongside my head and blowing my brains out while I slept."

"I thought of that, too," says this gent. "I thought of that, of course, but then I decided that it would be sort of worth while to wait around and see how you would take this—waking up and seeing me here."

"And?" said I.

"Oh, it's worth it, I think," says he. "You got your nerve."

"I would say the same by you," said I, a little peeved. "For an amateur, you seem to be doing a pretty good job."

"Do I?" says he. "Yes, I'm an amateur, but I'm a hard thinker, y'understand? I mean that I always plan things out, and the only reason that I ain't made a success of farming is because the harder you think, the worse that the weather plays against you."

"Sure," says I, "farming is like roulette, only worse. Because the cards is always stacked against a farmer, but *some* roulette wheels don't have a brake."

He nodded.

"We had better be fetching our way back to town, I think," says he. "Because Ma will be missing me a good deal and raising a ruction with all of the neighbors. How can she tell that I'm out gathering in the best crop that I ever harvested?"

And he grinned a little broader. You could see that it wasn't possible for that man to laugh. He could just smile a little more, and that was all. Misery was wrote out big and plain all over him. And there you are! I would as soon of taken a chance with that gent as with a man-eating shark, and no sooner!

"What shall I do?" says I.

"You had better get your hands up, about shoulder high," says he. "And then twist them around behind you, while I fit these on. That is, if you don't mind!"

And he kicked a pair of manacles that he had at his feet—a pair of old, rusty handcuffs, strong enough to hold an arm, I should of said.

I looked at them, and I looked at this farmer, and for the first time I begun to really think that I was beat.

23

Now, when I was fixed up with those rusted old irons locked over my wrists, I says: "What's your name, stranger?"

"Name of Solomon Rapp," says he.

"Hailing out of Massachusetts?" says I.

"Connecticut," says he.

"Well," I asked him, "what will you be doing with Cherry Pie?"

"The mare? I dunno that I'll get her. She belongs to the state, I suppose. I ain't up on such things, but if she comes to me, I'll auction her off to the highest bidder."

I was hoping that maybe he would be interested in horses, because what I aimed to do was to get him started talking for one minute—long enough to let his attention wander. Then I would try my hand at getting loose from him.

But horses wasn't the theme that would start his tongue to wagging.

"She would be as good as anything for your saddle work," I suggested to him.

"I would look fine, wouldn't I?" says he. "I would look fine draped over a thing like her! No, son, mules can cart me along good enough. I ain't ever in a hurry, and my looks don't bother me!"

He started me off down the valley, marching ahead with him behind, his sawed-off murder-gun hooked under his arm. But when Cherry started to follow us, Solomon Rapp halted us.

He says: "This bothers me a little—I mean, your horse following along like this. Because, from what they tell me, you and her work like partners, and do surprising things. Well, Dickon, I'd hate to be surprised and have a ten thousand dollar harvest hooked out of my hands, like this!"

I stopped and started to turn around, but he sang out in a voice that clinked like steel against steel:

"Face forward, Dickon! I hate to talk like this, but if you halt up like this again, I'll be likely to touch off the triggers of this here Salvation Gun. Y'understand? Because after all, Dickon, you're worth as much dead as living!"

I understood him. He was willing to talk kind and friendly, but under the surface he was hard as nails, and he meant to take no chances. So that my heart sank down another league or so into my boots. I about gave up all hopes. But I called to Cherry and made her go back, and she stood among the trees, whinnying after us, real anxious, while me and old Solomon Rapp trudged along through the forest.

I hunted around for something new to talk about.

"This'll be a grand day for you and your wife, Rapp," says I.

"It'll be a fair day," he allowed.

"The best you've had, I s'pose?"

"A good deal the best," says he. "As a matter of fact, this'll save me and put me up on my feet again, I don't mind saying."

"Ay," said I, "I suppose that you'll be putting the money right slap into the bank?"

"You suppose wrong," says he. "Because banks is made for wise folks to run and for fools to run to."

He chuckled a little. You could see that this man Rapp had his opinions about most things and was used to having them listened to.

"How is that?" I asked, real brisk and cheerful, and interested. Because it began to look as though I had him on the sort of a thing that he would open up and talk about.

"I'll tell you," says Rapp, "I used to think a good deal about banks. But afterward, I learned. What have they got in a bank? Nothing but a sure thing. Five per cent, maybe. But you're sure of that five per cent. But you take your money out and put it in some other thing that you know, and that money brings you in six, eight, ten, twelve, maybe twenty per cent!"

"Whew!" says I. "You seem to know a good deal about this business, Rapp!"

He was willing to swaller that.

"I ain't as much of a fool as some folks think," says he. "Because I've had my bad luck, here and there, it ain't any sign that I was born all dumb."

"Certainly not!" says I, very polite.

He was feeling so good, after this, that he started to whistle a little. I brought him back to the subject.

"But ten thousand, if they've priced me at that, is a good deal to soak right into a business," I suggested to him.

"Maybe it seems so to you," says he, quite superior. "But eighteen hundred of it goes to wiping out the mortgage. Won't the gents in the bank be surprised when I walk in and pay them back? No, damn it, because they'll know beforehand about how I caught you, and they'll be expecting me to pay. I hate that, old-timer, because I'd like to surprise them a little, the damned, uppity, sleek-haired, fat-faced, pink-skinned pigs!"

He used this just to warm up on, and then he damned the whole tribe of bankers, beginning with the first of them and leaving out none.

You could see that he had had some bad passages with that mortgage of his.

"Ay," said I, "but eighteen hundred don't more than scratch the surface of ten thousand."

"No," says he, "it don't, and that's a fact. But the next thing that I do is to buy in sixty acres next to mine. There's a fool there that has been trying to farm his land for the last twenty years without summer fallowing none of it. And now when he tries to raise a crop, he gets about one spear of wheat to the square foot! A thick head, he is! But he's give his land a bad name, and I can rake that in for twenty-five an acre!"

"Good," says I. "But that's only fifteen hundred more."

"You're right," says he. "The next thing that I do is to take a little trip south. I know where there's a run of mustang mules so damn mean that even growed-up cowpunchers busts down and cries when they think of trying to handle them. But *I* can handle them! I can buy those mules for fifty dollars a head, by taking the weedings. I'll get me four full eight mule teams. And half a dozen extras to fill in when the others get laid up with sore shoulders and lameness, and such—"

"Only," said I, "harness will cost a lot."

"I know of a place where there's tons and tons of good second-hand harness. Don't look pretty, but when you get it patched up it will hold pretty well. You keep a couple of coils of baling wire along with your outfit, and you can always keep right on slugging away!"

"That's right," said I. "And what would the whole layout cost you?"

"Well," said he. "Then I'm going to a couple of sales and lay in some second-hand ploughs and mowing machines, and such things, y'understand?"

"Yes," said I.

"And if you pick your spots, you can buy a hundred and fifty dollar ploughs for five or six bucks, at a sale, and a two hundred dollar mowing machine for ten! Why, man, pretty soon, I'll be all ready to work four full eights, and the whole thing won't cost me more than twenty-five or -six hundred dollars."

"That sounds good," I told him, seeing him warm up every minute, "but what about these light-weight, low-quality mules? How will they pull compared with good stock?"

"They do enough," he told me. "What does a regular first-class team of eight pull? Why, they plough about eight acres in a full day, if the work ain't more than four inches deep. Why, with these little ratty mules of mine, I'll plough a good six and a half acres."

"That much?" I said, doubting it a good deal.

"All of that, and maybe more. The great thing is to know how to swing the blacksnake, because leather fed into the skin of a mule does it more good than barley fed into its mouth."

He enjoyed this, pretty much, and I joined him, laughing, though it went kind of against the grain to do it.

I said: "That leaves you only six thousand out, and a lot of ground covered. Mortgage paid off, good chunk of land added to your farm, and enough stock to cultivate your own stuff, and then hire out—"

"That's it!" said he. "Hiring out—that's what brings in the coin! Besides,

I'll have four thousand left. What'll I do with that? I keep two thousand laid by, so that when the fall prices for hay and grain ain't good, I can keep the stuff stocked over until the next spring. And then the prices is *always* up! I'll make fifteen per cent better prices all around, that way. I've noticed how it runs, all of these years, but I've always been ground down so bad that I never was able to wait. I always had to turn in my crop as soon as I got it."

"That leaves you two thousand," says I, "to blow on your house and fixing up yourself and your wife—"

"Ha!" says he. "The wife, eh? Blow money on her? For why, I ask you? To improve her looks, maybe? No, God didn't make her for a decoration! Besides, it'll do her more good to know that money is working for us than to be wearing silks. We'll live the same way that we've started living. And the extra two thousand I'll lay out in a piece of good truck land down by the edge of the river. There ain't any reason why all of the vegetables that's ate in these parts should be hauled in all the way from McCormack. And I'll bring a gang of low-down Portugee to work the land for me on shares."

"Why Rapp" says I, "the fact is that you're a sort of a genius in business, ain't you?"

"Well, I ain't a fool," says he, thawing out all the way down to his toes.

"And you'll wind up with a few millions in your checking account, when some of the spenders are—"

Now, right there, I planted my right heel, and spun around on it, and I swung my hands at Mr. Solomon Rapp's head.

24

WELL, it was a mean sort of a trick, to get a man heated up talking about himself, but it had worked for me a couple of times before, and I always aim to believe that there's no way that you can put a gent into a sleep and start him hypnotizing himself so good as by getting him to talk about what a wonderful sort of a man he is.

This Rapp was a hard one and a sharp one and a restless one, but even he got a mite bleary-eyed. And right in the middle of his bleariness, I whirled around and swung at his head.

He had time to say: "Damnation!" and jerked the gun straight to blow me to bits. But he hadn't quite time. While he was still swinging the muzzles around toward me, those heavy, rusted handcuffs clinked alongside the head of Rapp, and he was done.

But as he fell, his fingers pulled the triggers of that gun, and it roared right along my side.

The swing that I had landed backhanded on Rapp was hard enough, but the way that gun kicked was a terrible thing to see. Because the butt of the shotgun hit a glancing blow that made a couple of Rapp's ribs break like clamshells, and then it kicked right on back and landed six feet away!

As for the loads of shot, they had ripped away the whole side of my coat under my arm, as though a cat had clawed at me, and had almost got me!

I thought for a minute that Rapp was dead, he lay stretched out so still, with a little trickle of blood smeared around his left temple. But when I leaned over him, I saw his breast rise a mite. He was still living, but knocked cold.

I felt into his vest pockets and located the key that I wanted, right away; and with that key, it was sort of backhanded work to get at the lock on the handcuffs, while my hands was still in them, but I managed to do it, because it's a trick that I had spent a good deal of time learning. The locks gritted and snarled at me, as though they hated to let go, but pretty soon I was a free man, sitting down beside poor Rapp, who was just coming to.

He had nothing on him by way of a weapon except one of my own revolvers, which he had taken away from me before we left my camp. Now I held that again, and as he opened his eyes, he looked up to me and to the gun and wagged his head.

"Counting chickens before they was hatched," says Rapp, as quiet as you please.

"You have a couple of busted ribs from that shotgun," I told him, "and so you'd better go easy!"

"Thanks," said he. "But I think there's more than two gone!"

He felt at his side with his hand, but there wasn't even a wrinkle of pain in his face. He was spent and done but he wouldn't howl, and I liked him a lot better than ever before.

Because, after all, whether a man is good, or bad, or kind or mean, or stingy or generous, or whatever else he might be, the main thing first of all is for him to be a man.

And that was this Rapp.

When he captured me, he hadn't crowed none.

And now that he was beat, he didn't whine. I can tell you, that, though I knew that he was mean, and I guessed that he was a skinflint, I felt a lot sorrier for him than I ever had for a lot of others that was better men than he would ever dream of being!

So I lingered on there beside him, for a time, though I was mighty uneasy, being as I was in enemies' territory, as you might say, with probably lots of other folks out for my scalp, and Cherry Pie so far away.

That Rapp, he as good as told me that I was a fool to stay there with him.

He says: "You better slope. There's a lot more that are out trying to get rich quick, the same as me." And he smiled a little.

He was looking a shade or two greener than usual. So I give him a swig of brandy out of a little flask that I always kept with me and never used except when I was pressed to the limit. He thanked me for that. And then I helped him to stand up and got him into the shade of a tree, because the sun was about due to get up in the east, and then there would be heat on him, and you couldn't tell how long it would be before help would come to him. Walking he couldn't do. I opened his coat and his shirt and I looked at those ribs of his, and they was a puffed and gory mess, I can tell you.

I told him to lay quiet there and that I would take a chance and show myself at the first shack that I come to and send him help. He thanked me for that, too, but then he said with a queer grin: "I don't think that I'll be needing your message, though."

"What do you mean by that?" I asked him.

'You'll find out in a minute or two," says he.

Just then, though I didn't hear nothing, it seemed to me that there was a sort of a quiver that run all through me, from behind, and jerking my head over my shoulder, the first thing that I seen was Wally Ops riding out of the trees full speed not two hundred yards away, and beside him there was a dozen more that was spreading out to each side and coming zooming down at me as fast as they could spur.

Wally Ops!

I said to myself that the rest didn't count. That it had always been a case of just him or me. That these here years of chasing had got to end—

And I jumped my Colt up, shoulder high, for a long shot at him. My hand was good and steady, and I was mad enough to see as clear as you please, but when I had that funny figure of Wally riding at me down the sights, and slanting in his saddle, the way that he always rode when he meant business, somehow I couldn't pull the trigger.

I jammed the gun into the holster at my hip and I spun around on my heel to run for it, and Solomon Rapp, he says, as calm as you please:

"You're a fool, after all, Dickon!"

A fool not to shoot, he meant, and perhaps he was right.

Behind me, there was a thicket, and I made for that. In a minute, the briars was tearing at me and I was groaning for Cherry Pie. But there was no Cherry to save me now, the way she had done so many times before. Without her, I was only half of myself, and that half was pretty well beat, I began to think. However, I pulled straight ahead.

The thicket rolled up a hill and headed for a great big mass of lodgepole pines, beyond, set so thick together that a horse could hardly make any progress through them. I sprinted for them, hoping against hope, with the brush making such a loud crackling around me that I couldn't hear more than a murmur of the sheriff and his men; and what direction they was making for I couldn't tell, so I headed straight on, as I was saying, and in another two hundred yards I come to a clear gap of not more than twenty steps, between me and the outskirts of that forest which meant safety to me—for the time, at least!

But the minute that I jumped into the open a rifle whanged and a bullet ploughed through the ground ahead of me. And another pair of rifles cracked, and I seen five men zooming along down that gulley.

I had thought and acted as fast as I could. But on foot I couldn't match up against those men on horses, and besides, they had Wally Ops to do their thinking for them.

I ducked back into the brush with bullets coming thick around me. And there I lay quiet, for a minute.

It was hard to think, with the sweat streaming off of me, and the dust from the brush settling on my skin, and the scratches from the million thorns stinging me.

But all the time I could hear the voices of the posse, as they called to each other, and spread out. They didn't make any effort to rush me in the jungle, there, and they was wise not to, because every one of the six shots in that gun could of made a dead man.

But after a time I saw that the one thing that remained for me was to try to work down through that brush and come toward the willow marsh that lay along the sides of the river—that same bottom land that Solomon Rapp was just in the midst of truck-farming with his Portugees at the time when I turned around and slugged him.

Down there by the river there was a pretty fair chance for me to work away. And if I could dodge them until night, then I might be able to drift down the river in the dark—

I thought of that while I got to my feet again, and started in working my way along, moving as noiselessly as I could. And I think that I had gone on for maybe ten minutes when a warm puff of smoke come rolling toward me through the shrubbery.

I stopped short and stood tiptoe, and then I seen what was happening.

Straight ahead of me there was a wall of blue smoke spotted with yellow fire, and it was marching slowly up toward me. I only needed one look, and then I knew what had happened. Wally Ops had seen a card to trump my best ace, and that was setting fire to the brush. Because it was only a long, narrow neck, comparatively, that led down toward the marshes, and now the fire was already burning clean across the neck of brush.

The wind was against me, too. And every instant, that fire was walking closer, and beginning to raise its head high and red.

So I knew that there was only one chance in ten that this wasn't the last of my chances. I was being burned out like a snake from tall grass!

25

IT didn't seem right.

I don't mean about being taken. Because any gent that had lived the sort of a life that I had followed has got to take good chances along with the bad ones. And this was sure my turn to suffer a little. No, it wasn't that which bothered me, but it was the idea that me, Larry Dickon, that had done what I had done, should be snagged at last in this low-down way!

Cherry Pie! My God, how I did long for her!

I raised a whistle as high and as loud and as long as I could make it. And after a minute, far away, I heard a whinny. And I knew that Cherry was coming for me.

Why, I got to admit that the tears come stinging into my eyes at the thought that she wasn't laying down on me.

But then I heard a voice screeching, and I recognized the voice of Wally Ops:

"Dickon!" he was hollering. "If you call for Cherry Pie and she comes, we'll shoot her down as sure as you're an inch high!"

Why, that come of letting one man chase you so long. Any other place, if I had whistled like that, what would the gents outside have been able to guess? But Wally Ops had trailed me for so long that he knew my mind a good deal better, in lots of ways, than I knew it myself!

I wished, then, that I had ripped the liver out of Ops one of the half dozen times when I had had a chance to do it. But it was too late for that wish, now.

I crawled to the edge of the thicket, and just then I seen my Cherry come dancing out of the woods and stand there in the morning light looking like the queen of the world, with her head up, and her ears pricked, looking this way and that, and listening and trying to locate me good.

But between me and her there was four gents, and two of them was covering her with their rifles. And any minute one of the swine might pull his trigger.

Why, it yanked my heart up into my throat. They knew that if she ever got to me, even on three legs, they would never have me in their damned jail. And so they was ready when Ops gave the word. Or would they even wait for that?

I couldn't stand it. Besides, fire was burning hot and close, and so I yelled out: "Don't shoot her, boys! I give up! I surrender!"

I chucked that Colt away from me, and I walked on out of the smoke with my hands up over my head. And they came running to get me. Cherry Pie come running, too, till Ops barked at me: "Keep back the mare, Dickon! You keep her back, or we'll drill her, by God!"

Why, what could I do?

I hollered to Cherry, and she shortened her racing gallop to buck-jumps, and then to a high trot, and finally she stood there lashing her flanks with her tail like a tiger, and sort of begging me to tell her how she could help.

Poor girl, there was no helping of me, then!

They come spilling in all round me, yelling and yiping, and calling in their pals. And yet, when they got up close, they only milled around me, with their guns all out, and covering me, and each man telling the other to go in and take me.

But none of them come forward. You would think that I was fire that would burn their hands, or poison to breathe, or something like that.

Then here came Wally Ops and they sang out:

"Go on in, Wally. You know how to handle this sort of a job—"

Wally, he come in through the circle of them.

He rode up and dismounted and he looks me in the face with a very queer expression.

"Well, Dickon," he says, "it's pretty hard for me to believe that the long trail is over!"

"All right, sheriff," says I. "You win. But you win by threatening to shoot horseflesh, y'understand? And that's low-down, Ops. I want you to remember that I hold that against you!"

"Ay, Larry," says he. "I know. It went agin the grain. But if that devil of a mare had got to you, we would of had all of these years of work to do over again. And the county don't pay me like I was a member of the Society for the Prevention of Cruelty to Animals. I had to do it."

"All right, sheriff," says one of the gents, bustling up all white with excitement. "Here's the handcuffs! And here's the irons for his legs—"

Wally Ops turned around and looked at him.

It was a good long look, too, and it seemed to make the young gent wince a little.

He says: "Thanks, but I don't think that this is that kind of a game."

He turned back to me. "Larry," says he, "will you give me your word of honor not to try to escape?"

I only smiled at him.

"I mean," he hurried up, "until we get you inside of the jail. Otherwise, I'll have to put the irons on you."

I looked around at those faces.

It was queer, somehow, to be so near to gents—near to so many of them, I mean, and them honest men, and me not with a gun in my hand. They was different. I had almost forgot the feel of being with decent gents. And they looked at me—why, as though I wasn't made out of the same kind of flesh as them.

"Thanks Wally," I told the sheriff. "I'll keep my hands free, if you don't mind."

It seemed a pretty big relief to Wally. He pulled out his bandana and mopped off his forehead.

"Good!" says he. "Damned good! You can have Cherry, then, old-timer, to take you in."

I called, and Cherry come floating up to me and laid back her ears and looked around at those other horses and those other men, as though it hurt her pride to have such common dirt circulating around her boss. She was an airy one, was Cherry. If she had been a lady, she wouldn't of been popular with the other girls, I can tell you!

As I got into the saddle, one of the boys sung out:

"For God's sake, sheriff—he ain't even given you his word of honor!"

And the whole gang of them seemed a good deal upset, but the sheriff, he only drawled:

"Aw, Charlie, shut up, will you? D'you want me to swear him in on the Bible?"

He says to me: "Will you ride up here along with me, Larry?"

I rode up alongside of the sheriff.

"You boys can run along home," says he. "I won't be needing you any more."

Why, that seemed to paralyze them. They asked him if he meant it, and when he said that he did, one of them told him that they couldn't take the responsibility of getting him murdered.

Wally Ops, he cocked a finger at the gent that said that.

"Barney, you damn fool," he said, "did you ever hear Larry accused of murder?"

Barney chawed his lip and seemed put out, and the result of it was that they reined back their horses and followed along maybe fifty yards behind us, while the sheriff and me rode along like pals, as you might say, into the town.

And oh, how proud Cherry Pie was that day! Because it had been a long time since she went through a town right in the broad light of day with all the folks to admire her. And you would think that she was a circus horse with the band playing, to see the way that she waltzed along, changing her gaits every second, from a rocking canter to a fast walk, to a trot, to a pace, to a rack, to an amble—and sweating all the while till it dripped off of her, as though she was afraid that she wasn't doing enough to show off her boss.

But Cherry wasn't the only thing that I watched. For the news, it run in ahead of us, somehow, and as we went down that long main street, the children and the women, they run out to look at us; and the mothers, they caught their little ones close to their skirts and gaped at me, and the men, they all run out carrying guns, I dunno for why, and they watched us go by with their teeth set.

All in front of us, that street was more silenter than a grave, and all behind us, there was a regular riot, with the folks spilling out and waving their hands and shouting and laughing and praising the sheriff so much that he should of blushed.

But he didn't. For a gent that had done that day's work, he seemed terrible quiet. It was only now and then that he looked at me from the corner of his eye with a glitter that told me how mighty glad he was that this was the whole end of the trail.

We got to the jail, and there a gent come running to meet us.

"You'll hang, Dickon! Damn you, you'll hang!" he yells at me. "And if you don't, *I'll* take charge of the justice of this here case!"

"Who is that swine?" says I to the sheriff.

"By name of Larson," says he.

"Ah," says I. "Related to Sandy, then?"

"A brother," says the sheriff.

There would be others, too, to hate me extra special for the way that I had carried on. And all at once, I was almost *anxious* to get inside the door of that jail, because I couldn't help remembering that the lynching habit hadn't never got stale in this part of the world, and that maybe they would get some arm exercise, before long, in the stretching of *my* neck!

26

HAVE you ever been in jail?

The reason that I would say that is because there is something you may never find out about unless you get there.

Well in all of my ramblings around, the one place where I never *had* been was a jail, and now I stood up in front of a gray-headed old sap who sat behind a desk, and who says to me: "What is your name?"

I sort of smiled at him.

"I suppose that you don't know?" says I.

He just smoothed down the page of the great big ledger that was spread out in front of him.

"What is your name?" says he, as patient as could be.

"Look here, man," says I, "is this a joke?"

He glanced up at me, then, and there was a wonder in his eyes.

"Joke?" says he. "Joke?"

"Why, damn it, don't everybody know that I'm Larry Dickon," I asked.

"I don't know anything," he told me. "I put no words in your mouth. You speak for yourself, now. What is your name?"

Why, he was the sort of a gent that, if he had met me in the open, would of turned around and scooted for cover. Most likely he had never handled a gun in his life, or a horse, except some six-mile-an-hour dog-trotter. He was the kind that you see going down to work in the morning about a quarter to nine, leaning back on their heels, and their stomachs so big that it makes wrinkles in their coats up the small of the back. And you see them, later on, walking around past the windows of the courthouse, wearing gray alpaca office coats. And they know how to smoke a cigar and smile out of one corner of their mouth and talk out of the opposite corner.

I tell you, that I had always looked on 'em not as humans, really, but just as things that you have got to find, like palm trees on a courthouse lawn in Arizona. These gents, they come out once a year about election time and stand on soap boxes and make speeches with tears in their eyes about what grand men their bosses are.

This was just that sort of a man, if you can call them men. But now when he looked up at me, it sent chills wriggling down along my spine. Because those dull eyes of his was as calm as a lion's looking at me. And all at once I felt like I was back in school, and the teacher peering at me through his spectacles, and the strapping leather hanging from the corner of his desk.

I mean, it was a very queer thing, y'understand?

You take a teacher, it's not him that you fear so much, but it's the things that are behind him. He's there paid by the state, and he has your parents behind him. They pay taxes, and the taxes pay him, and he's sort of a part of a machine that works on you. If you're good, all right. If you ain't, whang comes the machine onto you.

It was just the same way with the old chap behind the spectacles and the desk in the jail. When he spoke up to me, I felt that there was something behind him so mighty strong that even to *think* of cracking a joke about it made him turn a little grayer. It was the law—you understand?—that filtered down my spine like ice. It was that law that made him so strong. And behind that fat-backed hand of his, splotched with brown speckles, there was a hundred million other hands—

No, it was a lot worse than facing guns even in the hands of good shooters.

I told him my name as quiet as a boy that has been spanked. And then they took an examination of me about when I was born, and the names of my parents, and such. They told me what I had to answer, and they told me what I didn't have to answer, though they would be glad to know. Not that they talked kind, but just like a machine, they ground out certain words and phrases with no more heart in their voices than in the creaking of a wheel on an old axle.

It was the law, you see, that told them what to do.

Very queer. Now I could see through the heart of the thing. Those duty, hard-riding sheriffs and their posses, and all the printers that had pushed out posters telling the reward for my capture, and all the gents that had prayed and marched and fought to nab me, they was nothing, after all, except just little parts working for a thing that had a soul of ice—or no soul at all. The law!

I got thinking so deep about it that I hardly knew how I got into my cell. They was the law. So was I, too! I was a part of it. I was one of the hundred million hands. I was lending a finger's weight to the pressure that was closing the barred door on me.

It was the strangest thing that I ever went through.

And then I come to myself in the cell, so to speak, and looked around me; and I was scared!

The gent in the cell next to mine had hold of his bars and his face was pressed against them.

"Hello, Larry!" says he.

"Hello," says I.

"You don't place me?" says he.

He was a musty looking, ratty bird.

"No," says I, "I don't."

"I wasn't much, so to speak, along side of you," says he. "But one night when a fast freight was pulling into Santa Fe, I got into your way—you kicked me off!"

I remembered. It was a long time back, and this fellow was full of moonshine whiskey. It was a brisk little fight while it lasted, but finally he went off the top of the box car.

"Well," says I, "I never expected to see you again!"

"I never expected to see myself, neither," says he. "Not when I rolled off the top of that car. I thought that I was done."

Yes, and I remembered the screech of him as he dropped into the darkness, and the way he snatched at the stars as he went down, and it made me wriggle a little.

"Yes, that was me," says he, watching my face all of the time. "That was me, all right!"

"What's your name, bo?" I asked him.

"I'm Denver Charlie."

"How did you come through it, Charlie?"

"It did me in," says he.

He turned about and took a step, and his whole right side, it sort of crumbled up, and he almost fell down. He was crippled something horrible. Then he turned around and grinned at me again.

"It took me two years to learn how to walk even that good!" says he. "But now I manage!"

I looked at him and felt sorry. He was such a rat of a poor devil, and so cheerful about it.

"It was a bad night for you, Denver," I told him. "But you wouldn't listen to reason, you remember?"

He waved a hand.

"I don't hold it against you, Larry. Not a mite! I used to feel that, if I ever could, I would like to salt you down with lead; but after a while, when I seen how things was panning out for me, I didn't care much. My hard times was over, when I got out of the hospital. Because, me being smashed up like this, it's wonderful how it drags the money out of gents! They *can't* go by without giving me a handout! Had three square every day, except sometimes on the road!"

"What put you in here?" I asked him.

"Same old gag. Vagrancy. Y'understand? But I don't mind. Being in jail gives me a little publicity. I usually manage to get into the town papers through being in jail. And then the women will club together and give me some money, or something like that. Besides, I don't mind a good jail. Look how clean it is here? Tolerable bunk. And fair chuck, and very regular. Besides, it's restful. Don't have to do any thinking. Never have to care about tomorrow. Matter of fact, I *like* a jail!"

He added with another grin: "Maybe you don't figure the same way, eh?"

Not so good-natured, when he said that. No, some of the meanness sort of leaked out of him.

"What'll it be?" he went on. "Will they let you off with life, or will they hang you, Larry?"

"They'll retire me on a pension," I told him, "for clearing drunken bums off of the railroads!"

He only laughed, hanging onto the bars, with his head flopping back, an ugly sight to see. There was no pride in him. He didn't care how he looked. The worse he looked, the more money it was in his pocket, usually.

"Maybe they will, and then maybe they won't!" he told me. "Maybe they'll want to have a sight of you doing a dance with nothing under your feet. Or maybe—"

I pointed my finger at him.

"You curl up!" I ordered him. "You curl up and shut up. I'm tired of listening to you."

He only laughed harder than ever. It seemed to please him a good deal, because I got so mad.

"Go on," said Denver. "I like to hear you. It's funny to have you talk like this! Because in here we're all free and equal, though that ain't true any other place in the world! Jails, they're the places where you get your real democracy, old-timer. The sheriff, he's God. And everybody else is nothing! Even you, Dickon. Even you!"

And he rolled his head back again, with another laughing fit.

But it wasn't funny to me. The cold sweat, it streaked down my face. I felt pretty much done.

And when I turned my head, I found half a dozen other thugs listening very amused and watching me. They didn't drop their eyes. They were brave enough, now! And when they seen me stare back at them, they only laughed and shrugged their shoulders. It was as though you should stand in front of a cage in the zoo and find an animal that ain't afraid to meet your eye.

But there in the jail—the democracy—there was no fear. Not of other men. There was only one thing to be afraid of, and that was the Law!

I knew it then, I saw it was bigger and greater and finer than me. It smashed down the walls of my old ideas. It made me feel weak, and silly, and sort of new-minded!

27

THERE was a first class chance of me to get big-headed, about this time,
because the hullabaloo that was made about the taking of me beat anything
that you could imagine. Inside the jail, I couldn't notice much. There was
nothing but the crooks that was in with me, and some visitors that dropped
in, in a friendly sort of way.

I mean, old Choctaw came, of course, the first thing. You would think
that I was talking to him in my own house. He sat down outside the bars,
while the guard stood by to see that I didn't get anything from him. He
says: "You got no flies in here, Larry. That's a terrible big advantage! Pester
me all over the town, except here. Dunno why people will live in a town,
Larry, do you?"

And that was the way that he talked on, without a single word about the
way I had been taken, or about me being in jail, or about being sorry, or
about the trial that was to come.

Half an hour after he left, the sheriff came in.

He didn't have to have a guard watch *him* when he was talking to me!
He opened the door and came in to me.

"What has happened to that fellow Rapp—Solomon Rapp?" I asked him.
"Because he ought to get his share of the reward."

"Why?" asked the sheriff.

"Look here, Wally," I said, "would you ever have got your hands on me
if I hadn't been taken away from Cherry Pie?"

He admitted that that was right and he promised to see that Solomon
got his share and more.

"What I came specially to tell you," he said, "is that I want you to be
comfortable here. And I want to know what I can do for you?"

You know, when your brother or your father have died, folks stop you
and say: "What can I do for you, old man? You just let me know?"

What *can* they do? Sit down and hold your hand while you cry? Or go
to hell and bring back the gent that has just died? Funny what fool things
people say! And I just smiled at Wally Ops.

"Sure," said I, "you might put in a feather bed, and besides that, I'm
partial to good eats, and a steak at noon and chops at night, and half a
dozen fried eggs and bacon in the morning would come in pretty handy!"

The sheriff didn't take it as a joke. "You shall have it, Larry," he said.
"It breaks the rules, but damn the rules. Whatever I can do for you, I
certainly shall do it, right up to the limit. Only thing I'm sorry for is that
it had to be *my* county that you done so many of your tricks in!"

He left me, like that, and he lived up to what he said. I got the feather bed, which was so soft that it made me laugh to lie in it, and I got chuck that was fit for a king, while the other prisoners, they stood around and watched me and fair ached with envy.

Choctaw didn't end with a friendly visit. He came every day, and the second day he brought me a lawyer, and who was it but Jacob Israels? Of course you have heard of Jake and what he could do, and I had often read about him and seen his picture in the paper, but I didn't realize that such a smart gent could be such a weazened up little rat. His face came to a point at the tip of his nose. It curved back from that point to the top of his forehead and the end of his chin, which run down into his throat without any dividing line. He had black hair, brushed straight back with oil and showing the bumps on his skull, it was sleeked so close. And he had little, quick ratty eyes, and he was always looking at the floor and smiling, as much as to say: "I know all about it!"

"Here's your lawyer," says Choctaw. "You take to Israels."

"Not a chance," says I. "I haven't got your price, Israels."

He looked at the floor and smiled.

"Choctaw has fixed that," he said. "Now let's talk business!"

That was like Choctaw. How he got the money saved up, I dunno. But it made me ache to think of all the coyote skins and the wolf bounties that was being turned over to the lawyer for my sake by Choctaw!

"What have you done?" says Israels.

"Everything except murder," I told him.

He waved his skinny hand.

"I meant, what have you done that the state could get witnesses for? Nothing else counts?"

"It began back in Phoenix," I told him. "I had run into debt to a money-hound. He squeezed me so dry that I decided that I would take the law in my own hands, and so I blew his safe and took out of it enough money to pay him and—"

"Listen, Dickon," says the lawyer. "I'm not your confessor; I'm your lawyer! Being your lawyer, I believe that you're innocent, you see? All that I want to do is to get a chance to make a stand for a poor, downtrodden man, hunted by the law—y'understand? Have you got any women folk that could sit in the courtroom and wear black? Got any old mother with white hair, you know?"

I just looked at him a minute.

"My women folk stay out," I told him. "Whether it's hanging or life, I take what's coming to me."

"You don't understand, Dickon," he said. "The district attorney doesn't want justice. It's not justice that gets him his job. It's convictions! And I don't get my fees for justice, but for acquittals!"

"All the crookedness ain't outside the law, then?" I asked him.

"No," he answered. "That's just carelessness. The real fine work begins on the inside and stays there! Some robbers wear masks and work on the road. Some robbers wear the law and work in the middle of towns. You've been careless, Dickon. That's all!"

Well, that was the way that things were framed for me. But the best thing that could have happened to me was just having Israels, because when the district attorney found out that I had a smartster like that working for me, he boiled down his case and worked over it, not trying for the worst thing against me, but for the surest. And what did it all come to? Why, you wouldn't believe it! They picked out the case of Justin Carter, in the old town of Hannibal. There was nothing to it! All that had happened was that this Carter, who was a gambler, and a slick one, had sat in at a poker game with me, and had stacked the deck on me and the rest and had trimmed us proper. He got two hundred and eighty dollars from me, and cleaned me out, that time. But it happened that, while I was standing outside the door of a saloon the next day, the air was very still, after some gents had rode down the street, and I heard this Carter telling a pal of his how he had trimmed me the day before, and how he had stacked the cards and all that. I didn't waste any time. I went up the veranda to where he was sitting and shoved a gun under his nose. I got his wallet, counted out my share of the money he had taken, and then I backed away.

Very simple, you'd say. Yes, and no worse than he deserved. But the point seemed to be that, no matter what right you have to money, you got no right to use a gun when you go bill collecting. And as for witnesses—why, there was twenty men standing around that seen what I done and that knew me as clear as day.

Well, I could hardly believe that they would hang me up on that point, but that was what the district attorney did. And it made Israels very mad.

"Damn that fox!" he said to me. "If I had only had a chance to fight for you on something big—if they'd only tackled you on a gun-fighting charge—but sticking up a man for two hundred and eighty dollars—and with a dozen witnesses in hand—why, Dickon, I can tell you now that we're beat, and it's only a question of how I can cut down the sentence!"

I think that he might have got me off with one or two years, at that. But there was too much publicity. There were thirty reporters sitting in that court, every day, taking pictures and writing down stuff about me. Nothing I ever did in my life escaped without some sort of talk. They punished the telegraph wires every day and sent out junk by the tens of thousands. They had pictures of Cherry, of my rifle, of my Colts, of my gloves, of my hat, of my clothes, of my saddle. They had pictures of the place where I was caught and the jail I was in. And everything was labeled: "Gun of the famous outlaw." "Cherry Pie, the mare which has carried Dickon ten thousand miles in spite of the law!"

Why, in the face of all of this, the judge got excited. He couldn't keep himself from reading those newspaper accounts, and they made him feel that he would be laughed at if he gave me a light sentence. There was nothing for the jury to do. There were too many witnesses to swear to what they saw me do in Hannibal, that day. The jury had to call me guilty, and then I stood up in front of the judge and the old boy walled his eyes over the courtroom and bit his lip and said: "Seven years!"

I mean, he said other things, too, about making an example, and notorious criminals, and such—but the important words that sunk into my mind were just:

"Seven years!"

Well, I was thirty-four. Seven years would make me forty-one when I got out. Forty-one, with less than nothing done, with the prison shakes in me, and the prison stain on me! They might as well have said: "Hanged by the neck until dead!" Because it was the same as death to me, and I could never have started life over again.

I saw that in a haze, as I was led back to my cell, and how was I to know that the length of that sentence was the very thing that was to save me from any prison at all? That and Doctor Grace!

But I shouldn't be running on ahead like this. I ought to keep everything dark and show it just as it happened, but I can't help pointing out that the thing that saved me from going mad inside of a prison door was the fact that I had met up with Doctor Grace and come off best twice in a row. And the other thing was that the judge had strained himself a little to give me a big, fat sentence.

I should go back, first, to that minute in the court when there was a murmuring and a lot of talking, here and there, and folks saying: "That's pretty hard—for what he done to a professional gambler!" When all at once somebody sung out: "Look out! The old gent is dropping!"

I looked around and saw Choctaw, who had been trying to get to me through the crowd, turn white and topple over on his side along the floor.

I kicked one guard in the shins and knocked the second one down, and got to Choctaw before they could catch me.

He was living. It was only a faint. But as I heard him mutter and as I watched him open his eyes, and as the guards grabbed me and damned me as they pulled me away, I swore to myself that, if I ever got free from the law again, I would show the world that I could go straight. If I meant this much to any man, it was worth paying blood to try to run true to everything that was best in me.

28

SEVEN years!

You look backward, and it doesn't seem so much. You look forward and

it's everything. You look backward from eighteen to eleven. Well, that's a
good deal! But look forward from eighteen to twenty-five! So I went back
to the jail, and I had my picture taken, and was thumb-printed, and all
that. They might have taken me to the prison right away, except that no
more trains ran through, that afternoon. So they held me over until the
next morning. And that gave Doctor Grace and the long sentence a chance
to work for me. But that needs some explaining.

Nobody had heard anything from Grace for a long time. Weeks of silence
had come from him, since the night when he tried to snag me—the hound!—
at the house of Ham Turner. And I suppose that the world might have
known that he was most dangerous when he was most quiet. Except that
nobody could really have expected him to pull off a thing as black as this.

The first dribbles that come over the wire were pretty near nothing. Just
wild freaks. Then the real facts got across. And they sounded almost wilder
still. That news come so strong and so fast that not even the walls of the
jail could hold it out. It leaked through even to us crooks in the jail. The
old jailer couldn't help coming in and telling us the dope and damning us
all. And the half-wit, Denver Charlie, that had been hugging himself and
laughing like a fool ever since he heard about how I had got seven years,
even Denver Charlie sobered up and gaped.

It had happened up in Hookertown.

Hookertown was so plumb peaceful and easy-going that nobody but a
devil like Grace would of had the wits to think what could be got out of
the place in the way of money.

I mean, that Hookertown lay in Hooker Valley, with nothing but alfalfa
fields and orange orchards and lemons, and such, spread all around it,
and vineyards crowding up onto the foothills. And when you looked down
to it from the nearest mountain, why, it was like a checkerboard, all laid
out so level and so regular, and all that! And where the trees ran, some
days, you could see the silver streaks of the water in the irrigation canals,
or else the black shadows, which meant that it was mud, and the water had
just been run off. It done you good to see a place like that, I always thought.
And Hookertown itself was the finest place you could imagine, so neat,
and all the houses the same size, with lawns and maybe roses in front, and
even the backyards was neat. There was no big house, and there were no
big holdings in the valley. It was just a lot of little holdings, with everybody
working hard and putting away a few hundreds every year, and everything
prospering and going fine.

And that was what Doctor Grace knew. So, when he came out of his
silence it was to clean up the bank.

It was a mean-faced bank, humble and no-account looking. So that when
I went through that town looking for chances, it never occurred to me that
there might be anything worth while in it. But, for years and years and
years, that little bank had been putting away nine-tenths of the savings of

all the farmers in that rich valley. Four or five hundred a year ain't much. But you multiply that by a thousand, say, and it begins to seem something. That bank was soaking away hard cash for years and years and investing it in good bonds, and such, and its depositors were safe, and it was getting richer and richer.

Yes, it was good to think about!

Now, when Doctor Grace first got the idea into his head, it turned out later, he tried to bribe some of the gents that worked for the bank. But he couldn't get by with that, because the people in that valley were an honest breed. And then he lost his patience, and he decided to raise the devil.

You see he was plain mad and ornery. He had been slapped in the face twice by me. He had lost two of his best men, and then, when he heard that I was in jail and off his trail, he seemed to feel that he had a free hand. And this is how he used it!

He had his three regulars left with him—I mean, Dago Mendez, Little Joe, Lew Candy. All three, straight shooting, hard-riding, fearless gents— all of them wanted—and all of them wanted for things with murder at the head of the list.

Now, without wearing masks or anything, about ten one morning, that Grace jogged into town, and his men, they followed along after him. I suppose that they looked like any ordinary cowpunchers, come from over the hills and bound for the range farther north and west. Nobody would think to look under that dust and recognize the face of the Doctor, no matter how often they had seen it advertised in newspapers.

Into the main street, and up to the bank went Grace. There he stood on the sidewalk and rolled a cigarette and lighted it, as calm as you please, while the other three got off their horses and throwed the reins in different spots, not far away, and just as they dismounted, in walked Grace through the swinging door of the bank.

Altogether, in that bank there was five men at that minute, including the janitor, who sometimes worked as night watchman. He was a hard-boiled old gent about sixty, but straight and limber and handy, still. And when he had one look at the stranger strolling in, he yanked out an old-fashioned gat a yard long and hollered: "Hands up, Grace!"

No dust could save the Doctor from being recognized by old Grogan.

But before Grogan had that gun well up from his hip, the Doctor, who had one hand dropped into a coat pocket, pulled the trigger of a snub-nosed revolver that he was carrying there and sent a bullet through the lungs of Grogan. The old chap dropped, dead game, and, with his insides torn horrible by that bullet, he turned over, coughing up blood, and let drive at the Doctor.

That day, Grace was taking no chances. He might have kicked the gun out of the old boy's hands. Instead, he shot Grogan through the brain.

By that time there was more guns pulled in that bank. But behind Grace came in his three handy men, and after what they had heard, they came shooting. They killed the president of the bank, while the old man was lifting a big shotgun to his shoulder, and he fell over his desk. They killed the cashier as he was trying to close the door of the safe. That was three dead for a starter.

The other two were shot and wounded, but they dropped and played possum.

In the meantime, the roaring of those guns had alarmed the whole town, of course, and that wasn't the place to stand and ask questions. You notice that most really honest folks are brave when they get stirred up. It was that way with the men in that town.

They came swarming. They didn't even wait to get guns, a lot of them, but as they piled toward the bank doors, they were met with rapid revolver fire, and they had to give back, leaving four wounded men squirming on the pavement.

Right after them came the three men of the Doctor, carrying canvas sacks under one arm, and smoking guns pushed out before them. In the rear came the Doctor, a Colt in each hand—and believe me, he could shoot straight with two at the same time.

Before the charge of the four of them, that crowd split away. But it didn't run. It just sagged back, and when the crooks flicked into the saddles and started to gallop away, the men of Hookertown dropped down on their knees and opened fire.

But they had a lot of handicaps. In the first place, there was their own men on each side of the street, and they were afraid of hitting neighbors unless they fired very high. And besides they had moving targets.

Worst of all, they had *shooting* targets, because those devils, Grace and the rest, held their reins in their teeth, as you might say, and kept shooting on either side.

Well, they had plenty of targets, and the damage that a real gunman could do at close action was seen as they smashed their way down that main street.

They killed five men and they wounded sixteen before they got through the town.

They had left three dead and two hurt in the bank.

So the total casualties for that day ran up to twenty-six men!

On the side of the bank robbers, there was no surety that anybody had been hurt, but it was said that they thought that they had pinked Little Joe.

So he was the only one that they could even hope that they had so much as scratched, and when last seen, he was riding as fast and shooting as hard as any of the rest of his pals. That was what Doctor Grace had done in Hookertown. The list of the dead and the wounded, it looked like a train wreck.

And those twenty-six dead or wounded men had been the price of a real haul on the part of the Doctor.

He had a hundred and eighty-two thousand dollars in good hard cash with him, when he rode out of Hookertown.

The whole population that had horses followed the robbers, said the telegrams that kept coming in. It was felt that surely they would soon overtake Grace and his murderers.

I heard that and I couldn't help smiling. Because I knew what that meant. Everybody riding, everybody yelling and making dust and noise, nobody organizing things, and the result would be that this man Grace and his gang would ride right away from that mob, or else leave a little trail problem that would spoil the brains of the whole gang.

Nearly two hundred thousand dollars.

And now the borders were being watched. Trains were being searched. Even in San Francisco and New York, sailings of boats were kept under the eye. But that didn't fool me. I knew that Grace would never leave the country. The richer the pickings, the longer he would stay in it.

Well, that was the layout so far as Grace was concerned.

Now I have to show you how that happened to affect me, and the way that it *did* affect me is one of the strangest stories that you ever heard in your life!

29

WHEN old Choctaw dropped in the courtroom, there was a lot of fuss and pother over him, but when they had thrown some water in his face, and when he sat up and said: "Thank you, gents and ladies, I'm able to take care of myself!" they were all willing to take him at his word, and they went off about their own business—which was the watching of me into the jail.

There was only one that went to him and took him by the arm.

"I'm fit and fine, sir," says Choctaw. "Don't you go bothering about me! I just stumbled and tripped up and fell—"

"You're a terrible fraud," said Julie Ops, because it was her. "And I'm not a sir! You come along with me and mind what you're told to do."

"Ah, Julie, honey," says old Choctaw, "get me out into the air, because I'm main sick!"

Seeing that it was her, he put his pride in his pocket, and he leaned his whole weight on her, and she barely got him into the street. She fetched him up to her buggy, and when she was about to help him into it, he balked and stopped, though his knees was shaking under him.

"I wouldn't," says Choctaw, "sit in anything that belonged to the sheriff. God bless you, Julie, and you're a good girl, but for him, I hope that he lands in the hell that he was meant for, and I aim to tell him that, face to face, before many moons!"

You can see that he was heated up a good deal. But the anger helped to revive him a little.

"Will you tell me why you're so hard on Dad?" she asked him.

"Julie," says Choctaw, "you and me is pals, and all that. But I don't know even you well enough to tell you what I think of that father of yours. Only—I would like you to remember something. It's the yarn about the gent that fetched in the froze snake and warmed it beside his fire. And what happened to the gent afterward?"

"What has that got to do with it?" asked Julie.

"Nothing," says Choctaw. "Now lemme be. I don't want to see even you, today, Julie, I want to get away from the sheriff and all of his kin!"

Well, he started off down the way, and though Julie tried to stop him, she couldn't. Only she said: "Uncle Choctaw, is it fair to talk to me like this and then run away before I can talk back?"

"I got something else to think about," says he. "I got to think about a man that they've murdered, today!"

"Murdered?" says Julie. "Who?"

"You don't even know his name! Him that come back here and run his neck into the noose all for the sake of trying to see you once more—and that hung around giving money to the gent that you lied and said you was to marry—until he got himself caught—"

"I did exactly what you *told* me to do!" cried Julie.

"Did you? Well, then, I hope that you have no luck! Lemme be alone! I'm sick!"

And he broke away from her.

So she went back home alone, thinking all of the way, and when she started thinking, she was sure to get to some pretty good result. She usually could see her way clear straight before her to the finish of a thing.

So that girl was as fine as could be to her brother and her father and all of them, but when it come to the little time after dinner, when they sat down and Wally Ops says: "Julie, give us a tune and a song, will you?" then she says: "Daddy, I can't very well sing."

"Are you down with a cold?" he asked her.

"I'll tell you," says Julie. "I've been worrying about one thing and I have to tell you about it."

Everyone in the family was excited, by that time. They watched her and the sheriff says: "Had you and me better talk it over alone?"

"No," says Julie, "I think that the whole family ought to know about it! Because it's a dreadful thing!"

Why, they sat up as stiff as pieces of wood.

"Go on!" says the sheriff.

"I've been insulted!" says she.

"Ah!" says the sheriff through his teeth, trying to smile and looking like a death's-head.

"I've been insulted on the open street," says Julie, "by old Choctaw!"

"That miser'ble old scum!" says Mom Ops. "My pork and beans was never good enough for him. I didn't put in mustard, he said, and—"

"Mom, Mom!" gasps the sheriff. "For God's sake, will you let up? Say, Sis, what happened?"

"I met that wretched old man, and he told me that you were a snake!" cried Julie.

"He did?" said the sheriff, looking black.

"And when I asked him, what do you think he said?"

"I dunno?" said the sheriff. "But I aim to find out!"

"He said," went on Julie, "that you were the death of a man who had taken you in and warmed you with his own life blood!"

"Ha?" says the sheriff. "Does he mean—does he maybe mean that—er—Dickon?"

"He meant just that man!" says Julie. "Did you ever hear of anything so ridiculous?"

"Pah!" sneared Mom Ops. "A robber and a cutthroat—"

"*Has* he cut throats?" says Julie. "I think that he's wicked enough to!"

"Humph!" says the sheriff. "Cut throats? Damn nonsense! He's decent, of course."

"A decent robber!" spouts Mom.

"I asked Uncle Choctaw what he meant—he said that he wouldn't sit in your buggy—he'd never come near your house—he hoped that you'd go to the hell that you had prepared poor Larry Dickon for—"

"Julie!" sings out her mother. "What kind of langwidge—"

"Mom!" yelled the sheriff. "I stood about enough from you. Now, by God, you leave your tongue out of this talk, d'ye hear me?"

"I hear you," sighs Mom. But after that, all she did was grunt, now and then. Thinking wasn't the main suit of Mom. Cooking and eating was!

"Of course it's all ridiculous," says Julie.

"I should say it is!" yipped Lew.

"Ay, lad," says the sheriff, "even a boy can see that old Choctaw has been talking like a fool!"

You see, he was taking his comfort even from a lad like little Lew!

"Of course it's nonsense," went on Julie. "Just because you happened to be at the mercy of an outlaw for a few minutes—why, you helped him to save Cherry Pie, at least, in reward for letting you go—"

She said that with a bright smile, as though it settled things, but the sheriff winced a good deal, and young Lew twisted up his face, trying to think things out.

"Wait!" said Wally Ops. "You got to remember, Julie, that a sheriff is a man with his oath took to do his duty—"

"Of course!" said Julie. "And that's what I told poor old Uncle Choctaw. But he didn't seem to understand. He seemed to think that even an outlaw is a man—just like any other!"

The sheriff got up and began to walk up and down the room.

"What else could I do?" he groaned at last. "What else could I do? I had to play the game the way that I saw it. Besides, what does Choctaw mean by saying that this is death to poor Dickon?"

"Seven years in jail—that will be the end of him. He'll never be able to start a decent life, after that. You can't put a man together after he's been once crushed, Father—"

"Ay," groaned the sheriff. 'It's true, God knows!"

"Wally!" yipped Mom Ops. "What's in your mind? What are you going to do?"

He didn't answer.

He picked up his hat and ran out of the room, and that was the last that they saw of him until late that night.

In the meantime, I saw him at the jail.

And now you begin to see how Grace and Choctaw were working together to save me. Because, as the sheriff went down the street, one of the best men in the town stopped him and took his arm.

"A pity," says he, "that the man you have in jail isn't that murderer, Grace, instead of a clean gent like Dickon."

Not that I ever meant anything to him in the past or would in the future, but after what Grace had done, the sort of a crook that I was looked almost like an angel.

Anyway, it hit the sheriff in just the right spot for me, at just the right time. He went on to the jail. And all the way, he was hitting the ground with his heels hard and thinking.

When he got into the jail, he found that they was just turning loose that half-wit tramp, poor old Denver Charlie. He had served out his little term, and he wanted to stay and make a speech to the sheriff and say how much he had enjoyed that little old jail, and how much he hoped that he would be able to come back to it some day. But the sheriff wasn't in a mood for listening none.

He up and damned Denver and turned him out, and then he went up and down his office for a few turns, and he tried to light a cigar and burned his fingers, and threw the cigar out the window, and then he turned around and he filled his pipe, and it wouldn't draw. And he damned all tobacco and all human nature after it.

He was heated up, a mite, as you could guess, by this time. But finally he yelled to the guard:

"Go bring out that murdering scoundrel, Larry Dickon. I'm gunna have a talk with him!"

The guard was scared stiff.

"In irons, sheriff?" says he.

"Damnation!" yells the sheriff. "Ain't you been working in this jail for eight years? Don't you know how a crook like that man Dickon had ought to be handled? Sure you put the handcuffs on him, and put them on big and strong! And then bring him in here by the nape of the neck, damn his heart!"

The guard was so scared that when he come to me he said: "Now, God help you, Dickon, because the sheriff is in there asking for your blood! He means something close to murder! What have you ever done to him?"

I didn't know. It worried me. Because I had always thought that the sheriff was sort of friendly to me, and only against me because he happened to be a sheriff, and I happened to be a yegg, as you might say!

30

WHEN they brought me into the office of the sheriff, he yelled at the guard: "Now, you get the hell out of this and leave me alone with Dickon, will you? And what's that rat doing in here?"

Because, there was Denver Charlie, that had started out of the office a minute ago, but that had squeezed back in, when he heard that I was to be brought onto the carpet.

The sheriff was terrible mad. He made a run at Denver and took a kick at him that would have busted him in two, but Denver hobbled out again, laughing back at me over his shoulder. And a damn mean laugh that Charlie had, at that!

That left me alone with Wally Ops, and he sat down and studied the carpet for a long time.

"It might of been life, Larry, eh?" says he at the last.

"Yes," says I. "And they may make it life still, by the time that they get through trying me for the different things that I've done. They've got enough of them!"

He nodded at me. All of the noise had faded out of him.

"That's true, too," says he.

"And now what's up?" I asked the sheriff,

"I'll tell you, Larry," says he. "I got a terrible worry on my mind tonight!"

"And about what?" I asked him.

"About a funny thing," says he. "I spent my life trying to build up a reputation, ain't I?'

"I dunno," said I, "that you've had only one string to your bow. Because it seems to me that you've done a good job in finding a wife and a prime cook, rolled into one. That's enough of a career for most men, getting a wife like that."

"Ay?" says the sheriff, a little dazed.

"And you've made a whopping success of your farm," I told him. Because I sort of took pity on him, seeing him so down, when he ought to of been so up.

"Ay," says the sheriff. "I suppose that it looks as though I have."

"And you've got a fine daughter and a whopping good son. What more would you want, old-timer?"

"I got money, I got a good honest wife, and I got a fine son and a daughter, but I tell you, Larry," says he, "that I would throw them all away and start in with nothing—a damn beggar, with no family, no nothing, so long as I could get a chance to make myself a really big reputation."

"Why, man," I told him, "what are you talking about? What do you want to be except a sheriff?"

"Nothing!" says he.

"And who has ever been a better sheriff, Wally, you little square-head?"

"Ay," says he, "I ain't been so bad, son, eh?"

"The whole world knows about you," I couldn't help saying, and it was sure the truth.

"Do you think so?" says he, as wide-eyed as a child.

"Yes."

"Well, Dickon," he sighed, "tonight I'm giving up a life work. I'm throwing my ambition away!"

"Go on," I asked.

"What good does it do for a man to be famous outside, if he ain't famous *inside* his house?" says poor old Ops.

"Well?"

"The point is, Larry, that they look at me as if I was a low hound dog, inside of my house!"

"The devil they do!" said I.

"My daughter," says he, "has got herself ridiculous. She has fitted up a pair of wings for you!"

"For me?" says I.

The sheriff leaned back in his chair and closed his eyes. I felt that I could of stepped in and slammed him over the head with the handcuffs—I mean, I felt that I could of done it if it had been anybody except such a hair-trigger gent as the sheriff. But I knew him, and I took no chances with a sleeping cat.

"She's started collecting all of the scrap that she can get hold of about you," says the sheriff. "Doggone me if she ain't got more than a hundred pictures of you in her big scrap book, by this time, and God knows how many yards of stories that has been wrote about you, chiefly lies."

"Humph!" says I.

"Disgusting, ain't it?" says the sheriff.

"Oh, I don't know!" says I.

"Why, son," says he, "I seen her sitting up till midnight and poring over that bunch of newspaper clippings. She has got pale. She looks as if she cries. It's plumb ridiculous! Did you ever hear of any such fool thing as that, Larry?"

"Oh, I dunno!" says I.

Because I began to feel pretty good, between you and me!

"Well," says the sheriff, "the fact is that the whole family has got me wrote down for no better than a hound dog, and the reason for it is that you've been the gent that could have blown my head off, and you didn't do it! Now they tell me that I'm—"

He stopped, choking.

"Tonight you go free, Larry!" says he.

"Tonight I go free!" says I. "Man, what are you talking about?"

"I'm talking about two fool women and my boy, Lew," says he. "I won't dare to show my face in my own house if you go to jail. And what they're thinking, why, a lot of other decent folks are thinking, too! So I got to chuck you, and I chuck my reputation with you."

He looked white and sick.

"Why, Wally" I told him "I wouldn't take my freedom from you when you feel this way about it!"

The sheriff jumped up and smashed his hands together.

"Shut up!" he shouted.

I backed up, and I shut up. He was sort of wild, just then. He took a turn or two up and down his office.

"Larry," says he, "you got to tie and gag me. That's all that there is to it!"

I said nothing. It seemed dangerous to talk to him, one way or another, just then.

"Yes," gasped the sheriff. "You got to twist me up in a rope, and you got to put a gag in my mouth—damn your heart! And then get out of this jail and don't you ever lemme lay eyes on your face again, or I'll capture you once more, Dickon, and I'll fry you over a damned slow fire!"

You see how crazy he was talking?

But I let him talk.

Then he says: "Here! Gimme your wrists!"

I held them out to him, and doggone me if he didn't unlock those cuffs! I couldn't believe what I heard and what I seen. There was my own hands hanging at my own sides, and there was no sign of bars around me—not even at the office windows.

I sort of inhaled a new idea of life.

All the time, I had been thinking that I would sure never take my liberty from a man that hated to give it away to me as much as that sheriff did. I was going to say something pretty fine about not being a beggar, even for my freedom. But I tell you, when I felt the steel slide off of my wrists, I thought of only two things—how terrible bright the stars must be shining in the open sky, on a night like this, and how terrible clear they would glitter back from the eyes of Cherry!

After seven years in prison, what would Cherry Pie of been like?

Ah, well, I was a lot weaker than I though that I was.

The sheriff had slumped down into a chair.

"You have slipped the cuffs off of your supple wrists and hands," says he from the corner of his mouth, like a sick man, "and then you have leaped on me, and we've struggled hand to hand, like a damned book. And—"

Here he took hold of his coat and ripped a couple of the seams of it, because he was very strong in the hands.

"And then you got the best of me and you tied and gagged me—and hurry, before I do it to you!"

Did I hurry over there to take advantage of a gent that—

Why, to cut it short, yes, I did. I did walk over to him and tie him, but before I gagged him, I says: "Where's Cherry?"

"She was sold up the country near Granite Corners, to a horse lover, by the name of Delaney."

"I know him!" says I. And then I fitted in the gag.

The sheriff looked pretty funny, maybe, as he lay back there in his chair, but knowing what this meant to him, you can bet that I didn't smile none!

I collected two good Colts, a hat, a gunbelt filled full of first class ammunition such as a gent like Ops would keep, and I picked a fine Winchester off the wall, and I started for the door.

31

I WAS clear outside in the street before I remembered that I hadn't said one word of thanks to him. I was about to risk going back and saying what I had ought to say, and then I remembered what sort of a gent Wally Ops was, and that chatter didn't mean very much to him.

So I forgot about that, and I headed down the street, walking close into the shadow by the jail wall.

So close that something dropped on my head, as I sneaked along, and I was flattened to the ground, while a gent that sprawled on top of me yapped: "Help! Help!"

You shouldn't hit a half-wit and you sure shouldn't hit a cripple. But I got to confess that when I heard that voice I felt a terrible lot of satisfaction in picking out the point of his chin and hanging a nice right-angled hook on it with everything in my right forearm and shoulder, and everything in my heart, too!

Mr. Denver, he went down against the wall, sliding, like a balloon that is letting out air fast.

And I went along down the street again, and at the first alley mouth a couple of gents come charging out.

"What was the screaming?" says they.

"Fool back there trying to scare his wife," says I, and I walked on, while they stood stock still.

They were not tumbling very hard for what I had just said, and I was willing to start sprinting. Or else, I was willing to slow up and not enter the broad blur of light that came out from an open doorway and showed all the hoof-hollows and wheel-ruts in the dust of the street.

But if I hurried up, or if I slowed down, I knew perfectly well that I should get that pair of gents suspicious, and so what I did was to walk through that dim slant of light, busy rolling a cigarette.

That's an old gag, to show that you ain't nervous, but somehow, it always pops into my head in a crisis. Well, just as I went to the farther side of that slant of light, I heard a soft pounding and, glancing back over my shoulder, I seen that pair running after me as hard as they were able to sprint, and pulling at their guns as they went.

Confound the eyes of a cowpuncher. They're so used to looking a mile off and spotting the difference between a two-year-old and a three-year-old as it goes switching its tail up a hillside, that there ain't much that slips by them, when they care to turn loose and look.

I didn't stop to ask questions, and I didn't stop to explain. I took the first turn to the left, which happened to be right down a path between two houses, and as I run through, the gents on the front steps of both houses, they stood up and says: "Hello, what's this?"

But I didn't wait to explain to them, neither. In three seconds there was a yell went up behind me that tore that town in two.

"Larry Dickon is loose!"

It even made *me* feel sort of scared and chilly, just hearing it!

I hoofed down that path like blazes. There was a seven foot smooth board fence straight ahead of me. It would of taken a bit of climbing, usually, but I just dived over it, this here night. Then I sprinted down the next alley, and whirled around to the following street, feeling that I sure must of got that gang guessing.

Not a bit. The first thing that I knew, I heard the dust puffing under running feet behind me, and I glanced back and I seen two gents running almost shoulder to shoulder after me.

I knew them at once. They was a boy from the town that had come back for a vacation from college and that had brought along a chum of his. They was both footballers. And they looked like the cover design of a magazine, or an Arrow Collar ad, or something like that. And as they came running, their hair blew straight out from their heads, they came so fast. Why, they was sprinters, and what was I but a poor, broken down shack of a cowpuncher that had taken up yegging sort of as an excuse because the cow business was too much for me?

I had a mean feeling, just then, that I might have to kill those two pretty college boys before long, and so as I started running again, I fired a shot right between their heads—a real pretty, placed, snap-shot.

But when I looked back again, there they were, running harder than ever. Like the coach had said: "The one that makes this touchdown first, he gets an ice-cream cone—"

Maybe you know what I mean—there ain't any fool as bad as a college fool. Or finer either, if you want to look at it that way. Always ready to die for something or nothing—usually nothing. And never singing a song, except about how they hope that they'll get a chance to lay down their lives for Alma Mater—

Well, I seen that it was either them or me, unless God put a fast horse in my way—because even an ordinary cowpony would of been sprinted down by those two long-legged fools, you know!

Why, God, or Luck, or whatever you want to call it, just that minute put a couple of horses in my way and says: "Choose, Larry Dickon!"

Of course, after the mare, they both looked like nothing at all, but any sort of horseflesh was better than nothing. Two husky mustangs, they come in a hard gallop right around the corner, and as they slowed to take it, they headed *away* from me.

That was perfect. The speed that I was running at brought me right up beside them. I did a circus trick that I had often practiced on Cherry, when I mounted her at full speed. I landed in the saddle behind the left-hand man quick as a wink, and at the same time, I give him a cross-body sling and heaved him in the dust.

They was both heroes going out to see what had happened to Larry Dickon, and before the second man could say, "What the hell!" I slapped his face with the long side of a Colt forty-five and he gasped and went down, too. So there I was, riding one good horse, and another galloping wild right beside me. It didn't seem so bad for me, take it all in all!

The two college madmen, they come tearing up from the rear.

"Remember the Blue, Ed!" yips one.

"Till I die!" says the other, and they both headed for me.

Somehow, I'm sort of ashamed to say that I didn't have the heart to throw lead into those two young jackasses that thought they was making touchdowns for their football coach, still. I didn't even have the heart to hack in their skulls with the butt of the Colt. Instead, I leaned back and twisted around and gave the leading man a full-armed swing that landed on his snoot, and he fell, sidling right into the path of his companion. Down went the two of them. And the last I seen of them, a block later, they was scrambling to their feet again and heading after me for the sake of the dear old blue!

Take them by and large, I suppose that a pair of pretty cowpunchers was spoiled on the making of those students.

I had something else to think about right then and there, however, because the whole town was raging after me, too terrible cut up and rambunctious for words, when they found out that Larry Dickon was really getting away from their hands, after having been with 'em so long.

And as they headed after me, the first thing that I found out was that I did *not* have Cherry Pie under me.

No, sir, it was a good mustang, but no racer, and there *were* racers in that pack behind me.

As we left the town behind, and as we streaked up the valley, I saved every ounce of the speed and of the strength of that pony; but in spite of all that I could do, half a dozen long-legged real runners come out of the pack and settled down in a cluster, gaining on me fast.

I left the straight when I seen that I was beat, there.

I took to the rocks, and dodged in and out among them, and so I managed to just keep away in "living distance" but never out of their sight or of their hearing, and I can tell you that they were foaming fast behind me all of the time.

Now, when I seen that things was this way, I slackened up just a little, and then I changed from the first pony to the second one.

It hadn't been carrying any weight for that first killing half hour. And so it had a good edge of running left.

I had worked the chase out of the levels and into the rough and the steeper hills, by this time, where long legs and plain, flashy speed didn't count so much, and now, with a half-fresh horse under me, I made every mile a winning one.

I suppose that they fired a hundred pounds of lead at me, that night. But they didn't hit me, and they only grazed the rump of my first pony. And, after that, I was drawing away from them steadily.

Well, the minute that I had as much as a quarter of a mile clearance of them, I didn't try any clever tricks at trail weaving and problem making. I just swung around and I skidded as fast as I could skid for the place where I hoped to find Cherry Pie.

Because, man alive, there was nothing else in the world that I wanted half so much as I wanted her! With Cherry working for me, I could of pranced away from that gang in no time at all. But how they had worried me through the hills, and as I came up the valley toward the house of Delaney, I could hear a horse neighing wild and free behind me.

And by that, I could pretty well guess that the chase that had missed me in the hills had, or a part of it at the least, turned around and made a chance guess that the first place that I would head for would be my mare.

I damned again, heaved over every extra weight, and spurred that mustang until it bled fast.

So I shot over the ridge and had the lights of Granite Corners down before me, and a little to my left.

Somewhere out on the edge of that town there was the place of Delaney. I didn't know it well. A big, skeleton of a windmill, and a tall tankhouse, and then a rounded bushing of trees with a house somewhere in it. That description doesn't mean much. It would serve for almost a million Western ranches.

And I only wondered, back in my mind, whether there would be an instinct in me that would take me to the right place. I didn't try to think. I just left it to an extra sense that most of us have, if we'll only give it a chance to work for us.

So I tore down into the hollows, feeling sort of ghostly, and apart from myself. And pretty soon, by the grace of God, I seen something like a long arm, standing up out of a flat field.

I didn't have to guess any more. Them was the clump of trees. There was the tankhouse. Just a little different from the outline of a thousand other ranches that I had seen against the night stars. And as I rode, I could of laughed, there was such a happiness in me.

If only Cherry was there, safe enough!

I whistled the call as shrill and as high as I could pitch it, and it went shrieking off ahead of me, like a flying hawk.

Ay, true and clear the answer came back to me, the long, shrill whinny of Cherry, saying: "Hurry! Hurry! Hurry! Oh, I'll be glad to see you!"

I whistled again, and this time there was an answer that was no nearer.

And I knew that, hard as she was trying, Cherry wasn't free to get loose and come. Poor girl!

Delaney had that much sense. He didn't trust that the jail might keep me from coming to call her.

Well, I spurred the poor mustang, and the pitiful brute winced and staggered with every thrust of the spurs. I saw the barn loom up, long and low near the trees. I saw the tangle of the corrals close by. I whistled again, and this time there was the answer right straight before me—Cherry, waiting for me, calling for me, God bless her!

I made at her with a yell that would of been enough to wake the dead and raise 'em.

And as a matter of fact, it *did* raise a shadow along the bars of that corral where Cherry was kept all by herself. It raised the shadow up, and a voice called: "Who's there?" And the same instant a rifle clanged, and a bullet sizzed across my face.

32

THEY were pretty well fagged behind me. I mean, the ones who were riding so red-hot along my trail. And there was really no hurry about this job. I could of taken my time and gone up more slowly, and maybe warned this gent away from guarding the mare so hard. But he was, as you might say, expecting me, because, the minute that I got loose from the town, somebody telephoned out to him and told him: "Delaney, Larry Dickon has got loose from the jail and left the sheriff tied and gagged behind him. They are hunting him, but likely he'll get away, and if he gets away, he's fairly sure to make a straight run for Cherry Pie. If you want her, watch her close, Delaney!"

That was what Delaney was doing—watching her close. And, with the warning that he had had, it was a wonder that he didn't have a regular trap set for me. But it happened that everything favored me. That night, there was only one other man on the place with him, and Delaney tried to get his neighbor by telephone, and then rushed that hired man over to get help.

In between, I came, and I found nothing but Delaney himself between me and the mare. Could one man stop me? No, I had used up my share of bad luck, to last me for a while. I shot low for Mr. Delaney. And the very first bullet sent him down. It was only a clip through the calf of the leg, as I happened to find out later, but it sent him down, and before he could grab his rifle and pump bullets at me again, I was out of the saddle and at him. I got the rifle away from him, and I told him that he had better get back to his house and tie up his hurt. But he was Irish. He preferred to stay and talk to me.

I let the gate open, and Cherry came dancing out to me and pranced and danced around like she was crazy, because we had never been separated as long as this, before. But I made her stand still at last, and I shifted the saddle onto her.

Says Delaney, sitting holding his wounded leg: "They're hoofing up the valley for you pretty fast, Dickon."

I looked down the valley, and just then I seen the procession headed over a rise in the road and streak one by one against the stars.

"All right," I said, pulling the cinch up tight enough to make Cherry grunt. "All right. I understand that they're coming, but they won't catch me. My wings ain't clipped, now! By the way, how much did you pay for Cherry?"

"There was nobody on hand for the bidding when she was auctioned off," says Delaney, "and I raked her in for a measly four hundred and eighty dollars!"

"Dirt cheap," I told him. "I'll tell you this more, from me. When I get a chance, I'll send back the money that you paid for her."

Says Delaney:

"Don't you bother about that, because when this leg of mine is fixed up enough to stand the strain of a saddle I'll come to collect the coin!"

Nervy, you see, that Delaney was. I had to laugh as I swung into the saddle. So I said goodnight to him, and I dropped his rifle at a little distance and jogged Cherry out onto the road.

The air was crystal clear, and all the stars was busting themselves to shine bright, so that the leaders of the posse could see me fine, but clearer than they could see me, they made out the silver mane and the tail of Cherry Pie, and they let out a yell of sorrow, because they knew that they'd rode all that distance for nothing. However, there was a few of them that had a little speed left in their horses and they gave Cherry a run up the valley.

It wasn't even close enough to be fun. I just spoke to Cherry and she spread her wings and flew the first mile in about a minute, and after that, the road was clear for me.

I cut across country to the first good camping ground that I knew about, and there we put up, Cherry and me, and had a fine time getting to know each other again. And all night long, I couldn't sleep, but I kept waking up and looking for her, and always she was no more than a step away. And when I woke up in the morning, she was lying down like a dog at my side, with all of the grass eaten off the ground in a circle in reaching distance around me.

I shot a rabbit for breakfast, and then I circled back through the hills and I had to have another rabbit for noon. But by evening I was tired of rabbit meat and wanted something different. I hankered for flapjacks, and I knew that Cherry did too, so I struck away across country for the first lights that I saw, and I walked in on a camp of half a dozen cowpunchers and their boss sitting around a table in a chuck-wagon, with a Chinese cook handing out the chow to them.

I stood in the door of the wagon with a gun in each hand, which scared some of those boys a little, but the boss spoke up as cool as you please.

"Are you out of chuck, Dickon?" says he. "Come in and rest yourself, will you?"

If there had been three, I would have chanced it, but not with six. So I said:

"Thanks, but if you'll have John put up a snack for me, it'll do me fine."

The boss said the word, and John Chinaman began to put together some self-raising flour and some bacon, and salt, and such things, stopping every once in a while to grin at me, while the rest of the boys went ahead with their meal, but making sort of stilted motions, and now and then one of them would steal a hand toward a gun, but think better of it, and go on eating.

But the boss was not trying anything against me.

He said:

"You've done a lot of clever things, Dickon, but we all want to know how you happened to be smart enough to bribe Wally Ops? How could you do it? Because everybody in this part of the world would of swore that Wally was the straightest man in the world! Give us an idea how much cash you had to pony over, will you?"

I stared at him. It gave me cold chills, to hear that.

"I bribed him with a gun held under his nose and rope to tie him up, and a gag to choke him down," I said. "Didn't they find him that way?"

The boss laughed.

"Of course they found him that way," he said. "But you don't think that this gag can be swallowed, after what the tramp saw?"

"What tramp?" says I.

"Why," says he, "Denver Charlie, of course!"

Denver Charlie!

Now it came back to me in a heap, and I felt that I was a fool not to have guessed something before. I mean, how Denver Charlie had been climbing down from the wall and had fallen into me as I went by.

"Good God," I said, "what did Charlie have to say?"

"A funny story," said the boss. "Said that he was kicked out of the sheriff's office, when you was brought in last night, and that he was pretty curious to see what it was that made the sheriff so hot against you. And he swears that he went around and climbed up to one of the sheriff's windows, afterward, and looked in while you was talking with Wally. And he says why, that he saw the sheriff unlock your handcuffs, and then, after you was free, set himself down and let you tie him hand and foot and then gag him."

I busted out: "Look here, would the word of a damned no-account bum like Denver Charlie—"

"And how, when he was climbing down," went on the boss, "He fell into you, and you soaked him when he hollered. Is that all wrong?"

I hunted about in my mind for some few words to say that might have a little meaning in them. But words didn't come easy, just then. I looked from side to side and I wished that I was dead.

"Are they jailing the sheriff?" I asked the boss at last, with a pretty weak voice.

"They will, probably," says the boss. "But just at the present time, they're thinking the thing over, because Wally Ops has always stood pretty high around here. But, anyway, Denver Charlie's story is ruining all the work that Wally ever did. As a matter of fact, we believe Denver, Dickon. We believe that Ops is too much of a fox to let anybody slip handcuffs and take him—without him so much as firing a shot or hollering for help."

I hadn't thought of those little details, and when I did think of them, they made me rather sick. Because, as you can see for yourself, it made things look rather bad for Wally.

I couldn't help thinking back to that other night, long ago, on top of a box car, and how I wished that I had killed Denver Charlie, before he had a chance to make all this trouble for the whitest man that ever walked!

But it was the sort of a thing that couldn't be explained.

And I was dumb for a minute.

Then I said: "No matter what Denver Charlie seen, or says that he seen, I'll tell you something on my word of honor."

"Why," says the boss, as serious as you please, "if you'll talk to us on your word of honor, we'll all believe you, Dickon!"

"Then," says I, "I want you to believe that I never handed the sheriff a penny; I never promised him a penny; and in my whole life, I've never tried to offer him a bribe, and I've never dreamed of offering him a bribe, or of trying to influence him to be crooked in any way *at* all. And that's straight, so help me God! Now, whatever Denver Charlie may say, will you remember this?"

The boss was a red-faced, round sort of a man. But there was something to him under the fat, and he looked me straight in the eye.

"Give Dickon the package, John," says he to the cook. "Yes, old-timer, I'm willing to believe you, for one. But how the devil is the thing to be explained? Why should Wally Ops want to turn you loose unless he thinks that he can get credit by capturing you again?"

Now, what could I say to that?

I only thought of one thing, and a sort of a fool thing, at that. I said: "I'll tell you. There's things that can't be talked about now, but when they're known, you'll see that there's nothing at all against Wally Ops, and what he done was all for the best. Gents, I'm thanking you kindly for the handout!"

I backed out of the door, and I left them sitting quiet behind me as I climbed into the saddle on Cherry and rode her off into the dark.

In a camp that I made that night, I made flapjacks and cooked them, and Cherry sat down as clever as ever and begged for them like a dog. But while I fed her, I got no pleasure in it. I was sick. I was sicker, even, than when I slept in a jail.

33

WHAT I was going to do, I didn't know. That night I was half asleep and half awake all the time, worrying and wondering, and the next dawn I started out, not knowing where or what to head for. I had to do something for the sherrif. I knew that much, but what it could be beat me.

If they didn't have him in jail, it was because they didn't need to. He was being punished enough by having to live and endure all of the blame that they was heaping on him, and all of the slander and the hate that would be around him. When a big building is rooted up, you find mud and bugs and snakes that have burrowed under it. And when a big man falls, you find that there are heaps of enemies that have never dared to show their heads while he was standing big and fine, but now they crawl out of their holes and sink their fangs in him.

It would be the same with poor Wally Ops, and I was as keen as a knife to see what I could do.

I was riding up a ridge, with cañons dipping down on either side of it, and the trees piled like shadows in the heart of the ravines, and a bright, cool morning sun, and everything that a man could wish, with Cherry dancing and laughing back at me and asking me to please let her show me how she could run a thousand miles without ever stopping, now that she had me on her back again. But even that couldn't make me happy.

Pretty soon, I heard voices whooping in the distance. I took out my field glass and looked down at one of the ravine mouths, and there I seen seven or eight punchers riding hard after one stray horse. It was easy to follow that stray, because it was a gray—almost a white; and the sun turned him to silver, except for his black stockings. He came floating across the plain and the gents behind him scooped him into the mouth of the ravine. And it looked to me like they had him boxed up safe and sound, because that was a blind cañon.

The stray horse seemed to know it, too, just as he got into the mouth of the draw. I could see his head toss up, and he whirled around and made a charge on those punchers.

That glass was strong, the air was clear, and the sun was shining just right, so that I could see even the flicker of the ropes that they throwed for him. But only one of those ropes got a hold on his neck, and all it did was to snake the gent that throwed it, horse and man, right down to the ground. The stray turned a somersault with the shock of it, but he whirled onto his feet and was running again. And it was a grand thing to watch him go for it, now that he saw freedom ahead of him, once more!

I thought that he was free and away. If it hadn't been that I owned a Cherry Pie, I should of wanted to take up the hunt of that horse myself.

But just when I thought that the gray was off for good, so far as that set of gents and that day was concerned, I noticed one puncher streaking up on a little paint horse. He had been hanging away back in the rear, all through the hunt, and never pressing things, but just sort of lagging along. But now he seen his chance, and you never seen anything go the way that mustang went!

For two furlongs, the fastest thing on four feet ain't a blood horse. It's a common mustang with maybe a dash or two of the hot blood in him. And this paint horse was a real quarter runner. He flashed after the big gray; they measured against each other for a minute, then the paint horse crept up, and crept up, and gained, and gained, and suddenly the gray knew that he was beat and he tried to dodge.

He might be able to dodge most nags, but the pinto was a regular cutting horse, by the way that he handled himself. He dodged with the gray, and then the rope went glimmering out, the pinto set back pretty on his haunches, and down went the gray with a crash. I seen the dust cloud puff up, but through that dust I could mark the little cowpuncher jumping off of his saddle quicker than a wink and laying into the gray with his rope.

And when the dust cloud blew away, the trick was turned and the fight was over, and there lay the gray all roped up, and the puncher sitting on his head, and fanning himself with his sombrero.

It was a pretty thing to look at, and I was a mind to go down and congratulate that gent for as pretty a piece of riding and roping as I had seen in a long time; but after all, I had to remember that I was Larry Dickon—and that cowpunchers wear guns and know how to use them.

So, I just drifted along that ridge, again, but what I had seen had put my head up and made me feel pretty good all over. I could think, now, hard and fast, and what I was thinking was that there might be some way for me to apply the thing I had just seen as a sort of a lesson. If you got a real gift, the best way for you to get on in the world is to keep using it all the time. If a gent is a nacheral hand on a farm, the thing for him to do is to keep working the ground and not run off and take a flier, say, at banking. Well, I had been born with a few nacheral talents, and they had never done anything but keep me in trouble. I had a straight eye and a quick hand, and I could shoot a little better than most—even than most of the good ones. I didn't mind a fight, and I liked a free life. There was my special talents. What did I do with 'em? Why, I let 'em run me into outlawry.

But as a matter of fact, there was something else that I might of tried. I hated the crooks that I had met, mostly, and I liked the honest men. And now I could see, as clear as crystal, that I should of been on the side of the law, instead of opposite to it, all these years!

It seemed so clear and so simple that I couldn't help laughing a little. And suppose now that I was to try to take the side of the sheriff and the law, what was the thing that I could do for him, and set him right?

It come flashing home to me sudden and surprising.

I could go out and do what the little gent on the paint horse had done. Where the rest of them had failed, he had made his sprint at the right time, and he had captured the stray for them.

And here I was with the best horse in the world for the mountain work, and nothing but time on my hands, and nothing but guns to play with— why shouldn't I go out and try to tackle the great Doctor Grace, him that was now riding so pretty with a fifth of a million just hauled in—and a lot of reputation to his credit!

It was an idea so big and so staggering that I stopped Cherry Pie and let it shudder home in me. Long ago, I had swore that I would never stop hating Doctor Grace and his gang. But I had just meant that I would fight them when I came across them and had a good chance. But now I meant that I would worm them out, no matter where they was hid.

And that was the thing that I set my mind to.

It was a big thing to tackle. They say that Napoleon when he was quite a young gent started out to tackle the whole doggone world and lick them, and make them like it. Well, sir, I sat down and I thought this here thing over and it seemed to me that Napoleon's job didn't have nothing on mine!

First of all, I had to lay down a plan of campaign.

I did what I could in the way of thinking the matter out, but it seemed to me that I would be pretty foolish if I tried to handle this job just with my own wits and with no others. And so I said to myself that the thing for me to do was to light out and get to Choctaw, and to let me have his help. Because when it come to thinking, he had nearly everything beat.

Well, I went along and scouted down through the hills until I got to Choctaw's house late that afternoon. If I had ever gone up to that house careful before, it was nothing to the way I went up to it now. I had had bad luck, the last time that I visited, and I was dead set on not having bad luck again. It took me a whole hour to work around the place through the last quarter of a mile.

Well, I come up, at last, and found the house empty. So I took the mare to her feed of oats. I sat down to the cold chuck that was waiting for me, and with a rifle lying over my knee, I just waited for Choctaw to come along.

When he came, he was carrying an axe over his shoulder, and across his back was his rifle slung, and in his hand he was carrying the pelt of a big wolf. He was so full of the killing of that wolf that he could hardly pay any attention to me.

"Why, Larry," says he, "it's just the same rascal that sneaked down and killed my brown yearling, last May. Damned if it wasn't the same. Got the same missing toe on his left forefoot, and the same spread, too. Doggone me, if that ain't a beauty?"

And he spread out a yaller-white pelt and laughed and rubbed his hands again, just like a Jew is *supposed* to do when he makes a haul of gold. Which my experience is that Jews are a damn sight more generous than the gentiles.

However, old Choctaw was running along:

"I been trapping for him all these months. I've trailed him and I've back-trailed him. And I've tried to study his habits. But this here is a sort of a campaigning lobo. He does his butchering over about ten thousand square miles, and he's perfectly at home all over that spread. Fat—look at the quality of that hide, will you?

"But today, when I was looking at the bait on a coyote trap I had laid out, I looked up quick and thought that a shadow had ducked behind a rock on the side of the hill just above. Give me a chill, at first, and throwed me back into the old Injun days. I jumped sideways, my rifle ready—and then I seen this here lofer wolf scooting up the hill so fast that his hide rumpled from his tail to his withers, every stride.

"I didn't have much time. In ten more yards he would of been over the top of the hill, so I had to take a quick snap shot. And by God, boy, I broke his back with that shot, and he give a death yell and jumped into the air and then come rolling over and over back down the slope to me. Right down to my feet and lay still, there, with a quiver!"

"All right," says I, "but how is that going to help me catch Doctor Grace?"

"Hey, hold on!" yipped Choctaw.

Even he was impressed by that name.

"You ain't forgot that the sheriff is down and out on account of me," I explained to Choctaw. "Now, I'm going to set him up again. I'm going to bring in Grace, dead or alive. And then I can tell folks that the sheriff only turned me loose so's I could go and catch that Grace, for him!"

"All this for the sheriff?" says he.

"For Julie, that made her father turn me loose. Maybe chiefly for her. There ain't any more like her."

"Ay," says Choctaw, "every girl is the most wonderful woman in the world, once in a while. I married three of 'em, one time or another."

But he says after a minute: "She *is* uncommon fine, Larry, ain't she?"

I didn't answer. The things that I thought about Julie couldn't be wrote down or spoke out. And so I let Choctaw drift back to my problem which I wanted solved.

34

How would you of gone about a thing like this?

What old Choctaw did was to lie down and light his pipe and take a puff and look at the blue of the sky, and close his eyes, and take a puff, and look again.

"You tell me a couple of stories about bank robberies, will you?" says he, after he had finished trying to tell me that I was crazy if I chased the Doctor and his gang, single-handed.

I said, "You know a lot more about robberies than I ever shall."

"Don't argue," says he. "Just you start in and talk!"

I obeyed him, because old experience had taught me that he knew such a lot more than me that it was better to be bossed by him.

He lay there, then, in the cool of the shadow, smoking and thinking, and only listening to a few words about what I had to say, and then breaking in: "All right, then tell me another!"

And I would do what he told me.

Finally, after pretty near an hour of this, I had gone down through most of the list of the robberies that I had heard or read about—I mean, the bank robberies that had been successful. And then Choctaw, he sat up and he said:

"Look here, old-timer. What does every son of a gun do after he has cleaned out a bank, including yourself?"

"Run like the devil," says I. "Run away, of course, and get as far away as he can!"

"And in all of the yarns that you've been telling me, they've always scooted, that same fashion?"

"Yes."

"Now with this here Grace, they've been out and they've combed the whole country to locate him?"

"They sure have. They've spent money by the tens of thousands to get him!"

"What sort of a reward have they hung out for him?"

"There's twenty-five thousand dollars on him, now."

"Dead or alive?"

"Yes."

"Now, look here, son, don't it look like a reward of that size had ought to raise some sort of action against him?"

"It does," I admitted.

"But why ain't they had any trace or sign of him?"

"I dunno."

"Lemme tell you why. It's because they've begun all of their hard hunting at a distance. They've started at San Francisco and El Paso and New York, and such places, and they've been working back along the main-traveled lines, trying to see where the Doctor would try to get out of the country. But, lad, lemme tell you that they're all wrong, and that the end they should start looking at is at no place at all except Hookertown!"

Of course, I was a good deal surprised at this.

I sat up and I said: "What sort of a tip have you had, Choctaw?"

"Shut up," says Choctaw.

Then he went on, sort of dreamy: "After the robbery, this Grace says to himself that he'll lay low, and keep quiet, and he lays low and keeps quiet right under the noses of the whole damn gang up there in Hooker Valley. How many crooks is handy to Hooker Valley?"

I told him that it was a very clean country and that there were extremely few crooks around Hookertown, so far as I knew. But that only made him snort.

"As a crook, you ain't much account, son," says he. 'No, you really don't count a great deal. Now lemme tell you that no part of this here country, or maybe this here world, is without its crooks. If you don't know Hooker Valley and the country around it, I do."

He did, too.

He sat up straight and he made a little map on the ground, as usual.

"Here's where the Hooker River rises, and here's where it runs; these here are trees, that I'm stabbing in; here's the mud flats, and here's the lake; and here's Hookertown; and here's the irrigated lands and here's the big place of the Malones—"

Well, he went rambling along like that. And though I hadn't seen the valley for a long time, it all rolled back into my mind as clear as day.

I couldn't help admiring that old codger, the way that he worked along through his plan of that valley, until he had everything all set down. And then he went outside of the valley, and through the mountains around it.

"No," says Choctaw, "when I knew that part of the country, there was about five crooks around there. There was—"

"Hold on, Choctaw, what was you doing, when you knew that part of the country?"

"Leave me be," says Choctaw. "I was figuring on a terrible murder about the time that I knew that country—"

"The devil you were!"

"The devil I wasn't! It was my second wife. I kept figuring for two whole years how I could get rid of her, and whether the pleasure of murdering her would be equal to the misery of being in danger of hanging for it. Not that hanging was so bad, but that to hang for *her* sake would of been pretty terrible! Those was the times when I knew Hooker Valley!"

Choctaw was always that way. He would dodge out of your way when you tried to bear down and find out things that he didn't want you to know at all. I admired to see the way that he done it!

Says I: "Choctaw, you go ahead. I ain't going to ask no more questions. You just tell me where I'm to find Doctor Grace, will you?"

"You will find him," says Choctaw, "right here!"

And he stabs the end of a stick into the ground so hard that it broke off and left a jagged pin of wood standing in the dirt.

I looked down at that place as hard and as startled as though there was a chance of Doctor Grace and his three crooks rising side by side out of the ground where Choctaw had struck.

"Choctaw," I says to him in a whisper, "can that be the straight of it?"

"It can and it is!" says he.

"All right," says I. "I'll believe you. Tell me what the place is?"

"I'll tell you all about the place. It's run by a family by name of Donaldson. I forget or I never did know which one of them might be alive and at the head of things now."

"Hey, Choctaw," I asked him, "ain't you guessing?"

He looked at me, and he shook his head.

"I may be wrong, son," said he. "But there ain't no surer way of *making* me wrong than to start by disbelieving what I'm telling you, and there ain't no surer way of making me *right* than by believing every word that I tell you."

"How could me believing or not believing in you change things?" says I.

He got up both hands and waved them over his head.

"My God, Larry," says he, "sometimes you're so damn stupid that I dunno how you ever kept away from being hung for so many years!"

"All right," says I, "I believe everything that you say to me."

He quieted down a little and wiped off his forehead. He was all heated up, you see.

He says: "Now, where was I? I'm all lost!"

"Describing about the Donaldson house."

"The Donaldson house? Right. You come through a pass between the mountains—you tell it by one of the mountains being all whitish, sort of, in the evening, on the western side of Hooker Valley—"

That sounded like crazy talk, to me. A mountain turning white in the evening, on the side of a valley!

Well, I didn't say anything. I just nodded my head, and maybe blinked a little, and he went on: "The pass lies on the south side of that white mountain, And you'll find it a narrow, twisting, rocky way, with not hardly more than enough room for you to get through alone. There ain't a hundred yards in a mile, where gents could ride two abreast."

"Go on, Choctaw. I'm believing you—my God, how hard I'm believing you!"

"Then you come on out through the pass and you find yourself right over a long, broad, gradual fall of land, that looks almost level enough, and the soil plenty deep enough, for farming. And that's the bottom of the whole story!"

"Why the bottom?"

"Because, son, the Donaldsons used to be something back Kentucky way, but they lost a part of their property in a lawsuit, that perhaps they should have won, but the law turned against them. Well, they come out West, because they was disgusted with Kentucky, after that. They come out to the West and there they looked about for a good location, and old man Donaldson, he hit on that spot under the face of the white mountain, and when he seen the depth of the soil, he was sure that he had struck the right place, because he knew all about farming. Well, lad, the trouble seems to of been partly with the soil, because though it was deep it wasn't rich, and partly with the slope of the soil, because it let the rain wash down so fast, that that rain would wash out seedlings by the roots, and would smash down standing grain into a damn, muddy, mouldering tangle. And that rain itself—why, when the clouds come zooming across and hit the white mountain and turn into rain, it comes down by the bucketful!"

It sounded pretty good to me, all of this. It sounded like Choctaw knew some sort of facts and wasn't only dreaming.

"Now," he went on, "when the Donaldsons tried to farm that land and they couldn't make a go of it, what did they do? They didn't blame themselves, because they were strong and industrious and they used plenty of brains in the farming of that steep slope. They couldn't blame themselves, and so they blamed the lawsuit that sent them out of Kentucky, and so they blamed the law, and so they come to feel that the law owed them something—"

"And," says I, getting excited.

"And if the Donaldsons that are living up there now got it into their heads that they could make some money by cheating the law out of a man that the law wanted, would the Donaldsons hesitate? No, son, they wouldn't hesitate at all. A whole lot of things have been suspected against them— from moonshining to counterfeiting. But they still carry themselves like gentlemen. And the law ain't hardly got the face to be too rough with them, y'understand? And right up there, now I come to think of it, is the spot where you'll find that Grace and his gang has taken shelter!"

35

Now, there ain't anything in the world as important as confidence, and listening to the things that Choctaw said, and the way that he said them, suddenly I felt that he must be right.

He went on: "Somewhere near the valley, Grace is lying up. Then he's lying up with crooks. And what crooks is bold enough and strong enough, near the valley, to shelter him? Why, nobody but the Donaldsons. And so that's another way of working the thing out. And both answers, they check up one against the other, and so I must be right!"

He made it almost mathematical!

I says: "Choctaw, you're a great man, and that's all that there is to it!"

"Am I?" says Choctaw, grinning.

"Sure you are, and the only thing that I wonder at is how comes it, Choctaw, that you ain't made yourself a millionaire or something."

"I'll tell you something, son," says Choctaw. "There is some that can use their brains for themselves, and there is some that can only do their thinking for others. Now, you run along and get your head blowed off by the Donaldsons and Grace, and his gang!"

That was the way that he put it, and I couldn't help feeling that most likely he was right.

However, half an hour later, I was drifting away through the evening on the north trail toward the Hooker Valley.

I took things very easy.

I wanted to have the mare in the slickest possible shape, when I got to the valley, because I couldn't tell what sort of traveling she would have to do when she left that place. Most likely it would have to be fast work and long work, and I had had too much experience not to know that the best horse in the world can be spoiled by a little overwork.

So it took me three whole days lazying along toward the north. I made a detour around, and late in the afternoon, finally, I come out on the eastern side of the Hooker Valley, and there I unsaddled the mare and waited for sunset. Because I wanted to see one of the mountains along the opposite wall of the valley turn white.

It didn't seem possible, at all. It sounded, now that I was on the spot, sort of like a pipe dream of old Choctaw's. And he *was* old, and maybe he was getting a little simple.

I thought of that and smoked a pipe and waited, while the sun dropped lower and lower, and the air got more chillier, and finally the sun was out of sight.

Not that it had set yet, really. There was no rose colors in the sky, but the old sun was just out of sight behind the western peaks, and the minute that that happened, one of those mountains turned white!

No, sir, it don't seem a probable thing, to set it down in black and white, like this. And I don't mean to say that the whole mountain turned as white as a sheet, or anything like that. What I mean to say is that, while the sun was shining down from above, all of those mountains looked either brown or gray. But when the sun went behind them, then they all turned black as could be, in the distance, except for one, different from the rest. And all the sides of that mountain, as far as it lifted its head above the body of the range, turned pale and glimmering like dull chalk, until it seemed as though it was sort of shining by its own light, like the eyes of a cat when a lamp throws a ray against them.

So that mountain seemed to me, and I knew that it was what old Choctaw meant.

I can't hardly tell you what it meant to me. It seemed like this first glimpse of the truth must make *all* of what Choctaw had said right.

And it made me happy and scared at the same time—happy because I felt that I was on the right trail for Doctor Grace, and terrible scared because I thought sure, now, that before long I would be standing up to that gang, gun to gun!

Altogether, it was a queer mixture of misery and happiness that I felt.

When it was dark, I rode across the valley, because it would save me a lot of ground, and because riding by day would mean a big chance of being spotted, because it was said that Hooker Valley was plumb alert and ready for trouble, ever since the Grace raid.

I reached the western front of the valley, safe enough, and there I scouted along until I found the very pass that Choctaw had told me about, and then I was sure.

He had been right twice, and the third thing would be Grace!

So I found a fairly good camp and put up there with Cherry, and that night I rubbed her down and made her comfortable, and then I turned in myself and slept, the way that you sleep when you know that you got a hard day's work laid out ahead of you—when you *have* to sleep, in short.

All the rest of that night, and all of the next day I spent in that place, bothered a good deal by gnats, because the day had turned off close and hot, in spite of the height, and the gnats, they seemed to rise up in clouds out of the valley, and all head for my direction.

And it's a queer thing how much little things like gnats can bother a growed up gent!

Somehow, that miserable day got to an end, and when the end come, and the dusk began, I saddled Cherry Pie, and I rode her down through the pass, and as we rode along, a glimmer come behind me, and I turned and looked back and seen a half-moon rising through the eastern sky, and covering the mountain with a soft light.

And, somehow, I was terrible comforted when I noticed that that moon had been looked at over my right shoulder. Not that I'm superstitious, but in a pinch, you might as well have all of the luck fighting on your side.

We got through the little pass and I looked down on the land that Choctaw had told me about.

There was two or three square miles of it, all spread out down the side of the mountain, and it was crisscrossed with working roads, and it was all checked out by fencing, but even by the pale moonshine I could see that there was a lot of repairing had ought to be done to those fences, and it looked to me as though the attempt at farming had been given over, and as though that whole big ranch had been turned over to cattle that was grazing here and there by the moonlight, or lying down, with a steamy cloud of their breath rising from them.

Yonder, sort of at the side of the mountain, there was a house, tucked away among a growth of big pines and such, and I knew that that was the Donaldson place.

I rode all around it in a circle, and then in a smaller circle, and then in a smaller circle, still, because the best thing that I could do would be to know the whole layout of the land, as fine as could be. And when I was pretty sure that I had mapped down in my mind every wrinkle on the face of that place, then I got off from Cherry Pie and hooked the reins over the horn of the saddle, and I left her in a clump of young firs.

She would stand like that, once I had staked her in a place in this shape, for half a dozen hours at a stretch, and as long as the reins was hooked over the pommel of the saddle, she wouldn't even try to budge. Why, you could teach Cherry anything, if you only once got on the good side of her.

After that, I was all ready to go in and see what sort of a chance I would have with my luck.

But first I turned around and I gave a good look at the world around me, because once I got inside the shadow of the trees around that house, God alone knew if I should ever be able to come out again, and Cherry Pie might still be standing there, waiting for a dead man, until the Doctor went out and found her, and made her his horse.

Ay, and what an eagle Grace would be, once that he had a horse like Cherry under him!

I thought of that, and for a minute I was half of a mind to chuck the whole job and ride away. Because, what business had one man against so many?

But, after all, when you start at a thing, there is a sort of a force that pushes you along and never stops driving until you are through with it, and if you slacken up on the way, that force comes along and takes you by the nape of the neck and tells you to go ahead again.

It was like that when I stood there on the rim of the trees, rubbing the nose of Cherry Pie and telling myself that I could never go ahead with this deal.

But I *had* to go on.

So, finally, I took one deep breath and I started out straight for the house—straight but slow! Because I don't suppose that I went much faster than a scared cat across a strange street, where there is a danger of dogs any minute. Every whisper made me stop, and there was plenty of whispers, because the wind was rising through the sky, out of the west and humming through the trees, and now and then making a branch groan against another one. And when I looked up, I could see the half-moon washing through the clouds like a ship through high waves that threaten to sink it every minute.

I felt like that—mighty desperate, and close to the rocks!

Well, I worked along through the sheds until I got to the house itself, and one look at it was enough to send a chill through me. It was a great big building. It had a deep, long veranda in front with great, big wooden pillars to hold up the roof of it, and there was carved work here and there, looking fine and stately behind the moonlight. But you could see that the place hadn't had good care for a long time. Two or three of the windows had their shutters gone and were just boarded across. And a couple more of the shutters hung down where they had fallen when the last storm pried them loose. Now and then the wind partly stirred them, and they creaked on their hinges, very dismal. But when I circulated around past the front of the house, I could see that the rest of it had fallen right to ruin. It had two big wings. And one of those wings was almost down to the ground, with the roof fallen in. And part of the wreckage had been eaten away, and part of it still lay where it had fallen. So that I guessed that the Donaldson boys was using up that timber for firewood. It was a horrible sort of a thing to think about!

36

By this time, I didn't have any sort of a doubt about Choctaw being right. I could almost see Grace and his three lying up in the tangle of this old junkyard. I looked to my guns.

You never can tell when the best old gun in the world will fool you by sticking to its leather, just when you want to make a fast, snappy draw. So I pulled mine out a couple of times and jammed them back, until I was sure that they was working as slick as though the holsters had been greased. Then I sneaked ahead and made for the top of the house. I climbed up one of those straight pillars by the veranda. At the top of it I had a bit of a job hooking myself over onto the roof above. But I got there, and I climbed onto the roof and then tried the windows until I found a loose shutter. I worked that off and got through into a room as dark as mud. But I felt my way across it, got to a door, and went through that into an upper hall. There I crouched, listening, and waiting. But if you wait long enough in an old house, like that, you can hear anything that you wish for. It was the same with me. I stayed there on my knees until I began to get a chill, and then I got up and went on exploring, no matter how many footsteps went running tiptoe up behind me, and how many voices groaned out a warning around me.

I got to a flight of stairs big enough to drive four horses abreast down them, and along those stairs I went, keeping close to the wall, where my weight would have the least chance of making a creaking.

There was no use searching the upper floor, because just to listen to it and smell of it, you could be sure that nobody had lived there for ten years, maybe. But when I got down to the main floor, it was different. There was a faint smell of cookery and stale tobacco smoke hanging in the corners. So, of course, I went more cautious than ever, and yet not quite so scared. I was too busy keeping my eyes and ears open to have so much chance for being afraid.

Then a door sighed open and a man's voice sounded very loud in my ear, almost:

"Hey, close that door, Sam, will you?"

"Damn the wind! No, you close it yourself!"

"All right. Stay here and leave it open, then, and be damned."

"Where you going?"

"Down to the shack to see what's—"

"Look here, Charlie," says the voice of Sam, "you stay away. Ain't they cleaned you out already?"

"I can go down and watch, though."

"You can go down and get into worse trouble. I wish to God that we'd never let them come on the place!"

"Didn't they pay enough to suit you? Didn't you root for it, then?"

"Here, you can't talk like that to me! Come back here!"

"Oh, I'll come back. You don't think that I'm *afraid* to come back, do you?"

"Why, kid, if—"

Whang! went the door, and that was all that I heard of them and their talk.

It was the Donaldson boys. I wasn't too dumb to guess that. Here was the pair of them, jangling and wrangling at one another, and the drift of what they said was easy enough—one of them wanted to go down to a "shack," where he had been trimmed before, and where he would just look on, now. The other one didn't want his brother to go, and he wished that they had never let "them" come onto the place.

Why, this was just as clear as the brightest sunshine!

Old Choctaw was as right as a prophet. Somewhere on the place was a shack where Grace and his gang were holding out, and amusing themselves by gambling, and the Donaldson boys, after taking money from these crooks, had tried to take more money at the cards but had got themselves trimmed, instead.

Anyway you looked at it, it was a pretty bad mess.

But right then and there I was glad of one thing—that I was to tackle, not a lot of gents that was fresh from the riding of the range, with their brains blowed clear of cobwebs and their hands steady, but four that had been lying up and gambling the coin which they took away from the bank at Hookertown.

First of all, I faded out of that house by the same way that I came into it, and mighty happy I was to be safe and sound on the ground. Because, somehow, that had seemed a desperate bad place for a fight—that old, tumble-down house where everything was going bad and where it would be extra hard to do a good thing.

And this, take it by and large, was the one good thing on a big scale that I had ever tackled. I had done maybe a good turn, here and there, but here was a chance for me to wipe out all the scores that was wrote against me on the slate and stand up and say to the whole doggone world: "I've paid you back! For all the hundreds of bad that I've done, here's thousands of good! Here's a dead Doctor Grace!"

Why, if I could turn such a mountain of a job as that, the whole world would forget what I had done. I would no longer be on the outside. I would stand right on the inside of the law, and all its strength would fight for me, and every honest man in the world would be ready to shake hands with me—

Now, here as I write this down, I got to confess that it still makes me feel a little woozy, which you won't understand because you ain't been through what I've been through, nor had the lonely years on the trail behind you.

However, I straightened out and began my hunt, but though I circled three times around that outfit, there was nary a sign of a light that I seen anywhere. And how could they gamble without a light to do it by?

When I had thought that all out, I went back to Cherry Pie. She was ridiculous glad to see me again, and I had to choke her to keep her from whinnying. But, after I had patted her a minute, I started on my trail once more and hadn't gone fifty yards before I crossed a scent of woodsmoke and bacon mixed together, the oldest camp-smell in the West.

Certainly it couldn't blow from the house to where I was walking, and the only other place that stood between me and the wind was a little blind, black shed with a scattering of trees around it, sticking down in a hollow. But though my eyes told me over and over again that Doctor Grace and his outfit couldn't be in that place, dark as pitch, still my nose kept telling me that there was humans, down there, so I went to investigate.

I mean to say that I commenced to make circles around it, like a buzzard does, when it comes up the wind, sighting for a thing that it guesses at but can't see. That was the way that I sneaked around that shack; and pretty soon I seen something else that was very much worth noticing, and that was the shadow of a man striding along toward the hut.

Was that young Donaldson going down to watch the game?

No, as I sat behind a tree, staring, there was no sign of a door opening, and pretty soon the same figure come into sight, swinging along with big strides between me and the house—a great big tall man with a step that an ostrich might of envied a good deal.

Well, something told me that here was something that I could afford to get closer to. For that looked from the distance terrible like the big bulk of the nigger, Little Joe.

I flattened myself against the ground, and I was a snake, twisting along close and closer, until I was behind a rock, very close to the circle that he was walking in around the shack. The next round, he come by me within two yards, and he could of seen me easy, if he had thought of looking at the ground.

But Little Joe was all heated up over something, and he walked along, damning soft and continual to himself.

When he got to the shack, he paused for a second in his round, and he stepped up and leaned over against the wall, and pretty soon there was a single ray of light that come stabbing out.

They had that house battened down so snug and so tight that nobody could of known that there was so much as a spark inside, but Little Joe had moved something, so's he could take a glimpse inside.

Whatever it was that he seen, it didn't seem to improve his feelings none. The next time that he swung around the house, he was damning even louder than before, and shaking his head. And as he got madder and madder, something flashed in his hand as he strode along. The nigger had pulled out his knife and he was carving the air, now and then, as though he was promising that sort of treatment to somebody, before long!

It did me no good to see the size of him and the mile that he measured across the shoulders, but it pleased me a lot to see the humor that he was in.

But what else can you expect, when you coop up four cutthroats in a chicken pen for weeks together? The air is sure to get thick with lightning ready to flash. I wondered at Doctor Grace. He ought to of had better sense, you would say. But then, that's forgetting how things were at that time, and the way the head-hunters were still trailing across the mountains every which-way, anxious for a glimpse of that same gang. Another few days, and matters would be settled down about enough to let him go loose again and raise the devil in some quarter where he was least expected.

I thought of that as I saw the big nigger coming, but right away I thought of something else, because I seen that this time Little Joe, as he was walking guard, was marking out a bigger, looser circle than he had traveled before, and he was aiming to come right outside of me!

That way, he couldn't fail to see me. I hadn't any chance to move. The moon seemed brighter than any sun—and with Little Joe not three strides off, I rose up to my knees out of the ground, as you might say, and I showed him a gat in either hand, one trained on his body and the other aimed for the head.

I was afraid of two things—that I would have to shoot, or that he would holler. But he didn't do either. He just dropped the big knife, so that it tinkled on a rock, and was still. Then he raised his hands above his head, which made him look twice the giant that he was, ordinarily.

And he said: "My Gawd A'mighty! It's Dickon!"

So *that* was over!

37

I GOT him under the trees as fast as I could. There I felt pretty safe. I shoved one of my guns into its holster. I pulled out my skinning knife and I flashed it in the shadow.

"There is two ways of keeping you silent, Little Joe," I told him. "And one of them is this!"

He said nothing. He was a game coon.

"The other way," says I, "is chancier for me. It means tying you up and trusting to a gag to keep you still."

"Dickon," says Little Joe, "you ain't a murderer. You'll gimme my chance."

But his voice wasn't quite as sure as his words. He was scared, and he had a right to be, because just at that time the life of one of the crooks wouldn't of kept me thinking very long. However, you can't be too rough on a gent that trusts you. I stood over Joe while he cut his own coat to shreds, the way I told him to do, and while he was working, and while I was tying him, afterward, with those tough strips of cloth, I says: "How's things with you and the boys?"

"How would you guess them?" growled Joe.

"Bad," says I. "Because you need more elbow room than you got there."

"Bad," says he, "but how *damn* bad, you don't guess."

"What do you mean?" says I.

"You find out for yourself," says he. "I don't blab. Only I hope to God that you get that skunk, Grace!"

It sounded good to me, him talking like that. It was really as much as if he had told me a whole bookful of talk.

I simply said: "They've cleaned you out of your share of the loot, Joe, eh?"

He only grunted.

And so I gagged him and I gagged him proper, so that he had just about a chance each way, of choking to death or getting enough air to breathe. Then I went on to the shack, and I peeped through the place that Joe had opened for himself to look in.

It was what I expected. There was a swirl of tobacco smoke, and an old oil lamp leaning sidewise, and around the table there was Doctor Grace, sitting right facing the window, and on each side of him Lew Candy here, and Dago Mendez there, and all of them looking set and hard. I mean, all except Grace, because nothing could of changed him. His mustache was trimmed as neat as could be. There was no sweat on his pale face, though the others were streaming. And I couldn't help noticing how slick his hair was combed, and how neat his necktie was, with the diamond pin in it. He was a flash, was the Doctor!

He was dealing, just now, and the glimmer of his hands was faster than you could follow, hardly. He had two cards in the air all the time and in an instant he had dealt the round.

Dago Mendez threw down his cards.

"Same thing!" he said. "The same damn thing!"

Doctor Grace says in his deep, soft voice: "You'd better take a breath of air, Mendez. You have no luck tonight!"

Mendez started to say something in return, but just then a blast of wind hit me between the shoulders and knocked me forward against the shutters, with a little crash.

I was almost afraid to look through the peephole again, and I saw two of them on their feet. It was Grace, of course, that kept his place.

"Sit down, boys," he said. "It's only the wind."

One of the few mistakes that have ever been wrote down against the Doctor.

The others sat down but they still kept looking at the window now and then, for a minute or two.

"Those shutters'll blow right open, in a minute," said Mendez.

They would, too, if I hadn't held them. Because the bump of me against them had worked the fastening loose, and now the wind was like a steady hand pressing against them all the time.

"Let them blow," says Lew Candy. "Let them blow. Gimmee three!"

He was holding up a pair, and I saw the Doctor keep up three. There wasn't very brisk bidding—for that gang, loaded with cash as they was. But even at that I think there was ninety dollars on the table that the Doctor took in with three sevens.

He gathered in the coin, very thoughtful. Then he says: "Boys, you're not in a winning streak tonight. What I say is, let's call off this game until tomorrow, and then—"

"Call it off until the luck had left you and come back to you again?" barked Lew Candy. "I guess not! We'll stick right here!"

I was surprised at Lew. Everybody knew that Candy was an intelligent sort of a gent, but you could see that the long hours of gambling had worn his nerves down fine. He was simply trembling while he sat there and looked the Doctor in the face with blazing eyes.

"All right," says the Doctor. "I can't stop the game while I'm winning, but just the same, I think that if we got out and took a turn around the shack, it would do us all good!"

You see what he was taking from them, and what a light hand he was driving with! Oh, he was a fox, that Grace!

"D'you feel your luck running out?" sneered Candy. "No, Doc. We'll sit right here. I've still got three thousand left, and the game doesn't stop till that's all gone!"

Three thousand left—and they'd taken how much apiece?

Why even if you split a hundred and eighty thousand six ways and give three of them to the Doctor, that would leave thirty thousand apiece for the rest of the gang. And here was Candy, the smartest of the lot, with only three thousand left!

I was plain surprised! You would think that the Doctor would never be such a fool as to trim his men of *all* of their coin. But from the way that Little Joe had talked, it looked as though he was even nearer to broke than Candy, and Dago Mendez didn't seem much better off.

Oh, what a man the Doctor was, sitting so easy and quiet with murder on each side of him, and Little Joe, for all he knew, circulating around through the outside air, ready and willing to shoot through that same shutter at any time!

Why, I wondered that such a set of nerves as the Doctor had could of been given to any man! But still he was as cool as a cucumber.

I could hear him say, in spite of another flurry of wind that almost
dragged the shutters out of my grip:

"All right boys. You shall have as much of this stuff as you want."

And out went the cards again, with a little smile on the lips of Grace as
he dealt.

But that smile told me a lot. He wasn't as steady as he seemed, or else
he wouldn't have insulted that pair of thugs by seeming to smile to himself,
like that.

No, I could suddenly see that the Doctor was as tight as a violin string,
in spite of his quiet. There was nothing but death in the air, as he flashed
those cards across.

The fall of the cards seemed to be bad for Lew Candy. You could see
that he aimed to throw down his hand, but he changed his mind, kept up
one card, and drew to it. Of course, that was baby talk, and he got nothing
and he deserved nothing. He threw down his hand and leaned back in his
chair, smoking a cigarette, with his eyes closed, and his face thrown far
back. But by the arching of his chest, you could see that every muscle in
his body was getting tense and hard.

A mean looking critter was Lew Candy, just then!

Mendez had kept up two, and so had the Doctor. And when Mendez
had made his draw, he turned his cards a bit as he arranged them and I
saw that he had filled out his pair of queens with three deuces!

A very neat draw, that is. And though it happens now and then, it sure
is a sweet shock to fill from a measly little pair!

I looked to see Mendez bet fast, but he didn't. He just sneaked out five
dollars. And the Doctor raised him right away, by ten. Back comes Mendez,
covering the ten and raising it five more. Foxy, that Mendez was, and now
I was so interested and excited in that game that I forgot why I was standing
there, and I forgot that young Donaldson might be coming down from his
house at any minute to see the fun, and I was only hoping to the Lord that
Mendez could work up the stake to a rich one and then rake it in with his
full house.

Well, he seemed to be managing it, pretty well. In another minute him
and the Doctor was raising each other back and forth, a hundred at a time.
Easy money always goes like that in poker, and I suppose that any money
is easy when you've only paid for it with blood!

Suddenly Mendez said: "I'd like nothing better than to keep on with this,
Doc. But I'm done!"

And he set his teeth until his jaw-muscles bulged.

At that, forward rocks Lew Candy, and he slaps his wallet on the table.
"There's three thousand that you're welcome to bet, Dago!" he says.

Of course, offering a loan like that right in the middle of the hand was
like buying more chips in the same sort of a time. All against all the rules
of the game, and Candy knew it, and while he made his offer, he looked

at Grace with his face all pinched and white with meanness, and he had his right hand gripping the butt of a Colt so hard that his whole arm shook.

Mendez was watching the boss, too. And I never seen two men look more like a couple of terriers about to run at a stray dog.

Why, Grace was wonderful about it.

"You fellows can make your own rules to play by," says he. "I'm not going to interfere. Take Candy's money if you want to lose it, Mendez!"

And he smiled again.

Good Lord, how that made them twist in their chairs and show their teeth. I could guess that they had seen a good many of those quiet little contemptuous smiles, in the past few days. And they were filled with the poison of them right up to the lips.

However, right away that betting began again. Mendez used up the three thousand of his partner, a thousand at a crack, and every time that Candy saw one of his last thousands pushed out, he winced a little, but he stood the punishment, game enough. And always his eyes would flash over from face to face, trying to read them. You could read Mendez's, easy enough. He was red and swollen with meanness and eagerness to win, but the Doctor had nothing but that damned little mocking smile on his lips.

And then came the call!

38

THE wind at that instant whacked against the shutters so hard that they were almost torn out of my fingers, and only by the tips I was able to keep them from flying open.

"You'd better look to those windows, Candy," says the Doctor.

"Damn the windows!" says Candy. "You been called! You been called! Let's see the color of your cards?"

"I think that I did the calling," said the Doctor, polite but icy. "We'll, have a look at Mendez's cards, and all the time we'll remember that the men that are not betting are not in the game, Candy."

That was a slap fair in the face for Candy, and he looked wicked enough to jump at the throat of the Doctor, I can tell you. But he was too interested to stop even for a fight, much pleasure as it would of given him.

"All right," says Mendez. "This is what I had before the draw."

He laid down the pair.

"And this is what I did the betting on."

He laid down the three of a kind, and it made a pretty picture, that full house laying there under the shadow of the thousands and thousands that had been piled up in the middle of the table.

"Very good indeed," says the Doctor, and I thought what a good loser he was. "Very clever, indeed. But I think you'll find this better!"

And doggone my soul if he didn't put down a flush of spades, as neat as ever you seen!

I saw it coming, almost before it was down on the board, as you might say, and I saw that this was the time to make trouble among them—now or never. If I put a bit of grit into that mill, it might wreck a fine machine, just at this minute.

So I let the shutters slip away from the grip of my fingers, and the wind, sliding through, flacked every one of those cards of the Doctor's right off the face of the table and rattled them against the farther wall.

"Well," says the Doctor, "I thank you for all of this money, boy, which you insisted on giving to me!"

And he put out his hand for the stakes.

"Hold up!" snarled Lew Candy. "I didn't see what you had."

"I beg your pardon," said the Doctor, "but you were not in the game, and it was not necessary for me to show my cards to you. Mendez, however, saw that I had a flush of spades."

I thought for a minute that Mendez would never dare to face those steady eyes of Grace and lie, but those were his last thousands on that table, as well as the last ones of Lew Candy.

And he growled: "I seen nothing! The wind was too fast for me. Keep your hands off that money, Grace, or by God—"

Now, of course nobody could take that. Not even Grace, though he had proved that he was a pretty patient man. It meant gunwork, and it meant it so surely that I felt my own fire fingers itching. Mendez and Lew Candy saw what was coming in the same flash and went for their guns as though at a signal. But before there was any steel out of leather, a gun boomed beneath the table, and Mendez screamed and grabbed his stomach in both arms. He dropped out of his chair to the floor, and lay doubled up, screeching and kicking, very horrible.

Lew Candy was a flash faster with his Colt, and I always wondered why the Doctor held his fire for a while, unless it was because he thought that maybe Lew had too much sense to try to fight it out with him. When I say he held his fire, I mean that he didn't fire the second bullet for about a tenth of a second, until Lew's own gat flashed above the table. The wait of the Doctor didn't show so much in his gun as in his eyes, where I could see a shadow of thought flick across. Then he shot Lew through the heart, and Candy fell back, sending his own bullet through the ceiling.

The Doctor first gathered in the last stake on that table and dropped it into his pocket, saying: "Poor Lew. Not *quite* enough intelligence, after all!"

And then—well, I hate to write it down. I've seen cruel things in my days, but never anything like that—

Anyway, what he done next was to lean down and put his gun against the head of Mendez—and he pulled the trigger as I yelled—I couldn't help it—"You devil, Grace!"

And I raised my own gun to shoot.

I was late. I should of fired, perhaps, instead of shouting. But still, I couldn't help that. The Doctor dropped straight to the floor, and out of my sight, and as he dropped, he sent his fourth bullet smashing through the lamp and left that room in darkness.

I heard a door crash.

It was certainly toward the front of the shack and I rushed around that way to intercept him, but I was only in time to hear a sound of feet running from the rear of the building.

It was just a child's trick, but it had worked as smooth as silk.

He had simply banged a door at the front of the shack, and while I sprinted in that direction, he slipped through the other way and as I tore around in that new trail, I seen the shadow of a mounted man charge out of a shed that stood near, mounted on one horse and leading another—

Well, of course him being what he was, he and his gang would have horses standing saddled night and day ready to hit the high spots in case of an alarm.

I raised my Colts and took the best aim that I could. I emptied them after him, but he was running his horses in a weaving course, and the only thing that I damaged was a few streaks of moonlight.

Then he was gone out of sight behind the nearest trees, which he was heading for.

My thoughts spun around and around in a tangle. I didn't know which way to be turning. I thought of the nigger lying tied and gagged under the tree, and I thought of young Donaldson—it was queer that he didn't show up—

Why, there he was now—coming streaking along, with a gun glittering in his hand. There was no use in meeting him. I wanted no gunfights with gents that was supposed to be keeping the law. Besides, when he got to that shack, he would have enough on his hands, to explain how they got there, though I supposed he would simply say that the gang must have taken possession of the shack for that night, without him or his brother knowing anything about it. Sometimes a slim lie will save a gent's neck from the penitentiary!

Anyway, I faded out in the direction of Cherry Pie, and once I was in the saddle on her again, I knew what I wanted, and that was Grace— nothing but the Doctor!

Even as I loosed the rein of Cherry and she went bounding down the mountain side, I wondered how it was that he could possibly have got away from me! I had had him all those minutes under my gun! But still, when you're used to standing up and fighting in the open, it goes hard against the grain to have to shoot a gent that doesn't know that you're within miles of him!

I went down that mountain side, then, with all holds loosed, until, a couple of minutes later, I saw that I was acting like a fool.

For what could I do, riding like this blind on a blind trail? I would be sure to miss him, or even if I hit the right trail, he would hear me coming, and wait with a rifle for me. And this moon was bright enough to make good rifle practice!

So I pulled up Cherry to a dog-trot, and while she skimmed along soft and smooth, I worked the thing out in my head.

What I finally arrived at was this here conclusion: The best way to solve the riddle was to act the way that old Choctaw would of acted in the same place. And it seemed to me that what I should do was to stop the mare, get off of her, and sit down and plan the thing out with a map.

Maybe it seems foolish to you, seeing that seconds counted, then, and that Doctor Grace, the smartest man that ever rode through the mountain-desert, was streaking off ahead of me, with a change of horses, gaining distance with every breath.

However, what I did was to sit on the ground and draw a little map on a sandy place, and there I lighted a match, because the moon wasn't clear enough to please me, and I worked it all out and says to myself that the chief landmarks that counted was the pass back into Hooker Valley, and the way down the river, at the bottom of the slope where the Donaldson farm stood.

There was two ways of figuring it, from the viewpoint of Grace. If he went for Hooker Valley, where he was so known and hated, he would be laying himself open to the hardest sort of going, unless he got through before the daylight. But at the same time, that would be all the less reason for me to try to head him off in that direction, if I was a quick guesser. But on the other hand, he knew that I wasn't altogether a fool, and if I took a second thought, I might figure that he would do that very same hard thing, and go straight for Hooker Valley, danger or no danger.

So, thinking that, wouldn't he just streak on down the river?

It was the nacheral thing to do. It was the handy thing to do.

And if I tried to be clever, I would be riding hard for the Hooker Valley, while he was heading in the opposite direction.

I saw all of that as I drew the map in. And it seemed to me that there was too much logic in a clever head like the doctor's to take the Hooker Valley way.

So a minute later I was in the saddle on Cherry Pie, and driving along the line of the river.

He had a good start. And he knew right where he was going. And he had a change of horses, to keep shifting back and forth on, when one of them got tired. All that he *didn't* have was Cherry Pie. And I hoped that that lack would be enough!

Now that I had made up my mind to go down the river, I had a clear and simple goal. For down the stream there was one ford. It was fifty miles away, but between this point and the ford there was nothing but a rough trail laid along the floor of a cañon, with sheer walls going up to the south, and white water on the farther side. When he got to the ford, where the water spread itself out across a great big sand-bar, he would nacherally want to turn out of his course, perhaps to the north, but up to that point, I could depend upon him driving straight.

So I rated my mare to make her run straight for that ford. She had lost a lot of time, she was working against two, and they would be carrying a lighter weight than her—but still I trusted to Cherry Pie. There was only one thing that made it bad—that I had to make that ride without really knowing whether or not the Doctor was scampering along ahead of me.

39

I GOT Cherry Pie going in great shape.

Fifty miles ain't a sprint, so I never used that long, raking gallop of hers at all. On the dead level, I let her canter. On the uphill, or the downhill, or weaving around through very broken rocks, her trot was good enough for me. And so she snaked the miles away from in front of her and threw them one by one behind her.

I had lightened away every ounce that I could. I kept one Colt and the Winchester, both loaded. More than that number of shots wouldn't be wanted. But once more all my pack and my spare guns and all of my extra ammunition, they lay along the trail behind me.

It was a terrible strain. Every time I saw a headland of rocks striking down from the cañon walls toward the river, I told myself that yonder was Doctor Grace, laying in wait, with his rifle cuddled against his shoulder. And every time I thought of that, I told myself that he would never waste time waiting for a gunfight that he could possibly avoid.

Three times, toward the end of the ride, I gave Cherry a breathing space and a swallow of water at the edge of the river, and sloshed the water up over her steaming body. And three times she went on again, a little lighter and fresher than before.

But all night long, she ran like a swallow flying. And a dozen times my heart sank, and I told myself that I was a fool, sure, and that Grace was sure floating along through the fine, level roads of Hooker Valley, by now, laughing at half-wits like me; and a dozen times I looked at the little pricked ears of Cherry Pie, and talked to her, and told her that I loved her, and watched her shake her head and try to gallop faster against the pull of my reins.

She was a pal, was Cherry Pie, God bless her!

The moon begun to get dirty and dull, after a long spell. I thought that I was getting tired and my eyes going back on me, but when I looked at my watch, I seen that it was near time for dawn. Yes, and pretty soon the light freshened until the moon was no more than a tuft of silver cloud in the sky, that you had to look for twice before you could find her. And after that, she was blushing and rosy like the other clouds in the sky, while I turned around the elbow point of the last long down grade, and there I saw the waters smooth themselves out enough to take the image of the sky, and there I saw, too, how Grace was driving on before me with his two horses at a trot!

Lord God, how my heart jumped up into my throat. I had to thank something. I threw up my arms, and I raised my face to the sky, and I thanked God, for the lack of something better at hand.

Choctaw, for instance!

There was not much left in the horses of the Doctor. I could tell that by the way that his rear nag hung back and pulled back on the lead-rope and I knew that he must be driving his spurs into his other nag, cruel deep.

I loosed the rein of Cherry—and oh, she answered like the blowing of wind—no effort, free as a treat! Why, she just began to eat up those two horses in front.

I hoped that he wouldn't have any sign of me, but the nerves of that hound was set as fine as the best balance scales in a dentist shop. He twitched around in his saddle, all at once, and when he seen me, I could see him look first to the river, and then to the cañon walls and he knew that there was no hope for him there.

If he wanted to get away, there was only the ford.

He turned loose the nag he was leading. He leaned over and began to jockey his horse with whip and spur—but when he looked back, he could see the mare eating him up like a lion!

I wondered why he didn't stop then and turn and make a fight of it. But it seemed that he was too set on chancing the ford. And then, we all knew that the Doctor never chanced a fight if he could possibly get away from it—just as he never failed to kill when there *was* a need of it.

The water broadened beside him. He didn't wait till he was flush with the smooth part of the ford, but he jumped from the side of the bank into the white water. I saw him dip out of view, and then he came in sight again, his horse trotting on the sand bar, and him turning dripping in the saddle, with his rifle ready to use on me.

Well, I checked Cherry Pie for one minute and covered him with my Winchester. I had a dead bead. It was only the pulling of a trigger—but somehow it was like murder to kill him this way. And what I wanted was to fight it out with him, and pay, really pay, for what I turned over to the law.

So I sent Cherry down at the ford, and she flew at it like a bird.

He fired back at me three times, and I didn't believe it possible for any man to shoot so straight and true at a moving target, when his own mount was floundering and jerking so terrible. But three times those bullets kissed the air right beside me, very mean and waspish, and three times I ducked my head at something that was already a thousand feet past me.

I think that the fourth time he would of split the difference of his other misses and nailed me, but just then his horse went down into a hole in the center of the ford, and when it came up again, there was the Doctor clinging in the saddle, looking half drowned, and his rifle gone!

But Cherry Pie didn't stumble, neither did she falter, but she went on straight and true, a wonderful thing to see, and a more wonderful one to feel, with all of her fine body working and whipping along beneath the saddle!

I needed comfort, then, closing in on a devil of a man like the Doctor. And so I sang out to Cherry Pie, and Cherry nickered back to me, and man, man, you wouldn't believe all the heart that it put into me! As if she was saying: "There ain't nothing to fear! He can't stand up to you!"

I begun to feel that the horse knew me, and knew what would happen. And the fear it run out of me, and it left my heart beating steady, and swelling big.

Just close to the farther shore, the current deepened to swimming, and that was the reason that Grace couldn't turn and pick me off easy with his Colt, as I closed on him.

He had his hands full, working away as he swam at the side of his mighty tired horse, which was barely making headway. But Cherry? Oh, I wish that you could of seen her head with a leap into the deep, fast current, and breast it, and beat it, and walk right up on the Doctor, while I trailed swimming at her side.

The roar of the river was in the ears of the Doctor. And he had his eyes strained forward to the bank, which was only a stroke or two away from him; and if he had any strength and attention left for other things, there was the dying strength of his horse, which could hardly keep bobbing against the current.

And so it happened, I guess, that the Doctor didn't have any glance for me until suddenly the head of Cherry Pie, dark with the wet and shining, come cutting through the river just above him. He turned on his back in the river, then, with a shout of surprise, as though he couldn't imagine what had happened to bring us up with him. Even the Doctor, you see, wasn't able to understand all that was in Cherry!

I could have pistoled him then, dead easy. Instead, I simply gave him my fist on the point of the chin. Then I reached through the water and gathered him in and dragged him to the shore.

His own horse didn't have the strength to get more than its forelegs out of the stream, and there it stood half awash, its head down, and its eyes glassy, because Cherry had run the very heart out of it.

The Doctor was still dead to the world, so I took a second to get the horse out of the water and to drag off its saddle and bridle, and whip a bit of the heavy water out of its hide, because it didn't have even enough energy to shake itself.

But now the sun was coming with a rush, through rose and golden clouds, and pretty soon its good honest warmth would begin to bring the life back to the Doctor's horse. I thought of that, and I was glad, because I aimed to ride him into town on his own horse!

He was still in a dead faint when I went through his clothes. I got a wallet and a money belt, both loaded and crowded with coin. And then I found a little notebook in his pocket, but when it chanced to fall open, I seen that it was interleaved with good paper currency, and all in big denominations!

Why, he was crowded with money, that Doctor was! You couldn't touch him without coming away with a hundred dollars or so.

I didn't have to ask how much was here. I knew that he had on him the entire loot that he took from the Hooker Valley Bank, with the exception of what he might of paid to the Donaldsons for protection. And even the most of *that* price had mostly gone back into the pockets of the chief, from what I had gathered in the talk that I had overheard between the Donaldsons, themselves.

Yes, it was a rich haul, and it would of tempted me a lot just to finish off the Doctor and go on with the stolen money in my pocket, if it hadn't been that I wanted something more than what coin could buy. A new start— a sort of a new soul was what I wanted.

And just then, the Doctor opened his eyes, and he smiled and sat up.

How would you expect that he would act?

I hardly knew, but I expected something quick and desperate, because it didn't seem wrote on the books that I should be able to take the greatest of them all and bring him safe and sound into the hands of the law without some sort of a desperate fight.

But I tell you that the Doctor simply sat up and smiled. He said: "Well, Dickon, I've been dodging you for a long time, but now you've proved that I *have* to take you into full partnership, my friend. Perhaps as a senior member, because there isn't any doubt but that you've beaten me fair and square!"

That was the way that he talked, as near as I can put it down, except that there was always something in the Doctor's way that was hard to describe and impossible to imitate. Even if you put in all of the words, you would be sure to leave out the most important part, which was what he was, himself.

There he had been lying on the bank, looking like a ringer for a dead, drowned rat, one minute, and now with a flick of his hand to straight back his hair, and to put the right curve in his mustache, he was pretty close to as neat and easy as ever he could of been in the past.

40

I ADMIRED the Doctor, and I couldn't help wondering over him a good deal. But, all the same, I knew that he was a hound.

I said: "Now, Grace, I don't want to be hard with you, now that you're down on your luck. I'm simply telling you that you're going in to town with me, and talking won't help you none."

"Tush, man," says the Doctor, and he even laughed at me. "I suppose that you mean *you* are going to take me in?"

"I mean just that," says I. And I said it in such a way that he couldn't help believing, in spite of himself. He gaped at me, because it hit him pretty hard.

"I see," he says suddenly. "I'm the price that buys you off from the penitentiary sentence you've just escaped. If that triple-plated fool, Ops, had not let you get away—"

I thought that I might as well try my new lie on him, and so I said: "Before you start calling Wally Ops such a fool, you got to understand that it was him that set me loose, by coming to an agreement that I would trail you until I caught you, and failing of catching you, I would come back and give myself up to the prison authorities."

The Doctor grinned at me, and nodded.

"That's likely," he said. "Come, come, man, you're not serious?"

"Am I not?" says I.

"Hold on," says the Doctor. "Then I suppose that you're going to bring me in, and bring in all the money you took from me at the same time? You're going to turn over that grand fortune, my lad, when you take me back to the—er—impatient arms of the law?"

"You've read my mind," I told him.

It turned Grace pale. Because he could see all at once that I meant what I said.

Still, he would try his hand once more. He says:

"What you haven't been quite able to understand, Larry Dickon, is that I propose to let you right in on the ground floor. You know that I'm the sort of a fellow who detests a lone hand and likes to have plenty of company around him. My great mistake was in associating myself with a group of murdering rascals, who had nothing to recommend them except that they had no fear. Even with them, you'll have to admit, I went a long distance. But with you, Dickon, there would be no stopping me. Us, I mean! Because, what I couldn't accomplish, you would! Between us the world would be our nut, and we would crack it open and eat as often as we pleased!"

Why, to listen to him saying it, you could see a picture of the whole list of Broadway banks flying open and lying at our feet with their safe doors wide, and us able to take what we wanted, and when we wanted it!

But I just shook my head and smiled down at him.

"It's all right, Doctor," I told him. "You mean it right. You figure that I got to have something up my sleeve. But that's where you slip. There ain't a thing. I haven't got a palmed deck, somewhere. I'm just a plain sort of a sucker, Grace, and luck and a fast horse have given me a hard hold on you, and I aim to keep that hold as long as I can!"

Well, I thought that he would never have done staring at me.

"Look here, my friend," says he at last, "there's a girl in this."

I nodded that there was.

He fell silent again. Then he said: "Tell me this. Did you open the window and let the storm in to upset the cards?"

I nodded again.

"I thought so," says the Doctor to himself. "You are a clever devil, in your own way, Dickon. But I haven't been able to figure out just what way that may be. As a crook, you're ridiculous, a poor scarecrow riding about over the hills and getting nothing for your pains. Nothing but a little space in the newspapers! But a fellow who can make a dicker with a man like Ops—get free—and then keep his agreement, and give up two hundred thousand dollars—by God, Dickon, I have the clue to it! You've never been a crook at all. You're simply an honest man!"

I grinned at him.

"Thanks, Grace," said I. "That's the best compliment that I've ever received. We'll start rambling, though, if you don't mind. Your horse can walk along behind us, until it gets its second wind."

I tied his hands behind him and marched him down the valley until inside of an hour the sun was getting fairly high and fairly hot. Then I made up a snack for breakfast and we had something to eat. After that, his horse was in shape for riding, again, so we went ahead in the saddles, his nag tied to the pommel of my saddle.

We rode, off and on, a little short of three days, keeping to the nakedest parts of the range, because, though I could have ridden into Hooker Valley and given up Grace, I knew that there was about two chances out of three that those people would lynch the Doctor, and I didn't want him murdered, much as I detested him. But it was a very hard march, and during the whole time I don't think that I closed my eyes once. You can't sleep when you have a tiger along with you, even when the tiger has its paws tied and wears a muzzle.

So, in the hot middle of an afternoon, we came out on the top of the hills and looked down on the town and the valley where Wally Ops had once been king of the roost. He was the underdog, now, but he would be something more of a king than ever, if I could only get my man in, safe and sound.

But when I looked down at the last dusty miles of the trail, my brains spun around and turned black. I simply couldn't ride that little distance without falling out of the saddle. I had tried black coffee and black coffee until there was yellow spots before my eyes, but there wasn't any strength in the stuff to keep my eyes open any longer. All that I could do was to sleep. If only for two minutes, I had to sleep!

So I took my rope from the horn of the saddle, and I tied the Doctor to a tree, swathing him all around. His hands was tied behind him, his feet was tied in front of him, and I had him lashed to the tree trunk to keep him from rolling in any direction.

Then I stretched out in the shade of the next tree, lying flat on my back, with my arms throwed out to the sides, and I closed my eyes and set my teeth, and said: "Only two minutes. Fix that in your fool head, Dickon. In two minutes, you wake up and start for the town!"

And then I was gone, as though somebody had slugged me on the head with a club.

They tell me that nurses have stayed awake for three days running, but then, all that they have to do is to stay beside a bed, setting easy. But I had been riding hard through rough country, those three days, and I was spent down to the last ounce of strength that was in me,

So I lay there, more than half dead, and hours went by like seconds.

And after a while, a dream came to me. And I seemed to see myself down in a deep, black well, and somebody was calling to me to get up out of it, because the water was rising—and that water was hot as boiled steel, and it was creeping up over my feet, and over my knees, and over my body, and it had reached my chin, and my nose, and then it dazzled and burned against my eyes—but still I was too numb and weak to move—

That instant I opened my eyes again, and found the slant, westering sun was flaming against them and the black shadow of a man leaning over me and reaching a gun out of the holster at my hip—

I was still too dazed to make out very much. But suddenly I knew that it was Grace, and that he had got himself loose from the bonds, and was aiming to finish me off, so that he could take back the money, take Cherry Pie—and ride away to be free forever!

That jumped flish-flash across my brain like lightning, and I grabbed for his hand and got it.

I got his wrist, well enough, but I was still weak. He snatched his hand and his gun away from me with an oath, but by this time I was wide awake, and that little sleep I had had, had rested me and given me a wonderful lot of strength back.

I whipped myself over and threw my body at him, more like a snake than a human being, I suppose, and I struck the Colt up, just as he was firing.

The bullet scraped across the top of my left shoulder.

And the sting of it did me a lot of good. I slammed at the Doctor with my right hand, and back he staggered.

He was on his feet, getting his balance again, and I was on mine, snatching for my second gun, all in a second. And so it happened that each of us got a fair stand-up chance to fight it out.

That fighting lasted two seconds. I mean, two counts. The first count was a forty-five caliber slug from the Doctor's gun, meant for my heart but aimed a bit low, because he was in too much of a hurry. Instead of going through the middle of me, it cut nice and neat through my thigh and knocked the pins out from under me.

The second count was my own answering shot, as I fell. I intended that shot for the heart of the Doctor just as much as he had intended his for me. But the difference was that my aim was perfect. It was *too* perfect, because it hit his Colt on the way to his heart, and spent all of its force in knocking that gun back into his face and flooring him.

I crawled over and gathered in the fallen gun, and then, as the Doctor came to, I laid my back against the trunk of the tree, where the frayed ropes was still lying, that he had wore through against the rocks, in the time that I had been sleeping. I leaned against that tree, and I covered the Doctor with my two guns and made him put a tourniquet on my leg beneath the hip until the bleeding was stopped. And then I had him put on a bandage made of his own shirt.

Afterward I was ready for the march in.

But it was a terrible hard job. If you never been without the use of one leg, you dunno how it damages you. And even when I got into the saddle, I was as sick as a dog with the pain of my leg against the saddle leather.

However, that was the way of it as we rode down the valley in the dusk, the doctor ahead of me, with his head all the time turned back over his shoulder, waiting and waiting like a wolf for the time when my pain and my weakness would be too much for me, and I should faint.

But before I fainted, I had made up my mind that I would kill him first!

It seemed a thousand years and a thousand, thousand miles. The world turned black. I thought it was faintness coming over me. Then I seen it was simply the night on the world. And after that, a century or two of agony, and then here was the lights of the town!

41

I THOUGHT, when we rode down into the deep dust of the village street, that the Doctor would swing around and try to get at me. And once there was a twitch of his shoulders that looked very much as though he meant business. But he changed his mind. He was long-sighted was the doctor, and why should he take any foolish chance with my two Colts when there were still lawyers and plenty of money between him and hanging?

I suppose that that was the way that Grace figured it out, and he went into the town as meek as a lamb, until a gent came galloping by us at a rocking canter and seen me with two gats out herding a gent before me— and then, as he drew up, there was something that he recognized in the back of the head of the Doctor—but there was something more that he recognized in me.

And he yelled, as he pulled his gat: "It's Larry Dickon! Help!"

"You fool!" I yipped at him. "I'm Larry Dickon, but that's Grace. Which do you want the most?"

Grace was ready to sink spurs into his horse, but he seen that it was no use, because I was paying no attention to the new gent, and just keeping both my cannon trained on the murderer ahead of me. I have never in my life shot a man in the back, but if the thing had to be done, why, there was nobody that I would sooner of drilled than the Doctor, and he knew it!

However, that first gent that come up saved me a lot of trouble. He was one of these nacheral noise-makers, and he had a crowd around us in no time.

"Dickon, surrender and drop that gun!" he called to me, when he felt that he had enough backing.

"You wall-eyed son of a Texas steer," I bawled back at him. "Fetch the sheriff. I've come in to surrender to him!"

"Are we gunna break open the jail in order to get the sheriff out and let you surrender to him?" says the other.

Get the sheriff out of jail!

Why, that was a good deal of a blow for me, and when I thought, somehow, of what that must of meant not to the sheriff only but to his wife and his son and to Julie, with her head high in the air—why, it took my breath.

I think that there was a hundred or more armed men milling all around us, as I went down that street, but none of them could quite make up their minds about what to do, because when they looked at me, and decided that they should jump me, then they seen Grace ahead of me, and then in a minute there was a yell:

"It's Dickon bringing in Grace. Bringing in Grace! And it was Dickon, then, that killed the other three—"

"Shut up!" I yelled at them, "and clear the way! I ain't nothing but the sheriff's agent! Get out of my way!"

Why, when they had made out exactly what was going on, they treated me like I was a king, and they herded around Grace, and some of them rushed ahead to get the jail open. And they did it, and they shouted as they started off that they would have the sheriff out to welcome us.

And all the time, as I rode along, gents was singing out at me, and hollering very loud, and telling me that I'd never regret the work that I was doing, on this day. And another section was always hollering that they couldn't believe that any one man could ever of hunted down the whole Grace gang!

But here is where I've got to pause and explain the things, exactly as they happened, because a good deal more had taken place than just the capture of Grace.

When young Donaldson run up to the house where the two dead men lay, and when he seen the blood, and the smoke, and all of that, he was scared to death, because he didn't know what to do in order to explain his having two dead men on the place.

Exactly what happened, then, I don't know, but what I've always guessed very free was that he called his brother in and they talked the thing over. They decided that it would be foolish to try to get rid of the two bodies and cover the thing up. Altogether too dangerous. And then, when they looked around the place, they found the nigger. And the nigger knew all about what had happened, and he also knew all about how the Donaldsons had sold out to his chief. So, to cut a long matter short, they must of pistoled poor Little Joe in the coldest of cold blood.

Because the report that come down to the town was that the Donaldsons had heard shooting, and that they had got to a shed in their place from which the sound came, and that there they had found three of the Grace gang dead.

Who had killed them? It was figured that it was just a feud in the gang, at first, and that the Doctor had murdered the rest of his men and gone away with all of the loot, which filled the mountains with men hunting for him.

But then, when I showed up in the town with the Doctor, they changed their minds, and all at once they gave me the credit for that triple killing. It was all over the range at once, and though I denied it in public and in private and in print, still, that yarn keeps going the round, and if you ask any old ranger what become of the Grace gang, he'll tell you, nine chances out of ten, that Larry Dickon killed Sandy Larson first in a knife fight, and that I shot Missouri Slim in getting away from the house of Ham Turner that night, and then that I followed up the gang and killed Little Joe and Lew Candy and Dago Mendez all in one bloody fight!

But the fact is what I've wrote down here clear and plain, that I didn't do anything like that at all, and that all I did was to kill two out of the whole lot, outside of taking in the Doctor. Which was the hardest job of all.

I have stopped here and tried to straighten this thing out for the last time, and still I know that I'm talking in vain. And it makes me sick the way people will swallow a fool story, just because it's an exciting one. It ain't the probable lies that go down, but the neat ones. And what is neater than to say that Larry Dickon started out after the Grace gang and killed the five of them, one by one, and finally rode down Grace himself and brought the Doctor in alive? So that when I ride into town today, nine chances out of ten, as I get into the post office, I'll hear one of the gents that are lazying near the door say: "There goes Dickon."

"Jiminy!" says a stranger. "Is that the gent that killed the five gents in the Grace gang and brought in the Doctor?"

"Yes," says the other, "and what's more—"

It used to sort of please me, that sort of talk, but when you get older, you want to be liked and praised not for what you might have been, but for what you really are. The facts count when you're over fifty!

However, I've been using up a lot of words right at the door of the jail, so to speak, with me and the Doctor riding through scores of mighty excited men that was only gradually getting the drift of what had happened.

But enough of them had tumbled to the facts right off. And a dozen of them had gone rushing ahead. They beat open the doors of the jail. They kicked a couple of guards out of the way. They tore open the cell of the sheriff, so savage that he thought that they was gunna take him out and lynch him.

And when he was too proud to ask any questions, they dragged him out of his cell real savage mad and to the door of the jail, and he looked down and seen a swirl of excited, yelling men—

Well, when there's enough folks around, its hard to tell their happiness from their anger, and so the sheriff made up his mind that they had decided finally to really string him up to the first tree, and he took a last look at the brightness of the stars.

But just when he got that idea fixed in his head, a couple of happy maniacs on each side of him, they snatched him up and planted him on their shoulders, and they went whooping and yelling down the street, and dancing, and waving their hats, and everybody trying to crowd his shoulder under the sheriff, hollering: "Who called our sheriff a crook? Wally, hey, Wally! We're gunna make you governor. We're gunna make you president, by God! Who says that Larry Dickon bought his way out of jail?"

It was more exciting than you would ever of believed, and I couldn't help shaking and gagging a little bit you understand, while I pressed up close behind the Doctor and urged him along through the gang.

And then, here I seen the sheriff being carried right up to me. And you can bet that I didn't need any sunshine to see the brightness of his face, and how he took my hand and God-blessed me—why, it was enough to pay me back for everything that I had gone through in the past three days, no matter if they hung me the next moment.

But I managed to tell the sheriff that I was come back to give him the Doctor and to surrender myself up to the jail, again—

Lord love me, there was a mess of cheering and whooping and hollering, at that.

They wouldn't have me in the jail. They would have me in the best doggone room in the hotel and stay there at the town's cost as long as I pleased—

But they didn't reckon on the sheriff, at that.

He says: "Dickon, he's an escaped prisoner. I have been taken out of my cell by force. And the Doctor, I suppose, ought to have a cell, also. But into the jail we go, all three of us, and wait for the law to take us out or leave us in, in due course!"

No matter what they said, he would have his way, and when he pointed out that there had already been enough trouble over one illegal happening in that jail, you can bet that they hung their heads, a good deal.

And that was how it happened that we all went right up to the door of the jail, and it was there, when I tried to dismount, that they discovered that I was wounded.

Well, sir, that put a tin hat on everything.

It is queer how blame ridiculous gents can be when enough of them get together and get excited about something. But nobody can tell how much worse everything is when the women get mixed up into it.

And, of course, there being a wounded man to take care of, that let the women in. It took about a dozen of them to assist the doctor in getting my trouser leg cut off, and taking off the old tourniquet—with about half of the dozen fainting when they seen the blood and the flesh all blotchy and purple, where the tourniquet had stopped the circulation in the thigh. And then them that fainted, of course they come to right away, because they didn't want to miss anything. But if it had only been the men, why, I would just of been a pretty good plucky gent that had done a good turn by bringing in Grace. But the women, it was them that made me a hero!

42

WELL, sir, it would be fine to be able to lean back and say honest that I seen through all the chatter then as plain and clear as I do through it now. But the honest fact of the matter is that I was so tickled that it sent the chills up and down my back, and the voices of them women, blubbering over me, and praising me, they plumb choked me with self-pity, which is about the most meltingest thing in the world.

And, on the whole, I suppose that there was never anybody that was so thoroughly mauled and hauled and patted and petted and admired as I was, until I half expected that I would fall to pieces. Fall to pieces inside, I mean. Because it was terrible weakening, being made so much over. They talked so big about what I had done that it almost scared me to think of riding any little mountain trail at night, let alone racing it at the full speed of Cherry Pie. And when it come, after a few hours of this coddling, to thinking about ever having stood up to such a gent as Doctor Grace, why, I felt as if I had stood up to a train in a butting match!

I'll give you an example to show how all round foolish everybody acted about me. The sheriff wouldn't let me out of that jail without the order from the governor pardoning me. And, by Jiminy, if a lot of gents didn't tear down the bars away from the window of my cell, which was the extra prime best cell in that jail.

Yes, and they cheered as they jerked each bar away, and then they brought up Cherry, and she stuck in her head and said how do you do to me, as fine and kind as you please, while all the women they stood around and wept about it and said how wonderful it was, and could there be any harm in a man that a horse loved so much?

Why, it was wonderful to hear how silly they was. I could of told them how his horses loved old Hank Jeffreys back in my home town, and how Hank was a prime wife-beater and all the rest. But I didn't. I was getting a little too weak to do much talking, because all of this excitement had settled in my head, and there was spells of dizziness that took me and whirled me a mile into the air and then let me down with a jerk.

But finally the doctor come alone and sent all the women away, and hushed up the jail, and hushed up the folks in the street, and he give me something to drink that cooled me off a little. And so I slept.

I mean, I started to dreaming, and I dreamed for so long that pretty soon I got back to the last nightmare that I had had, I mean the one about being down a well. Except that this time it was different. I was climbing up a long, shaky, swinging ladder, and up at the top of the well, there was Julie, bending over and smiling down at me, and I kept working like mad to get up to her, but all the time that ladder kept slipping and slipping down, and the harder I worked, the more it kept slipping. And finally I began to holler: "Julie! Julie! I'm trying to get up, but you're so damn far above me that I can't get to you and—"

And here I woke up with my own voice ringing in my ears, and then I seen, what do you suppose? Why, that my hands had hold of the cool hands of Julie, and she *was* leaning over me, and smiling.

"Lord, Julie," I said, "have I been swearing a lot?"

"Not a word," said Julie, "that I wasn't glad to hear. Are you feeling better, now?"

"I'm on top of the world," I told her. "Are you gunna be able to stay here a minute—I mean, in case I should slip back down that well—I mean—I was screaming about being down—"

"Hush," says Julie. "I understand. And I won't leave you."

"I'm slipping," I says to Julie. "I can feel myself dying, Julie, unless you hold onto me tight, will you?"

"I won't let you go, Larry dear," says she.

And she held me in her arms, and the black weakness fell away from me and left me as clear-headed as a bell. And then I went to sleep in real earnest and I didn't wake up again until nearly twenty-four hours later, when I come to myself and what would you think that I seen?

Why, it was the sheriff, sitting there smoking his pipe, very peaceful. And he winked at me and pointed. And there was Julie, sitting asleep in a chair right close to the head of my bed, looking tired, with dark circles around her eyes, but more beautiful than any other woman ever looked since the beginning of the world.

"You better send her home to bed," says I to the sheriff.

"Humph," says the sheriff. "I dunno that I seem to have any more influence over Julie. It ain't nothing but escaped crooks that she minds! Maybe *you* could send her home!"

And he got up and stood at the window, and talked to Cherry.

But the minute that I so much as whispered to Julie, she woke up with a start and caught my hands.

"Is it the dream again, Larry?" she says.

"The finest old dream that ever come over the pike," says I to her, "and I hope that I won't never have to wake up out of it, Julie. Y'understand? I sort of hope that it might be permanent!"

"Oh," says Julie, "you're *not* delirious any longer!"

"I'm talking the best sense that I ever did in my life," I told her. "And what I mean, Julie—"

"There are people looking," says Julie. "You mustn't stare at me like that or what will they think?"

"They'll think that I love you, Julie. And let them think it, because it's true!"

Then I reached out and got both her hands.

"Tell me, Julie," says I. "Or would a clean shave help you to feel kinder about me?"

"You haven't touched a razor for a week," says Julie. "I can't say that you're a *pretty* outlaw, Larry. But you're the sort of one that I like!"

And she leaned over, I tell you, with no less than about twenty reporters standing outside of the bars of my cell, and she kissed me, did Julie, in front of them all.

Then she stood up and she whirled around and faced them, and she says:

"Don't you dare put *this* in your papers, or Larry will get you, one and all!"

And she went out from the cell, while they give her a cheer, and at the door, she turned around and she gave me a smile that they all could see— the sort of a smile that stayed with me for the rest of my life and made me happy.

Now, if you don't know by this time what sort of a clean-shooting, honest-injun, hundred per cent sort of a girl Julie was, I say, God pity you, because you'll never be able to know nothing about good women. But there wasn't a one of those reporters that didn't seem to know and they all kow-towed to my Julie and she went out from the jail. And out in the street, the boys cheered her again, which was the sweetest sort of music to my ears, you can believe!

The sheriff, he came back to me, then.

"You seem to be able to handle her, son," says he, very gentle. "I hope that you're going to keep the upper hand all the way through, because she's always been too much for me!"

"Send the reporters away first," says I.

"How can I?" says he. "I ain't been reinstated as sheriff."

"Don't talk like a fool, Wally," says I.

"Shut up," says Wally Ops. "This is something from the governor for you to read."

And he handed me a long telegram with the governor's name at the bottom of it, which said:

"I am glad to pardon Dickon hereby, but wish that you could let him escape once more to clean up the rest of the crooks in the state before he becomes an honest man."

"It means the end of the trail," says Wally Ops when I had finished reading that telegram for the tenth time. "And the devil of it is, son, that this trail of yours ended without me having my hands on you."

He was a good game one, was the sheriff, and after that affair had cleared up, and the smoke and the talking, as you might say, then there was nothing in the world that could of persuaded the gents in our country to vote for anybody but Wally Ops for sheriff. He had a sort of a strangle hold on the law and order in that section of the mountain-desert.

Well, that was the way that trailing of the Doctor ended up, that had started so many months before on the night when he stole Cherry Pie. And as you might of noted, it was Cherry Pie that had beat him in the wind-up. Because all the human brains in the world can't match up with a good horse.

43

LIFE on a farm, and sowing and mowing and reaping; and marrying and having children; and house-building and such, well, they make good living, but they don't make good telling. I have noticed how most books end up with a marriage and the reason is that after a gent has got the right girl for himself, then there ain't anything for him to do except to be happy, and happiness ain't interesting to those that are outside the front door of your house. If it wasn't for panics, and murders, and robberies, and politicians, and such, newspapers would be terrible dull reading, you know. So here is where I have got to stop talking about myself and say a little about Doctor Grace.

I feel, somehow, that I've been so busy talking about my own affairs, all of this time, that I never have been able to give the Doctor a square deal. By which I don't mean that he needed honest treatment, but more space and cleverer writing than I can manage. Because of all the gents that I ever met up with, the Doctor was the most smart, and the coolest head, and the steadiest hand. And all by myself I could never of beat him. It was Cherry Pie, as I said before, that turned the trick for me.

If I was able to follow on with what happened to the Doctor after I brought him to the jail, I could give you a clearer notion of the strength that was in him.

In the first place, the papers was full of nothing except "outlaw, murderer, robber, brigand, assassin," and such names when they mentioned the Doctor. And everybody took it to be just a matter of course that he would be convicted quick and put out of the way with a rope around his neck.

But the Doctor had plenty of money stuck away in odd corners of the world, and he pulled some of it out to fight the law, now. He hired fine brains to help him make his fight, and the first thing you know, he had got a disagreement in the jury!

The papers put up a terrible yell, and there was another trial right away, and the second time they convicted him. But then they had an appeal, and at the end of a year there was still fighting and wrangling over that case, but it was no longer very interesting to folks in general. They sort of took it for granted that the Doctor would get what was coming to him, and they did't care just when it happened.

It was while his second appeal was hanging in the air that he made a new move.

All the time after I brought him in, he had been a real model prisoner, so that the lady reporters which write up the "human interest" stuff for the papers always had columns and columns about him. His game was "repentance," which is always interesting for suckers to read about. He repented a terrible lot. And he told stories about how he had been led into crime. And all he wanted, he said, was a chance to get justice, and to prove that of the bullets fired in Hookertown, none of his had done any killing. Just wounded a couple of gents, you see!

This was his game. And it seems that he sort of convinced his jailers and they stopped watching him so extra careful as they had done at first. You can't be so hard on a gent that keeps on smiling for a year and a half, you know!

And so, when they got a little careless, he took the first good chance and sawed through two sets of bars, caved in the head of one guard, took the rifle from a second guard and left him for dead, climbed over the outer wall, and got away to where there was a car left standing by the road, nobody knew by whom!

And at the rate of fifty miles an hour, that car rattled him off toward the mountains that he knew so well.

And that was the very last that was ever heard north of the Rio Grande about Doctor Grace.

A murderer, nacheral and plain and simple was what Doctor Grace was, but along with all of his faults, he was brave, and I think that he could of been faithful, too, if he had ever found pals who would of kept their nerve and their heads through thick and thin.

I've never had any doubt that, when I finally caught him, he was in earnest when he suggested that we team it together. And if he had found me without any thoughts of Julie in my mind, I suppose that I might of weakened and taken up with his offer.

In that case, by this time I might be a rich Don south of the Rio Grande in the land of "mañana." Or maybe I might be sleeping in my grave for these long years, with the knife of somebody stuck between my shoulders. But, in that case, I think that it wouldn't of been the knife of the Doctor.

No, in a way I think that him and me was cut out for one another. He would of furnished the brains. And I would of furnished a scrap of decency that he lacked. But by the time that we met, he was a little too far gone in blood one way, and I was too far gone in love another. And we never could go back and start together.

However, I'm glad that Grace got away.

He was meant for a bad end, of course, but I don't think that he was meant for a rope.

And my favorite dream, by night, is of how the Doctor sat in the cabin at that poker game so cool and so steady, with a killer on each side of him, and how he handled all the breaks of the game and the situation when it looked the blackest for him. And I notice that when that dream wakes me up, it always wakes me up smiling.

FLAMING IRONS

1

A Fine Pair

IF the colt had stood still and taken things calmly all would have been well, and they could have worked it out in time. But the colt was not much over three years—just old enough to have its strength and not old enough to have full sense. Except to one person, it was as wild as any unsaddled mustang from the farthest range of the mountains. And when it found itself caught in the treacherous mud at the edge of the water hole, it began to flounder and fight with a terrible energy.

Tarron and his older boy got a lariat of stout rawhide over its head and tried to pull it out in that way, but it was sunk much too deep.

Then they ventured into the slush and tried to quiet the fine gray, but their presence only made the handsome fellow more wild with fear.

It was down to the shoulders; then down to the very withers, and such were the furious efforts which it made that its strength was rapidly ebbing, and before long its exhausted head would sink.

A horse is too intelligent in some crises. A mule, when in a tight corner, will stand quiet and trust to Providence whose special care has always been mules. But when a horse cannot solve a riddle, like many a high-spirited and high-strung man, it gives up, surrenders completely, and so is lost.

A very little more and the gray would surrender in just that manner, and Tarron knew it.

He was desperately put to it. From his little place, where he managed to provide for his family only by dint of the most constant exertions, he could not afford to lose a sheep or a calf, to say nothing of the finest horse that mare had ever foaled in those mountains.

Suddenly he cried: "Where's Les? Where's Les? Get Les down here, Joe!"

Joe, with a nod, leaped on the back of his cow pony and spurred over the hill.

When he reached the house he shouted, as he sprang from the saddle, "Where's Les?"

Mrs. Tarron, dishcloth in hand, came toward him in a flurry.

"Poor Les has a dreadful headache. He's still in bed, I guess."

"Oh, dash his headaches! The gray's drowning in the tank!"

And Joe Tarron hurried up the ladder to the attic room.

It was still semidark in that room. The atmosphere was close, and in a corner an outline could be dimly discerned under a huddle of bedclothes.

"Les!" Joe yelled.

There was no answer.

Hurrying to the huddle of clothes, he tore them off the prostrate form of the sleeper.

"Les!"

There was a faint groan, and then a feeble voice muttered: "Sick, Joe. Can't get up—"

"Damn you and your sickness! Get up! Get up! I know the kind of sickness that keeps you in bed on frosty mornings!"

Les Tarron groaned softly again, and, turning on his side, his heavy breathing announced that he was already falling into soundest slumber.

His brother, in an impatient fury, stretched out a hand to strike, but something withheld him.

"You fool!" he shouted. "It's the gray, your own colt, bogged down at the edge of the tank—"

You would have said that he had struck some vital nerve, not of a man, but of a cat, so quickly did Les Tarron spring to his feet. He was past his brother in a bound. Half dressed, his long hair flying behind him, he dropped from the trap door, disdaining the ladder—fled through the kitchen, and, springing into the saddle on the mustang, rode furiously away while Joe afoot labored heavily behind.

When he got to the edge of the tank, he could see his father keeping the lariat taut, but it was patently a useless effort to maintain the head of the colt above the edge of the slime. The eyes of the gray, usually so fiery bright, were now glassing over.

"Jim!" called the rescuer.

The mud-covered ears of the colt pricked, and he uttered a feeble whinny, as Les Tarron jumped from the saddle and stood on the edge of the tank.

"In bed—by heaven, I might of knowed it!" sneered his father. "Now save the gray, or it's the last day that I keep and feed your useless carcass!"

Les Tarron hardly seemed to hear. He reached one hand over his shoulder and plucked away his shirt. The garment, not coming free at once, was ripped in twain by the force of that grasp. A strange thing to see, for the shirt was of stoutest wool, and one would have guessed that the united strength of two men could hardly have accomplished so easily what a single gesture had done now. However, now that the shirt was off and the sun glinted on the naked torso of Les Tarron, the explanation was not far to seek. He was no giant in bulk, but Nature, which makes so many forms in slipshod haste, had here worked with the delicate hand of an artist and composed all in a perfect harmony and a perfect balance. The muscles stirred and moved like living snakes beneath his skin.

He had come barefooted. Now he stepped straight into the slush.

"Keep a pull on Jim's head," he directed. "Not too hard, y'understand, but hard enough to take advantage of what I'm gunna do."

"What *are* you gunna do?" asked the father, seeing his son already sunk hip-deep in the mud.

Les did not answer. Bending low, he seemed to find a grip on the horse and made an effort to move him.

It caused the muscles along his neck to stand out like knotted fists, but it only drove Les Tarron shoulder-deep into the mud.

"Steady!" shouted the father in alarm. "It's no good! Anyway, you ain't fool enough to think that you can lift the weight of a horse, are you? Get out of that mud before you're drowned, you blockhead."

Still Les Tarron made no reply. He squelched through the mud. He straddled a little farther apart and felt a firmer bottom beneath his gripping toes. Then he took a great breath, and, leaning over, he sank shoulders, neck, and head beneath the surface of the slime.

In the filthy darkness beneath, his hands fumbled, and presently he found his grip—both hands and wrists thrust under the barrel of the gray behind the elbows.

Then he began to lift, with flexed legs that stiffened and straightened, and with bent back that struggled to straighten also.

A groan from the colt told of a body half crushed by the gigantic pressure. The gray tried to rear to avoid the pain, and so some of its weight was transferred to the hind quarters. Suddenly he was thrust up, head and neck, clear of the mud.

There was a shout of triumph from the shore. Then beside the colt rose the mud-covered head of Les Tarron. He had to tip his head up to clear his face; then, wiping away the filth from mouth and eyes and nose, he breathed a great gasp of relief, and waved a blackened arm toward his father and brother.

"Great work, Les! Now, get out of that and come ashore. I thought that you'd never come up again. You were down a whole minute!"

"Leave me be," said Les Tarron. "He ain't cleared yet!"

The colt had begun its desperate struggles once more, but now a single word from its master quieted it. Back to the sunken hind quarters went Les Tarron, moving with desperate flounderings. Once more he sank beneath the surface of the mud. Once more he bent and strained—and now the colt was fairly dragged out from the deeper mud which had imprisoned it.

The strain on the lariat could tell, from this point. The struggles of the gray itself were helpful, and last of all was the gigantic strength of Les Tarron moving the horse and lifting it forward.

In five minutes the rescued colt was on firm ground, and stood with sinking head and trembling legs while all three washed off the thick layers of mud with water.

Once clean, a horse was revealed eminently worth even such efforts as these had been, a compactly built, powerful animal, with legs which mean speed.

"My, but ain't you a mess?" sneered Joe at his mighty brother.

"That's nothing," answered Les.

He ran down to a point where firm ground came to the edge of the little artificial lake. There he plunged in, and presently he came up white, freed from the black mud. He stood, dripping, beside the dripping colt, and his father, with a sort of happy sadness, admired the magnificent group.

"Ah, Les," said he, "if you could ever come into yourself and be worthy of sitting in the saddle on that horse, what a man you'd be! But there ain't much chance of it, I'm afraid. And one of these days you'll just be bogged down and lost—like Jim here nearly was. Lost doing something useless and foolish, and men are gunna be glad that you're done for!"

These bitter words seemed to slip unregarded over the youth's head. Now that the limbs of the colt had ceased to tremble Les Tarron leaped up and sat sidewise on its back. There was no need of bridle to guide Jim; a word or two and he broke into a gliding pace that carried them softly over the hill, horse and rider, still dripping wet, flashing like a precious stone in the morning sun.

"Watch 'em go," said the rancher to his older son, "watch 'em go! And where would you find a finer pair than them, Joe? Where would you ever see a finer horse—that won't cut a cow, or work with a rope? Where would you ever see a finer man—that won't ride herd or handle a lariat or a branding iron or a pitchfork? Aye, strong enough to lift a horse, as you and me have seen this day, but what good'll his strength be put to, I'm asking you? And yet they say that God made all things with a purpose— even the flies in the air!"

"Aye," said Joe bitterly, "and He made Les so that we could have our foretaste of hell on earth!"

2

A Successor to Samson

LES TARRON left the colt in the small paddock near the house. It followed him along the fence, whinnying piteously, for it knew as clearly as a man would have known that it owed its life to the intervention of its young master.

At the kitchen door, Mrs. Tarron raised her work-reddened hands.

"Les Tarron! What d'ye mean running around the country more'n half naked to make folks think you're a monkey or something? And what—"

The boy walked lightly past her. It required a good deal to rouse him from his habitual apathy, but the enormous effort he had made to free the colt had set his blood in circulation, and he was stirred even to the point of mirth. He smiled at his mother, and going into the front room measured the distance from the floor to the trap door of his attic, took a running step, and leaped. He missed his hold with one hand, but the left gripped the edge.

"Les Tarron!" cried his mother, following him to the door. "Did you hear me speak to you? Did you—oh, land love us!"

She paused in the doorway and looked up to him, where he hung swinging by one hand.

"Les! Wait till I move the ladder. You'll fall and hurt yourself!"

"No, leave the ladder alone. I'm all right."

"Wait one minute! Can you hold yourself with one hand?"

He merely laughed.

"Oh, I can hold myself I think—if you move quick!"

Panting with haste and dread, she dragged the heavy ladder close to him.

"Can you manage now, son?"

"I'll try," said he.

And then, with one arm—

You young man who have chinned yourself with both hands often, have you ever chinned yourself with one? And have you ever hung at the full strength of your single arm and then drawn yourself up head high? And, worst of all, have you let yourself dangle for a couple of minutes and then tried to make your numbed muscles work?

Les Tarron lifted himself slowly, still laughing down at his mother, and hoisted himself through the trap door into the attic above.

His mother, staring up at him a-gape, grew furious as she saw that he had been making a mock both of her and of his danger.

She stood beneath the trap and hurled angry words up at him until she heard a blithe and unconcerned whistle rising from the room over her head.

Then, quite at a loss, she shook her fist at the gap in the ceiling and went silently back to her kitchen work. She was the only member of the family who had the slightest sympathy for Les. He was her son; therefore, while the others called him fool and sluggard, and though she could not deny that he was both, at least she would reserve the right to love him still.

She did not understand him. Most people thought that there was nothing worth understanding in the youth, but his mother felt that he was a mysterious problem that might be solved by a wise head at some future time.

There had never been a half-wit on either side of the family. She could trace her own blood back for several generations, and all her kin had been mentally alert. The same was true about the line of Tarron.

Whence, then, this anomaly had come?

She could not tell, she could not even guess; but she was fond of watching and waiting, and when she saw her lazy boy developing into a lazier man, and a worthless idleness consuming all his days, she still would hope that one day he would change, and rouse himself to better things.

Today, however, she despaired. She knew enough of men and of their physical prowess to feel sure that few persons would have been able to do the thing which she had seen her son accomplish with such ease.

It did not rouse her admiration. Rather, it filled her with awe and unrest.

She remembered that when Les was a mite of seven he could master his tough, work-strengthened brother of ten. And thus far throughout his life, when he cared to call upon his reserve powers, he could accomplish things which were beyond the capacity of other men.

So thought the mother, working in her kitchen while, meantime, she listened to the whistling of her son.

It was a pleasant sound, but quite unlike the whistling that one hears from the average boy in the morning. One could not call it a tune, but there was rhythm and music in it. The whistling stopped, and through the window, far away over the fields, she could hear the song of birds, unseen among the shrubbery.

Mrs. Tarron dropped her dish mop with a soft exclamation and glanced over her shoulder in terror, for it seemed to her that the song of the distant birds was like the echo of her boy's whistling.

Just at that moment, there was the soft padding shock of a heavy weight falling upon the floor of the next room, and she winced again. When Les dropped from the trap door of the attic, the shock sent a crash through the entire house. And it had never before occurred to her that when her lumpish younger son did the same thing it was like the muffled fall of a cat.

Now, Les came yawning into the doorway, and as he stretched, and the old clothes which he had donned cracked at the seams, she lost her momentary awe of him.

"Go comb your hair!" she commanded. "You look a sight."

"Hungry!" he responded. "Lemme have something to eat."

"If you eat in this house, young man," she replied, "how often have I told you that you'll have to be on time for meals?"

Raising her voice, she added harshly: "And what about the cows? What about the cows? Ain't you going to take them down to the pasture, you lazy good for nothing?"

"Eh, yah!" yawned Les Tarron.

He opened the bread can and took out half a loaf of stale bread. Munching that, he walked away contentedly. His mother stared after him, shaking her head over him for the ten thousandth time. For, certainly, he was not like the others of his kin. There was no resemblance. She had had to cater to her husband and her first son with meticulous care. Good cooking and plenteous fare were essential to them, but this wastrel could get on as well with dry bread as they could with beefsteak! Aye, and he throve better than they on any diet. He could eat like a wolf, and then curl up and sleep for twenty-four hours; and could go for three days thereafter without tasting anything but water. And if—

But she closed her mind upon such memories. They were too upsetting. About everything else in her family she was fond of gossiping to the neighbors, but about Les she never would say a word; because she feared lest the uncanny thoughts which she herself often had about the boy should spread abroad and be reflected in the minds of others.

In the meantime, Les Tarron had gone down to the corral and called out the cows.

He did not drive them before him, as a cowherd should; but waited until the great red bull, the master of the little herd, had lumbered through the gate. Then with a bound he seated himself astride the fleshy hump across the shoulders of the monster.

The bull lashed his tail fiercely and lurched his head from side to side, with deep-mouthed bellowing; but he had attempted to shake off this clinging pest many a time before, and now he quickly gave up the battle and rolled on down the road with his accustomed majestic gait.

The cows followed. Sometimes the calves would race ahead for a short distance, keen to get the good grass of the pasture, but Les Tarron paid no heed.

He sat on the bull's back with his eyes closed. Stretching forth his arms blindly, once more he tensed his arms and smiled with joy as he felt the slight ache in his muscles.

The bull stopped before the pasture bars. The boy swung down, pitched off the bars, and let the herd through.

It was a difficult task, this of herding in the pasture. For one half of the ground had been summer-fallowed, and the other half was covered with tender green growing wheat. On the summer fallow the herd was welcome to reach for the bits of grass beneath the plow furrows. But there was the constant temptation of the tender wheat field beyond.

Young Les Tarron selected a pleasant shady tree at a corner of the pasture, and there stretched himself, his eyes half closed. The bull made straight for the wheat field, with the whole herd behind him, but as he came within half a dozen paces of the forbidden land a sharp, biting whistling from the herdsman stopped his majesty.

The bull paused, changing uneasily from foot to foot. But after pawing up the dust a few times, he turned sullenly and rambled back into the plowed area. The herd followed his example; and Les Tarron, secure in the knowledge that no one of the dumb brutes would dare to disobey his whistled warning, completely closed his eyes.

Not to sleep, but to see more clearly.

For it was the very greatest day in his life. He had known that he was stronger than other men, but the greatness of his strength he had not realized. Now, for the first time he had put forth his utmost might, and the sure consciousness of his muscular prowess sent a tingle along his blood and through his heart.

It had been a great joy. And perhaps—who could tell?—there would be other occasions before very long in which he could use all of his powers; use them to their utmost!

So he lay there on his back, enjoying himself in these reflections, until a voice called from beyond the edges of his daydream:

"Hello! Boy! Oh, Boy!"

He opened his eyes, but he did not sit up.

"Hey, boy! Hey, kid! Come here!"

Les Tarron closed his eyes again.

"You sassy brat! Will this fetch you?"

And a bullet sung above his head and spattered solidly into the tree trunk!

3

By Process of Deduction

HE looked up with mild interest at the smoking gun in the hand of the rider.

Then he turned and regarded the neat round hole which had been drilled through the tree.

"Come here, you young fool, or I'll send the next one through your thick head," came the ringing invitation from the roadway.

Les Tarron stood up and regarded the strangers with a closer attention. There were five of them altogether, mounted on dripping horses; and though he was used to seeing the roughest mountaineers, he thought that he had never before seen such a set of fellows ready for anything.

He smiled at them. For all strong, swift, sure things appealed to Les Tarron. The eagle above the peaks or the mountain lion beneath the forest shadows brought a thrill to his heart.

Like five lions, or like five eagles, were these men; all brave, bold, powerful, and cruel. His own life, he felt, came tinglingly close to the tips of his fingers—a thing to be given away with hardly a thought.

He thought, also, of the revolver at his hip. But he did not touch it.

Instead he walked slowly forward to the fence and leaned against it, still smiling his appreciation of the riders.

"We got all day, maybe?" queried the leader of the five furiously. "Why the deuce can't you come when you're called?"

"I was thinking about coming," said Les Tarron, unconcerned; "but I took a while to get here."

"He's a half-wit, Ingram," said one of the men. "Take it easy with him, or you'll scare him to death."

"No, you won't, Bert," said another. "He's too foolish to be scared."

The wild rider, Bert Ingram, who had during these seconds eyed the boy up and down in a sort of contemptuous disgust, now growled: "Did somebody come down this road?"

"When?" asked Tarron.

And he looked absently past the questioner into the distant heart of the sun-whitened sky, where a buzzard had been sailing the last time he noticed. It was circling there no longer. But from all corners of the sky came other black specks, tiny with distance, swinging through the heavens in loosening circles.

"When do you think I mean?" barked Bert Ingram. "Yesterday or last month? No, I mean inside of the last hour or so!"

"You're kind of rough, ain't you?" remarked Les, looking Ingram in the eye.

He did not stare in fear or in anger, but with the same curious intentness which he had first displayed. For anger and fearful danger did not seem to horrify or appall or disgust him; it merely fascinated him to the bottom of his soul.

The leader, however, had not time to take further note of the peculiarities of this youth. He now declared, with a savage vehemence:

"Talk out, kid, or I'll have a rope throwed and daubed onto you! And then we'll teach you a lesson that you had really ought to of learned at home!"

Les Tarron said: "Wait a minute!" Dropping his chin in his hand, he seemed lost in thought.

This curious vagueness seemed to irritate the leader more than ever, and he roared: "Half-wit, did you call him! I tell you, the kid ain't got a brain in his whole head!"

Les Tarron looked up and nodded.

"You agree with me, eh?" asked the leader, and there was a roar of laughter from his companions.

"A man went by here a while ago," said Tarron.

"How long?"

"About forty-five minutes."

"You remember seeing him, do you? What sort of a man, then?"

"Big man. Pretty big, I'd call him."

"Aye, aye!" cried Ingram, his eyes flashing. "I begin to think that there's *some* sense in you. Yes, if it's the fellow that we're after, he's big enough for two. Go on!"

"What else?" asked Les Tarron.

"What sort of horse was he riding?"

Tarron's eyes wandered a little, and then lighted as though in memory.

"A big brown horse," said he.

"Good! One big brown horse! I think that I know the one!"

Tarron added: "With white in the tail, too."

"That's it! You've named it! What shape was the horse in?"

"Near tired out," said Tarron.

There was a yell of delight from the entire group at this news.

"We'll have blood before night," said Bert Ingram, rolling his eyes at the neighboring mountains as though his fierce thoughts were already busy roaming there in search of prey. "You say that horse was tired out?"

"Tired so bad that when he got to this little grade here, the big man jumped down and walked and he had to drag the horse after him, the poor nag was so dead beat."

Bert Ingram growled in utter satisfaction.

"I never heard anything better than that!" he said. "Kid, seems like you got some sense, after all. And now tell me one more thing: What shape was the big man in?"

"He seemed to be hurt bad," replied Tarron.

"Hello! What makes you think that?"

"Because he was bending over and walking with short steps. He seemed to be in a lot of pain."

"Darn him!" shouted one of Ingram's followers. "I told you that I nicked him back in the old draw."

"Kid," said Ingram, "I think that you sure enough did, and I'll just make that the luckiest shot that you ever fired."

He turned back to young Tarron.

"How was he armed?"

"He carried a double-barreled shotgun."

"Hey?"

"A double-barreled shotgun."

"You lie!"

"No, I don't lie."

"Boss, I believe it. He must have stole it at the last farm that he touched up. So he's carrying a double-barreled shotgun? It means that Dorn is meaning to fight like sin if he's cornered. You savvy that, boys?"

"Sure, that's pretty likely."

"Now, kid," said the leader, "you say that the horse and the man was both pretty near done for?"

"Down-headed and dragging their feet, both of 'em," said Tarron.

"Better and better. What else?"

"Half blind with tiredness and hurt," said Tarron, "so that they hardly knew where their feet were falling, y'understand?"

"Aye, and ain't I been that way myself, so bad that I could hardly wish the same for any other man in the world!"

"Except that hound!" exclaimed one of the followers with an oath.

"Aye, except for Dorn. That swine—he needs all that he gets. And now tell us one last thing. Which way did he head?"

"I don't know," said young Tarron.

"Hey?"

"I don't know."

"Well, kid, did he bribe you to tell everything but that? But you can't keep secrets from me, young man. You don't know me, maybe? I'll let *you* in on a secret, then. I'm Albert Ingram. Will that be news enough to start your tongue working to tell us all you know?"

Les Tarron shook his head.

"Look there," he said, and pointed to the side. "The trail splits down yonder. I only know that he went that way."

"Through those rocks!" exclaimed Ingram. "How can a trail be followed here?"

He turned to his men.

"We got to get to that trail and split. I'll go down one side with Chet. The rest of you take the other, and you can make your own choice of which side you'll travel on."

"No good, chief. We'd come to another split in the trail, and then we'd have to divide up again, and what would happen then? We can't comb all the trails in the mountains."

Ingram, his face dark with discontent, scowled and tugged viciously at his mustache.

"This kid could tell us more, if he would," said he.

"Not me," said Tarron.

The leader yanked a revolver from his holster and thrust it suddenly under Tarron's nose.

"You lie, you sneaking brat!" he shouted.

Les merely glanced at the revolver; then he laughed in Ingram's face.

"It don't seem to bother you much—a gun?" asked Ingram, sneeringly, as the coolness of the youngster brought a murmur of astonishment and admiration from the members of the band.

"Why, it sort of tickles me," confessed Tarron.

"You've told all that you know about this gent?"

"Yes, about all."

"About all? What's the rest? Out with it!"

"Only that his second horse died in that valley, yonder."

"Hello! He stopped to talk to you, then?"

"No."

"You mean to say you know that he had a second horse that dropped dead in the other valley, yonder?"

"I guess that was it."

"And he didn't tell you that?"

"No."

"What are you getting at, kid?" said Ingram. "If he didn't tell you, how could you possibly know?"

"How could he tell me," asked Les Tarron, "when I didn't so much as see him?"

This statement reduced the group to a dead silence.

"Hold on, chief," said one of the men, "he's just simple, as I was telling you before. I wouldn't hold it too much against him!"

"The sneaking little rat—" began Ingram who was a burly fellow. "If you didn't see him," he added, "how do you know so much about him?"

"I seen his trail, not him," said Les Tarron. "And I made him out of his sign."

4

A Minor Prophet

THE leader snorted contemptuously.

"You seen him in his sign, did you?" he sneered. "That told you the color of his horse, maybe? Why, you—"

He raised the quirt in his hand; Les Tarron stood alert and watchful, his eyes not on the impending lash but on the face of the man who wielded it.

"Wait a minute, Bert," put in one of the other riders. "This kid ain't so simple as he seems. Let's hear how he can explain things to us!"

"Explain? What explanation could there be?" cried Ingram. "But I don't mind. We're losing time, but I'd like to hear what the young liar has got to say for himself."

"That's right," said the other. "What's your name?"

"Leicester Tarron."

"Les, just you up and tell us how the tracks of that horse told you that he was brown and that he had a white patch in his tail, and that he was a big horse?"

"He must have stopped beside the fence here," said Tarron, "and rubbed against it."

He tapped the outside of the fence, where a tiny patch of brown hair could be observed.

"Say, but that's pretty thin, kid!" exclaimed Ingram. "However, we'll let that go. You've got enough behind it that I might want to hear explained. The white patch in his tail, for instance?"

Les pointed toward the shrubbery at some distance.

"There's a white hair tangled yonder," he said.

"Hello! Where?"

"Right there."

"Go look, Charlie."

The delegate returned with a hair almost a yard long, which he was winding around his forefinger.

"The kid's right. He's got uncommon sharp eyes, though. Uncommon queer. But you've only started, kid. You said that this here horse was tired out."

"Sure he was tired out. Right here where he rubbed against the fence, he stopped and staggered. Look at where those tracks are doubled."

He pointed down.

"Where?" asked Ingram. "I don't see—wait a minute. By heavens, I think the kid is right!"

"A horse don't stagger for fun," said Tarron calmly.

"You're right he don't. But, go ahead! You said that the man was fagged out and hurt."

"There's his trail on this side, closest to the fence. Look at his steps. By the way that the heel-marks show, he's a big man; but his stride is short, and in some places it's a lot shorter than in others. He's a big man, and he's able to step out and walk fast, but something holds him back and ties him up, and what could that be except that he's been hurt and weakened inside so's he's not himself?"

The five regarded the youth as if he were a sort of minor prophet. The sneering smile had left even the face of Bert Ingram who, dismounting, crawled along the ground upon his hands and knees and scrutinized the marks with a careful eye. Others of the troop followed his example, and there were frequent murmurings.

"And he seen that without even bending over!" exclaimed the man called Charlie, as he stood up. "Is there any Indian in you, kid?"

"I don't know," said Tarron.

"No," said Charlie, "I reckon that you ain't interested, either."

He wagged his head, as though this remark concealed some profound meaning.

"Go straight ahead with your yarn," ordered Ingram. "I'll swallow most of the rest of your bunk, but I want to know about this stuff of the double-barreled shotgun! Just lemme hear how you knew that! By the way he limped on his right foot?"

And he grinned with a curious malice.

"Now," said Tarron, "there's nothing queer about that. You see the moss along this streak of the fence, don't you? Well, that takes an impression pretty easy. And look here!"

He indicated two tiny indentations, each a little curve, very difficult to see.

"When the horse stopped for a minute, the man stopped too, and he leaned his shotgun against the fence here."

"Hang it," shouted Ingram, "he's got his answer all pat for everything! But, just the same, I'd like to know one last thing, and if he can build us an answer out of the trail, I'll eat half of my hat. Look here, kid, didn't you tell us that the horse of this gent—the second horse, I mean—had dropped dead in the other valley?"

"Yes, I said so."

"And how did you know that?"

"I didn't *know* it. But the buzzard that was sailing over that spot has dropped, and there come the rest of the buzzard family, traipsing up this way!"

He indicated the specks sailing through the heavens.

"That valley," Les continued, "ain't nothing more'n a bowl of rocks and sand. Nothing living goes through it except men, so far as I know; and only men in a terrible, desperate hurry, at that. The buzzard dropped because there was some dead thing in the valley floor. What dead thing would be there? Not likely a man. More likely a horse. And that's the only thing that was behind my guess."

He paused and yawned broadly, as though already tired by his unusual exertions.

"It's good," pronounced Bert Ingram, staring fixedly at the young mountaineer. "I hate to say that I'm beat by any man, and especially by any kid, but this kid beats me. I'd like to see the faces of his ma and pa. There's something queer somewhere!"

"Sure there is," agreed one of the troop. "But what a heap of use this kid would be to us if we had him along on the trail!"

"Aye " agreed the leader, with much unction. "And why shouldn't he come? Look here, son, there's a dollar and a half in it for you."

"No," said Les Tarron.

"Why not?"

"I can't go without that horse of mine, there."

"Well, take your horse along, kid. Why not?"

"I don't own him."

"You don't own your horse? Then who does?"

"My father."

"Wait a minute. You don't own him, but your father—well, what do I see in this?"

"Make me a present of that horse and I'll do what I can for you."

The leader whistled softly.

"How much?" he asked.

"Dad turned down a hundred and fifty for that colt the other day."

"Aye, it's a likely looking piece of horseflesh. I pay you a couple of hundred dollars for a couple of hours' work?"

"That gent that you're trailing," said Les Tarron, "has so much nerve that it's worth spending a little money to catch him."

"You know that much about him, do you?"

"Yes, anybody that's willing to tackle the valley yonder with a fagged horse, has got a lot of nerve. Most folks are afraid to try it even with a fresh one."

Ingram again whistled softly.

"You'll do what? Bring us up in sight of that fellow?"

"Yes."

"And if you fail to do that?"

"Then you take the horse for yourself—and I walk home!"

"This gets better and better," said the leader. "Did I say that this kid was simple?"

He added sharply: "Suppose that there was a brush along the way and that we needed another fighting man. Would we have to take care of you, or could you take care of yourself?"

"I don't know," said Tarron quietly.

"I mean—can you shoot?"

"I got a gun."

"Let's see it!"

Bert Ingram took the revolver and chuckled over it.

"Kind of loose," he estimated. "Rattles in the head and shaky in the heel and wore out in the teeth—well, fifty years old, ain't it?"

"I dunno," said Les Tarron. "My granddad owned it."

There was a burst of laughter.

"Give him a good gun, chief, if you're going to try him," advised Charlie, who seemed to be a second in command, a sort of lieutenant to Ingram.

"Let him try his hand with his own gun," decreed Ingram sternly. "Hit this!"

He waited until Tarron, unabashed by the ridicule, dropped the revolver back into his pocket; then, scooping up a piece of gray slate three or four inches in diameter, he tossed it into the air.

"Hit it, kid!" he ordered, as the stone sailed through space.

Young Tarron stood with his fine head thrown back, his dull, vacant eyes apparently lost in a study of the blue heavens above him. As for the spinning stone—surely nothing so near and so small could arrest his attention!

But just as the stone reached the crest of its rise and poised for the fall, the Colt flashed in Tarron's hand. There was a loud explosion; a puff of old-fashioned black powder smoke.

But the piece of slate had disappeared.

It had been snuffed out in mid-air. In the brush near by, an instant later, there was a light rattling, as though a handful of sand had been thrown upon the foliage.

Mr. Ingram, for some reason, dropped his quirt on the ground and trod upon it. And he flushed redly. Could it be that he was remembering how he had raised his whip, and how the mild, blank eye of this handsome boy had watched indifferently the impending stroke?

Mr. Ingram winced—as though it was his own soul he had heard rattle like a handful of sand against the foliage.

5

Across the Hills

MR. TARRON, SR., coming slowly in from the plow, saw a little cavalcade advancing to the house, his son among them, riding the gray colt. He forgot the service which Les had rendered that morning. As a matter of fact, it was his habit to be angry first, and to think afterward, and truly this boy of his had given him ample provocation.

So he shouted: "Les!"

"Aye?"

"What do you mean by leaving the cow pasture?"

"These gents want to buy the gray," explained Les quietly.

It put only a slightly better face upon the matter, however. No mountaineer could refrain from a horse sale or a horse exchange, to be sure; but Mr. Tarron had great expectations for the colt.

"I ain't selling him," he said to the leader of the riders. "I'm keeping him for a while till he gets more mature. Then I'll try him."

"I'll make allowances for him being young," replied the leader. "And the man who's to ride him ain't a heavyweight. Come on! Let me have a price on him, will you?"

He turned his head a little and looked frowningly toward the crowded peaks of the range, amid which the lamed, weary, wounded fugitive was struggling.

Yet, with all a Westerner's love of a good horse trade, the big man would not allow his impatience to show; for there is no better way of losing all advantage in a sale than by letting it appear that one is in a hurry.

"I'll tell you something," said the farmer, with an expectant grin. "There was a fool the other day that offered me only a hundred and fifty dollars for that horse!"

Bert Ingram drew a long face.

"A hundred and fifty?" said he. "Why, man, that's a lot of money."

"A lot of money it is, and I ain't denying it," said the farmer. "Yes, sir," he added darkly, "I never paid that much for a horse myself in my whole life."

"Then," snapped Ingram, "tell me how you happened to have such a colt as that foaled on your place?"

"There's a story behind everything," said Tarron, rubbing his chin with pleasure as he thought back to that older day. "I had a fine gray mare. She was the best thing that I ever had in horseflesh. And once I drove her down into the valley—they was having the races there, y'understand—I seen that the big stallion that had been shipped in from the East and that had won the main race and a whole fortune in betting—why, I seen that that horse was pastured out in a five-acre lot—and the fence around that lot was particularly shaky—and, tell me, partner, what harm was there in putting the gray mare to pasture near the weakest part of the fence?"

He laughed joyously as he remembered the trick, and even Ingram could not help laughing also.

"You paid no fee, and you got yourself a good colt," he said.

"Yes," said the farmer, "and a lot better horse than ever his father was in his palmiest day, and that father won lots of good races."

"Hold on," said Ingram, "it's a good thing to see a man admire a horse, but I dunno about this colt. His legs are a trifle short for real speed."

"Are they?" snorted Tarron. "Mind you, I ain't showing him off in the hopes of selling him. His price is too high for most. But what makes his legs look short is because his hocks is let down so far, and because he's got something in his shoulder. Hold on! Seeing is better than hearing. Just let that partner of yours on the brown take a spin up the road, and back, and my boy will catch him on the gray."

"The brown has made quite a march today," said Ingram craftily. "It ought to get a handicap."

"Well, I ain't particular about that," declared Tarron. "Run to that white tree and around it and back. And you can have a start of from here to that black stone."

Ingram was surprised.

"Hello!" said he. "D'you mean to say that the colt could beat the brown in that distance with such a start?"

Tarron bit his lip nervously.

"The brown is a good one, I see," said he. "Well, I'll stick by what I said, though. And if the gray feels like galloping today, you'll see him run right over your horse."

"I have fifty dollars," said Ingram, "that says he won't."

Mr. Tarron's face turned actually gray.

"Fifty dollars?" he echoed huskily, for very little hard cash really passed through his hands in the course of a year.

Then he remembered a sock filled with savings that was hidden away in the house against some great crisis in their life.

"Wipe out that handicap," he said, "and I'll take your bet."

"You've got a fresh horse against a tired one," insisted Ingram.

"Then, damn it, I'll take your bet as it stands!" cried Tarron. "Go on, Les, and if you ever woke up in your life, wake up now!"

Les Tarron was already on the gray. A surcingle furnished him with a seat, and for a bridle there was a light bitless halter on the colt's head.

"Get in place, Harry," said Ingram to his man, "and ride that brown out like the wind. You know what she can do. Look to it that you get all the possibilities out of her!"

Harry needed no more encouragement.

He glanced rather contemptuously at Les, hunched ungracefully on the gray stallion. He looked at the rather coltish body of her gray. Then gathering his reins, he shouted over his shoulder: "I'll win this, and I'll win it without a handicap, too!"

"Do your talking afterward," said Ingram. "Are you both ready?"

"Ready!" they called.

"I'll shoot twice to start you. If there's only one shot, keep on your mark. Understand?"

"Yes."

"Around that birch. Now—go!"

He saw that at this moment Les Tarron had turned his horse to the side, and as he spoke, he fired twice.

The brown was off in a flash. The gray started floundering behind him.

"It's no race!" screamed Tarron. "It's crooked, and I won't pay. Jim didn't get a fair start—that fool boy—I'll skin him alive for this!"

"Go it, Harry! Go it, you little brown devil!" shouted Ingram entranced by the success of his trick.

The brown mare was already far in the head, and to the white birch and back was, after all, only a short race.

It seemed as though the brown was gaining, under the flogging whip of her rider. But expertly as Harry jerked the cow pony around that birch and started her back, the gray gained wonderfully in the maneuver, and as the animal straightened out for the home run, the watchers could see Les Tarron, lying along the back of the gray, laughing contentedly.

"By heavens," cried Ingram, "the kid thinks that he can win still!"

"He will!" shouted the father. "The lad never makes mistakes about horses. He'll win, too!"

There was not the slightest doubt of it. In half a dozen long bounds, Jim was up with the mare and went by her with his ears pricking, perfectly in hand. Les Tarron was easing his mount at the finish. And Harry came by well to the rear, eating the dust of the gray.

"She went lame!" yelled Harry, furious and bewildered. "She stopped for nothing, after she got around the tree."

"No," answered the leader, "she ran her race, and she got beat by a better horse. That's all. Now, Tarron, what's the price of this stallion?"

"Name something," said Tarron, grinning. "You've seen him run!"

"Wait a minute. Is he trained for cutting?"

"He's a young horse," said the other defensively.

"Good with a rope, then?"

"Young to train," said Tarron gloomily. "I'll sell a horse. Him that gets my colt can train him."

"Thanks," grinned Ingram. "You got a horse here that can't cut a calf, and that can't work with a rope, and you're asking—how much?"

"When I seen that gray foaled," said Tarron, narrowing his eyes, "I went back into the house and I told my old woman that we was five hundred dollars richer than when the day was an hour younger."

"Hello!" cried Ingram. "Five hundred dollars?" And he whistled.

"That's what my wife done when I told her," said Tarron. "But I've stuck by it even since. And I've laughed at them that offered me less."

Ingram turned his head once more toward the distant mountains, and back again toward Les Tarron, whose services were now placed at such a high figure. But he had had proof enough of the value of both youth and horse, and now he was eager to finish the transaction and carry the pair off with him.

From an inner pocket he drew a fat wallet, and out of that counted five crisp, new, hundred-dollar bills. He placed these in the hands of the astonished farmer and then called: "Get ready, Les. We start now!"

"Hey—what! I ain't through!" cried Tarron, who began to suspect that he could have obtained a thousand dollars from this affluent stranger with as much ease as he had drawn five hundred. "And what d'you mean about Les? Les, what're you doing?"

Les had come from the shed carrying a battered old wreck of a saddle, which he now strapped on the gray's back.

"I'm leaving," said Les Tarron.

"Leaving?" cried his father. "Les, d'you know anything about this man that wants to take you, and where he wants to take you?"

"I only know that he's taking me away," answered Les Tarron. "And any place over the hills is good enough for me."

He was already in the saddle.

"Hold on!" cried Tarron in genuine alarm. "I ain't gunna let you go. Your ma— Why, Les!"

"Lemme be," answered Les. "I been a fool at home all my life and now I want to see if I can't be something better on the other side, across the hills."

6

Like a Gallon of Water

MR. TARRON would not have ended his protests here. He was a comparatively slow man, but now, as he realized that his son was on the verge of riding away with strangers, his voice and his temper rose to a high pitch.

The huge form of Bert Ingram rode in before him.

"Get under weight, Les," he commanded. "I'll handle your father."

"I'm coming back, Dad," said Les Tarron. "I'm coming back to put everything right for you and Ma. Goodbye!"

"Les!" cried the father. "And you," he added to Ingram, "who are *you?* Where are you going? What work do you want Les for?"

"Work that'll keep him warm enough," replied the other. And he grinned gloomily at the farmer. "I've bought your horse, and I've bought your boy; be glad that I ain't touched a match to what's left of your family. So long!"

He turned the head of his horse, and rode instantly in pursuit of his companions.

They had turned the shoulder of the mountain, when he came up to them, and Les Tarron on the gray was in the lead. The others, having seen the matchless trail craft of the boy, were quite willing to give him precedence now, unchallenged.

He rode along at a swinging gallop until he reached the place where the trail near the cow pasture forked into two branches.

There he dismounted, and examined the ground with some care.

"He hasn't gone fast," said Tarron, in answer to the anxious question of Ingram. "And he took the upper trail here. That was foolish, because the rough ground will kill off his tired horse. And we'll surely have that horse before it's gone a mile and a half."

"If we have the horse, we have the man!" exclaimed Ingram. "Scatter out a little, boys. Let the kid work out the trail, because he can make a better job of it than all the rest of us put together. Scatter out, and keep to cover as much as you can. If I thought that the trail would be so short, we'd never have lost so much time on the getting of the gray horse. Scatter out, and go careful, because the man that Dorn sees is a dead man, as you all ought to know by this time!"

Under these instructions the men spread out, and so they advanced up the gorge, always slipping cautiously from tree to tree or from rock to rock, and sweeping every atom of the country before them.

"The kid said a mile and a half, and we've already gone a mile," said Charlie to Ingram.

"Wait a minute," chuckled the leader. "He ain't a prophet. He's only a queer kid, working out a hard trail. What does he find on those rocks, will you tell me?"

"He's got microscopes for eyes," declared Charlie. "Now tell me if *he* wouldn't be a hard one to follow and catch, particularly since he's got that gray under him?"

"As soon as this here trail is over, Charlie," asked the leader, "how long is the kid to keep the gray?"

"I thought that was his price?"

"He said he couldn't go with us unless he had the gray to carry him. That was all."

"I see." Charlie grinned. "And then he can walk back, after we've found Dorn?"

"When Dorn is dead, the kid can find his trail home without a horse," said the leader. "I've an idea that I could make use of that gray. It would carry my weight in another six months."

He added, as though some explanation were needed even to this ruffian follower of his:

"The kid was sassy when I first talked to him. Now he'll have to pay to learn good manners—with me for the teacher!"

In the meantime, the gorge along which they had been working narrowed and narrowed, and finally pinched away and came out on the side of the mountain.

The whole surface was dented with abandoned pits where miners in older days had sunk their shafts in search for precious metals. And, still surviving from the old time, a cable stretched across the sharpsided canyon to the farther slope. Along that opposite slope a roadway had been hewed roughly, and there the mule trains received the ore and carted it down to the smelter far away.

A very clumsy arrangement, but one which had turned hundreds of thousands of dollars' worth of metal into coin.

Now there was a sudden shout in advance:

"There's the horse!"

They could see the exhausted brute standing, head down, beside a trickling stream of water. The saddle had been torn from the animal's back by its master before deserting his mount; and now it was standing, with glazed eyes, intent on the difficult business of breathing and trying to keep erect on its trembling legs.

Whether it would live or die was a problem.

"And Dorn is somewhere yonder," exclaimed Ingram. "Now, go like cats. He ain't far off. The kid has been right about everything else—even when he said that we'd get the horse within a mile and a half. You would think that he knew the mind of a horse, wouldn't you? Go slow, now. Even if Dorn is hurt and sick, he'll still fight like a devil, won't he?"

These cautions did not seem exactly necessary, for the four riders who followed Ingram were stealing along like cats, keen for the hunt, but careful not to expose themselves.

There was another sudden shout ahead, followed by a humming, rumbling sound. At the same moment, the old ore car, which had not traveled across the line of the cable to the far side of the valley for half a generation, perhaps, came surging out upon the line and swayed with quickening speed along the wire.

"It's that devil Dorn!" growled Ingram. "Confound him, he's side-stepping us again! Plague take him and his tricks! Stop that ore truck! Who'll stop that truck? There's five thousand dollars for him that'll stop the truck and—"

His words died suddenly. From the racing ore car there was a spurt of flame, and, with a yell of terror, one of Ingram's men jerked his horse to one side.

The next instant all were in close covert, while five steady rifles opened on the speeding car. From its metal sides came back a rapid tattoo. But would soft-nosed rifle bullets pierce the stout old sides of that truck? And if they did, would the body of the fugitive be found within?

It seemed very doubtful, and even while he reloaded and fired, big Ingram was cursing steadily to himself.

In the meantime, however, another element began to work against the fugitive.

The ore car, which had run down the cable rapidly enough at first, quickly lost pace, and now, sweeping toward the farther wall of the ravine, it had to ascend along the slack of the ancient cable. The moment this point was reached, therefore, the way of the car decreased. It swung and staggered to and fro in the air, and a strong vibration could be seen running through the old cable across the gorge.

That brought a yell of expectant triumph from the watchers. Another moment, and the car came to a halt while it was still a full twenty or thirty paces from the end of its journey.

There hung the car suspended, and the man within was powerless to move his vehicle.

A figure came quietly up and sat down beside big Ingram, who was in a frenzy of joy and excitement.

"Kid," said he, "I ain't forgetting how much of this I owe to you. I ain't forgetting. It's the end of Dorn. It's the absolute end of him, and may he burn forever!"

He looked round at his young companion and found that Les Tarron, far from showing the slightest interest in his words, had turned up his face to observe the rapid flight of a hawk which, having gone to shelter in a treetop during the shooting, now took advantage of the lull in the firing to flash across the gully and high up into the blue of the sky at a pace which made the eye move rapidly to follow.

"Horses are pretty good," declared the boy. "But no horse can move like that. Not even Jim!" he added softly.

"I'm talking about Dorn," said the leader grimly. "Look here, kid, d'you mean to say that you're not giving a rap what happens to him? Ain't you even got any care for a man that has to hang out there and starve to death, unless he takes it into his head to throw himself out of the car and break his fool neck on the rocks under him, yonder? By heaven, I hate Dorn and I've let the whole world know that I hate him, but I've never seen a fellow in such a dirty corner as that, I can tell you! I'm sorry for him—almost. And I should think that a kid like you would feel your blood run cold!"

"Cold blood? Run cold? Never heard of that," said Les Tarron as he shied a pebble accurately, and splintered it against the face of a small rock twenty feet away.

"You don't care whether he lives or dies, eh?"

"Why should I care?" said Les Tarron. "What's he to me? Did he ever gimme a meal? Did he ever hand me a piece of good advice. Nope, he's nothing to me, dead or alive! Unless he should do something pretty fine, and it don't really look like he would."

The curiosity of the leader had become intense.

"What do you mean by that?" said Ingram. "What do you mean by 'Something pretty fine?' "

"I'll tell you now," replied the youngster. "When we was on this trail, I thought that this gent was holding out so well that maybe after I'd lived up to my contract with you and brought you into sight of him, I would just slip over and give him a hand to get away from you."

"You thought that, eh?" snarled the leader, his keen eyes narrowing.

"I thought that. But now I see him hanging out there in a bucket neither up the well or down, and such a fool as that don't deserve nothing except to be spilled out like a gallon of water!"

7

"Something Pretty Fine"

IT reminded Ingram very much of the attitude of a wild beast—of a wolf, say, which has regard only for the things which it may prey up, and those which it may not. So it was with this youth. There were in this world certain things to be feared. The first were of account, the others were worthless.

In what other manner would a beast of the forest think, and how else would it act?

There was only one sharp point of divergence. It seemed that one capable of a "fine" performance would gain the hearty respect, almost the friendship, of this singular youth.

"Just tell me, kid," said Ingram, "just lemme know how this here Dorn could have done anything finer than he worked while scooting up the valley ahead of us. What else could he have tried?"

"I'm willing to tell you that," responded young Tarron. "In the first place, he would have left his horse a way back and hid him in the trees."

"Would that have puzzled you any?"

"No, but it would have puzzled you. And he don't know that I'm on his trail. He don't even know that there's a fellow like me in the world. He should have hid his horse to hold you up. Then he should have hiked along up the valley, and at this point, maybe where there's plenty of water and good shade and berries to be had—he should have laid down; then he should have washed his wound, and rested, and waited for you to show yourselves. And when he got a chance he should have killed at least one of you."

"Supposing that he could!" cut in Ingram, who was nevertheless intensely interested in the recital of possibilities.

"He could have done it, well enough," answered Les Tarron. "He has the steady nerves, and he ain't unused to shooting at folks it seems."

"That would have left five of us to surround him!"

"No, he couldn't know about me. For all that he know, there was only five of you. He kills one. Maybe he wounds another. Anyway, at the most, that would leave only four of you. You have to circle around through the rocks. There ain't any place from which you could fire down on him, and there ain't any place from which he couldn't fire down on you. That would have made a good deal of difference."

"While we sent one of us to hunt chuck, and the other three watched him, and he starved to death here!"

"You think so? No, he could live for a couple of weeks on the roots of these here, and on the berries. Dry 'em on the rocks in the sun, and grind 'em up, and they're thick with seeds and stay your belly almost as good as bread."

Ingram frowned a little and bit his lip. He felt that he knew wilderness men and wilderness ways, but this youth was introducing him to a stratum of knowledge far beyond his ken. Far below it, too, perhaps.

He said finally, with a shrug of his shoulders: "He's badly wounded. That would have made it impossible for him."

"Not so badly hurt that he couldn't keep you all busy following him— and not catching him so very fast, after all. He could have stayed up here for days, until his wounds got better and he was all rested. And, in the meantime, you four would be having your dead man to bury and your own chuck to rustle, and you'd be pretty miserable after a while, because gents like you ain't very good for that kind of work."

"Just what kind of work? Fighting?"

"No, watching. The cat sits by the gopher hole. You know what I mean? You want excitement. That's where you're pretty weak. I would have laid up here and never made a sound. Finally one of you would have had to come up closer. You couldn't help it. You'd say: 'Maybe he's died of his wounds. Maybe he's dug a hole for himself and got away. Maybe he's asleep.' You would have thought like that, and felt pretty bad, and finally one of you would have come sneaking up to see. And after that," concluded Les Tarron, "there would have been only three of you to watch this here place, and that three would have been feeling pretty sick, and beginning to think about home, and bacon and eggs!"

"It's easy to kill men in daydreams," said Ingram.

"And in fact, too," said the boy.

"Did you ever kill a man, kid?"

"Oh, no. I never wanted to. But I could, easy enough."

"You got no doubt about yourself?"

"Nope. You see, it's easier for me to shoot straight at a living thing than it is at a dead one. I'm not so dead certain shooting at a rock. But a bird on the wing—I like to shoot at that!"

He nodded and laughed a little, rubbing his strong young hands together.

"I believe you with all my heart," said Ingram. "I believe that some day you'll be wanted. I believe that some day you'll be chased by a thousand men. Well, when that time comes, good luck to you! And if—hey—what in damnation!"

He broke off thus suddenly because of a shout from Charlie followed by a rapid firing of rifles.

A voice was crying at them from near by: "Wake up, chief. Dorn has left the ore car, and he's hauling himself toward land hand over hand!"

It was evident at once that this was exactly what had happened and that the man in the car had not the slightest intention of hanging in the air like a bucket of water to evaporate. Rather, he would leave the car and trust to the strength of his weary arms, hauling himself hand over hand toward the farthest side of the ravine.

The ore car, in the meantime, released from his weight, began to swing from side to side and to bounce up and down on the cable, not rapidly, but with sufficient vibration to make it extremely difficult, no doubt, for Dorn to keep on his way.

However, the oscillations of the car served one good purpose with Dorn. For at the very moment when a rifle was trained upon him, the ore car was sure to swing between him and the muzzle and the bullet sped not into his flesh but into the metal sides of the car.

Instead of having a certain prize in his hands, big Ingram now was confronted with the danger of losing his man altogether; for if Dorn could reach the farther side he would have gained valuable headway over his pursuers—so impracticable would be an attempt to cross that ravine.

Ingram's fury and impatience boiled over.

"Scatter to the sides, you fools!" he screamed at his men. "Scatter to the sides, and then you can plant a bullet in the hide of that—"

A wild stream of profanity followed. The men hastily scattered to this side and to the other, rifle in hand, until they could see before them the almost naked body of the fugitive flashing in the sun; for Dorn, in his last terrible effort to escape, had as a matter of course, stripped off practically all of his clothing. He dangled from the cable, swinging himself along with rhythmic sweeps of his arms, and in this crystal-clear mountain air, one could even see the play of the sunlight upon the gigantic muscles which covered his back and shoulders.

Big Ingram shouted suddenly: "Hold back, all of you! By heaven, nobody's to have the pleasure of killing that swine except me! Don't nobody fire a shot, you hear?"

They heard, and they stayed their eager hands.

"Dorn!" shouted Ingram. "Dorn! It's me! It's the fool kid and blockhead that's got a gun trained on you. Will you turn around to take the bullet in the breast?"

Another half dozen efforts and Dorn would have been at least close enough to the edge of the ravine wall to have thrown himself toward the brush which lined its slopes and trusted to chance.

Now that voice of enmity stabbed him and all at once he hung limp, dangling at the full length of his arms. The heart had gone out of him, and Ingram, sighting down his rifle, laughed with a black exultation, for of all the sweets in the world, there is none so entrancing as the knowledge that your foeman confesses your conquering hand before he dies.

Spirit was snatched from Dorn, it seemed, after his long and daring struggle for life, and yet, no—he could still make another effort. Gathering himself with all his might, he flung back to Ingram a defiant shout, and swayed his heavy, sun-polished body on toward the ravine wall.

That shout seemed to find an audible echo on the nearer shoulder of the mountain. There was a ringing cry of admiration, shrill and high, and the next instant Ingram's hat was lifted from his head, and, caught by a passing gust, whirled away over the liquid shadows of the ravine.

He started back with a cry of terror.

"Who—what—" he began, when another bullet sang through the air not an inch from his nose.

He asked no more questions; but his wild eyes, sweeping his men, saw them scattering hastily for the rocks, and shelter. He himself leaped for protection, and at the same moment his thundering voice announced: "It's that devil-born brat—it's that young hound, Les Tarron! He's betrayed me! Oh, send him through fire and back again!"

Thus wailed big Ingram, as though sure that this sudden flank attack would give his foeman safety.

Taking shelter under the lee of a rock, he pitched the rifle to his shoulder. Yonder was Dorn, still struggling toward safety with weary, heaving shoulders;

but as Ingram curled his trigger finger ready to launch the bullet, he saw his target suddenly drop downward.

Dorn had tumbled into a mass of shrubbery against the farther wall, and five rapid-fire rifles poured a hasty hail of lead at the spot where he had disappeared. There was still at least one good chance out of two that they would nail him.

But Ingram was too furious, for his part, to aim straight. A black mist of fury kept swinging across his eyes.

"May I get 'em both!" he sobbed, in the ecstasy of his anger. "May I get 'em both! *Charlie!*"

"Yes?"

"Did the kid really get the gray colt, too?"

"I don't see the gray anywhere."

"Ten thousand damnations!" shouted big Ingram. "That gives us ten times as much work for getting him!"

8
A Drifting Log

LES TARRON, among the rocks, was amusing himself to the top of his bent. Five men were attempting to force their way across the mountainside toward him, but he had in his hand Charlie's Winchester, an excellent and new gun, and around his hips was the cartridge belt of another of Ingram's riders. So that he was supplied with a gun and with ammunition.

He was not shooting to kill; he was not even shooting to wound. For this appeared to Les Tarron only a game—a complicated and dangerous game, to be sure—but, nevertheless, one to be mightily enjoyed.

He had three problems before him, while retreating. In the first place, he must keep under cover. In the second place, he must break that cover to observe his advancing enemies. In the third place, he must break that cover to fire upon them.

He managed it with the greatest possible adroitness. The gray colt, Jimmy, had been sent on ahead, and like an obedient dog the fine horse wandered in the lead, now and then tossing up its head with a snort as bullets whined through the air close by. Behind the horse came the master. He was never in one spot long and, shifting constantly to one side or another, or drawing back, he never showed himself twice in the same spot.

All that was to be seen of him at the best was a mere flash of face at the corner of a shrub or a stone, and in a single instant he had seen what he wished to see. Or else there was a single flash of rifle or revolver, and a bullet sped down the mountainside to clip within half an inch of a head, or to cut through the sleeve of a man who hardly dreamed that he was exposed.

The five men, infuriated by this tantalizing fire, and never dreaming that these bullets were not intended to kill, grew hotter and hotter for their work and in their eagerness to close with the foe, for each of them felt that he had escaped death at least once by the merest hair's breadth. Yet they had learned caution, and not one of them dared to advance except on hands and knees from shelter to shelter, or even like snakes, wriggling forward.

Whenever the faintest chance offered, they sent a hail of lead at the fugitive. But they scored no hits, and they knew it; for ahead of them, time and again, they heard a burst of half-manly, half-boyish laughter, as Les Tarron slipped away before them.

Who has not felt the joy of a game of tag, and the thrill of passing just under the tips of another's fingers? But Les Tarron was to be tagged with a slug of lead from a Colt .45, or a large caliber Winchester.

When he was halfway down the slope, he suddenly increased his rate of retreat. He caught the gray colt, sprang to his back, and sent him scampering to the rear. It was a singular thing to see Jimmy running like a mountain goat along the steeply angled hillside; but he had been raised among the mountains, and he had learned to jump from rock to rock and hold his footing by turning up his toes and letting the spongy frog of the hoof do the gripping.

So Jimmy carried his young master lightly down the hillside and before Ingram had the slightest idea of what was happening there was a rattling of stones toward the bottom of the ravine. Then, spying down among the shadows, he saw a bright, fleeting glimpse of Jimmy as the good horse passed into the densely sheltering thicket of the river bottom.

In the meantime, what had become of Dorn?

Unless he had been pierced by one of the bullets that were showered at the point where he disappeared into the brush, he by now had had a fine respite, and it might well be that he had moved on. But in what direction? Had he gone on over the ridge, or had he turned back and wandered up the headwaters of the creek? Or had he simply blundered feebly downstream?

But there had been no question of further walking with Dorn. He had been thoroughly exhausted already, and the strain of swinging himself along the cable by hand had completed the wreck of his forces.

He had rolled down through the thicket more like a log than a man; then he had lain on his back and, while gasping in his breath, had looked up through a gap in the treetops and watched the spitting guns on the hill above him—five guns against one!

What mysterious enemy had arisen against his pursuers then?

He was too enfeebled even to think. When he could rise, he staggered to the edge of the water, not because he had any plan, but simply because it was downhill.

There he saw a half-rotted log stuck against the shore. It gave him a thought. He thrust it from the bank and lay face down upon it, embracing it loosely with his nerveless arms. In that fashion he floated down the stream.

Had the water been swifter, it would have spun this natural raft like a top. Had it been shallower, he would quickly have grounded on any one of a hundred banks. But the water that day was neither too high nor too low, and kind gods who had watched the persecution of Dorn now came to succor him.

He thought neither of gods nor men. He thought not at all. Utter exhaustion had blanked his mind, and now he relaxed like one who has been pierced by a bullet.

Pierced he had been, but no wound he had received could compare with the dreadful drain of his fatigue.

His eyes closed. He slept, with his hand trailing into the snow water and growing frozen, and with the sun burning into his back. He slept, and every breath during his sleep was a deep moan of relief.

And, in his sleep, he only knew that he was constantly drifting on and on. It was no longer the legs of an exhausted horse to which he had to trust. It was no longer to his own failing power that he had to commit himself. The river at its own pleasure carried him softly on and left his enemies, if it pleased God, far behind him.

Such was the sleeping mind of the fugitive, when it seemed to him that the sun passed behind a cloud, and the motion of the river ceased.

All that had kept him unconscious during that hour of drifting had been the sense of motion. Now, as that sense was lost, he roused himself suddenly and sat up on the log.

It threatened to roll over with him. The trees wavered before his eyes. And then he saw that before him there was a new enemy—a man sitting on a rock at the verge of the stream, while a gray horse stood near by, picking at the green, tender tips of the shrubs and watching the shining face of the water and every shadow that dappled its surface.

Dorn rallied himself.

He had slept for only an hour, but with what an incalculable value had been invested that brief time of rest! For now he could think and feel. Life, which had hardly been more than a blurred mist, was now a desirable thing. The taste for it had come back. Yes, with a violent passion he saw that he loved life as he had never loved it before.

And, having slipped through the hands of the terrible Ingram and his band, he was now confronted by a youth of less than twenty, surely.

Here was something hardly to be feared. Rather was it not in the nature of a gesture from heaven itself? This man had been sent across his way to provide him with clothes, weapons, ammunition, with everything that he had thrown from him when he made the attempt to leave the car and get to the valley wall.

So Dorn, lifting his bearded face from the boy, smiled at the stranger.

"Hey—hello!" said he. "It looks as though I've been asleep."

"Aye, it looks that way."

"Have you been sitting here watching me long?"

"Not more'n half an hour."

"What? Half an hour?"

"Yes, about that long. You started to wake up as soon as you got into the shadow. But it took you a long time to come around."

"Half an hour here?" echoed Dorn.

He stretched out his naked arms. One could see, then, the strength which had defied Ingram through the long pursuit. Dorn was not a young man; he was all of forty. But at that age, when some men grow soft and flabby, others grow mightier than ever. The head is a little slower and the step a little heavier. But the eye is more steady, and the hand has an enormous weight which it lacked in younger and more athletic years.

So it was with Dorn. He had been a mighty man in his youth. He was a mightier man now. If he had not quite the lightning foot and hand which the boxer needs, he had the cunning and the vast weight of power which the wrestler requires.

And now Dorn schemed only how he might be able to lay his grip upon this young man. That was all! Once that grip was established, he would master the youngster, strip him of those possessions which were necessary to his own existence, and then he would pass on, leading that gray horse over the rough, and riding it over the smooth. If only that horse had looked a little more powerful!

In the meantime, was this boy simply a country yokel, or was he a member of the Ingram gang, keeping post here, while Ingram and the rest rushed up to close in their arch enemy?

He would not ask questions. With that resolution, Dorn worked his way to the end of the log until his bare feet touched the muddy bottom; then he waded for the shore.

When Dorn stood up, he looked larger than ever, for he stood several inches over six feet, and thirty or forty pounds more than two hundred were distributed on his magnificent frame. He had been hurt, too, and one could see in his bare side the half crimson, half purple gash which a bullet had made in raking his ribs. But one hardly thought of such an injury seriously enfeebling him. For so great were his strength and his bulk that such scratches were merely like small indentations on the broad trunk of an oak.

9
Slippery Shores

ONE long stride brought Dorn to the shore. There he slipped a little in the slime and the mud and staggered. The youngster on the bank instantly extended a hand which Dorn grasped, and, drawing himself up, he changed his grip from that hand to the body of his assistant and flung himself with all his power upon the smaller and younger man.

He saw a hand flash down toward a gun, and he seized the forearm and began to twist the arm with all his might. In just such a manner, taking a clever purchase, he had once broken a strong man's arm. But now he felt muscles leap out like steel ridges beneath the covering skin. The arm twisted out of his grasp. He threw his whole might into a bear-hug that should have fairly broken the back of the smaller man. Instead, the comparatively slender body of Les Tarron swelled with prodigious power, and then—

Dorn could never exactly understand how it had been done. But all at once he was lifted and whirled; then he lay upon the ground.

Over him leaned a face as cold as iron, and eyes like the eyes of a tiger blazed down at him. A clawlike hand closed over his throat—

Then he was raised swiftly and lightly to his feet.

"I guess I understand," said the youth. "You didn't have much, and you thought that you might help yourself to what I've got. Was that it?"

Dorn smiled suddenly and frankly.

"You've taught me a lesson, lad," said he. "I came down this creek nearer dead than living, and I acted as other desperate men might have acted. The fact is that I'm more than half starved, pretty badly hurt, nearly naked, as you can see for yourself; and behind me are five fighting men, all well mounted, and wanting nothing so much as my scalp. Now, if I haven't made an enemy out of you, too, I want to know what you'll do for me? Have you anything to say? Anything, I mean, beyond the fact that I've tried to treat you like a snake?"

"Get on that horse," said the youngster. "He'll take you along; you can't travel overland with bare feet, you see."

With a foot already in the stirrup, Dorn asked almost fiercely: "Will you trust me with this horse, lad, after what—"

"It's not much of a trust, as a matter of fact," Tarron smiled. "You simply couldn't ride Jimmy away if you tried."

"Hello! And why not?"

"Because he'd come back to me if I called to him."

"Even if I used a whip to him?"

"That would only make him buck you off. Come here, Jimmy!"

Dorn pulled back on the reins with all his might, but the stallion shook his head and trotted up to his master.

"The confoundedest thing that I've ever seen," said Dorn, panting with his effort. "And now what do we do?"

"Ingram is coming down the valley," said Tarron. "But he's still a half mile away. That gives us time. You ride Jimmy in the water there where the water's shallow and the sand is firm. You can tell by the clean face of the sand and the way that it shines back at the sun, like gold."

Dorn obeyed without a word. And, combing his thick beard with his fingers, he found himself being carried down the course of the stream smoothly and easily, while his young guardian followed on the bank.

"They must be coming close!" cried Dorn at last, growing tense with impatience.

"Listen!" said the boy.

He raised his hand, and Dorn, straining his ears, could hear the crashing of the brush farther up the valley.

"They're coming," gasped Dorn. "And if—"

"Don't do it," said the boy. "I've got a rifle and a revolver, as you see, and I could kill you easy with either of them. And I'd do it, too, as sure as I'm standing here. You understand?"

Dorn stared into the calm, quiet face, and nodded.

"I understand," he said gloomily. "But what are we to do?"

"They'll slow up pretty soon when the trail goes out."

"They're the very devil in following hard trails. I know by experience, my lad. They may cast straight ahead and so come on us here!"

"I don't think that they will, though. Ingram is too hot to kill you, and he won't take chances of overrunning your trail. You can depend upon that!"

"You know Ingram?"

"I know him today. I know that he wants your scalp!"

"Aye, and he does, though," said Dorn. And he added through his teeth: "But he'll never have it. He's chased me and hounded me for a long time, but he's never had me. And he never will have me—only what's to be done now? Something quick! Something quick! Let me just give this good horse his head—"

"No," said the boy firmly.

"Wait!" said Dorn. "I'll buy him from you."

"There was five hundred dollars paid down for that horse today in hard cash," said Les Tarron.

"What's your name?"

"Tarron—Les Tarron."

"Tarron, I'll give you a thousand! Take it out of this wallet and if you help yourself to an extra hundred or so, it will do no harm—but this horse has got to be mine!"

The wallet was not taken.

"I won't sell," Les said calmly.

"Rent him, then!"

There was a sound of horses breaking through the underbrush along the stream. It threw Dorn into a panic.

"Tarron," he cried, "rent the horse to me! Take the thousand, take two thousand if you like, and let me go with him."

"You don't mean that much to me," said Tarron coldly. "I want you to win, and I'm taking my chances with you. But I won't let you take the gray. And if you try to make a break—I tell you, I can shoot straight!"

One last frantic glance was cast at him by Dorn, and then the latter surrendered.

"Have it your own way. Whatever you decide on, I've got to do; but remember that if Ingram finds you with me, you're the deadest lad in these mountains."

"Ingram find *me*?" said Les Tarron. He laughed.

"No," he said, "whatever happens, Ingram won't find me! Ingram is pretty blind, you know."

"Ingram blind—a poor trailer, you mean? Well, young man, let me see what you do. I have my own opinion about what that fiend of an Ingram can do at working out trail puzzles."

"Here we are," said the youngster, as they came to a point where a slender rivulet wandered down into the main creek. "Turn Jimmy up here and keep him going."

Dorn hesitated only an instant, then he rode the horse up the little run of water.

"We're hemming ourselves in against the wall of the valley," he complained. "There's no way out if they catch us here."

"They won't catch us. They're too hot on the trail."

"But if they miss me, they'll still have your footprints on the bank."

"No," said Tarron. "Because I'm leaving no footprints that they can read."

Dorn, glancing askance at him to see if this were a joke, noticed that as a matter of fact the boy's foot never fell on the sand. Where grass grew short and compact, there he stepped with wonderful lightness; or on stones, or on fallen tree trunks. Sometimes he had to bound from one place to another; but the older man began to understand how it was that even a keen eye would hardly be able to decipher the trail which he left.

A scant hundred yards from the start, the rivulet was found to tumble down the sheer wall of the canyon.

"Now?" inquired Dorn.

"We'll stop here and rest," said Tarron.

"Stop here, right under their noses?"

"I hope that they ain't going to find us. For their own sakes I hope that!"

"Five to two!" said Dorn. And he added: "One of us hasn't a gun!"

"Are you straight with a rifle?" asked the boy.

"I've done a great deal of shooting."

"Favor your left hand a little," said Tarron. And he passed the rifle to his companion. "It shoots a trifle to the left. If you try anything over a couple of hundred yards, allow about two inches to the left. But shorter than that, it hardly matters much, unless you're trying for the head."

Dorn swallowed hard.

"That leaves you what?" he asked.

"This," said Tarron. And he drew out a Colt. "Take Jimmy out of the water," he ordered.

Dorn obeyed. Then, dismounting, he watched the horse take position behind its master.

They were in a little bracken of tall ferns and short shrubs. The trees before them made a thin screen, but anyone who advanced within fifty yards of them was sure to see the horse, at least. No; a word from the boy made the stallion lie down. And now Dorn began to breathe a little more freely.

After all, there seemed good reason to hope that the party would pass on down the stream. But if they turned aside, with odds of five to two—

He hardly cared to think about that.

In the meantime, the horses and the voices of the pursuers were passing down the canyon. Another moment, and they were at the mouth of the runlet. There, instead of passing on, they paused.

Dorn cast an anxious eye at young Tarron, but the latter smiled back blithely.

"It may be a party, after all," he said.

Dorn gaped. A party! Was that the opinion of this youth concerning a battle of two half-armed men against five fully equipped with weapons?

Then they heard the ringing voice of Ingram shouting: "Scatter and hunt!"

10

Five Riders Searching

ALMOST instantly they could hear the sound of horses turning toward them.

"They've got us cornered here!" gasped Dorn. "And if they sight us, how can we get away?"

"That's why they'll never look too close in here," said Les Tarron. "Lie low. And keep your rifle ready. If you'll take one, I'll take the other. And always remember that if two come together, you take the right hand man. If only one shows us, I'll take him!"

He snapped out these orders like one accustomed to command; and although Dorn was a fellow who had been through many a bitter fight, still he accepted the orders unquestioningly, with the instinctive subservience of a man who realizes that a superior authority is present.

They lay in the ferns. The gray colt was stretched out like a dog in the grass, his eyes glistening and his ears sharply pricked, as though this were a great game to him.

Glancing aside at young Tarron's face, Dorn saw that there was an equal joy in his eyes, and all the while he was smiling a little to himself. It made Dorn shake his head in wonder, but it also helped to steady his battered nerves. A companion who looked upon battle with a sort of hungry joy was just the man for an emergency such as this!

Then through the brush ahead of them, and not twenty steps away, loomed a rider.

Dorn set his teeth, expecting his companions' gun to bark at once, but there was no sound. He glanced at Les Tarron and saw that his face was suffused with blood and that the triangular muscle at the base of his jaw worked rapidly in and out. Plainly he wanted to send a bullet into yonder fierce rider, and also plainly he was holding himself in check with all his power of will.

Another shape came shadowy through the trees. It was Ingram—Ingram in person, turning his stern eye here and there in quest of his quarry.

"They'll never be here," said the first rider.

"Why not?" snapped Ingram, in high bad humor.

"Why, it's a regular pocket; not even a fly could climb that wall of the mountain. And Dorn wouldn't be fool enough to try to hide in such a place."

"It ain't Dorn that I think about," said Ingram. "I've finished chiefly with him—for a while."

"What? Finished with Dorn?" gasped the companion.

"Aye," said Ingram.

"Finished with Dorn, and the belt that he wears?"

Dorn's hand instinctively went down to his belt, which circled his body above the hips and against the skin. But young Tarron had not seemed to hear.

"I'll have the belt in the end," said Ingram. "But before we can ever get Dorn, we'll have to tag the kid with a slug of lead."

"That won't be hard," replied the other. "He's a smart kid on a trail, but he's too young to amount to much."

"Too young, you say!" snarled Ingram, and he added: "I'll tell you this, bo. Some gents get old in one way, and keep young in others. I've seen a lot of men that was wise and old in their own front parlors and was worse'n infants in the wilderness; and I've seen gents what was fools in town that was Solomon himself in the mountains. And this kid may be one of them!"

"You rate him high," said the other carelessly. "But one slug of lead would finish him."

"And five slugs would finish us," declared Ingram. "And maybe the kid is the one to shoot 'em!"

"Anyway," said the other, "two men can't ride one horse—when one of the men is the size of Dorn!"

"Aye, and I thank God for that! We got 'em in our hand. If only we can find how to close our fingers over 'em! But the worst day's work that we ever done was when we took the kid along to help us on the trail."

"It was," admitted the other.

"It'll take a lot of undoing, that job will. Go ahead, there, and ride through that shrubbery."

"All right."

Ingram's companion started forward; but, at that moment, there was a sudden series of shots and a yell farther down the stream. The riders whirled about and spurred their horses hotly in the direction of the noise.

Dorn relaxed on the ground with a gasp.

"I thought that we were gone just then!" he admitted.

"Did you think so? *They* were nearly gone, though. And, look here! If you hate Ingram so much, and if you need to get rid of him as bad as he needs to get rid of you, why not take a chance and kill him out of hand?"

"And let the law into this game, my young friend? No, no, I've dodged the law so far and I intend to keep on dodging it!"

"Seems to me," said Tarron, "that you'd have a pretty good proof of self-defense."

"What good would that do me? If they could bring a charge and get me arrested, that would hold me quiet and steady. And then a bullet through the jail window, or when I was being brought into the courtroom to the judge—why, those things could be handled so easily by them that they would ask for nothing better!" He added bitterly: "Besides, what difference would it make to me if I were to kill Ingram. He's only a unit. There are others. And the one at the top could hire twenty men as good as Ingram. They know that he's headed me off, so far. And that's the only reason that they keep him in command. But if he were dead, maybe there'd be a dozen they could get that would run me harder than even Ingram has done!"

He said this with an utter conviction that could not be gainsaid. Then he went on: "What's happened to call Ingram away from this spot?"

"Luck!" said the boy. "We're getting them puzzled. They don't know what to make of us, quite. And they're beginning to be nervous. That's why they started shooting. One of them thought he saw a shadow move like a man, I suppose. He began to use his gun. Listen to them chasing down the canyon! Him that started the shooting is ashamed to admit that he didn't have anything real to shoot at. And now all that we have to do is to go up the back trail for a ways."

"Leave the shelter here?" asked Dorn.

"Aye, leave the shelter. You can't win any sort of a game by sitting still, you know!"

"Yes, I know that, of course. I'll go if you say the word, Tarron!"

Forth they went, but new ideas were beginning to form in the mind of Les Tarron. He knew the face of Dorn and the face of Ingram. He knew that they were trying to kill one another. But their motives were all obscured utterly. He could tell that Ingram hated Dorn, but it might very well be that there was no foundation for the hatred other than the fact that he was trailing the man.

In the meantime, other items had been added to Les Tarron's stock of information concerning this singular affair.

In the first place, there was a motive for the hunt in something contained in the belt which surrounded the hips of Dorn. In the second place, there was a power behind Ingram which thrust him on along the trail. So much so that if Ingram fell Dorn declared that a dozen others could be hired to take his place. In the background, undiscerned and distant, there were powers which pulled the strings that caused Ingram to ride with his four stanch fighting men. Who and what were those powers? Who were "they"?

However, these ideas did not trouble Les Tarron's mind a great deal. They merely occupied him more and more. He had lived in a dreamy world of little meaning. Now he had been brought out into the real world, and that first contact with danger and excitement was like the taste of fresh air to stifled lungs. And he was utterly contented. He did not care where the trail led. It was sufficient to him that he was actually on the way!

Now he turned down the little rivulet, which masked the trail of Jimmy, as it had masked the trail before. They went straight up the margin of the creek for another hundred yards or so, and then Tarron at last gave the word to the big man to ride his horse up on the firm bank.

Behind them, Ingram and his followers had at last made up their minds that there was little to be gained by continuing the hunt downstream. They had turned back, and the noise of their horses could be plainly discerned to the rear. For all sounds were magnified and made much of and wonderfully prolonged in the echoing heart of this canyon.

"Let him jog along," said Les Tarron. "I'll follow along behind you."

Dorn, accordingly, loosed the rein and the stallion broke into a long, freely striding trot. It seemed to Dorn that he had never been conscious of more delicious motion than that which carried him with such fluid ease away from Ingram and his men. And when he glanced behind him, he saw Les Tarron running lightly in the rear, not at all embarrassed by the speed or by the grade up which they were climbing.

Such a man hardly needed a horse to help him!

So thought Dorn, and shook his head again. For the whole affair of this day was beginning to look more and more miraculous. It was as though the heavens had opened in his time of greatest need and sent this rescuer to help him. It looked, indeed, like the very hand of Fate.

Dorn began to relax all through his spirit, and, sitting back in the saddle, he abandoned himself to the superior guidance of this creature of the wilds.

In the meantime, they were coursing swiftly up the valley. They climbed past the point at which the cable and the old ore car crossed the ravine; and they could see the car dangling above their heads, now trundled a little from side to side in the rising wind. They climbed still higher. And then the ravine melted away and came to a point where the stream which had carved it joined the side of the mountain.

There the two fugitives paused. They looked behind them down the valley, and when Dorn raised his glasses to his eyes, he could make out in a clearing of the woods, five riders searching slowly for their prey.

And it seemed to Dorn a miracle that he was not down there still, and in the shadow of their danger!

11

For The Lost Cause

LES TARRON stood on the top of a hill where the last light of day was clinging, though the valley at his feet was deeply drenched in shadows. And through those shadows he watched the glimmering lights of a town begin to shine in greater and greater numbers, like golden bees coming forth to taste the sweetness of the night.

He turned back to the huddled heap of manhood; Dorn, lost in a profound sleep. For the brief slumber of the afternoon had not appeased the enormous fatigue of the big man. It had simply given him the little added strength which was necessary before he could be able to make the final effort to escape. All through the afternoon he had been failing, and a dozen times he had nearly fallen out of the saddle, so deep was his slumber. Now he lay prone and nothing would wake him. It seemed to the boy safe enough to leave his companion.

When the black waves of slumber were about to overwhelm Dorn, he had roused himself for a last moment and unbuckled a belt from about his hips. He passed it to his youthful companion.

"If anything happens to this," he had said, "I'm worse than done for.

I'm a ruined man. I'm too exhausted to keep my eyes open, and I'm going to ask you to take care of it for me until I wake up again. Will you do that?"

Les Tarron nodded.

"Mind you," continued Dorn, "there are fellows in this world who would shoot you down like a dog if they knew you had that belt in your possession."

Tarron nodded.

"Ingram and his men would forget all about me, if they knew that you had it. They would turn off my trail and never take it up again so long as they thought that you had the belt and what's in it!"

"I'll believe that," said Les Tarron, "but when I was with Ingram last he seemed tolerable keen to have your scalp."

"You were with Ingram then?"

"Yes."

"When?"

"Today. I helped him to work out your trail up the valley."

There was a faint shout of amazement from Dorn.

"Aye, aye! I thought that he was following me very close—for him! I thought that he had taken a new set of wits. And it was you, lad! But how did you ever happen to work for him?"

"For the fun of it—and the price of the gray."

"What? Jimmy? Did he give you Jimmy?"

"He bought him for me."

"But what made you leave him?"

"I told him that I'd bring him in sight of you, and I did it. I didn't tell him that I'd help him to capture you. And when I seen you swing out of the ore bucket and start for the valley wall along the cable—why, I seen that you was worth saving. So I just slipped off to the side among the rocks with Jimmy, and I cut loose at them with the rifle that I'd borrowed from them. That made them hunt cover. And before they could open up on you again, you'd dropped for the brush."

"God be with me! God be with me!" murmured Dorn. "I see how it came about. I see it and I understand it! I could almost have sworn that heaven had sent you down to me, lad. But I see, as a matter of fact, that it was only your own sporting sense of fair play that made you fight for me. Am I right?"

"Call it what you please," said Les Tarron. "I seen that it would be a better game helping you to get away from five men, than helping five men to get you. That was all there was to it!"

"Aye, lad," murmured Dorn. "Some day, when I'm out of this, I'll have a chance to thank you. I'll have a chance to tell you—"

But Les Tarron held up his hand. In his heart of hearts he was strangely bothered by such talk as this. He was not at all accustomed to it, for at his home whatever he could be forced into doing, was taken as a matter of fact and course. There was never any gratitude spared for him. And when big Ingram came along he bought the services of Les Tarron for a price.

This, however, was something very far different. For here was a man overwhelming him with thanks, and in a deeply moved voice, like one who means more than he can find words for. And Tarron felt a new sense of pain that hurt him more deeply than anything that had ever happened to him.

He said: "Don't talk like this. I don't want to hear how—"

He paused. He felt that he had spoken with a too brutal abruptness. But Dorn seemed to understand and added: "I understand, old man. We'll let it go, then! Only, I see how decent you are; and, after all, the decent fellows are always on our side of the matter. They hardly ever start with the others; but even if they do, they switch over to us, and stay with us to the finish— God help them!"

He added with a sudden burst of frankness: "Give back the belt, Tarron!"

He fairly snatched it, and added: "I was a hound ever to let you have your hands on it. So far as I know, they may have marked you down already, just because you've been with me this long and have been helping me. Because all of us that work—we've been marked down by them, and one by one they get us!"

These words sank deep into the heart of Les Tarron. He guessed at some enormous mystery, but what it was lay far beyond his understanding. It was a cause which good men supported.

"Then it ain't you that they're chasing?" he said to Dorn. "It's something behind you?"

"Me?" laughed Dorn. "Chasing *me?* No, I'm only the tool. I'm a mighty small thing, lad! But better and stronger and finer men have tried to do the thing that I'm trying to do now, and they've all failed! Ah, I've known a few of them, and I've known what's happened! People thought it was a little odd when poor Chivveley was burned in the barn. A man like Chivveley! But the two doors of that barn were locked, and oil was scattered to make the fire spread! Poor Chivveley—a hero, and yet he went out like that! And it was a queer thing, too, that Rogers should have fallen out of the big boat and drowned! I knew Rogers. He wasn't the sort to fall out of a boat, and he could swim like a water rat! I knew Barrister, too. Barrister grew dizzy on the edge of a cliff and fell and was smashed to a pulp. Another accident! Accidents will happen, you say? Three accidents, then. But odd that all three men should have been doing the big work that I'm doing now. Very odd, I have to admit! But it was no accident that stabbed Lucas. Suicide? He was the brightest-souled man in the world. Suicide? I always laughed at the idea. But I never could laugh when they said that Margent had been a suicide also. Margent of all the men in the world! Margent! Would he have taken poison, if he had wanted to end the thing? No, no, Margent had heart enough to use a gun and leave word behind him that the thing was his doing, so that no innocent man could be blamed. But they all knew— they all chose to risk their lives in the great work—and they all went down.

And I suppose that I'll go down, too! Today should have seen the last of me!"

Les Tarron was tingling to the tips of his fingers.

"But why not let me know?" he asked. "Why not let me know? I've wanted some sort of work—that wasn't work. I've wanted something that wasn't roping cows and cutting firewood. Something sort of bigger and better and harder—y'understand?"

The big man smiled sadly, and kindly and wisely, too.

"I understand," said he. "I was in such a mood when I undertook the thing. And I'm a dog to have talked to you so much about it now. As a matter of fact, the thing will never be done. But men will still try to do it, just because it's impossible! That's what makes it attractive—knowing that it cannot be done! And if I were to open my mind to you and tell you what I know and ask you to join, I can tell by the fire in your eye that you would. You're the meat that feeds the tiger—volunteers for the lost cause. No cause is great that isn't lost. Nothing is worth doing that can be done. Nothing is worth having that can be had. So we shoot at the star. Any star. The one that we see first, when our hearts are big. Your heart is big now. You want to try this way up the mountain. But I tell you, keep the humor. Find something else. Something that'll bring you glory, even if it kills you young. But in this work, you died—by accident. And people forget who you were and where you fell—"

He paused, his gaze fixed far above him, as though in fact he were staring at some distant star in the heavens.

And Les Tarron actually turned his head and stared in the same direction. Those who knew Tarron in the after days felt that nothing could have made him tremble. And yet trembling he certainly was at that moment. He hardly knew what the thing was which had taken possession of him. It was an ache of the heart and a blindness of the eye and a fierce, determined eagerness.

"You think I'm just a kid," said he. "Well, I am just a kid, I admit that. But I can do things. I don't know much—except about the mountains. But I'll take my chances like a man, I think. If you give me leave!"

"I've said too much," retorted Dorn aloud, and he nodded. "I should never have said so much as this. Never! But—what is it you want?"

"To help you guard the belt, for one thing."

"You really want it?"

"Yes, tonight—while you sleep. You'll be a dead man till morning!"

Dorn covered his eyes with his hand. Then he extended the belt again with a sudden gesture.

"After all," he said, "why not? Who am I to do the picking and the choosing? They would take you and use you, if they could see. And they're better and wiser than I am! Take it, Tarron—and God help you, and forgive me!"

That was what had happened, and five minutes afterward Dorn was asleep on the top of the hill, leaving his young companion to clutch the belt in his hands and turn it back and forth, and squint at it curiously, and fumble the little buckled compartments which composed it from end to end.

Strange things were passing through the mind of Tarron, and a roll call of names hummed through his ears: Chivveley, Rogers, Barrister, Lucas, Margent had died by poison, the knife, a fall, a drowning, and fire. They had passed away mysteriously—men who had devoted their lives to the service of "them." They had been destroyed by the long arms of the other "them" to whose service Ingram and many another man were committed. And was it all for the sake of this old money belt which had been given to him by Dorn?

Tarron, determined, on the instant, to examine that belt and see what it contained!

12
A Belted Knight

WHEN I think of Tarron on the crest of the mountain, examining the money belt by covert matchlight, other pictures come into my mind; and I see the young new-made knight watching all night over his arms—the shield which is to defend him and all who are defenseless, the sword which he is never to draw, save in a faultless cause, and the spurs which bid him never to sleep upon the trail of his duties. That is what I see, for I know what was passing in the heart of Les Tarron, sanctifying him, subduing him.

As he opened each pouch of the belt, a shudder of mysterious horror and dread and delight passed through him. There was no sense of guilt, for he had not been told to leave the belt alone. It had been placed in his hands to guard with his life, and had he not the right at least to see that for which he was willing to fight to the last drop of blood in his body?

Aye, and he felt that he was giving himself not for a moment, merely, but for all of the days of his life; accepting peril, devoting himself to some distant cause, great and good. Later, in the fullness of time, enough would be explained to him—all that he deserved to know, at least!

So thought Les Tarron, as he went through the pouch slowly, reverently, but with his heart on fire. And at every moment he lifted his head sharply and looked about him across the darkness of the valley beneath and to the darkness of the mountains above.

But no foes crept in upon him. And there was only the gray body of Jimmy, glistening by starlight through the gloom.

What did he find in the money belt?

In the first compartment, he discovered nothing more than a minutely folded letter of Dorn's mother to him, complaining because he was away so long, and begging him to return soon to his home and to her and to his wife and his children. It sobered young Tarron to read this, and to realize how full was the background of this man who now lay stretched in full exhaustion so complete that he drew every breath with a slight groan.

In the next compartment of the belt there were a few of the more delicate working parts of a Colt revolver—a wise precaution to bring them, to replace any that might be damaged. Next he found some silver money—not more than three dollars in all. After that came a rough sketch, which appeared to be a map, and Tarron was beginning to feel that he had utterly wasted his time in this matter when, in the last compartment of all, he found something of much greater value.

There was half a handful of uncut stones, green and red, and though Les Tarron knew nothing about jewels, yet he felt certain that these were gems of great price. If they were cut and polished—better still, if they were genuine rubies and emeralds—they would be worth a huge fortune, for each one was of considerable size.

What they might be worth, he could not guess even remotely. He poured them into his hand. There were eleven of them altogether—six red and five green; and he felt sure that the smallest of them, once put into a remarkable condition, would bring at least five thousand dollars.

This was the rudest sort of a guess. And in his heart he thought that he must have far underestimated the value of the whole.

He felt that he had the explanation of the mystery now in his hand. This was a fortune large enough to cause many men to risk their lives. On the one hand, there were people to whom these jewels belonged and who hired brave men to transport them; on the other hand, were people who coveted the stones, and who hired others to intercept the convoy.

Yet this explanation made the very soul of Les Tarron shrink. For a great cause he had been willing to risk himself. But for the sake of mere money—why, that was a very different matter!

However, when he reflected on the thing, he decided that what had been enough to command the services of such a man as Dorn must surely be worthy of all his strength also. And then there were those others—Chivveley, Rogers, Margent, Lucas, Barrister—all of them had given up their lives. And even though it were only for money, yet perhaps it was for money which was to be used in some great and mysterious good cause.

Tarron rebuckled the compartment flaps and belted the thing about his hips. Then he considered the problem that lay before him.

If he left Dorn, danger might come upon the sleeper. If he did not leave Dorn, they would find themselves in the morning very short of provisions, with the necessity of shooting game; and guns made a fatal noise in this empty wilderness. Moreover, they would have to continue their march with a single horse, and that would be out of the question.

The lights of the town, by this time, had reached their full number and their full brilliance. Complete darkness covered the sky, and the handful of little yellow stars huddled in the valley beneath promised to the boy everything which he and his companion could need. Les gave a final look to Dorn, made sure that the big man was absolutely unconscious; then he started down the slope, mounted the gray stallion, and galloped rapidly for the town.

It unrolled before him, in the starlight, into a handsome little village, with the rush of a mountain stream through the midst of it keeping the air in a tremor of sound throughout the central ravine.

Les Tarron left the gray in a cluster of trees, and, making the stallion lie down—assured that the animal would stay there without moving until he returned—the boy started for the village.

He did not go at once to the main street. He preferred to slip along through back yards, growled at by a dog now and then, but never betrayed. At kitchen windows and beside back porches he listened to fragments of talk, until he was sure that the fight and the escape in the valley across the mountains had not been reported in this place as yet. Otherwise, some reference to it would surely have been on the tongues of some of the people upon whom he eavesdropped.

In the meantime, he needed a horse above all other things. And he had that fat wallet which Dorn had entrusted to him and never asked back.

He went boldly to the hotel veranda, which he knew would be the established gathering place of all of the gossips in the town.

A fat, coatless man, in the doorway, with a cigar in his mouth, Les took to be the proprietor, and he went up to him.

"My dad is back up the valley with a wagon," he said. "We busted down. Our sorrel mare, she turned dead lame. Dad told me to go on ahead and see if I could buy or hire a horse to get us into town."

"Hello!" said the fat man. "It's kind of queer that he wouldn't have come in to do the buying himself!"

"Yes," said Tarron, "but he stayed out there to rub the sorrel down with liniment. He says that it's a strained muscle in her leg."

"What kind of a horse do you want?" asked the proprietor.

"A biggish sort of a horse," said Tarron. "And if—"

"Can't hire a horse to you, son," said the fat man. "I dunno that I ever laid eyes on you before. And if you got the horse, maybe I'd never lay eyes on you again."

"Well," said Tarron, "I'd buy a horse if I had to—a goodish sort of a horse, y'understand, if I have to buy it."

"I got some horses in my corral," said the fat man, "but I ain't got a thing under eighty-five dollars."

"That's all right," said Tarron, "what I want couldn't be bought for that price."

He was led out behind the hotel, and a little group of men followed to watch the transaction.

Lanterns were bought. A full dozen of horses lifted their heads and their bright eyes glistened out of the darkness toward the light.

"I'll tell you what I'll do, kid," said the proprietor. "You stand up there on the fence and take your choice. My own horse is in that lot—my special riding horse. But if you can pick him out—why, I'll sell him to you!"

"All right," said Les Tarron. "But what's the price?"

"We'll settle that later on."

"I pick the horse, and then you ask whatever you want for it? That's a good bargain for you!"

"Come on, Jeff," said one of the bystanders. "If you want to see if the kid knows horses, you got to give him a chance. Give him a shot at a bargain, because there ain't much chance that he'd pick out your Monte!"

The proprietor writhed.

"Well—three hundred dollars kid!"

"Hold on!" cried Tarron. "Three hundred for the horse that I pick out?"

"Mine is worth twice that, kid!"

"Three hundred for the horse I pick if it's the wrong one. But if I pick your Monte a—hundred and fifty."

"What?" yelled the fat man. "Not in a thousand years, I tell you!"

"The chances are twelve to one against me," said Tarron.

"That's true," spoke up an outsider.

The proprietor turned the matter over slowly in his mind.

"I feel kind of creepy," he said at last, with an embarrassed laugh, "at the idea of losing my Monte for a hundred and fifty dollars. But I ain't a four-flushin' cheap sport. I'll take the chance with you. You stand to bust three hundred dollars open if you don't get the right one."

"That'll do for me."

"Go ahead, then, and make your guess."

"Gimme a lantern, first, and I'll go have a look at them."

"All right! Here you are. Careful, though, because they're a wild bunch!"

"I'll risk it. If I can get close enough to talk to 'em!"

And he climbed through the bars, lantern in hand, and approached the little herd.

They swept together in alarm at his approach, throwing their heads high, their nostrils quivering.

Les stretched out his left hand, palm up, and then went gently toward them.

The horses quivered, they shrank, but they did not scatter and flee.

"Look, Jeff," said someone. "You better begin to shake. This kid has handled horses!"

13

A Way with Horses

FOR Les Tarron went among the horses with perfect ease, and those high-spirited mustangs which would run like deer if a man dared to enter the corral gate now quieted themselves and let him pass among them.

"What's he doing?"

"Looking at their backs."

"What the devil can he tell by their backs?"

"And looking at their feet, too."

"Yes, look at him handling the hoofs of that roan!"

"I see it! What does he expect to learn by that?"

"I dunno, but it looks as though he's got some system."

"Well, here he comes."

Les stepped out from the herd of mustangs and came back toward the corral fence.

"Well, kid," said the fat man, "have you come up for air and a second start?"

"No," said Les Tarron, "I've made my choice."

"You've made it?"

"Yes."

There was a breathless silence.

"You mean, kid, that you think you've picked out my Monte?"

"Yes. You say that Monte is in that caviya?"

"Yes, he's in there."

"Then I've found him."

"You have!" gasped Jeff in consternation. "Which one do you pick?"

"It's the mouse-colored gelding."

Silence fell upon the crowd, and then an impatient bark from Jeff: "Some one of you hounds done me dirt and told him!"

"Nobody told me, mister."

"Then how could you know so sure?"

"Why—"

"Monte ain't nothing to look at much."

"I didn't pick out a horse for looks," said Tarron. "I just picked out *your* horse."

"Go on, kid. You're getting kind of mysterious."

"No, I can prove that I had reason behind what I done."

"Prove it, then."

"You ain't a lightweight, mister?"

"No, not since I was a lad. What about that?"

"Well, a heavy man in a range saddle sometimes rakes a good deal of hair off the back of a pony."

"Yes, that's pretty true."

"Another thing—most fat men don't ride a lot."

"That's right," said one of the bystanders. "They hate to tuck their stomachs inside of a pommel, even a high one."

"So, naturally," said Les Tarron, "I just went out to see if I could find a horse with heavy saddle marks on his back, and shoes that hadn't had much work. And there was the mouse-colored gelding, with white spots all over his saddle, and his hoofs growed out long over shoes that ain't been changed in a long time."

"By the Lord," said the fat man, "I thought that there was something queer about it, at first. But now you can all see that there wasn't nothing to it."

He added, to show the direction in which his thoughts were drifting: "You can't expect me to give up my horse for a fake like that! A measly hundred and fifty dollars for a nag that's worth a thousand?"

"Wait a minute," said another, "there's a lot of things that look pretty simple after they've been done, but they're hard enough until the way has been showed. And I figure that this kid has a head on his shoulders. Let me see any of the rest of you make them nags stand while you paw them over and lift up their heels like you was their granddaddy!"

This remark seemed to have a great deal of effect, and Jeff, with a reluctant groan, had to nod his assent.

In the meantime, above the heads of the crowd, young Les Tarron heard a sudden sharp voice exclaiming: "It's him!"

He thought that that voice was more than vaguely familiar to him, and he would have hunted for the speaker at once, at any other time. However, he had the matter of the mouse-colored horse on his hands at the moment, and the price had not yet been paid down. He merely scanned the faces in the crowd, and recognized none of them.

He paid down a hundred and fifty dollars for the gelding; and an additional thirty for a secondhand bridle and saddle, with a saddle blanket thrown in for good luck.

"Where did you say that you hailed from, kid?" asked big Jeff, mournfully eyeing the gelding which was about to depart from his ken.

"From over Buxton way."

"Did you know Chris Buckley?"

"I've heard about him."

This questioning did not please Les Tarron. He knew where Buxton lay, and that it was in the direction from which he must pretend that he had come with his fictitious father.

But as for people in that town, he hardly could connect a single name with it.

"But the father of Chris was the great old boy. You knew him, I guess?"

"Oh, sure."

"And the way that he used to crack his jokes about his wife?"

"Of course," said Les Tarron, strapping the saddle on the back of the gelding.

"Folks used to say that he would have been a pretty dull man if he hadn't been hitched up to a patient woman like her that was too deaf to hear his talk."

"I've heard that," said Les Tarron.

"All right, sheriff," said Jeff in a tone of greatest satisfaction.

At that moment, having jerked the bridle over the head of the mouse-colored mustang, Tarron turned to swing into the saddle and ride from the town, for he had decided that there was no use wasting time in this place in buying provisions. It was much too dangerous. Too much talk. Too many questions.

So thought Les Tarron, and was prepared to leave straightway. But, as he swung about, he saw a little wide-shouldered man standing with his feet well apart, a brace of Colts in his capable hands.

This sawed-off cross-section of Hercules called out: "Just shove 'em up, kid!"

"Hello!" said Les Tarron, looking over his shoulder. "Who's wanted?"

"You are," said the sheriff, smiling grimly. "You dunno why, I suppose?"

"I got no idea in the world."

"Put your hands up over your head and maybe I can tell you about yourself."

Tarron's hands rose reluctantly as high as his hips.

"Up, up! Get 'em up!" said the sheriff angrily.

Very slowly, Tarron's hands crept toward his shoulders and hung there, twitching nervous.

"He don't like to get them up," said the sheriff, calling the attention of the bystanders to the obvious mental struggle through which the boy was passing. "I'd say that there was something of the nacheral gun fighter about this kid, by the way of his hands. Get those mitts up above your head!"

The last was delivered in a savage roar, and as he spoke, the sheriff took a long stride toward Les Tarron.

The latter submitted to the inevitable and hoisted his hands slowly to a level with his ears.

"Up higher!" commanded the sheriff.

But there the hands of Tarron stuck, as though it was beyond his power to budge them farther.

In the meantime, directed by the sheriff, the willing hands of the fat hotel proprietor relieved Tarron of his Colt.

"Pat his pockets," said the sheriff, unwilling to give over the search so quickly. "And frisk him thoroughly. That kid has an ugly way with him, and we don't want to take chances!"

The fat man was wonderfully thorough. He brought out at last a formidable hunting knife, but there his researches ended without a further profit.

"I want to know why I'm stopped here!" exclaimed Tarron.

"You'll have a chance to tell everything to the judge," said the sheriff.

"I want a fair chance," said Tarron. "There's my father up the trail—"

The sheriff cut in briskly: "Your father? We've had your father on the wire on the other side of the mountains. It ain't likely that he's flown over here in the last few seconds, is it?"

That retort caused a stir through the listeners, and a sudden widening of eyes. The crowd gave back before the prisoner and his captor.

"What's the charge, sheriff?" asked someone.

"Charge?" said the sheriff. "Oh, it's bad enough. You'd think that such a young kid wouldn't have the nerve for it. But this one did. Horse stealing, boys! Rank horse stealing, at that!"

And Les Tarron saw surprise and sympathy fade out of all faces and instead, hard sneers of anger and of contempt appear.

Horse stealing? Of all the crimes in the world, he and his whole kind considered this the meanest and the most detestable vice. Horse stealing?

"Aye," someone remarked, "I could believe that. He's got a way with horses, and we've all seen him use it. Don't let him get through your fingers, old-timer!"

The sheriff laughed at this exhortation.

"I'd rather let a murderer slip than a horse thief," he said. "Keep back and give me room and don't bother me none. I'll handle this kid and I'll handle him without gloves!"

And Les Tarron knew that the man of the law meant what he said.

They approached a low, squat building, and as Tarron noted the steel bars which crossed the windows, he knew that it was the jail.

At the same time the sheriff called: "Here he is, Bert. And I think that was a good tip that you passed to me. I've got him, you see!"

And Tarron, glancing quickly to the side, saw the harsh face of Bert Ingram, now wreathed with broadest smiles of triumph.

14

A Cornered Wild Cat

Now those two things together might have stunned an older man than Tarron—the appearance of Ingram and that charge of horse stealing. But Les Tarron remained perfectly calm.

Clap your hands at a wild cat and it may flee a mile. Corner it, and it will fight as though possessed by ten devils. And Tarron was cornered.

At the door of the jail he said: "Will you tell me what the charge is, sheriff?"

"I'll tell you when I get you locked up safe. I understand that it ain't exactly wise to take chances with you, kid, and I never was fool enough to play anything but a safe game with crooks like you."

"I ain't a crook till I'm proved a crook," said the boy.

"Kid," said the sheriff, "I dunno but what you've got the law against me on that point. But I've never yet heard about a gent being accused of being a horse thief if there wasn't some sort of fire behind the smoke. Ain't that right, in your own experience?"

He brought Les Tarron into the interior of the jail.

The sheriff had been a busy man. He was always a busy man. But nevertheless, there were cobwebs in the corners of the jail's room. For the work of the good sheriff, like that of many another Western supporter of the law, was too often performed across the wide face of the desert, and the chase ended in a gun fight that brought death to the fugitive. Or else, the man of no law escaped from the man of the law and wandered off into the inaccessible deeps of the mountains, while the sheriff turned back to wait for a better chance and a fairer time. So that the work of his hands rarely had brought home a harvest to the jail.

Cobwebs gathered, then, and yet that jail was to be known among other things more for the fame of having held this same young unknown lad, Tarron, than for having such a sheriff as he who really brought the victim in.

However, that was a matter to be established in the future; and for the present the sheriff regarded his companion with a mixture of hatred, disgust, and wonder.

"You don't look like a snake," he confided to Tarron, after the latter had been locked behind the bars of a cell. "You don't look like a snake and you don't particularly act like one. But a snake you are, young feller, and if I had my way about it, there would be only one way of punishing a horse thief, and I'll tell you what that would be, if you would like to hear."

"I'd like to hear," admitted the boy.

"Well, kid, I'd take that there horse thief, and I'd take the clothes offn' him, and I'd tie him hand and foot, and then I'd lay him out an I'd stake him down where he couldn't budge too much; and after I'd done that, I'd lay a trail of molasses from him and smeared all over him to the nearest ant heap, and then I'd go off and I'd wait and watch. And pretty soon, when he came to be black all over with the ants, and when they was wandering into his eyes and out again, and into his mouth and out again, and into his nose and out again, then I'd holler out and I'd ask him what could I do for him? And when he told me what he wanted, I'd tell him that hell would be a lot more miserable for a skunk like him than the place that had been laid out for him there. Because I'll tell you this, kid, that God sure hates a hoss thief worse'n He hates the old devil himself. Because a hoss thief, he's more ornerier and meaner and lower and sneakier, and blacker, too, by heaven!"

He said this with a ring of honest enthusiasm that might have made Les Tarron smile had he been a little older; but young men are serious men, and Les Tarron was very, very young.

Besides, he had been jailed for horse thieving in a section of the world where it was considered the best of good sport and fair play to take a horse thief from a jail and hang him up to a limb of a near-by cottonwood.

Les thought of this, and he said: "Sheriff, I want to tell you something."

"Go ahead, kid. I guess I don't have to warn one of your kind that everything that you say now can be used again' you!"

"You don't have to warn me of that," said Les Tarron, "only I'd like to say to you that I've never stole a horse in my whole life, and that I wouldn't want to begin now."

The sheriff merely smiled.

"It's all right, kid," said he. "I can see that you're young, but you've already got the hang of things. You've got the face for it. I understand."

Young Tarron leaped to his feet and strode to the bars and pressed his face against them.

"I swear to God," said he, "that I never stole no horse!"

The sheriff pushed back the hat from his head. He scratched that head, regardless of the hat falling upon the floor.

"You never stole no horse?"

"Never!"

"Why would Ingram tell me that, then?"

"Ingram? Why, I'd tell a man that that ain't very hard to guess straight through to the end. Ingram? He hates my innards worse'n if I was a snake. He hates me that bad!"

"Why should he, you being a kid?"

"Because I beat him out of capturing or killing the man that he hated most in the world—hated most until he run up to me!"

The sheriff waited. But no more was said. There was no fierce or tremulous outpouring of emotion from Tarron. Instead, there was a controlled and patient endurance in his face and such bright, keen eyes were fixed upon those of the sheriff as he had never seen before.

"I think you mean something, kid," he said at last. "I'll tell you what. I'll give you a chance to meet this here Ingram and have a talk with him in front of me."

"I'd like nothing better," said the boy.

The sheriff left.

Les Tarron did not wait for the return of the man of the law; instead, he looked hastily and carefully about him. He tried everything in the room. A strong wrench at the cot, which was bolted down, brought one end of it up with a creak. A tug at the other end, and it was clear.

Tarron nodded with a short, gasping breath of satisfaction.

What did the looseness of that bed mean? Nothing, except that he had matched his strength against the strength of things in that jail, and he proved that he was the stronger—in one respect at least.

He stepped in some eagerness and confidence to the bars, and tried his strength on them. But there was not so much as a creak of protest from them. He tried his shoulder, prying against the bars with all the might of his body.

The faintest of creaks answered him.

But that was not enough. For the present, at least, he would have to admit that the cell was stronger than he. But something might be evolved later on for beating even the strength of those steel bars. So he stepped back, rubbing the coiled pad of shoulder muscles which had been pressing against the bar.

A moment later the sheriff came back, with the long form of Ingram striding beside him.

"Where's the kid?" asked Ingram.

"In here."

Before the cell the tall man took his stance.

He raised his long arm and pointed.

"Kid, where did you put my gray hoss?"

"Your gray—whose gray?"

"Listen, sheriff, he don't seem to me to be in a very fancy lying mood tonight. Is that the best that you can do, kid? I suppose now you'll say that the horse don't belong to me?"

"It don't!" cried Tarron hotly.

"All right! All right!" said the other. "I ask you—did I pay down five hundred dollars to your father yesterday?"

"You done that," admitted the boy.

"And did he give me the horse at that price?"

"Yes, he done that, too. I know that as well as you do."

"You admit it, do you?" asked Ingram. "Dog-gone me if I didn't think that you'd try to disprove that; because if you don't, where does the rest of your case lie? You admit that you seen me pay five hundred for that horse, and that I took the horse. Wait a minute. Maybe you think that I got five hundred back from this kid, sheriff?"

He turned to the man of the law, but the latter shook his head, bewildered.

"He just don't talk like a liar, though," said he.

"He's got brass. I ain't denying that," said Ingram. "Oh, he's got enough brass to furnish an army of beggars with, that kid has. That was why I give him the run."

"You gave me the run, did you?" asked Les Tarron.

"I took him along for a chore boy, y'understand, sheriff?" explained Ingram. "And dog-gone me if the kid didn't slip away with the gray horse that I had bought from his father. Done a clean and neat get-away."

"What's your story, lad?" asked the sheriff.

"He wanted me to help him on the trail. I wouldn't leave home without I had my Jimmy horse with me, and so he bought Jimmy, and told me that if I brung him in sight of the other gent, I should have the horse."

"Hold on," said the sheriff. "Sight of what gent?"

"One that was pegging up the valley on a spent horse. But his trail was near lost in the rocks. I got an eye for trails, and when I spotted this one, Ingram said that he wanted me and wanted me bad."

"By Gad," burst out Ingram, "it sort of riles me, sheriff, to hear the little runt talk as if I could ever have had any need of him. If it wasn't that you got him under your wing, I'd give him a lesson! But he knows that the bars protect him!"

Tarron sprang against the bars.

"You dead-eating buzzard!" he shouted. "Open the door of this here cell, sheriff, and let him and me have it out with bare hands, and I'll show you how much I'm scared of him! Or with guns or knives or any way that he dares to fight me!"

Ingram switched suddenly to a new track.

"There's your young, innocent kid that couldn't have the nerve to steal a horse!" he said. "Look at the face of him, sheriff, and look at the hell in his eyes."

The sheriff whistled.

"Aye," said he. "It's a picture that would sort of scare even his ma!"

15
Vain Search

THE sheriff began: "You claim that Ingram needed you on the trail? Shut up, Bert, and let me handle this."

"Yes," said the boy, "I claim that very thing."

"And he offered you the horse if you was to bring him in sight of the gent that was ahead of him?"

"I claim that."

"I've knowed Bert Ingram for a long spell," said the sheriff. "And I would say that he's as handy on the trail as any man that I ever come up again' in my whole life!"

He paused, and Les Tarron made no answer.

"What become of the man that was being chased?" asked the sheriff suddenly.

"He's off in the mountains with the gray."

"How come that?"

"He was fagged out and wore out. He had to sleep. And I come down here to get another horse, if I could."

"And then there ain't anything in your yarn about your pa being down in the valley?"

"No."

"Then you admit that you lied about that?"

"I admit that I lied about that."

"And where did you get the money to buy 'Fatty's' horse?"

"The gent give it to me."

"He's kind of large and freehanded, ain't he?"

"You ask me all of the questions, but just ask Ingram what did he offer me to go with him?"

"What *did* you offer the kid?" asked the sheriff.

"What would you offer him, sheriff? I offered him three dollars a week and keep for coming along with us and doing the fire building and the dish cleaning, and such, when we made camp. Besides, he said that he wanted to go south with us."

The sheriff nodded.

"That's all pretty reasonable."

He turned to Tarron. "Anything else that you want me to ask him?"

"Yes, ask him what he was doing with his four fighting men in the hills?"

"I don't mind telling you," said Ingram. "We got tired of Montana falls and winters, and when the nights begun to get a snap in them, we decided that we'd head south and try for a place along the—Alcazar."

There was just a trace of hesitation before this word.

"Sure!" said the sheriff amiably. "I know what it is to get tired of the long snows. Well, kid, are you talked out?"

"I've finished," said Les Tarron.

"As if," chuckled Ingram, "I would offer that kid a five-hundred-dollar horse to help *me* work out a trail!"

The sheriff laughed loud and long.

"And see the face of him," he said. "Dog-gone me if he ain't a sassy one! I got to go downtown, Bert. Will you come along?"

"I'd rather stay here," said Bert, "and have a chat with this kid. I dunno. Maybe he ain't so bad. I'd like to find out just what sort of a kid he is. Because maybe—why, maybe I wouldn't press the charge against him, that is, if there was any decency in him."

"That's talking like a white man, Bert," agreed the sheriff. "Every young fellow is a young fool in lots a ways. But they can mostly use a second chance pretty good. Take this key. Let yourself into the cell and sit down and have a chat with him, will you?"

"Thanks," said Bert Ingram.

The sheriff departed, and Ingram lighted a cigarette and leaned against the bars, smiled at the prisoner.

"You see how it is, kid?" remarked the tall man. "You got a sort of brains, but not enough to stand up again' a real man."

The prisoner was silent, watching and waiting.

"The jug would cool you down a bit," remarked Ingram. "It would probably do you a lot of good. Be a sort of college education in patience for you. But I hate to cut too deep. You're young. And if you'll gimme that belt that you got around you, I might call it quits."

Les Tarron blinked once, as a cat blinks at a sudden blinding light; then he continued to stare calmly at his enemy. Under that gaze Ingram grew restless.

"You know what it would mean, I suppose?" said he.

"What what would mean?"

"A jail term for horse stealing?"

"I dunno."

"About ten or twelve years. The judges in this part of the world are pretty hard on that sort of a deal."

"I didn't steal the horse. I done what I said I would do. I brought you into sight of Dorn."

"And then you quit me like a skunk and went over to him?"

"I had a right to do that."

"You got a right to stay in jail, too!" declared Bert Ingram.

"You don't scare me," said the boy. "I ain't going to give you the belt."

"You admit that you got it, then?"

Again Tarron blinked. Then his teeth clicked shut. Ingram laughed contentedly.

"Hard to keep from talking, ain't it?" he remarked. "Mighty hard, I'd say, when you got a man that knows how to draw out the words. But lemme have that belt and I'll call off the jail business."

"You can't bluff me," said Tarron.

"Bluff? Does this here look like a bluff?"

"It takes time to push through a thing like this," said the boy. "You got to have lots of time. Have to be a witness against me when the trial comes off—have to stay around here. And you won't stay around here. You're afraid to."

"Why am I afraid?"

"Because if you stay put they'd find you, and that would be the finish of Ingram."

"Who would find me?"

"You know what I mean, I guess."

"Lord!" breathed Ingram, "that fool Dorn has talked to you—to a kid like you!"

He seemed partly wrathful and partly amazed.

Tarron was silent.

"There's nothing for it," said the tall man. "I've got to come in and talk to you!"

He opened the door and stepped inside, holding a naked Colt.

"I'll have that belt, son," said he.

"You will?" asked Tarron calmly.

"I'll have it or sink you, son!"

"It won't work," said young Tarron. "You ain't going to leave a dead man behind you."

The tall man set his jaw and glanced hurriedly over his shoulder.

"I don't want to do it," he said soberly. "I hate to do it, as a matter of fact. But if you make me, there's nothing left. Don't fool yourself into thinking that I won't, if the pinch comes. The sheriff's gone. He won't be back for a long time. I put a bullet through your head, and then I cut loose and take my horse outside the jail and ride off. How'll they get me? Inside of two days I'll be where no man in the world can put a hand on me!"

He laughed sneeringly.

Tarron studied his face. Suddenly he nodded.

"You get the belt," he said.

"That's sense," said the tall man. "Unbuckle it, will you?"

Slowly, his eyes upon the door as though he hoped that the sheriff might return, Tarron unbuckled the belt. He handed it to Ingram. After all, it was better to live and try to get back the belt than it was to die and lose life and belt also. Even Dorn would agree that this policy was the correct one.

Ingram, in the meantime, had backed to the door, as though eager to leave. But impatience overcame him. He could not wait. He had turned pale. His eyes had grown wonderfully brilliant, and his face glistened with moisture.

Rapidly he unbuckled the compartments of the belt, took out the contents— and suddenly dashed the belt upon the floor.

"It ain't here!" he snarled. "You little rat, it ain't here! Hand it over before I—before I rip it out of you!"

Tarron closed his eyes and opened them again.

He could not help smiling at the thought of the apparent candor and frankness with which Dorn had given him his belt to guard. But now it seemed that that had been a mockery. No, the jewels, if they were real, were certainly something. But the treasure which was of such interest to "they" was vastly more important—so much more important that Ingram did not think the loot in the belt worth another glance. Not even Ingram, a man keen for money!

The secret cause for which Dorn and all the others had fought, and which Ingram and his peers had attacked, was now elevated once more to a position of commanding importance. It was once more a vast mystery, and the blood of young Tarron leaped.

He laughed in the face of the furious Ingram.

"I ain't got it," he declared.

"Why, you little fool," said Ingram, "do you think that a lie like that is enough to bamboozle me? No, no! Come out with it! I got no time to fool away over you! No time at all! Come out with it, or I'll find it for myself!"

"I'll never hand it to you," said Tarron suddenly. "If you want it, take it with your own hands. I'll never have Dorn say that I gave it to you!"

"All right!" nodded Ingram, as though this were a reasonable point of honor. "I'll tell them that want to know that you done your best to guard it. But lemme know—what pocket is it in?"

"The inside pocket of my coat."

"Stand fast—take off your coat—no, never mind. But stand still while I get it, or I'll finish you, kid, at the first twitch that you make!"

As he spoke, he came close, and ramming the muzzle of his Colt into the prisoner's stomach, he thrust his long fingers into his inside coat pocket.

"Golly," Ingram muttered, "this day'll make me a great man and—where is it?"

He reached deeper.

Les Tarron struck at that instant.

Ingram's Colt knocked away from his body. At the same instant it exploded and sent a bullet scorching along Tarron's side. But the shot had missed; by a miracle it had missed. Or was it rather the unreasonable stiffness of that trigger?

16
Breakfast for Two

INGRAM, with a moan of rage and fear, jerked at the gun to bring it into position for another shot, but he found his hand caught in a crushing grip, whose like he had never known before. At that moment a fist like a club of steel smote him beneath the heart. Darkness exploded across his brain— darkness lit by red, tearing flashes. Ingram dropped upon his face and lay writhing feebly.

Tarron paused to scoop up the fallen gun. He had no time for anything else but that and the rescue of the belt, for outside the jail he heard excited voices.

He leaped through the cell door and raced for the entrance. Crouching beside it, he heard hurrying footfalls and the voices of two men, one of whom was the sheriff.

They strode in.

"Bert!" cried the sheriff, hurrying on. "Bert—what in—"

A shadow rose from against the wall just behind them and sprang through the doorway swiftly and silently. Yet it did not fail to catch the attention of the sheriff.

He whirled on his heel, with two guns working before he was really facing his mark, and sent three slugs, not through human flesh, but through the stout oak of the door, which had been slammed as the fugitive darted through. Slammed—and locked with swift, deft fingers.

The yell of the honest sheriff was like the scream of a mountain lion in agony.

Outside, young Les Tarron was already in the saddle on the sheriff's own horse. He turned it down the street and hammered his heels into its ribs. It settled into a rapid gallop at once.

Straight down the street went Tarron, straight back toward the heart of the little town. He flung the horse through a tangled crowd of cowpunchers who were mounting in front of the hotel. He leaped from the saddle and confronted the fat proprietor.

"What are you doing here?" shouted that worthy, his face purple with surprise. "And on the sheriff's horse—"

"I've squared it with the sheriff. He sent me down here as fast as I could come—Ingram's trying to murder him in the jail—" Half a dozen shots in rapid succession and a roaring of voices in the distance seemed to reinforce his words.

"Help! Send him help!" yelled Les Tarron.

He did not need to urge haste. The cowpunchers who were idling on the veranda of the hotel had already gone for their horses when they heard the first shots. Now they swept up the street like a volley of arrows, with the fat proprietor and all other pedestrians sprinting to keep up and get to the scene of the tragedy as quickly as possible.

And young Tarron in the corral was busily throwing the saddle and bridle which he had scooped up in the shed upon the back of a rough-looking, mouse-colored horse!

For, after he had saved himself from Ingram, he had no wish to surrender the animal for which he had paid honest money earlier in the evening, and become a self-confessed horse thief by riding away on the sheriff's property.

The saddle was on and cinched. The bridle was on; the throatlatch drawn up, and now he heard hoofs pounding down the street again in the direction of the hotel, the half hysterical voice of one man dominating the rest—a man insane with fury.

Now the sheriff's voice was deep and harsh, ordinarily, and this voice was the voice of a yelling baboon, yet young Tarron knew that it came from the lips of the maddened man of the law. It came from him, and he would have blood to repay him for the insult which his pride had endured on this night!

Tarron listened and understood; and then, slipping into the saddle, he galloped the mouse-colored horse to the back of the corral. He paused there to throw down the bars. And now, across the front of the hotel, a dust cloud rolled, with horses and men boiling out of it.

"He's there!"

"No, here!"

"Look yonder across the corral—by heavens, that's him!"

A living screen had formed behind Tarron as he galloped Monte through the gap in the fence. For the other horses in the corral, alarmed by the clamor in the street and glad of this opening for escape, now swept through the exit behind the fugitive. And, like any Indian brave, Tarron had thrown himself along the side of his racing pony. Bullets, to strike him, would have to drive through the bodies of half a dozen horses running behind him.

There were fences behind him to be cleared by the mounted crowd, and cow ponies are not fond of jumping. They have neither the legs for it nor the knack of it. Gates have to be opened for them, and bars let down before they can burst through. And a running horse covers a thousand yards in a minute!

Before the ponies were well away, there was only a cloud of dust far before them, Les Tarron doubtless riding in the midst of it. For that goal they set themselves, but Tarron was already out of their ken.

At the first draw the herd of stampeded horses crossed, Les turned Monte to the side and cantered him easily up the depression. He reached a group of trees and, pausing there, laughed joyously to himself as he saw the dust cloud of the horses and the dust cloud of the sheriff's pursuit rolling behind the other across the country, leaving a long pale stain of dust through the air behind each sweeping body.

He was contented. He was more than contented.

To an ordinary man, there had been enough excitement and action to last for the rest of his life; but to the slaves of the mysterious power which Dorn and others served, such an evening was as nothing at all. A mere commonplace!

Tarron was still laughing softly as he turned his mouse-colored gelding up toward the distant hills.

Now that he had gained one object, he had no mind to return without executing the rest of his proposed mission. So he swung from his straight course toward the lights of the first ranch house that he saw.

He left the gelding, with thrown reins, at a little distance and, stealing up to the house, he saw a Negro cook in the act of finishing the evening dishes.

Five minutes later, the cook left a darkened kitchen, and Tarron entered to take what prizes he could.

A side of bacon, flour, salt, baking powder, some tinned jam, matches, and such incidentals as a great mince pie and a few other decorative details made up his plunder.

He slipped out a side window. Then, sitting beneath the trees, with the mouse-colored horse grazing near by, Les ate the pie with infinite relish, watched the lights in the house go out, and saw the stars gleam brighter and brighter in the central sky.

He was very contented. He had no flaws to find in this world or in the entire starry universe which the Creator had planned, as it seemed to him, so that brave men might ride abroad and win joy and mince pie at the risk of their precious necks. Such were the reflections of Tarron.

Then he mounted and continued on his way toward the rendezvous where Dorn must be waiting. Waiting and sleeping!

Prone on his back, his arms thrown out sideways, it seemed to the boy, at first, that Dorn was a dead man; and he leaned over him, half in fear, expecting to see the dark splotch where the knife had been driven home.

But Dorn was not dead. He slept the sleep of perfect exhaustion, however.

Tarron, curling himself into a knot, like a cat in cold weather, presently slumbered in turn; but he wakened at the first touch of gray in the sky, perfectly refreshed, perfectly alert, perfectly rejoiced with the work which might lie before him in the service of that mystery which Dorn followed.

And Dorn himself still slept, and continued to sleep while the boy prepared breakfast for them; and slept on until the eastern sky was a red blaze of glory, and the strong, sharp scent of boiling coffee attacked his nostrils.

Then he roused himself with a groan, and at the sight of Tarron, automatically grasped his rifle.

He recovered himself at once.

"Tarron!" he said. "God bless me, if I hadn't forgotten about you while I slept—and such a sleep! Such a sleep!"

Tarron grinned at his companion.

"All's well?"

"Yes."

Dorn's brain was still befogged. He staggered to a runlet of water that trickled out of the slope a little farther down, and bathed his face and hands. When he came back, his eyes were clear and bright.

"Where did you get this stuff, lad?" he asked, pointing to the food.

"They give away chuck to hungry people in this part of the world," said the boy.

Dorn cast a sharp glance at him and smiled in turn. He sat down to his meal without another word. But presently he cried: "Hello, there! Did that horse stray in here?"

"Strayed in," said young Tarron. He lowered his eyes to his coffee. "Strayed in and took his saddle off and made himself at home."

There was another keen glance from Dorn, but still he would not commit himself.

He finished his breakfast. Then he asked quietly:

"You have the belt, son?"

"Here."

Les handed it to the owner.

"Look inside," insisted Tarron, as he saw Dorn hesitate.

"Thanks," said the latter. "I will."

He examined the little series of pouches carefully and then looked with a smile at his companion.

"It's all right," he said. "I guessed that it would be, and it is!"

"And here's your wallet that you gave me."

Tarron handed it over, adding: "There's a hundred and fifty dollars out of that."

"Hello! Lost it?"

"On the horse, yonder."

"You went where?"

"To the town, yonder."

Les waved toward it. In the morning mists of the valley below, it looked a great deal farther away than it had during the night when the lights were shining from it so brightly.

"You went down there?"

"Yes."

"And got that horse for a hundred and fifty?"

"Yes."

"Is he a good one?"

"I made a bargain with the owner. Yes, it's a good horse. Not up to Jimmy, but strong enough to carry you; and fast enough to keep you away from trouble, I think."

"And you had no trouble?"

"Outside of Ingram, not much."

"What? Ingram?"

"He had me arrested for stealing Jimmy."

"The infernal—"

"The sheriff jailed me, but I managed to get away."

"Broke jail?"

"They left Ingram to guard me."

Les drew out the revolver which he had taken from Ingram and juggled it, a faint smile on his lips and a dreamy, far-off look in his eyes.

"On the way back, I picked up the chuck. I figured that it was owing to us, y'understand?"

"You killed Ingram!" gasped Dorn.

"No. just pasted him and left while he was sleeping."

Dorn leaned back against a rock and whistled long and softly at the morning sky.

17
What Flies by Night

AFTERWARD he said: "Lad, I'll tell you what I can do for you, and then I'll tell you what you can do for yourself. First of all I want to say that if I hadn't been sick and helpless with weariness and this wound in my side—why, I would never have let you tie yourself up with me for a moment. But now, I'll give you two thousand dollars that I have in this wallet. Never fear, it'll leave me still plenty of money for myself. After that, you can take your Jimmy horse—unless you'll sell him to me for a fat price, because God knows I'll need his speed—and ride for the nearest railroad. When you get to it, try for the first train that passes. Build a bonfire on the tracks. Do anything to flag it. And when you've managed that, get aboard and go wherever it will take you—north or south or east or west. Keep traveling until you come to the limit of this country; and when you get to Canada or Mexico don't stop there, but keep straight on. Keep flying. Put an ocean between you and the States. Change your name. Grow a mustache. Take up a new business. Change all your habits. Never mention the place you come from. And—if you do all of these things—you have a fair chance of living. But even then the chances won't be much more than even. They got Chandler in Java, and they killed poor Richards in the hills of Brazil. But it's worth your try. Life, Tarron, life is what you'd be flying for!"

"All right," murmured the boy. "If I run that way, which way will you run?"

"Ah," said Dorn, "I've committed myself. I've tasted the fire. It'll always burn in me until I do my work—or the work does for me. I can't give it up. I've gone too far. But you're only on the threshold."

"Well," said Les Tarron, thoughtfully, "there ain't any doubt that you mean what you say. You want me to pull out!"

"I want nothing more. I'd be haunted, youngster, if any harm came to you because I'd led you into this mess."

"I'll tell you about myself," said the boy. "I've been a lazy hound all my life. Never no good at anything. Nothing but a waste around the farm. But now I've hit something that I'm interested in. Peace, it don't interest me much. Money don't bother me none. Good chuck I can do without. But I been living all this while waiting for something to wake me up. And I think that you've brought the thing along with you. Because if it hadn't been for you, why, one of these days I would have got a gun and gone out hunting excitement on my own account."

His glittering eyes looked straight at Dorn.

"I've had thoughts of doing it often!" he added slowly.

Dorn, sitting bolt erect, frowning with interest, nodded.

"I don't ask no questions," said the boy. "You can use me for anything that you want me for. And I'll help to push you along your trail, wherever you want to go."

"La Paz."

"I dunno much about it."

"It's south and west, in the mountains."

"We'll head for that, then."

"Do you mean what you're saying?"

"Nobody ever meant nothing more!"

"Without even knowing what the trail is for, and what the thing is that I carry?"

"No."

"Whether in my hand or in my mind?"

"No."

"Then shake hands with me, Tarron!"

"I'm glad to do that."

"We'll finish the trail together?"

"We'll finish it together, Dorn."

"And in a day or so, when I know you better, I'll try to tell you what it's all about."

"I ain't impatient," said Tarron. "Things happen along this trail, and that's all that I'm interested in."

The sun still shone upon the mountains above the little town of Santa Trista. But the town was already in darkness, except for the mountain glow which was still reflected upon the big square bell tower of the church.

The town of the "sad saint," under the burden of the premature dimness, was preparing for the night. Dinners had been cooked and eaten. Men sat in the doorways with their cigarettes. Behind them, the women worked in their kitchens to clean the supper dishes. In the streets before them, dogs and children and rooting pigs worked through the dust, raised it in clouds, and filled the air with dirt and noisy merriment.

Into this town rode Dorn and Leicester Tarron. They threaded their way through the winding streets, with all the city turning dark around them, except for the still glimmering gilded cross above the church of the saint. They reached the hotel, and led their horses to the stable behind it. Water was pumped into a triangular wooden trough. The men stood side by side and watched their tired horses drink.

"How old it is, Les!" said Dorn. "Old, and sleepy, and forgotten by the world. A man could rest here. A man could rest here and forget even his sins, I think. Look! There are no electric wires for light or even for the telegraph. A century or two have slipped past them in this nook of the mountains. Perhaps they have heard strange tales of the other world which has managed to force its way up into the other valleys. Strangers like us have come in among them now and again. But I suppose they won't half believe what they hear. It becomes a fairy tale. There was a time, Les, when the horizons of men were more limited. They could not see so far. They did not have such accurate maps. The world was still a big and strange place. Much was still to be discovered. Passes were inaccessible in winter. Electricity had not taken time by the throat. And everything that lay over the hill was a fairy tale, and a miracle. This is such a place, Les. Poor devils! you say. And it's true that such a place as this will breed a thousand fools. But at last it will put forth a wise man; and his wisdom will surpass all the work of the machine, all the efforts of steam and gas and electricity, and all the cleverness of the magazines and the newspapers. You would not have to tear down a forest and make it into paper in order to print all the thoughts that can be born in a village like this, but some few of those thoughts may be worth more than all the standing forest, and all the words that could be printed on the paper made out of it! Do you believe that?"

"A bit less than half," said Les Tarron. "I dunno that I like the smell of this place."

Dorn laughed.

"That's true," he said. "There is one thing that time improves and sensitizes, and that is the human nose. The world is more fragant today than it ever was. But perhaps there are even better things than soap and water. You can wash the skin clean, you know, but what does the skin really matter. You remember that the old saints did not make a virtue of cleanliness. You may think they were fools. But perhaps they weren't. Perhaps they were a bit right in despising their bodies for the sake of something else."

"For the sake of what?" asked Tarron.

"I'm raving a bit, Les. Forgive me."

"It's all right," said Tarron. "When you get to talking like that, sometimes I understand a little bit of what you're saying. Like things that fly by you in the night, you can't tell whether it's a night hawk or an owl, y'understand? That's the way when you start in to talking the way you've been doing. But it's a quiet little town, all right, if that's what you mean."

The other hesitated.

"Yes," he said at last, "that's what I chiefly mean. And tonight we'll have a chance to enjoy a meal cooked and served by the hands of others."

"Perhaps," said Tarron. "But if I was you, I'd prefer to stay out in the mountains. They're safer a lot!"

"Tush!" said Dorn. "There's a place for caution, and there's a place where chances have to be taken."

"I suppose that Chivveley took a chance, and so did Rogers?"

"No more of that. I say that we'll wash ourselves with good hot water and soap, even if the soap is only homemade; and then we'll have roasted kid for supper. And, after that, we'll each have a separate room, and a fine large bed to sleep in."

"I hope that we'll not wake up with a knife in the back," said Tarron.

18
What the Moonlight Showed

LIKE a lover of the sun, long imprisoned in the arctics, and newly returned to the southland, Dorn expanded and relaxed under the influence of this quiet little town.

He was so gay and cheerful during dinner that Tarron could not help smiling and laughing in his turn. But all the while, the younger man was observing certain precautions, such as keeping his back to a corner of the room, and his revolvers ready at his belt; for by this time he and Dorn were both armed to the teeth with the finest and newest models of firearms. Moreover, he watched everything that happened with the keenest of eyes; not a shadow crossed the window that opened onto a little narrow balcony without bringing a glance from Tarron; and when the fat waiter entered the room with a burden of roasted kid or another flask of wine, he was constantly under the attentive eye of the boy.

Dorn, noticing this, laughed long and largely.

"Do you think, lad," said he, "that the news of us can have come even to this place?"

"I'd take no chances," said Les Tarron.

"You're a young fox, lad," said the older man. "But this is a place where you can curl up and sleep with both eyes closed. There are no dogs to chase you. Why, my son, they hardly know that there are steamers on the sea, they hardly know that trains are running on iron rails; and they're probably referring to powder and lead as new inventions. You don't know what these little Mexican mountain towns can be like. But I do. I tell you that when we topped the head of the trail yonder and dipped into this snug little valley, at that very moment we left the old world which we knew and our horses stepped across several centuries. We entered a region where there is only one dimension—that of space! Do you hear?"

"I hear you."

"Aye, you hear me, but all the while your eyes wander from door to window and from window to door. And you are even searching the ceiling and the floor. Now, what could be wrong with the ceiling, lad?"

"There are some little holes between the bricks."

"Certainly! And the good and sufficient reason for that is that the old house had settled a bit on one side and thereby has thrown everything out of kilter—the bricks have moved a bit. And so those chinks appeared. I noticed them as we came in."

Tarron was silent.

"Come, come!" said Dorn, tapping impatiently upon the table. "You

mustn't be quite so gloomy. It's not fair, my son. This is our cheerful hour.
Here, for a moment, we lie basking in the sun. Danger has left us. We are
free and alone—"

"Alone," agreed Tarron, "unless some gent is lying up there watching
us through a chink in those same bricks, or listening at them. He could
hear every word we speak."

"A great deal of good would it do him," said the elder man. "I hope
there *is* an eavesdropper. I'd be pleased to have some one listen to us and
write down what we say. I took a trip to the Himalayas one year with a
notebook fellow who always had his pencil out whenever—I say, Tarron,
I wish you'd let that mangy dog go out of the room! What do you see in
the starved, sneaking cur?"

Tarron, with a shrug, shredded away a portion of a tortilla from his
plate and offered it to the ragged brute, and the dog's starved eyes melted
with joy as he devoured it.

"You never can tell," said Tarron. "A dog can often be a lot of use to
you!"

"Tush! I think you've given him a taste of everything that was on your
plate!"

"Well," said Tarron, "make a friend of a dog, and the least he can do is
die for you."

Dorn struck the table lightly with his fist.

"By the Lord!" he said, "this is a great deal too much! You think that
some of this food may be poisoned, and you're trying it on the dog?"

Again Tarron shrugged.

"I don't mind wasting a little time," he declared. "And it makes things
taste better."

"Well, let it go," said Dorn. "I won't argue the point with you—but pass
me that platter of kid again."

So dinner went joyously to its close, and afterward they stroled through
the narrow streets of the town and watched the moon rise, broad-faced
and yellow, and cover the mountains with a soft, transfiguring light. Then,
back to the inn, and to bed; Tarron in a little chamber on the ground floor,
which he declared was plenty good enough for him, though it had only a
single small window; and Dorn, in the room just above, which was large,
comfortable, with an ample balcony stretching across its big window.

From that balcony, the scent of strong cigar smoke curled down to Tarron
as he lay awake for a time watching the single star which hung before his
window. But at last his eyes closed, and he slept.

It was a fitful sleep. For many nights, now, he had been sleeping out
under the sky, with the four winds blowing across his face; and the stifling
air in the little room half choked him, and he roused again and again with
a thundering heart and a sense of oppressive fear.

The third or fourth time this happened Les remained awake, listening to a new sound that sent a chill through his body. A small, soft sound, that seemed to steal across his room and stand beside his bed.

No. It receded. It seemed to stand in the middle of the room—

Gun in hand, Tarron raised himself softly on one elbow and stared about him. His concentrated gaze gradually pierced the gloom. Bare walls on all sides of him—there was nothing in the chamber with him to be feared! And yet, the sound continued, more slowly. It was hardly like a footfall, but rather like the dropping of water, falling slower and slower.

He slipped from his bed and dressed. After this, he knew that he would not sleep again that night. Moving gradually forward, his left hand held before him, he felt a drop splash suddenly upon that extended hand.

He drew back hastily—and at that moment something stirred the handle of his door.

He sank upon one knee against the wall, a gun in either hand, this time, and waited. Very slowly the door opened. When it reached half its width, it remained motionless, and a faint radiance penetrated the room—as from a lamp burning at a distance.

A moment passed. The stealthy sound of dripping water was no longer heard in the room. Tarron began to slip toward the door. A snake could not have moved more stealthily. He reached the opening, peered cautiously around the corner of the door—

There was no one to be seen.

Perhaps standing in the hall, waiting to lure him past the doorway—

More stealthily and cautiously still, he peered farther out. But the hall was still and empty, and only a single candle smoked and burned dimly in a bracket some distance away. He chanced to look at the back of his left hand, and saw upon it a bright smear of crimson.

He touched the stain—it was blood!

He turned hurriedly and lighted a match. There in the center of the room was a little dark-red pool; it had dripped from the ceiling through a chink in the bricks.

And above him was the room of Dorn!

Now Les moved like lightning, but softly as a hunting cat. He left his chamber, not by the door, but by the window, small though it was. A moment later he drew himself lightly onto the balcony above.

Standing full in the moonshine, Tarron peered into Dorn's room. A broad shaft of the silver light entered ahead of him and showed him what he had to see.

Dorn lay face downward on the floor, both hands curled above his head. Instantly Tarron kneeled beside him—turned him over—and saw his throat wide cut, from ear to ear, and dead, fishy eyes staring blankly up to him.

Dorn was dead! After his long, long trail! Big Dorn was gone, and all his high hopes with him. And the great work unaccomplished! The blow had been struck in this small, sleepy village, to which time was a stranger!

Instinctively, Tarron glanced over his shoulder. It seemed to him that a shadow had crossed the door to the balcony, but when he leaped noiselessly to it, he found the balcony empty; and before him lay the quiet valley, beautiful under the moon, and the sleeping houses, their windows glinting like black, living eyes.

He went back to Dorn, and lighted a match; because the moon's light made the dead man's face so dreadful to see. But the light of that match showed Les something which was worth a keener attention. Where the hand of Dorn had lain on the floor—the dead right hand—some words were written in a red smudge.

As he lay dying, he had written on the floor with his own blood, until death stopped the sentence. Then, falling forward, in his fall he had rubbed out most of what he had inscribed.

A few brief words remained.

"—tall and scar—"

All before and after was indecipherable.

"Tall and scar—"

What might that mean except a description of the murderer, as Dorn had seen him, his eyes unclosing from sleep, the steel already in his throat?

A tall man with a scarred face, then?

So much for the murderer. But what of the great work? Tarron reached for the belt which Dorn wore ever buckled about him, night and day. The belt was gone!

And so Dorn's life-work was undone forever!

Unless, indeed, this mountain-bred youngster who had joined forces with him could carry on the great battle!

19
Like a Gale of Wind

YOU must understand that there had been so little spare time on the farm of the elder Tarron, and every day had been so filled with labor, that no one had ever had a chance to teach young Leicester Tarron how to pray; but when he kneeled beside that fallen hero and looked through the open doorway past the balcony and the treetops to the moon-flooded heavens, God could never have misunderstood what was in his silent heart.

After that, Tarron went out to the stables and found, as he expected, that both the gray stallion and the mouse-colored gelding were gone.

He remained for a moment in thought; then he went back into the house and tested his landlord's door. It was fast—locked! However, he gave his shoulder to the door, the inside bolt was wrenched off by his strength; and at once he strode into the room and found the landlord standing in the middle of the floor, half dead with sleep and bewildered with fear and wonder.

Tarron took the rifle from the hands of this worthy man and pitched it through the window. Then he took him by the hair of the head and dragged him to the window.

"Merciful God! Merciful God!" moaned the landlord. "Spare my life! Spare my life!"

"I am not God. My name is Tarron," said the boy. "I brought you to the window to study your face, and I see that it is like a book with only one page. Tell me: Who was it that murdered my friend this night?"

There was a loud scream from the doorway. The wife of the landlord had crept like a ghost from her bed after her husband was attacked. But when she came to the threshold of safety, her terror escaped in a screech, and she fled away down the hall, crying out for help.

"Listen, señor," breathed the landlord, "you hear that woman! She will raise the entire town. They will tear you to pieces! Flee now, and I shall show you a safe way out of the house!"

"Do you swear that?"

"I do swear it."

"Good. Then tell me first the name of the murderer—"

"Kind saints! Murder! Murder? In my house?"

"You rat!" said Les Tarron. "You small-eyed rat!" He shook the landlord until the wretch's teeth rattled together.

"Tell me!" he commanded.

"Señor, señor! There is nothing that I can say. You cannot pour wine from an empty jug!"

"Suppose that I put in a little wine first—can't you make it grow into a jugful? Suppose I tell you of a tall man with a scarred face—"

The landlord ceased his wrigglings and his prayers. He hung motionless between the hands of the boy and gaped at him.

"Very well," said Tarron. "I have not said that I am going to kill you. I've asked you if you'll tell me the truth!"

"Listen!" cried the landlord. "They are gathering! Do you hear them running? They are coming in hundreds. In another moment, even *I* cannot save you, for my wife will have shown them how to block the secret way."

"Friend," said the boy, "you have spoken well. But you can speak much better."

He laid the keen point of his hunting knife against the hollow of the landlord's throat and moved the handle so that the moonlight flashed up and down the blade.

Men who know their weapons have a certain way with them; it was not hard for the landlord to tell that Les Tarron loved knife-work.

"Señor," he gasped, "how could I tell? I only knew that he commanded us to keep in our rooms and lock our doors upon us. I could not disobey!"

Tarron saw a cord hanging round the landlord's neck and, snatching it, he burst open a little knotted rag at the end of the string. Half a dozen broad pieces of gold fell out and rolled across the floor—the frantic eyes of the landlord strove vainly to follow the direction of each one.

"Justice of God!" moaned he. "They will drop into chinks between the stones! They will be lost forever! They will do no more good in the world!"

"They will murder no more men, you mean to say," said Tarron. "But I've waited too long. Have you a prayer to say before you die?"

"Señor! Kind and wise young señor! Hear me!"

"Speak quickly."

"Had it been any other man, I should have turned him away from my door. But who could have refused Don Quexada?"

"Is he one who can command here?"

"Does an eagle command crows and pigeons? Señor, I begged him to do nothing in my house. But he commanded. I—I could not resist. I asked my wife. She agreed with me that there was nothing I could do but obey. So we went to bed at the appointed time—"

"Who stole the two horses?"

"Stole the two horses!"

"Speak, man! Do you *want* to die?"

"It was he!" breathed the landlord. "It was Don Quexada, again, so that if he did not manage to kill you both, neither of you could pursue him!"

"Good!" said the boy. "I begin to understand. Now come with me out of the house!"

"I shall show you the secret way. Go before me—this way through the hall—then down that flight of steps—"

"Listen to me, friend. I am young, but I am not a fool. If my friend had been of my mind, he would be still alive. Walk before me, now. If you look to the right or the left, your wife can have a new husband."

The landlord said no more.

Down through a winding way he led. The clamor of rapidly approaching voices swarmed above them and then grew faint. The landlord began to ascend again. He pushed up a trapdoor, and they were in a field behind the stable.

"Tell the stable boy to catch and saddle two horses. No, the boy is gone. We will catch them ourselves. Mind that I watch you every instant. And my gun never misses, even by moonlight."

The landlord was far too exhausted by terror to object or to attempt to escape. Mutely he submitted. The two horses were caught and saddled just as a fresh clamor began in the tavern and spread outward like rings in a pool after a stone has been dropped into the water.

By this time they had mounted.

"Now, where?" gasped the landlord. "Where do you take me, kind young señor?"

"This Don Quexada has ridden off. Which way?"

"Up the valley, señor. Shall we not follow? Yes, this way!"

"We'll not follow. Which horse does he ride?"

"The mouse-colored gelding, señor."

"You saw him away, I see! Was there blood on his hands then?"

The landlord cringed as though his backbone had turned to paste.

"Now," said Tarron, "I'm gunna get up with Quexada. I dunno how. But you know. Maybe there's a short cut. I leave that to you. If you bring me up to him by dawn, you can ride back here to your home and forget that there was ever a man named Tarron or a man named Quexada. But if you don't show him to me by dawn, I'll kill you. I'll tie you up by the wrists and cut off little pieces of you and feed them to that mangy dog that wants to follow us!"

The landlord rolled his eyes at the dog, and moistened his fat, trembling lips.

"Brave and wise and good señor! I am to die, then?"

"As you choose!"

"But there is no way! I swear—by the sweet saint—"

"Hush!" said Tarron. "Maybe you can still pray your way out of hell, but not if you lie about this!"

"Come," said the landlord, setting his teeth. "We can never overtake him, because he rides like the wind. But I don't think he'll try the upper pass. Oh, God pity me! God pity me! It's only through the upper pass that we could stop him!"

The landlord waited no longer, but turned his horse's head down the valley, just opposite to the direction he had first suggested. He rated his pony at a good, hard gallop; and with set face he pointed their course at a cleft in the upper mountains that looked now like the tall ears of a mule, leaning away on either side from a dark and narrow gap.

Mile after mile they rode; not a word was said, until the landlord suddenly turned in the saddle to his companion, who was always a significant length behind him.

"Have no fear, amigo. Ride up beside me. I begin to wish that you win. I begin to wish that Quexada should die. I have seen the times when I've ridden that pass. No one else dared to try it, but I could do the thing. I was young then, and no Quexada would have dared to treat me like a dog, as he's treated me, and as he treats all of the rest of them!"

"Bueno!" said Tarron. "I see that time may have made your hands a little dirty, friend, but your heart is still clean."

"Clean as a bone," said the landlord, taking more heart, and raising his head to the fresh, sweet wind of the night. "I shall spend half of the gold Quexada gave me for Masses. In that way, I shall do good for the heathen soul of your dead friend, and I shall also save my own soul from danger. I shall not forget you, either."

"A little gold to spread out a long distance, it seems to me," said Tarron. "You've ridden this pass before?"

"When I was a boy, señor, I would have taken Quexada by the beard and laughed in his face. Look! I bought that big tavern with money that I made before I was twenty-five. Well, how is so much money made so early in life? Not by lying in bed at night, you guess? And you're right! Holla! I was abroad, and I rarely came home without something in my pockets. There are ways for brisk young men to push on in the world! Come on, and on! We'll go through the pass like a gale of wind—God willing! God willing!"

20
In the Dust of the Trail

SO with this villainous landlord to guide him, Tarron entered the pass.

They had not climbed a mile into the back throat of it before Les could understand why even fugitives would not willingly use this pass. For a cold wind screamed through the heart of it continually, and a stream had cut a narrow ravine through the center of the gorge. Along the edge of that stream they had to ride, and fifty times they had to cross and recross the white water, never knowing when one of their horses might lose footing and go whirling down the torrent with his rider.

Nevertheless, Tarron was contented, for he guessed that they were cutting across the neck of a long loop around which this Quexada must be riding. What amazed him most of all was the fine spirit with which the plump landlord undertook the task. Never once did his heart fail him, though twice his horse slipped and nearly cast him into the boiling water.

But presently they reached the crest of the divide, and from that moment the going began to be infinitely worse, for the slope pitched down at a terrific angle. Rain was falling. The stones were slimy and wet, and there was not a ghost of a trail to follow. Even now, the landlord kept on with a brave spirit. And as the wind howled, he howled and shook his fist back at it.

"We'll teach Quexada to murder men in their beds!" he shouted. "We'll let him know what happens when he dares to shame honest taverners and their taverns! This should be a day marked with red on the calendar. I shall do such a good deed that I shall not have to spend money in Masses for my soul. A good mark against a bad mark—and that strikes a balance! Holla! A fig for the wind and the rain! Are you there, señor? Shoulder to shoulder, brave heart, we'll win through together. We'll come down on Quexada like two thunderbolts. We'll strike him from the face of the earth! Oh, the midnight murderer!"

So trolled the tavern-keeper, passing into such a joyous ecstasy, that

Tarron could not help smiling more than once in spite of the hardships of that wild passage of the mountains.

Drenched and cold and stiff, they came down from the upper pass; and as the dawn began, they saw before them the rolling hills, and the white road looped loosely across them.

"That is the place!" said the landlord. He drew rein and looked anxiously ahead of him, screening his eyes with his hands, though there was not yet light enough to dazzle even the eyes of an infant.

He had lost a great deal of his enthusiasm. And Tarron understood.

He said grimly: "Wait up here. I'm going down. There's Quexada now!"

He pointed, and plain in sight was a horseman, riding one animal and leading two. The silver flanks of Jimmy glistened in the early morning light.

"God be with you, señor," said the tavern-keeper. "And what becomes of the good horse of mine that you are riding?"

"I ought to take him," said the boy fiercely. "And I ought to take the one that's under you now. And I ought to turn you out of your clothes and send you back naked!"

"*Madre mia!*" gasped the other. "What a tiger you are! At one word, you have your teeth in a man's throat! Forgive me, señor. Keep that horse. I make you a free present of him. I wish you joy of him."

But in spite of himself he could not help making a wry face.

"I don't want your horses," said Tarron. "I'm gunna head down there for Quexada. And after he dies, I might leave you this horse of yours and the horse that Quexada is riding, too. You can have them free of charge. But when you get back to your house, you see to it that the body of my friend Dorn is buried all right and proper. You hear me?"

"Señor, señor!" gasped the host. "You carry me away with your great kindness. You make me like dust under your feet."

"You're a liar and a scoundrel," said Tarron, "but I can't help laughing at you! I see that you ain't so sharp for getting at Quexada, now that he's in sight?"

"Señor," said the fat man, making a wide gesture with both hands, "you see how this thing is? I have not had guns in my hands for a long time. Besides, why should I go to help where no help is needed? Is it fit for a thing like me to take the credit from a hero like you?"

"Wait here," he said, "and keep yourself out of sight."

And he rode straight down the nearest draw that pointed toward the distant road.

Before he came to it, he entered a little grove; and, while he was under the shelter of the trees, he heard a distant sound of shooting coming from the direction of the pass.

Could it be that the treble traitor, the innkeeper, was striving to betray to Don Quexada the danger in which he was riding?

Tarron pushed suddenly out on the road and saw before him, not fifty yards away, the form of a tall rider mounted on Jimmy, with the other two animals in the lead.

It was Don Quexada, peering to the side toward the mouth of the pass, where the innkeeper was firing his gun rapidly to attract attention.

Quexada took the warning; he was in the act of reining his horse sharply to the right when Tarron's challenge met him from beneath. He whirled Jimmy back into the road. But the good gray had seen his master, and in an instant he had bolted to reach Tarron's side. The lead ropes snapped like twine, and a frantic buck, high in the air, flung Don Quexada out of the saddle and rolled him in the dust.

Before Quexada could rally himself an iron grip was on his throat and a Colt pressed against his temple.

"Will you lie still?" asked Tarron.

The latter nodded. And still as a stone he lay while Tarron took from him two Colts, and a long, murderous hunting knife. Even the cool nerves of Tarron could hardly endure the sight of it, with the faint blur of blood about its shaft. He tossed it into the long grass and went on with his work, which was to pinion the arms and the feet of his captive, and last of all, to remove from his hips the long belt.

Kneeling in the dust, with rapid fingers he went through the compartments of the belt, and found that all was there even as he had last seen it, except for the middle compartment at the back.

This had been empty when he examined it before. But now it was completely filled by a small steel box, black with age and covered with fine engraving. It was perhaps three eighths of an inch in thickness, and three inches long. The moment it lay in Tarron's hands, somehow he knew that the prize was in his grip.

It had been this little trifle that Dorn had abstracted from the belt before he dared entrust it to Tarron.

"Open it," said Quexada bitterly. "There is death in it. I looked within last night, and I die this morning!"

"Last night," said Tarron, "you murdered for it, eh?"

"Murdered?" repeated the Mexican, raising his brows. "Murder? Is not everything fair in this war?"

He spoke as though in perfect innocence.

"And do I reproach you," he said, "because I am to be murdered this morning?"

"I took you man to man, with the sun to show you what I intended to do," said Tarron.

"A horse bucked me off his back, young man," said the Don. "Or else you would be at the gates of hell now!"

"Good!" said Tarron.

He leaned back and rolled a cigarette.

"It looks to me," he said, "as though you have your share of nerve. I suppose that they would have given you a pretty stiff price for this job?"

"Ingram could not do the thing that I did," said the Mexican.

He had the air of a man who has performed some admirable deed. There was no trace of shame in him for the foul murder he had committed, and yet he had all the appearance of an intelligent human being. His forehead was high and well proportioned; his eyes big and well placed, and only the length of his mustache and the sharpness of his beard gave a sort of old-fashioned stiffness and fierceness to his aspect.

"Ingram couldn't do it," admitted Tarron.

"I followed him," said Quexada. "I followed where the tracks led, and where the tracks were not. I outguessed Dorn. I knew that he would never keep on the straight road to La Paz, no matter how hot he was to see her. And there he was—so near, and yet what a distance from her! What a distance! Ha! At the very time when he thought that he was ready to stretch out his hand to her, the knife ended him! And then the devil sent you to bring me bad luck!"

"Was it the devil?" asked Tarron. "However, all your work is nothing. Here am I to take the thing on to her."

"Do you think that you are as near to the end as he was? Then ride ahead! Try your best. You will soon see! You will soon see!"

His laughter was like the croaking of a raven in the boy's ears.

Two touches of a knife set Don Quexada free. One of his own Colts was tossed into his hands as he rose in wonder to his feet.

"I swore to myself that I would forget everything until I'd found you," said Tarron. "But I can't butcher you like a dog. There's a gun. Now fight for your life, Quexada!"

"*Madre de Dios! Madre de Dios!*" gasped the Mexican. "Do you give me the victory after all?" And almost before his eyes had been lowered from the sky, he notched up the muzzle of his gun and fired.

A neat shot, well-aimed; but Tarron had spun around sidewise like a top jerked by a string. The bullet hummed past his head. His own shot struck fairly between the eyes of his opponent. He saw Don Quexada take three great strides toward him, and then fall headlong in the dust of the trail.

21
As Time Is Measured

WHAT passed in the heart of Leicester Tarron when Quexada fell dead at his feet?

It was the first time he had actually aimed a shot at a human being. It was the first time that he had slain. And yet Tarron regarded the dead man with a calm unconcern. There was too much on his hands for him to waste time in sentimentalizing over death. First of all, he went through the clothes of Don Quexada with meticulous care. A well-filled wallet he appropriated without the slightest qualm of conscience. And the filled ammunition belt of the dead man he took also. He found nothing more of interest except, within the wallet, a letter which might well set him musing.

It was written in a clerk's fine, scholarly hand, rapid yet well formed:

> My dear friend Quexada: When you receive this, you will know that the box is being brought into your territory by Dorn and a companion, a boy named Leicester Tarron. The box is actually carried by Dorn. You will take your measures accordingly. But by all means try to dispose of the boy also. Do not be deceived into softheartedness or neglect by his youth, because of the two he is the more important.
>
> You have heard something of Dorn and his work. He has carried the box actually closer to the finish than any other man. He has worked like a hero, and he has given us more cause to worry than all the others combined. However, young Tarron is even more dangerous. At this time he knows very little about the box, even if he has heard of its existence. He has attached himself blindly to Dorn as an adventurer, and you may know that from such careless adventurers a great deal is to be feared. Therefore, do your best to destroy the boy if you wish to secure your retreat in safety. If you must leave him alive behind you, be sure that he will follow you, no matter how faint a trail you leave. If you leave him in your rear, ride by the shortest route, and kill your horse if you must. Tarron will be coming like a storm after you.
>
> I give you this detailed warning because I feel that the matter is being placed in your hands more completely than it has ever been placed in the hands of any other person. It is now in your power, Quexada, to end this long struggle at a blow.
>
> Do your best, and the matter will be over; and I shall see that you receive such a reward as even you cannot imagine easily.
>
> Start instantly. Omit no care. Adios.

In place of a signature, there was a little impression of a seal. Beneath, was written hastily:

> I open this letter in a hurry to impress upon your mind, finally, how vastly important it is that the boy should be disposed of.

With that, the missive ended.

There was enough in it to flatter the heart of young Tarron with a most pleasant warmth; but there was also enough to make him shake his head in concern. Here was proof positive that he had been marked down by the enemy and that they would spare no effort to cut him off.

But what interested Tarron more than all else was that "they" should have gathered so much information about him so quickly; unless, indeed, the tale of what he had done in escaping from the jail had been magnified in the report to the man whose seal was affixed to the letter. It showed him, on the whole, that he was face to face with a carefully elaborated system of spying. His enemies' informants were everywhere, and they made instant and copious reports. He could not help but be somewhat discouraged. For, when he had faced the great adventure, he felt that perhaps he would gain some advantage from his youth. Men do not expect great things of a boy as a rule. And he had hoped with all his heart to take "them" by surprise.

That was not to be. "They" had written him down at his full value, and perhaps something more than his full value. Yet it cannot altogether displease a young man to find himself regarded with dread by formidable foes.

Turning back to the consideration of the letter, he tried to make something of the seal. It looked to him at first like a wheel, but then he saw that what seemed the spokes were naked arms projecting from a common center; and what seemed the rim was composed of swords, hard gripped. A very curious thing as a seal. Tarron, knowing nothing of such matters, strove to make head or tail of it.

He could not decipher its meaning, except that it had been used in the place of a signature. It came, assuredly, from one of Dorn's enemies—one of his own enemies! Somewhere in the mysterious city of La Paz, man— or perhaps woman—had pressed that seal upon the paper, and the order had gone forth to destroy young Tarron.

It remained for Tarron to discover the whereabouts of that town, first of all; and, secondly, to learn who were the rightful owners of this little steel box which so many people had tried to deliver, and tried at such a dreadful cost.

In the meantime, his fingers had been constantly busy at that box, but it would not yield to his hand. Halfway down the side, he could make out the lips which joined in the closing of the box. But he could not pry them apart without using so much force that he feared to break the box.

And that might be a calamity! Whatever was in the box, mere exposure to the air might ruin it, and undo all the labor of having brought it so far and so cleverly.

Les did not fail to press every inch of the surface, in the hope of finding some secret spring; but he had no success.

When he studied the design engraved on the box, he had no better luck. It was covered with the most elaborate arabesques: except for a central frieze of tiny horses, men and dogs, chasing a stag. The work was done with such a delicate and admirable art that when he scrutinized the thing more closely, the more he saw of the vitality of the men, the straining of the horses, the fierceness of the dogs, and the terror of the stag at whose haunches the leaders were already leaping.

Altogether it was a dainty thing; but Tarron made up his mind that what the box contained was the important matter. He tested the weight. So far as he could judge, the steel was not very thick, and certainly there was nothing like gold within—the whole was much too light!

Never was a lad more thoroughly baffled than was young Tarron, and yet he almost rejoiced that his wits had not been able to penetrate to the heart of the puzzle. It left a greater work still before him. Drawing up the cinches on the gray stallion, Jimmy, Les swore to himself that he would never give up the trail until he had won; or until the enemy had crushed him, as Dorn and all the others had been crushed.

In the meantime, La Paz! He must find the city.

The dead man, Quexada, had said that the end of the quest had been comparatively near when Dorn and he were in the sleepy little mountain town where Dorn had been overtaken by the murderer's knife. Therefore, Tarron intended to ride in that general direction once more. Not that he meant to pass directly through the village again. That would have been too completely headstrong and foolish; but since La Paz lay yonder, in that way would he journey.

So he made all ready, looked his last upon the dead man, and rode on down the valley. And it occurred to him that Quexada himself would have been hurrying back to reach La Paz and so bring the work to an end. Therefore, it was wisdom enough to ride down the valley.

A common goal for both the pursued and the pursuer!

Tarron marveled at this, but he had determined not to puzzle over seeming incongruities which might not be incongruous after all in the long run. In the end, all would be explained by a single word, no doubt!

He rode for perhaps two miles, and the sun was beginning to grow hot, when he passed a shepherd—a grizzly old man sucking at a black pipe, trudging slowly after his flock.

Tarron drew rein beside him.

"Good morning, father."

"Good morning, boy."

"I'm looking for the road to La Paz."

"La Paz?"

"Yes. Is this right?"

"This is right for Callahar and Santa Maria. La Paz? I never heard of that place."

"You've just come into this district, then?" said Tarron.

"Well, in a manner of speaking, I've not been here overlong."

"Is there any house near where I could learn?"

"No; nobody knows better than I do."

"What?"

"Well, why should they?"

"Man, man, you've just admitted that you haven't been in this district long."

"Boy, boy, that's as you want to measure time. But I've been around here longer than any of the rest."

"Very well, then. Let me know where La Paz is, will you?"

The other raised his skinny hand, uncertain and shaking with age, and pointed to the sky above him.

"It's there, and no other place!" said he.

"You like your joke," sighed Tarron.

"I'm too near that place to joke about it," said the shepherd. "Good luck, lad."

He pushed the sheep on, and went wearily along behind them.

But Tarron reined Jimmy back across his path.

"Listen to me, old-timer. You're making a lot of riddles for me, and I'm no hand at getting the truth out of such hard nuts. You say that you're traveling toward La Paz?"

"Toward La Paz. Yes, of course. And so does every sensible man that I ever heard tell about. But they never find it on this earth. The trail to it goes out in air, sooner or later, and you've got to die to live in La Paz!"

"You mean to say, then, that there is no such town as La Paz in these mountains?"

"I do."

"Then how long have you been here?"

"Only a matter of fifty-eight years, son!"

22
A Man with Three Horses

THE way to Santa Maria and—what was the other town? Callahar?

Tarron stopped in his path. He let the shepherd who had known these hills and mountains for fifty-eight years go slowly down the road and out of sight around the bend. And then he watched the dust cloud which the sheep had raised hang long in the windless air, but at length dissipate.

This was not the way to La Paz. A man who had lived here for more than half a century had never heard of the name of such a town. As for the other two towns, he knew nothing of them.

Might it not be the name of some hacienda, then? At that thought, Tarron whirled Jimmy round, and with the two led horses galloping behind him, retraced his way at full speed.

He found the shepherd settling himself for a brief rest on a stump at the edge of the road, while the sheep scattered in search of the best grass.

"Look here," said Tarron, "there may be some other place that bears the same name—some house, some hacienda; even a river or a mountain—anything you know of that carries the name of La Paz?"

The old man shook his head, and yet he smiled kindly on the anxious enthusiasm of the youth.

"Set down and think," said he. "Thinking will get you farther than fast riding in this here world. Set down and think it over and take council. That's what our elders used to do."

Tarron, gaping at him, wondered what in all the world could be elder than this white-bearded grasshopper of a man.

"You've never heard of anything like that name?" he said.

"Nothing like La Paz," said the gray beard. "I know this here country better than a book. The doctor tells me that I'm gunna be plumb blind in another few years. God willing, I'm gunna be dead before my eyes die on me! But even if I have to go blind, I could still move about. I know every fence post inside of a hundred miles. I could walk blindfold over the worst of the mountain trails. So that it ain't likely that stream or mountain or town or hacienda could be called by any name that I really wouldn't know, is it?"

"No," said the boy sadly, "it ain't very likely, I suppose."

"Nor trail nor path nor pool," said the old man, "and some of the trees and the hills have their names, but nothing like La Paz. It ain't a name that would ever be popular around here. Why should it be, seeing that there ain't never been very much peace around these parts!"

Tarron, in his eagerness, had dismounted. Now he swung into the saddle again with a loud groan of vexation.

"It's no use, then," said he. "I've got to hunt some other way."

"Hunt any how you please," said the ancient, "you'll never find what you're hunting for. Not in this part of the world. Not peace in fact nor peace in name. It all looks dreamy and quiet, but there's all hell everywhere just under the surface."

So Tarron went on down the road again.

But he was tremendously ill at ease. Had there been even the shadow of a ghost of a trail for him to follow, he felt that he could have worked it out as well as any man under heaven, for he knew his powers, and recently they had been tested severely enough. But there was only a name which no man recognized.

How could he turn, then, and in what direction?

To go on vaguely and blindly might be to override the mark, and never know that he had passed it. And as he advanced, most certainly he would be advancing into danger—danger from men whom he did not know—antagonists to whom honor was a mere name, and who would shoot him from behind, or slash his throat in the night with no pangs of conscience.

Poor Leicester Tarron turned his problem back and forth and found no solution. But he felt that the shepherd must be wrong, in spite of all his fifty-eight years of experience.

Dead men do not dally with the truth except for a grim purpose, and Quexada, when he spoke of La Paz, had been no better than a dead man—death, according to his expectations, lay immediately before him. Therefore, he must have meant what he said when he declared that La Paz lay close to the little town in which Dorn had died.

Looking back up the slope toward the mouth of the dark pass, Tarron could see his host of the night before riding in desperate haste, leading behind him the pony which Tarron had borrowed and had turned loose for the sake of the better animals with Quexada.

There was an easy explanation for the actions of the innkeeper. The latter had felt his spirits mounting as they forced their way through the dangers of the mountain forge. But when they came out into the daylight, and when the familiar form of Quexada was in view, caution and policy had overcome the fat man's bravado. He had tried to give the Don warning, and he had almost succeeded.

However, Tarron thrust away such memories. He dared not dwell too much upon the past. It had all been so confused, so filled with terror, that to contemplate it was to make him despair of the future, and with despair no man can mate and win a game.

This knew Tarron, but as he wandered on down the valley, he felt like a rudderless ship.

The three horses were an embarrassment of riches. He could not manage them as well as he could manage two; and, for that matter, he half felt that it would be much better to dispose even of the mouse-colored gelding, and keep only the gray. In that manner he would be more free in his movements, and it was unlikely that any pursuit would tax the powers of Jimmy to the utmost.

There was only one thing that Tarron could do as he pursued this journey, and that was to keep wide awake to every possible ambuscade. And, in the meantime, he could map out the country in his mind, studying the face of each mountain as he approached and passed it. For land lies very differently to those who come and to those who go. If he retreated in haste through these valleys, he must know them as well as possible. And every creek he crossed must be jotted down in his memory as easily fordable, or difficult to cross, and its exact place remembered accurately. All of these details might become matters of life and death, later on.

It was not long after noon that he saw a slanting stream of smoke rising from behind a hill.

Instantly he reined his horse into the brush. For a smoke column was one of the oldest of signals, and might still be used in a region where the telegraph was strung only here and there, at wide intervals.

He made a semicircle around the base of the hill, and thus rode into view of a small house, tucked in a hollow of the slope, with a little garden of vegetables extending in brilliant green behind it. A broken-down horse cropped the scanty grass in the pasture; there was a pair of cows, and the cackle of geese and chicken came thickly on the air. But otherwise there was scant token of how a living might be eked out in this wilderness.

In front of the door sat an old man, with a silver beard that flowed down almost to his waist and flashed in the sun like metal.

Once more Les determined to dare the dangers of approach to a habitation. Information he must have, and quickly. And better a danger ventured here, than a greater danger risked later on. There had not been much time, perhaps the mountaineers had not all been warned against him. But before long the enemy would have spread a net for him everywhere. He knew it perfectly well, and therefore he rode up the slope with the sangfroid of desperation.

When he dismounted, he found that the old man's eyes were shut beneath a gray mist of brows. But as he spoke, the ancient one looked up.

"I, señor, am Pedro Gregorio. Put up your horse. Come to sit here in the shade for a while. Dinner will soon be ready. Lucia! Lucia! There is a friend to eat with us!"

"Friend?" cackled a voice within the house. "Friend? What one of your begging, worthless cronies is it this time?"

A stalwart woman of middle age came into the open doorway. Her formidable arms were brown and bare to the elbows, and there was a scowl on her brows. Yet she was a rather handsome creature, in a way, and perhaps not so fierce as she at first seemed, for a big, yellow cat came with her to the door and rubbed fondly against her dress.

"If you can spare me food," said Tarron, in her own Mexican tongue, "I am happy to pay for it, señora!"

"A man with three horses!" said the old man. "And you call him a beggar?"

The woman fell silent, staring at the new guest, and Tarron waited, hat in hand.

At length she started, as though out of a dream.

"No one ever comes here except some of his penny-clipping companions," she said by way of apology to Tarron. "You'll find crushed barley in the corner bin in the horse shed. Give some of that to your nags. And then come in. There'll be a dinner ready in ten minutes."

He gladly did as he was told. Grain for Jimmy was more priceless than gold just now, for the extra strength it gave his horse might be the saving of his master's life before the world was much older. Tarron brought his three animals to the stable, unsaddled them, rubbed them down with straw, gave them a generous feed of barley—wondering the while that such a place should possess such a luxury—and then, when he had added a portion of hay apiece, he came back to the house.

The old man had come hobbling back on a crutch and a cane to watch his guest wash face and hands at the spring, where the water slipped eternally out of the breast of the mountains and overflowed a little basin chipped in the rock.

"Keep your hands in the water above the wrists," said the old fellow. "That cools you off. After you have been soaking up this sunshine it needs water to soak it out of you again. Oh, and the back of the neck. Keep water on that, too, and it'll clear your eyes wonderfully."

Nothing pleases people so much as to see their advice followed, even in the smallest matters. It makes them patrons. They become straightway tender of the affairs of the veriest stranger. And Tarron was scrupulous in taking the directions of this tottering sage.

23
Where Lies La Paz?

"WHAT brings you through this part of the world, child?" asked the old man as they sat in the cool shadow of the pine tree before the house.

"I'm on the heels of an old yarn," said Tarron.

"Following a story?" The Mexican smiled genially. "I have followed them, too. I have had gold in every valley of these mountains!"

"You lie!" cried the woman from within. "Let me see some of it, then!"

"I've had the hope of gold," said the old man, after making a little pause so that the harsh echo of the woman's voice might die away. "Following the gold is better than having the gold, some say. If that's true, I haven't wasted my life."

"It's not true, though!" barked the woman.

The ancient sighed. But he did not look toward the door from which these ringing accents poured. He merely moved off a little farther. And Tarron replaced his stool for him on the farther side of the pine tree.

"But you're starting for the same thing?" asked the Mexican. "You're following gold, too? Ah, boy, you'll have years of happiness—and very little money, I suppose!"

"You've been here a long time?" asked Tarron.

"In one more year I shall be ninety."

Tarron breathed deep. He had never before seen a man so old. And never had he seen one who so perfectly filled the picture of what age should be—mellow, quiet, dignified, and wise, with all the bitterness of ignorant prejudices rubbed away.

Not all of these thoughts were formulated definitely in the mind of Tarron, but he felt them all, and he could not look at the old man without smiling, half-affectionately. Old men and children have little pride; therefore we may show that we love them. But most strong men had rather be feared than loved.

"Ninety years," said Tarron quietly. "Well, it's a grand thing to be that old!"

"Do you think so?" said the seer. "And why?"

"Why," said Tarron, "ain't it better to be a filled bucket than an empty one?"

This speech the other considered for a moment, stroking his beard placidly. And then he laughed, and his eyes shone blue and bright beneath the white brush of his brows.

"The pleasure's in the filling of the bucket," said he, "not in being where only a few more drops can be added!"

"Ninety years!" murmured Tarron. "And most of them spent on the mountains, here?"

"I've lived in a small way," said the other. "Small as people around here count distances. I've prospected over ten thousand square miles—a thousand square leagues, if you want to put it in another way. But I've never gone outside of the country that I was born to."

"You were born in the mountains, then?"

"Lad, my father built this house with his own hands. When I was eighteen, I chipped out that bowl in the rock beneath the spring."

"Ninety years in this place!" murmured Tarron. "That's a fine long time!"

"Fine and long or dreadful and long. There's two ways of looking at every day—or every thousand days. What's done in them, or what's lived in them! Lucia thinks only of what is done."

He added suddenly: "You keep three horses?"

"Yes."

"And two saddles, too?"

Tarron was silent. He had not expected this sharp and sudden turn to the talk, and he could not help letting his eyes wander for a moment.

But when he glanced back, the old man had raised his hand.

"Don't explain," said he. "Never talk except about things that make you happy. We have long winters to make us remember the summer. I talk of summer in winter. And Lucia does not understand. But you will understand— with your extra saddle!"

And he smiled kindly, straight into the eyes of his guest. Yet Tarron had no doubt that, in this moment, he had been vitally weighed. He had been adjudged a fighter, a man-killer. And the empty saddle was, to Pedro Gregorio, the equivalent of a story of war and death. And yet the old man did not start or change color. His voice remained as even and as kind as ever, and Tarron could guess that it was not the first time that this mountaineer had had to do with deeds of death and those who dealt them.

"I'll tell you frankly what I've come for," said Tarron, with a burst of confidence. "If you'll not talk about it afterward?"

"Son," said Gregorio, "it is a kind thing to trust a stranger. And if you can trust me, I think that I can trust myself."

He added: "Tell me what you wish."

"Is there anything about these mountains that you don't know?" asked Les.

"Uncounted millions of things that I don't know. What makes that poplar grow twice as fast as the other? Why do the squirrels bury all their nuts beneath that tree and never beneath this pine? And a million other things I can only guess at."

"I don't mean about trees and squirrels, but about people."

"People? Yes, I have known a great many of them."

"And the towns?"

"Oh, yes. I have been in all the towns. Except the new towns on the San Jacinto. They were built only thirty-five years ago, and I haven't been there since then. My first son died in that valley," he added absently.

"You've heard of lost mines?" said Tarron.

"Many, many times. Are you on the trail of a lost mine?"

And he smiled gently, understandingly, pityingly on Tarron.

"No, no," said Tarron. "I'm on the trail of a harder thing."

"What can that be?"

"A lost city."

"Ah!" said the old man. "A lost city?"

Something in the idea seemed to interest him immensely.

"A lost city?" he repeated.

"A lost city," said Tarron, studying himself with a frown, as he saw that it sounded like nonsense. "I've heard of the place and when I asked for it, they told me that there was no such city."

"What was the name of it?"

"La Paz."

He waited, breathless, but the old man slowly shook his head.

"I never heard of that name," he said. "La Paz? No, there's no such name!"

Tarron could have groaned. Why had not Dorn, who had told him so much, not told him the vital bit more that he needed to know?

"I thought that it was hopeless," said he. "Because an old man who had lived here most of his life told me that there was no such thing. But when I saw you, I hoped that you might know better."

"Had he lived here long, then?"

"Wonderfully long. Fifty-eight years in this very country."

"So! Fifty-eight years?" said Gregorio rather contemptuously. "Well, that is not the age of a boy, to be sure! Fifty-eight years in this country—an old man, did you call him?"

"He is much older than that. He is a shepherd—"

"That would be young Gonzales."

"No, not young. He can barely totter with his years."

"I call him young, my son, because when he first came to this country he worked for me, and I taught him to shoot. But there was always a curtain across his eyes. He never could understand the hard things. And mountains are hard. Such a man could live all his life in a single room and not know the faces of the things that are in it!"

"I believe it," said Tarron gloomily, "but still he knows what I wanted to find out. There is no La Paz in the mountains!"

"Wait!" said the other. "If it is important, it is worth thinking back!"

He leaned against the trunk of the pine, half-closing his eyes.

"Our minds are like old junk heaps," he said. "We can sift and search in them for a long time. We pick up one little memory and then another. Turn it over. See that one side is twisted out of shape and the other quite strong and fresh. Perhaps I shall pick up something about this La Paz."

He closed his eyes again.

"Father!" shouted a strong voice.

Tarron turned with a start, and he saw that the woman was more than halfway down the path from the house to the tree.

"We are coming, child," said Gregorio. "I hope you'll have that good soup for him?"

"He'll get what he finds," said she ungraciously as ever.

"Ah, ah," said the gray beard, "a kind word is better than butter on dry bread. Well, Lucia, you are still young—God be praised!"

"If my soup were like your talk," said the daughter sourly, "it would be as thin as water!"

She turned her back on them and marched into the house.

Tarron was surprised to find everything neat within. His own mother was a meticulous housekeeper, but even she could not have improved upon the cleanliness of the rolled and swept dirt floor. All was in good order, and a meal for two was on the table. The yellow cat was curled beneath it, waiting for a portion.

"Where's Lorenzo?" said Gregorio. "Where's your boy?"

"Gone to the village with the goatskins this morning, as you very well know."

"Ah," apologized Gregorio, "it is that way with us old men. Tomorrow is clearer than today. There is always a mist over the present. And you, Lucia?"

"I have to get the cows in to water. I ate my share while I cooked."

"Time, time, time!" sighed Gregorio, taking his place before a bowl of bread and milk. "Well, since you worship time, may you surely have enough of it!"

"Here, Lady," said the woman at the door. "Come, come, you little fool!"

The yellow cat, as its mistress clapped her hands in fierce impatience, rose from beneath the table and stalked slowly to the door. There, as it paused to lick its whiskers and glance forlornly back at the steaming food on the table, Lucia reached down and swept up Lady, and marched away with her.

24
The Pillars of Smoke

Now that they were left to themselves, Tarron saw that he had before him a plate of boiled beef, a sharp contrast with the bread and milk of his host.

And he said at once: "You've taken the wrong chair, father. That should be my place."

Gregorio smiled on him.

"This is enough for me, my friend. And when you are old, like me, you will soon forget your appetite. For an old man, meat in the stomach is like a day's labor laid on the shoulders. And I do not wish to be like some old people, having all their life in their bellies and no strength left for their brains."

"I understand," said Tarron, and he took his place.

The big, yellow cat, which must have slipped away from its mistress by some dexterous sleight, now ran into the room and leaped up into the third chair which stood by the table; and there she sat in all her feline gravity, the end of her long tail twitching with interest as she eyed Tarron's plate of meat.

"She's hungrier than I am," said Tarron, smiling.

And he gave her a piece of the meat.

It was too large a piece for her to swallow at once. So she held it between her paws, very like a monkey, and ate it bit by bit, while Tarron watched her, delighted at her daintiness.

"I've never seen a cat like that!" he declared.

"Lucia has taught her tricks," said Pedro Gregorio. "If she would spend half the time on her son that she—"

He paused with a sigh. Then he added: "Your food is growing cold, señor."

Tarron prepared to eat, but at that moment some thought or memory occurred suddenly to Pedro Gregorio. He said: "La Paz! La Paz!"

And he closed his eyes and leaned back his head, as though the effort to clear his mind were very painful.

"It's lodged somewhere back in my mind," he said. "I don't know where, exactly. La Paz! Where have I heard it before?"

Then as Tarron, forgetful of his food, listened in intensest interest, his eyes glued upon the face of his host, the latter added with a sigh: "But that is the way with us old people! For so many things have been crowded into our minds that we hardly know how to distinguish between what we know and what we think we know. We feel that every face has been seen before; every story has been heard before; and every name is one we know. It is the same with this La Paz, perhaps, and yet something tells me that I have heard it. Somewhere a long, long time ago! I wish that I could think back to the day and the place. That might help me to remember the facts."

He shook his head.

"There's no use forcing the memory," he said. "It is a servant, of course, but a very stubborn one. When it pleases, it will supply you with what you need. But it will take its own time and act in its own way. And you—you are not touching your food!"

There was a good appetite in Tarron, and now that his hopes were postponed by Gregorio, his knife and fork were instantly busy with the meat. He had not brought a bit of it to his lips, however, when the voice of Lucia was heard calling Lady, and calling her with such a stormy voice that it was plain the golden cat was a very disobedient truant.

"Where *is* the cat?" asked Gregorio.

"She was on this chair," said Tarron, politely beginning to search.

"No, continue your dinner. Poor boy, you haven't touched your food, between a talkative old man and a cat! I'm heartily ashamed. Let me look for Lady—"

There was no need to look. A pitiful moan came from the corner of the room at that moment, and peering into the shadows behind the stove, Tarron saw great, round, burning eyes look back at him.

Then Lady, hearing the voice of her mistress, crept out from her warm shelter.

She was much altered. Her tail lashed her sides, and every hair on her back stood erect. Halfway to the door she paused, stood stiff-legged, and then fell in a fit, biting at the air, biting her own body, and striking out in an agony with her unsheathed claws.

"Lucia! Lucia!" shouted Gregorio. "Lady is sick!"

Lucia's formidable bulk appeared suddenly in the doorway. She was panting with haste and anger and fear. When she saw the cat she pointed suddenly at Tarron.

"You devil, what have you done to her? What have you done to her?"

"Lucia, Lucia!" cried the father. "My friend was only kind to her. He's even fed her from his own plate—"

"Curse him!" cried Lucia.

Her face wrinkled in fury and hate, and she dropped on her knees beside the writhing cat. Regardless of striking claws and dangerous fangs, she gathered up Lady and carried her out into the sunshine.

"Colic," said the old man, shaking his feeble head. "But I've never seen a cat taken so quickly and so severely with it—"

"That kind of colic," said Tarron, "doesn't take long to work."

"It'll soon be over."

"Yes," said Tarron, "I think it will. It will soon be the finish of the cat."

"The finish, señor?"

"Don't you see, Señor Gregorio? This is poisoned meat!"

And he stood up and pointed to the boiled beef.

"*Madre de dios! Madre de dios!*" breathed the old Mexican. "How can I believe that? What devil could make Lucia think of such a thing? Oh, God defend her from—"

He paused, staring white-faced at his guest.

"There is no harm done except to the cat," said Leicester Tarron. "I'll do her no harm in return, for your sake, señor. But there *is* a devil in that woman!"

"Disappointment, hunger for money, love of easy living, envy of the successful—those are her curses," said the father; "but what special fiend could have pointed you out to her? Would she have murdered you for the sake of your three horses? God forbid!"

He added: "And yet—when she saw you she was suddenly kind—ah, what a soul is in her!"

He buried his face in his hands.

"Hush!" said Tarron. "She isn't so much to be blamed as the ones behind her, because you mustn't think that she determined on this murder of me without having it suggested to her in the first place! No, she knew that if she could kill me, she'd have whatever she wanted, up to thousands and thousands of dollars! I could tell you more than this. There's no reason why you shouldn't know, señor. But I'm trying with all my might to find this lost city of La Paz, and the others are trying to beat me back from it. And poison is pretty welcome to them, if it'll stop me. You understand?"

"I understand that you are attempting to do a dangerous thing in these mountains. Ah, son, where are your helpers?"

"My friend that rode with me is dead."

"And he didn't know La Paz, either?"

"He knew, but he hadn't told me. He still wasn't sure of me."

"How did he die?"

"A knife across his throat."

"That is his horse?"

"One of them is his horse."

"And the second spare horse?"

"That was ridden by the man who murdered Dorn in the night."

Pedro Gregorio closed his eyes. Then, as he opened them, he said:

"I was going to give you advice that would usually be wise—to leave these terrible mountains, son. I know them well enough to understand the perils that are in them. The rider who came to the house this morning and spoke to Lucia—he must have been spreading the alarm about you; and by this time every eye in the mountains is searching for you, or waiting for you, and knife, gun, and poison will be out against you. But I won't advise you to turn back. Heroes cannot give up an enterprise they have undertaken, and it's better that they shouldn't, for otherwise the common men would have nothing to steel their nerves—no great examples!"

He paused, and then added: "How heartily I wish to God that I could help you! *La Paz! La Paz!* Oh, lad, to ride through these dreadful mountains in the hunt for a lost city of peace! *La Paz! La Paz!*"

He seemed to have worked himself into a mild agony in his effort to remember. Sweat stood upon his forehead, and young Tarron, leaning across the table, stared hungrily, intently, into the face of the older man. He saw that face grow blank.

"Alas, alas, my boy, if you can wait, and if I can think of other things, then perhaps I shall be able to remember!"

"I'll wait," said Tarron resolutely.

He picked up a piece of dark bread and, walking to the door, he looked up and down the valley.

"I'll wait," said he. "I have to wait, because—"

Here he paused suddenly, for to the side and on the farther head of the hill he saw three thin pencil lines of smoke rising, and thickening each moment. And why should *three* smokes be going up side by side?

He broke off short and hurried from the house, went around the edge of the hill, and into sight of three small fires, which Lucia was even now covering with green leaves to make them smoke more heavily. On the ground beside her, limp and dead, lay the golden cat.

At sight of Tarron, she shrank away with a gasping sound, like a great cat spitting. Fear and hate and malice distorted her face unbelievably, but Tarron had seen all that he wanted to know.

Somewhere, far off among the mountains, those three columns of smoke could surely be seen rising against the sky; and as they were seen, so surely were men swinging into the saddle and riding hotly toward this as a rallying point.

The word was out, and it was high time for him to be gone. Here and there through the mountains he would soon have to be fleeing like a frantic deer, and malice as fierce as that of this woman would be pursuing him.

25

The End of a Famous Man

IT would be pleasant to say of Tarron that, no matter how thoroughly he understood the malice of this woman, he still treated her as men should always treat the opposite sex; but the fact is that Tarron looked upon people in very broad categories—as friends or enemies, as young or old, but hardly as men and women. Women were not of much interest to him at this period of his life. And as he looked at Señora Lucia, her femininity was the only thing that kept him from killing her.

So he strode up to her. Realizing that she could not flee fast enough to escape from him if he cared to pursue, she shrank a little away, but laid a hand on the knife which was carried at her girdle, and prepared to stand her ground.

In spite of the knife, Tarron stalked up to her and laid a finger on her shoulder. That finger was like a heavy rod of steel, and she winced under its pressure.

"I've stopped," said Tarron, "long enough to tell you that I understand. That meat was for me, of course. The poor cat died by chance. And if the old man had taken some of the meat from my plate, you would not have cared a lot! The sooner he is dead the better, you think. It'd leave you free. I tell you, you she-devil, that I'm coming back this way; and when I come, I'll stop in here to see how things are, and when I call, I'll make it a point to find out how the old man's been treated. You understand?"

Her lips writhed back like the lips of a snarling dog, but she said not a word, and Tarron went back to the stables. There he left the fine horse which he had taken from Don Quexada. It was a swift and sturdy creature, but it seemed a little soft in flesh; and a soft, delicate animal would never do in the campaign which Tarron might now have to wage.

The mouse-colored gelding, Monte, was of proved worth, hardy as mustangs are apt to be. As for Jimmy, he was as tough as wire, could run twenty hours a day, and in the remaining four do his resting, and dine heartily on cactus and thistles, if nothing better were available. His appetite was not fastidious.

With Jimmy on a lead, to save his strength for a critical burst of speed, Tarron rode Monte to the house and found the old man beneath the tree, an expression of bewildered suffering still on his face.

"About the cat—and the rest," said Tarron, "don't you bother about that—just let it go. But if you could only remember about La Paz—why, that would do me a lot of good!"

Gregorio struck his fist against his forehead.

"I've been trying to remember," he said. "I've tried and tried, but the idea won't come back to me! I can't remember! But, every day, I'll attempt to remember. I'll keep it in my mind, and sooner or later I'll have the thing. Can you come back again?"

"I may come back," said Tarron, "if I can't learn in any other place. Goodbye, father."

"Goodbye, my son! God send you good fortune."

"Thanks for that."

"I shall remember you in my prayers."

And Tarron rode off, selecting for his course not the road out of the valley but the road straight into the mountains. For somewhere, yonder, lay La Paz, the mysterious, vanished city of La Paz!

You can understand, now, why Tarron gritted his teeth and scowled at the heavens. If he only knew what object he was to attain, he would risk his life to get to it; but he was thrown into the playing field for a dangerous game without even knowing where his goal lay! What is the use of dogged persistence when one is ignorant of the object to be reached? Baffled, bewildered, tired, but grim as death, Tarron felt the spirit of battle rising higher in his breast the more perfectly he became convinced that he could never solve this riddle by his unaided wits.

He kept up the valley, then, until he saw straight before him a thin cloud of dust, moving rapidly across the tops of some trees. At that sight, he reined back and to the side and found shelter in a little ring-shaped copse. He had no sooner gained that shelter than four riders burst into view, with half a dozen led horses behind them. They were only range mustangs; but range mustangs, for the rough ups-and-downs of mountain work, are as good as the best mounts in the world, and these men rode as if they knew what spurs are meant for. They galloped past in silence, but their eyes searched the country before them and upon each side. And Tarron did not have to be told that they were riding in response to the triple column of smoke which had been raised. Three white hands of smoke clutching at the heart of the sky, saying in language which would be well understood: "The man is here! Come! Come fast, and guns in hands!" These four had rushed to answer the summons, and it was well that they had not gained an open view of their quarry!

Grim-faced, tight-lipped, Tarron watched them go. And he could not help fondling the butt of his Winchester. At this short range four well-placed shots—

But he pushed the idea away. Bulldog ferocity would not win his goal for him. There were more enemies in this range of mountains than he could ever destroy!

So decided the boy, growing months older with every moment of this desperate existence. He saw the horsemen dip out of view into the valley, and then himself rode forward on the trail with a rising hope that perhaps he would be able to slip through the cordon of his enemies by this very loophole which the four riders had made.

Yet he was far from any blind confidence, and as he swung down a sheltered slope his keen ears heard the pounding of hoofs on the opposite side of the narrow grove. Deep dust, perhaps, had muffled the sound from his ears; but he had not time to reenter the shelter and so escape detection before two more riders shot around the lower elbow of the woods. Take a wolf by surprise in broad day, or an owl on a moonlit night, but never hope to surprise a mountain-bred Mexican. His nerves react more quickly than the nerves of a cat to water, or of a bear to noise. And as the two riders shot into view, that instant their guns glittered in their hands.

It is harder to shoot downhill than it is up. Moreover, Tarron was trying to turn his pair into the forest. But, letting go the reins, he whipped a Colt into either hand.

His first shot beat either of their guns. Oh, welcome were those long hours of practice at the draw with which he had killed time at home in the days when his father raged and his mother wept because he would not work in the field. Make a plow horse and spoil a racer!

That first bullet, fired hip-high from Tarron's fanned weapon, hit the first rider and dropped him dead from the saddle. A hornet sang past Tarron's ear before he could plant a second bullet; and, as he fired, he saw the horse of the other rider rear. The broad frontlet passed across the line of the slug and the mustang, rearing higher, flung itself back with a human screech of pain and pinned its rider to the ground.

Tarron was on the spot in an instant. The dead man needed no attention, but when he had helped the second fellow from beneath the dead horse, he was glad to note that the man was not badly hurt, but shaken, shocked, and a good deal bewildered by the sudden ending of this battle.

Two excellent and time-hardened cavaliers mounted upon good horses and armed to the teeth, flash upon their single quarry as they make a turning in the road. And in two minutes all of their excellence comes to naught and they are laid along the road, one dead and one helpless. So unnerved was this wounded man that Tarron did not even tie his hands or his feet. He simply took two revolvers and a pair of deadly knives from the Mexican, and a wallet each from him and from his dead companion. Then, rolling a cigarette for himself, he tossed the makings to his new-found companion. The latter rolled his smoke with trembling hands to which the heavy dust of the road still clung.

There was no threatening with a pointed revolver. No, from time to time Tarron actually turned aside from the captive in order to examine more carefully the dead rider's mustang, standing in the near distance; or to note the signs up and down the valley—chiefly down, where the three thin columns of smoke were still rising in close pencil strokes against the sky.

"It was that, eh?" he said in Spanish.

"Yes, señor."

"And you and your friend came to answer it?"

"Yes."

"How are you called?"

"Venustio."

"And your friend, there, who had the bad luck?"

"Señor, that is a famous man. That is Silvio Oñate."

It is never well to make a man explain his superlatives.

"I have heard of him," said Tarron, lying politely.

"Of course! How he happened to fall, I cannot tell!" sighed Venustio, and he looked half angrily and half bewildered at Tarron. "He should not have failed. He never fails! To ride at the side of Oñate into a battle is as safe as to ride at the side of lightning. He blinds men. They fall down as soon as they see his face—and there—Lord! Has he gone?"

"He has gone," said Tarron soberly.

"How—and in what manner? But you were waiting for us—no, you were trying to turn into the trees—we had seen your horse through the woods—we were ready—and yet he failed. He was beaten. Your gun was quicker than his—and straighter—it is a world of many miracles! And you, señor! What is your name?"

"My name is Tarron!"

"Ha! Tarron!"

"Then you've heard about me, too?"

"Tarron! It was you, also!"

"Who did what?"

"It was you who murdered poor Quexada—poor Don Quexada! Murder me, too, but still you will never leave the mountains alive!"

26
All the Money in the World

ODD things and exciting things and desperate things had happened to Tarron before this, but nothing quite so singular as being threatened with death by a man who was at that very moment helpless within his power. Moreover, there was the fire of fearless accusation in the eyes of the Mexican. He pinched out his cigarette and stamped it under his heel, as though even the tobacco which he had been tasting was poisoned, now that he knew the name of the man who had given it.

"I'm a devil, then?" asked Tarron.

"Yes!"

"I murdered Quexada?"

"Yes, yes!"

"How?"

"You stole behind him and shot him through the back."

"How does it come, then," said Tarron, "that the bullet hole was through the head, and that the bullet entered between the eyes?"

"It did not!"

"How do you know that?"

"The people of the mountains know the truth."

"Well," said Tarron, "you're talking like a fool. Maybe you want me to go ahead and murder you, eh?"

He could not resist flashing his revolver, but Venustio scowled back at him, unafraid.

"You have taken a better man than I shall ever be by your trickery this day," said he. "Why should I hesitate to follow? I do not hesitate. Hear me, Silvio!"

He raised a hand and looked upward—a wild fanatic—as though the dead Oñate's spirit, flown from earth to heaven, could lean down and hear his voice.

Tarron dropped his revolver back into the holster.

"Very well," said he. "I'll not live up to what you expect, then. I murdered Quexada by shooting him through the forehead, face to face, giving him the chance for his life after I had him in the road as helpless as you are. I murdered Silvio Oñate in the fashion that you saw. And if you wish to die honorably, there is a revolver, friend. Pick it up, and fight for your life! I will show you how I murder!"

He tossed a Colt to the feet of the other, but the Mexican did not regard it. He stood stiff and straight, frowning at the American, violently striving to readjust certain ideas which had been upset, or seemed likely to be upset.

He said at last: "Can it be that they have lied?"

Tarron broke in: "You did not know my name?"

"No."

"But you came to hunt me?"

"Why not?"

"What were you told?"

"To chase a scoundrel with at least three horses—one mouse colored, one a fine gray. And it *is* a fine one, I see."

His glance flashed appreciatively toward the colt.

"And the signal was three smokes?"

"By day, and three fires by night, of course."

"I hadn't thought about that. Tell me who gave you your orders?"

"I have talked enough. Perhaps I have talked too much. I am ready to die, señor. I am not ready to talk any more."

"If I tie you and gag you in the forest there," said Tarron, "you'll starve to death, or a mountain lion will take you before the morning."

"Yes," said Venustio. "That's true. What of that?"

"But if you take that gun at your feet and fight me, that will be murder, too."

"Murder? I am not a child with a gun, Señor Tarron. I warn you of that!"

"I know," said Tarron, feeling suddenly too old and wise. "You're a good hand with a gun. But I know the way that they talk. You see?"

He smoothly tipped a Colt out of its holster. It spoke. There was a light crashing through the branches above, and the headless body of a squirrel dropped between them with a thud into the deep dust of the road and lay there already more than half buried.

Venustio opened his eyes.

"That," said Tarron, "is not a trick."

"Señor," said Venustio, "I see that I have been told lies. You do not need to murder from behind!"

"Then," said Tarron, working out the problem painfully, "what am I to do? If I tie you in the woods, you die horribly. If I fight you with a gun, it is worse than murder. And if I turn you loose, you ride up the valley and tell your friends where I have ridden. You bring them all after me!"

The Mexican frowned in thought. But he attempted no answer.

"Damnation on all of you!" cried Tarron suddenly. "Take that horse and go!"

The Mexican mounted the dead man's horse at once. But when he was in the saddle, he swung suddenly around on Tarron.

"Señor, I begin to believe that you mean it."

"Mean what?"

"To let me go."

"What else do I mean, man?"

"*Madre de Dios!*" said the Mexican, "after I have said such things to you? And tried to shoot you down?"

"Your bullet missed," said Tarron, "though it was a close thing. And the words didn't hurt, because they weren't true."

"Listen to me, brother," said the Mexican with a sudden burst of emotion. "I wish to serve you. Tell me how!"

"Do you wish to serve me?"

"With all my heart."

"Then tell me where is the thing that I wish to find."

"If I can."

"I am hunting for the city of La Paz."

"The city of peace?" murmured the other. "You are not joking, señor?"

"I'm in terrible earnest."

"La Paz! I've never heard of that name."

"You know these mountains?"

"I've ridden through every inch of them."

"Ah, well," said Tarron, "it can't be helped; there's nothing more that you could have done for me."

"Señor, think again. I have friends. I could send you through the mountains with a written word—"

"You would? No, Venustio. What good would it do? They'd sell me out in spite of you. And you'd be ruined, too. Only tell the others when they find you, that when I met you and your friend here I fought square. Will you do that?"

"Before God, señor!"

"And that the last you saw of me, I was riding up that rocky draw."

"I shall say all of that. And what more?"

"There's nothing more. Adios!"

"Adios!"

Venustio started his horse slowly up the valley, but paused and turned.

"Search your mind, señor. There is something more, perhaps, that I can tell you."

"Yes. How many more of you are riding to catch me?"

"I don't know. There may be two hundred men riding through the mountains on the search."

"Two hundred!"

"Yes."

"Where did you start from?"

"Santa Maria."

"Where is that place?"

"Straight through the pass, between the mountains, by the side of the lake of Santa Maria. You'll see the lake flashing like silver as you come through the pass."

"I'll remember."

"And there is much money promised. A hundred pesos to every man who sees you close enough to shoot. A thousand to the man who brings you down. A thousand to every man in that party!"

"Very good!" said Tarron. "And you know that you can trust the ones who promise that money?"

"Ah, why not?"

"I'm a fool," said Tarron. "I should have asked you before. Who are the people who promise the money?"

"Ah, but you know that!"

"On my honor."

"Well, señor, you wish to make a child of me."

"I swear to you, Venustio—"

"By your honor?"

"Yes, by that."

"I have to believe. But who would start riding a race when he knew not what roads to follow?"

"I can't help it if the thing seems strange."

"I'll tell you the name. It is Don Roberto."

"Don Roberto? Who is he?"

"Ah, my friend, you are surely laughing at me!"

"No, no."

"But the whole world knows about him!"

"I never heard of him."

"Not of Señor Langhorne?"

"Is that the rest of his name?"

"Roberto Langhorne!"

"A Mexican?"

"American."

"And he's offered the reward for me?"

"Yes."

"Now," said the boy, "make it all perfect by telling me where Langhorne lives."

"That's hard to tell. He has several places, but mostly he is at Santa Maria, in the old town house in the center of the town."

"Did you say the center?"

"Yes, you may see the trees of his place behind the church. Only the trees. The house is too old and low. It is covered by the trees."

"Thank you. Armed men around him?"

"A hundred, I suppose!"

"Rich?"

"He has almost all the money in the world."

"Good," said Tarron.

"And now," said the Mexican, waving his hand in farewell, "wherever else you may go, you will know enough not to try to go near the house of Don Roberto. He is greater than the devil!"

27

Enter Juan Cordoba

WHEN Venustio left, Tarron rode straight down the road; but before he had gone a half mile he heard the telltale drum of horses' hoofs before him, and turned in haste into the wood.

A moment later—almost before, it seemed to him, the dust which his own horse had raised could have settled—a compact body of riders went by, eleven men on good cow ponies, all well armed. It took Tarron's breath to see such mustering of armed forces against him. He decided that he would wait until dusk gave a veil to his progress. Then riding deeper into the forest, he picked out a quiet place and rested there until the sun was down, and the shadows were thickening through the trees. After that, he worked his way quietly to the edge of the wood with the two horses.

It was still too bright to take any risk. So he delayed until he saw the stars begin to peer faintly from the sky. Then three level rays of red light struck down from a hill farther on in the pass—three rays close together. On a hill on the opposite side of the pass, there were three more in a close group. He understood as they flashed at him, three from each side. Three columns of smoke in the day and three shining fires by night were to give the signal. They were calling the men together to watch him in the throat of the pass.

Very greatly Tarron wanted to pass that line and get to the town of Santa Maria beyond it. He stared up at the high faces of the mountains on either side. There might be some way of cutting through them, and so avoiding the pass. Or, for that matter, he might be able to steal straight down the pass.

The enemy could hardly expect that he would attempt to press through there by night; they were simply gathering their forces to attempt to head him off the next day and spread the search for him.

Mighty was the power of this Robert Langhorne who could at will call up a small host. All the country swarmed with his creatures—dangerous fighting men, as Tarron had had a chance to learn. No wonder that even at a distance he had been able to make his hand felt through the campaigning of such resolute fellows as Ingram. And Ingram himself must be working up this trail as fast as horses could carry him and his associates. When he arrived, if he were not on the spot already, the trouble would thicken perceptibly.

And yet Tarron's heart did not shrink, but rather swelled to meet this emergency. He had weapons which were all that heart could ask. He had two chosen horses at his disposal. And he was willing to play the game even against such odds. If only he could have a little clearer knowledge of exactly what he could expect to do and where his hand should strike as he progressed. Armed with such knowledge as Dorn, for instance, had possessed, he felt that he could have worked out a reasonable campaign. But as it was, he only had learned that Robert Langhorne was an arch enemy, though perhaps even he was no more than an outpost of the main forces of the foeman.

Tarron formed this resolution: He would press on toward Santa Maria, attempt to get to the house of Langhorne, and, once there, he would leave everything to the spur of the moment, learn what he could, and then determine his future course from that point.

There was, however, one great difficulty. Jimmy's color made it very difficult to execute a secret night march through the midst of foes. His gray, even in starlight, became a glimmering and easy target. The eye could catch it, and what the eye could catch a bullet could strike. Monte, on the other hand, was a perfect color—neither too dark nor too light, one that would blend into the vague light of the open spaces. It was heart-breaking to leave the fine stallion behind him, but so fiercely eager was the boy's desire that he would not let even this sacrifice stand between him and his work.

He put Jimmy on a lead rope at the edge of a stream that trickled through the woods, where there was a plentiful growth of grass. Unless the horse betrayed his presence by whinnying when a searching party was near by, the chances were that he would go undiscovered in this place for a considerable time. Perhaps for several days he could live here untroubled, except for the saddle, which Tarron decided not to remove.

So Jimmy was left in the little forest, and Tarron issued from the woods on the mouse-colored gelding. Straight up the main road he went into the pass and had ridden two miles into the gorge, which became increasingly narrow, when a voice shouted from the ground before him:

"Who goes there?"

He answered in good Spanish: "Friend!"

"Friend to who?"

"Señor Langhorne."

"What are you doing here?"

"Who are you that asks?" replied Tarron with an imitation of honest heat.

"I've got a right to ask," said the man. "Stand up! This fellow wants proof!"

"We got proofs enough," said a second man, rising like a shadow out of the bush. He brandished his rifle in the dim starlight. "What are you doing here?"

"You're part of us, I suppose?" said Tarron, as though reluctant to admit their authority.

"Oh, there ain't any doubt about us, but what about you? Just cover this man, friend!"

The other leveled his gun instantly.

"I've been riding my horse into the ground all day," said Tarron. "I've been hunting that Tarron, and all that I'll have will be a fagged horse if I hunt for a month."

The guard hissed with the violence of his agreement.

"He turns into smoke," said he. "He turned into smoke, too, after he murdered Silvio Oñate."

"What! Did he kill Oñate?"

"Aye! You haven't heard that?"

"What chance have I had to hear things?"

"Well," said the guard who had spoken first, "he murdered Oñate."

"Shot Silvio through the back?"

"No. Through the head. But there must have been some trick about it."

"There was no witness, then?"

"Venustio. But poor Venustio's horse reared, and that coward of a Tarron killed the horse."

"Ha!" cried Tarron. "What a devil! Then he murdered Venustio, too?"

"No, Venustio cleverly pretended that he was killed in the fall; and when he got a chance he mounted Oñate's horse and came away safe with Tarron chasing him."

"But they say Tarron has a fast horse."

"Well, judge for yourself. Venustio galloped away from him safely enough."

Tarron smiled in the darkness. It was plain that Señor Venustio was equipped with an ample share of imagination. However, he could forgive the man for that. At the time of the battle, the Mexican had shown courage enough and good heart, also.

"Where did it happen?"

"At the mouth of the pass."

"Then Tarron must have turned back."

"That's what we think; but no, we have to stay here. Another man has come who hunted Tarron in the north, and he says that Tarron will always do exactly the opposite of what people expect. So we are kept here to guard the pass."

"Well, I'll go in and get food. Where?"

"Go straight up the pass. What is your name?"

"Juan Cordoba."

"Cordoba? Adios, Juan Cordoba."

Tarron rode on, very well pleased. He had passed through the first peril, but he was a little disturbed by the resolute manner in which these fellows had questioned him. Suppose that one of them had come close enough to discover that his horse was neither hot nor covered with the salt of a day's sweat?

But he was past the first cordon, at any rate; and he went on, very cautiously, scanning the brush on either side. Working away from the main road, he came to an obscure bridle trail through the brush, which he followed for a short distance; but even that was certain to be watched, and therefore he left it, and began to move gradually forward, taking his course from tree to tree and rock to rock. Monte worked at the game with a catlike eagerness, as though he understood exactly what was expected of him. Once three men loomed through the darkness. Tarron checked Monte in the shadow of a low tree, and the three went softly ahead, talking quietly to one another. When their voices faded, he moved forward again; and presently, with a feeling that he had crossed the second line of defense, he saw before him what was unquestionably the main danger.

Straight across the throat of the valley there was a string of small campfires, with the black shadows of men around every one. Beyond, the ground dipped away, and Tarron knew that from this point the pass declined and the valley widened. Here the forces of Langhorne were massed. If he could pass this critical point, he might easily win down to Santa Maria.

But to steal through that mass of men? He saw at once that it could not be done. Above him, to right and left, blazed the triple signal fires, still recalling to the pass all the outlying forces. An excellent system. And yet it seemed rather strange to Tarron that the enemy should have chosen to block him by main force away from gaining passage through that valley rather than to attempt to snare him here at its entrance.

He had not time to work out such riddles. He determined straightway upon his course. If he could not advance farther by stealth, he would attempt to go ahead by brazen boldness which will often win when caution and skill have failed.

He looked at revolver and rifle, to see that all was ready in case of emergency. Then he touched the mouse-colored horse with his heel and went forward at a brisk jog-trot. And as he rode, the better to mask himself, he called attention to his way with a cheerful whistle.

28
By Starlight and Firelight

TARRON aimed his course at the space between the two campfires which threw the least light into the intervening space. And yet, all seemed terribly bright. He reassured himself by remembering that his eyes had been accustomed to the deeper darkness of the open night, and that to watchers who had been long near the fires the light would seem dim indeed. He went straight on, therefore, abating neither his whistle nor the pace of his horse.

He saw before him a half dozen men walking restlessly up and down, as though they were already tired of sentry duty. One of them called something to him which he did not understand, but he waved his hand to them and went on. His heart leaped. He saw himself already through the last line of watchers, when he was hailed brusquely from the side, not in Mexican, but in the clearest English: *"Who goes?"*

"Amigo!" called Tarron, waving his hand as he jogged along, and resuming his shrill whistling.

"Stop!" yelled the voice. "Stop when I holler, or I'll drill you clean!"

Tarron saw a leveled rifle, and he drew Monte to a walk.

"I don't mean a walking horse; I mean a stopped horse!" thundered the voice.

Tarron eyed the space before him. He could see no one. The light of the bonfires was dying out. Straight ahead there stretched a dark, deep, and empty region, with the valley widening at every stride. But that leveled rifle meant business, judging by the voice of the man who carried it. If his opponent had been a Mexican, Tarron told himself that he would have rushed ahead to force the lines. But he was not a Mexican. He was a white man, and a white man with a cold heart and an angry temper. Monte was brought to a reluctant halt.

"Well? Well?" snapped Tarron. "Do I have to make a speech to you?"

"He's only a greaser," said one of three men who now drew near. "Let him go."

"I'm gunna stop him and I'm gunna talk to him," said the first speaker. "He sasses me! I'm gunna teach him that no greaser can sass me!"

"Easy, Jerry!"

"Oh, leave me be! I know my business, old-timer. Leave me be with him. Hey, greaser, get off that horse and come talk to me!"

Tarron's gorge rose high, but he checked himself. Leveled rifles are wonderfully eloquent. He hesitated.

"Jump!" yelled the other. A bullet sang not an inch past the brim of Tarron's sombrero.

Jump he did, and landed on the ground by the side of the gelding's head. There was a loud yell of laughter from all three. This was apparently the sort of humor which they were able to enjoy to the full.

"It's only a kid," said one. "Let the greaser kid go, Jerry."

"That Tarron's only a kid, too. I'm gunna have a look at this one. Kid, step up here, will you!"

"Yes, señor!" said Tarron mildly.

"Listen to him, will you?" said the first speaker.

"He's left some of his sass behind him, ain't he? He's learning to talk pretty and polite already. Oh, it don't take long to teach 'em, if you can only catch 'em young. That's the main difficulty, y'understand?"

The others chuckled. Now that they were committed to this game of torment, they seemed to like it nearly as well as their leader.

"What's your name, kid?"

"Juan Cordoba, señor."

"Juan Cordoba, what are you doin' wandering around through the night like this here?"

"My mother sent me up here, señor."

"Up here to do what?"

"To find my father, señor."

"Who's your father?"

"Also Juan Cordoba, señor."

"Hey, he's simple minded, ain't he? Listen to what he talks like!"

The stern voice of Jerry broke in: "What was you to do for your father?"

"Bring him eleven pesos and some made cigarettes, señor."

There was a roar of laughter at this simple remark.

"How far did you ride from?"

"Twenty-two miles, señor."

"Leave the kid go, Jerry. You've pestered him enough."

"Wait a minute. I'm gunna talk till I'm tired of talking, and I don't give a hang what the rest of you say. I'm just gunna find out about a lot of things."

"About what?"

"Why does he pack a rifle if he's so simple and such a kid?"

He stepped beside Monte and dragged the rifle from its case.

"My mother told me to take the rifle, señor. She thought that my father's other gun might have been broken, if he fired it too fast in the first day's fighting."

There was a grim chuckle from Jerry.

"Look here! Your father is a kind of a hero, maybe?"

"Señor, he is the bravest man in the world!"

Another chuckle, which ended in a snort.

"He's brave enough to own a brand new Winchester—and in tiptop condition, too!"

"Hello!" said one of Jerry's companions. "I think that it *is* in tiptop shape. Never knew a Mexican to take such fine care of a gun. Lemme have a squint at it. Bring it over to the fire, will you?"

"We'll all have a look at it."

"Bring the kid over, too, and his horse. There's something kind of queer about him."

And "Juan Cordoba" found himself led straight toward one of the big bonfires to the side, with the frieze of black silhouettes around it.

"Careful, señor, señor!" said he, as the carrier of the rifle swung it around. "It has a hair trigger."

"Why didn't the brat tell me that before?"

"He hoped that you'd put a bullet through yourself, that was all!"

Glancing to the side, Tarron saw far off down the valley the twinkling lights of the town of Santa Maria. If he could get to the gelding and make a break in that direction, perhaps he could escape a following fire of bullets. But even while the idea of making a frantic break in that direction came to him, he saw all hope of such a move snatched away.

A line of no fewer than twenty men came riding up from the heart of the broad valley of Santa Maria; and, as they came, their fresh horses pranced and danced beneath them, and their riders were shouting and singing like so many children.

There was no longer a possible retreat in that direction. Suddenly the brain of the boy reeled, as he saw himself completely shut off from all escape.

That confusion did not last long. A leveled gun clears the wits. And the extremity of the crisis braced Tarron at once.

"While you're looking at that gun," he said, "might I have something to eat?"

"The kid's a good kid. He's hungry," began one of the trio.

At that moment, the gelding snorted and shied at a white rock. There was an oath and a crash. He had sidled into one of the three men and sent him spinning to the ground. Tarron instantly leaped into the saddle.

"I'll quiet him," said Tarron.

"Leave the horse be," roared Jerry, swinging around, Tarron's rifle in his hand. "I want to look at the gun and at you, too! What in—"

The gelding, goaded in the tenderest spot on his flank by Tarron's heel, leaped ahead. A fist with the weight of Tarron and the running horse behind it struck Jerry's nose and flattened it against his face, and, as he fell, the borrowed rifle was torn from his hand.

Two of the little party were down. The third had two Colts out by this time and blazed away at the target not twenty yards off. Nothing but chance could save Tarron—chance and upset nerves. And chance and upset nerves kept the bullets away.

As a roar of shouting and confusion rose behind him, he drove the gelding for the nearest cover, a little circular copse of trees. Flattened along Monte's back, Tarron raced into that covert. Heavy branches struck at him and tore his clothes. But now he was through. The stars flashed above him once more, and to left and right the red, triple eyes of the signal fires shone threateningly down at him.

"Who's there!"

Straight before him, rising from the ground, two figures start up, gun in the hand of each.

Les had shoved the rifle into its case as he plunged away in his first flight. Now in either hand he held a Colt, spouting fire. With knee and voice and sway of body, Tarron could guide the supple gelding easily, though he had not over this horse the absolute control that he possessed over the gray. He fired at those riding shadows from either hand. He saw them go down. And as he galloped onward, he heard one scream from beneath Monte's hoofs.

Bitter work—but if with rope or bullet they can catch Tarron, they will do worse to him than this! So he gives no thought to anything behind him. Let the proved speed of Monte answer the flying hoofs which are beginning to follow! His guns will take care of what lies ahead. And the God who directs the shining of those stars take care of him, and prosper the right!

29

Goodbye Monte!

SUDDENLY there was a flash of silver water under Monte's nose. He had no time to dodge. Everything must be taken in full stride or not at all. A single swerve will throw him back into the teeth of the lion. So both heels cunningly wound the gelding, and Monte, frantic with pain, flings himself forward with a squeal. In midair, his hat whisked from his head by the wind of the gallop, Tarron sees the broad, metal face of the water shining beneath him. A spurt of red fire darts from the opposite bank and a bullet whispers in his ear, then follows the crash of the explosion. Another miss! The devil is confounding these marksmen in the service of Robert Langhorne and giving fortune to the bearing of the steel box! Down shot the gelding from the height of his great leap. The black shore rose up before him— he struck, staggered, then the ground gave way sickeningly.

On the verge of that sheer bank, Tarron hung for half a second looking ruin in the face. He thought of flinging himself clear of the saddle and abandoning the horse. Before that thought could be put into execution the gelding, scrambling like a tiger-cat, had clawed his way up to a firmer footing.

"It's Tarron! Shoot, for Heaven's sake!" a voice was yelling in perfectly good English. And three guns unlimbered on his left.

A red-hot finger flecked across Tarron's forehead, and the blood ran down his face. But that was nothing. Monte was already under way. He silenced the fire of the three marksmen with a shot that crumpled the central figure with a groan, and the other two scuttled for cover, yelling for help.

Tarron did not waste bullets. No matter how many lay dead behind him to attest his prowess, the living still in front of him down the threat of the pass—who must have heard this uproar of voices and guns, and who would be nerving themselves for the battle—it was they who counted! He sent Monte down the narrow gorge at furious speed.

"Good boy!" called Tarron.

His ears jerked forward in acknowledgment of the praise, Monte rushed on. The pursuers were coming fast and furious behind him. The swiftest horses in the mountains bore them. The water jump had weeded out all except the most daring riders and the finest animals, and these, unembarrassed by crowding numbers, made every jump tell.

But before them Tarron rode like a jockey on a race course. He had come up this valley in the darkness, noting every feature of it. And that knowledge surely served him well enough now.

If only the race had been against those who were already in the rear! But there are many ahead! Tarron had only passed the first and second lines of Langhorne's men; the outposts were still to be overcome, they throng down to meet the fugitive.

Tarron entered a long and straight neck of the pass. Surely it would be lined with men! But not a gun spoke, and the trees lay silent and dead before him. Only for a moment!

Behind him he heard a triumphant yelling. He feared he had run into a trap, and as he turned to glance behind him, a voice shouted: "Now take him, boys! Don't shoot too high!"

And half a dozen rifles spoke.

But it was the same story. Try shooting at *any* target when there is nothing but starlight to direct your bullets. Then imagine shooting at a racing horse with a rider bent low, jockeying his mount over rough and smooth, and dodging among the obstacles of the trail. Tarron was not touched—and the blood was already stopping its flow down his forehead.

He turned the next winding of the path and saw suddenly the veritable trap into which he had put his head. The trees were hedged close together on either hand. Even an unmounted man would have found it hard to make way among them, and for a horseman the wood was impenetrable. Before him they had heaped up fallen trees and brush into a mighty mound.

Higher than his head, even as he sat the mustang, towered the mass; and the cries of triumph along either side of the way had certainly their meaning. He was bagged—unless he could turn back. Not even that, for the riders behind had entered the narrow way between the groves.

He swung back toward the mound. Now that he was closer, it seemed far more imposing than before; and solid enough, too, bristling as it did with the butt end of logs thrust forth from the mass. All but the central and the highest portion—for through that mass he could see the dim twinkling of firelight burning on the farther side of the barricade.

Well, one chance in a million is better than no chance at all! Riding for liberty and a ghost of hope, the blood of a man runs faster and his heart is stronger than at any other time.

So it was with Tarron. He had ridden hard at the water, but he had not had the chance to gather his horse beneath him and bring it gradually up to a mighty effort; but now he could settle down, hand riding the gallant gelding, and whipping it into its most desperate stride.

Twice Monte, seeing the obstacle before him, buck-jumped and shuddered with fear, as though his master were riding him at a wall of rock.

But then, whether because he, too, saw the light glimmering through the upper tiers of the center of the barricade, or because of confidence in his master and of glory in his own might and speed, Monte straightened true as an arrow for the barricade and flung himself high into the air. Never a hunter behind the pack of hounds leaped an obstacle more gallantly!

It was as though gigantic wings had thrust the mustang upward. Will he not go over? No, you cannot ask the impossible even of Monte. He strikes the upper part of the heap—but strikes it solidly, head on, without flinching—and before him, what had seemed solid, but was really merely a pile of brush, gave way. Head over heels pitched Monte, flinging Tarron from the saddle at the first impact. Down they smash, but down clear of the wreck of the barricade. Screams and shouts surround them; but as the gelding regains its feet, a little dizzy from the fall, Tarron vaults like a tiger to the saddle. The roar of guns behind and before—the hot tang of gun-powder burning his nostrils—and the gelding is once more into its stride.

Gallant Monte, undismayed and stanch of heart! Never a truer run than this! Let them search all the old tales of Arabs and of racers, they will find nothing finer. He was at his work at once, gathering his power, shaking his head, still half stunned by the fall. But the voice of the master is strength running into his heart, and down the reins the master's hand is sending electric power.

On goes Monte, sweeping through the trees ahead. Now more open country sweeps to right and left. No despair, now, but a real and burning hope with the knowledge that the worst is behind them. If they have done such gigantic and impossible things, never to be believed, can they not accomplish easily what lies before? Only a scattering of men and horses intervene between them and that spot in the forest where the peerless gray waits to take the weight of his master from the tired loins of the mouse-colored hero.

So away goes the fugitive. Never say that Monte did not feel the thrill of his master's call in that final spurt. Never had his heels flown so fast. And there was need. Through the gap in the barricade which their heroic leap had opened, the finest heroes and horses of the pursuit have leaped and followed without so much as breaking their stride; and therefore they are closer.

Tarron leaves the woods to the rear and flings into the open. Let the pursuers be cautious how they try to close that gap between them and their prey!

For Tarron rides with a Colt swinging in one hand, and his eyes are flecked with red.

A rifle flashed before him!

Another miss! All misses! No! Rising out of the very ground a man shows down to the waist and fires.

Monte staggered.

It seemed to Tarron, that the hindquarters of the gallant mustang had fallen away beneath him. No, he gathers himself again, and lurches ahead. And, as he gallops, the red blur of fury and despair and grief clears from Tarron's eyes. Into the shadow he fires, and the half seen man bobs down. He whirls past. The man is seen from a new angle, trying to creep away.

No mercy, now, Tarron! Again, again, and again he fires, a devil in his heart! He sees the creeper stop; sees the poor fellow writhing on the ground. He sees that writhing stilled.

A wicked and a cruel thing, to be sure! But there is no sorrow or compassion, Tarron. Only a swelling, aching, bursting heart. For beneath him, running almost as true as ever, he knows that Monte is dying, and that every stride he takes is marked with heart's blood!

30
A Light Shining

THERE was no staggering, no reeling, no blind pitching, mind you. But only, as the gallant mustang ran, a little faltering, showing that though his great heart was driving him forward as earnestly as ever, somehow the body was failing to give a perfect response.

Tarron looked back. He saw a wide semicircle of horsemen sweeping behind him, each a proven man, each on a proved horse, each worthy of being termed the pride of a country. No little Eastern county, but one of those vast Western kingdoms of the desert, few in men, great in manhood.

But Tarron felt no admiration. The man in him was down; the tiger up. A rifle jerked from its holster and closed against his shoulder. He fired instantly, and saw a fine animal in the center of the semicircle leap high into the air and come down a crumpled heap, its rider flung head over heels to the side. And he shouted with a savage satisfaction.

A wail came from the rest—a wail of wonder and dread. It is not often given to men so to shoot from the back of a galloping horse, at a moving target, and by night. But miracles, to the desperate soul and the iron hand of Tarron, were as trifles, now.

The followers checked their headlong pursuit. They were falling back, and the faltering gelding gained a little.

He gained, then staggered and almost fell, and a moment later swept into a strong and furious gallop.

Tarron felt that effort with a breaking heart, for he knew that it was Monte's dying struggle translated into terms of gallant speed and true running.

On they went, the ground flying back beneath them and the trees spinning past with a whirl and a rush. They reached the edge of a little wood where the gray had been left. Was he alive? Had the wolves found him tethered there and cut him down? Had men discovered his lurking place and captured him, and left a guard on the spot, in case the master should return for his priceless charger?

These were things to think about, but Tarron thought of none of them, for all his heart was occupied by the plight of Monte!

If there was a God who watched man, could there be a God who did not watch horses? Surely not! And what justice was there in this thing? What was the sin of Monte save in serving too faithfully!

They pressed on, wavering and faltering, and on the edge of the clearing where the gray waited and raised a ringing challenge, Monte fell.

Tarron, on his knees, his arms close around the sweating head, his voice calling into the ears, saw them flicker forward, felt the quivering of the nostrils, and then—

Monte had gone to whatever heaven waits for good horses and true. God keep them all!

Grief has its place and its time, but this was no place or time for Tarron to indulge his. He was on Jimmy's back with a bound. He dared not wait to slip on the bridle. He could not even wait to untie the lead rope by which the gray was tethered. A touch of the hunting knife and they were free.

And what a freedom! Monte had been fleet, but what was his fleetness compared to this? As the leap of a deer to the flight of a hawk. And every note of Tarron's voice, every pressure of his knee and sway of his body had a meaning for Jimmy. He had been raised by the hand of Tarron and the very thoughts of his master sank into the soul of the stallion. And he burst from the copse like a storm cloud into a calm sky.

Now, Jimmy, what speed is yours? For the foe comes on the left and on the right. They have lost the edge of their gait by their rush down the valley; but upon the left are four riders and upon the right are three, and every man of the seven is shooting as he comes. Chosen horses, and chosen men, the best in the mountains!

What speed Jimmy had, he showed at once, but in a strange direction, for Tarron swung the stallion straight around at the trio to the right. And he rode with a yell that would have done credit to some champion of the dreadful Cheyennes in the old days of glory on the plains. His knees gripping the sides of the gray, his feet loose in the stirrup, his body part of the racing horse, his hair blown back from his head, the broad band of crimson drying like paint on his brow. I wish that you could look with me upon that picture of Tarron, charging his foes!

And if you could see him, as he was, you would almost forget that each hand held a flaming Colt. For the three before him well-nigh forgot his weapons.

All that they saw was the terrible man on the silver horse dashing at them like personified death. And for half a moment only they stood their ground.

Then a bullet crashed through the head of the best and bravest warrior. And the remaining two scattered, one to right, one to left.

Tarron scorned to pursue them. He thrust the Colts into the holsters and held the stallion into an easy gallop. It would have been well-nigh a racing gait for an ordinary horse, and it was sufficient to leave behind him the men from the pass, fagged as their horses already were by the effort of following the wonderful run that Monte had made that night.

And having failed to capture Monte, how could they capture this silver ghost, this twinkling will-o'-the-wisp? There was little joy in Tarron at his reunion with Jimmy, however. It was of Monte that he thought constantly. And when he saw that the pursuit had died and scattered hopelessly behind him, he doubled back like a fox to the place where Monte lay dead. There he laid bare the face of a birch, and with a pencil he scrawled on the shining bark:

> Here lies Monte, that was the finest and the truest of them all. You punchers, you pray for a horse like him, but you'll never get his like.

He felt better after he had written this. Then he remembered that he should sign his name, lest there be the slightest doubt as to the identity of the writer.

He then took from the case the rifle which he had left with the gelding and, remounting Jimmy, went on his way. He felt very much better now that he had paid proper tribute to the dead horse. And, he reflected, in what manner could Monte have died better?

There would be one more comfort for him in the future. He would find the owner of Monte, and would tell the fat man how gallantly Monte had made his last run and died.

Now Tarron came out from the shadow of the trees once more and checked the stallion in the light of the stars. Pursuit, for the moment, he no longer feared.

He had Jimmy beneath him, and he was willing at any time to stake his life upon the strength and blazing fleetness of foot of the gray.

But one thing had been demonstrated beyond all doubt. He could not cross the pass. And what else remained for him to do?

Yes, and could he even be sure that when he got through the pass he would gain any advantage by slipping into Santa Maria? Perhaps that had been merely a wild goose chase, from the beginning to the end.

La Paz! La Paz!

Where was the city of peace? What a name to give to a town that was to madden those who hunted for it through these solemn mountains! Must the hunt be in vain?

And, in the midst of his distress, he thought of the one man he had ever met who possessed invincible peace of mind and utter calmness. He thought of old Gregorio—and his tiger daughter.

Perhaps, by this time, the mist would have lifted from the memory of the Mexican, and he could tell Tarron definitely the whereabouts of the lost city. So, at least, Tarron would have something to do on the following day—and a sufficiently dangerous thing; for all along his trail he knew it was most likely that men would be watching for his reappearance. Particularly since the old Gregorio might well have remarked that the wanderer intended revisiting him to ask his question.

So he headed back up the valley, and across the hills, aiming his course for the dwelling of Gregorio.

As he rode, he began to wonder a little at himself.

How long was it since he had tasted food or drink? How long was it since he had slept? What matter? His body was not faint, his nerves were not shattered. His strength was as great as ever, and his heart was marvelously light.

He touched his face with his hand. It seemed to him that the outlines of his cheek were flattened and that he was sharper and leaner about the jaws. But he could never read by touch the real alteration that had come to him.

He had passed out of his boyhood at last. Far behind him lay another self which he had sloughed as a snake sloughs an old skin. A newer, cleaner, stronger, keener, better self was this of the man Tarron. So, as he faced toward the cabin of old Gregorio, what wonder that his self-confidence was brimming, and that a whistle trembled on his lips?

He had long arrears of living to make up, and he was living fast and gloriously.

Through the night, he maintained the stallion at a steady, sweeping dog-trot, covering the miles in the tireless manner of a wolf, until, rounding a headland that jutted down into the valley floor, he saw before and above him the house of old Gregorio, and in its window there was a light shining.

A light shining—yet the hour was late! It seemed proof positive to Tarron that something must be wrong in the house. So he left the gray behind him in the trees and started forward on foot to stalk the place.

31
Brave Talk

TARRON could hear the sound of men's voices when he was still at a little distance. From that point his approach was more stealthy than the creeping of a wolf. By degrees he came near the door. He could see Lucia waiting upon four caballeros and giving them wine as they sat about the table. They had finished their dinner, but still drank and ate crusts of bread to fill up the crevices of their great appetites.

"Call the old man again," said one of them in Spanish.

"There's no use in that," said Lucia. "He's said all that can be drawn out of him, the fool!"

"Well, there are ways of getting more from him."

"You think so," said the woman. "But I know better. When he was a young man, he did enough to make stories which they still tell through these parts of the mountains. Once he followed a wounded wolf into a cave, and a mountain lion sprang on him in the darkness and knocked the rifle from his hand. That great white scar on his forehead is the result of her leap. He got out his knife and stabbed her to the heart. Then he went on, found the wolf, and came back with the pelts of both the animals."

"That was when he was young," said one of the men.

"Aye," replied Lucia. "But though his body is old, his heart is still stubborn. Oh, don't I know? He makes my life miserable. What can I do with him? Nothing!"

Then another voice spoke from the back of the hut, and Tarron started in alarm for it was the unmistakable deep bass of Ingram, speaking execrable Spanish:

"You told us that he said Tarron would come back. Didn't he say when?"

"No, he didn't say that. And he won't say that."

"Perhaps he doesn't know," remarked one of the others. "But the best thing is to lie low here and wait for him to show his head."

Ingram laughed.

There was such an ugly sound to that laughter that the others turned their heads perforce toward the big man.

"Why do you do that?" they asked.

"You think that this boy will walk into your trap?" asked Ingram with a sneer.

"Why not?"

"You sit here laughing and drinking. He could hear you a mile away. That lad has the ears of a wolf, I tell you! Besides, by an extra sense which he has he would know that there is danger here."

He added: "Probably he is now up the hill talking with the old man! And laughing when he hears our voices below him!"

"I'll go and see!"

A handsome young Mexican sprang into the doorway.

"Come back!" called another. "How could even he ride up here from the pass?"

"No, that's true. Not after the work that his horses have done. And not after the work that he's done himself. He'll be asleep somewhere in the woods! Lord, Lord, it would be a thing to find him asleep that way!"

"Yes," said another, "If you could shoot before he opened his eyes."

"Let me have my gun pointed at him, and I don't care when he opens his eyes. I'll finish him!"

"Your hand would shake like a baby's, Pedro! There is a devil in him, beyond question. Ask Lucia. She's a sensible woman, and she's seen him and talked to him, which is more than most of us have done. Just see what she says."

"That's true," said Lucia with an air of importance. "I've talked to a great many men, but I've never seen any like him. He's a devil. Ah! I shudder when I think about him! I wouldn't like to meet him again. When the darkness came tonight, I began to tremble. Don't laugh! I never trembled before for anything! He has the evil eye. When he looks at you, he turns your blood cold!"

"Ghosts, ghosts!" said another, laughing. "Let's tell ghost stories."

"He'll make a ghost of you, my boy," said Lucia sternly. "Well, laugh like fools. I don't care."

Said Ingram slowly: "You, Pedro, you had the telephone message. How many was it that died?"

"Four are dying, señor, and they think that a fifth man will die surely. And there are six wounded. Nothing like that fighting was ever done before!"

Said another: "He must have gone down through the pass like a starved lobo through a pack of strangling dogs. I would have liked to see that!"

"From a distance, Manuelo!"

"Well, from a distance. I'm not ashamed of that. It would take a madman or a fool to want to stand up to such a fellow!"

"That's true. There was never anyone who could fight like that. You can see that he could not do such things except that the devil points his guns."

"Nevertheless," said Ingram, "there has been much greater fighting than this."

"Tell us one man who ever did more!"

"I could tell a lot of them. I'll give you one example, though: When Wild Bill Hickok was in a shack, ten men went to kill him. They rushed the shack under fire, and he fought them hand to hand. When he was full of wounds, three men who were left alive ran out of the shack and tried to get away. Two of them did get away, both wounded; but the third man was shot off his horse by Wild Bill. Now tell me, was that a greater fight than this boy made?"

There was a moment of awed silence.

"Yes," said Pedro, "that was a wonderful thing, and a hard thing to believe!"

"That is the truth. Everyone knows that—everyone in Texas, I'd say."

"Well, I should like to have seen the face of the man that did that thing!"

"He wasn't like Tarron. Tarron looks like any boy, except that he's a handsome brat. Wild Bill looked like what he was. A king! Well every desperado looks tremendous until he goes down. And when I've caught this Tarron, you'll see that his claws are not so long!"

There was another moment of silence, and then the voice of Lucia asked coldly: "A great many brave men have tried to catch Tarron. You seem very sure of yourself, señor."

"I am," said Ingram. "I feel in my bones that I'm the man to corner him, one day. Besides, I have the horse that will do it."

"Your black horse is very fine, that is true. And he *may* run down the horse of Tarron."

"The finest thing that ever stepped, that black. And he cost a price! Arab blood and thoroughbred mixed. He has the flint of the Arab in his bone; and he has the size and the stretch of a thoroughbred, y'understand?"

"He is a grand horse to see."

"He moves like running water."

"What was the price?"

"There was twenty-five hundred dollars paid for that critter, my friends!"

A general shout of wonder came from the listeners.

"Oh, he could win on a race track," said Ingram proudly. "And besides he's been toughened all his life to mountain work. You will see something when he begins to run."

"Besides, the best horse of Tarron has died."

"No, the gray's better than the one that died."

"Better?"

"Aye, a marvelous horse. You'll see him run, one day. I hope that you'll have a chance to watch the black catch him, though."

"What do you call your horse?"

"Name of Benedict. I call him Ben for short."

"Where is the sheriff, Señor Ingram?"

"Which sheriff? There's two of them on the trail. They'll be working up different trails. They'll never catch him, because they'll be working too slow for him. But they all help. We've got these mountains filled with hornets, and one of 'em is sure to sting this dragon fly sooner or later."

"Dragon!" broke in Lucia. "That's a good word for him!"

"They have raised the reward," said another.

"To what?" snapped Ingram eagerly.

"It is eight thousand dollars, now, and more offered nearly every day."

"The little fool!" exclaimed Ingram exultantly. "To get the law on him like this!"

"For horse stealing. That was bad enough. Now for murder!"

Ingram whistled.

"We'll soon have an end to him. Oh, for one fair run at him with Benedict! Oh, for a fair chance!"

"Aye, señor, but suppose that your black horse should carry you too far ahead of your friends—"

The questioning voice stopped in the very pitch of malicious interrogation, and Ingram answered calmly: "I'll be ready for Tarron. I know that he's as brave as a lion and as secret as a snake. But something tells me that I'll down him. We'll have to wait and see!"

This remark was greeted with another silence, rather of wonder than of contempt, for it was plain that Ingram was speaking out of actual conviction rather than a mere empty boast.

"How did you come to hate him so much, señor?"

"Because the first time that I met him he made a fool of me and stole my horse—that same gray. And ever since, I've wanted to get at him. God's gonna turn him over to my hands!"

A sort of religious conviction thrilled in big Ingram's voice, and even Tarron, waiting and listening in the darkness, shuddered a little. He felt that, if possible, he would like to avoid an encounter with this man, because when a Western fighter feels that fate is on his side, he is apt to be invincible.

So it was with Ingram, now. He was not in an ecstasy of excitement. He was simply, calmly, bent upon his purpose. And a little rare chill of fear persisted in the heart of Tarron for a moment longer. He would decidedly like in some way to throw this big, grim fellow out of the chase. The power of Langhorne, the power of the law, the hundreds of free lance hunters for his head, they began to seem nothing to Tarron compared with the persistent malice of this enemy. Twenty-five hundred dollars for a single horse!

32
Light Feet on the Mountains

Up on the hill he found a dark figure seated on a rock, and he could discern, even at a little distance, the glimmering silver beard of the old man.

"I shall not come in, friend," said Gregorio sternly, as he saw the boy approach. "I shall not come in. I am better here, and I have talked enough. Too much, perhaps, for the welfare of my poor young friend, Tarron."

"Ah, señor," said Tarron, "you need not be afraid that I'll ask you to go into that house!"

At that voice, Gregorio sprang up with a wonderful lightness and agility and coming in haste to Tarron he caught his arm with hands that trembled with excitement and with age.

"Dear heavens, my child," said Gregorio, "how have you come back here, so wonderfully?"

"I'm here, and I'm safe," said Tarron. "That's all. Don't worry about me."

"And the dead men who lie behind you?"

"Well," said Tarron, "they had almost conquered me. I had to fight back."

"God's will be done!" said Gregorio. "It has been a glorious day for you, and after this, youths will stand straighter and have bigger hearts, remembering the great things that young Señor Tarron performed in the pass of Santa Maria!"

"But I haven't come back to boast, father."

"You have come back for what, child?"

"You can guess if you'll try, I think. For answer to the question that I asked you before I left."

"Questions? My poor old brain forgets nine tenths of the things that happen today. Only the old, dead years are clearly before my eyes."

"That may be true. But now, try to think. I'd asked you about La Paz. Where is there such a city in the mountains?"

And Gregorio answered slowly: *"Santa Maria de la Paz?"*

"Ha!" cried Tarron. "You have it! You've remembered it, then? The name of La Paz!"

"There has never been a city of that name."

"What was the name that you just used?"

"It came off the tip of my tongue by mistake, I suppose. Let me see— what did I call it?"

"Santa Maria de la Paz."

"Yes, yes, but—ah, now I remember! In the old days, men called it by the whole name—Santa Maria de la Paz! What was it!"

"Aye, and sometimes they shortened it to La Paz?"

"Yes, perhaps. In the very old days. I've almost forgotten. But somewhere— when I was a child—someone has told me, surely, of the days when it was called Santa Maria de la Paz."

"That's the place. That's what it must be. It's the only chance!"

"The only chance of what?"

"That I may find the lost city."

"Do you mean to go to Santa Maria de la Paz?"

"Yes, yes, if I can get there!"

"Ah, lad! Don't you understand what a thing it would be to cross those mountains where the head-hunters are waiting to snare you?"

"I understand. I've had a taste of them. But perhaps they won't be expecting me to try that way again."

"They will, they will! There is this tall devil of an American—this Señor Ingram. He seems to know beforehand just what you'll do, and he has been swearing that you'll try again to get through the pass."

"Ingram and I—" began the boy, and then he paused and left his sentence incompleted.

"He is the great enemy, is he not?" said Gregorio. "Ah, and there he sits with the rest of the bloodhounds, and they have drawn down the law on your head, lad!"

"I don't mind the law!"

"You think not, because you are very young. But the law never rests. And eventually it will win. Time is nothing to it. It waits ten years and then takes you while you sleep. It is a panther creeping through the dark and never stopping."

"Well," said Tarron, "but Santa Maria de la Paz is what I want to talk about."

"Only I know that, somewhere, I have heard that it was called at one

time Santa Maria de la Paz. Some old man must have told me when I was
a boy. That's all. What does that mean to you?"

"You can't remember that it was ever called only La Paz?"

"No."

"Then I'll have to run down this thread. Back to Santa Maria! Back to
Santa Maria! Señor Gregorio, for the love of God tell me of some other
way across the mountains—some way except the pass!"

"There is no way except where even a goat would be dizzy!"

"I'll try that way."

"No, no, lad! You could only cross it by foot. You would have to leave
your horse."

"Then I'll leave the horse, and get another when I pass the mountains
into the valley of Santa Maria."

"But the others will surely know about the pass, and they'll watch for
you there."

"Perhaps they will; perhaps they won't, if it's a place where a horse can't
go. I've got to take the chance."

"So, so, so!" sighed the old man. "I also was filled with hot blood when
I was young. But I was never quite like this. It is true that a young man
cannot remain in his own front yard and conquer the world. But still—
well—if you die you will be remembered. You have done enough this day,
child!"

"The pass, the pass!" cried the boy. "Tell me how to get to it."

"You start straight for the pass of Santa Maria. And a mile from the
mouth of the pass, you'll see a stream leaping down the face of the mountain
to the right—"

"Yes."

"That is it."

"I remember that stream. What about it?"

"That, child, is the place where the pass of which I speak begins."

At that even Tarron paused, his breath gone.

"Has a man ever crossed that pass?" he asked.

"The Indians have a legend of a hero who once crossed it. That is why
Langhorne may have the pass watched."

"I remember the spot," sighed Tarron. "And I thought that even a goat
could never have got up it."

"No, it would be hard. But I've seen, with my own eyes, a goat climb the
pass."

"Then I'll try it."

"Then may God be with you!"

"Señor Gregorio."

"Yes."

"I have one other thing to ask of you."

"Ask it, in God's name!"

"Señor Ingram came riding a fine black horse."

"Yes. It was a glorious animal to see."

"Where is it now?"

"Ah, ah! Must you do that, my son?"

"He is the devil on my trail," said Tarron gloomily. "I've no desire to murder a horse. But—I've got to stop Ingram. After I've done this job, then I'm willing to meet him and fight him. But until the work's finished, I want to keep away from him. My blood turns cold when I think about him!"

"It is always that way," murmured the old man. "The greatest and the bravest are always afraid of one thing. There is one spot where they may be wounded. And with you, it is this Ingram?"

"Yes."

"Then you'll find the black horse in the little corral behind the shed. There is no other horse with him. He's a stallion and very savage."

"Well, so much the better. Father, good-by!"

"Good-by, child. Will you come back to me again?"

"Yes, if I live through the next ten days."

"You cannot tell me what takes you to Santa Maria?"

"No, because I hardly know myself."

"You hardly know!"

"Good-by!"

"Good-by, son. God grant you fortune!"

Tarron went hastily down to the rear of the stable, and there he saw the horse at once.

A lighthouse standing on the shore could hardly have been more conspicuous, even among the shadows of the night, than was this monster. He rose a full seventeen hands. His great eyes glistened in the starlight, the shaking of his mane in the wind was like a threat to Tarron.

Les stepped to the edge of the corral, and the big horse flattened his ears and lowered his head with a snaky and ominous movement.

"I'll have no advantage of you," said Tarron. "My knife only against your four hoofs, and we'll fight it out!"

He slipped through the bars of the corral, knife in hand, and had barely straightened when the black monster was upon him with a rush of hoofs. Had he been attacking an ordinary man, it would have been instant death, but Tarron was no ordinary man. His leap to the side enabled him to avoid the reaching teeth and the battering forehoofs.

He stood for an instant with poised weapon at the side of the monster. And then, lowering the weapon, Tarron whipped around and vaulted over the top rail of the corral. It had not been in his heart to take the life that was in this mighty king of beasts.

And the wicked devil raged up and down the bars of the corral, furious because this prey had been snatched away.

In the meantime, a voice, the familiar voice of Ingram, was calling:

"Who's out there? Who's bothering my horse?"

A footfall approached. Tarron hesitated. Now he could do the thing pat, waiting until the tall man's form loomed before him in the darkness. Taken by surprise, bewildered by the sudden challenge, big Ingram would be half beaten before he began to fight.

No, that was not the way. They were too magnificent a combination, taken together, for Tarron to wish to meet them except in the brightness of the day, man to man, hoof to hoof.

So he slipped into the shadow of the shed, and saw Ingram come to the bars and curse the huge stallion affectionately, and the stallion came and laid a head on the shoulder of his big master.

33
Over the Precipice

IT was a very strange thing to Tarron, you may be sure, to see this demonstration of affection between man and horse; to hear the low, smothered voice of Ingram speaking to the black monster, and to see the ears of the stallion pricked forward.

He waited to see this; then he slipped away through the night, went past the house, and stood for a moment at the side of the gray stallion, watching the light pouring through the door of the old shack and spilling down the hillside.

In that moment, Tarron came marvelously close to giving up the work which was before him. The sounds of singing from the house and the cheerful knowledge that there was good bread and better wine in the place had nearly unnerved him and made him sharply and miserably aware of his own hunger and his own misery.

However, there is a force of habit which makes even hard things easier. We are carried along by instinct, as it were, in the course which has been first begun. And when Tarron turned Jimmy's head, he pointed it, almost against his will, toward the mouth of the pass of Santa Maria. However, the good gray had not taken a dozen steps, trotting down the valley, before Tarron's heart grew more resolute. He was ready to stick to his purpose now, and to stick to it with all his might.

So, in an astonishingly short time, he came again within the danger zone at the mouth of the pass.

Dawn was beginning to break at last over that night which had seen him pass through so much; and now, looking up the face of the rock, he watched the water bounding down with a rushing and roaring. It was no great body of water, but the distance and the sheerness of the fall made the noise like that of a plunging torrent.

He hardly dared to pause, because if he had waited his resolution might have slipped from him. He gave Jimmy a farewell hug, and then advanced to his work. He pushed through the scattering vines which masked the bottom of the rock. And within these, he found the precipice beginning. However, it was really not a precipice at all. Though the general lines of the rock were, at a distance, sheer enough to daunt any heart, still, close at hand, he found that the dashing water of the fall had, by centuries of patient labor, broken a way through the solid rock upon either hand, so that the foot and the hand found an easy stairway prepared. He had climbed a hundred feet with great speed when a frantic neighing beneath him called him back toward the stallion.

Jimmy stood beneath, whinnying as though his heart would break to bring his master once more to his side. Tarron glanced anxiously up and down. He could not tell when that clarion summons would bring suspicious spies to investigate the nature of the disturbance here. There was nothing in sight, but still he was greatly worried; and he had to shout to Jimmy until the good horse became quiet once more.

Then Tarron turned to the task before him. Every instant it grew easier. The hardest portion seemed to be the first ladderlike stretch of rock. In most parts of the world, this might have been a commonly used path, but here in the West, where men lived on horseback, it was a different matter. Only where a horse could go would men travel.

He gained the top of the first ascent, and looking before him, he saw that the dreadful pass which old Gregorio had described was, in reality, nothing more or less than a long, high, ascending plateau, which stretched away toward the west and south. And he laughed aloud in the pink of the morning light as he thought of the dreadful prophecies which the old man had made.

He tightened his belt, and as he did so, a big mountain grouse rose from a shrub. It did not fly far. The empty stomach of Tarron lent him speed and he brought the Colt from his holster with a swift gesture. As the gun exploded, the grouse tumbled from the air through which it was slanting upward, and fell heavily upon the ground.

Tarron's attention was taken from his prey for the moment, however, for now he heard a great scratching and scrambling over the stones behind him, mingled with a heavy snorting; and turning in haste and in some dread he saw the magnificent head of Jimmy rising above the edge of the rock wall!

Whinnying with joy, the fine gray bounded to him. Tarron went back and looked over the edge down the ragged, broken ascent. Looking down, it seemed surely that no horse could have managed the thing. But here was Jimmy in the flesh, more beautiful than ever, and arching his neck as though perfectly conscious that he had done a wonderful thing deserving of the highest praise.

Jimmy was turned out to graze in the patch of grass at the top of the cliff, and there, on the verge of the height, Tarron devoured the dead bird "neat." That is to say, it went down uncooked, and to the famine-sharpened maw of the young man, there had never been any meal so perfectly delicious— or so without the need of cookery.

Sleepiness and a trembling fatigue came over him the moment he had finished his meal. He found a deep dell among the rocks, and there he concealed himself among the brush, leaving Jimmy like a watchdog, free to graze, or rest. Sure that the stallion would give the alarm, Les curled himself up and slept.

What a sleep, with hard rocks for a couch!

Many a long hour later he wakened, with a ringing in his ears and a sense of pain in his stomach. It was only returning hunger which tormented him. His body had absorbed the last meal as the face of the desert absorbs a cupful of water.

By the time he had washed his face and hands in a runlet, he was himself again. His head was clear. The pain left his stomach. And here was the stallion, in the evening of the day—for he had slept the clock almost around— as fresh as a daisy and ready for any work he might have for him.

God bless the mustang stock in that indomitable horse!

Now that Tarron was rested, he only wondered at one thing—that he should have felt the slightest awe of Ingram on the preceding night. But he attributed that to the bewildering effect of weariness and hunger. Therefore, he dismissed the qualm which had bothered him, and vowed that the next opportunity that offered would find him flying at Ingram's throat. There was no slightest doubt in him as to the result of such a battle.

Tarron had been well blooded by this time, and he was as keen as a hunting knife for the work which lay ahead. If there were danger, he would welcome it as another might welcome a banquet.

But now for Santa Maria! Now for the house of Señor Langhorne. And once in it, let God be his guide and plant his feet in the right steps!

You will wonder how such a profane young man could come to call Divinity to his aid. But so many strange things had happened to Tarron during the brief period since he had left the house of his father, that it was forced upon him and he felt, in spite of himself—that he had been selected for some great accomplishment.

Perhaps that consciousness of the ever-working hand of destiny is a great advantage, for it urges a man forward with calm nerves and no strength is wasted upon vague forebodings. Danger is accepted as it presents itself, and as a thing which must and will be conquered. Such was the state of the mind of Tarron, and no more ideal state could have been found.

He mounted the gray, and continued his journey in the most leisurely fashion, for he was not at all anxious to get to the valley beyond before the evening of the day had well closed in. As a matter of fact, it was deep in the dusk before he came to the edge of the table-land, and there he found beneath him a dangerous and shelving slide. It would be almost impossible to ascend, and perhaps fatal to descend. On the verge of it, he paused again and looked about. The lights of Santa Maria lay beneath him, gradually growing in numbers as the householders kindled their lamps. Beyond went up the dusky mountains, and on the forehead of one of those heights gleamed a triple eye of red. No stars were ever so angrily bright and threatening. No, these eyes must be made by the hand of man.

Les Tarron caught his breath with a gasp. What a half wit he had been not to have guessed at once—not to have seen that light the instant that he came into view of the inner valley.

It was the signal prearranged to summon the mountaineers to that place to search for Tarron and to guard against him. And it told him, in no uncertain words, that the men of the valley were forewarned, forearmed. His coming was expected!

Had they, perhaps, trailed up the ascent near the broader and easier pass? Les groaned with rage and despair and disappointment.

If he descended into that valley, he would be like a wingless fly, committing itself to the deeps of a great, smooth-sided bowl. He did not know the mountains and their passes which ringed the valley round about. He did not know them, and he did not know what snares were laid for him beneath. But of one thing he could be doubly sure, that the house of Señor Langhorne must be heavily guarded at this very moment. Perhaps half a hundred men were there at the disposal of the mysterious leader who had already thrown so many obstacles across the path of Tarron.

But yonder lay, in some fashion, the solution to the mystery. There was the seat of his enemies. There, also, must be the stronghold of his friends, if he could only learn their names. Yonder was the rightful possessor of the little steel box. Yonder, also, were the cunning wits and the cruel hands which would sacrifice ten thousand lives to keep the box from its rightful owner. Above all, yonder was the solution of the puzzle.

Tarron, with a thrust of his heel, sent the stallion over the verge of the semi-precipice. Down they went caroming, like a rock cast loose from its moorings. Down they went! Behind him a small avalanche was loosed and began to crash around them, rattling volleys of stones. And then, before him, sweeping through the darkness, Tarron saw riders emerging from the trees!

34

A Beggar Afoot

THE mind can go to Sirius and back again while a dog is snapping at a fly. Tarron had time to look back to the probable reason why this approach to the valley was watched. Someone heard Jimmy neighing at the farther end of the crossing. There they had found torn brush at the bottom of the ascent, and at the top, scraped and freshly broken rock. So they had simply sent on word to the inner valley of Santa Maria, and the result was that the exit was watched.

Heavily watched, too!

Tarron swung the gray to the right. Like lightning they sprinted. And from the brush riders rose every instant and swarmed after him. He doubled Jimmy around, for the stallion could twist about like a dodging jack rabbit, and back along the edge of the rock rubble at the bottom of the long slide the gray horse flashed, running as he had never run before. Even Tarron was amazed by his lightning speed.

Men were not fifty yards to his right, now, and as he rode back, he emptied two revolvers—not at them, with aimed shots, but toward them, firing simply with a blind haste, so that they might hear the humming of the bullets, and perhaps be turned and dazed by the whir of lead.

There was a moment's hesitancy even in that half dozen of men. As a football team stands amazed when it sees some daring opponent dash away on an unexpected flank run, so stood these men of the valley of Santa Maria.

They wavered only an instant, and then rushed in pursuit, their guns roaring. But Tarron had already been near the brush, and now he was into it. The men behind him shrieked in their madness of disappointment. They fired blindly into the woods as they galloped, and more than one in the hysteria of angry haste was knocked from his saddle by an unexpectedly low limb of a tree. Before that crowd of horsemen the gray slid through the forest like an oiled swimmer through the waves. The noise of his going was utterly drowned by the tremendous crashing behind him. Each second he was gaining yards upon the riders in his rear. If only he did not find new enemies before him!

No, in this direction the entire guard seemed to have been massed at the very point of the danger; as though they made sure that their hands would be so strong at this place of contact that they could not fail to catch and crush the fugitive.

Not fugitive, either! Rather a single wild-hearted gadfly attacking an army of tigers; flying into their den, goading them with a poisoned sting, humming its wings in their faces, scoffing at them and scorning them, and passing through their savage ranks to do some harm—some dreadful harm— against which all their powers and their trained watchfulness could not defend them and their king!

That was the feeling that came into Tarron's heart and with it, came again that thrilling suggestion of the hand of fate thrusting him forward and controlling him.

He reached the edge of a small creek. The water foamed down the center of a little gorge with banks ten feet high. Down that rocky bank went the stallion, and then whirred rapidly along, covered by this as in a sunken trench.

Les Tarron heard the noise of the pursuit break from the covert and roar into the open. Then a sudden burst of firing and the noise rolled far off to the right. They had begun to pursue some fleeting shadow in the hope that it was Tarron.

Tarron now drew up the gray and walked on with him, laughing in spite of himself, for there was not a wound of any kind upon his body except that scratch across the forehead. He had made a bandage for that hurt, and therefore he was in perfect comfort. Behind him lay utter confusion and bewilderment. Before him lay—well, what lay before him?

"They" had tried to knife him as he slept; to murder him on the way with poison. "They" had set an invincible guard in two places. Through the first he had nearly slipped, and, baffled there, he had returned again, paralyzed them with his daring as a wasp paralyzes a doomed spider, and flying into their faces he had cut through them and ridden on straight toward the heart of the town of Santa Maria.

Well, what were "they" thinking?

Were "they" now in the house of Robert Langhorne, hearing the report which some panting fellow telephoned in from the battle front—another report of failure? Did they not, then, turn their heads and stare at one another? Did they not wonder if the lonely rider might not break in upon them in spite of their strong walls and their watchful guards? Would there not be terrible though quiet misgivings among even the stoutest hearted of them? Would not the guards themselves be above all unnerved? For their fellows had watched faithfully in the distance, and Tarron had ridden through them as the prow of a ship rides through the waters.

The lights of Santa Maria were close before him when he rode Jimmy up the bank of the stream. Studying the outline of the town, he distinguished the tall front of the church at once. Behind that would be the house of Langhorne and his first goal.

In the meantime, he must secrete Jimmy, and at that thought his heart sank. Ride him into the town he hardly dared; but if he left him in some close copse near the verge of the city, there would be a great distance between the Langhorne place and Tarron's line of retreat. That was a danger which he must endure, he decided. So he set about finding a wood in which to leave the stallion. Not a furlong away, between two small houses, he saw a shadowy growth of trees and started for it. As he moved behind the first house he tripped over the shafts of a cart. He stopped to nurse his barked shins and swear silently, shaking his fist in a boyish fury at the cart. Then a new thought came to him.

He had no time to examine these inspirations in detail. He stripped off his riding boots and socks. That left him barefooted, but bare feet were a small hindrance to him, for in his home shoes had been more or less of a luxury. He took off his hip holsters and slung a Colt under each arm, where, after all, they were even more conveniently placed for a quick draw. After that, he unsaddled Jimmy, and entered the little shed at the side.

There he found a broken, tattered harness, patched with bits of rope. This he placed on the stallion, and Jimmy, with turned head, watched this proceeding with amazement and disgust. He had never borne such a weight on his back before.

After that, Tarron took the bandage from around his head and washed his wounded forehead in a pool of rain water. Next he ripped and tore at his sleeves, until they were dangling shreds that reached no lower than his elbows. His hair he rumpled and combed down with his fingers until it fell across his eyes.

Now Tarron hitched Jimmy to the cart and shook his head in concern as he saw the fine animal shudder with dread and crouch between the shafts. In the cart he placed the saddle, with the rifle in its case. Some rubbish from the shed was heaped over the saddle, and on top of all Les placed a thick layer of charcoal which he found in a corner of the little outhouse.

Thus equipped he went to Jimmy's head, took the lead rope in his hand and whispered. Jimmy started, felt the tug of the lumbering cart, and lurched ahead in terror, snorting. The cart followed, with a prodigious rumbling and squeaking of wooden axles on wooden hubs.

"Hello!" cried the voice of one within the house. "Who is that?"

"Drunken Felipe, most likely," said another, "getting home late."

Tarron, holding his breath, thanked the kind Lord who had brought him safely past his first danger. He led Jimmy fast growing accustomed to the new work but still from time to time nosing at his master by way of assurance through a winding way among the trees and then he saw before him the first dimly lighted street of Santa Maria.

At the same moment, from the bell tower of the old church, bells began to clang and crash, not with the slow and rhythmic tolling which calls men to a Mass or funeral or wedding, but with a rapid, hurried, uneven beating, one wave of sound rushing out on the heels of the other and overtaking it and smashing against the ear in continual discord.

No call to prayer, as Tarron very well knew. No, it was a call to arms. An alarm bell, the rope tugged at by frantic hands, to send out the summons far and wide, floating above the roofs of the town, and drifting far off to the hills beyond. All would hear it, and all would answer.

There was no doubt in Tarron's mind as to the nature of that call. "They" had received the news that he had broken through their lines and was approaching the town itself, and now the danger signal was pealing. In the far distance, at either side of the valley, the triple red lights blazed forth from the foreheads of opposite hills.

The valley was roused. It was prepared to do its utmost. And even the heart of Tarron quailed in him. How can one man defy an army? But he was somewhat reassured, as he headed steadfastly down the street, leading his gray stallion.

"They" were looking for a dashing rider, on a brilliant gray horse, with a bandage about his forehead, and guns at his hip, and the hair blown behind his head by the speed of his going. What a contrast between that alert figure and this barefooted peon trudging through the dust of Santa Maria's streets, with his eyes glittering behind his tousled mass of falling hair! And as for the gray horse, how could its beauty be better disguised than by the ugly, broken, patched and rope-mended harness, while he tugged a lumbering, screeching cart behind him?

Tarron, with a steadier pulse, led Jimmy forward. But at the first turn of the street, half a dozen men swarmed out at him. Never had he seen more savage-looking fellows. And one who seemed in control stopped him with a sharp:

"Boy, did you hear the alarm bell? Where are you going?"

35
Captain Courageous

As if to remove all doubts, at that moment the alarm bell crashed again from the church tower and filled the air with an uneasy dinning, and Tarron blessed the noise of the bell, for it covered his confusion and gave his wits time to clear a little.

When the noise had subsided, he answered, gaping: "Senor, what can a poor boy do?"

"Take a stick or a knife," said the other, "when the bell rings. You know that?"

"Ah, señor, how gladly would I take stick or knife, but my father takes his rifle and goes off and leaves me to drive the cart. I don't want to drive the cart, señor. But what shall I do?"

"Leave it standing then, and be ready for work. The devil is loose tonight!"

Tarron crossed himself.

"Señor, señor," said he. "I shall be beaten by my father if I don't drive on with the cart!"

"Stuff!" said the other, while his companions grinned. "The law is the law. No matter for your father! Where does the cart go?"

Tarron thought swiftly. If he imagined a name, would it serve. No, this city was not so large, and a lie of that sort might bring a sharp questioning that would ruin everything.

He knew only one name in that town, and now he used it.

"For Señor Langhorne's house, señor."

There was an instant change.

"For that great house? Why didn't you say so before, young fool? Make way, there! For Señor Langhorne's house!"

And suddenly Tarron was free to go on down the street.

No, not free, for this fellow who was in charge insisted on accompanying him, and down the street they went, the pseudo-captain shouting in a great, important bellow: "Way! Way! Casa Langhorne!"

That word worked like enchantment. Even wildly galloping riders swerved respectfully to the side and sheered past the clumsy cart.

The "captain" was full of words.

"That is a good horse, my son," said he. He looked more closely. "Ha, what is such an animal doing pulling a cart!"

The heart of Tarron rapped against his teeth.

"Our good horse is sick," he declared, "and my father had to put in this poor thing."

"What? 'Poor thing?' Don't I know a horse when I see it?"

"See, señor. It is broken down in front, and notice how it hobbles!"

"Of course," said the captain, changing instantly. "I saw that at the first glance, but I wanted to learn if you knew anything about horseflesh. Well, I say it is a cruel thing to use such a beast for cart work. It should be turned loose in pasture, or put out of misery with a bullet through the head, it would make food for dogs."

"Aye, señor, and sometimes for men, too?"

The other indulged in a little laughter.

"Yes, for men, too. Well, lad, you are well out of this trouble tonight!"

"I hear," said Tarron, "that everyone is terribly excited."

"Tush! There—they are ringing the bell for the third time. There has never been such excitement since the rebellion—the revolution I mean to say!"

He made that addition hastily with a side glance at Tarron, but the latter pretended not to understand.

"What will be done?" asked Tarron mildly.

"Too many men! Too many men!" said the other, with a shake of the head. "These things should be left in the hands of a few brave and determined men—and God to help! God to help! I could name some of the men, some who have proved themselves!"

Thrusting out his chest he said this.

"Ah," said Tarron, "I think that my father has pointed you out. You are—let me see—"

"Juan Pilotte—he's pointed me out?"

"Yes, yes. Juan Pilotte. Señor Juan Pilotte."

"Well," said honest Juan. "A man's work will speak for itself in spite of modesty. It will talk out at the last and make itself known."

"That is true."

"If I could have a dozen men of my naming, I think that we'd handle this wild devil of a Tarron."

"Yes," said Tarron, "I should think that one such man as you would be almost enough."

"Do you think so, lad?"

"Because this Tarron—after all, he's only a man!"

"You may say that who have never stood guard against him. But I tell you, I saw him ride down the valley, crushing men like eggshells!"

"Oh, I would have liked to see that!"

"You would? You would have run home to hide your head under a blanket. I have never seen such a thing!"

"Yet he was not very big," said the son of his father.

"So you say! So you say! Well, he's not many inches over six feet in height, and he's got a horse that's about eighteen hands, at least. You may call that a small man. You may call it a small horse, too! And as for fighting, he kills men at three hundred yards with a revolver, shooting from a horse at full speed."

"Is it possible!"

"Isn't it, though? Have I eyes in my head? Can I see?"

"Of course, señor, you have judgment."

"However, bold as he is, I would face him—with a little help from man and God. Just a scant half dozen honest fellows I could name—and we'd stand to him."

"That is brave!"

"Why, a man can only die once. Only once! Better to die fighting bravely!"

"But he'll never dare to enter the town!"

"Won't he? He may be in it now!"

He shuddered violently, and cast a sharp glance over his shoulder at a tree they were passing, a tree which had an odd shape almost like a man on horseback.

"In the town now!" gasped Tarron. "And here I am in the open streets—thank God that I have you to protect me, brave Señor Pilotte!"

"Tush! Have no fear! I shall bring you right up to the door of the Casa Langhorne!"

It was the last thing that Tarron wanted, and a frown of thought came on his forehead.

"Yet," he said, "how could a man dare to come here—look!"

Down the street came rushing a little cavalry charge of half a dozen caballeros, armed to the teeth, naked rifles flashing through the dust which their horses raised.

"Let them go! Let them go!" exclaimed Pilotte. "And don't cry out suddenly again, like that. It rubs all the ends of my nerves raw!"

"Pardon me, Señor Pilotte! But that a man could dare to come into such danger!"

"He would dare anything! He dared to ride up the pass in spite of many brave men. I was there, and I had friends with me! And there were others. But fools got in our way. We could not get at him. Besides, he had magic in his horse. It went over everything, or through anything like running quicksilver! Dare to enter this town? Tush, he would dare anything! Hello! Hello! Are you going past the gate?"

They were passing a tall, wrought iron gate, flanked with powerful stone pillars. Beyond loomed a gloomy woodland.

"True! true!" said Tarron, cursing his carelessness. "But I was too interested, listening to you, señor."

"Well, turn in."

Jimmy brought the groaning cart to the gate, and there four armed men crossed the way.

"What's that?"

"Charcoal for the house."

"There was charcoal brought only yesterday."

"Well, they will burn up a load a day in that great place, I suppose. Hello, don't you know me, Olivero?"

It was Pilotte, taking charge of the whole matter.

"Juan, are you delivering charcoal? Have you gone into that business?"

"Not I. I bring this boy with his cart safely through the streets, and that is all."

"Well, nothing goes through these gates. There are orders."

"His father will beat him if he brings it back."

"Let him speak for himself."

"Alas, Señor Pilotte, if you cannot win me through, what can I do for myself?" pleaded Tarron.

"Well, that's true. You'll see that I have some authority. Listen, you— Leon!"

"I hear you."

"I know this boy. He is my nephew. I have known him all my life. And the house needs charcoal. You'll sweat for keeping him out."

"Well, let him go through. Drive on. Let me take a look at the charcoal, first."

The sharp eye of Tarron measured the distance to the trees. If the odd nature of his load were discovered as the hand of the inquisitor reached into it, he decided that he would flee for the trees and trust to God to be able to get out again, for after the alarm was given, he would never be able to enter the house. That much was sure.

However, the guard merely peered at the black heap in the cart.

"A small load," said he. "But go on. Everyone gives a short measure and a long price to Señor Langhorne. Pass on!"

So the cart passed up the driveway, and Tarron thanked his companion.

"That is nothing," said Pilotte. "A man's life is not lived in vain. We have some authority, thank God, over our fellows! Hush! What is that?"

"Where?"

"Yonder—a shadow among the trees!"

Tarron caught quickly at the fancy.

"Senor!" he whispered. "Could it be a horseman? Could Tarron have come so soon?"

Pilotte stopped with a groan of terror. Then he mastered himself.

"Go on," said he. "You will be able to see the lights of the house around the next bending. Go on! I'll return where danger may be and I shall be needed!"

And he turned and hurried down the path.

36
A Curtain Raiser

WHEN Tarron was left alone, he laughed until he was weak, but then a memory of where he was and what he had before him struck him sober. It was well enough to have passed so many dangers almost miraculously. And now he had entered the very grounds of the great house. But what of the house itself? How was he to manage that?

Well, let every bridge be crossed when it was come to. In the meantime, he must bring his horse somewhere close to the great house and leave the cart hidden in the trees, as close as possible to Casa Langhorne.

As for the cart, that was a problem soon solved. In another ten yards there was a gap among the trees and into it Tarron drove Jimmy. Deep in the woods he unharnessed and unhitched the stallion, and put the saddle on his back. Then he started straight for the house, Jimmy following.

Tarron had not gone fifty yards before a group of figures loomed before him, and he stopped. Jimmy, behind him, turned to a statue of stone, and the group crossed not a dozen yards away, but some low brush helped to screen Tarron and his horse. Yet he could not help worrying.

Suppose that while he was in the house the searching patrol which was combing the woods in front of the house should come upon Jimmy—then the flight of Tarron would be cut off utterly, and he would be ruined.

Or suppose that the searching patrol found the cart and its disturbed load?

Well, let the past bury its dead, and the terrors of the future take care of themselves, one at a time!

Now, as he went ahead, the trees began to thin, and through them near rays of light commenced to break, so that Les realized he had brought the stallion as close as he dared. He did not choose a circle of trees, but in a nest of deep shrubbery he made the stallion lie down. There he was lost to view, and there he would remain like a trained dog until the voice of Tarron spoke to him again.

For a moment he remained beside the good horse, patting him and whispering in his ear. Then he slipped softly ahead, noiseless as a shadow, drifting rapidly from tree to tree and bush to bush, until he came out before the lofty face of the house of Langhorne.

There were three stories, each tall, and each faced with long windows. There was a balcony for each story and never had Tarron seen such a number of ways of entrance to a dwelling. It was a rest to his eye to examine the monster place and see in how many manners it could be attacked.

What he chose was no flank maneuver. And his reasons were excellent. Here in front of the house two great oil lamps threw a daylight blaze that revealed every detail of the surroundings, and up and down across the front of the mansion constantly paraded four men.

Four men here; therefore twice or thrice as many for the other and darker sides of the building. But it was not light that Tarron feared. It was the number and look of the guards, and above all, the way that they did their work. As for these four, they took it for granted that their numbers and the flare of the light cut off all chance of an approach to the mansion from this direction. And Tarron wanted nothing better. Danger there was, but danger had been so much his of late that this seemed nothing at all.

He saw his plan at once. Just before the main entrance and its towering portico was a circular bed of flowers, surrounded by good-sized shrubs, and the moment that the guards had passed it and marched on, arm in arm, chatting with one another gayly, Tarron slipped from his shelter and ran to this circular bed. There he crouched behind a big bush and waited until the quartet had passed him again, moving toward the farther end of the promenade. Then he was up and away like a flash and behind their backs reached the garden which fringed the foundations of the building.

After that all was easy. The crowded pillars of the portico were made to order for him. Barefooted, mighty of hand, he climbed up between two of them and gripping the edge of the cornice, swung up, and up, and drew himself onto the balcony above.

He dared not wait there long. From those windows in front of the Casa Langhorne others were watching, from time to time. But there was an open door before him, and at a stride he was through it, and crouching in a corner behind a curtain.

He had passed the barriers one by one. He was in the Casa Langhorne. It still remained to find the man he wished to confront. But that was a piece of detection which could surely be accomplished were Señor Langhorne here.

Ah, for a little more knowledgei Ah, for just five minutes of such talk as Dorn could have poured into his ears! But where should he go now, and what should he do?

He was in the second story. Most likely the master of the house was below. And he was to get there, too. This chamber in which he now crouched— as the flare of light from before the house enabled him to see—was a bedroom, beautifully furnished. And for one article Tarron gave thanks—the deep rich rug which covered the floor.

Even a heavy-footed monster could have moved over such a surface without betraying himself by a single sound. And as for Tarron, not even a whisper was roused as he crossed the room and listened at the door. There was no sound from beyond.

Little by little, he turned the well-oiled lock. He let the door move gradually open, and glancing out, he saw before him a spacious hallway—the central stairway of the mansion climbing up around the edges of a monstrous well. He saw this—and he saw two men leaning upon—no, not rifles, but sawed-off shotguns! He closed that door in great haste and fell back, biting his lip.

He had expected precautions, but these were a little more than might have been anticipated. For when he has established such advance guards as Langhorne had provided, even the most careful of men would hardly be expected to arm his very house in such a manner as this. But, as he sat in a corner of the room, resting, and rallying his thoughts, Tarron told himself fiercely that this, after all, was for the best. The most timorous of men would not have guarded himself in such a fashion. That was certain. Therefore there must be something in this house exceptionally worthy of being protected.

Tarron sighed, and set his teeth. What was the treasure? Man, woman, child? Or some priceless document?

One thing at least was determined. The hallway outside could not be used as an exit. There remained the big windows. He crossed to the farther one, which was standing open. Outside of it stretched the balcony, broken along its length by the potted shrubs at its edge, and by the rising pillars which supported the balcony of the story above.

Tarron did not hesitate long before he ventured out on it. He stepped boldly out—too boldly, alas!

For, as he passed, the door swung in a little, and the knob caught in his belt. There was a light ripping sound, and then the clang of falling metal.

He looked down, his heart stopping and saw on the floor of the balcony the little steel box, lying face up—and open! In its fall it had struck the spring which he had been unable to find, and now its secrets were exposed to him.

He did not pause to examine it, but scooping it up he sprang back, tigerlike, within the chamber, for the noise had been like a blow on a gong.

Behind the same curtain which had sheltered him before he crouched now, a Colt in his hand. Instantly there was a sound of footfalls—and voices spoke at the window which he had recently left.

"Go on in!"

"Give me the lantern. There we are!"

A bright shaft of light flashed up and down the room, and Tarron held his breath.

"Go in, I say!"

"You go first."

"You're commanding. So you've got to lead the way."

"Well, let me have a look first."

"You've had your look. You can't see behind those curtains from this distance."

"Well, I suppose I've got to."

They stepped through the window. Tarron made himself small behind the curtain; still, it seemed certain that he must make a bulge in the bottom of it.

He could see a sudden brightening of the material just before his face. A ruddy red, like blood, showed through, and he knew that they had turned the brightness of the unhooded lantern straight upon his hiding place. That moment he gave up all hopes of succeeding in his mission. But if he could shoot down these two—gain the window—slip down to the garden and from there bolt to the place where Jimmy waited for him—then God help him to the rest!

"That's something there."

"Where?"

"Behind that curtain. It moved."

"That's the wind, you fool."

"I say I see something."

"Go look, then."

"And get my head blown off, maybe?"

"Look here, you blockhead, do you really think that Tarron is in this room?"

"Why not? Didn't we hear something?"

"Well, if Tarron were here, would he sound a gong to let us know it?"

There was a moment of breathless silence.

"Anyway, I'm going to look."

Steps crossed the floor. The curtain was twitched out, and Tarron, looking up, leveled his gun into the face of a handsome young Mexican.

"You don't see a thing!" said Tarron in a whisper.

And with a shaken voice, his eyes starting from his head, the seeker called out: "There's nothing here!"

37

'Gainst Solid Steel

HE who stood at the door answered briskly: "Come away, then. I told you there'd be nothing."

The other remained staring blankly at Tarron, who shook his head.

"Face him, but don't leave!" whispered Tarron.

The handsome youth turned toward the door.

"I'm going to wait here a while," said he.

"By yourself, and be a hero, eh?" said the man at the door.

"Why not?"

"What would you do if Tarron showed up?"

"I'll handle that chance," said the young Mexican.

"You talk like a fool. Stay here if you want to! Remember what the orders were—to keep walking the rounds."

"Don't mind about me. I'll worry for myself."

There was a stifled oath, and the light flashed out. At the same time, the iron hand of Tarron fell on the shoulder of his captive. There was no escaping from that grip.

Stepping from behind the curtain, he was able to see that the other guard had passed on. The blackness in the room was like a blanket of secrecy around them.

"Hands above your head," murmured Tarron.

He was instantly obeyed. While the victim's hands were raised at arm's length, Tarron went hastily over his body. The fellow was well enough armed. A Colt and a double-barreled pistol, short and huge of bore, rewarded the search, to say nothing of a deadly little stiletto.

"You can put your arms down," said Tarron.

"Yes, senor."

The arms obediently came down. But it was plain that the man would attempt nothing. He was trembling like a leaf.

"I'll do you no harm," said Tarron, "if you'll play square with me."

"I shall do what I can. I have no wish to die, señor!"

"You have sense. Tell me first, where can we go to talk? How can we get out from this room?"

"Through that window onto the balcony. Or through that door and into the hall."

"With guards at either place?"

"Yes, señor. There are many guards at both places."

The man had spoken the truth, as Tarron knew, and he began to feel more confident.

"What is your name?"

"I am Felipe Morales."

"Felipe Morales?"

"Yes. And your name, señor?"

"I'm Leicester Tarron."

"Oh, God receive my sinful soul!" breathed the captive, and sank limply upon his knees.

"Hush!" said Tarron, almost laughing in spite of himself when he saw what terror his name inspired. "I'll not murder you."

"No, señor. I pray God that you will not. I have an old mother, a wife, and little children! And what would one more death be to a hero like you, Señor Tarron?"

"No hero. You may be able to tell me things that will be well worth hearing."

"My very heart is open to your questioning, señor! But by what miracle did you bring yourself here?"

"By taking chances. And by taking more chances I hope to do something before I leave the Casa Langhorne."

"I shall tell you what I know."

"Sit down here in the darkness, in this corner. So."

"Merciful God!"

"That's the muzzle of a revolver against your ribs. But I'll do you no harm with it. It's only to make sure that you keep the peace."

"I believe you! I believe you, Señor Tarron, my friend!"

"I shall ask you questions as though I knew nothing."

"Very well."

"In that way I shall know whether you are speaking the truth or not."

"I understand. But you must know, señor, that in this house of mystery there are only a few things known even to me. And yet I know more than almost all the others!"

"Good!" said Tarron, his hopes rising. "Tell me, then, why I am here?"

"That, of course, I can say. You are here to reach Antonio Lopez."

The name rang in the ears of Tarron most unexpectedly.

"Lopez? Lopez?" he thought to himself. "Why can that be? How does he enter the case?"

"And who sent me?" he added aloud.

"Andrea Alvarado, of course."

Another name! And yet both this and the other had come instantly from the lips of the prisoner.

However, it was a great step forward. God bless this man who knew so much! Andrea Alvarado, it seemed, was one of "them" who had financed and employed big Dorn and many another man to go to his death in the carrying of the steel box.

"Does Alvarado know that I am here?"

"Alas, señor, can I tell that? I know he must guess that you will have done more than all of the others. But I cannot tell you what is in the mind of Señor Alvarado, even though he is in this city!"

Again young Tarron's heart leaped.

"Where is he in this city?"

"If he is not in his house, God knows, and not I! I don't think that he would dare to leave his doors in such a time!"

"And where is his house?"

"Señor, you mock me!"

"I must test the truth that is in you, friend. Where is his house?"

"Of course. It is the low, broad white house on the western hill."

"Very good. I see that you tell the truth!"

Looking back into his mental picture of the town, Tarron could remember a tree-crowned hill to the west of Santa Maria de la Paz. And through the trees there had been touches and streaks of a white façade. There lived Alvarado, and to know that was, really, to know everything. Or so, at least, it seemed.

"I think that you are telling the truth," said Tarron. "But I must make sure."

"May the thunderbolt strike me if I leave the truth a single half inch to the side of me in what I speak."

"Why am I here instead of at the house of Alvarado?"

"Ah, señor, and what could you do there to advance the cause of Alvarado? No, we all know that the secret is to be had from the lips of old Lopez."

"And who is Lopez?"

"Well, señor, who should he be but the father of that poor, murdered Miguel?"

Murder! More and more Tarron felt that he was closing down upon the heart of the secret.

"How was Miguel murdered?" he asked.

"If I knew—well, of course I don't!"

"Tell me what you know?"

"There is very little to say. I was in the house at that time, however. I was here, and I know how Miguel had gone out into the mountains with young Carlos Alvarado. I know how he came back, too, in the night. And he and his father and Señor Langhorne went out into the little summer house in the garden. All that I know is that the shot was heard there, and young Miguel was killed by the bullet. All men know that."

"And who fired the bullet? Was it Langhorne or the father?"

"Señor Langhorne? Of course he does not have to do his killings with his own hand. And would a father murder his own son? But as for what happened, I know nothing. Only that Antonio Lopez lost his wits afterward. And it must have been a dreadful thing that could have turned his head!"

"Do you think his wits are turned?"

"Hush, señor! I dare not say! I only know that I knew him first when his hair was black, and now it is white, and Señor Langhorne has sworn that his wits are addled. That is all that I dare to know."

"And what do you guess?"

"I guess—ah, Señor Tarron, you have guessed it also!"

"And what?"

"That he is not crazy more than you or I. And that he is kept here so that Andrea Alvarado cannot speak with him. And for what other purpose, God and the steel box know, as the saying runs."

"The steel box?"

"Yes, señor. I have heard the saying, but what it means, I cannot tell."

"Morales, I believe that you have said nothing except what you know or think."

"May heaven strike me otherwise."

"Then tell me how I may reach Antonio Lopez."

"Alas, I knew that you would ask for that. But also I knew that I could not give the right answer. How can I tell you how to leave this room without being seen? And to be seen is to be shot at. The men are instructed to shoot first at strangers and to ask afterward."

"I understand. Tell me at least where I shall find Lopez if I can leave this room?"

"You know, of course, señor. He is always kept in that same room, where the sun can never reach him. But still his spirit is not broken after five years! And it will bend, but never break. For the old man is all steel!"

"And what room is that?"

"It is the cellar room, señor."

"Of course. How may it be known?"

"On the second floor down in the cellar, I myself have seen the door of it—all one slab of strong steel. It will turn the edge of a chisel."

"Do they trust to the strong door now?"

"Not since you have come near the city. No, no! Two men are in the room constantly, and they are changed every four hours."

"At what hours?"

"The next change is at ten, señor."

"Then lie down on the floor, my friend. And lie still. I am not going to choke you, but only to tie and gag you. Do you protest? Look! One slip of your old knife and I could put you on the floor, past all speaking!"

38

Three on the Lookout

HE left young Morales, the honest man, lying swathed in strips of velvet curtain and securely gagged. Not a finger or a toe could the fellow move.

But now that Tarron was free of hand once more, he hesitated at the window. He had, at last, enough information to act upon. He knew who was to be reached in this house. He knew where to find Alvarado, the man who had sent out the steel box. And this was a treasure of information to him. However, what was he to do with it?

First of all, he must get from the room and to the cellar. And that was a task for a giant. Tarron chose the most roundabout method. To go down or around would be tremendously dangerous, but having gone thus far up the side of the building, he trusted that he might be able to go still higher— and then to pass down over the roof, and to the rear of the Casa Langhorne.

He had to shrink back into the dark of the room the next moment, as a guard walked down the balcony. Then, crouching where the light from the strong lamps outside the house threw a reflection into the chamber, he took the steel box from his pocket and examined it.

His heart almost stopped! For within the box there was nothing except a soiled, tattered, much rubbed piece of paper; and when he unfolded it, he saw nothing upon it other than a crooked line checked with a few crosses.

He felt frantically in the pocket into which he had dropped the box after its fall. But the pocket was empty, and now Tarron guessed that the real treasure which the box had held had bounced out when it fell on the balcony and had dropped to the ground below. There, no doubt, it had been buried in the soft muck of the garden strip which ran along the wall of the house. It was lost, and lost in a place where he could never expect to search for it!

Bitter moments have come to other men, but surely there was never any more completely heartbreaking than this of Tarron's, when, come at last to the door of his quest, he found himself empty handed!

The pain of the old wound in his forehead, which he had utterly forgotten, now stabbed through his very brain; and all at once he felt sick with weariness, trembling with the weakness of hunger.

Little by little he mastered himself. And, although he might lose everything by unlucky chance, still he determined to force his way ahead. In that cellar room, closely guarded, was Antonio Lopez, by whom many mysteries might be unveiled. If he reached the place ten minutes before the hour for the change of guards; if he knocked at the steel door and demanded entrance as the new guard, stepped through with a pair of guns leveled and—

Ah, well, it was a chance more desperate than any that he had yet taken. But he was determined to push on. He was too far committed in his own mind. He could not turn back!

He slipped out of the window now, and slid like a ghost down the narrow balcony to the pillars that ran sheer up the face of the house. Once more they served him as a tree trunk serves a monkey. Bare toes and talonlike fingers gripped securely the deep flutings of the wooden columns, and Les has climbed rapidly to the top. He swung himself up over the eaves and now lay panting at full length on the gutter of the great house. Turning his head aside, he glanced down a dizzy distance to the garden beneath and the four guards who still strode confidently up and down, not knowing that the fish had passed through their net long ago!

His danger was so terrible that it cleared his mind, and the weakness and the fatigue passed from him. The first ridge of the roof arose above him, and over the tiles he crept until he had reached that vantage point. Peering over, he saw that the uppermost reach of the roof was occupied by a rectangular platform, a sort of captain's bridge, from which the eye could command the entire town and the valley beyond it.

He made for that point, and while he was lying just under the narrow balustrade that fringed the edge of it, he heard a sudden grating as of a door opened, and then a noise of steps and a burst of voices.

Flat upon the tiles went Tarron, and lay there, hardly daring to breathe. The first eye that looked over the edge of that balustrade and down upon the roof would find him! With a soft but swift movement, he drew himself up still closer and lay stretched out just under the rail, a motionless, formless shadow.

"There isn't much wind," said a voice in perfect English.

"I thought it would be blowing more, señor."

"No, it's very comfortable. Look at the lights! Our fellows are everywhere!"

"They are, señor."

"Do you think that this young devil, this will-o'-the-wisp Tarron could break through?"

"You see for yourself, señor. If he is not entirely mad—surely he will never even attempt it!"

"Aye, but we know that he did attempt it this very evening, and that he probably broke through into the village."

"What good will that do him, señor?"

"That is true. I try to imagine what good it will do him to be in the village."

"If he is in Santa Maria, then he's lying low like a rat with ferrets prowling around it."

"That's very likely. I believe that even the old man would give up hope if he were brought here."

"I think it very likely, señor, when he sees your power shown as it's shown tonight in all those lights!"

"Send one of your men down to the guards. Tell them that Lopez is to be brought up here at once."

"Señor!"

"Don't gape! Do as I say."

"But he has never—"

"Never had so much liberty before? It will do him good, perhaps, to see so much of the thing that he doesn't possess. Go at once."

"Señor Langhorne, I do as you say. I trust there will be no evil consequences."

There was another stir of feet, and Tarron heard someone whistling. The great Langhorne, no doubt, taking his ease on that lookout station, was enjoying all the beauty and the majesty of this valley of which he was the overlord. Such a man was like a king and nothing less.

Langhorne standing just above him—Langhorne within the stretch of his hand. Tarron held his breath in sheer amazement. But the monarch was surrounded by stanch fighting men; and one could wager that only the best of the keen warriors of the mountains would be trusted so near the person of the king.

He heard the whistling end, after a time, and then footsteps coming upstairs, and a heavy panting breath.

"Here you are, Lopez!" said Señor Langhorne cheerfully.

"I am here, señor," said the voice of an old and broken man.

Then, after a little pause, the same voice added: "There is a God over us, after all. I had forgotten the stars. Are they not the face of God, Langhorne?"

"Tush!" chuckled Langhorne. "Isn't it better to be addled than completely poetic, like this, my friend?"

"And therefore," said Lopez, continuing his own thought, "God is watching you. That's enough to make you tremble, I should think!"

"Not a bit!"

"Perhaps not. Well—why have you brought me here?"

"Guess, my friend."

"To give me a glimpse of the stars and the beautiful open night, because that will make the filthy room in the cellar more horrible to me!"

"Not filthy, Lopez!" broke in the other sharply.

"No," admitted Lopez. "Not filthy, except that the darkness is always foul. What other purpose could you have in bringing me here?"

"I'll tell you, presently. But I think that we can make this a very short interview. I am going to convince you, at last."

"You could never do that, señor."

"We'll see. Look out yonder. There are stars of heaven—and earth stars, also."

"You mean the lights—from the fires?"

"Yes. The watch fires."

"Well, there are enough of them. What are you watching against, now?"

"I'm going to tell you that. Lopez, in these years that you have been here, you know that the Alvarados have made great efforts to get at you?"

"Yes."

"And they've sent the steel box by clever messengers—"

"Yes. You've told me that to torment me."

"And I haven't waited. I've reached out and stopped them at a distance."

"You have—so you have said."

"But finally, my friend, a young man took up the work and came like lightning through every danger up to the pass. He rode into the pass, where my men were waiting for him—"

"And was shot to pieces?"

"No, wait for the end. He rode in, was stopped, got away, and galloped like a madman down the throat of the pass again. He escaped by a miracle. He left five dead men and many wounded behind him."

"God be with that young hero! Is he still alive, señor?"

"He came straight back, having failed at the pass. He crossed the mountains by a forgotten trail and dropped down into the valley. And there he was waited for by an ambuscade, but he slipped through them like a ghost and rode into the town!"

"A hero, Langhorne."

"Beyond any question. But this is the point. Now he lies somewhere in that town, surrounded by danger, hardly daring to breathe, and my men hunt for him everywhere. You understand? He has done more than all of the others. But still the best that this wild man, this brilliant fool, could do, was to place himself hopelessly within the trap. There are my men in my city. There are my outposts far away. And when he tries to get away, he will be lost. He has not eaten food for two days, I think. He is starving, weak, worn out. Soon he will be snapped up, and the last of your hopes will go with him. I've brought you here and told you the sheer truth, Lopez. Now, like a reasonable man, capitulate!"

39
Close to the Clue!

"HE has smashed through everything, and actually got into the town!"

"Yes."

"And there he is lost?"

"Ask your own reason."

"And for that reason I should surrender?"

"Well?"

There was a sudden soft cry from the old man.

"Señor Langhorne, listen to me. If I had been in that devilish prison of yours seventy years instead of seven; if I were worn out and crushed and broken and about to surrender, and if then I heard that such a hero in such a manner had come into the valley to rescue me—a man whose face I have never seen and who has never seen me—I tell you, señor, that I would then have the strength to endure for another seventy years. There are many causes in this world that are not worth a snap of the fingers. But if I am a cause worthy of such a hero, he will not die for me any more quickly than I will die for him!"

"By the Lord!" murmured Langhorne. "Too old already—too soft-witted to understand simple logic!"

"You have always scorned me," said the Mexican. "But nevertheless you have never broken me!"

"Tonight, however, I am going to convince you, my friend."

"God give you greater strength of persuasion! I stay here and enjoy the shining of the stars and the nearness of God. You cannot tempt me, señor!"

"We'll see," retorted Langhorne.

He gave orders:

"Tie the hands of this old man against the central post, there. Then go down below and wait in easy calling distance, but not closer than the first landing. I do not wish to be overheard. Do you understand?"

"Yes, señor," came the answer, and presently there was a noise of many feet retreating. The sound of a trap door shutting heavily on a cushion of air, and then Langhorne and his prisoner were alone on their platform high above the town.

No, not entirely alone, for another man lay listening. And what a man! Rather call him a tiger as he lies in the shadow, his eyes burning!

It was all miraculous and unbelievable to Tarron. He had come so far and done so much and fought always against such dreadful odds, and now, by a contrivance of kind fortune, the two men whom he wished to have in the hollow of his hand had been placed there. Old Lopez, the mysterious prisoner, was within arm's length! And with him stood this king of the valley, Langhorne, whose agents had caused so many men to die! Both in his hand! For, with his two guns and all his craft, could he not take Langhorne utterly by surprise?

Yet Tarron lay still for a while longer, anxious to hear what he could and delaying the stroke, very much as a cat plays with a mouse—tasting his power and unwilling to use it.

Moreover, when Langhorne was helpless in his hands—what next? Of what avail to have the lord of a castle in one's power, when one stood at the crest of that lord's castle with all his armed retainers between one and freedom?

But Tarron did not care to look to the future. The present, the present only, would he cling to with a grip of iron and let tomorrow take care of itself.

"You understand, Lopez," said the master, in a quiet tone of argument, "that you have made a moral issue out of a practical affair."

"The death of a man's son," replied Lopez with feeling, "is something more than a practical affair!"

"That is an attitude," said Langhorne, "that I can sympathize with, of course."

"You cannot," replied the other, "for you have no heir, and never have had one."

"Well, well!" snapped Langhorne, apparently touched in a sore spot. "There is no need to dwell on that. However, let us meet even that point in your statement. That one concerning your son. Tell me, my friend, how your dead son benefits by your present misery?"

"How would he benefit by my surrender to you?"

"How would he be harmed? That is the question."

"Because he had committed a great sin, I must do what I may to undo his sin."

"He paid his penalty. A life for a life. No code can ask for more than that!"

"It is true. No code can ask for more than that. But I can ask for more, and I shall do more than that!"

"They killed your boy with a bullet through his back while we sat in the summer house. What could be more dastardly than that?"

"I shall tell you something more dastardly. My son went with a friend to undertake a great adventure. It was young Carlos Alvarado who had worked out the problem of the lost mine and unraveled the mystery of the chart. He had spent years on the thing. Then, out of the greatness of his heart, he asked my boy to accompany him in that final search."

"I admit that, Lopez."

"He went with young Alvarado, and when they had actually discovered the mine and the enormous wealth of it, he allowed the wealth to madden him. He killed his friend and benefactor—because Alvarado had sworn to give him a third share in the profits if their search succeeded."

"I remember all of the details."

"I say that the murder of Alvarado by my son was far fouler than the murder of my son by the men of Alvarado. If they had killed me, also, there would still have been a debt against our name! And now you wish me to tell you what I know, so as to place the mine in your hands. No, no! That is not my conception of justice, my friend. And I shall never do what you wish. You may be sure of that!"

"Be reasonable, Lopez."

"I am trying to be reasonable."

"Then you will see that your case is hopeless."

"I have thought so until this night, when you told me of what that young man, that young hero, has done to reach me. His name?"

"Curse him and his name! Who would think that such a story would make you credulous! Do you dream, Lopez, that any human being can break into my house and carry you away with him?"

"He does not need to carry me away. Let me see the chart, and with one word I can give him the clue to its working!"

There was an oath from Langhorne, and then the sound of his footfall, as he strode up and down.

Tarron lay breathing fast, for the veil was being quickly torn from the face of the mystery.

"After all," said Langhorne, "your son may have dreamed of what he saw in the old mine. He may have dreamed it, and even if we should find the mine there might not be much in it!"

"So you say! But in your heart you feel otherwise. You believe so thoroughly in the report that my son made that you have been haunted all these years by the wish to get at the place. You have searched every inch of the mountains, and you have not found it. And still you keep searching!"

"One day I shall have it," said the other bitterly; "in spite of you I shall have it!"

"That I doubt."

"I shall hunt until not a mouse could be hidden from me!"

Lopez laughed.

"You have a space of ten thousand square miles to hunt over," he said, "and in any part of that space the entrance to the mine may be. Are you so sure that you can find it?"

Another snarling oath from Langhorne. Then he changed his tone.

"My friend," said he, "you must not think that it has not been against my conscience to keep you confined as I have done. It has haunted me—"

"Hush," said Lopez. "Hypocrisy is the most damnable of all sins."

"Well, you will not believe me until I give you the proof. This is it! I have offered you your freedom for your information. Now I offer you more. I offer you the third share that your son was to have had in the mine."

"Blood money!"

"Man, man, are you past all reason? What blood money is there in it?"

"I tell you, Langhorne, that even if I wished to, I could not help you. I know one of the landmarks, yes, two of them, which my son pointed out and named to me, while you were closing the door of the summer house just before the shot was fired. But, for all that, I could not connect the plan, unless I saw the chart once more."

"Give me the names of those landmarks. I remember something of the shape of the chart. I remember the scale of miles by which they said that they had worked. And with that memory, I think that I could work out the solution just as your son did. I am not a fool! No, my friend, tell me those key names, and I'll do the rest if the wit of man can accomplish it!"

Silence.

"Like a fool," said Langhorne, "you are going to cling to your darkness?"

"Perhaps so. I shall not speak. I shall not take the least chance that you should profit by anything that I could tell you. The information which I could give belongs to the Alvarados. They know it. For that reason they have been making such vast efforts to reach me. And by the pleasure of God they will win in the end! The devil cannot favor you much longer."

"Then go back to your cellar and let the darkness breed more madness in you," gasped Langhorne, choking with rage. "And yet I'll try one last argument to convince you that—"

There was sudden hoarse shouting from beneath.

"Señor! Señor Langhorne!"

Tarron took advantage of that clamor to cover the sound he made in rising to his knees along the balustrade. Opposite him stood old Lopez, but as he saw the light glitter on the barrel of the Colt in Tarron's hand the old man made not the slightest sign and the expression of his face did not alter.

"Señor Langhorne!" came the cry from beneath.

"Yes?"

"They have found in the garden the gray horse of Tarron! He is now hiding among the trees!"

40

If Fortune Favor

Señor Robert Langhorne, as Tarron now saw him outlined against the brilliant stars, was a tall, slender man. On either side of his cheeks was outthrust a thin pencil of shadow—the ends of his well-trained mustache. He paused for a moment as he heard this hoarse cry from beneath, and then exclaimed softly: "The devil takes care of his own. This Tarron must be the archfiend! Has he actually brought a horse into the grounds of the house?"

He called aloud: "Send every man to search the grounds. Search them inch by inch, and in the meantime, throw a cordon around the house."

"Si, señor!"

A sound of retreating footfalls.

"You see, señor," said the prisoner, "that he was able to break through your guards, after all."

"Broke through and into the trap, like a frantic rat," said the tall man calmly. "In another ten minutes I shall have him here face to face, unless they kill him when they take him. I hope not. I want to see him—hear his voice. Odd thing, Lopez, that such a boy should have been able to give me so much trouble. But he's the desperate sort. He'll die fighting, and I'll never have the pleasure of sending him down to share your cell. Better still, I'll never have the pleasure of using him for my own work."

"Could you hire him?"

"Why not?"

"After he has killed so many of your best men?"

"That is nothing. The wheels of life turn more smoothly because there have been a few sacrifices."

"But are you not afraid? Suppose that this Tarron had broken through your line and into your house?"

"Impossible! Men are marching up and down in front of Casa Langhorne and on every side of it. The devil himself could not fly into it without being seen."

The Mexican threw back his head and broke into laughter. In the meantime, a general hubbub resounded in the garden beyond the house. But the wind was rising, and the shouts and the commands came only blurred and faint to this lofty platform.

"Why do you laugh?" asked Langhorne grimly.

"To think of your confidence, señor!"

"And what of that?"

"When you may be already in the hands of your enemy?"

"You talk like a silly fool with a weakened brain. I must send you back to your damp shadows forever!"

"No," exclaimed the Mexican. "A price has been paid for my life. Did you not say that five men died yesterday? Are they not a sufficient price even for my life?"

"Your wits have gone wandering," said Langhorne.

"Prosperity has maddened you," replied Lopez. "I have seen you come into this land without a penny in your pocket. Your success has turned your brain."

"By that brain I made my fortune grow, old man."

"By your deft fingers, rather, which helped themselves to many pockets."

"Scoundrel! Insolent dog, how dare you say that?"

"Ah, Langhorne, because I closed my eyes then, it does not mean that I was quite blind. I know how you began operations with money stolen from me. Why, señor, the salted mine that you sold me in the beginning—was I such a fool as not to see through that? But you amused me. The loss did not ruin me. I waited, hoping that I might find a way to gain back what I had lost!"

"I wish," said Langhorne, "that you were twenty years younger. But I cannot fight you. I can only show you what a dog I've always felt you to be."

Stepping closer, he struck the Mexican heavily across the face with his open hand.

"Señor," said Lopez calmly, "that is the worst folly that you have ever committed—except one other."

"What was that other, Lopez?"

"To stay here alone with me—without a guard—when you knew that Tarron had already come as far as your garden!"

"Was that a folly?"

"Yes, because it placed you in his hands!"

"That is a pleasant riddle. Explain it!"

"You would never believe my words."

"Perhaps not."

"But would you believe your own eyes?"

"Ha?" cried the tall man, starting convulsively.

"Then turn around, and see for yourself!"

Langhorne whirled about, but at that moment Tarron was stepping across the balustrade, and the master of the house fairly thrust his breast against a leveled revolver.

He did not cry out. Never did man show a more wonderfully steady nerve.

"Tarron, by all the gods!" he murmured. He waited.

"There are two things that we can do," said Tarron quietly, drawing a knife with his left hand and holding it against Langhorne's breast. "We can kill this cur and take our chances of escape. Or we can make him go with us, and have the pleasure of hearing his own voice order his own men away from us. Which do you choose?"

"My son," cried the old man, his voice trembling, "God has sent you, and God will not let you shed unnecessary blood. Do not kill him."

"Listen!" said Tarron to Langhorne. "Do you hear? You who struck him! Do you hear?"

Langhorne said not a word. In the silence, Tarron stared into the keen, burning eyes of the older man, and wondered at his quiet. Devils must have been raging in his soul, yet he made not a sound.

"Put up your hands!" commanded Tarron.

Langhorne raised them slowly above his head, but when Tarron searched him, the only weapon he found on his person was a small penknife.

Tarron turned his back on his prisoner.

"Watch him!" breathed Lopez. "He will throw himself from the roof—"

"No," said Tarron. "There's still too much that he hopes to live for! He won't do that."

He undid the bonds which fastened the hands of old Lopez.

"Now," said Tarron, "we'll walk in single file. Señor Langhorne goes first. He doesn't like it a lot. He'd be glad to make a break. But he knows that I'm walking right here behind him with a gun, and my hand on the trigger. He knows that if he makes a false move, I sink a .45-caliber chunk of lead through him. And he knows that I'd almost die myself for the pleasure of polishing him off!"

He added: "Señor Lopez, you come behind me, and as we go along, keep looking back, to see that nobody swarms too close behind us!"

"I understand."

"Langhorne!"

"Yes."

"Start down through that trap door—and go carefully!"

"My boy," said Langhorne, taking a deep breath to rally himself, "this is one of the finest things that any man ever accomplished. But it won't do! You could never get through the grounds. And if you could, what would be your advantage? Who would ever do as much for you as I'd do?"

"You'd hire me?" asked Tarron.

"At a grand salary. I don't offer you a little post. A position, not a job. Ten thousand a year, say. A groom to take care of your horses—a servant to look after your wants—freedom to do as you please—a house of your own, furnished and paid for by me—ground of your own, to farm if that eases you, or a range stocked with cattle if you prefer. And all I'd ask from you in return is allegiance to me. Now and again—once in three years, perhaps—some small thing to do for me—"

"Like a murder, say?" suggested the boy.

Langhorne was silent.

"I know you, you rat," said Tarron. "I've been on a trail that you've made hard for me."

"Ah, my son, would you have had me throw away what is most—"

"Don't talk," broke in Tarron. "Why, it makes me sort of mad to hear you. Don't talk! There's ways of playing even the hardest sort of a game. And you ain't been playing that way. You've played crooked. A finer man than you ever was I've seen lying on his face on the floor in the moonlight with his throat cut. It was your knife that did it, Langhorne!"

"What? A midnight murder? I never put my hand to such a thing."

"You lie! Because your men done it for you! And you sold 'em the sort of work that you wanted done!"

"Tarron, will you listen? The stake we played for was possible millions. What's a life or two in such a game? And they fought me as I fought them— with every weapon that they could imagine!"

"They never poisoned. They never cut throats by night. And they never hit old men in the face—old men whose hands were tied. Now get down the stairs. I've listened to you for the last time! Get down the stairs, and if one of your men comes toward you, tell him to stand away because you're busy and can't be bothered. But if you let one of 'em come too close—I'll kill you, Langhorne; and I'll do it with a lot of pleasure."

"And then die?"

"I've got through your lines before. I could get through 'em again. And how hard would your men work for you, once they knew you were lying dead? Will you tell me that?"

Something in this last speech seemed to strike a responsive note in the breast of the older man, because he suddenly winced and without a word faced around to the trapdoor.

Down the narrow descent they went, with old Lopez struggling clumsily behind them.

They reached a door at the bottom of the stairs which opened on an upper hallway. Into that same hallway Tarron had looked earlier in the night, but now he found it empty. The guards had been stripped away and sent by the master's own orders, to search through the garden, and guard the house from the outside.

If fortune favored them, they might now pass entirely through the house without being detected!

41
Through the Tall Gateway

THEY actually passed through the lofty chambers of Casa Langhorne without being seen or challenged by a soul, and at the rear of the house Tarron paused and considered a new idea. To leave that place on foot was a difficult task. But to gallop from the grounds on a horse would be comparatively simple.

He said to Langhorne:

"If you call through the window, señor, one of those men would bring up my horse and two others."

"He would," said Langhorne, looking askance at Tarron as he understood the meaning of the suggestion.

"Well," said Tarron. "Give the order."

"To whisk me away with the pair of you on horseback?" said Langhorne, scowling.

"And why not?"

"Am I a rank fool, young man, to give orders such as that?"

"Think it over," said Tarron, eying him grimly. "Killing you or letting you live is pretty much the same to me. There's never a job I've had in my life that I'd like half so well as to polish you off, Señor Langhorne. There's poor Dorn lying in a Mexican grave yonder in the mountains. When I think of him, I want to be at you. Is that reason enough for you to do what I want—and to ask no more questions?"

Even then Langhorne needed a moment to consider. He went to the window. But what he had commanded had already been done, and while some of his men beat over every corner of the park around the Casa Langhorne, others were drawn in a compact line around the big place.

"Orvetto!" he called.

"Señor!" answered a ready voice.

"Orvetto, have Tarron's horse brought here, and two others with saddles on them, and at once."

"Instantly, señor. Tarron's horse is already close!"

In the pause, the trio within the house could hear the many voices of the searchers through the park, and now it seemed surely beyond the range of possibility to force the owner of the house from his place against his will. Yet Langhorne was black of face as he stood scowling with folded arms, his back to the wall. Plainly he foresaw that the very worst was still a possibility.

In the meantime, the horses came. There were two black beauties, one as like the other as peas from a pod; and with them Jimmy, unkempt of mane and tail, weather stained, and seeming somewhat long and low in contrast with the others. Tarron's eye lighted with sudden joy when he saw the young stallion.

"And that's the horse!" said Langhorne, taken from his musings by the sound of the hoofs outside the window. "That's the horse with which you broke into the valley. No wonder the others couldn't take him. That's a racer, my son."

"Thanks," muttered Tarron, whose hatred for the older man was growing apace during every moment he was with him. "Now tell them to leave the horses and scatter to their work. Send everyone of them about their business, searching through the woods. Order the men from around the walls."

Langhorne set his teeth and hesitated, but again necessity was plain to him, for Tarron's eye, with murder in it, never left his face.

"Leave the horses there. Now scatter through the park, you rascals. You've let Tarron into the park. See that you get him again, or there'll be reason for some of you to remember today as long as you live. Go!"

Langhorne let his rage come into his voice, and there was an instant scampering of frightened feet in response to his order.

"That ought to do," murmured Tarron. "Can you ride now, father?" he added to old Lopez.

The latter answered with a faint smile:

"I could rise from the grave to ride any horse like one of those three. I shall be at your side, my son, if the horse I'm on can keep me there. Are you ready?"

"Ready, yes!"

"Then lead the way out, Langhorne. And still watch yourself, and remember that my gun is on you every second!"

There was no answer, but the tall man obediently stalked forth in the lead. Just outside the door he hesitated for an instant and turned his grim face from side to side while he scanned all the woods of the park near to him. But his thundering command had effectually banished his men from that vicinity and they would not soon return to beard the lion.

Langhorne took the central black, Lopez the other, and Tarron was instantly astride the gray. Down the winding drive past the house they went. They had not entered twenty yards into the park before a dozen men spilled into the way before them and shouted "Who goes!"

"You dogs!" thundered the master. "It is I! Do you know me?"

And he reached for the nearest with the quirt which he had snatched from the bow of his saddle.

"Softly, Señor Langhorne! Softly!" said old Lopez. "One more move such as that, and you invite your soul up to the center of heaven—or hell. You were almost gone, then! Señor Tarron's finger was curling on the trigger."

Langhorne turned his head and gave Tarron the most baneful look that the latter was ever likely to receive even in a long, long life which had not been without its trials and tribulations.

"That is enough," said Tarron. "I'll give you a fair chance, Langhorne.

Something better than a dog's chance. Unless I doubt you. And then I'll let my gun do my thinking!"

They passed on down the drive. Twice again they were challenged, and twice the master of the house freed them from danger. And they came to the great gates, now closed, and guarded by a score of rifles.

"Send them away, and have them open the gates before they go," commanded Tarron. "Send them into the woods to hunt."

His orders were obeyed. Langhorne vented some of his tortured feelings in an outburst of rage at the guards which made the latter fling open the great leaves of the gate in terror and then fly.

In the meantime Tarron said to Lopez: "Now, señor, tell me how Alvarado has managed to live in the same city with Langhorne all these years when the man was the enemy of the other house?"

"Ah," said Lopez. "You do not understand. Men work for Langhorne because though he is a stranger, he can pay them for what they do. But was not Alvarado one of the first Conquistadores? They follow Alvarado for love, which is stronger than money, God be praised! They would go to hell for the money of Langhorne, but still he could not bribe them to harm an Alvarado."

"But if you and I rode to the house of Alvarado?"

"We would be as safe as though an ocean lay between us and this devil."

"And if we took Langhorne there?"

"What difference would it make? Yes, I should like to see that!"

"Then we'll do it. Keep to the side as you ride through the gateway. There's too much light, here, and more people coming!"

So said Tarron, for the tramp of many horses now passed down the road, approaching the gates. No doubt these were men who had been called in by the alarm from the Casa Langhorne. Now they were passing through the gates, Tarron to the right and old Lopez to the left of Langhorne, when the black which the latter was riding suddenly reared and struck, and the horse which carried Lopez reared in alarm, and sent his startled rider toppling from the saddle.

Back went Tarron like the flash of a whip and caught Lopez before the latter could fall—caught him with one hand and caught the bridle of the rearing horse with the other—and as he brought them straight again, he heard a rush of hoofs, and looked to see Langhorne darting away bent low over his saddle.

Oh, childish trick, and how well had it worked!

As Langhorne rode, Tarron heard him shouting: "Ingram! Ingram! Faster! Faster! Tarron is behind!"

Ingram! It was a name of fear to Tarron.

"Now ride, if you want to live," said Tarron to old Lopez. "Straight for the house of Alvarado, and I'll be at your heels! Straight for the house of Alvarado! Spur every foot of the way!"

The old man did not pause to apologize for the clumsiness which had let Langhorne slip through their fingers. He bent to his work like a jockey, and set his black flying through the gates.

That instant, plunging toward them up the road at the head of half a score of followers, Tarron saw big Ingram riding, with Langhorne rushing toward them, and now safe in their midst.

Langhorne safe, and Ingram coming like an angel of vengeance! Tarron himself was riding away at the heels of the old man. He could have left them far behind in no time, but his speed was by his honor limited to the speed of Lopez, and he gritted his teeth as he saw Ingram constantly gaining. This would be the shrewdest cut of fate, if Ingram rode him down at the moment of his victory!

"Faster, Señor Lopez!"

"The black can do no more! On, Tarron, and forget me! Save yourself!"

Brave old man! Even now, he was willing to give up his precious liberty and return to the prison rather than jeopardize a comrade. But Tarron had no thought of abandoning his post. He whipped about and fired— then waited to see big Ingram crash backward in the saddle.

But Ingram did not fall!

Les Tarron fired again, aiming just beneath the brim of Ingram's hat. And still the broad-shouldered monster followed close. Twice had he missed, and now a cold sweat bedecked Tarron. He changed his aim, fired lower, and saw horse and rider pitch to the ground.

But only for an instant. Ingram was up again, raving: "Go on! Ride like the devil! Take him! It's Tarron himself! It's Tarron, do you hear?"

That word did not seem to spur his followers forward, however. Instead, Tarron could see them frantically drawing rein. He watched Ingram snatch one of his followers from the saddle and mount the horse in turn. But too late! Next moment Jimmy had whisked through the tall gateway of a garden, and now they could see looming before them the front of the Casa Alvarado, gleaming white among the trees.

42
A Dark-Eyed Maiden

WITH his Winchester in his hand Tarron kneeled in the patio. Servants were running here and there with lanterns in their hands. Lopez was clasped in the arms of a dignified gentleman with long white hair and a white, pointed beard. Then Tarron saw the latter walk out the patio gate and meet the raging mass of riders which Ingram had led. He heard his calm, clear, unhurried words:

"Señor, you must be a stranger to Santa Maria de la Paz. Otherwise you would know that men do not ride uninvited through my gate. No, not even the men of Señor Langhorne! I see that your men understand and are willing to leave. Do I need to invite you to follow them?"

There was a frantic burst of cursing from Ingram. But his riders were melting away behind him, and presently he himself wheeled his sweating horse around and galloped off. And after that, Tarron stepped into another phase of life, so new and so strange and so sweet to him that it seemed like a taste of heaven brought down to earth. He found it hard, afterward, to remember all that was said, and all that was done. He was only clear on one point, and that was when he met Alvarado returning to the patio and said to him: "You are Señor Alvarado?"

"Yes."

"I don't know who this belongs to," said Tarron. "You—or Lopez."

The steel box was in his hand.

"You had Dorn working for you?"

"Yes."

"And you know he died for you?"

"Yes. God be kind to him—he was a brave man! If he had remained with you that night—he would still be living, Señor Tarron. But we'll talk of him another time. Now we must talk of miracles—of yourself!"

"No," said Tarron. "I don't want to talk. I want to get rid of this—before more men die!" And he gave the steel box to Alvarado.

"It is open!" cried the tall man, and added next instant: "But the chart is here! Lopez, Lopez, the chart is here!"

They could not wait to reach the inside of the house. There in the patio they pored over it eagerly by lantern light.

Lopez said excitedly: "I remember that my boy put his hand on this cross. 'That is Mount Santa Anna,' he said. 'And this is the Santa Anna trail.' Ah, fools. That we should never have looked there!"

He turned to Tarron.

"It is in our hands! Brave Tarron! God witness that you shall not suffer though you have given up the box without asking a price first! Name it now! What will you have?"

"I don't know," said Tarron slowly. "What I want most is a bath. A good hot bath, and then something to eat!"

He began now to feel himself weakening. Pains slipped through his body, and bewildering shadows flocked across his eyes. For he had had one meal in several days, and one sleep in the midst of what labors, and how long had all his nerves been drawn taut as bow-strings!

He heard, dimly, kind sympathetic laughter, and someone saying that that was a small price; and then he was suddenly in a room where house mozos were pouring steaming water into a granite basin. He lay at length in the delicious water, and the ache was passing from his body, from his soul. He dressed. In place of his blood-stained, battered, tattered rags were beautiful, soft, smooth-fitting clothes, such as he had never owned and never so much as dreamed of in all his days. He donned them, wondering. When he left the room, he had about him only two familiar things—a pair of Colts, carried in little holsters beneath the arm, slung cunningly so that they did not bulk beneath his coat.

All the house seemed to be waiting for him; shining eyes were fixed upon him, and everyone was smiling.

He entered another room, where were Alvarado and Lopez, who broke off their conversation to rise and meet him. With them was a slender girl of seventeen or eighteen, with dark, serious eyes, and a smile that passed through Tarron as lightning passes through the heart of the sky.

Then they were pressing around him, taking his hand. What would he have? What could they do?

"I'm hungry," said Tarron.

Was it by magic that he found himself at a long table spread with all dainties and before him a plate flanked by a darkly shining glass of wine? In the background, many moved with smiling faces, to attend on him. And in the foreground were Lopez, Alvarado, and the slender girl. And even they were waiting upon him, offering him food.

"What is wrong?" cried Alvarado. "There is something you wish, my child, which you don't see?"

"No," said Tarron. "But it's all queer, you know. Like Christmas! Like Christmas!"

He ate while they laughed. Not mocking laughter. Nothing that he did but seemed to rejoice them. And those Christmas faces pressed closer, watching, nodding, and beaming on him like mothers watching a famished child.

"You have not touched this cold chicken! And that ham, boiled in sweet white wine! Let him have some of those sweets. Here, my son, is the pride of our kitchen—jugged hare!"

What eating! At what a table! At what a time!

Tarron stopped.

"What is wrong? Are you ill, señor?"

"What is your name, señorita?" he asked.

"I am Anna Maria Alvarado, señor!"

He nodded as she curtsied.

"You've got a voice like your name, and like your face, and like your hands," said Tarron. "Wonderful, I mean!"

They laughed again. Was there nothing he could say that would not make them laugh?

He could eat no more. The wine cast a comfortable warmth of happiness into his very brain.

"There's no danger?" asked Tarron sleepily.

"No, none!"

"*You,*" he said to Anna Maria, "*you're* not afraid of anything just now?"

"No, no, Señor Tarron!"

"There's something I want to say to you. I'll try to think what it is."

People were nodding and smiling, looking at him and at the slender girl. Her face had grown wonderfully rosy. But she was smiling and nodding at him, too, and what eyes she had for darkness and brightness and kindness!

He put his head on his hand to think. Voices withdrew to a distance. He seemed to be surrounded by whispers. And then he slept.

When he wakened, he was in a great bed, and the soft warmth of clean linen sheets embraced his body. He put out his hands. His strength had come back to him, it rippled through his body like a mountain torrent. And he laughed aloud. Let Ingram face him now, if he dared!

"Señor!" exclaimed a voice from the corner of the room.

He sat up on his elbows and saw in two corners of the room two armed men, rifles across their knees.

"Hello!" cried Tarron, grinning. "What's happened? Am I a prisoner here?"

"Prisoner?" exclaimed one of them. "We are only your guards, señor. And we are ordered to obey you as though you were the patron!"

He understood. There was still much danger in Santa Maria de la Paz. Therefore the sleep of Tarron was watched by his kind host. But let danger come as it would and when it would. He had a mind for it, a taste for it. And his strength had been given back to him.

It was afternoon. He had slept more than twelve hours, and when he strode into the next room, smiling and joyous, he found them all waiting for him—Alvarado, Lopez, and Anna Maria, smiling shyly toward him before she slipped from the room. Well, if God were willing he would find the time to see more of her hereafter!

Meanwhile there were other things to think about, other things to be done. In five minutes he stood at the topmost tower window of the house and looked forth with Alvarado on the city. In the house they were free; they could not be attacked. But how would they escape to find the mine, now that they had the chart, and the key to the chart?

"We cannot go out with a cart, as you came in," said Alvarado, and smiled. "And yet now that we have you with us, I feel that this mine is already ours, and the wealth of it in our pockets. But your share? What shall we say about that before we start?"

"I'm interested in the fun of it," said Tarron seriously. "Never mind about my share."

"Shall we say a half?"

"That's too much. I want men, first. I've gone through their lines before. Have you any men who would ride with me?"

"I have men, Tarron, who think that you could go safely through hell and back. They would follow you anywhere. And if they shouted your name, I think that they *could* ride through."

"Would you trust yourself to me and ten more?"

"I would. Tonight?"

"No, today!"

"*Madre de Dios!* By daylight? However, you know best!"

So through the bright, golden sun of the afternoon a round dozen horsemen rode down the path of the garden. They were near the gate when they heard a heavy, regular, rhythmic tolling of the great bell of the church, and a moment later a panting messenger sprang to them.

"It is the end, señor!" cried the man to Alvarado. "Señor Langhorne is dead. His heart is broken, they say, with pride and rage and shame. He died in his bed, shouting in his sleep: 'Help! They have murdered me!' Señor, let God be thanked! Our enemy is dead!"

"And his men?" asked Alvarado.

"They are scattering already as fast as they can ride. They fear you now, every one of them. Half of them are already whirled out of Santa Maria like dead leaves in a wind. The danger is over at last!"

43

One Reaches the City in the Sky

NOT a shot was fired, not a hostile face was seen, when Alvarado and his troopers cantered out of Santa Maria de la Paz that day, with Tarron beside the master. And the townspeople flooded out and cheered their old patron and forgot the gold with which Langhorne had bought them.

"The name?" said Alvarado to Tarron. "It was called La Paz, many generations ago. It was only a village, then, an Indian village; there was not even a church. When the church of Santa Maria was built, the name was added; and finally the last part of the name was lost, and only the first part remained. That is the secret. But Dorn and some of the others had heard the old story, and they used the forgotten name when they talked of the place to which they were taking the box. God rest them all—brave souls!"

They took to the mountain trail.

"A hundred thousand hours have been wasted in the search of these mountains," said Alvarado. "Now let us see if my boy died for nothing, or for a priceless treasure."

And as they went up the trail, following the little, dim chart to which his dead son Carlos had provided the key, Alvarado told how his son long ago had discovered this document and had gradually ferreted out its history which went back to the days of the Conquistadores. When they first came with fire and sword, the Indians had fled before them; but before they fled they had closed the entrance to a vastly rich mine—so the story went—which was the very cause that had brought the Spaniards to La Paz.

The secret of the mine was never betrayed, so the legend went, to the invaders. Finally, all the Indians who knew the secret died, and a new generation came, which had only heard of the lost mine of La Paz, but knew nothing of the place where it was actually to be found. Carlos Alvarado, by years of careful study, finally deciphered the key to the little chart done on Spanish parchment, yellow with centuries, which he had found in some Indian relics. With young Miguel Lopez he had gone to the trail. Lopez had murdered his companion, and returned, stricken with remorse, to tell his father and Langhorne what he had done and beg their protection. But it was learned that Miguel had come back alone, and an old servant of the Alvarado family, going to Casa Langhorne, had overheard the confession of murder in the summer house, and fired the fatal bullet through the window.

Such was the story to which Tarron listened while they rode up the mountain trail, and as they went, he repieced the old tale and made the figures live before his eyes. In the meantime, he was giving heed to the chart, which ended abruptly between two signs—a cross and an arrow. The riders stopped at the edge of a precipitous slope.

"Along this edge, then," said Alvarado, looking anxiously up and down the barren plateau over which they had ridden.

"Down!" said Tarron without hesitation. "That arrow at the end points down, which means that at the end the trail goes down, too. We must follow in that direction."

"Lead!" said Alvarado. "I have no right to question you in such matters as these. You have but to order, and we to obey!"

Down they clambered, leaving the horses, for no horse could follow them on such a path. A hundred yards beneath the brow of the precipice, one of the Mexicans shouted suddenly, waved his arms, and then disappeared.

When they rushed to the place, they found that there was a narrow, dark opening into the middle of the mountain. Then a light gleamed, which the Mexican had struck inside. Another shout! As they crept into the place, thrusting aside the debris that blocked the entrance, Tarron saw a great depth of tunneling before him, narrow and ancient, where a man could not stand upright. They advanced farther. There was a frantic yell from the leader, and hurrying up they saw the Mexican wildly gesticulating before such a sight as never gold miner had seen, save in some world-famous bonanza. It struck across the face of the cut like a yellow blaze—like a bit of artificial gilding—a rich, rich thread of purest gold, and above it a thick ledge of the finest gold-bearing ore!

Tarron was ignorant in such matters. But he understood, as he stared at the gleaming line, why so many lives had been lost. The riches of Croesus were under their hands, waiting ready for the pick and the drill!

What Tarron did afterward would take long to tell. It was not the end of the trail for him, in many years, but the real beginning. He went back to the North to his father and mother and brother, and rode away again, leaving them wealthy for life.

He labored over books, with a stern tutor who ruled him with no gentle hand.

And Tarron married!

One would like to describe how he went in person and found Gregorio and brought him back to that valley of heart's desire and strove to make him rich and joyous; and how old Gregorio stole away in the middle of the night and went back to the home on the mountain side to wrangle and jangle again with his savage daughter.

But there is one matter which must be described.

It is said that a big and dark-faced man rode into Santa Maria on a day, and saw, as his horse drank from the watering-trough in the center of the village, a gay young caballero dash merrily past.

The flash of a gold-trimmed Mexican jacket, the glare of crimson sash, the sheen of a silken, shining silver stallion which the stalwart youth bestrode!

"By the eternal God!" said the stranger. "Who is that?"

"That?" cried half a dozen. "Why, that is the son of Alvarado!"

"I thought Alvarado's son was dead?" said the stranger, frowning more blackly than before.

"Oh, his own son, of course. But that is Señor Tarron—the great Tarron, the fighter. He is like a son to Alvarado now. He married into the house, you see!"

The stranger remained for a moment in black thought. Then he gave a broad-faced silver peso to a youngster who stood by.

"Go to the Casa Alvarado. Tell Tarron that I want him at the crossroads, yonder, beyond Santa Maria. You understand?"

"And who shall I say sent me, señor?" asked the boy, stricken with amazement at the peremptory tone of the big man.

"Who'll you say?"

He glowered at the boy, as though bewildered that anyone should not know his name.

"Say Ingram," he said.

And the boy fled at his bidding.

Beside the crossroad, drawn carefully out of the dust where he had fallen, they found this same stranger the next day. His body had been carefully bestowed. His hands were folded across his breast. His eyes were closed, and there was a smile of peace on his lips. Between his eyes was a purple splotch, round and even.

So was he buried, and money from an unknown source paid for a marble headstone to mark his grave. No questions were asked. None were raised in that region as a rule, when a man was found with the wound in front. Moreover, who was there in the valley of Santa Maria that cared to spread stories abroad about Señor Tarron? He was almost an Alvarado. Some considered him something less than a member of that grand old family. But there were many who considered him a great deal more.

Perhaps for Ingram there was no fitter end imaginable. He had sins enough to deserve his taking-off, and yet it was almost pitiful that Tarron's should have been the hand that ended him. For it was Ingram who had called Tarron out of his sleepy youth and given him to the long trail of the lost city and all that lay there waiting for Tarron's hand.

THE MAN FROM MUSTANG

1

The Prairie Fire

ON the brow of the last hill that spilled from the knees of the mountains toward the prairie, under the last tree, "Silver" sat with his knees hugged in his arms and watched the rider in the distance, and the prairie fire behind him.

Parade, with bridle off and saddle on, grazed near by, biting off the short, sweet grass close to the roots, eating greedily, as though he knew that the taste of this pasturage was much sweeter than the tall, dry grasses beneath him. Now and then he jerked up his head and looked suddenly at his master, and then all about him, with pricking ears, for he understood perfectly that to the wolfish keenness of his scent and to his quickness of ear and eye, Silver looked for warning if any danger came his way. Parade was a combination of stallion and sentinel, the guardian and the servant of the man.

The day was hot and dry. Silver had taken off the big sombrero as he sat in the shade, and thereby exposed the two marks of gray hair above his temples that looked like incipient horns sprouting, and had given him his universal nickname of "Silvertip." Now he made himself at ease. He had been long enough in the mountain wilderness which he loved, and it seemed to him a typical irony of fate that as he turned his face back toward the dwellings of man he should see a rider on the plain and a grass fire at the same time. For among men there was always danger.

The fellow who jogged his horse quietly along seemed unaware of the coming of the fire for a long time. It had begun as a small point, like a dust cloud, rolling. It increased. Evidently a wind was favoring it, and finally a gust of that breeze went whispering through the leaves above the head of Silver.

By this time the grass fire had gathered both speed and frontage, and was leaving behind it a widening wedge of black against the pallor of the prairie grass. At the same moment the lone rider became aware of the danger behind him. Silver laughed to see the man bring his mustang to a gallop and flatten out along the neck of the horse.

It was high time, but time enough, for the horse could move a great deal faster than the fire itself, though that was now galloping like a thousand wild beasts, wallowing, plunging, throwing forward a leaning wall of smoke, as though a dense mass of skirmishers were running forward with rifles firing constantly. Fast as the wind blew, pressing the smoke forward, the speeding flames ran almost as quickly. Now they rushed down a hollow with a slower gait. Now they leaped up a slope, and at the crest hurled upward a gigantic cloud of fire, as though in excess of strength. A god seemed to be rioting in that flame, bounding between earth and heaven, trailing his cloak of smoke high up in the sky.

The fugitive, in the meantime, was gaining rapidly on the wall of danger, when all at once, as he came close enough for Silver to make out that the horse was small and the man big, the mustang went down and hurled its rider far away, spinning head over heels.

The horse tried to rise at once, but a dangling foreleg prevented it. The man, on the other hand, lay perfectly still, face down, twisted as though his body had been broken in the middle.

Silver had the bridle on Parade almost before he had finished noting these things. For both horse and man lay directly in the path of the fire.

With the throatlatch unfastened, he sprang into the saddle. The big golden chestnut got under way like a frightened deer. Down the hillside he streaked, across the green like a meteor down the blue arch of the sky, and struck the level, where the tall prairie grasses whipped like splashing water about his shoulders. That impediment could not slow his speed or shorten his stride.

And angling straight toward the danger point, Silver rode him between the fallen horse and the fallen rider.

It would be a near thing. Already the running flame put out an arm of crimson and smoke that enveloped the struggling horse. The poor beast screamed with agony. Silver, twisting in the saddle, put a bullet through its head from his revolver.

Right behind him came the sweeping fire. The wind that hurried above the flames dropped a shower of sparks and whole bunches of burning grass that seemed to have been uprooted by the force of the draft! And little new fires caught hold on the dryness of the grass even before the main body of the flame had rolled to them.

One of these spots of fire was spreading at the side of the fallen rider as Silver came up. He called out. Parade stood on braced feet, and Silver, without dismounting, leaned far down from the saddle.

He took that burden under the armpits and hauled it up. The head fell back as though on a broken neck, to show Silver a young, brown face, almost absurdly homely. There was enough nose and jaw for two ordinary men, yet what the face enjoyed in length it lacked in width. But the forehead was good, and what Silver saw first and last was the frown that lingered on the brow. A dead man's face would have been smooth, he told himself, but here was the promise of life!

With that limp body in his arms, he called again; and Parade went like a flashing gesture through the tall grass, back to the shorter growth on the hillside.

There Silver deposited his burden. He had to spend a minute beating out sparks that had begun to ignite his clothes. Parade was dancing because of a smoking place on his mane. When that was out, there were more burning spots on the clothes of the stranger.

In the meantime, the roar of the prairie fire went by, leaving acres of glowing red behind it, and the black, smoking heap where the mustang lay dead.

The unconscious man now stirred suddenly, and sat up with a gasp. He said nothing for some time. First his eye marked the distant rush and roar of the conflagration. Then he looked down and actually patted the short green of the grass on which he was sitting. At last he marked the place where the dead horse lay.

At that he started to his feet with an exclamation. It seemed to Silver that he was about to run down into the grass toward the dead horse, though there were still flaming bits that far behind the head of the fire. Silver caught his shoulder and held him.

"You'll burn your boots, and spoiled leather won't help that dead horse," said Silver.

"No, you're right," said the other slowly. He looked at Silver with a dull eye of suffering. "He's eaten enough right out of my hand," said he. "And now the fire's eaten him—right off the ground."

He smiled. His whole face twisted with grief that he fought again.

"He was a good-looking horse," said Silver gently.

"He was a right good one. He was a cutting horse," said the stranger, wiping his hands on his leather chaps absently. "You put him on the tail of a calf and he'd follow that calf to kingdom come. Yes, sir, and head it off before ever it got there, in spite of anything. That's the kind of a cutting horse he was. But the fire got him—fire!" He shuddered as he said it.

"I put a bullet through his head just before the fire ate him," said Silver.

The stranger looked Silver up and down, but saw no gun. A gleaming gesture made a big Colt with three extra inches of barrel on it appear from beneath the coat of Silver and disappear again.

"I'm thankin' you," said the stranger. "And you didn't have no lot of time on your hands, neither."

He looked down at the spots on his own clothes, some of which were still faintly smoking. Then he eyed the damaged costume of Silver. Suddenly he grinned.

"I'm goin' to be owin' you a suit of clothes in exchange for the skin that I'm still wearing," he said.

"All right," answered Silver.

"Poor old Jerry!" said the man under his breath. "I'll tell you what he was," he added suddenly. "He was a partner. You know?"

"I know," said Silver.

The stranger glanced toward Parade.

"Yeah, you know, all right," he agreed. "Maybe you know even a lot better'n I do. When I was camping out, he'd watch over me at night like a dog. We've been on desert marches when he ate half of my bacon and drank sugar and milk. We been on marches when I've boiled his oats and halved 'em with him. Jerry," concluded the stranger with a broad sweep of his hand, "was a horse!"

"He was," said Silver. "Right up to the end, he was trying to get to you and tell you that the fire was coming."

"What happened?" asked the man.

"He put his foot in a hole in the ground, I guess," said Silver. "He broke his leg when he fell, and he couldn't get up."

The stranger took off his sombrero and wiped from his face sweat that was never produced by the heat of the sun. He swallowed hard. Then suddenly he faced Silver.

"I don't know your name," he said. "Mine is Ned Kenyon."

Silver took the hand.

"People call me Jim," he said, "or Arizona Jim, or Arizona. I don't care much what I'm called."

A slight shadow passed over the face of Kenyon, but it was gone at once.

"Any name is the right name," he said, "for me to tell you that I've had my hide saved by you. The day before my wedding day, too!"

He grinned broadly, and the ugliness disappeared from his face, it was so lighted.

"The luck stays with a plumb happy man," said Kenyon.

"It does," agreed Silver.

"Look," said the stranger impulsively. "I want you to see her right away. I want that you should know you've done more than save my hide; because maybe you've kept a lot finer person than me from trouble. I want you to see her."

He jerked a flat leather case from his inside coat pocket, and then paused, and his blue, small eyes lingered wistfully on the handsome face of Silver, as though asking for permission.

"I want to see it," said Silver. "Let's have a look."

That was enough.

Ned Kenyon opened the leather case and displayed the picture.

"It don't do her justice," he said, sidling around to Silver. "But you just get a sort of general idea, is all."

A small, stinging shock had passed into the brain of Silver as he looked. A queer numbness spread in his mind. For as he stared, he told himself that there was only one thing under heaven he could be sure of, and that was that such a girl as this could never marry Ned Kenyon.

Silver saw her in profile, but he could tell the bigness and the straightness of the eyes, and the refinement of the mouth, and the proud lift of the chin. A king could have married her proudly, and not for her beauty only, but for things of mind and spirit that spoke out of her face.

Half squinting, Silver called up the image of the man beside him, the long, gaunt body, the long, gaunt face.

No, he decided, the thing could not be. Perhaps the poor fellow had this mania—that being unattractive to most women, he had picked up the portrait of some reigning beauty of New York or Paris, and carried it about with him, to boast pathetically of his triumph.

"She's very beautiful," said Silver gravely, giving back the picture.

Kenyon took it in both hands and shook his head.

"It ain't the beauty that counts. It's the heart underneath it," he said. "She's a clean-bred one. Oh, she's as straight as a string, let me tell you!"

"I'll put my money that she is," said Silver.

"Brave, and honest, and sort of simple and quiet, and about perfect," said Kenyon slowly.

He put the picture back inside his coat.

"To-morrow at noon," said he, "we're going to be married in Mustang. And I wish that you were going to be there, partner. That's what I wish. That you were going to be there, so that she could thank you face to face. I'd like to have you hear her voice—just once. Because it's the sort of a thing that you'd never forget if you lived for a hundred years."

Silver looked at the vanishing smoke of the prairie fire, far away, for it had been running like wild horses all this time, cleaving a greater and greater wedge of black through the pale prairie grass.

The thing could not be. Every instinct in him spoke against it. She could not, being what she was, marry this lean grotesque of a cow-puncher.

"How far is Mustang?" he asked.

"Only twenty miles!" said the other eagerly.

"Then I'll go there with you," said Silver. "It's a long time since I've seen a wedding."

2

The Simple Man

THERE was no doubt of one thing—that just as firmly as Silver was convinced that the wedding would never take place, just so firmly was Ned Kenyon assured that on the morrow he would be the happiest man in the world, and that this girl would be his wife.

He was ready to talk of her. Words about her overflowed his lips.

She was only twenty. Her name was Edith Alton. All the perfections that God could give to a woman had been showered upon her.

Perhaps, thought Silver, it migt be an old acquaintance, one of those deep affections that grow up from years spent together—as, for instance, Kenyon might have been for long the foreman on her father's ranch. Or perhaps there were hidden qualities in this man—he might be, for all his rather ungrammatical language, an artist, an inspired poet, or a philosopher such as Silver had met in the West more than once, filled with wisdom that seems to rise like sap from the ground.

"You've known her a long time?" asked Silver.

"Seven days!" said Kenyon.

Again the numb incredulity spread through the brain of Silver. Seven days!

"That's not long," remarked Silver. "Love at first sight, I suppose?"

"No," answered Kenyon. "Not for her. For me, yes. But not for her. I saw her at the railroad, and I drove the stage that brought her up to Mustang. I hardly kept the wheels on the road, because I was turning all the time to look at her. And then the next day was my day off the driver's seat, and I went to a dance, and there she turned up, and I danced with her, part of a dance.

"But she wanted to talk more than to dance. And she asked me to take her outside. We walked up and down under the pine trees, into the black of the trees, and out into the white of the moon. Mostly talking. Mostly me talking. And she listening, with her head a little on one side. It's dead easy to talk to a girl like that!" he exclaimed. "And there was me, that never had found a girl in the world that would pay no attention to me! And there was me, with the queen of the world, as you might say!"

Silver, as he walked along at the side of his companion, the stallion following without the need of a lead, sighed a little. The problem was beginning to grow more and more unfathomable to him. Behind it there lay a mystery as profound as a pit, a darkness which his eye could not penetrate. But with every step he made at the side of this man, the more convinced he became of the man's steel-true honesty and worth. There was not a crooked bone in his body, not a shadowy thought in his brain.

"You talked of a lot of things?" asked Silver.

"We talked about me," said the stage driver. "She seemed a lot interested in that. I told her about being a kid on the farm in Dakota, and about the way the winter lasted, and the way the spring came up, and the way the snow first melted, and the spring skating, and a lot of things like that, and how I came farther west, and about prospecting, and all that, and how I started to drive the stage, and got along at that because I got a way with horses. And she listened like a baby to music all the time, with her head a little over on one side, and now and then turning her head, and smiling at me a bit. In a way," said Kenyon, "that I couldn't tell you about it. Just a kind of a smile that soaked into you, like spring sunshine!"

He was no poet, either, thought Silver—just a fine, honest, decent fellow, with unprobed virtues of courage and decency. But a mate for that girl in the picture, with her lifted chin and her straight-looking eyes, and the sensitive nose and lips?

No! Whatever happened, it could not be that she intended to marry Ned Kenyon.

"You go on and ride," Kenyon was saying. "I don't mind walking. I'm pretty good at it. And with Edith to talk about, I could walk to the end of the world."

Something jerked at Silver, something pulled him up in revolt even to hear Ned Kenyon call the girl by her first name—and yet he was to marry her on the morrow!

"If you could ride half the time while I walked," said Silver, "it would be all right. But this horse doesn't like most people, and he'd be fighting every minute to get you out of the saddle."

"Would he?" murmured Kenyon.

He gave the brim of his hat a jerk.

"I ain't boasting," he said, "but the fact is that I'm pretty fair with horses my own self. I'd like to try him, if you don't mind, stallion or no stallion!"

"Would you?" said Silver, smiling. Then he laid a hand on Kenyon's bony shoulder and added: "Don't do it. He's a trickster. He knows a thousand ways of getting a man out of the saddle, and the worst of him is that when the rider drops, he has a way of trying to savage the unlucky fellow. I'd be on hand, but I might not be close enough to call him off in time. I don't doubt that you're a good rider—but I'd rather not have you try him."

Ned Kenyon looked wistfully at the golden stallion, and then he sighed.

"You know your own self and your own horse better than anybody else," he observed. "And it's the seeing of a man like you, Arizona, with a horse like that, that makes me wonder how Edith can look at me once and want to look at me twice. But I remember folks saying years ago that the likes of men for women and women for men there's no accounting for. Only, when I think of you, riding on a horse like that—well, I can't help thinking that Edith may shake her head a coupla times. Only I know that there's nothing in her but faith. For what would the world amount to, Arizona, if there was anything behind a face and an eye and a voice like hers except truth and honesty, and the kind of love that won't die in a long winter?"

Silver, listening to this speech, which was drawled out with a good many pauses, while Ned Kenyon found proper words to express himself, looked several times down to the ground, and several times with his narrowed eyes peered into the horizon like a hawk.

He said at last: "A man or a woman that lied to you, Ned, would need a hanging; and I'd be glad to pull on the rope!"

"Would you, Arizona?" asked the simple man. "I think you mean it, too. I think it's been a great day for me, Arizona. Because, look here—a man can't live by a woman only, but he needs a friend, too. And I don't know that I've ever had a real friend in all my born days."

"Never a friend?" asked Silver, starting. "Do you mean that, Kenyon? Do you mean that you've seen through the lot and found them all a worthless gang?"

"Looked through them?" echoed Kenyon. "Man, man, who am I to be looking through folks? No, no! There's three out of four or four out of five that I would be glad enough to have as friends. I'm no one to make big pretendings. Any right man is a good man for me to talk to and keep to. It's not my choosing, but the choice of the other people, that doesn't fall on me. Unless they want to cheat me out of money, or talk kind to me to-day just in order to make a fool of me to-morrow. And so it's come about that I've never had a friend in my life, until to-day it sort of looks as though *you* might be a friend to me, Arizona!"

He slowed his step and turned his frank, open eye on Silvertip; and the heart of Silver swelled in him.

He put his hand again on the thin shoulder of Kenyon and said carefully, weighing his words: "I've had few friends, too. And most of those I've had are behind me somewhere." He made a gesture, as though dropping something over his shoulder. Then he went on: "But I think that you and I could pull together as long as we're traveling in the same direction. I'd like to tell you this, Kenyon, that I hope you'll be able to trust me in any pinch— as long as I'm around your part of the world."

Kenyon held out his hand. It was taken in a firm grasp by Silver as they looked fixedly into the eyes of one another.

Then Kenyon began to laugh out of pure pleasure.

"It's been a lucky day for me—a right lucky day—if only poor Jerry hadn't gone! But Jerry was twelve, and every year it was harder for him to do what he wanted and live up to himself. Well, there he was, out fighting on the danger line, and that's the way that he would have chosen to die, I guess. And I'll tell you what, Arizona—the Indians all used to believe that when a brave went up to the happy hunting ground, he was sure to find his best horses there before him, waiting."

He laughed again in some embarrassment, as though he disclaimed a belief in any such superstition. But for a time, as they walked along, his eyes went upward and roved the sky with a blowing rack of clouds, and with such a smile on his lips that Silver knew suddenly what thoughts were running in the mind of his simple friend.

Silver made a fierce and a deep resolve to give mind and heart and hand to this man until that call which moved him irresistibly across the face of the world reached him again, and drew him he knew not where across the sky line.

He was still thinking of this hours later, when they came over a hill into sight of a town, and down a trail not far from them a woman was riding.

"Look!" cried Kenyon. "There's Mustang—and there's Edith Alton! Do you need more'n a sight of the way of her to tell that there's no other woman like her on earth?"

3
Edith Alton

MUSTANG was a flourishing center of trade, as was proved by the five roads that led into it, all whitened by constant travel, to say nothing of the irregular trails that were traced threadlike over the surrounding hills. Mustang Creek darted through the midst of the town, with two bridges over its narrow banks, and scattered groves of pines came down from the hills and right into the town itself. What more could the heart of any mountaineer require than such profusion of wood and water? Moreover, the town was placed where it could serve the great mountain region that tumbled behind it to the north and west, and also send out its freighters through the plains beyond the southern and the eastern hills.

But Silver gave that picture only a glance. Neither did he regard the huge wagon, drawn by fourteen mules, that was rolling down one of the white roads toward Mustang, sending the screech of brakes, like the screaming of hawks or bagpipes, through the still air toward him. What he watched was the girl who came pitching down a trail on the other side of the valley, swerving her horse through brush and among boulders, with the wind of the gallop fanning the brim of her sombrero straight up, and her bandanna fluttering behind her neck like a flag.

"And that's Edith Alton?" said Silver thoughtfully, shaking his head a little. "She's a Western girl, then, Kenyon?"

"No more Western," said Kenyon grinning, "than Boston and New York. But she's the sort that knows how to do what other folks do, wherever she goes. She could ride Eastern, and it don't take much for them to learn to ride Western. I've stood and seen her, Arizona—I've stood and seen her thrown four times hand running from a pitching broncho, and get up and take the saddle, and never pull leather till that mustang fitted to her like a silk glove and said 'Yes' and 'No' just the way she wanted! And there she goes, sailing. And that black mare of hers is a piece of silk all over, too. I'd know that mare, and I'd know that girl, by the sassy way they've got about them!"

Silver let this talk slip easily through his mind while he studied the disappearing rider. She rode, in fact, as though she had been raised in the saddle. Some of the dark suspicion went out of Silver's heart, for what Western man can resist the sight of a woman who knows how to ride "straight up and hell bent"?

"She looks like one in a million," he said to Kenyon. "I suppose you've wanted to paint her or do her in words!"

"Paint her? Me? I can paint a barn; I wouldn't aim to even paint a house except on a bet. Words? I've written ten letters in my life, I guess, and that's about all!"

It seemed to Silver that the last possible way of understanding Kenyon's hold on this girl had been removed. If there had been mystery before, it was doubly dark now.

They came down into the village, Kenyon explaining why he had been riding across country. He had gone to the nearest railroad to telegraph to his distant parents the news of his approaching wedding, and to buy in a larger town a suit of store clothes that would be a credit to him when he "stood up in church." But when he and Silver had examined the pack behind the saddle of the dead Jerry, they had found it almost totally consumed.

"It don't matter so much," declared Kenyon. "She ain't the kind to care much about clothes. They wouldn't make much difference to her! It's the other things that count with her."

Every word he spoke, every expression of trust and faith, pulled at the heart of Silver as though he heard them spoken by a child who was about to be disillusioned in this savage world of facts.

They went to the hotel.

"The time you get straightened up," said Kenyon, "I'll tell her that you're coming in to eat supper with us in the dining room. She'll be right glad. There's only one other thing. She wants the wedding to be a surprise to everybody back home; everybody that knows her. She don't want it to be talked about here. You'll understand how it is, Arizona?"

Silver nodded and smiled, but his smile was very faint; and as he heard this, something rang like a bell in his mind, and made him surer than ever that the whole thing was a cruel illusion which was being built up around his companion.

After watering the stallion, Silver put Parade into the stable behind the hotel, and saw that he was well-fed with clean hay of barley and wild oats. After that he took a room in the hotel and went up to shave and wash and brush his clothes clean of the dust of the long walk.

He was not tired. That body of his was furnished with steel springs so tempered that no ordinary strain could make an impression on him. And now, with a light step, he went down into the lobby and waited in the little square hall.

The girl came first. He watched her down the stairs. If all the features of her picture had been blurred, he told himself that he would have known

THE MAN FROM MUSTANG

her by something high and proud in the carriage of her head. And though she wore a plain khaki riding skirt and the most ordinary of blue silk blouses with full sleeves that ended at the elbows, she seemed dressed for the pleasure of the most critical eye in the world.

She was a smiling girl, of the sort that people like to see even in a stage or a railroad carriage, or in a ballroom, or on a street, merely. Glances trailed after her, and strange expressions of homesickness appeared for a fading moment in the faces of the men in the lobby.

She seemed to know the names of most of them, and she spoke to them all. In another part of the world she would have been surrounded at once, but in the West a woman generally "belongs" to some man, and outsiders are not in haste to rush in and make fools of themselves. She came straight across to Silver and held out her hand.

"Ned told me about you," she said. "You're Arizona, and you don't bother about other names except Jim. And he told me how you saved him from the fire, and that you're going to have supper with us so that I can thank you."

He looked straight back into her eyes. As far as he could penetrate them, there was nothing but candor. And yet there was a trick somewhere. It could not be honest. It must be a sham. She had blue eyes, a little stained with shadow on the lower lids, almost as though with a cosmetic. Her brow was as clear as a sculptor's marble. He could not find a place to put his finger and say that this or that might be the sign and the symbol of deceit. And her beauty drew at him like the first day of spring after a long, white winter.

"I don't want thanks," he said. "I've had a chance to talk to Kenyon, and I've learned to know him a little on the way here. That's better than having thanks."

She sat down beside him, explaining that Kenyon would be with them later. It seemed to Silver that perhaps she had turned to her chair a little too quickly, when she heard this deliberate praise of her fiancé. She went on to say that it generally took Ned a good bit of time to get his hair in order.

"It sticks up like fingers around the crown," she said, and laughed a little.

Silver did not laugh. He was looking back into his brain, running over his memories of other women. There had been none that gave a clew to her. There was an air of perfect calmness, of self-possession and strength, that set her apart from the rest.

She was talking again, in spite of his silence. Her whole attitude was one of gratitude and almost of reverence, though she would not touch again on the thing he had done that day for Kenyon.

Outside, the sunset was drawn red across the window. He wished that the full light of the day were striking about them, and that he could keep studying her face. But perhaps it was better this way, for he could face almost away from her and still regard her from the corner of his eye. That is an art. The cultivation of it had saved the life of Silver on more than one day.

She was saying: "Ned tells me that you don't talk about the past; that it's all future with you, Arizona. But I suppose that you've been what every one is out here, part prospector, cow-puncher, lumberman?"

He turned up the palm of his hand. The fingers were straight and lithe, as the fingers of a child. There were no callouses. Labor never had deformed that supple hand.

"No," he said simply.

And for the first time he had touched her. It was only a single upward flash of her eyes, and perhaps she felt that she was shielded from his observation because he was not directly facing her. But in that flash he thought he read suspicion and sudden fear.

He explained his simple negative. "I'm one of the drifters. I'm one of the idlers. I've daubed a rope on a cow now and then; and I've chipped rock with a hammer, too, and swung an ax now and then. But business never has interfered with pleasure."

"And pleasure?" she asked.

"Pleasure?" said he. "Oh, it comes in its own form. I never can tell where I'll find it, or what it will be like. To-morrow I ought to find it, though, when I see you stand up before the preacher with my friend, Kenyon."

She did not wince. She did not blush. She began to nod a little, and she kept on smiling. But he felt that the smile was a trifle frozen, a trifle too fixed.

All of his suspicions took him by the throat. What she could possibly gain from a marriage with Kenyon he could not guess. But in that instant he was convinced that it was not the man she wanted, but something else that she would reach through him.

And all her beauty seemed to drop away from her suddenly, as though a hailstorm had swept across the spring day of which she had reminded him, darkening the skies in a moment and battering grass and flowers into a common mud. So it was for Silver in that instant, and he could face her now with his own faint smile, that seemed to come from nothing except sunshiny content of the heart. It would be a contest between them, and in the angry mood that possessed him, he almost pitied the girl who sat there, still smiling, still making pleasant conversation. The ice already must be entering her heart. She had guessed that he was hostile. She must be choosing the weapons with which she would fence.

Far back in his mind he cast, to find some possible goal of the deception she was practicing on poor Ned Kenyon. Silver could think of none unless it were a matter of property. And what property would a man like Kenyon be apt to have? He must make inquiry about that.

Kenyon came down. They went into the dining room together. They sat at the table, and made conversation amiably until poor Kenyon fell into a silence and merely stared hungrily at the girl.

If she were embarrassed, Silver helped her at that moment, for he began to tell stories of old Mexico that soon had both of the others agape with excitement.

Afterward they went out onto the veranda to watch the moonlight that poured down into the valley, making the upper branches of the pines a luminous mist. Kenyon went to buy tobacco for his pipe. And she said to Silver, in the shadow that covered them:

"Why are you against me? Why are you hating me? Why are you getting ready to crush me in the palm of your hand?"

He merely looked down at her and said nothing. Then he drew on his cigarette to complete, in this way, the perfection of the insult, and so that by the glowing tip of the cigarette she would be able to see his face dimly lighted, and his smile.

4

At the Lone Star

AFTER Ned Kenyon returned, the girl remained with them only a short time. When she had excused herself and said good night, Silver was left alone with his new friend. He found Kenyon overflowing with questions. It was not that the man doubted the beauty, the grace, the wonder of the girl, but it was simply that he preferred hearing Silver reassure him, because there was no other subject in the world of half so much importance to him. It was for the moment the subject that was most on the mind of Silver, also; but he wanted silence to think the thing over. He was glad when Kenyon suggested a drink.

They went across the street diagonally into the Lone Star Saloon and found a dozen men leaning their elbows on the bar. Luck favored them in finding a vacant space at the extreme end. Silver put his back against the wall.

It was the ordinary type of saloon, the room long and narrow, with a few tables against the wall, and a strewing of sawdust on the floor.

Silver had barely taken his place when he heard a voice say:

"Is that Kenyon?"

"That's him," said another. "Wanta be introduced?"

"I don't hanker to have nobody introduce me to a skunk," said the first speaker. "I'll introduce myself with the toe of my boot. Because I'm goin' to kick some new wrinkles into his spinal column."

By this time the attention of the entire saloon was focused on the fellow. He was one of the "picturesque" Western types, with blond, saber-shaped mustache, and a lean face a little too pale to belong to an honest man in this part of the world, unless he had just risen from a sick bed. He wore the finest of shopmade boots; his shirt was of yellow silk; and above all, his revolver had a handle of shining pearl. Yet it was apparently not a tenderfoot's gun worn for show, but a useful tool. The way the holster was buckled about the thigh showed that, and the low pitch of the gun, angling forward a trifle so that the butt would be conveniently ready for a whipsnap draw. If ever this fellow worked, it was fairly apparent that his business must have to do with Colt revolvers.

He was coming forward now, and Silver took heed of Kenyon as the acid test was about to be applied to him. There are few grimmer moments than that in which a man is asked to defend his personal dignity and life from the attack of an armed stranger.

Ned Kenyon turned gray with fear and shuddered so that the heart of Silver sickened. He closed his eyes for an instant, to shut out the picture of that terror.

And *this* was the man that Edith Alton had said she would marry the next day?

The bartender glanced at Kenyon and then shook his head.

"What's the matter, Buck?" he asked gently. "Kenyon never makes no trouble for nobody!"

"Buck" kicked a chair out of his path. It caromed across the floor and crashed against the wall.

"That's what *you* say, you square-headed fool of a beer-drinking Dutchman!" cried Buck. "But I say different. And I got in mind right now to ask Mr. Kenyon to up and say is he a sneaking skunk or ain't he?"

Ned Kenyon turned around slowly. Silver half expected him to bolt for the door. Instead, his voice came out thin and sharp through the nose, but with a tone steady enough.

"I don't know you, Buck," said Ned Kenyon. "And I guess you don't know me. But anyway you look at it, I'm a peaceable fellow. I don't want trouble."

"I'm askin' you," said Buck, "are you a hound, or ain't you a hound? And if you ain't a hound, how you goin' to prove that to me? Hey?"

He thrust out his head. His lips twitched back to show the yellow line of his teeth. He was cold sober, and he was doing his best to work himself into a fighting rage.

Kenyon sighed very audibly.

"Well," he said, "I take everybody to witness that I'm not hunting for a fight. I never have in my life. I never so much as pointed a gun at any man. But on the other hand, I guess I never took water, that I can recollect, and I don't aim to start taking it now."

Silver, bewildered and delighted, could hardly believe his ears. Buck, also, was so amazed that he halted for an instant. Then a swift flash of joy crossed his face. For after this speech of Kenyon's, the fight that was to be would be in the nature of a fair battle, fairly accepted—the sort of thing which too often passes as "self-defense" west of the Mississippi.

At the same time, the men along the bar who had been looking on curiously, now scattered rapidly back toward the wall, to be out of the line of a possible gun play. The bartender prepared to duck.

It was strange to see how calmly every one took this incident. Mustang, to be sure, was "wide open"; but even if the inhabitants had not seen gun fights before, they had heard of them often enough to brace their nerves for the shock.

Ned Kenyon stood straight and stiff. The straightness pleased Silver. The stiffness told him beforehand that his friend would die.

He took Kenyon by the shoulder and gently, irresistibly, pulled him out of the way. His left elbow was leaning on the bar. He continued to lean there, at ease, with his right hand resting on his hip.

"Buck," said Silver, "if you want to talk, talk to me, will you?"

"There ain't anybody that I won't talk to," said Buck. "Who in the devil are you?"

"I'll tell you a part of what I am," said Silver, "In a way, I'm your sort of an hombre, Buck. I spend a lot of time every day practicing with my guns, just as you do. I'm an expert. I'm such an expert that I know the average fellow, who does honest work with his hands, can't possibly stand up to me. Ned Kenyon, for one instance, probably couldn't stand up to me, any more than he can stand up to you."

It was perhaps the oddest speech that was ever heard in a Western barroom. It struck every whisper out of the air. Winter frost could not have stilled all life more completely. Only the mouth of the bartender gaped and closed again, like a fish on dry land, making its last gasp for air.

"You're goin' to put yourself in his boots, are you?" said Buck. "You're goin' to prove that he ain't a skunk? You'll have some proving to show me what *you* are!"

"Wait a minute, Arizona," said Ned Kenyon. "This here is mighty fine of you, but I aim to fight my own fights when they come my way."

"Take your hand away from my shoulder!" snapped Silver, sharply, so that Kenyon jumped back. "And don't speak to me again. This rat here is likely to try his teeth on me the first instant he thinks that I'm off guard. Do you hear me, Buck?"

"Hear you? Well, yes!" shouted Buck. He smote the floor with the flat of his foot and swayed forward a little. Then curses began to spill out of his mouth.

"Were you hired to do this?" asked Silver.

The cursing stopped.

"Because," said Silver, "every time you swear, it's going to be harder on you. I thought at first that I might have to pull a gun and put you to sleep, Buck. But I can see now that I won't have to go that far, because you're only cursing to keep yourself warm, and you wish, this minute, that you were out there in the street in the kind darkness."

Buck tried to laugh. "Just a big bluff and a blowhard," he cried. "And when I break him in two, you'll all see yaller!"

But no one nodded. No one smiled in sympathy with Buck's laugh. It had been too hollow and manifestly false.

"I'm going to ask you a few questions," said Silver. "If you don't answer them, I'll give you a quirting. But in the first place, I'll have to take your gun away from you. Put up your hands, Buck."

He said this so quietly, with such assurance, that the spectators gaped and craned their necks, and could hardly believe that Silver did not have his man covered.

"Why, you fool!" shouted Buck. "You think I'm crazy?"

"You don't think that," said Silver. "You know I'm right, and that I'll do what I say. You know that I'm a faster hand and a surer shot than you are, Buck. And your poor little soul is shrinking and dying in you. There's a sort of pity that grows up in me when I see you turn white around the mouth, as you're doing now. And a disgust when I see your eyes begin to roll."

He stood straight, and commanded in a harsher voice.

"Put up your hands!"

It was a frightful thing to see that armed man, that gun fighter, that slayer of men—Buck—standing wavering as though a whole regiment of soldiers had drawn a bead on him. But all that threatened him was the empty hand and the pointing finger of Silver.

"You hear me?" said Silver, and took a half step forward.

A queer, bubbling sound broke out of the throat of Buck. His mouth yawned. His lips started to frame words, and could make only a hideous gibberish.

And there before the eyes of the crowd the miracle happened, and his hands started to rise from the level of his pearl-handled revolver to his hips—would he try to whip out some hidden weapon, then?—and so on to his breast, and up to his shoulders, where they fluttered for an instant in feeble revolt, but then continued until they were above the top of his head.

The sickening thing was not finished. Silver stepped forward and pulled the pearl-handled gun out of its sheath, and as he drew it, a great groan of despair came from Buck. He had allowed an act of shame to be performed on him that would make him a very legendary figure of shame, a horror of which no man would gladly speak.

Yet all of those men who watched with pale, fascinated eyes, stared less at Buck in his disgrace than at the terrible face of Silvertip as he pulled that gun out, and then laid it on the bar. And more than one man wondered, if the face of Silver were before him, if he would have had the nerve to do anything other than Buck had done.

Hypnotism was what it seemed like. No man exchanged glances with his neighbor. Each man hoped that his own horror was not being observed, and each knew that the coldness of his skin meant a definite pallor.

"You can get the gun afterward," said Silver. "I'm not going to take it and keep it. And I'm not going to harm you in any way, Buck, so long as you tell me, frankly, the name of the man who hired you for this job. You *were* hired, I take it?"

The jaw of Buck dropped. He gasped, "Yes! Hired! Oh—yes, I was—"

One long breath was drawn by all the men in that room. The bartender stood straight for the first time since Silver had begun speaking.

"Who hired you?" demanded Silver.

"Who? A gent by the name of Alec Wilson."

"You lie!" said Silver. "Kenyon, get me your quirt, will you?"

"Not Wilson!" groaned Buck. "What I meant was, the gent that hired me was really—"

There was an open window at the side of the room. A gun glinted beyond the sill, now, and the explosion of the shot tossed the mouth of the revolver a little up into the air.

The head of Buck dropped over on his shoulder. He slumped into the arms of Silver, slipped out of them, and spilled onto the floor.

5

The Murderer's Name

SILVER went out of that room like a cat after a bird, but as he turned the front corner of the building he heard the rapid beating of hoofs begin behind the saloon, and knew that the quarry was on the wing.

Oh, for five minutes of Parade, then—to loose the golden stallion like an arrow at the mark—or for any horse, for that matter. But there were none except down the street, at the hitch rack on the farther side of the hotel, and that was too far away.

He went gloomily back into the saloon. Half the men had scattered to look for the murderer; half had remained to look at the victim.

He was dying, beyond doubt. The bullet had cut straight through his lungs, and Buck was already in his death agony. He kept rising on one hand, and turning his swollen face and his terrible, starting eyes from one man to another, mutely asking help.

But there was no help to be given. The finest doctor in the world could not assist, though messengers had gone to fetch all the physicians in Mustang. Buck himself seemed to realize that there were only seconds to him. Then he tried to speak, and that was the worst of all.

Silver, the indirect cause of his death, was the man he wanted most to talk to. He came clawing across the floor and reached up and caught Silver's hand in his. He tried to speak, but only a rapid succession of red bubbles burst on his lips. He was strangling. He was biting at the air, and getting none down to his lungs.

Others drew back from that sight of agony, but Silver slipped to the floor and sat by the struggling body.

"Write it, Buck!" he called loudly. "Write it on the floor! Write the name, and I swear that I'll try to get him for you!"

Buck was beating on the floor with his feet and hands, in the last struggle between death and life, but he understood Silver. He flopped heavily over on his side, dipped his right forefinger into the thick pool of his own blood, and commenced to write. Then death caught back his red-stained hand and turned him on his back. He seemed to be making a last effort to speak as he died. One long shudder ran through his body, and he was gone.

On the floor beside him was written: "Nel—" followed by the sweeping stroke of crimson where his finger had been snatched from the writing.

Silver folded the hands of the dead man across his breast and closed the half-open eyes. When he looked up, he saw that men were standing by with their hats in their hands, and with sick faces.

He stood up and took off his own hat.

"Does anybody here know a woman named Nell, or a man named Nelson?" he asked.

"There's a woman that does laundry," said the bartender, instantly.

Silver shook his head.

"There's Digger Nelson, the prospector," said another in the room.

"What sort of a man?" asked Silver.

"A regular rock chipper. He patches the seat of his pants with flour sacks and—"

"No!" said Silver. "He's not the man I want. He's not the man who hired Buck to pick a fight with Ned Kenyon, and shoot it out. He's not that sort."

The first of the doctors came hurrying in. The sheriff was just at his heels. Silver took Ned Kenyon by the arm and led him out of the barroom into a back room, closing the door behind them. They sat down at a table.

Mustang was now well awakened. Scores of footfalls were padding up the street, or pounding loudly over the board sidewalks. Horses snorted in the distance under the spur. Voices were gathering toward the saloon like buzzing bees toward the hive. Presently the sheriff would be sure to want both Silver and Kenyon, but Silver used this interim to pump Kenyon as well as he could.

"Ned," he said, "do you know what to make of all this?"

"I'm flabbergasted," said poor Kenyon. "I can't make head or tail of it. But it looks as though you know the inside workings of everything!"

"I wish I did! I'm only guessing. I'm reaching into the dark and getting at nothing. That's all! Nothing! Ned, listen to me!"

"The way I would to a preacher," said Kenyon, with a naïveté that made Silver faintly smile.

"What does this fellow Buck hitch with?"

"I don't make that out, either. I never saw him before. I don't suppose that he ever saw me. He says that he was hired—"

Into this stream of meaningless words Silver broke sharply.

"What's the thing we can catch on?" he asked. "There's something you have, or that you're about to have, that other people want—or want to keep you from. Now tell me out and out—have you anything worth money?"

"Not even a horse," said the stage driver sadly. "Not even Jerry, now!"

"You have some land, somewhere," suggested Silver.

"Father has a patch—a quarter section. That's all there is in the family."

"Where? In the mountains? Some place where pay dirt might be found? Gravel, for instance? Near an old creek bed, perhaps?"

"Pay dirt? The clay runs down about a thousand feet. The old man works that ground about sixteen hours a day, and he hardly makes a dollar a day, clear. I never saw worse clay. We've dug wells. We know how far that clay goes down."

"Wait a moment," said Silver, violently readjusting the course of his suspicions. "There's another chance. You've been around the world a good deal, partner. And you're sure to know a good lot. You've looked in on some queer things in your time. You've seen men in odd positions. You have up your sleeve something that some one would be pretty glad to hush up. Think, now. It must be that!"

Kenyon thought. After his fashion, he took his time, fixing his eyes on distance, and thoroughly combing his memory. At last he said: "No. There's nothing that I can put a finger on."

"There must be," insisted Silver. "There has to be something! Think again."

"No, Arizona—or Jim, if I can call you that—there's nothing. Nothing ever happens to me—or nothing ever did happen until—"

"All right," said Silver. "That brings us back to Edith Alton, as far as I can see. You're going to marry her to-morrow morning. And some one hates the idea of that. Somebody wants to stop you. Somebody with a first or a last name beginning with Nel. Who could it be?"

Again Kenyon shook his head. "I don't know. It beats me."

"It beats you? It'll *kill* you before you're many days older!" said Silver.

"Man, man, are you sure that you don't know any one whose name begins with those three letters?"

"Well, Jim," said Kenyon, "don't be mad at me. I'm trying to think, but there are not many people whose name begins with those letters."

"No," said Silver. "There are not many. That's a good point in the deal. It'll narrow down the hunting field."

"You *look* like a hunter," said Kenyon, rather over-awed. "But by the jumping thunder, Jim, I'd hate to have you on my trail with that look in your eye and with that set to your jaw!"

"I'm not on your trail. I'm on the trail of murder," said Silver. "I can smell the murder inside my nostrils. I can taste it against the roof of my mouth. Murder—*phaugh!*"

The door opened. There stood on the threshhold a man with a stocky body and a long, triangular face.

"Murder is what we been talking about, in there," he said. "Maybe I can talk to you two boys in here about the same thing."

Others were about to follow this stranger inside the room, but he closed the door in their faces, and they did not try to open it behind his back.

He came across the floor, opening his coat to show the badge that was pinned inside it.

"Name of Philips," he said. "Or maybe you'll introduce me, Ned?"

Kenyon started up and sawed the air with his hand, embarrassed.

"This here is Sheriff Philips. Bert Philips," he said. "And this is a friend of mine that's got into a lot of trouble on my account, this day. He's Arizona Jim, sheriff. And he—"

He paused. The inadequacy of that nickname seemed to fill the throat of Kenyon, at the moment that he spoke to the man of the law.

"Glad to know you, Arizona," said the sheriff. "Ned, who killed Buck?"

"I don't know. I wish—"

"Ever have a grudge between you?"

"Never. I never saw him before he—"

"Ned, you walk out and buy yourself a drink. I want to talk with Arizona."

Ned Kenyon went out hesitantly, as one who feels that he may be deserting a friend in a time of need, but the calm smile of Silver reassured him until the door was opened and closed again.

Then the sheriff pulled out a chair and sat down opposite Silver. He said: "You know what I've got on my knee?"

"Yes," said Silver. "A gun."

"Does that mean anything to you?"

"It means that you're rather young," said Silver.

The sheriff frowned. Then, suddenly, he grinned.

"You're all they say about you,—Silver," he said.

Silver said nothing at his identification by the man of the law.

"A dead cool one," continued the sheriff. "Now, you tell me who killed Buck."

Silver smiled.

"Go on!" urged the sheriff.

"Otherwise you'll shoot?"

Suddenly Philips raised the gun into view and shoved it back inside his coat.

"Maybe I've been a fool," he said. "I thought for a minute that I'd call your bluff. But now I almost think you mean what you've been saying. That right?"

"It is."

"You're Kenyon's friend?"

"Yes."

"Do you make anything out of this mess, then?"

"Only guesses."

"Let's have them, Silver. I don't know just how to take you. There's some call you a crook and a man-killer, and others say that you're the whitest man on earth. Anyway, you have brains, and you've been a friend to poor Ned Kenyon. Now, tell me everything you think."

"I think," said Silver, "that some one wants to stop a thing that's due to happen to Kenyon to-morrow."

"What?"

"I can't tell you. I've promised Kenyon not to tell."

"Stop him by killing him?"

"Gladly, if there's no other way."

"Silver, how much do you know?"

"Hardly more than a baby."

The sheriff laid hold of his chin with a big brown hand and gripped hard, staring over his knuckles at the face of Silver.

"It's hard," he said, "but I'm going to believe you. I want to know this: Are you working with me?"

"With all my might!"

"Good!" said the sheriff. "And if you have an idea, you can call on me night or day."

"I'll have an idea before the end of to-morrow," said Silver. "And then I may call on you to blow up half this town!"

6

Dawn Riding

SILVER went to his room, dipped a towel in cold water, tied it around his head, and waited for the whisky fumes to disappear. He had had only two drinks, but he felt that they were too many. He sat in the darkness, without a lamp, watching the moonlight inch its way across the floor, reach the feet of a chair, and crawl up the varnished legs.

But still he could find no answer to the questions which were whirling in his mind.

He took off his boots, left his room, and went down the stairs. The outer doors were all locked. He opened a window, got onto the veranda, and stole down it until he stepped onto the pine needles beneath the grove beside the building. There he sat with his back to a tree, not even smoking, and watched the moonlight shine on the windows of the house as on pools of black water.

The moon grew dim. Its shadows no longer made a pattern of jet and white on the ground. The dawn came, with a chill that started his flesh quaking, and then he heard the loud rattling of iron on iron, as some one began to work at the kitchen stove. Immediately afterward, a door in the back of the hotel groaned faintly.

Silver got up, and walked behind the trees until he could see the small form of a woman hurrying toward the barn. He knew her by the walk— the girl who was to marry Ned Kenyon before noon of this day.

He rounded to the back of the stable. Two seconds after she led out the black mare he was on Parade. He was saddling as she turned down the main street of Mustang, and he was able to note the direction. A half minute later he was riding west, also, but keeping behind the most outlying houses of the town. In that way, he rounded into the head of the valley in time to see the rose of the morning bloom on all the snow-clad peaks of the distance. A solitaire was singing as though the beauty of the dawn had filled its heart. And in the distance he saw the black horse slide into the shadows of a big grove of pines.

He followed only a short distance up the valley, for he was reasonably sure, for a definite reason, that she would ride up the same trail by which he had seen her descend the evening before. Kenyon had told him that she loved to ride out by herself—generally toward the west. That was her favorite, the zigzag trail down the western hills, Kenyon had remarked.

But it would be very odd if she preferred that trail to others that were ten times more beautiful. And if she was, as Kenyon said, merely a girl tenderfoot trying to see the West for herself unimpeded by too much chaperonage, it would have been more natural for her to take all of the trails, one by one. Some singular attraction had kept her until deep into the evening of the day before among those western hills. Perhaps the same thing—not the beauty of the morning—was taking her out there before the day had well begun.

Silver rode up the slope to the left of him to the water divide above. The black mare was fast, but she could not keep pace with the cat feet and the winged stride of the golden stallion. Parade was well over the ridge and coming through a group of trees, when Silver saw the girl swinging her horse at an angle across his line. And he sighed with content. He was on the right trail. And if she were ten thousand times more beautiful than she was, he would find her share in the mystery and lay it bare.

So he shadowed her, moving Parade with care from one covert to another, half guessing the probable course of the girl a dozen times, and always hitting it correctly.

She dipped into a narrow ravine, at last, and Silver had to halt his horse on the brink of the steep ground, then rein it well back to wait for the black mare to climb out up the farther bank.

He waited a sufficient time, until a pinch of suspicion stirred him. So he dismounted, put Parade in a clump of tall brush, gave him the word that would tether him in place more strongly than ropes, and went forward on foot to investigate.

He had to lie flat and peer over the rim of the canyon, before he could see what he wanted. But the sight was reward, and a rich one. For in a clearing among the trees in the middle of the ravine he saw the girl walking up and down with a young man in a gray felt hat with a brim foolishly narrow for Western weather, and with a quick step, and nervous gestures. That was all that Silver could make out.

The stranger seemed to be pouring out a tirade, to which the girl listened most of the time with a bent head. She seemed then to be making gestures of denial, and at this he fell into an attitude of earnest argument and persuasion, until the very ears of Silver ached to hear the words.

Whatever they were, they were sufficient. Presently she was nodding in agreement, and then she was putting her head up in its characteristic fearless poise, as though she were ready to outface the world.

A few minutes later, the two disappeared under the trees, and then the black mare mounted the farther slope and tipped out over the rim of it beyond his view.

There remained the fellow in the ravine. Silver worked down the sharp slope toward him, moving more like a snake than a man. It was hard to make that descent with any surety that he was unseen, for a dozen times he was without real cover. He was perhaps twenty steps from the bottom of the valley when a rifle clanged, a bullet spatted against the ground beside his face, and he had to dive into the shrubbery before him as into water.

He was worming his way through that cover, with his revolver in his hand, when he heard the rapid thudding of hoofs that ranged up the ravine, and knew his quarry had taken to flight.

Gloomily he went on until he came to a small clearing in which a mere dog tent was pitched. There was a heap of empty cans at one side. There was a rudely put together fireplace built of stones. And under the cover of the tent he saw a bed made down, the blankets rumpled, together with a book or two and a few magazines.

Silver went around the camp with a furtive step. This camper had been on the spot for a week, at least. He was not used to a life in the open, or he would have built his fireplace better. He was no fisherman, for he would have worn a trail along the side of the little brook, and particularly down to the edge of the broad, still pool not far away. He was, in fact, nothing but a tenderfoot.

Silver sat down on a stump and smoked a cigarette. He had plenty of facts, and he could make a few deductions.

The girl who was betrothed to Kenyon came to this place daily, so it seemed, in order to talk with a light-stepping, active young man who apparently was able to persuade her against her will on matters of importance. This young gentleman, instead of going to the hotel in the town, preferred to live in the wilderness, though he had neither talent nor apparent liking for that life—for no one who liked it could have put up with the arrangements of that camp. In addition to these things, there was the further fact that the stranger actually had tried with his rifle for the life of a man who was stealing upon his camp!

The component parts made the picture of one who could not be other than a criminal, it seemed to Silver. And if he were, it was a fact that threw keen light upon the character of the girl.

But with this much gained, Silver had to return to Mustang. He went back to Parade, and took a leisurely way to the town, his mind crammed with thought every inch of the way. In the stable behind the hotel, he put up the stallion and paused to look over the mare. She had been taken flying home. She still was head down, panting hard, and the sweat was still running on her sleek body. It was apparent that the girl had wished to be away from the hotel as short a time as possible.

Silver went up to his room, undressed, slipped into his bed, turned on his face, and slept soundly for two hours. Then the striking of the breakfast gong roused him.

A wash in cold water wakened him thoroughly. He dressed, and went down the stairs humming softly, and into the dining room, where the girl and Ned Kenyon were already having bacon and eggs, with a sooty pot of coffee beside them, for service in that hotel was not of the most polite.

"A good night, Arizona?" asked the girl cheerfully.

"One of the best," said Silver. "Did you sleep right through?"

"Like the dead!" said she, and smiled at him.

It was a good, direct smile, with open eyes that met his, easily. He wanted to say to her: "You lie well. I know the types of liars, and you're one of the best!"

Yet, as he sat there with them, as he heard the softness of her voice, as he watched the clear beauty of her face, he found himself saying, against his better judgment, that she must be all right. It would be an irony, a sarcasm of nature, if she were other than honest and true.

Poor Ned Kenyon, who dwelt on her with his eyes, who devoured her every gesture, every word from her throat—what would he say if he knew of that visitation to the stranger over the hills?

Silver had a chance to find out, a few moments later, when the girl finished and excused herself from the table. As she rose from her place, her glance lingered for one serious, penetrating instant on the face of Silver. Then she went out hastily, as though not trusting the words that she was tempted to speak.

Afterward, Silver said, to the rapt face of Ned Kenyon: "You love her, son."

"More'n breath," said Kenyon simply.

"If she turned out to be a counterfeit—would that stop you?"

Kenyon did not smile. He merely looked out the window for a moment, as though to contemplate the immensity of that suggestion in a calm seriousness.

Then he said: "You're a swimmer, Jim?"

"Yes," said Silver.

"You know what it means," said Kenyon, "to fetch under water for a long distance?"

Silver nodded.

"And the way your lungs burn—and all? Well, suppose that you came up to the surface and there was no air to breathe! And it's that way with me. It ain't what is right or wrong about her, any more. It's just that I couldn't live without her in every day of my life—either having her, being with her, or knowing all the time that she belongs to me. You see?"

"I see," said Silver.

"Murder," said Kenyon quietly, "not even if she'd done murder, it wouldn't stop me. It'd matter, but it'd matter as though I'd done it myself. That's all. But what was in your mind, partner?"

"Well, I was just thinking, was all," said Silver. "I simply wanted to know how you felt."

"In a couple of hours," murmured Kenyon, "there's a new life waiting for me. I'm not thinking about that. I don't dare. It's like thinking of walking on water, or walking on blue air. But you'll be there, Jim. You'll be there to steady me. That's what I'm counting on."

Silver got out of the room like a blind man, fumbling. For he knew that to tell his friend of what he had seen this morning would be like pouring acid on a man already incurably ill. He could not speak!

7

The Wedding

THE church was a little square frame box with a steeple tacked onto one side of it, like a forefinger lifted above a fist. The preacher was a good, hard-working man who covered all parts of his parish both winter and summer, climbing among ice-clad rocks in winter to places that no horse or mule could ever reach. Only a small percentage of Mustang attended his Sunday services, but there was not a man in the district who would not have fought for the sky pilot.

Silver looked on him with wonder. He was regarding all things with astonishment, at that moment, for he could not believe that Kenyon and the girl were actually standing in front of the man of God, about to be joined in wedlock. The hotel proprietor was one witness. The keeper of the general merchandise store was the other. As for Silver, he had dodged the duty. In case he served, his real name would have to be written down, and that name he preferred to keep unknown.

He stood in the back of the empty little church, acutely aware of the four windows that looked in on the scene, and prepared any instant to see the gleam of a gun outside the glass, for if they had killed one man in the cause of preventing the marriage, did it not stand to reason that they would kill another?

So, with a sense of the two revolvers that hung beneath his armpits, Silver waited, and watched, and was all eyes rather than ears. Yet he could hear the responses, too, and he could be aware of the surprised face which the minister kept continually turning toward Kenyon. Even that unworldly man could see the absurdity of such a match.

All had been done quietly. Not a soul in the village knew of what was to take place. That was the reason why the church was not crowded.

He heard the preacher saying: "You promise to love, honor and obey—"

Silver saw the girl turn her head suddenly, and flash her eyes at Kenyon before she answered in a forced, barely audible voice: "I do."

Poor Kenyon!

It was over, suddenly. In turn, the witnesses bent to sign the little book. The preacher was shaking hands with the bride and groom. And out of a few spoken words there had been established a bond which should last until death. But would it last for even a day?

Silver watched them come down the aisle. Kenyon was a man walking above the surface of this earth. The girl was pale, with a frozen smile. A careless eye might have put her pallor down to mere timidity, but Silver saw, or felt he saw, that it was an agony of the mind that moved her.

Silver himself avoided shaking hands with them, first by opening the door for them, then by saying that he would hurry to the hotel, and see that the buckboard was ready. For the plan of Kenyon was to take her at once out of Mustang, and then over the green plains and up to the little town where his mother and father lived. It would be a simple honeymoon, but it was all that his purse could afford.

At the hotel, Silver harnessed the span of mustangs which Kenyon had bought to the small buckboard. He heaped in the baggage behind the seat, while Kenyon came out of the hotel to help where he could. But his hands were helpless, and his small eyes were continually lifting to the sky, and being dazzled until they filled with moisture.

The girl would be down in a moment from her room, Kenyon said.

But she did not come for five minutes, for ten minutes, for half an hour.

"Women have always got fixings to go through," said Kenyon. "It don't matter. I'd rather wait for her here than dance with anybody else while a band was playin'."

Silver said abruptly: "Perhaps I can help her about something."

"No. Leave her be. Let her take her time," said Kenyon.

But Silver was already through the door of the hotel. Once out of sight, he moved fast, up the stairs, and to the door of the girl's room. He knocked. There was no answer. He pushed the door open, and no sign of Edith Alton was inside. Only a wraith of white smoke hung in the air above the little round-bellied stove that stood in a corner. And on the table was an envelope, sealed, and addressed in her handwriting to Edward Kenyon.

Silver went down to the back of the hotel and found the cook.

"See Miss Alton go out toward the barn?" he asked.

"Half an hour ago she rode her black mare out of the barn and went up the valley," said the cook. "She was traveling fast, too, like she wanted to catch a train."

Silver came through the hotel to Kenyon and took him by the arm.

"Ned," he said crisply, "you've got bad news. She's left you."

Kenyon straightened. It reminded Silver of how the man had stood the night before, in the saloon—straight, ready to meet his fate, but unable to struggle against it.

"She's left a letter for you upstairs," said Silver. "That may do a little explaining. I'll wait for you down here."

The stone-gray lips of Kenyon parted stiffly. He put a hand on the shoulder of his friend.

"If you wouldn't mind, Jim," said he, "if it wouldn't be wrong for me to ask, I'd like to have you come up there with me."

That was why Silver climbed the stairs again, suddenly feeling old and weak.

Yet there would be a sufficient strength in him, he thought, if he could lay eyes on the girl, or on that fellow in the hills, who moved with that alert and springing step.

It seemed to Silver now that he had done everything wrong. He should have spoken his suspicions to Kenyon at once. At least he should have demanded from the girl an explanation of her morning visit to that rifleman in the hills—that young fellow who was so ready to try his hand at murder!

But now there was a ruin, and it was entirely in the life and the heart of poor Ned Kenyon.

When they got into the room, Kenyon paused a moment at the door, and took off his hat, breathing deeply.

"Kind of fragrant, Jim, ain't it?" said he. "I mean the air. Kind of like her. Like flowers, eh?"

He actually smiled at Silver, to invite his agreement. But Silver, jerking his hat a little lower on his head, stalked to the window and looked down to the ruts in the dusty street, and across the roofs of the houses, above which the heat waves were shimmering and dancing. He could have drunk hot blood.

He looked sidewise, curiously, at the stove, above which the wraith of smoke was dissolving. In winter weather in Mustang there would be plenty of need for stoves, but hardly at this time of the year. He opened the door. On the fire grate there was a ball of gray-and-white fluff, the ashes of small bits of paper which had been wadded together. Now the draft took hold of them and blew them dissolving up the chimney.

He opened the lower door to the ash pan and pulled the pan out. As he had expected, several of the small bits of the paper had dropped through. He picked them up. It was contemptible to read them, but the girl was no longer fit to be treated as a decent human being. She was a criminal, and she had committed her crime in the most detestable fashion, against the most helpless of men.

So he stared at the few words which he found. Several of the scraps were covered with words written in the more smoothly flowing and smaller hand of a man. None were in her own writing. But of them all there was only one out of which he could make any sense. It contained the words:

out fail in Kirby Cr

That could be pieced out a little. "Without fail in Kirby Creek," was perhaps the true sense of it. Suppose one went back a little and filled in: "Meet without fail in Kirby Creek."

If that referred to the past, it was nothing. If it referred to the future, it might be everything.

"Maybe you better read it," said Kenyon. He was holding out a letter toward Silver. Then he drew back his hand, murmuring: "I dunno, Silver. Seems to me maybe it wouldn't be fair to her, hardly, if I was to show her letter to another man?"

"Fair to—*her*?" asked Silver hoarsely.

"Ah, but don't be too hard on her," said Kenyon. "She ain't very old, Jim. And she ain't very used to the world, and you'll see that the world's been hard on her, poor girl!"

"Well," said Silver, in a voice of iron, "do you want me to read the letter, or not?"

"Not if you talk like that," said Kenyon, drawing back his hand.

Silver laughed, in a sort of despair.

"Give me the letter," he said. "I need to read it. I *have* to read it."

"Well," said Kenyon, "I don't think that she'd mind. Only this morning she said to me that I must always stick to you, because there was no other friend that I'd find like you, in the whole world."

"Did she say that?" asked Silver sharply.

"She did, and she had her heart in her voice, and a kind of a pity and a kindness for me in her eyes, Jim. So I guess she wouldn't mind you seeing what she wrote to me. Here it is."

Silver, taking the letter, for a moment could not look at it. His mental preoccupation was too great, as he pondered over what the girl had said. For she could not have been in doubt that he was her enemy, heartily and forever.

He went back to the window and saw, first of all, pinned to the top sheet of the letter, a check made out to Edward Kenyon for ten thousand dollars and signed Edith Alton Kenyon.

Ten thousand dollars!

Some of his walls of reservations were knocked flat as he saw the sum. If she had done Kenyon harm, she had intended to do him good, also.

The letter ran:

> DEAR NED:
>
> To-morrow I expect that we shall be married, unless your friend Arizona Jim finds a way to prevent the ceremony; because he loves you, Ned, and he guessed from the first moment when he saw me that I was not honest
>
> And I'm not. If you're reading this letter, it is because I have married you, and left you, and this is the farewell message.
>
> I suppose that it's human nature to wish to defend ourselves. That's why I'm going to say that I don't think another woman in the world could have stood out against the terrible necessity that was pressing on me. It was a question of life or death. Not my life or death, but that of another person, infinitely of more importance to the world than I am.
>
> I can't even explain farther than this. I only knew that I had to be married, at once. I knew that I had to be married to a kind and honest man who might never forgive me for having wronged him, but who would not pursue me.
>
> That was why I knew I had found some one who could be of help to me when I found you. I thought of even telling you what I wanted and of asking you to marry me, and then forget me, and divorce me. But I couldn't risk that. You might say no, and then there would be no time to find another man. I had to talk with you, persuade you into asking me to marry you, and then go through with the ceremony.

Then it seemed to me that you were really growing fond of me. And my heart ached to think of it. But I've rushed through with everything, hoping that God would understand that I meant what is right, even if kind, honest, gentle Ned Kenyon would not be able to understand, ever.

I'm leaving a check with you. It isn't hush money. It's simply that I want with all my heart to help you to the thing you wish to have—a small ranch and a chance to lead your own chosen life. I would make it five times or ten times as much, but I know that you would never take the money.

Forgive me, forgive me.

Edith.

8
On the Trail

SILVER, as he finished the second reading of that letter, ground his teeth together in a helpless rage. There was a certain ring of honesty to the words. But he would believe nothing. Her troubles were unknown, distant. The grief of Ned Kenyon was a present and immediate thing. Behind her there was certainly a power of wealth. Ten thousand dollars—which she could have made fifty thousand, she said, if she had dreamed that Ned Kenyon would accept it! It argued piled treasures somewhere in her background.

He gave back the letter to Kenyon.

"What do you think, Jim?" asked Kenyon.

"I think," said Silver, "that you're the straightest fellow I ever met. I think, Ned, that I could cut her heart out, and enjoy the job. As for the letter—man, it's easy to write words! Dead easy, I tell you!"

"You won't believe that she's honest?" asked Kenyon.

"Never in the world," said Silver. "She knew that you loved her. A woman can never go wrong about that! And still she went ahead."

"There was a matter of life or death," argued Kenyon.

"Bah!" said Silver. "You'd believe that a frog croaks in a marsh!"

Kenyon shook his head, picked up the letter, detached the check, and put the letter itself into his pocket. The check he tore into small pieces, and threw into the stove.

"She knew that you'd do that, too," said Silver bitterly. "She knew that you'd never take the dirty money. Ah, Ned, you're going with me to find her, if we have to travel around the world. You understand? I'm staying with you until we find her, if it takes the rest of my life!"

"Follow her?" said Kenyon, with a look of mild surprise. "No, no, Jim. I can't follow her. She doesn't want me, and I can't bother her. I can't go after her."

"Are you going to sit down and take your licking—from a pretty little female crook?" demanded Silver.

Kenyon turned slowly toward him.

"You're bigger, stronger, and faster than I am, Jim. But if I ever hear you say a word against her again, I'm going to try to knock your head off! I'm sorry to say that, but it's what I mean."

Silver groaned. "What are you going to do, then?" he asked.

"I don't know," said Kenyon. "Back to driving the stage, I guess, and take up where I left off. The boys will guy me a little, when this marriage is known. But I come from the part of the world where they grow good hickory, Jim!"

He smiled, as he said this, and tears suddenly stung the eyes of Silver. He took the hand of Kenyon and gripped it hard.

"You're a better sort than I am," said Silver. "I'm getting out of Mustang. One of these days I'll see you again. I'm going on a trip and—so long, old-timer!"

He walked out of the room quickly. When he reached the head of the stairs, he could hear the voice of Kenyon calling after him, but he ran down rapidly. His trail was outward. There were many things to fill his mind, from that man who had hired Buck, whose name began with "Nel," to that light-stepping friend of the girl, and there was the girl herself, and that matter of life and death about which she was so wrought up.

He paid his bill, went out to the stable, and saddled Parade. He was outside the barn before he heard the voice of Kenyon raised high in the distance, calling:

"Arizona! Oh, Arizona!" But he put Parade into a hard gallop.

He cut back into the main street of the village, after a short distance, and stopped in front of the blacksmith shop to make his inquiry, for blacksmiths, next to bartenders, know more news than any one else in the West.

The blacksmith came out, busily tying a bandage about a bleeding finger.

"Where's Kirby Creek?" asked Silver.

"Kirby Creek?" said the blacksmith. "Never heard of it."

"There's a place of that name," said Silver.

"Kirby Creek? Never heard of it."

"Anything else that sounds like Kirby Cr—"

The blacksmith grunted with the profundity of his mental effort. Then he said: "There's Kirby Crossing, if that's what you want to know."

"I *do* want to know," said Silver. "Where is it?"

"Fifty mile back into the hills. Yeah, right back into the mountains. You take the northwest road. You foller along it for twenty mile, and then you come to a trail that branches off to the left and—"

Silver listened to the directions, carefully. He repeated them after his informer and was pronounced letter-perfect. After that, he would never forget. The words would stick like glue in his memory.

So he took the northwest road, keeping Parade along the edge of it where there was no dust and the footing was therefore firmer. Gradually the hills rolled up about him in greater and greater dimensions. He was climbing into the mountains when a rider with a pack mule tethered to the pommel of his saddle came down a cross trail toward the main way on which Silver was traveling.

He was a very big man, with a shag of beard covering his face almost to the eyes. And one of those eyes was covered with a great black leather patch. The size of that horseman made the mustang he rode look hardly bigger than a goat.

Silver, seeing that he was noticed, drew rein, and waited. He had reason to wait, he felt, unless he wanted a bullet through his back, for he had recognized "One-eyed Harry" Bench, from whom, not so very long before, he had taken two good riding horses by dint of not so much of the cash he paid down for them as of a bullet through the soft of One-eyed Harry's shoulder.

So Silver waited at the crossing, in doubt.

Those doubts were scattered in a moment, as big Harry Bench let out a whoop and spurred his mustang to a canter, the mule dangling back grimly on the end of the lead rope. Pulling his tough pony to a halt, One-eyed Harry reached far forward and caught the good right hand of Silver in a grip that threatened to break bones.

"Silver!" he shouted. "Curse me black and white if I ever thought I'd lay an eye on you ag'in. How come, you old rattler, that you're in this part of the range? I thought you was away far north, or away far south. What brings you around here?"

"Just drifting, Harry; just drifting. How are things with you?"

"Better'n ever before," said Harry Bench. "The grouch I had at the world was all let out with the blood that run when you slid that chunk of lead through me, Silver. I done some hating of you, for a spell. But when the news got around to me, and I found out that it was Jim Silver himself that had nicked me—why, there ain't no shame in being put down by Silver himself, is there? Not to my way of thinkin'. The day has been, since then, that gents have seen me stripped and wanted to know where I got the scar on the shoulder, and when they hear that it was a bullet out of Silver's gun, I get a considerable pile of attention, Jim. And the boys, they most generally tell me that I'm lucky not to be wearin' that scar right through the heart, and make no mistake about it. Where are you bound?"

He poured out the words in a hearty torrent, and in a thundering voice that plainly had been rarely confined to the echoing walls of a room.

"I'm bound for Kirby Crossing," said Silver.

"Kirby Crossing?" exclaimed the giant. "And what would a gent of your size be doing in a place like Kirby Crossing, I'd like to know?"

"I'm a lot smaller than you are, Harry," said Silver.

"Across the shoulder, maybe, but not across the brain," said the big man cheerfully. "It would sprain Kirby Crossing in the small of the back and both ankles, to have a gent of your size of name inside of it, man!"

"I'm not wearing the same name," answered Silver. "I'm a Mexican, when I go in there."

"Hold on!" cried One-eyed Harry. "You mean that you're a bare-footed greaser in rags, like you were when I first seen you, Silver?"

"That's it. Something like that."

Harry grinned. "What's the little game in the wind now?" he asked.

"Would you help me?" asked Silver curiously.

"Me? And why not? Sure I'd help you. And how?"

"By being my boss," said Silver, "and letting me drive that mule into town for you, as though it were my job."

The mirth of One-eyed Harry thundered through the air like a roaring cataract in a narrow valley. "Me with a servant?" he said. "Me with Silver for a servant? And why not? But hold on, Jim Silver!"

"Well?" said Silver.

"There's another way of lookin' at these things. What kind of hurricane are you goin' to raise when you get into Kirby Crossing? And after you raise it, how you goin' to ride it? Have I gotta sit on top of the same kind of a wind that you like?"

Silver smiled. "I don't know what's ahead of me," he declared.

"Something like Barry Christian and his thugs?" asked One-eyed Harry.

"I hope not."

"No," said the big man, "it ain't likely that you'll ever crash into anything as tough as Barry Christian, if you live to be a thousand. They ain't hung Barry yet. You know that?"

The face of Silver darkened. "I know that," he agreed.

"And it doesn't seem likely to me," added One-eyed Harry Bench, "that they ever *will* hang him, because it don't seem likely that the rope was ever braided or wove that'll hang a neck like his. But about the things you're after in Kirby Crossing—tell me, Jim Silver—ain't it a blood trail?"

"Why do you ask that?" said Silver, frowning.

"Because," answered Bench, "I've heard more'n one gent say that you never ride on no trail at all unless it's a blood trail? Is that true?"

"I hope not," answered Silver. "I hope I'm not such a devil as that, Harry."

"Well," answered Bench, "there's a good many men have seen you at work here and there, and they all say that they never hear of a trail of yours that wasn't spotted with red before the end of it. Is there a killing in your mind, in Kirby Crossing?"

"There is!" said Silver, suddenly and grimly. "And you can count yourself out of the party, Harry. It may be more than you'll want to swallow."

"A mean gent that you're after?" said Bench wistfully.

"A man whose face I wouldn't know," said Silver.

"Not know?" cried Bench. He groaned with curiosity. Then he exclaimed: "Ah, well, I can't live forever. I'm goin' to be a fool for once more in my life. Count me in, Jim. I'll stay as long as I can!"

9
Kirby Crossing

THEY expected to get into the town that night, but when they reached the place they found that Kirby Crossing was no crossing at all, for the bridge had gone down in the flood that was still roaring through the ravine. Disappointed teamsters were piling up on the two sides of the stream, waiting until the bridge could be built again, and helping earnestly in its construction. It would be another week before the flimsy structure could span the creek, though the big stone foundation for the central pier was still in place and undamaged, and though the biggest trees were being felled and dragged down to build the understructure of the bridge.

The only other way of getting over Kirby Creek was to go nearly another fifty miles up Kirby Run, and then come down it on the farther side of the stream, after reaching the ford. However, that ford was only practical for men and horses, and active men and horses at that.

Silver and big One-eyed Harry camped for the night opposite the little mining town, and then went upstream the next morning. It was nearly sunset of the third day before they got into the place. A strange outfit they were, and no one had a glance for anything other than One-eyed Harry. His picturesqueness took all glances away from the big-shouldered, long-shanked Mexican who trotted along bareheaded, a mop of shaggy black hair falling down over his forehead, as he led on a shambling mule and a chestnut stallion that looked fit for riding, but which carried nothing but a big pack saddle.

The big horse had the legs and the look of speed if one cared to examine closely; but it was covered with dust and had a very sad limp in a foreleg. Not a man in all of Kirby Crossing but would have laughed if he were told that this was that famous outlaw stallion, Parade, which had defied capture so long and caused such a wastage of money in the hunt for him that at last he became known as the hundred-thousand-dollar horse. It was too incredible.

The little group paused in Kirby Crossing only long enough to buy flour, bacon, a few canned goods, and get the latest papers. But the newspapers were far less important than the word that ran from lip to lip.

The State penitentiary, hardly eighty miles away, had been the scene of a cunning escape. One David Holman, then lodged in the death house, had cut through the bars of his cell, gained the prison yard, and climbed over the guard wall by the aid of a ladder of silk equipped with fine aluminum grapples at one end. Finally he either had drowned in the lake in the middle of which the penitentiary stood, or else had swum the long distance to the shore on a night when a veritable hurricane was blowing. Only one thing was certain—that some of the guards must have been bribed to look the other way. But so far the investigation had convicted no one of guilt.

It was One-eyed Harry who spent an hour or more buying the food and getting the gossip. Silver, in the meantime was slipping along securely in his Mexican disguise from group to group and from window to window, until at last he had peeked into every saloon, and examined the people in the dining room of the hotel, and in the restaurant. He was searching for a man with a peculiar birdlike alertness of head and manner, and a singular lightness of step. Or if the man could not be found, he hoped to get a glimpse, perhaps, of Edith Alton Kenyon.

But he was disappointed. He had to rejoin One-eyed Harry, who, in the presence of a few yawning spectators, cursed him as a lazy greaser for being late, and threatened to flay him alive if he were ever tardy again.

Then they went up the valley, and camped between the edge of Kirby Run and the trees that crowded the valley. They chose the site of some old diggings. Gold was everywhere in the sands of the creek. The only trouble was that it was scarce, and there were few places where a man could wash a day's wages with any ease. However, One-eyed Harry Bench was willing to stay there as long as Silver needed him.

"If it hadn't been for you routing me out with a bullet," said Bench, "I'd still be out there in the desert, eating sand with my bacon and hating the whole world! I'll camp anywhere you say. And what could be better than this here?"

It was a good camp, in fact, with plenty of food and water, and a view of big mountains before them and behind. Kirby Crossing was only a little over a mile away.

They built a lean-to the next morning, and Silver left his friend arranging the stones for an outdoor fireplace, while he slipped up into the town again. There were other Mexicans in the town, and one saloon at the end of the street was their gathering place. Into the brown horde Silver went, to let his disguise be thoroughly tested. But he had few doubts that it would pass muster; a dozen times he had used it in old Mexico itself.

In the saloon he kept his eyes down and his ears open, while he drank tequila. But he heard nothing that had any bearing on his quest. There was only talk and more talk about the prison break. It pleased the Mexicans to know that the government and the law had failed. Their rattling voices rose to crescendos; they laughed heartily, flashing their eyes at one another.

But what was the prison break to Silver? He left the saloon and resumed his search through the town. His eye was so trained that half a second's pause in front of a window could show him all the faces inside. And a few side glances were enough for his study of whole groups as he passed among them. But he had worked up and down the street twice before some one caught his eye.

It was a man he had seen before, seated in the back room of a saloon, playing poker and chewing nervously at a cigar. But only when he walked out onto the street did the attention of Silver fall seriously on him. For he had a quick, lightly rising step, like that of a sprinter in the pink of condition for a race. As he walked, his head had the same birdlike alertness that Silver had noted in the unknown companion of Edith Alton, that morning in the ravine. The farther the man drew into the distance, the more convinced was Silver that he had found his quarry.

A warm little glow ran through him. He had to set his teeth to keep from laughing aloud.

The stranger mounted a horse tethered in front of the saloon, and rode out of town at a dogtrot that freshened to a lope as he gained the open beyond. But Silver was not far behind. He kept among the trees that bordered the narrow road closely on either side, and his long legs flew over the ground with the easy stride of a natural runner.

He had a chance to note several things on the way. The first was that he was behind a good horseman. The second was that the stranger was by no means used to the Western style of riding. And finally his conviction was that in spite of the cow-puncher outfit, time-rubbed as it was, his quarry was quite a stranger to the West and Western ways.

He was inclined to take the reins in both hands, for instance, instead of reining across the neck. And when they came to a runlet that ran across the road, the rider pitched forward in the saddle and hunched over, as though expecting the mustang to jump the barrier. Instead, being Western, that cow pony calmly trotted through the water.

It was not a long run. In twenty minutes or less the rider turned off toward the creek, and halted in front of an old, disused cabin, on the front of which a flap of canvas had been hung to take the place of a door. A burly young Mexican with a mustache that glistened like black glass came to take the horse of his master, throwing down the ax with which he had been chopping wood.

The rider disappeared into the cabin, while Silver sat on the edge of the woods and watched the Mexican put up the pony in a lean-to that was attached to the end of the cabin. This was only until saddle and bridle had been removed, and hobbles fitted. After that the mustang was turned loose to graze on the good grass.

When this had been done, the Mexican returned to his ax. Silver, who was now breathing easily again, came out from the trees and stood to watch. The other gave him a wave of the hand, and then went on with his swinging of the ax.

"There is no chance to talk, amigo," said he. "That gringo has the eye of a hawk and the ear of a grizzly bear. He keeps me working all day. Except for the good pay, I am only a slave. If you have something to say to me, wait for me to-night in the saloon in Kirby Crossing, where all of our people meet."

"The fact is," said Silver, "that this work is too hard for you, friend. It needs a stronger man."

"A stronger man?" said the Mexican, scowling. "Who sent you out here to trouble me?"

"I came of my own accord," said Silver. "I have a kind heart. I never want to see a man working beyond his strength."

"You, perhaps," said the Mexican, "could do this work very easily?"

"No doubt," said Silver.

"You could cut the wood, do the cooking, wash some gold out of the creek sands? You could wash the soiled clothes and sweep out the cabin, and then find spare time to shoot fresh meat for his table?"

"I could do all of those things," said Silver. "What's more, I *shall* do them."

The Mexican stared. Then his eyes glassed over with rage. His chest swelled, his chin sank. "Fool of a stone-faced half-wit!" he roared. "Get out before I cut you in two with the ax!"

"Don't lift the ax," said Silver, "or I'll have to take it away from you."

A voice spoke suddenly, sharply, from the cabin doorway, and there was the master of the house.

"What's the matter out there, José?" asked he.

"Matter, Señor Lorens?" said José. "Here is a crazy man who says that this work is too hard for me, and that he is going to take my place!"

Silver turned to Lorens and gave him a deep bow.

"A bright day to you, señor," said Silver. "May the sunshine fall on your heart; may the gold gather for you in the sands."

This flowery outburst, in swift Mexican, set Lorens chuckling.

"This fellow is a poet, and poets are the devil, José," said he. "Does he say that he is going to take your place?"

"He may be a devil," said José, grating his teeth together, "but even a devil will feel the edge of this ax."

He gave it a swing as he spoke.

"What's your name?" asked Lorens.

"Juan," said Silver.

"Juan, I like the look of you," said Lorens. "Your hair might be mowed or tied back from your eyes, but you look able to do something."

"I can do everything that that man can do, and then twist his neck," said Silver.

"Do you hear, Señor Lorens?" said José, trembling with rage. "This is one of those fools who boasts and thinks that his loud talking will be the thing that weakens the heart of another man! Away with you, you lying, stealing, ragged thief! Would an honest man wear such clothes? Look, señor! His trousers are not long enough to reach his ankles, and therefore he keeps them rolled up to his knees. There is nothing on his body but that cheap shirt. See the sandals on his feet! Señor, let me send him on his travels again!"

"If you can," said Lorens calmly. "Drive him as far as you please—if you're able!"

10
A Man of Talents

JOSÉ, when he had received this permission, gaped at Silver with a sudden joy. Then, weighing the broad-bladed ax in both hands, he advanced at him with short, quick steps, like a boxer.

"Hold on!" called Lorens. "An ax against a man with empty hands?"

"Señor," said Silver, "I have a knife, but I shall not use it. Who will use weapons on children, señor?"

José uttered a short howl, something like that of a dog when it starts to bay the moon. Then he came with a skip and a leap and a swing of the ax right at Silver.

In José there was no such folly as would lead him to try a downright blow that might be side-stepped. Instead, he feinted at the head, and then swept the ax around in a mighty circle. The edge of the blade flamed with keenness. It could have cloven deep into the body of Silver if it struck fairly home. Instead, it merely brushed through the top hair of his black wig as it swished by, for he had crouched suddenly close to the earth. The weight of the stroke turned José half around. He knew that he had missed, and that his failure was apt to be his ruin. Even while his arms were carrying his body around, his head turned toward Silver, and his face was desperate. But there was nothing that he could do. The blow that found him had the weight of Silver leaning straight behind it. José fell in a heap.

Silver took the ax from those numb hands and swayed it lightly into the air.

"This poor rascal," said Silver, "may come back to steal, señor. But if I tap him across the back of the neck until the bone snaps, then I can weight him with stones and drop him into the river. With this current he will soon be rolled to bits. In five days, if they have dragged the river, they would be able to find no more than a finger bone of all of him."

Lorens began to laugh heartily. He was a handsome fellow, a little too thin of face, a little too bright and active of eye; now he was alight with appreciation.

"Don't kill the poor rat, Juan," said he. "Do you think he'll come back if you tell him that you don't want him around?"

"I must talk to him in a special way," said Silver. "Permit me, señor, and his face shall never be seen around here again!"

"Talk to him any way you please," said Lorens. "I have any idea that you're going to work for me, Juan."

"Ah, señor," said Silver, "to hear you say that is already as good as roast kid and frijoles in my stomach. Hey! José!"

José, coming to his senses by degrees, was startled by this cry to his feet. He stood wavering, looking wildly from Silver to his master.

"The honorable and rich señor," said Silver, "is tired of wasting his money, tired of spending the kindness of his heart on a poor thickwit, a wretched fellow who knows nothing of cooking, who leaves the floor of the house dirty, who has no luck in finding gold, and who cannot make the smoke of the fire blow away from the house. He sends you away, José. And he tells you that if you are seen near this house again, to beg or to steal, he will make you disappear—like this!"

At that he picked up a small stone from the ground, hurled it far into the air and when it spun, hovering, at the height of its rise, he flashed a revolver into his hand and fired. The glimmering stone and the bullet met with an audible impact, and the stone disappeared.

José still was blinking in the direction of that spot where the little rock had hung in the air. Now his mouth opened slowly.

He had seen something that was worth more to him than a thousand hours of explanation and lecturing. He backed up a few steps, turned, and fled dodging, like a snipe when it goes winging against the wind to avoid the gun of the hunter.

"You see, señor," said Silver, "that when we deal with children, we do not need weapons except to frighten the silly fools!"

"Juan, you speak good Spanish," said Lorens, standing in the doorway, with his chin on his fist and study in his eyes.

"I learned it, my master," said Silver, "in Mexico City itself. I was in service there."

"What sort of service?"

"Shining silver, and taking the small dogs out for their walks."

Lorens smiled, but there was still dubious thought in his eyes.

"How do you wear that revolver?"

"Here under my left arm," said Silver. "Most people don't expect it to come from that place. So I have a chance to surprise them, and to please myself, and that means that everybody is happy."

"Or dead," suggested Lorens.

"Or dead, señor," said Silver, bowing.

"A fellow with your talents," said Lorens, "ought never have to work with his hands."

"Observe my palms," answered Silver. "They are smoother than the hands of a young maiden, señor."

"Ah?" said Lorens. "Then why are you taking a job here with me?"

"I am not in my own country, where I would be known," said Silver. "If I were there, señor, there are villages where the men would stop everything the instant that I appear, and the women, without being bidden, would at once begin to cook. One would roast a kid. Another would seethe a chicken. Another old woman would bring out her finest cheese, packed in wet salt grass, delicious in the mouth with wine. I should sit, señor, in front of the fonda, and drink with the head men of the town, and then eat, and ask one or two of the notables to sit down with me and taste my food. And when I had finished eating, I should pay them all ten times over by telling them three true stories of three days of my life. They would give me their blessing, follow me to the edge of the town, fill my saddlebags with food, press a canteen of good red wine into my hands, place a little bottle of tequila in my coat pocket, and tell me to hurry back to them again!"

He delivered this long speech with a sort of lordly flourish.

."Well," said Lorens, "Mexico is still in the old place. Why aren't you there?"

"Because all of my countrymen are not so kind and so true," said Silver. "There are some rude fellows that you may have heard of."

"The rurales, perhaps?"

"The señor," said Silver, "sees at a glance to the heart of everything. The rurales know that there is a price on my head. Therefore they hunt me with more passion, señor, than the Americanos of your country will hunt a wild duck—though they may have plenty of tame ducks waddling about in their back yards!"

Lorens laughed again, but very shortly. "Look here, Juan," he said. "You won't want to be working for me very long as a cook and a hunter and a fire tender."

"Señor," said Silver, "you will not very long be camped by this river, pretending to hunt for gold. And before you leave this place, you may have found better ways to employ me."

"What do you mean by saying that I only pretend to hunt for gold?" asked Lorens.

"What do I mean? Nothing! If the señor is angry, I mean nothing. I know that the señor has eyes enough for two, and ears enough for two, also, and a tongue that is capable of speaking for all his affairs."

"No, but tell me why you think I only pretend to look for gold?"

"Because I saw you playing poker, señor. And after I had watched you shuffle the deck three times, I knew that you could dig more money out of the hands of men with a pack of cards than strong miners can earn by digging and blasting at a mountain of rock all their lives!"

Lorens tapped his rapid, slender fingers against his lips, looking over his knuckles at Silver critically.

"Juan," said he, "you're an impudent rascal, and you see too much."

"It is true," said Silver calmly. "The señor does not want a blind José, but a Juan with two eyes, perhaps. Yet if you tell me to close them, I am blind."

"I know what you mean," remarked Lorens. "You're able to see anything and remember only what I want you to know."

"The señor understands," said Silver.

"Juan, you have killed men in your time."

"I have had that joy, señor," said Silver. "I have seen the faces of my enemies turn black under my hands."

Lorens shrugged his shoulders as though to get rid of a feeling of cold up his spine.

"What money do you want?" he asked. "How will you have it?"

"I shall be paid according to my services," said Silver. "If it is to cook and clean and hunt for the señor, the scraps of food that are left will be food and pay for me. But if more important matters come, and they are put in my hands, then the señor himself will know how to reward me. It is not for money alone that I work, but for pleasure, señor, and to fill my hands with the name of a man!"

This speech seemed to please Lorens more than all the rest put together.

"You're a hard bit of steel, Juan," said he. "You'll take an edge and keep it. I want to know one thing from you. Did you ever hear of a man named Silver—an American?"

"The Senor Silver?" said Silver, looking down. "I have heard of him and seen him."

"Tell me what sort of a man he is?"

"A man to beware of. He has done certain things. He shoots very straight, and he shoots very quickly. And he has killed men, señor—a great many of them."

"A fellow like that, Juan—a fellow who answers the very description of this man Silver, may be on my trail. I don't know. I'm not sure that he will follow me. But he's one that I should like you to have in mind. Dream of him as he was, Juan. Look for him in the shadow under every tree. Listen for his voice. Watch for the flash of his gun!"

"He shall be more in my mind than my own self," said Silver.

"Tell me this," said Lorens. "Would you stand up to a fellow like Silvertip, do you think?"

"Perhaps he is a larger man than I am," said Silver. "But I should hope to stand up to him. A brown hand can be as quick as a white one, and a white skin does not turn bullets."

"Juan," said Lorens seriously, "you and I are going to get on together.

You don't need to make a slave of yourself. If you can shoot fresh meat and cook it, that will be enough for me, along with some coffee. And I suppose you know how to cook frijoles?"

"You shall be glad I am with you," said Silver, "every time you eat the food I cook."

He bowed again, and, looking up through the overhanging shag of his forelock, he studied the face of the man who within this week had sent a rifle bullet inches from his head. There was murder in that thin, handsome face. There were infinite possibilities of treachery in the uncertain brightness of the eyes. And behind all, there was a quick flame of intelligence. If he were to pull the wool over these eyes continually, Silver knew that he would have to be on guard constantly. He would have to live like a dog with a wolf, never knowing when the teeth would be in his throat.

But behind this man, somehow and somewhere, loomed the form of the girl. Perhaps it was in the handwriting of Lorens that the words had been written: "—out fail in Kirby Cr—" And perhaps through this man, also, Silver could come in touch with him who had encompassed the death of Buck, and whose name began with "Nel—"

Danger breathed now out of the very air, but opportunity was in it, also.

11
The Reward Poster

LUCK favored Silver in the execution of his first domestic duties for Lorens. He took the rifle of Lorens, a beautiful weapon, and walked ten minutes, straight through the woods, when a stag sprang out of a covert hardly twenty yards from him. Silver let it run until his bead was perfect, and then sank the bullet behind the shoulder.

The stag was young, but when all the less choice parts were discarded, there remained more than two hundred pounds of good, edible meat. Silver loaded himself with half of it and brought it close to the shack of Lorens. He went back and got the other half. After resting, he put the whole crushing burden on his shoulders. He stepped out from among the trees and came up to the shack with a swinging stride.

Lorens was sitting cross-legged under a tree, smoking a pipe. He sprang up with an exclamation.

"Venison, man? Venison, Juan?"

"It is not veal," said Silver, putting down the load.

"That's something José could never get for me," said Lorens. "He said that the deer were all frightened out of the valley, long ago."

"You know, señor," said Silver, "that we never find what we do not hope for. But I, Juan, will keep you in venison."

"There's enough there for a whole camp!" exclaimed Lorens.

He tried to pick up the burden and it slipped out of his straining hands.

"Great guns!" said Lorens under his breath, and with profound awe stared at Silver askance. He had heard the rifle crack in the far distance; he had seen his new man come swinging in with a light, long stride, carrying that weight and hardly breathing under it. He began to look now at the lean shanks of Silver.

"Some men are different," Silver heard him mutter. "The way mules are smaller and stronger than horses, or cats are stronger than dogs!"

On venison steaks broiled to crust outside and of a melting tenderness within, they dined that night, with potatoes fried crisp, and cress from the edge of the running water, and thick, strong black coffee. And Lorens declared that he had not properly eaten since he had left—

The name of the city remained unspoken, but Silver did not think it would be hard to fit in the name of the metropolis where this gambler had been plying his trade. For all his good looks, the man had the manner and something of the look of a rat that had lived underground most of its days.

He said, as they sipped coffee—Silver sitting farther from the fire than his employer as though out of respect, but in reality because he wished to have his face studied as little as possible: "Juan, tell me something of your old life down there in Mexico, will you?"

Silver pretended a distress which was not altogether unreal. Then he said: "Ask me for my blood, señor, but do not ask me for my past. The old days are rope that is made; the new days are rope that is in the winding; my past may not please you, but the new rope may be what you want."

"For hanging myself?" asked Lorens.

The question was so apt that Silver started, but Lorens was already laughing at his own remark.

"You're right, Juan," said Lorens. "The fellow who talks about his past is not likely to have much of a future. Here's a poor devil who's had a past, I suppose. A batch of these posters came to town to-day. Fast work on the printing press, eh?"

He put on the ground before Silver a picture of a man of not more than thirty, with a strong, dignified, even a refined face, with every capacity of thought and feeling indicated in it. But the big print offered a reward of five thousand dollars for the apprehension of this man dead or alive. The name was David Holman, and Silver remembered hearing that this was the criminal who had recently broken out of the penitentiary, less than a hundred miles away.

"What d'you think of that face?" asked Lorens.

"He is too strong to be only a little good, or a little bad," said Silver. "He must be everything or nothing."

Lorens picked up the poster, and looked from it suddenly and piercingly at Silver.

"You're no fool, Juan," he said.

Then he added, half to himself: "Dead or alive! Dead or alive! Think of that! These fellows around here will hunt for a week, every day, for the sake of bagging a timber wolf that only has a ten-dollar bounty on his scalp. Dead or alive, and five thousand dollars for the lucky fellow who draws a dead bead and pulls the trigger! Eh, Juan?" he said, making his voice suddenly cheerful. "That would be a handsome bit of money to have down yonder in Mexico, where things are cheaper!"

Silver shook his head with real distaste.

"Blood money, señor!" said he. "I have killed men, but never for money."

"No?" said Lorens.

"No," said Silver. "Never for money. And I never shall."

"But five thousand dollars! That's a fortune!"

"It would all taste of blood!" said Silver.

Lorens began to brood again, the lower part of his face propped up in the flat of his hand, and his eyes lifting suddenly, now and again, to his companion. At last he said: "Juan, I have to be in two places at once to-night."

"Yes, señor," said Silver.

"One place is in Kirby Crossing. One is right here in this camp. Understand?"

"A man's body cannot be in two places at once," said Silver.

"One of me will have to be you."

"Yes, señor."

"Juan, I've known you only for a few hours, but I'm going to trust you. I want you to go into Kirby Crossing and at ten o'clock stand across the street from the hotel. You hear me? At ten o'clock. And stay there the rest of the night if you have to. Can you do that without closing your eyes?"

"Once," said Silver dreamily, "for four days there were men around a little nest of rocks. If I so much as nodded, they knew it, and crawled closer."

Lorens grinned, a quick contortion of the face that became still again at once.

"As you wait there," said Lorens, "two or three times an hour you'll be smoking a cigarette."

"Yes, señor."

"Well, then, every time you light a cigarette, take two matches under your finger and scratch them both—so that the two will burn at the same time."

"I hear you, señor."

"After a time—I don't know when—I think that a woman will come up to you. She will ask for Charlie. You'll tell her that you come in his name."

"Does she speak Spanish, señor?"

"Enough to understand that."

"How shall I know that she is the right woman?"

"If she's young, pretty, and holds her head high, with her chin up a bit, you'll know that she's the right one."

"I understand," said Silver, his heart beginning to beat fast. For who could it be except Edith Alton Kenyon, that cunning trickster? And he wished, in a sudden moment of savage rage, that poor Ned Kenyon could be sitting here to listen to the words from Lorens.

"You can go now," said Lorens. "Buy two horses and two saddles. How much will they cost—two mighty good ones?"

"Five hundred dollars apiece," said Silver.

Lorens grunted. "That's worse than blood money. I mean something around a hundred and fifty dollars."

"It can be done, señor. There are horses for gentlemen and there are horses for Juan. I shall buy two horses for Juan."

"That's it. Put the girl on one of 'em, and bring her out here."

He took out a wallet and counted the money, while Silver scowled at the fire. He liked this very little. The man was, in fact, trusting him. And to betray the trust even of a fellow who had tried to put a bullet through his head, went sore against the grain.

"Here's four hundred," said Lorens. "And that's a lot of money for me just now. Do your best with it."

"I shall bring a hundred dollars back," said Silver, "and still you'll be satisfied."

"I don't want a hundred back. Spend all of it. Or if you can satisfy me with less, put the change in your pocket. You can go now. Buy the horses, and be opposite the hotel at ten o'clock, ready to wait there until the morning, if it should so happen you have to."

"In all things, as you please, señor," said Silver.

He took the money and counted it, and rose to his feet.

"One more thing," cautioned Lorens harshly. "I'm giving you enough money to tempt you a little, perhaps. But you remember this: You've been a big man in your own country, but you're not a big man in this one. And if you try to run out on me, I'll have the scalp off your head and the marrow out of your bones—I'll have it, and there are plenty who'll help me to get it!"

His thin face wrinkled like an old leaf with sudden malice as the mere thought of his promised vengeance passed through his mind.

"Señor," said Silver, "only a fool promises. A wise man waits to have judgment passed on his deeds."

"All right, all right," muttered Lorens. "You sound like a copy book. I'll see what you bring home to me from Kirby Crossing!"

12

Silver's Game

SILVER went back to Kirby Crossing on the run. He only slackened his pace
to walk with his long stride through the town, and he lingered an instant
to watch the strange spectacle of the building of a bridge by night, for the
work was being pressed twenty-four hours a day. Lanterns hung in a long
festoon over the timbers. The great underlogs were being wedged and
bound in place, and the bridge began to look like a skeleton of what it
would finally appear.

Silver went on past it. He entered the dark of the open country in the
lower part of the valley, and here he sprang again into his Indian trot that
shifted the ground rapidly behind him. When he was not far from the
lean-to which he and One-eyed Harry had put on, he whistled. And from
the dark of the brush sprang Parade, and came racing, with a whinny.

He went round and round Silver like a bird in the air about to settle on
a nest. He was dancing and snorting, with the hand of his master on his
shoulder, when big Harry Bench came out of the lean-to. In the dark he
looked more gigantic than ever.

"Silver?" he called. "Man, man, that hoss has been about crazy while you
was away. He's come smelling around the shack, and he's still-hunted your
trail down the valley. Where you been, brother?"

Silver went into the lean-to and sat on a homemade stool in the corner.
The stallion stood with head and shoulders intruding through the doorway.

"I'm up the valley on the other side of the Crossing," said Silver. "Take
a look at me! I'm Juan, the greaser, who works for a fellow named Lorens.
I've got two minutes to spend here, and no more than that. I have to get
back. I'm working for a fellow with an eye like a hawk and the wit of a
prairie coyote. One day, when I was wearing a white skin, this same Lorens
put a bullet inches from my ear and then ran out on me. Just now he
doesn't know me, but if he guesses that I'm lying to him, or that my skin
is not as dark as it seems to be, he'll take the first good chance to shoot me
in the back."

"What in the nation do you wanta waste your time on him, then?" said
One-eyed Harry, lifting his huge voice.

"Because," said Silver, "I'm on the outside edge of a regular whirlpool,
old-timer. Lorens is the edge of the whirl, and if I stick to him, I think I
may be drawn into the middle of the pool."

"And who the devil wants to be drowned in a whirlpool?" demanded
Harry, staring.

"Call it a dance instead of a whirlpool," said Silver, "and all of the dancers wear knives, and I'm blindfolded, and I never know what tune they'll strike up next, or where they'll step. But there's a lying crook of a woman, a murderer, and somebody who's tried to murder *me*. They're all elements in the job, and I don't know how many other forces are behind 'em. You can see that it's a pretty picture, Harry!"

"You like it!" exclaimed One-eyed Harry Bench. "Doggone me if you don't like it a lot. Kind of makes your eye shine just to think of that dance, eh? That kind of a job is just like pork and beans to you, ain't it?"

"Like it?" said Silver, surprised. "Of course I don't like it. I'm likely to lose my hide any minute, and my head along with it."

"You like it," said Harry Bench, pointing with his huge, grimy hand. "That's the game for you, the way poker is the game for the small-time gambler. You ain't happy, by thunder, unless your life is on the table as the stakes."

He took a step toward Silver and shook his hand at him. A sort of horrified realization came over that rugged face as Bench said:

"You're goin' to keep after them, you're goin' to keep playin' that game till you're killed. You know that, Silver? You're goin' to play with the fire till you're burned to the bone. What makes you such a fool? You can't keep ten knives in the air all your life. One of 'em is bound to fall sometime and stick right into your heart. Hear me talk?"

"Hear you?" said Silver, apparently irritated. "Of course I hear you, and you're talking like a half-wit, Harry. I'm not up there with that tiger cat, Lorens, for pleasure. I'm up there because there's a crooked game in the wind, and because a friend of mine has suffered on account of it already. That's why I'm there!"

"If you're not in that mess, you're in another one. It's always the frying pan or the fire for you, Silver!"

Silver started to deny the charge, but as he parted his lips to speak, his glance went inward upon his life and showed him the crowded story of his past in such pictures that he was suddenly mute. It was true. All of his days he had played with fire. He could tell himself that he was simply following the courses which chance led him into, but why was it that every trail he put his feet on was a trail of danger?

So he was mute for an instant, seeing those pictures, and out of the past reading the future. For what big Harry Bench had said was indubitably true. No man could continue to play with fire without being finally burned to an ash.

Gradually he drew himself out of the dark humor and scowled up at One-eyed Harry. Bench was pacing back and forth, taking the breadth of the little room in three strides, and whirling on his heel and toe. For all the size and the bulk of that man, he was as active as a big cat. Silver vaguely admired the magnificence of that physique, so swift and yet so massive. He himself had the strength of two men in his arms, but he knew that in the grasp of this giant he would crumble like sand.

"Somebody had oughta watch out after you," said Bench. "There had oughta be friends to keep you hobbled. Even your hoss has to stay and worry about you!"

Silver looked toward the sooty muzzle, the beautiful, deerlike eye of the stallion, and smiled. "Harry," said Silver, "maybe there's a lot in what you say. The more I think about it, the more I agree with you. I've got to stop my crazy ways. And I'm going to do it. Believe me, partner? This is the last job that I take over on my hands, no matter how the luck tries to drag me into trouble."

"Sure!" growled Harry Bench. "That's what you say now. But you'll be changing your mind one of these days. If you got sense, you'll stay here and let Lorens go hang."

"He won't go hang, and I want the job of the hanging," said Silver. "If I don't hang him myself, I want to point him out to the hangman, and turn him over with his hands tied behind his back, if he's the sort that I think I can prove he is! Now stop talking about me. I want to ask you a question."

"Fire away."

"There's a fellow named David Holman—"

"That just escaped from the death house at the prison. Yeah. I know about that."

"I've an idea that my friend, Lorens, up the valley, has a sort of an interest in Mr. Holman. What put Holman in the death house? What did he do?"

"Oh, nothin' much," said One-eyed Harry. "He come out from the East to be a cashier in a bank over in Tuckaway. Pickin' up experience, you see? But he wanted to pick up some hard cash, too. And he took it out of the vaults. After a while he was pretty far in the hole, and so this here Holman, he planned to have the bank robbed, and, of course, the robbery would cover up what he'd stole.

"So he got a pair of yeggs to work with him, and one night him and them robbed the bank, all right. But it happened that Sheriff Bert Philips was riding back into town that night, after chasin' a half-breed hoss thief a coupla hundred miles and never sighting him. And he seen three men sneakin' out from the rear of the bank, and he hollered out to them. They ducked away to their horses and ran for it. He followed and yelled for help, and some gents who were havin' a late night of it at a saloon, they come out and joined in the chase. And then there was a long run, and the three of 'em got away for the time being.

"But the chase was so long that this here Dave Holman didn't have a chance to fill in his plan, which was to be back in his home in bed when the day begun, with his split of the stag stowed away somewhere safe. He was still on the run at sunup. And then he says to himself, that as long as he's goin' to be found out, he'd better be caught for a sheep than for just a lamb. So he ups and murders them two gents, and takes their share of the loot, and lights out with it. And the sheriff and his posse comes along while there's still a spark of life in one of the dyin' gents, and this feller tells about the holdup, and how Holman had planned it, and how Holman had murdered them. And the sheriff, he follers on, and gets a sight of Holman on a dead-beat horse, and runs him down and hauls him in.

"When it comes to the trial, this here Holman, he puts up a cock-and-bull story about how the two thugs had come to his house in the middle of the night and forced him at the point of a gun to go to the bank with 'em and open the safe, and how they'd kept him under their guns, and made him run with 'em, and how he'd taken the first chance to get hold of a revolver and shoot the pair of 'em. And why did he run when the sheriff came up after him? Well, it was because all of the swag was on him, and he seen that it would be hard to explain things away and prove that he was an honest man. It was a pretty far-fetched story, and the whole jury, it busted out laughin' in the middle of the yarn, they say. So they made him guilty of murder, and there you are!"

Silver had listened attentively to this story, and now he nodded his head. "What that has to do with Lorens," he said, "I don't know. But Lorens has a lot of interest in that fellow Holman, I think. Now, Harry, there's one thing more for me to say to you. I'm going back up the valley. I'm going to be in Kirby Crossing for a while, and then I'm going on. Every day I'm going to try to get in touch with you. If I don't manage that, I want you to start on the trail for me, because it may be that I'll be needing help. Will you do that?"

"I'll do it glad and willing," answered One-eyed Harry. "You're going back into the fire, are you?"

"This one job is the last one, but I've got to finish it," said Silver uneasily. He stood up.

"Try to keep people away from Parade," he cautioned. "There are more men who know that horse than there are who know me. And if Parade is spotted people will know that I'm not far away—and that will complicate everything. This disguise business is thin ice to skate on, and it won't take much to make me break through. I'll put Parade in the woods, and he'll stay there till I come back. Just see that he has water and grain. And so long, Harry."

Harry followed his friend out into the night.

"I hate to have you go, partner," said he. "It seems to me that there's a lot of trouble pilin' up in the air around us."

"Perhaps there is," said Silver. "But this is the last time for me, Harry."

"The last time you hunt trouble?" echoed Harry. "You couldn't stay away from it. No more than a dope fiend can stay away from his dope. But so long, Jim. Will that hoss stay there without no hobbles, even?"

They stood together in the dark of the trees near the lean-to, and Silver spoke to the horse and patted the silk of the neck.

"He'll stay here till he hears me call or whistle," said he, "I think he'd stay here if the brush were set on fire. But your job, old son, is to keep people away from this neck of the woods during the day. Mind you, if anybody puts an eye on the horse, I'm next door to a gone goose!"

13
Perry Nellihan

SILVER ran back to Kirby Crossing and went to the biggest horse dealer's yard. It was out on the edge of the town—a little shack of a house, a sprawling shed, and a tangle of corral fences all within sound of the flowing of the river. The proprietor was eating his supper alone in his kitchen when Silver tapped at the open door and saw a face swollen with fat and red-stained by whisky lifted from a platter of jumbled food.

"How much of a pair of hosses do you want?" asked the dealer sharply.

"Four hundred dollars' worth," said Silver simply. "Horses and saddles."

The dealer ducked his head and coughed to cover his grin of satisfaction. Five minutes later Silver sat on his heels with his back against a corral fence, and watched a wrangler run half a dozen horses into the lantern light of the inclosure.

"No, señor," said Silver. "It is not four hundred dollars' worth of horse meat that I want, but two horses at two hundred dollars apiece."

"Here!" exclaimed the dealer. "There ain't a pair of this lot that ain't worth two hundred bucks."

But though he blustered, he realized that he was not dealing with a fool. He brought in new selections. It was not until twenty animals had been brought before him that Silver elected to try one. He took the one he tried. And twenty more went before him before he selected its mate. Then he had a good gray and a roan. Neither of them was a picture horse, but each promised to be full of service. It rather amused Silver to note that he was using his best endeavors for Lorens, who would eventually be his open enemy. But the instinct of the bargainer had control of him.

By the time the horses were secured, the dealer lifted his lantern and shone the light of it into the eyes of Silver.

"If everybody bought hosses like you do, stranger," said he, "I'd have to go out of business or turn myself into an honest man!"

Silver took the horses with the flimsy, battered equipment that was included in the sale price, and led the pair to the long hitch rack in front of the hotel.

It was nearly ten o'clock, so he went to his designated post opposite the hotel and sat down on his heels again, with his back leaned against a wall.

There were few people in the street. Only about the doors of the saloons appeared the forms of men entering or slipping away. Those lighted doors seemed to be attracting the inhabitants as lamps attract insects on a summer night. But most of the houses down the street were already darkened, because the town dwellers of a small Western community retire early and begin the day betimes. Even in the hotel, only three windows above the ground floor were lighted. And at ten o'clock the veranda was empty, and the hanging lanterns that illumined it were put out.

Silver stood up, stretched his cramped legs, and settled down on his heels again. He was perfectly content. Sometimes invisible whirlpools of dust brushed against him, and the taste of alkali came into his mouth. But in his nostrils there was the fragrance of adventure, and the light in his mind was more than lamps could shed.

The minutes went by him like stealthy feet. It was eleven, or close to that hour. Only a single window in the façade of the hotel was lamplighted. One of the saloons had closed for the night. And Silver, for the third time, lighted a cigarette, scratching two matches, so that both came into a blaze for a moment, though he held them in such a way that none of the light could fall upon his face.

Then a form came across the hotel veranda and rapidly across the street toward him. The starlight showed clearly enough that it was a woman. After her came a long-striding man, a queerly made, light-shouldered fellow who took immense steps.

The girl turned sideways from him and started to run. She thought better of it and turned suddenly to face him.

The two of them were close, by this time, and Silver had slipped back into the thicker shade of an inset doorway, where he was almost invisible.

He heard the girl saying: "You can't follow me. You can't bother me like this, Perry. It's no good! It won't do. I won't have it, Perry. You have no right!"

"Why, I don't know," said the man. "Maybe I have right enough. Maybe I have a sort of duty, Edith, to follow a woman who's run away from her husband the day of the wedding. Maybe I have a duty to show up a fraud. That's what the thing amounts to. Fraud, Edith! You deceived a man. You led him on to marry you, and then you ducked out. Plain fraud, and there are laws that deal with it!"

"You ought to see him," said the girl calmly. "Go see Ned Kenyon, and ask him to open suit against me."

"You're confident in him, are you?" said the other, sneering. "Edith, there's no shame in you, apparently!"

"Shame?" said the girl. "Shame, Perry Nellihan? Doesn't the word blister your tongue a little?"

"Why should it?" asked Nellihan. "I've done only what any man would do to protect my rights! I was robbed of my rights. And you know it!"

"Suppose," said the girl, "that my father had known what you are, instead of merely guessing—what do you think he would have done?"

"The old fool is dead," said Nellihan. "I don't have to think about him. The fact is that he raised me like his own son all my life, and then he cut me off without a penny! Practically."

"More than two hundred thousand dollars—is that only a penny?" she asked.

"Compared with what you're getting!" said Nellihan.

"If I had told father what I knew, he would never have left you even that."

"The point is that you didn't tell him what you knew. That's where you were a fool."

"Very well," said the girl. "Take your hand from my arm, Perry. I don't want you to touch me."

"I'm not good enough to touch you, eh?"

"You're not," said she.

"I've done my share of shady things, perhaps," answered Nellihan. "But I've never done a worse thing than you worked on that poor idiot of a Kenyon."

"I don't think you ever did," she agreed, with a sudden warmth that surprised Silver. "But you know why I had to do it. You know that you worked me into a corner from which I couldn't dodge! There was only that way out for me!"

"I arranged that pretty well," said Nellihan. And he laughed.

Everything about that man was offensive to Silver for more reasons than he could put into words. And the voice, high, thin, nasal, cut into his very brainpan and put his nerves on edge.

"Take your hand off my arm," she repeated.

And the striking muscles in the shoulder of Silver leaped into hardness that refused to relax.

"Where do you want to go?" asked Nellihan.

"That's my affair."

"Girl wandering alone in the middle of the night," Nellihan sneered. "Is your precious thug somewhere around here?"

Silver could see him turn his head suddenly from side to side in eager curiosity.

"If he were," said the girl, "you'd be shaking in your boots."

Nellihan laughed again. "You're wrong, honey," said he. "I'm no saint, but I'm not a coward, either. And when it comes to gun work, I'm not afraid of any man in the West. You ought to know that."

"I only know that you're detestable!" she exclaimed.

"Listen to me, Edith," said he. "You're trying a hard game, and I can spoil it for you. You'll have to talk turkey to me."

"You mean that I'll have to talk money to you?"

"That's what I mean."

"I'd rather give you my blood than a penny of father's money," she answered.

"No matter what you'd rather do," answered Nellihan, "you'll have to talk turkey. I've got you where I want you, and you're a poor fool if you think that I'll let you get out from under before you've ponied up the iron men."

"You haven't a finger's weight of hold on me," she told him.

"No?" said Nellihan. "Don't you suppose that I can put poor Kenyon on your trail? He can make plenty of trouble for you! You'll disgrace yourself and your family—and you won't be able to do a particle of good for the dirty rat you love."

Silver heard her sigh—a long, long breath of disgust and weariness.

"I've told you before," she said "that you can't do anything with Ned Kenyon. He won't act against me!"

"He will, when I show him how much money he can get out of you. He hasn't enough brain to think in terms of millions, but I can teach him the way of it! I'll put a match to his imagination and set him on fire. Then he'll go after you! Before I did that, I wanted to have a talk with you. That's all. I wanted to show you that you're in my hands!"

"I'm not," said the girl. "For Ned won't act against me. It's hard for a poor, creeping snake like you, Perry, to understand that some men may be honorable!"

"Well," said Nellihan, overlooking the insults blandly, and going straight on, "let me tell you something. I have another hold on you. Do you know that Sheriff Bert Philips is in this town right now, looking for an escaped crook? Now, then, suppose that I tell him why *you're* up here? Suppose I tell him that, suppose that he gets on your trail—why, what will happen then?"

"You won't do that, Perry," said the girl slowly. "I know that you're bad. But you're not as low as that! You know that my life is smashed to bits. You know that there's no future hope for me. And you won't take away my last chance to find a few minutes of happiness?"

"Won't I?" said Perry Nellihan. He began his snarling, savage, nasal laughter.

"Oh, won't I?" he repeated. "Won't I squeeze you till I've got what I want out of you? Edith, don't be such a fool! You ought to know me better than that. The next thing I know, you'll be on your knees, begging. But words don't matter in my ear, Edith. Hard cash is the only thing that will talk to me!"

"It's true," she said. "And I *am* a fool to talk to you."

"On the other hand," said the man, "take a calm look at the business and see the simple and straight way out. I'm not going to try to take everything. I'm going to make a fair split with you. I'm only going to ask for what I should have by your father's will—one half of the whole estate. Your half will be more money than you can spend. You know that. Why should you grudge me my bit?"

The girl paused, and Silver waited, with tingling nerves, to hear her acquiesce.

Instead, she said in the same quiet way: "You don't quite understand, Perry. I've done one terribly bad thing. I've smashed the life of Ned Kenyon— for a little while, anyway. And that one bad thing is enough. I'm not going to do another. And the worst thing that I can think of would be to turn you loose on the world with money and power in your hands. The very worst thing! Better send a plague into a crowded city than put power in your hands!" She paused an instant. "I've told you what I think. Now get away from me."

"You're going to visit the sheriff with me, my dear," said he grimly. "You're going straight down the street with me till I find the sheriff, and I know where to look for him. Come along!"

He turned her with a violent jerk, so that she made a long, lurching step beside him. Then Silver came like a noiseless ghost behind them.

"Excuse me, señor," said Silver in Spanish.

Nellihan whipped about suddenly, and the force of his turn and the driving weight of Silver's fist combined to strike him down. He bent far backward and then dropped on his side with his arms flung out.

14
Baffling Problems

A MAN who falls like that does not rise suddenly. Silver gave him a single glance, and then said to the girl:

"Quickly, señorita! The two horses at this end of the hitch rack—the gray and the roan! Take the roan. I have shortened the stirrups for you!"

She nodded, saving her breath for her running. And, coming up with the hitch rack, she flashed into the saddle like a man, while Silver jerked loose the knot that tethered the ropes. In a moment he was jogging his horse beside hers down the street.

She had been about to break away at a mad gallop when he cautioned her:

"Señorita, a slow horse is never seen, but a galloping horse is a bonfire. All eyes find it!"

They were turning the corner beyond the next saloon before Silver, looking back, saw the tall form of Nellihan stagger to its feet. They were out of sight around that corner before a sharp, wailing voice began to yammer for help.

The girl bent forward and turned her face to Silver, as though asking permission to gallop the horse. But he made a signal of denial.

That was why they went calmly, unseen, through the town of Kirby Crossing. Only when they reached the upper valley road would Silvertip let the horses gallop. And as the windy darkness blew into his face, he set his teeth hard and tried to understand what he had just seen and overheard.

The whole problem remained vague and obscure in his mind, but he felt that this darkness might be that which goes before the dawn. Nellihan, it was plain, had been raised by the rich father of the girl as a member of the family, though it seemed that he had never been adopted. The man was a rascal, and Alton had suspected it; therefore Nellihan had been cut off with merely enough of an inheritance to support him in comfort. At the same time, Nellihan had managed to use his influence so that the girl's own inheritance was embarrassed. And that embarrassment had forced her, it appeared, to marry Ned Kenyon.

At the thought of Kenyon, the hot anger poured through Silver again, and yet, in spite of himself, he was unable to detest the girl as he had done before. Contrasted with Nellihan, she seemed a saintly figure, almost. And furthermore, what the springs of her actions had been he could not understand, and perhaps when that understanding arrived, he would be able to forgive her, in part, even for the blow she had given to poor Ned Kenyon.

She loved a "thug," as Nellihan had phrased it. Her life, she had said, was wrecked. She was fighting now to salvage from the ruin a few moments of happiness!

As Silver turned these words and ideas in his mind, he was more and more darkly baffled. She was young, beautiful, rich. How could her life be wrecked?

They were almost at the end of the ride when another thought struck like red fire through his brain.

Nellihan! There was a name that began with the letters he was searching for: "Nel—".

And why should it not have been Nellihan? The murderer of Buck must have been tied into this great tangle in some way. The whole thing seemed to possess minute inner relations. He ran over the names—Nellihan, Edith Alton, Ned Kenyon, Lorens, Buck, and finally perhaps some vague connections with the escaped convict, David Holman. These people had entered on the stage from various directions and at various points. When would they be combined in such a way that Silver would be able to understand the entire problem?

But one thing was clear in his mind. Nellihan, he could swear, was the man who had killed Buck. He had spoken of familiarity with guns. And he was exactly the type of slayer who would shoot from the dark of an open window.

These ideas, rolling across the brain of Silver, were ended by his arrival near the cabin where Lorens lived. He held up his hand as a signal to draw rein, and presently they were dismounting near the cabin of Lorens. He whistled, and Lorens himself came out, hurrying.

"Are you there?" he called.

"Here!" said the girl.

"Thank Heaven for that!" said Lorens.

He told Silver to unsaddle and hobble the horses. He even lingered a moment to look over the animals and he said:

"You got your money's worth, Juan."

Then he turned away beside the girl.

Silver heard her say breathlessly: "Is he here?"

"Not yet," answered Lorens, lowering his voice. "Not yet, but he ought to get here before the morning. Did you bring it?"

"I have it with me—plenty!" she said.

"Good!" said Lorens, very heartily, and they disappeared through the door of the cabin.

Silver went about the unsaddling of the horses, wondering who might be the "he" whom the girl desired to see, and what was the "it" that she had brought plenty of?

He had hardly finished hobbling the horses when Lorens called him.

"Juan," said the man, "can you navigate on very little sleep?"

"Señor," said Silver, "I can lay up sleep the way a cow lays up fat in summer for the winter."

"Can you keep your eyes open all night long?" asked Lorens.

"For three nights, señor, without closing my eyes."

"Good!" said Lorens. "Good man! The lady has told me about the way you handled Nellihan in the town. A very good bit of work, Juan. Come inside and have some coffee, and anything you want to eat."

"No, señor," said Silver. "I have had coffee enough; and I have eaten enough. Now I shall stay outside and watch."

"She wants to thank you, Juan," said Lorens. "Come in for that!"

It was the last thing that Silver wished to go through. He knew the clear, quiet eyes of the girl, and he did not wish to have them fall on him now. What men could not see, she would penetrate with her woman's glance, perhaps. However, there was hardly an easy way of refusing to face her, and he had to follow Lorens back into the cabin.

The girl sat at the wobbly little table in the center of the room, eating cold venison steak with relish. She looked up at Silver and smiled at him, while he stood with his head inclined, his feet close together, his neck thrust a little forward, and his shoulders bowed a trifle. There is nothing that confuses recollection more than a change of the habitual posture of a man. He could hope that she would never dream of the erect, straight-eyed, rather imperious "Arizona Jim," when she was talking to this awkward Mexican, with the shock of black hair falling down over his eyes.

"It was a very bad time for me, back yonder in the town, Juan," she said. "I want to thank you for helping me. Nobody could have done better. Nobody! For he's a dangerous fellow—that one, Juan. If you hadn't stunned him, he would have been shooting while he fell!"

Silver bobbed his head, made a vague, brief gesture with one hand, and then shrugged his shoulders, as much as to say that what was passed was forgotten, and that the whole affair was not really worth much consideration.

Her manner changed a little. Her head tilted a shade to the side. A certain quizzical look appeared in her face.

Then, rising, she held out her hand.

"Give me your hand, Juan," said she. "Because after we've shaken hands, you'll believe that I won't forget you. And when I find out what you like the most in the world, I'll try to get it for you."

Silver looked down at the palm of his right hand, shrugged his shoulders again, scrubbed his hand against the white cotton trousers he wore, and then glided forward to take the hand of the girl and make a little, ducking bow above it.

When he tried to withdraw his hand, she kept a firm grip on it.

"It was something more than saving my life, that you did for me," she said. "It was giving me a last fighting chance for happiness, Juan!"

"He's tongue-tied," said Lorens, laughing. "Let him go. He's a strong devil, and brave as steel. Juan, you can go outside now, and stand watch. Keep your eyes open. What I expect is one man and one horse. If you find more than one coming this way, give me the alarm. You understand?"

Silver nodded, backed through the door, and was gone.

When he was at a distance, he whistled a bar of a song to register the amount of ground that separated him from the cabin; then he turned and ran for it like a silent shadow, and paused close to the door in time enough to hear her say:

"You're sure about him?"

"Why not?" said Lorens. "He's done enough to prove himself, I'd say! He's worked well for you. He's bought me two fine horses for half the money that I would have had to pay."

"His eyes are light," she answered.

"You find plenty of light-colored eyes in Mexico," said Lorens.

"They must be the exception, though," said the girl.

"Well, perhaps they are."

"So this man Juan is one of the exceptions," said she. "He's an exception in lots of ways. He's bigger than most men. He has heavier shoulders and longer arms. Most peons look stupid, but he has a thinking face. There is a sort of fire of fierceness in him, but when he was standing in front of me, he tried to cover up everything."

"Come, come," said Lorens. "You know how that is—just nervous, just embarrassed in front of the beautiful señorita!" He laughed a little.

"It wasn't embarrassment," she answered. "There wasn't any embarrassment in his make-up. There was no blood warming up his skin. He was cool as a cucumber. And from the look or two I had at his eyes, it seemed to me that he was all set and intent on something, like a tightrope walker a thousand feet off the ground. He was watching his step."

"I don't believe that," said Lorens.

"I hope that I'm wrong," she answered. "But all the while it seemed to me that he was trying to prevent me from having a look at his mind. He hung his head and let his hair fall over his eyes. But it seemed to me that his natural position would be as straight as an arrow, and looking the world in the eye. That's what I felt about him. Perhaps I'm wrong. I know that I'm nervous enough to make mistakes. It's because I'm making my last play to win happiness, and I can't feel secure about anything. Perhaps I have an hour, or a day, or a week—if we're lucky, there may be a month for us. But that's the end! It's for that instant of happiness that I'm fighting and on the alert!"

"All right," said Lorens, his voice growing a little weary and cold. "I suppose I know what you mean. But this fellow Juan—he's all right. If he's not, I'll cut out his heart and take a look at the color of it!"

15
The Fugitive

IT is possible to be grateful even to a rogue. Silver was grateful to Lorens. He knew the man was a scoundrel, as dangerous as a snake with poisonous craft, and still he was grateful because Lorens had defended him.

But as Silver drew back into the night again, he kept wondering what might be that happiness for which the girl was willing to do so much.

Now he began to make his rounds of the place, sliding shadowy among the brush and through the trees, rousing up every animal instinct to the keenest pitch of alertness. Nervous hands, as it were, began to reach out from him, and make him aware of everything near by. And yet, for all his caution, for all his spying, when he saw the figure standing at the door of the shack, it was as though the form had risen out of the ground.

He started toward the cabin, swiftly.

For one thing, they had talked about a horseman arriving, and there had not been a hoofbeat even in the distance for a long time. Silver was halfway to the door of the cabin when the shadowy form slipped suddenly through the door into the lighted cabin. Silver had a sight of a man of middle height, of rather a strong build—and as the fellow disappeared from view, the voice of the girl split the very eardrum of Silver with a scream.

He came at the cabin as fast as a tiger runs at easy prey. Through the doorway he leaped with the Colt ready in his hand—and saw Edith Alton Kenyon wrapped in the arms of the stranger, while Lorens conveniently turned his back and had started toward the door.

When Lorens saw the drawn gun, he snapped out a revolver of his own with wonderful speed, but by that time it was apparent that Silver was simply amazed, not attacking. As for the stranger, his face was visible in profile, and it clearly showed the features of the escaped criminal, the pursued murderer, David Holman!

Silver drew back toward the door, entranced. Lorens was beckoning to him to go outside again. And the last he saw was that Holman had made the girl sit down, while he kneeled in front of her and kissed her hands, and looked constantly, hungrily, into her face.

Pale from the prison confinement, his eyes deeply sunk in shadow, it seemed to Silver that David Holman could easily be capable of a murder—but hardly a murder by stealth. It was as strong a face as Silver ever had seen. There was a stonelike quality about the flesh, and there seemed to be a stonelike quality about the stare which he fixed on the girl. He was not speaking. His jaws were hard set. But it seemed to Silver that he had never seen passion so mute or so powerful. That was the index and the key of the man—power, power, and more power!

Looking at him now, it was not at all strange that he had robbed a bank and killed two assistant thieves, but it was just a trifle odd that a sheriff and a posse ever had been able to take him alive, or that he should have told such a cock-and-bull story in his trial.

But there he was in the cabin—that happiness for which the girl had been working and praying; an hour, a day, a week, a month of David Holman had been her dream. And Silver, seeing her in the fulfillment of her wish, found her transfigured. She was crying with happiness; she was a child, and yet she was more profoundly a woman than any Silver had ever before seen in his strange life.

He went out through the door into the black of the night, dazed and confused. He heard Lorens saying, within:

"You two need to talk. I'll take the outer guard, and Juan will keep the door. You can talk right out. He only understands ten words of English."

He came out, calling: "Juan! Come here!"

Silver came slowly back to him.

"You stand here by the door, Juan," said Lorens. "You've made one mistake to-night—that is to say, it might have been a mistake if that had been any man other than Holman. Now, keep your eyes a little wider open. You won't find many as shifty as Holman, but there are others who have eyes, too."

"I shall watch," said Silver grimly. "But if I stay close by the door, I can see only half the night."

"Do as I tell you," said Lorens. "Stand right by the door, and be ready to shoot if anything strange happens. You know what this means, now, Juan. You know that Holman is hunted by the law, with a price on his head. But can you trust us to give you more than the law would give you?"

"Señor," said Silver, "the law has very seldom been my friend. Why should I work for it? And even if I could capture Señor Holman and bring him to the sheriff, ways would be found of cheating a poor Mexican like me. Besides, perhaps the law wants me, also!"

Lorens laughed.

"You're a useful sort of a fellow, Juan," said he. "And you'll be paid your weight in gold, before you're through with this business. There's money to be had out of this affair, and trust me, I know how to get it. This whole business is dripping with coin—dripping! And you shall keep your share. Keep your eyes open. I'm going to walk in a big circle around the house."

He went off into the darkness, whistling under his breath, and Silver pursed his lips in silence.

It was clearly apparent that Lorens was in this for the money, only. He had been the agent, the go-between who had helped the girl to free Holman from prison, in some way. He had distributed the bribes in the proper places, perhaps. And now that the two were together, Lorens intended to watch over them, serve them, and continually squeeze the purse of the girl for his own gain.

In the meantime, it was unpleasant to be an eavesdropper at the door of the cabin, but he could not disobey Lorens. He walked back and forth and tried to shut the voices from his ears, but they kept penetrating his brain constantly.

She was explaining: "Lorens knew one of the trusties very well. He had to pour the man full of money, but at last the thing was done. Some of the bribes were handed out, here and there. And that was why the guards looked the other way when you were escaping. But I don't want to talk about that. The thing's done. You're here. Nothing else matters."

"I want to have everything clear in my mind," said Holman's voice. It was deep, resonant, and yet very quiet. "Where did the money come from? According to your father's will, you were not to have any real income until you married."

Light shot at last through the brain of Silver, as he listened.

The girl said nothing.

"Is that hard for you to answer?" asked Holman.

There was more silence.

"Do I have to tell you?" she asked at last.

"No," said Holman. "I don't want to put a finger's weight of pressure on you. Tell me only what you please."

"Then forget everything in the past!" she urged him. "You know that we haven't long together. They are going to hunt you down. Every minute is one of the last minutes. How can we waste them?"

"Secrets will make shadows between us—that's all," said Holman.

"If I tell you," said the girl, her voice breaking, "you'll despise me!"

A sudden fierce anxiety broke out in his next words: "What thing *have* you done?"

"I found a man who would marry me," she said. "I found—"

"You mean to say that you're married, Edith?" breathed Holman.

"Only in name, only in name!" said the girl. "Listen to me! There was no other way to get the money, and without money I couldn't help you. I found a man—the simplest fellow in the world, only interested in ranching and beef, and such things. I was going to marry him, and then disappear, and leave him a large sum of money, so that he could go ahead and lead the sort of life that he wanted to lead. And when I failed to appear again, he could get his divorce without the slightest trouble because of desertion. Don't you see? Wanted to do him no real harm, but actually to help him, and chiefly, to help you!"

"You *wanted* to do him no harm," muttered Holman. "And then what happened to him?"

She had to pause to rally herself for a moment, apparently, but at last she said: "He grew fond of me. And he—Listen to me! You have to listen. You can't turn away like this. I know it makes you sick at heart. I know that *you* would never have wanted me to do it. But I couldn't dream—"

"Before you married him," said Holman, "didn't you have an idea that he might be getting in pretty deep?"

"I couldn't know for sure. He was such a great, gaunt, simple creature—a caricature of a man. Every one laughed at him—and I wasn't laughing at him. No, no, I was pitying him and liking him. I began to guess that he was fond of me, really. I couldn't tell how much, though."

Holman groaned. Silver heard the spat of a fist driven into the flat of a palm.

"David, what could I do?" cried the girl. "Look at me; tell me what I could do? I didn't dream poor Ned would be of such fine stuff. I thought he might feel one twinge of pain, and then forget all about me in the pleasure of having ten thousand dollars."

Holman's step began to pace the floor.

"What's his name?" asked Holman bluntly.

"Edward Kenyon. He—"

"I've kept my hands clean all my life," said Holman bitterly, "and only for this—to be a condemned criminal escaped from the death house owing to a fraud on the part of a woman. I'm a sponger—a sneaking, cringing cur! I live on a woman; I let her torture other men for me. Ah, that's a picture to remember!"

"If I'd opened my heart and told the whole thing to poor Ned," said the girl, "he would have gone through the form of the wedding. I know that, now, but at the time I was afraid that one whisper of the truth would get out and be the ruin of my plan to set you free, David."

"Hush!" said Holman. "I'm going mad. My brain's turning. I know you've done nothing for your own sake, and everything for mine. It seems that I'm put on the earth to make a fool of myself and a scoundrel of every one else around me. I've put a curse on the people I love. I've made a sneaking, contriving, lying criminal out of you! Out of you!"

Silver heard her begin to sob, not wildly, but a deep, choked sound that told how she was fighting like a man against her weakness. But Holman did not console her.

"About the money," he said. "How much have you spent, so far?"

"I don't know, David. I don't want to think of it. The money doesn't matter. Heaven knows I would have given everything for these moments with you, even if you've begun to detest and despise me!"

"Despise you?" said Holman, in a voice that made Silver stop short in his harried pacing to and fro. "It's myself that's being poisoned by every word that you've told me. I want to know the whole story. How much have you spent?"

"You have to know? You command me, David?"

"I beg you, my dear!"

"It's something over forty thousand dollars."

Silver heard Holman gasp.

"You paid that out to whom?"

"To Lorens, of course. He's handled everything."

"And how much of it is left with Lorens?"

"Nothing, David. He had to spend floods in the prison, through the trusties."

"He used up the entire forty thousand dollars? He didn't put anything in his own pocket?"

"No, David. Not a penny. He has hardly a cent in his wallet, now. He told me only to-day. But I've brought more. I brought another fifty thousand out—"

"Fifty thousand?" cried Holman. "Don't you know that it's enough to get you murdered? Fifty thousand dollars, carrying it around like pebbles in your pocket? But wait a moment. How much does he get of that fifty thousand? How much does he expect?"

"Nothing for himself, David. All that he wants to do is to see you safe. He's had trouble with the law himself, and he took pity on us, David. He himself offered to do what he could. I've never been able to give him a single dollar for his own pocket."

"He sounds like an ideal character," said Holman dryly. "But he doesn't look like one. Not by a mile! Go on, Edith. Tell me how much you'll need to spend now?"

"Just for the moment, a good deal," said the girl. "Lorens is going to arrange everything for us. He knows a section of the mountains where we can be safe, he swears. Perhaps not for days and weeks, but for years. He knows the sheriff of that county, and he knows several others who can be bribed to close their eyes and not know that we're there. It will cost a good deal, to begin with, but then—"

"How much?"

"About forty thousand dollars."

"Forty thousand? Forty thousand dollars, did you say? For a sheriff— and a few others? Who are the others?"

"I didn't ask him. I know that we can trust him. Why are you glaring like that, David?"

"Because the thief is bleeding you! If he spent ten thousand to get me out of the prison, he was a fool. If there's a sheriff to be fixed, either the man can be bought for five thousand, or else he couldn't be touched for five millions. And that's more apt to be the case. Have you given him that forty thousand, yet?"

"Yes," said the girl. "Because he— What are you going to do, David? You're not—"

Holman came to the door of the shack.

"Oh, Lorens!" he called.

"Here!" answered Lorens and came swiftly. "Anything wrong?" he asked cheerfully.

"I think there is," said Holman. "Come inside. I've been hearing about your money dealings with Edith. I've been hearing about your altruism, too. I've heard that you've just bled her for another forty thousand dollars, you cur! And I'm going to take that money away from you!"

Lorens flashed his hand for a gun.

Holman hit out with a strength that flung Lorens back against the wall and made him drop to one knee. He was half-stunned, but not enough to spoil his shooting at such a close range. And he meant murder. The snarling look in his face was like that of a wild cat about to put his teeth in red meat.

"You fool!" yelled Lorens, above the cry of the girl. "I've trimmed her. And now I'm going to trim you—and collect the blood money on your head!"

"No, señor," said Silver, and he shoved the muzzle of his Colt out of the darkness and into the verge of the light in the room.

16
To Aid an Outlaw

THE whole scene was in nice balance. The girl had caught up a Winchester, but dared not swing the muzzle toward Lorens, knowing that she would be too late. So she stood with the rifle in her right hand, her left arm flung out, her face white with fear, and strained in every muscle. Holman, obviously unarmed, was on tiptoe to rush in at the kneeling Lorens, but even Holman, though there was a savage fury in his face, kept himself from moving. And as for Lorens, he was tasting the kill beforehand, with an infinite relish.

But the gleaming of Silver's revolver was enough to change everything. It made Lorens glance to the side.

"You rat!" he yelled. Then he swung into smooth Spanish, saying: "Juan, you know the hand that feeds you. You know—"

"I know, señor," said Silver calmly. "And I know that it is the lady who will spend the money, and not you. Señor, I am sad but if you don't put down that gun, I shall have to shoot you through the head! Quickly, amigo!"

Lorens turned on Silver a frightful look. Then, in silence, his right hand jerked down inch by inch until the gun lay on the floor. Still his fingers worked on the butt, yearning to snatch it up for action. At last his hand was clear of the Colt.

"Now stand up, señor," said Silver. "Forgive me—but if you make one quick move, my poor thumb on the hammer of this gun will be frightened, and the hammer will fall, and you will go up to join the sky people."

Lorens stood panting, silent. He obeyed Silver's instructions, and turned his face to the wall with both arms stretched high above his head, and in this position, Silver searched him from his hair to the soles of his boots. There was plenty to find, but what mattered most was not the hidden knife and the hidden little two-barrel pistol, but the wallets. One was of good pigskin and rested in the inside coat pocket, but the others were simply a tissue of oiled silk inside the top of each boot.

In the first wallet there was intact exactly the forty thousand dollars which Lorens had been paid on this day. In the two silk swathings, there was almost thirty-two thousand more. Holman counted out that considerable fortune in greenbacks of large denominations.

In the meantime, Lorens was saying to Silver: "What a cursed fool I was! To-night I argued on your side of the fence, too. But I'll tell you, Juan— I'll find a way to come back to you. How you'll pray to die—how you'll beg for hell itself when my hands get to work on you, one day!"

"You hear him, Juan?" said David Holman, in very poor Mexican dialect. "He means poison. You've given me a life that's not worth a rap, but I'm thanking you for it. That's all I can do—thank you. But the lady will try to choke you with a flood of money. Tell us, in the first place, what we can do with this fellow Lorens?"

"Señor," said Silver softly, "what do we do when we find a snake?"

"Kill him? Kill him out of hand?" asked Holman. "You mean that, Juan?"

He stepped back a little, not horrified, but looking at Silver with a sort of pitying curiosity.

"Listen to me, señor," said Silver. "If you try to take him with you, he will escape. If you set him free, no matter what he promises, he'll have the hunters on your trail very soon. I shall not murder him. Let him have back his revolver. We shall both put our guns away, and then it will be fair and even at the start!"

"Good!" said Lorens, with a sudden cry of relief. "I'll do that, Holman! I'll take my free chance with him, first, and with you, afterward!"

Holman shook his head. He lifted a finger at Juan.

"Tie his hands," said Holman. "Then we'll try to think the thing out."

Silver obediently bound the hands of Lorens. He could hardly believe the work that his fingers were doing.

He had found the trail of this adventure when he came out from the upper mountains into view of the plains. He had encountered poor Ned Kenyon and followed him into a maze of strangeness. He had out-fronted Buck; he had seen Buck murdered on the verge of speaking the name which began with "Nel—" And he had become the "Mexican" servant of One-eyed Harry Bench, and then of Lorens, only to swing over to the aid of an outlaw with a price on his head!

"I'm wrong to keep him alive, perhaps," explained Holman to Silver, "because I know that he's no great gift to the world. But at the same time, we can't have people killed like that, Juan."

The girl came up close to Lorens.

"Why did you do it?" she pleaded. "I would have given you money. I would have given you anything you asked for. I trusted you. Don't you see, you were only harming yourself? *Why* did you do it?"

Lorens bared his teeth as he looked at her.

"Partly," he said insolently, "because I felt like doing it that way—because I wanted to make a fool out of you—because I intended to suck the blood out of your fortune and leave only a shell of it. And partly I did it because I hated the sight of your face, and the yammering about Holman. Is that enough reason for you?"

He was magnificent as is a fearless beast that is ready to fight to the last, and Silver dimly admired him for the savage that was in him. It was only strange, in the light of this wonderful courage, that the fellow had run away from him that day in the ravine, after firing the first shot. But perhaps that could be explained. There was no money, after all, in the murder of a stray rider, and why should such a man as the great Lorens needlessly leave dead men in his trail, so that the law could find them afterward?

"We'll have to talk things over," said Holman to the girl. "Come outside with me, and we'll make a decision. You, Juan—are you intending to help us?"

"And you shall have as much money—" cried the girl.

"Hush!" said Holman, lifting his hand. "There's something else. He's not doing this all for money."

"No," said Silver. "If they catch me with money, they'll soon know that Juan is a rascal. Let me be a poor man, señor, and when I leave you, give me only what you please. There is no spending of money when a man is buried, señor. And cold tortillas and stale beans are better to eat than lead; neither is it easy to swallow with a rope tight around the neck. Señor, they want you, and they have put a price on you. Señor, they want poor Juan, also. There are people who would pay a price for him, too. So I shall serve you, if you please. I only wish to run back into the town. In half an hour—in an hour, I come again."

"Very well," said Holman. "Trot along."

Lorens began to sneer.

"You see him now. When you see him again, he will have the head hunters along with him! Bah! When was there a greaser who could keep his tongue still?"

Holman merely said: "You can make a noise, Lorens, but you can't make a sound that any one of us wants to hear. Go on, Juan. I'll trust you. I'd rather be dead than give up the hope that there's an honest man somewhere in the world!"

That was what rang in the brain of Silver, as he raced down the valley toward the town again. The hope to find an honest man! It could hardly be mere hypocrisy. And was it true, therefore, that David Holman had been falsely accused, falsely sentenced?

17

An Unexpected Meeting

IT seemed to Silver that he was in a labyrinth. Now and then he found or thought he found a glimmer of light, but whatever passage he took, led him eventually deeper into profound darkness. But he had the sense of one verity which measured with the simple honesty and gentleness of poor Ned Kenyon—and that was the passion that existed between Holman and the girl.

Silver ran straight on through the town. The dawn was commencing, and the edges of the river were streaked with fire. For this one hour in the day, work on the bridge almost seemed to have ceased. On through the silence of the town, and down the valley he went at full speed.

But when he was still at a distance from the lean-to, he saw the huge bulk of One-eyed Harry in front of the shack, and the smoke of the fire he had kindled rolling slowly off on the wind.

Silver leaned against the shack, panting out words.

"Harry, what's your limit? Are you ready for anything?"

"What are you up to?" asked Harry Bench, the beard puckering all over his face as he pressed his lips hard together.

"Taking an outlaw and his woman where the headhunters won't find him."

Harry Bench grunted. "That's a mean job," he said. "It's been tried, and it don't often work."

"This time it has to work," said Silver.

"What do you get out of it?"

"I get a barrel of fun out of it," said Silver grimly, "and a chance to put my claws into one or two people who need trouble. *You* get any sort of pay that you want."

"Well," said One-eyed Harry, considering, "I've worked a lot for a dollar and a half a day, and there's been times when I've got two and a half a day, for a short job that was a hard one. But for a layout like this, I'd want double that. They'd have to come across with five dollars a day to me, brother!"

He shook his head to emphasize his demand.

"Ten dollars, call it," suggested Silver, smiling.

"Ten dollars?" said Harry Bench, his eyes gleaming. Then he shook his head again, but this time in denial. "It's too much. There ain't any man that's worth that much for the work he does with his hands. Five dollars a day does for me. No more, and no less. I ain't a hog, Silver!"

"Saddle up, then," said Silver. "Fix my outfit on Parade. Get everything together, and the pack saddle on Parade, and throw some dust on him to tame his color a little. I'm going to sleep a half hour, if it takes you that long."

He lay down on his back, closed his eyes, relaxed his body, his limbs. There was a nervous twitching of his right hand which presently was stilled in turn, and as it ceased, Silver was asleep. Through the noise made by the heavy stride of Bench, through the squeaking of saddle leather, he slept on, until Bench called his name.

Then they went up the valley together, as Bench protested.

"It ain't right to start a long march on an empty stomach, partner!"

"You can live on your fat, for a few days," answered Silver. "We're not apt to have much time for the cooking of fodder, or for the eating of it, either!"

"All right," said One-eyed Harry. "A gent can't expect to travel Pullman when he's collecting five bucks a day. Lead on, son!"

One-eyed Harry put his horse to a trot. Silver rode the mule with his own saddle on it, and Parade followed on a lead. That was how they got into Kirby Crossing just as the town wakened in earnest and the stores were opened. In the distance they could hear the shouting of voices, and the beating of hammers where the bridge was building.

"Go into the grocery store," said Silver. "We'll need more bacon and general grubstakes for four people. We're going to hit for the tall timber, and we won't be stopping to do any shopping on the way. Pick up what you want, Harry. I'll wait out here and hold the nags."

He sat down on his heels as Harry disappeared, made a cornucopia-shaped cigarette, and smoked with his back against a post of the hitch rack, and his eyes half closed. As a matter of fact, he was half asleep when a voice said:

"Arizona, are you goin' to forget your old friends?"

He turned his head, suddenly, and found Ned Kenyon standing behind him, smilng a twisted smile.

Silver rose quickly to his feet.

"How did you spot me? Who told you that I'd be in this sort of a get-up?" asked Silver, scanning the street up and down.

"Nobody told me," said Kenyon. "But there was a kind of a look about this here stallion. Four legs like those ain't put under every horse in the world, you know. And every man ain't got a pair of shoulders like yours, Arizona. Not shaking hands?"

"Do you shake hands with every greaser that you meet?" asked Silver.

The twisted smile of Kenyon appeared again. He was so worn about the eyes, his face was so sallow, that he looked as though he had barely dragged himself out of a sick bed.

"All right," said Kenyon. "No offense, Arizona. Shall I go along?"

"Wait a minute," answered Silver. "What brought you up here to Kirby Crossing?"

"There's a man by the name of Nellihan that I'm goin' to meet in a few minutes," said Kenyon. "He got in touch with me. I guess he's not much of a man, partner, but he has an idea about me making some trouble for Edith."

The eyes of Silver narrowed.

"Of course," went on the slow, weary voice of Kenyon, "I don't intend to do that. But I was thinking that through Nellihan, maybe, I'd be able to see her again. I managed to rake up five hundred dollars. I borrowed it here and there, and sold a coupla old saddles. And if Nellihan knows where she is, maybe for five hundred dollars he'd be willing to take me to her."

"Why do you want to see her again, Ned?" asked Silver, setting his teeth hard as pity for his friend mastered him.

Kenyon looked far off across the roofs of the houses. He pushed his hat back and scratched his head.

"Well, it's like this," he said. "If I could kind of tell her that there ain't any hard feeling on my part, and that I'm willing to go and get the divorce, if she wants me to, or keep on being married, if she wants me to, it would sort of ease me, a good bit. And more'n that, to tell you the truth, there's been some minutes—since that day—that I've sort of just wished that I could see her. Just only that. To see her and not say anything, that would be better for me than venison steaks and church music, Jim!"

Silver swallowed hard.

"Nellihan," he said. "Where are you to meet him?"

"Right over there, in that little shack down the street—the one that's got white paint on the front of it and no paint on the rest of it."

"Are you going there now?"

"I'm going there as soon as you're through talking to me."

"Listen to me, Ned. Nellihan is a bad hombre."

"He has to be," answered Kenyon, "or he wouldn't want to make trouble for Edith."

"You don't need to talk to him, if you want to see her. I can take you to her."

"You?"

"Yes," said Silver. He waited for the flush to finish burning the face of Kenyon, and when the pallor had come over it again, as quickly, he said: "But I wonder if it's the right thing for you to do, Ned?"

"Maybe it ain't," agreed Kenyon gently. "I been thinking sort of selfish about it. But maybe it ain't the right thing to do. You'd know better, Jim. If you think that it would hurt her to see me, I wouldn't go."

He waited, tense with anxiety, for the judgment. He was only a child, thought Silver, but never in the world had a more honest child existed.

"If you want to see her, you shall," said Silver suddenly. "I'll take you out there to meet her. But I'd like to lay an eye on Mr. Nellihan, first."

He said it in such a way that Kenyon started.

"What do you mean?" he asked. "You want me to take you over to him?"

"I want you to go over there and start talking to him," said Silver. "Because there's a chance that he knows the look of me, and if he does, he's likely to out with a gun and pepper me. I want you to go in and take his eye, and then I'll try to step inside and have a few words with him. Will you do that?"

"Does it mean guns?" asked Kenyon with a sigh. "I ain't any hero, Arizona. I ain't like you. I got nerves, and bad ones!"

"I don't know what it'll mean," said Silver. "I want to talk to him. You understand? I have something to say to him. That's all. He may start a fight. If he does, I'll have to try to finish it."

Kenyon bit his lip, then nodded.

"I'll go in first, then," said he. "You come when you're ready. So long, Arizona."

He went down the street with his long strides.

A moment later, big One-eyed Harry came out, singing from the bottom of his deep throat.

"Load up the stuff," commanded Silver abruptly. "Get the horses ready. And take them down the street, slowly, mind you. Don't go any farther than that white house, down there. When you get near that, find something to do about the saddle—a girth or something to fool with until you hear from me. Is that clear?"

"Clear as a bell," said Harry Bench. "What new kind of deviltry is up now?"

"It's all a part of one pattern that I don't quite understand, but it's almost clear, now," said Silver. "Do what I say. Be ready to chuck the mule loose, because we may have to start moving faster than a mule gallop."

By this time, the tall form of Kenyon had disappeared through the front door of the white-faced shack, and therefore Silver followed on at once. When he came to the steps that led up to the diminutive veranda, he was glad of the soft-soled sandals he wore. They carried him noiselessly to the door, and as he reached it, he could hear the voices inside.

The penetrating and disagreeable tone of Nellihan was saying: "Business is business, Mr. Kenyon. But to go back to the beginning, you've endured a terrible wrong. That wrong ought to be righted. A fraud has been practiced on you. A terrible fraud. That marriage should not lead to a divorce. It ought to lead to an annulment. As though it never had been. It was a piece of trickery on the part of that girl. And she should be made to suffer for it. Any man with a right sense of his own dignity would be sure to *see* that she suffered for what she's done."

The gentle voice of Kenyon answered, drawling: "I suppose that a lot of people would agree with what you have to say, Mr. Nellihan. But I dunno that I can see it that way. It ain't the money that—"

"Money!" said Nellihan, his voice suddenly lowering. "Money? Do you know what I'm speaking about when I say money? Have you any idea of what you intend to throw out the window?"

"Not any clear idea," answered Kenyon.

"Then listen to me—and I know what I'm talking about. It's my business to know—and I *know!* It's a matter of between eight and ten million dollars!"

Kenyon gasped very audibly; even Silver was shocked by the amount of the fortune.

"I'm putting my cards on the table, Mr. Kenyon," said Nellihan. "I have to say to you that I was made the victim of a crooked will, a piece of fraud engineered by that same girl, and I want you to know that if I can prove that her marriage was an act of fraud, I can have the estate sealed up, make her repay the money she's stolen from the bank, and have two chances out of three to have myself declared the full or the half heir of the whole business. There are my cards, sir. Now what do you think of 'em?"

His hand slapped the table, evidently, at this point.

"Well, partner," said Kenyon, "I dunno what I think. I only know what I feel when you tell me that you're goin' to accuse her of anything and try to prove it by something that I say or do. And I can tell you, man to man, with all the cards face up on the table, that you're an infernal rascal, and that I'll have nothing to do with you!"

"You fool!" gasped Nellihan.

And that was the moment when Silver pushed the door open and stepped inside.

18
The Alarm

THE gun of Silver appeared before his body, so the swift hand of Nellihan fluttered, but failed to complete its gesture. He stood in a rather ridiculous, namby-pamby attitude, as though he had been trying to shake mud off his fingers.

"Excuse me, señor, if you please," said Silver.

"Back up into the corner, Kenyon!" breathed Nellihan. "If we've got him between two angles, we'll make him jump! The greaser!"

Kenyon turned quietly to Silver.

"Shall I stay here?" he asked.

"Stand back here near the door," answered Silver, "and wait till I need you."

He kept his speech in Spanish, but Nellihan cried out in the same language:

"Is this a plot between the pair of you? Kenyon, are you a crook, after all? Here—you—what do you want?"

Silver looked at him with a curious penetration. He was seeing Nellihan clearly for the first time, and he thought the man's face was the most detestable he had ever seen. There was something about the entire makeup of Nellihan that was revolting—a sort of cross between the bird and the beast. He had a long, gaunt pair of legs with a pair of great feet on the end of them. He had a hunched back which forced his shoulders forward and kept his head thrust forward at a sharp angle. But no bodily deformity matched his face—a sickly yellow-gray.

The color was not all. The features could be called handsome, in a way, and a smiling way, at that, but there was a birdlike intensity of brightness about the eyes that turned the blood of Silver cold. The man was something more and something less than human. And if this were the antagonist of Edith Alton, Silver could pity her. It was no wonder that she had been driven to the wall.

"What do you want?" Nellihan was repeating.

"Señor," said Silver, "one night not long ago you killed, in a saloon in Mustang, a man named Buck."

"*You* say I killed him," said Nellihan. "Is there any reason on earth why I should have done it?"

"Yes," said Silver. "The señor hired Buck to murder Señor Kenyon here. And when Buck was about to confess that he was hired, and who had bought him, the señor fired a bullet out of the darkness. He stood safe in the night, and killed this man. But Buck lived to write on the floor!"

"He wrote three letters on the floor, and because they're the first three letters of my name, d'you think that that's a proof against me?" asked Nellihan. "What would the law say to that? He might have been starting to write 'Nelson' or 'Nelly,' or I don't know what!"

"There are not very many names that begin with those letters," said Silver.

"You poor fool," exclaimed Nellihan, "you think that you'll get reward money if you take me back to Mustang and lay the charge against me? Why, the whole town would laugh. There's no motive that could be charged to me!"

"No?" said Silver. "There was first the motive of hiring Buck—to prevent the marriage of the señorita with Señor Kenyon—and then the killing of Buck to close his mouth."

Nellihan leaned over and gripped the edge of the table with both hands.

"That's the case you'll talk up, my Mexican friend, is it?" said he. "You might raise a mob—that's all you could do against me. You never would have a grip on the law. The law would laugh at you. The sheriff would refuse to make the arrest."

A change came over Silver. He stood straighter. The mop of black hair fell back from his eyes, and let the sheen of them strike into the very soul of Nellihan.

"The thing is outside of the law, señor," he said. "But I, also, am outside of the law. I am going to put up my revolver. I know you carry one. If you can murder in the dark, perhaps you can fight in the light. Now, señor!"

Silver flashed his Colt back inside the looseness of his shirt, beneath the pit of the left arm.

But the fear that had been turning Nellihan to stone now was relieved, and the life gradually came back into his eyes. It had seemed to Kenyon, looking on at this strange scene, that the man had been taken into the hand of Silver's greater mind and greater emotion, and crushed. But now he recovered a little, rapidly.

"I see what you are," said Nellihan. "No more a peon than your eyes are black. No more a thug than a saint is. You're one of these romantic fools, are you? Well, I won't make a move to get my gun!"

"If you don't—" began Silver, and suddenly paused.

What could he do? There was nothing he wanted more than to rid the world of this poisonous monster. But he could not shoot down a man who refused to fight.

"I won't," said Nellihan, shaking his head, smiling and sneering. "Some other day—perhaps. Perhaps when I'm myself. But I've had a small shock, and I'm upset. Another day, when I'm myself, I might have the pleasure of putting a bullet through you—whoever you are behind your skin! But not now. I won't lift a hand—and *you* won't do murder!"

Silver stared hard. If ever there had been a temptation toward murder, it was working now in his blood. His breath left him, in the passion of his anger and his disgust, and it would have been hard to tell what his next act might have been, when a footfall sounded on the steps of the little house, and the door was flung open by—Lorens!

The gun of Silver flashed toward him, instantly, and seeing the full picture of Kenyon, Nellihan, and Silver gathered together, Lorens slammed the door again and bounded back down the steps, with a yell.

That yell went ringing through the air: "Help! Help! Guns this way!"

Silver rammed the muzzle of his Colt under the chin of Nellihan, and with a swift hand snatched away his two guns.

And he was saying as he "fanned" Nellihan: "There'll be another meeting, Nellihan."

"In which I'll send you to the devil!" said Nellihan.

He was perfectly calm about it. If there was no shame in the man, the lack of it was an added strength for him, it appeared.

"Get your horse!" called Silver to Kenyon. "Get your horse and ride like the devil after me. Keep the spur in its side!"

Then he leaped for the door and out into the street, in time to see Lorens darting into the hotel, still shouting.

The long legs of Kenyon bore him rapidly across the street, diagonally backward. Silver himself reached Parade, and as big Harry Bench mounted his own mustang, throwing the mule adrift, Silver flung himself on top of the pack.

He was working with both hands, as the great horse sprang away, and finally managing to reach down with his hunting knife, he cut the last strap that bound the pack and the saddle to the stallion.

The whole contraption fell crashing into the street, and left Silver on the smooth, rounded, powerful back of Parade.

Looking back, he saw Kenyon streaking a horse after him, with Harry Bench already midway between the two. Still farther back, there was a rout of men tumbling out of the hotel, and mounting their horses.

Silver thundered: "Harry, keep coming, I'm leaving you, but I'll meet you again in five minutes up the road!"

And he left them—yes, as though they were standing still, for at his call, Parade went away on wings. The green trees blurred together in walls on either side of the road, so great was his speed. It seemed hardly an instant before Silver found himself nearing the shack where Lorens had lived; and as he did so, he saw David Holman ride out on the gray horse into the trail.

Silver waved his arm frantically, as a signal for haste.

"The girl! The girl! Both of you start on the run!" he yelled.

Holman twisted that cow pony around as though he were an old hand on a cattle ranch, and as Silver checked the stallion opposite the shack, he saw Edith Alton swinging up onto the roan mustang. Then, in one well-formed sweep, the five riders broke away on the trail together.

Silver lingered near the front only long enough to call to Holman to learn how Lorens had escaped, and he was told that the man had been left securely tied, while Holman walked out with the girl for a few minutes. When he returned, just now, he found Lorens gone, and fearing that danger would come, he had saddled both horses and started to ride back a little down the trail to see that all was well.

The story was simple enough. The damage that was done by the fact might be the end of them all, and Silver knew it.

He reined back beside the girl. She gave him a sidelong look of agony out of her pinched face. Her look said to him, clearly: "You're Arizona Jim! You're the friend of Ned Kenyon, and you've brought him here like a curse on me!"

He answered that look by crying out: "I'm here to help you. So is Kenyon. We're for you, and for Holman. We'll see you through!"

He fell back still farther, and waved cheerfully to One-eyed Harry Bench, who gave him a tremendous scowl and a shake of the head, as though knowing that his weight would wear out any horse, in a long chase.

Still farther back, along the single file, Silver ranged up beside the white face and the shadowy, sunken eyes of Kenyon. That was what the sight of the girl had done to him.

But Silver shouted at him, almost savagely: "Go up into the lead! You know all of this country like a book. Go up and lay a trail for us that will shake off the men from Kirby Crossing! Go on up to the lead, Ned, if you're half a man!"

19
The Chase

THERE were many doubts in the mind of Silver, as he fell back to the place of rear guard on that procession, with the dust raised by the others whipping into his face.

With Parade beneath him, he could sweep away from all danger, easily; and the girl and Holman were well mounted, also. But the weight of Harry Bench was a ponderous load for a horse to bear, and Kenyon was a clumsy rider, and his mustang not very fast of foot. The speed of the party would have to be the speed of the slowest member in it, unless he could devise a way to split the group into sections.

What the men from Kirby Crossing wanted, of course, was David Holman, and the price that was on his head. If Bench and Kenyon, being the worst mounted of the group, could be shunted aside, it was not likely that any of the men of Kirby Crossing would tail after them. But now they left the trees and entered a great ravine where there was not even a bush or a rock to make a hiding place, and no canyons opened on either side. Perhaps a glacier, in the dead ages, had plowed out this enormous trench. At any rate, it seemed to Silver that Kenyon was leading the party into a hopeless trap, for the pursuers were rushing out from the trees in turn, and racing up the gorge.

He looked back, and gauged them. There were a full score of head-hunters who had answered the call of Lorens and joined in the chase. Except for Lorens himself, five thousand dollars, even if divided into twenty parts, would give a handsome sum to each of those fellows. And if Lorens despised a cash reward as small as this, he would be gratified by revenge.

They made a formidable couple, hunting together—Lorens and Nellihan. And behind them, no doubt, was a hardy assortment of fighting men. Silver, scanning them, thought that every one of the lot rode like a veteran horseman.

He ranged Parade forward to the side of Kenyon, who galloped in the lead.

"They're gaining on us, Ned!" he said. "Some of 'em are eating up the ground. We've got to get into cover or broken ground before long, or they'll scoop us up."

Kenyon pointed ahead.

"You can't see it yet," he said, "but half a mile ahead there's a ravine opening on the right. It twists back into the mountains, and it's filled with cover. Three men could hold off three hundred Injuns in that ravine."

Silver pulled back to the rear again. David Holman joined him.

"Go back beside the girl!" Silver commanded him. "I don't need you."

"You've turned from Mexican into white, Juan, have you?" said Holman. "She tells me that she's recognized you at last—that you're Arizona Jim—that you're the friend of—of her husband!"

His face twisted as he said that.

"Whatever I am, and whatever Kenyon is," said Silver, "we're in here to help you. You get back beside the girl."

"While you stay back and catch the bullets that fly?" asked Holman.

He smiled a little, then eased the Winchester that slanted in a saddle holster under his right leg.

"I'll stay back here with you," said Holman calmly.

Silver protested no longer. Those men from the town of Kirby Crossing were gaining too rapidly, and the mustang that carried the bulk of One-eyed Harry was beginning to labor and grow unsteady of foot. Loud yells came from the pursuit. Each man rode as if for a prize. And the cold sweat beaded the forehead of Silver as he heard the whoopings.

But there, on the right, opened the mouth of a narrow canyon. It looked not so much water-worn, as simply a crack in the rocks. Kenyon led the way into it, and from behind, Silver heard a redoubled shouting that seemed to be of triumph. He looked back. He saw waving hats and hands, and one of the punchers shooting a stream of bullets into the air.

That was the way men acted when they rejoiced, but why should they be triumphant now?

For the entrance to the ravine seemed to Silver to promise them an ideal retreat. The little canyon wound crookedly back into the highlands, and the floor was covered with shrubs and with rocks that had fallen from the walls. But as they turned the first elbow bend, a shout of woe went up from Kenyon.

Silver saw the trouble at a glance, and an explanation of the exultation of the men of Kirby Crossing. For the lofty wall on one side of the valley had been shaken loose by an earthquake, perhaps, and now the gorge was choked almost to the top with a mighty confusion of broken rock, great stones that had broken square or jagged, and were heaped in ten-ton fragments.

"Climb! Climb! Climb!" yelled Silver.

He took the lead to show them how to do it. There would be no time to dismount and gradually maneuver the horses up the face of that dangerous pile. The men of Kirby Crossing would be at them in no time, and Silver flew Parade right at the mighty barrier.

Right and left, like a mountain goat, Parade sprang up three- and four-foot stages. His feet were slipping; his iron shoes were striking fire at every move, but yet he went on swiftly. Nothing but his seventeen hands could stretch from one footing to the next, perhaps. But up to the top he went, dislodging a great boulder near the crest of the barrier.

Silver, dismounting, shouted the order that would make the stallion lie flat on his side, safe from rifle fire. Silver himself turned, rifle in hand, and dropped to his knees, for his first purpose in riding up the wall had been to get into a position from which he could cover the climbing of the rest.

He saw the boulder that had been dislodged leap down an irregular step or two, then bound outward. It missed the head of Kenyon by a hair's breadth, and smashed to bits on the rocky floor of the ravine. Kenyon himself was struggling up among the rocks. He had given up trying to lead his horse, which had promptly balked. In fact, only one horse of the outfit was climbing, and that was the gray which Holman had been riding. The tough mustang seemed to be cat-footed as it followed, though far less swiftly, where Parade had showed the way with a rider on his back. Big Harry Bench was leading in the climb, close behind the mustang, and David Holman was a little below him, helping the girl.

That was the picture at the feet of Silver when the leaders of the posse came sweeping around the corner of the canyon wall. He hoped, in his heart, that Lorens and Nellihan would be among the first, for he wanted with all his heart to put lead into them. But they were not among the leaders, and Silver could not shoot point-blank at strange men, whose hands might be clean.

He could fan their faces with his bullets, however.

Lying flat, with his rifle on a rest, he pumped six shots in rapid succession among the riders, and every bullet made some one of them jump or duck as though it had actually whipped through his flesh.

They whirled their horses, yelling, swinging forward like Indians along the necks of their horses, to make themselves into smaller targets. In a moment they were out of view, at the same time that the gray mustang gained the crest of the rock pile. Silver caught the horse, threw the reins, and let it stand. Then he lay down once more to guard the climbing of his party.

Presently, guns began to clang. The men from Kirby Crossing had dismounted, and lying behind rocks, or standing behind the edge of the elbow turn in the canyon wall, they opened fire. Two or three bullets sang in the air over Silver. Others thudded against the boulders farther down.

He answered that fire. He had only an occasional glance at the sheen of steel gun barrels, but a howl of pain answered his third shot.

An instant later, it was echoed by a cry of agony from Edith Alton. Silver looked down, in horror. It was not the girl that had been struck, however, but David Holman, who lay helpless, wedged between two rocks.

Kenyon saw that from beneath, and struggled up to help the wounded man. Greater help came from above, however, for huge One-eyed Harry sprang down, caught up Holman's body as though it were a sack of bran, and bore it unaided over the top of the rocks.

There was only one reason why every one of the climbers was not shot down, and that was the rapid fire which Silver opened on every glint of steel. Not a single rifle was answering him when Kenyon helped the girl up the last step, and the whole party ran stumbling forward into safety.

Silver looked back. He could see a red stain spreading over the back of Holman's coat, as Bench carried him trussed across his shoulders. The bullet seemed to have gone right through the center of Holman's body! He marked the place where it had entered; he marked the white agony in the face of the girl as she ran to her lover. Then he shouted his orders.

They were to strip Holman to the waist and examine the wound, and dress it as well as they could. While the girl and Kenyon did that, Bench would clamber onto the high ground on the adjoining side of the rock heap, and cut down two straight, light-bodied saplings for the making of a litter. He, Silver, would try to keep the enemy back while these preparations were made for carrying Holman with them in their retreat.

No one answered him by word of mouth. Each dumbly set about the execution of his appointed task while Silver turned back with a freshly loaded rifle and gave his attention to the ravine below.

The men of Kirby Crossing were not apt to try to charge forward from their angle of concealment. They were more likely to try to climb the wall of the gorge at their left, and so come out on a level with their quarry. They would not be in very great haste however. For they knew that Holman had been shot, and they would not be likely to imagine that the other three men would attempt to take the desperately wounded man along with them in the retreat. No, Holman was their prize, and Holman they would soon have!

Silver could not help agreeing with that thought. Hope had dwindled in him to a vanishing point, as he glanced back from his scanning of the valley and watched the girl and Kenyon at work. It was a strange sight to see the three together, this girl and the man she had wronged working with a single devotion to save her lover.

They had stripped Holman to the waist. He was still senseless. And now they were bandaging him with strips torn from shirts and the underskirt of the girl. Kenyon was lifting the body, and the girl was passing the long strips around it. She had made a pad over the wound where the bullet entered that body, and another over the more gaping mouth whereby it had torn its way out.

Were they bandaging a man already dead, or breathing his last?

Silver looked back toward the ravine again, when he heard the voice of Holman say distinctly:

"The rest of you go on. Arizona—and the rest of you. You'll get long terms if you're caught helping an outlawed man to escape. And I'm not worth it. The life's running out of me. In another hour it won't matter whether you've stood by me to the finish or not! Arizona, take charge— make the rest of 'em march on!"

20
The Rope Bridge

SOMETIMES to a lucky father there comes a moment when his son reveals by some word or some act the promise of a mind and a soul worthy of taking its place among the good and the strong men of the world. And in that moment all the pain of labor that has been spent, the anxiety, the fear, the groaning time of disappointment, are repaid, and a calm happiness comes over him.

So it was with Silver when he heard Holman speak. Much had been ventured for this fellow. Not only Silver's safety, but Bench and poor Ned Kenyon were endangered exactly as the wounded man had pointed out. But that danger mattered nothing now, because the words of Holman proved that he was worth all that could be done for him.

He heard Kenyon saying: "There ain't any use talking. Arizona won't leave you. And I won't leave you. And I reckon that Harry Bench won't chuck you over, neither. Here he comes now!"

Bench had duly brought back the stripped sapling poles that Silver demanded. The ends of them were tied to the saddle of Parade and of the gray horse. Across the center of them a blanket was lashed to complete the litter, and Silver helped lift the wounded man into it.

He made one final protest.

"Waste is a bad thing, Arizona," said he. "Why do you waste yourself and all the rest, Arizona? The life is running out of me. It's no good fighting when the fight's lost beforehand!"

He even turned to the girl, saying: "Tell them, Edith. Tell them that they've done enough already. If they try to go on with me, they'll simply be scooped in by Lorens and the rest. I'm what those fellows are after. They'll leave the trail if they get me!"

The girl said nothing. She kept her great eyes fixed upon the face of Holman and suffered silently.

"If you've got breath enough to chatter like this, you've got breath enough to live for a while," said Silver. "Harry, you can't lead Parade. He'd try to eat you. I'll have to take him along. Ned will see the gray doesn't pull back. Edith, you walk beside Holman. Harry, you're the rear guard. Watch yourself, because those fellows are going to be after us on horses before long!"

It was the logical danger. After the men of Kirby Crossing gained the high ground to which Silver's party was now passing, the pursuers would be sure to get at least some of their horses over the rocky barrier, and so be able to rush the fugitives.

There was one good feature. The whole of the upland was covered with boulders, with big brush, and with copses of pine; and if they could make a few trail problems, they might keep away from the pursuit until darkness gave them a real chance to slip away.

Behind them they heard not a sound as they began to climb the side of a mountain, and when they were well up, Silver looked back and halted Parade for an instant. They were among big pine trees, but through the trunks they had distant glimpses of the scene below, where the entire posse was at work bringing up unwilling horses to the top of the barrier. Already eleven horses were up. Two more came to the top, and instantly these were mounted, and the diminished posse rushed off in pursuit.

"Ned," called Silver, "they'll be on our heels in twenty minutes. Is there any way out for us?"

"There's no way except one that a horse can't walk!" said Kenyon. "There's nothing but the old rope bridge across Whistling Canyon. If the ropes ain't rotted away!"

No way except one that a horse could not take? It meant leaving the gray behind, then; above all, it meant that Parade would be lost. Silver, jerking his head suddenly back, looked up at the sky and groaned.

"You've done a grand piece of work and you've made a good try," called the voice of David Holman. "But it's no use. Put me down here, Arizona. Heaven bless you for what you've done, but drop me here and go on to clear your own heels before the fire gets at them!"

Silver answered harshly: "Save your breath, Holman. You may be needing it before night! Ned, which way to the bridge?"

Kenyon called the directions. Silver led the way, and they went slowly around the side of the mountain—slower, it seemed, than the crawling of a snail—while behind them horses were galloping on their trail! But now they came out on the side of Whistling Canyon and saw the bridge. It was a thing to take the breath, a fifty-foot stretch of ropes sagging across a gulch a hundred yards deep. And those ropes not only looked small, but they were whitened by long weathering.

The floor of the bridge was a mere cross-lashing of small ropes, stiffened by sapling poles to give a steadier footing. There was a guide rope stretched three feet above the frail bridge, and the whole supple structure was swaying in the wind that had given the canyon its name.

Silver set his teeth and looked across the span. Then he stepped on the edge of the bridge and strained on the ropes with all his might. They gave very little as he pulled up the slack. But though their strength might sustain his single weight, how would it support two men in the center, with the burden of Holman borne between them?

He dared not risk that. Two at a time would be the greatest weight that he dared to put on the ropes, he felt.

Quickly the litter was unfastened from the stirrups, and, lifting Holman to a sitting posture, Silver said to him: "Hang your arms over my shoulders. I'm going to carry you."

"No!" cried the girl. "You can't balance yourself with Dave on your back. You'll both—"

Silver raised his hand.

Holman said gravely: "You know what you're doing. I'm only a fool if I try to stop you. But Heaven help you, Arizona, when you get out there in the center, if the wind starts the bridge pitching!"

Silver grunted. The fear of the thing was already a cold stone in his stomach.

"Go first, Ned," he commanded Kenyon. "Sneak across and try it out for us. If it holds one man, we'll chance it with two."

Kenyon, yellow-green with terror, cast one glance at the girl, winced back a step, and then marched straight out onto the ropes! Silver watched him, amazed at the nerve power that the poor fellow had managed to rouse in the time of need. Right out across the bridge went Kenyon, with stealthy, short steps, one hand gripping the guide rope. He reached the center. His weight there, fighting against the pressure of the wind, made the whole bridge shudder violently. But still he went on, perhaps for no other reason than because to pass on was easier than to turn back!

And now he had leaped the last yard or so and lay face down, safe on the farther side.

Big Harry Bench came grunting up, exclaiming: "They're milling around down there on the side of the mountain, but they'll find the trail again in a minute. What the devil is this here? I been told I was goin' to die by the rope, but I never seen *this* kind of a picture of my finish! Here, Silver! I'll pack him over! I can do it more easy than you!"

"Pack yourself over—and shut up," said Silver, and rose with the feeble arms of Holman hanging over his neck. He gripped those arms with one hand. The other he placed on the guide rope, and the last he saw before he stepped onto the peril of the bridge was the girl on her knees, her face buried in her hands, unable to look on.

No, there was one thing more he saw, and that was the beautiful head of Parade thrusting close to his face with pricking ears, and eyes filled with mild inquiry. He tried to speak, but no words came to Silver. It was the end of the horse for him, no doubt. Those men of Kirby Crossing would pick up the great horse as their rightful prize. And they would soon learn that it was a prize worth more than the blood money they could collect on poor David Holman.

He stepped straight past Parade and started out onto the bridge.

Step by step he went on, his teeth hard-set. And at his ear he heard the gasping breath of Holman, for, of course, the man was enduring the most frightful agony.

Silver tried to keep his glance only on the floor of the bridge, but that floor was hardly two and a half feet wide, and again and again his eyes slipped over the side and reached the bottom of the ravine, where the waters of Whistling Creek were churning themselves white and sending up an ominous voice into the shrillness of the wind. He saw a blasted pine, a naked trunk at the edge of the water, and it looked hardly larger than a walking stick.

One false step—

And he could not trust to the guide rope except for the most treacherous bit of aid in steadying himself. He had to keep his balance almost entirely by his feet alone. It was hard enough at the side; it was a desperate business in the center, for the wind came in gusts and struck the ropes hammer blows.

But the center had been passed, and now his courage and his hope revived together. He was moving forward more rapidly when suddenly the body he carried slumped down, the full weight jerking on his shoulders as the knees that had gripped his hips lost their hold.

He staggered. For one instant he swayed far to the right. The hands which clutched the arms of Holman shuddered and almost relaxed their grip. It seemed that they were already falling, the two of them together— and then the wind knocked at the bridge and seemed to put it again under the feet of Silver.

He walked on. The feet of the senseless man he carried were dragging behind him. But there was Ned Kenyon waiting for him, holding out both hands, shouting with a white, distorted mouth, words of encouragement. So he made the last steps and stretched his burden safely on the ground.

A dead man? No, the lips of Holman were moving, though they made no sound. Neither had there been a fresh hemorrhage. And Silver began to breathe out loud groans of relief.

"Look at her!" he heard Kenyon saying. "There's no fear in her except for him. There's no care in her except about him, Jim! Look!"

She was already halfway across the bridge, moving more rapidly than any one who had passed before her. She seemed almost to run up the last bit of the way, and now she was dropping to her knees beside Holman.

Silver merely said: "He's living, and he's going to keep on living. I've forgotten the litter. No, there's Harry Bench bringing it. Ned, there's a man with a heart as big as his body!"

For Harry Bench, with the long poles of the litter balanced on his shoulder, was now coming steadily, smoothly across the bridge, and in a moment he was with them.

"Get him on the litter," commanded Silver. "Quick, Harry—take his shoulders—there we have him. Ned, cut the ropes at this end, and we'll leave a jump that the Kirby boys can't take!"

"Send him back!" shouted Kenyon. "Look, Jim! He's trying to cross the bridge to join you!"

Silver, whirling about, saw that the great stallion had actually started out on the bridge, and was already a little distance from the farther side. Crouching low, his head thrust far out and down, the golden horse was stealing like a cat across the bridge. And he could not be sent back; he was already committed to the crossing.

21
Holman's Story

A STUPOR came over Silver as he watched. Love drew the great horse to him, he knew. But that crossing could not be made. Even if the ropes could endure the strain of that great body, Parade could not keep his balance against the battering strokes of the wind, whose force was increasing now. He had no hand to place on the guide rope and help him across the worst moments of the way.

He would fall, and the creek beneath would grind his glorious body to shreds. There would be one crimson flowing of the water, and there the end of Parade! And Silver thought of the other days when he had made the great march behind the starving wild horse, and how they had journeyed up the burning valley, and drunk together from the same spring!

He had not conquered Parade. It had been simply that in the end they had given their trust to one another. And because of that trust, Parade was crossing the bridge, tremblIng, crouching with terror, feeling his way like a cat, but always with his ears pricked.

Silver heard the voice of Holman saying: "His horse, Edith—he's giving his horse for me, too—and he'd rather give up half his life than that!"

Then the girl was suddenly at Silver's side, holding his arm with both hands, looking not at Parade, but at the master of the horse. She was saying:

"He's going to win across. God won't let him fall! God won't let him fall!"

Silver heard her words out of a dream. She believed them, perhaps.

Parade was coming to the center of the bridge, while the ropes groaned loudly under his great weight, and the wind screeched like an angry fiend as it smote that frail structure. With every gust the huge body of Parade shuddered, and the whole bridge swayed.

If there were some way to hearten him; if there were something that could be done!

For Parade had stopped in the very center of the bridge, at last totally overcome by fear. The slight twist of his head to the side made Silver know that the horse had given up hope and was thinking of the way back. Thinking of that—and staggering and swaying, his balance going. And every hair of his golden hide was drenched now with the nervous sweat.

And Silver?

He broke suddenly forth with a hoarse singing, an old song that has comforted many a night herd when it was bedded down on the trail, a song that Silver had sung more than once when he and Parade were marching through the cold and the wind of some winter evening:

> "Oh, I'm riding down the river,
>   With my banjo on my knee;
> I'm riding down the river,
>   And no one else with me.
> Strike up that banjo, strike her!
>   A song has gotta be.
> Strike up that banjo, strike her!
>   That banjo talks to me."

As Silver worked into the song, his voice gained a ringing power and struck boldly across the canyon through the wind.

What meaning had it for Parade? Perhaps it meant for him as much as the touch of his master's hand on the reins, sending sure, calm messages from the brain of the man to the brain of the horse. For suddenly the stallion was no longer swaying, crouched till his belly almost touched the ropes. He was standing higher; he was moving forward with cautious steps; he was nearing the place where Silver stood with the agony in his eyes and the song on his lips. Now the outstretched hand of the master touched the head of Parade, and now the great horse stood shivering on safe ground!

The girl threw her arms around the wet neck of the stallion, but Silver merely laid his hand on the broad forehead of the horse and spoke words that had no meaning.

A moment later the knife of Kenyon had slashed the ropes, and the length of the bridge swished into the air and hung dangling from its moorings on the farther edge of the canyon.

After that Silver took up one end of the litter, and Harry Bench the other.

No one spoke. Something like fear was in their faces as they pressed forward among the rocks and the shrubbery, for they felt that they had been privileged to witness a miracle.

Hardly had the shrubbery closed behind them when they heard the beating of the hoofs of horses and the yells of angry men. The pursuit had reached the end of its tether for that day, at least!

They went on by slow stages to the end of the day, and so worked through the rough of the mountains to the projecting shoulder of a peak from which they could see the foothills sloping down in diminishing waves to the plains beneath. In the sunset time they could see the faint golden sheen of the Tuckaway River, that wound through the level, and the windows of the town of Tuckaway itself glimmer like distant fire for a few moments before the sun went down.

It was necessary to rest at this point, for though the wounded man endured the pain of travel without a word, he would have to have sleep. It was certain, now, that the bullet had avoided injuring any vital organ; neither had there been any great loss of blood. He was simply weak from shock, and time would be needed for the healing of the wound.

It was the plan of Ned Kenyon, who knew the whole district perfectly, to leave the mountains before sunrise and trek out into the plains—chiefly because the pursuit would hardly expect such a move, and moreover because he knew of certain obscure shacks here and there where they could lie up with little danger of being discovered. As Kenyon put it: "We'll sit down right in front of their door, and they'll burn up their horseflesh combing the mountains for us."

The choice of that particular mountain shoulder was largely dictated by a lucky chance, for as they reached the ledge and put down the litter to take breath, a mountain sheep was seen far, far above them, looking out at the sunset. Silver's rifle clipped that prize through the head, and the sheep came pitching and rolling the great distance down to the flat, where the party waited.

Food was needed, and this was a prize. Kenyon and One-eyed Harry cut up the sheep rapidly while Silver arranged half a dozen small fires, which he fed with the wood of dead and dry brush. The changing half lights of this time of day would make it very difficult for an eye even close at hand to distinguish the misting breaths of smoke that rose from those small flames, each a mere handful of brightness. And presently there was mutton roasting on wooden spits at each of the fires.

They had not even salt; they had cold spring water instead of coffee; but ravenous hunger after the day of labor made them eat like wolves. And they were sheltered from observation for this one night, at least. Somewhere, perhaps not a mile away, the men of Kirby Crossing were bivouacking. Or had they turned back and given up the hunt? That was hardly likely—not with Nellihan and Lorens among their number to urge them on. But for this night it was almost impossible that they could close in on their quarry any farther. To-morrow the peril would recommence. This was an interlude of peace to be enjoyed to the full.

Holman was the amazing man to Silver. With every hour he seemed to be gaining in strength. He ate a share of the roasted meat, and afterward he smoked a cigarette which Silver made for him. He had been bedded down on a soft pile of pine boughs, and after his wound was washed and fresh pads placed over the bleeding places, and the bandages again drawn into place, he seemed to be suffering no great pain. The girl sat beside him silently. There seemed to be no sky, no earth, no day and no night for them; they looked only at one another.

Holman tried to express thanks to Silver. He was cut off abruptly.

"If you've got any breath to waste," said Silver, "use it to tell me that the yarn I've heard about you is a lie. You didn't plan the robbing of the bank with 'em. What you told in the courtroom *was* the truth?"

Silver had discarded his black wig. He had scrubbed away the dark stain on his skin. And now, through the glimmer of twilight, the girl and Holman could see the points of gray in his hair, like an incipient horn growing up above either temple. That suggestion gave him a touch of wildness, and his ragged clothes intensified the strangeness—that and the way the stallion always grazed near by, sometimes coming over to sniff at the master, sometimes lifting a lordly head to study every scent that blew toward them on the wind. It was patent that this man was at home in the wilderness, and that he asked for no better companionship than that of the stallion alone. He seemed to Holman, particularly, like a wild, migratory animal which for a moment was crouched among them, and would presently be gone, no man could tell whither.

"What I told in the courtroom," said Holman, "sounded like cock-and-bull, but it was the truth. Truth has a silly face a good many times."

"Who was behind that pair of thugs, if you were not?" asked Silver.

"George Wayland. Buster Wayland."

"Who's he?"

"He used to be vice president of the bank. Simonson was the president, and Wayland the vice president. Now Simonson is out, and Wayland is the whole thing. He's the big boss."

"You hadn't robbed the bank of a hundred thousand or so before the safe was opened that night?"

"How could I have been such a fool?" asked Holman. "I have money enough of my own. I was working in that bank to get experience. That was all. I wasn't gambling. I wasn't buying stocks on a margin. As a matter of fact, my salary was small, but I lived inside of it."

"Who *did* rob the bank, then?" asked Silver.

"Wayland."

"Are you sure?"

"Yes. I saw him do it."

"When?"

"On the night when they put guns at my head and made me go down to the bank. There were not just the two of them. Wayland was along."

"If he wanted to rob the bank, why didn't he do it without you?" asked Silver.

"Simonson and I were the only ones who knew the combination that unlocked the safe."

"And they picked on you instead of Simonson?"

"Simonson wouldn't be apt to rob his own bank. It was in good shape. And besides, Simonson would have fought back. They picked on me because they knew that I was yellow."

"That doesn't wash," said Silver. "You're not yellow."

"Perhaps not now. But I was then. And Wayland knew it. He'd bullied me in small things, and I had lain down. As a matter of fact, when they put guns to my head, I was so scared that I could hardly move. They had to carry me out of the house I was in—or almost carry me. When we got to the bank, my hands were shaking so that I could hardly work the combination. But I opened the door of the safe for 'em—and because of that, I deserved everything that happened to me afterward. Oh, I doubtless deserved even more."

"No!" whispered the girl.

Holman went on calmly: "Wayland had a small interest in the bank, even though he was vice president. He wasn't much of a banker. And he saw his chance to make a stake for himself. Right there in the bank, they split the loot into three parts. Wayland took one part. The two yeggs took two parts. It was an equal division, except that Wayland took most of the hard cash and gave the others more of the securities. Then the yeggs went on with me. You can see how the scheme would work out. The bank robbed, the door of the safe opened, and with me gone from town, the whole suspicion would point at me. When I was taken, I might shout my head off accusing Wayland, but he would simply laugh at me. He could depend on the crooks to keep me away for a day or two, he thought.

"Well, matters went a little differently, but all the better for Wayland. The sheriff, happening by in the middle of the night, after Wayland had said good-by to the thugs and they'd started off with me, made things hard for them. Wayland got back home to his bed, but as he was turning in, the thugs were being run out of the town, and I was carried along by them. They were sticking to the promise they'd made to Wayland to the last. The posse came after us. Finally we got clear, and I saw that I was ruined unless I managed to do something.

"I got desperate enough to forget some of my fear. The two yeggs despised me. They had reason to despise me, you see. And so I had a chance to get a gun from one of them. I knew a bit about shooting. And I had them by surprise. I nailed them both, and then tried to get away with the loot they'd taken. My idea was that if I could get back to Tuckaway with the money, it would be proof that I'd been innocent. But when the sheriff and the posse hove in sight, I lost my head and tried to bolt again. I played the fool. They caught me. The money was on me, and when I tried to tell my story, I was laughed at.

"Now see how the thing worked out for Buster Wayland. As soon as I was brought in, he swore that if I had robbed the bank that night, I had been probably robbing it before, and covering up the thefts in my books. They made an accounting and found the bank terribly short. Of course, that was because Wayland still had his share of the loot! When the bank was found short, a run on it started. Simonson had no ready cash. When the funds in the safe were used up, Wayland was in a position to hold a gun to Simonson's head.

"Simonson had to sell out his shares in the bank for next to nothing. And Wayland simply stepped in and filled the breach with part of the stolen money. It gave him the name of a hero and a public benefactor, too. He wound up owning the bank; he'd established himself as an honest man and a strong one. The big ranchers and mine owners in the district, I understand, have been hauling their accounts out of other banks and depositing with the Wayland Bank in Tuckaway—because Wayland can now pose as the financial giant, the public-minded citizen, the man to whom honesty meant more than hard cash, the fellow who flung his private fortune into the breach and saved the widows and orphans. Simonson died of a broken heart. I was sentenced to die. And Wayland can loll back in his easy-chair and smoke some more of his fat cigars."

He ended without raising his voice. He had spoken rather as one who reads a story aloud than as one who tells it. It was almost pitch-dark, and out of the darkness came the voice of Silver, saying:

"I'll have to be taking a trip to Tuckaway tonight!"

Everyone protested, except One-eyed Harry. He said: "I ain't big enough to try to change his mind. Then how can the rest of you think that you got a chance?"

Holman said: "But I know the difficulties more than the rest of you. Arizona, let me tell you that Wayland keeps guards about him night and day. He knows how to win the faithful services of crooks, perhaps because he's such a crook himself. If it were Wayland himself—well, you might do something, though I don't see what!"

"I won't know till I'm on the spot," said Silver. "But I'm going to Tuckaway. Tell me one thing more. When the posse reached the second of the yeggs you had shot up, he was alive; and as he died, he confirmed the yarn that Wayland was to tell later. Why didn't he tell the truth as he died?"

"Because he wanted to be sure that he'd knotted the rope around my neck before he cashed in his chips. I'd killed him; he wanted to be the death of me; and he'd already gone over the story with Wayland in case of need."

"That's all logical," said Silver.

He went aside with One-eyed Harry and Kenyon, and said to them: "It's about an hour's ride from here to Tuckaway. That means two hours for going and coming back. Besides, I don't know how long I'll be in the place. It may be near to sunup before I arrive here again. Be on the watch. Lorens and Nellihan have brains in their heads, and they know how to use 'em. They're fighting men, too. And anything that a snake could do, *they'll* do. One of you had better keep on watch half the night, and one the other half. Ned, come and step away with me."

He led Kenyon aside and found his hand in the darkness.

"You're going through hell," said Silver, "but you're going through it like a man. I know you'll put up a fight if the pinch comes."

"I dunno," said Kenyon. "I ain't much of a fighting man, but I hope I'll do my best. And it ain't exactly hell that I'm goin' through, Arizona. The fact is, it's like bein' in the middle of a sort of a sad dream, but not wanting to wake up from it."

Silver wrung his hand and went to the girl. She moved slowly beside him through the darkness.

"Oh, have hope," said Silver. "There's luck with us, or we couldn't have lasted this long."

"We've had you from first to last," she answered. "You've saved us before, and I can't *help* hoping, so long as you're in the fight!"

"Perhaps the whole thing is for the best," he said. "Tell me one thing— were you very fond of Holman before he got into this trouble?"

"I was always fond of him," she answered. "But he seemed a little weak and soft. He wasn't what he's grown to be. But when I heard what he was accused of, only one thing crashed into my mind—that he'd fought two criminals and beaten them with their own weapons."

"I almost knew it," said Silver. "He never would have discovered himself if the big pinch had not come. And you would never have discovered him, either. There's Nellihan, though? What about him? Is he as much of a snake as he seems?"

"The lowest creature in this world!" said the girl. "He was even able to put in my father's mind some doubts about me—to make it seem best to my father that I should not come into the money till I was married. That was because Nellihan knew that I loved David Holman, that David was sentenced to death, that if he died I would never marry anyone. Don't you see? And Nellihan was the next heir."

"I understand," said Silver. "And in a short time he would have found a way to put you out of your misery. I have to leave you. Holman is going to live. Don't doubt that. And trust everything to Bench and Kenyon. I know how you feel about Kenyon, but I don't know what else you could have done. You tried to do a small wrong in order to do a great right. But I suppose that sacrificing one man for another is never a good business. However, that thing will be straightened out. Kenyon will do whatever you want. He'll get a divorce in Nevada, I suppose. And afterward I'll find ways in which you and Holman can manage to repay him."

"If you could do that!" cried the girl.

"Don't pity him too much," said Silver. "He's having his great chance to be a man just as Holman had his chance. Holman was remade. Kenyon is being remade, too. If he lives through it, he'll be able to respect himself for the rest of his life. He was simply a good-natured, haphazard, ramshackle cow-puncher and stage driver before this."

"And you?" said the girl suddenly. "What will you gain by all that you've done for Ned, for me, for David?"

"I'm having the fun of it," said Silver with a faint laugh. "And the rest of you are having the pain."

She did not try to answer him. He went back to Parade, saddled the horse, and rode him to the side of the wounded man.

"Heads up, Holman?" said he.

"Clear up in the sky," said Holman. "Arizona, I've tried to persuade you not to go near that devil in his own roost in Tuckaway. I know that you're going, anyway. But I want to say this last thing: Everything will be harder than you expect to find it!"

"Thanks," said Silver. "If you say that a thing is hard, I know that you mean it. But I've got to go. Holman, adios! We'll be together in a luckier time."

He turned Parade, and the stallion moved down the slope over the edge of the mountain shoulder. He went carefully, for the voice of his master was hushing him, and Parade glided through the brush like a hunting cat, making never a sound.

22
Wayland's Place

THE house of "Buster" Wayland had formerly been the house of the leading banker of the little town of Tuckaway. Simonson had taken an entire block, planted an evergreen hedge around the outside of it, and a grove of trees inside. Within the trees he had established a lawn, and within the lawn stood the house and the stables. The house itself was a frame dwelling, square, plain, and dignified, because Simonson had taste as good as it was simple.

Silver rode his horse right in through the big open gate, but turned aside from the driveway into a dark cloud of trees close to the lawn. There he dismounted and spent a few moments patting Parade and giving him those whispering injunctions which would make him stand fast until his master's whistle summoned him, or his master's voice.

In the meantime, Silver himself was taking breath, and clearing his wits, as it were, by deep breathing. He was still dressed, of course, in the ragged, stained white clothes which he had worn before. And therefore no eye could fall on him without suspicion. He would have to move invisible to the very moment when he began action. And even what that action was to be, he had very little idea. He was like an actor who walks out before the curtain to entertain a crowd, and who must improvise his speeches on the spur of the moment.

He left the horse at last and made a circle of the house. All along the front and rear and one side it was lighted. On the fourth side there was not a light showing.

The ground windows were low, and the first one that Silver looked through showed him the dining room, with Buster Wayland and three guests at the table, and a Chinaman, humpbacked with anxious effort, gliding about to serve them.

It was not hard to guess that the man at the head of the table was Wayland. All of his nickname of "Buster" showed in his big, florid face, in the sheen of his eyes, in his continual smiling or laughter. He was big. He was so big that he overflowed his armchair. His gestures and his voice were of the overflowing type, also, and as Silver looked at him, he could not help having a flash back at the wounded man who lay on the shoulder of the mountain with only the vaguest of hopes of giving him comfort.

As for the guests, they were men worth seeing. One of them was none other than Sheriff Bert Philips, whom Silver had last seen in the town of Mustang. The other two, it came instantly to knowledge, were deputies who were assisting Philips in the man hunt. They were talking of that, and of nothing else, and the banker was assuring the sheriff that there would be an adequate reward paid outside of the promise of the law once young Holman was accounted for.

"How he's kept away this long, nobody can make out!" declared Buster Wayland. He bumped the table with his fist. "But it's a certain sure thing he can't keep away much longer."

"It's nothing but Jim Silver, or Silvertip, or whatever you want to call him," declared the sheriff. "He's the fellow who has saved the scalp of Holman. And to think that I had him under my gun in Mustang, and didn't shoot."

"Aye, that was a mistake," growled the raw-boned young deputy whose fierce eyes faced Silver from the opposite side of the table.

"A mistake," agreed Wayland. "But I know how it is—a man wants to give the other fellow every chance, unless you're dead sure!"

"There's Silver's record, besides," said the sheriff. "He's been at outs with the law before this, but he always turns up right and the law turns up wrong. He proves his case, and it ain't always the law's case."

"One day he'll wake up dead before his proving is finished," said the deputy with the burning eyes.

"But there's money behind that crowd," said Wayland. "Silver, as you call him, may be honest most of the time, but that girl has money enough to bribe a saint."

"Maybe so—maybe so," said the sheriff. "But what counts with me is that Holman is still on the loose in the mountains."

"We'll hunt him out of there," said the second deputy, an older and a graver man, with a thick red neck and a bristling mustache.

"I think," said Bert Philips, "that maybe we'll do a good job if we simply keep a lot of men riding on the lookout down in the plains, not so far from Tuckaway. Remember that Ned Kenyon is with 'em, and Kenyon knows the lay of the land around here pretty good."

The truth of this remark pinched the memory of Silvertip. Whatever happened, he must get back to the party in time to warn them that Kenyon's suggestion would simply lead them into ruin. They must keep back among the mountains.

"If they're in the mountains," said Buster Wayland, "they'll soon come out on the run. That fellow Nellihan that came in and talked with me to-day, he's as keen as mustard, and he knows his business. He took all the best horses and the best riders out of this town when he scooted back for the hills. He'll work all night, if there's starlight enough to show him the difference between a rock and a bush."

"We'll get 'em," agreed the sheriff. "But only because Holman is wounded. It's a good thing that Lorens shot straight that time. Because if Silver's hands weren't tied down by the moving of a wounded man, I don't think that we'd ever see hide or hair of that party."

The second deputy put in: "What I wanta know is this—who had the nerve to tell the lie that a horse ever walked across the bridge in Whistling Canyon? I know that bridge. I've been across it, and it's made me sick at the stomach to go over. I've ridden twenty miles out of my way to keep from having to cross that bridge. And now some blockheads tell me that a big stallion up and crossed it—this fellow Silver's horse!"

"Aye, but that horse is Parade," said the sheriff. "You can't judge him by ordinary horses any more than you can judge Silver by ordinary men."

"How come?" asked Wayland.

"Parade was the hundred-thousand-dollar mustang that used to run wild up there in the Sierra Blanca Desert. Never hear of that?"

"Sure, I have!" agreed Wayland.

"That's the one. Seventeen hands of thunder and lightning, and all gold and twenty-four carats. That's Parade. They say he'll stand up and cakewalk when his master whistles. And it's a sure thing that he *did* walk that bridge, because he wasn't left on the near side with the other mustang."

"We'll have a drink," said Wayland. "Hey, Sammy, bring in another bottle of that rye. We're going to have a drink to the lucky man that crashes a slug of lead through the brain of that scoundrel of a thief, that David Holman. The man that has that luck is going to collect an extra two thousand dollars from me, and you're all my witnesses!"

They looked at one another, and Silver gritted his teeth. To cow-punchers who worked for forty-five dollars a month, two thousand meant a huge fortune. Almost anything would be done for the sake of that money. Now it was stacked on top of the original five thousand that had been hung up as a prize, and nothing could save David Holman—nothing but some way of proving his innocence.

Silver kicked off his sandals. Even their light weight would be in his way now.

He rounded to the front of the house, shinnied up one of the wooden columns that framed the Georgian porch, and so came to the second story of the big house. A balcony ran down the side of the building, and he could move at ease down this.

There were only two lighted rooms, one a big bedroom, and one an upstairs study with a big easy-chair in front of a fireplace, and a silk dressing gown and a pair of slippers laid out. Mr. Buster Wayland would probably take his ease here after dinner had been finished.

But the furnishings of the room did not end here—there was also a big steel safe in a corner of the room. It was hardly a decorative piece, but it had more interest for the owner of the house, no doubt, than all the rest of the place that Simonson had built.

The safe was not all. There was also an element of human interest, for in a corner of the room, seated beside the only lighted lamp in the chamber, was a guard.

Holman had said that Wayland knew how to attach thugs to his interest, and certainly this fellow was a perfect example and type of ruffian. He was reading a magazine with such interest that his brutal head was thrust far forward on his neck, and his face snarled with the emotions that worked in him.

Something that Silver did not hear in the least reached the ear of the fellow. Instantly he was out of the chair, crouching, a gun in his hand. He went cat-like to the door, opened it, and then came slowly back, his mouth still working, his eyes glaring.

He was not a man. He was simply a formidable beast. Once back in his chair, he remained for a time alert, in a singular way, reading, or pretending to read, and suddenly flashing his glance up and around the room.

Then the truth was borne in upon Silver. It was the gaze that he himself kept fastened on the gunman that made the fellow uneasy, the insistent force of that regard constantly bearing in upon his unconscious mind, and vaguely sending messages of warning to the consciousness itself.

The man wriggled and stirred as though he were seated too close to a hot fire. Never had Silver seen instinct work more powerfully and on so slight a cause.

Presently the man sprang out of the chair and walked straight across the room and to the window where Silver was watching. Silver flattened himself close to the wall of the house, raising in his right hand a revolver which he grasped by the barrel, the butt offering as the club.

And after a moment a bullethead came out through the window, not slowly, but with a quick, dipping motion so fast that the blow that Silvertip aimed at the base of the man's neck found the very top of his head instead.

The weight of that shock drove his face down against the sill, but did not quite stun him. Silver, following his attack with wonderful speed, saw his man on one knee before the window, with a gun coming gradually into his hand. There was no need for another blow. Silver simply tapped him across the forehead and the gun slid to the rug.

The whole soul of the guard was striving to fight, but the numbed body and brain could not react. The face of the man was a frightful thing to see. It was like the twisted mask of an ape trying to bite.

He kept shaking his head to clear away the clouds that were gathering over his wits. Silver tied the vaguely struggling hands of the man behind his back before sense enough to cry out came to the thug. He tilted back his head, and his chest heaved before he let out the yell.

It was never uttered. Silver simply stepped in front of him and put the muzzle of the Colt into that open mouth. The apelike creature clamped his teeth down on the steel and gasped.

Silver removed the gun and looked over his captive.

"What's your name, brother?" he asked. "And talk soft when you answer."

"What the devil is my name to you?" snarled the captive. "What I'm goin' to do to a sneakin' slick of a second-story worker like you when I get my chance—"

He paused, as though realizing the futility of threats at this moment. His breath came straining and rasping in his throat. The butt of the gun had cut his scalp a little, and a crimson trickle, having worked through the hair, spilled down beside his right eye, and gradually worked in a crooked course toward the chin.

"What's your name?" repeated Silver.

"Lefty some call me, and Soggy some call me," said the yegg.

"All right, Soggy," said Silver. "That name goes for me. Tell me when Mr. Wayland comes up to this room?"

"Why should I tell you?"

"Because he's going to be wiped out of this town, Soggy," said Silver. "He may be wiped off the face of the earth. I don't know. The fact is that if I have to drop him, your own name will be mud around this neck of the woods. Am I wrong?"

"Soggy" said nothing. He merely lowered his head a little and glowered at Silver from beneath shaggy brows.

"It would be hard to explain," said Silver. "Wayland is a big man in this town. If anything happens to him, it might be tough on his hired gunman. Lynching parties work pretty fast around here."

Soggy pursed out his lips in thought. He said nothing.

"I'm going to tie you into that chair," said Silver. "If I have to, I'll choke you with a gag, but I'd rather give you a chance to breathe comfortably. Walk over there and sit down. Remember, I'm giving you a better break than you'd give me. And if you try to yell, I may have to sink a chunk of lead in you."

23

A Forced Confession

SOGGY, without a word of protest, let himself be tied into the chair. And Silver even made a cigarette, lighted it, and put it between the lips of his captive. Thereafter, by ducking his head far down, Soggy could manage to transfer the cigarette from his mouth to his right hand, which was tied out on the arm of the chair in which he sat. Silver stood back and grinned at him, and Soggy grinned back.

"Hard lines!" sympathized Silver.

"I've seen worse," said Soggy. "I've seen worse birds than you are, too. What's your monicker?"

"I work with quite a batch of 'em," said Silver.

"I'll bet you do," agreed Soggy.

"Arizona Jim, some call me."

"Arizona," said Soggy, "you're kind of white. What's the game on Wayland?"

"He's a thug and a crook," said Silver. "He has a lot coming to him, and he's going to get part of it, or all of it, to-night."

"I like to hear you, kind of," said Soggy. "The while I been workin' for him ain't been so sweet. Easy money—but he's a bum. He's a four-flusher."

"He can fight," said Silver tentatively.

"That's what *he* says," answered Soggy. He added: "If you hand him the rap, do you give me a break to get loose out of here?"

"If you don't bother me," said Silver.

"I'll sit like a bird in a tree," said Soggy. "Go ahead and blaze away, will you?"

"I'll go ahead, and I'll blaze away," agreed Silver. "Know anything good about this fellow Wayland?"

"No. Nothin'."

"Don't even know when he'll come up here?"

"No. Maybe in an hour, Maybe any time. He comes up here off and on to see how things go. He's got his heart and his liver and his lights locked up in the safe yonder. Some mug that cracks that safe open will get a hand-out worth havin'! And if—"

Silver raised a hand for silence. He heard something on the stairs beyond the room. He heard a rhythmic thing—a pressure rather than a sound—coming down the hall toward the door. Stepping close to the door, flattening his body against the wall, he saw the door suddenly swing open. Big Wayland, with a step surprisingly light and fast for a man of his size, strode into the room.

His first glance was for the face of the safe. But while he was taking it, he saw his gunman tied into the chair, and the ominous gun in the hand of Silver, just beside him.

There was good fighting stuff in Wayland, after all. With his right hand he reached for his gun. With his left he drove a long, straight, whipping punch at the head of Silver. The latter let the blow go past him. He stepped in and jabbed the muzzle of his Colt into the ribs of Wayland. With his left he caught the gun hand of the big fellow.

So for an instant they faced one another, Wayland glaring, the eyes of Silver utterly cold and remorseless. The thumb of his right hand was trembling with desire to let the hammer drop and ease this crooked life out of the world.

Wayland saw the expression and seemed to understand it. He said in a low, guttural voice: "All right. You've got me. Who are you? What do you want?"

"They've been talking about me down at your table," said Silver. "They call me Silver, or Silvertip, but names don't make much difference. This is a business call, Wayland. Give me that gun!"

He took the gun. It was the only weapon the banker carried, as Silver discovered by sliding his hand rapidly over the body of the man.

When he was disarmed, Silver stepped back from him and said calmly:

"You don't need to hoist your hands over your head. Just remember that I'm watching you, Wayland. Now take a sheet of that paper, sit down at the table, unscrew your fountain pen, and write a little letter for me."

"What sort? A letter of credit? Is that what you're driving at?" asked Wayland.

"A letter to whomever it concerns," said Silver. "Saying that you hired the two crooks who took young Holman down to the bank, that you went with them, that you helped yourself to one third of the loot, that when you saved the bank afterward, you were simply using money that you'd already stolen from it for that purpose, and for buying out poor Simonson before he died of a broken heart. Is that clear?"

Wayland showed not the least surprise.

"Write a little story that clears young Mr. Holman. Is that it?" he asked. Then he turned toward the tied-up gunman.

"You let yourself be brushed out of the picture, did you, Soggy?"

"He socked me," said Soggy. "But I dunno that I'm sorry, if I'm goin' to have a chance to see him sock you, too!"

"You can't go through with this," said Wayland to Silver. "I have men down there waiting for me. They'll be up to see what's wrong if I stay here. Besides, you're only making a fool of yourself. You're going to force a confession out of me, and a forced confession isn't worth anything, and I've got Soggy here as a witness to the force used. Look here, Silver, you're a fellow with a bright eye. You're the sort of a man who ought to be able to tell on which side your bread is buttered. And I'm an open-handed fellow, Silver, if people approach me in the right way. You could have a fair—"

He stopped. Something in the face of Silver told him he was wasting time—a cold and profound disgust.

"Sit down," said Silver, "and write. Begin with the date line, and go down to the finish. Understand? I know what the form should be, and so do you. Now write!"

The big man sat at the table, his face shining with sweat, the fatness of the fountain pen looking actually slender in his bulky hand.

"You can't bleed me," he gasped finally. "You can't do anything with a forced confession. I can laugh at this to-morrow."

"You won't be here to-morrow," said Silver.

"Murder?" said Wayland, steadily enough.

"I don't think so—unless you fail to write," said Silver. "To kill you wouldn't be murder, Wayland. But if you write the stuff out, I'm simply going to take you downtown and see you catch the freight that's pulling out of the station in about forty minutes. You'll catch that train, and Soggy will catch it with you. When the confession is found in here and you're found gone, I think it may do something, Wayland. But because I know you'd rather die than tell the truth and lose all your loot at the same time, I'm going to give you another sort of a chance with that. I'm going to let you open that safe and take what's in it along with you."

"To become a fugitive of justice, eh?" said Wayland, narrowing his eyes.

"You've been that before, or my eye can't read straight," said Silver. "Start writing!"

One desperate glance Wayland flung around the room. Then he compressed his lips and began to write. The room fell utterly silent, so silent that the scratching of the pen seemed to be growing louder and louder, and Silver became aware of the ticking of the big clock that stood on the mantelpiece above the chimney place.

He was aware of something else, too, after a time, and that was the approach of footfalls up the stairs. Big Wayland stopped writing, and his face lighted.

"If it's one of your guests," said Silver, turning the key in the door, "tell him that you're busy. That you'll be right down. Understand?"

Wayland nodded. But a fugitive hope was glimmering in his eye all the time.

Presently a hand beat on the door firmly.

"Hello?" called Wayland, looking straight into the muzzle of Silver's gun.

"Hello, Wayland. This is Bert Philips. Wondered what was keeping you."

"Coming down in a minute," said Wayland. But there was a shaking huskiness in his voice that made Philips exclaim:

"Wayland! I want to see you, man!"

He rattled the knob of the door. He had found enough in the absence of his host, he had heard enough in the voice of that host, to alarm him. There was no doubt about it. Wayland would have to admit him; at least, see him face to face.

"You've been upset," whispered Silver to Wayland. "Tell him that. Go unlock the door and face him—but if you let him come into the room, I start shooting, and I shoot at you. You hear?"

Wayland rolled despairing eyes. Then he nodded, went to the door and turned the key. The door came instantly open, as though Philips were pushing against it. But Wayland held it by the knob, and the sheriff was saying:

"I'm worried about you, man. And you look green-gray. You're sweating. What the devil's the matter? May I come in?"

"I've been upset a little, is all. A little sick," muttered Wayland. "You go back and keep the boys entertained. I'll be down in a little while. Don't worry, I'm all right. Just keep the boys entertained for a bit, will you?"

"Well," said Philips uneasily, "well, I'll do that. But I'm worried about you. Sure that nothing's wrong?"

"No," said Wayland. "I'm all right!"

What torment it must have been for him to speak those words!

But they were spoken, the door closed against Philips, and the lock softly turned back.

Tottering in his step, his head hanging, Wayland went back to the table. Suddenly he said:

"Silver, I'll make you rich! I'll pay you—"

"Listen," said Silver sternly. "If you had ten millions in gold and you could give it to me with a wave of the hand, I'd still laugh at you!"

For one moment Wayland stared at that grim face. Then he resumed his writing.

As he finished it, Silver, looking over his shoulder, read the document, and knew as the signature went down that the thing was perfect. If anything could save Holman, this was it—if only Wayland could be removed, so that it would look as though conscience had forced a confession from him before he fled with a part of his loot.

He pushed the paper onto the center of the table, favored Silver with a scowl of the blackest hate, and then hurried to the safe. The combination wheel spun back and forth for an instant under his fat fingers. The heavy door opened with a faint puffing sound, and there was Wayland on his knees, at work.

He knew where every item of the highest value was to be found. Perhaps, crook that he was, he had the cream of his wealth collected there against just such an emergency as this. At any rate, in five minutes he was on his feet again, with his pockets stuffed. Silver, stepping to the side of Soggy, with a touch of the knife had made the thug free, merely whispering:

"Soggy, you're going to climb on board the same train with him. You know where the pies are. Maybe you'll be able to help yourself to some of 'em."

Soggy rolled up his face with a frightful grin distorting it, and a flare of the big, apish nostrils. Suddenly Silver knew that he could trust the man to work honestly with him during the rest of that adventure.

And he was right. He had no fear of the gun that he intrusted to Soggy. It was simply another proof that Wayland would not be able to get away. His figure was definitely settled.

They passed out along the balcony. Soggy went to the ground first. Wayland then with stifled grunts of effort followed, to slide down the pillar at the end of the porch, while Silver hung by his hands from the edge of the balcony above and then dropped lightly to the ground. That was how the trio reassembled, and started across the grounds. The thinnest sort of a whistle summoned Parade out of the trees to the side of his master, and now Silver walked behind the pair, occasionally spurring big Wayland forward with a word.

No one noticed the leading citizen of Tuckaway as he strode down alleys and across the little town toward the railroad station, or as he went under the guidance of Silver a little distance down the tracks to a point where a rising grade made it certain that the next freight could be boarded.

It was not until the train came groaning and thundering near, however, that Wayland realized a new feature of danger in his plight.

"You've given Soggy a gun!" he exclaimed. "It's the same as murder for me to get on board the train with him. He'll bump me off as sure as daylight! He's bound to!"

"I've got a spare gun for you, too," said Silver. "You can have it as soon as the headlight of the engine goes by."

"Hold on!" yelled Soggy. "Don't I get any edge on that big thug after I've—"

But the approaching thunder of the train drowned his voice. The headlight of the engine went by, printed the swinging shadows of the leaves of the bushes on the faces of the three men.

It was now that Silver put a Colt into the hand of Wayland.

"Now hop that train!" he shouted. "Because if you're still here after it goes by, you shoot it out with me!"

Then, kneeling at a gap in the brush, Silver, with poised gun, watched Wayland rush for the train. He saw Soggy leap like a monkey and catch with hands and feet. He saw big Wayland catch one of the iron ladders with almost equal agility. And then the train swayed on and passed out of view around the next turn, gathering speed all the while.

It was already shooting along with a speed which would break the neck of any man who tried to leap from it. And many and many a mile would be between Wayland and the town of Tuckaway before he could start the return journey. Day would have come again, and the news of his disappearance and of his confession, before he could get back. And with the news, there would be a run on the bank unless the directors of it closed the doors.

All the consequences were obscured before the eyes of Silver, except he knew that he had kept himself from shooting a rascal who needed killing— and that he had assured the safe return of David Holman to the ranks of the law-abiding citizens.

24
Kenyon's Sacrifice

HE had assured the return of Holman—if only he could bring help to his friends in the mountains before the cruel wits of Nellihan and Lorens had located the wounded man and his companions.

Silver drove Parade like a golden streak straight back for the house of Wayland. He checked the stallion in front of the porch. Inside the house, he could hear a heavy battering at a door. Were they at last sufficiently alarmed to beat down the door?

He rapped on the front door, in his turn. The Chinaman opened it before him, and then winced back at the sight of the tall body and the white rags it was dressed in.

"Is the sheriff here?" asked Silver. "Then go tell him that Jim Silver is down here waiting to see him."

The Chinaman fled up the stairs, his hands outstretched to help him, like wings, his head jerking over a shoulder, now and then, to cast furtive glances back at the big man who waited in the hall.

Upstairs, the battering paused for an instant, and Silver heard the voice of one of the deputies exclaim: "Mr. Wayland, if you don't open the door, we'll take it for granted that something has happened to you, and we're going to break it down!"

The voice of the Chinaman broke in on this. There was a sudden exclamation from the sheriff, then the stamp of his running feet on the hall floor above.

Silver sang out: "I'm down here, Philips, and I'm not fighting."

Yet the first thing that he saw come down the dimness of the stairs was the glimmer of a revolver, and then the dark outlines of Philips crouched behind the gun.

Silver put his hands up, shoulder high.

"I'm not fighting," he said. "Tell me if you know that Wayland has run out of town with all the cash he could get together. And then come down here and pinch me, if you want to!"

"Break down that door, Gene!" called the sheriff to one of the deputies. Then he came hurrying down and confronted Silver.

"Silver," he said, "keep those hands up till I've fanned you. You know you're wanted for knowingly and willingly and witting—or whatever the legal phrases are—helping that rat of a Dave Holman to escape!"

"Fan me, Bert," said Silver. "There's a gun under the pit of my left arm, and there's a knife on my left hip. Take 'em both!"

The door went down with a crash while he was speaking. Philips took him into the dining room, where the Chinaman remained quaking in a corner.

"It's the queerest layout that I've ever seen," declared Philips. "I've never known anything like it. I hope I never *do* know anything like it. Wayland has turned into a green-faced mystery. You say that he's gone out of town and—"

There was a loud shouting from above, and then the thundering of heavy feet on the stairs. The first deputy, he of the fierce eyes, rushed into the room, with the signed confession of Wayland fluttering like a white flag in his hand.

He slapped it onto the table in front of Philips and cried: "Bert we been ridin' all this way for nothin'. The scalp of this here gent, this David Holman, it ain't worth a damaged nickel—because the whole yarn about him robbing the bank was a lie. Here's the truth!"

The sheriff was not a slow-minded man, but when he had finished reading that paper for the third time, he said: "But what persuaded Wayland to confess? If he's been this much of a skunk, why should he ever have confessed?"

The deputy pointed at Silver.

"Him!" he said. "He must've done it!"

"We want Wayland, not Holman," said the sheriff. "Where did you say that Wayland is?"

"On a freight train bound east. You can telegraph ahead, but I don't think he'll arrive at the first station," said Silver.

"Why not?" asked Philips.

"Because he may have some trouble on the road," answered Silver. "Philips, if you don't want Holman, you don't want me."

"I don't want you," agreed Philips. "I might have known that you'd prove the law wrong, again! Poor Holman! Something ought to be done to make up to him what he's gone through!"

Silver had lowered his hands, slowly, while Gene watched him with starved, bright eyes, as though he hated to see this quarry slip through his hands.

"The great thing you can do," said Silver, "is to see that the men of Kirby Crossing don't mob Holman and the others during the night. Nellihan and Lorens are leading those men from Kirby, and you can bet your money that they'll keep moving all night. Philips, will you get on your horse and make a drive toward Kendal Mountain, yonder? That's where I left Holman and the other three—up on a shoulder."

"I know the place," said the sheriff. "I'll get there as fast as horseflesh is able to fetch me. I'll be with you in two minutes, as soon as we can saddle up."

Silver stepped to the window, and sent a whistle cutting into the outer night.

"I'm going on ahead," he said. "Parade will take me there ahead of you. There's enough moonlight for straight shooting, and I'm worried about what may be happening up there. So long! You know the place! Ride your horses to a finish!"

Hoofbeats sounded softly on the lawn, and came to a sliding halt on the gravel of the path beside the house. The sheriff saw the sheen of the golden stallion in the lamplight. Then Silver was through the window and into the saddle. He was gone in a flash into the night.

It was almost at that moment that on the shoulder of Kendal Mountain, Harry Bench laid his hand on his sleeping companion, Ned Kenyon. As Kenyon wakened, he heard Bench saying:

"They're coming, Ned! Get up and out of here, fast! They're not fifty steps away. Listen!"

Kenyon heard a soft crackling, as a twig snapped. He was up instantly, sweeping his blanket into a roll.

He saw, then, that the girl had not slept. She sat passively beside Holman. He had thrown out his hand, during his sleep, and she held it in both of hers. One gesture from Bench told her of the danger. She sprang up. Holman wakened with a start. In a moment Bench and Kenyon were carrying their wounded companion on the litter away from the little clearing.

The moon was less than half full, but it shed a light that seemed to be growing stronger and stronger, as though danger were brightening it. If those who hunted for them found the place where they had camped, might not they also be able to find the out trail they were following?

Kenyon carried the head of the litter and led the way. They went down the first slope until it entered the head of a ravine that wound on through the foothills, growing deeper every moment.

"This here—it's a trap!" said Harry Bench. "Suppose that they come down on us here, they'll just flood us away!"

"If we kept up there on the divides," said Kenyon, "they could see us miles away, under this moon. We ain't in this valley because we like it, but because there ain't any better place for us to go!"

That was the sheer truth. They went on silently and had put a good mile behind them when a gun spoke from the cliff at their right.

No bullet came near them. Three times the rifle was fired in rapid succession, and looking up, their frightened eyes saw a horseman wheeling his mustang away from the edge of the cliff, and going out of sight at a dead gallop. His wild Indian yell came whooping dimly down to them.

The men of Kirby Crossing had found them. They could guess that, and it would not be long before the flood of fighters came sweeping down into the ravine, as fast as horseflesh could carry them. They put down the litter and stared at one another.

Holman said: "It's all right, boys. You've done more than any other men in the world could have done. The luck's against us, at last, and that's all. I can take the medicine. Stand back and hoist your hands if they sight you. Or better still, try to climb out of the canyon and get away. They may rough you up a little if they find you with me; but if you're not in sight, they'll be glad enough to get me, and they're not likely to keep on hunting for you."

The girl said nothing. As usual, she merely looked at Harry Bench, for she was rarely able even to glance toward Ned Kenyon.

It was Kenyon who made the answer to that last remark, however. He said: "Harry, we're in the narrows of the canyon. One man oughta be able to hold back a crowd for quite a spell, here. And while he's holding, the other man and Edith can fetch Holman along till you come to some cut-back at the side of the ravine—some place where you can hole up and hide."

He took out a silver dollar, new-minted, flashing in the sun, and laid it on the back of his thumb.

"Call, Harry!" said he, and spun the coin high into the air.

Harry Bench looked up at the rising of the coin with despairing eyes. It was life or death, he knew, that was being tossed for. The man who remained behind, as Kenyon had so calmly suggested, would check the flood for a time, but it was sure to beat him down and roll on, before any long time.

"Tails!" called Bench.

The coin spatted on the palm of Kenyon. Bench leaned forward to look at it, but instantly the long fingers of Kenyon furled over it.

"It's tails," said Kenyon. "It's tails, all right. You win, and I stay here."

"I won't stand for it!" groaned Holman. "Go and save yourselves, both of you, and take Edith."

Confusion of mind and doubt bred something like anger in the voice of Harry Bench.

"She won't leave you, you blockhead!" exclaimed Bench. "There ain't any other way about it than this. Heaven help Ned—but the luck was agin him. Edith, pick up the light end of the litter, there."

He himself picked up the head of the litter. But the girl had run to Kenyon.

"Come on with us, Ned!" she said. "If anything happens to you, even if the rest of us lived, would our lives be anything but a curse and a darkness?"

"I ain't going to be killed," said Kenyon. "I feel kind of calm, and lucky. Say 'Good-by' and go fast."

"Come on!" cried Bench, "or I'll start draggin' him by myself!"

He began, in fact, to stride forward, trailing one end of the poles behind him.

"Go on," said Kenyon. "It's what I want you to do!"

Still, for an instant, she hesitated.

"Heaven will never forgive me for what I've done to you! But can *you* forgive me, Ned?" she asked him.

Holman was crying out wildly, ordering Bench to drop the litter, swearing that he would not accept a life given to him in this fashion. Kenyon took the girl by the arm and waved her toward Holman.

"He's a better man than me," said Kenyon. "Go help him. Forgive you? There ain't anything to forgive. God bless you; good-by!"

She seemed to Kenyon, suddenly, like a child that stared up with incredulous wonder, and awe. What she said, he could not understand, because her voice was choked. And then she was gone, and Kenyon stood looking down at the hand which she had kissed.

He saw her pick up the dragging poles of the litter, and so the group disappeared around the corner of the wall of the ravine, and the protesting voice of Holman grew faint. At the same time, the clanging hoofs of many horses came roaring into the upper end of the valley.

Kenyon looked up at the sky, where the moon made it pale with light. He looked down at the walls of the canyon, one black as ink, one shimmering softly with the moonshine. He felt that he was about to die, and this picture was in some manner entering his very soul.

There was only one bit of shelter for him—a fallen boulder that projected two feet or more above the sand. Behind that he stretched himself and put the rifle to his shoulder. And then he saw them come pouring—a great sweep of horsemen, darkly silhouetted against the moonlight wall of the ravine. He fired three shots and waited.

They were not aimed shots. He was no good with a rifle. Besides, he had no intention of shooting to kill. And he drew a great breath of relief when he saw the cavalcade split away to either side, suddenly, as though the prow of an invisible ship had cloven a way through them, pushing them back under the shadows of the cliffs. He saw one man dismount and begin to climb by a crevice up the sheer face of the ravine wall. That would be the end—when that fellow gained the top of the wall and could shoot down at an easy angle into the body of the man who blocked the passing of the ravine. But Ned Kenyon did not turn and run for his life. If there were fear in him, he could not recognize its presence, but all he felt was a calm happiness that had no regard whatever for the future.

25

The Show-down

IT took one hour for a horseman to get from Tuckaway to Kendal Mountain. It took forty minutes for Silver to rush out from the town on the back of Parade. As he reached the abandoned camping place, he heard the rifles open in the ravine below. So he swept down from the heights like a hawk from the upper air, and came into the narrow ravine where the guns boomed like small cannon. Then, at an elbow turn of the wall, he had a chance to view the scene in detail, without being looked at himself.

Close under the walls of the ravine, chiefly on the side where the shadow made a black apron, a dozen or fifteen men were taking shelter behind brush, or behind fragments of rock that had fallen from the cliffs above. Their rifles spurted little jets of fire, now and then. In answer to them there was an occasional shot from a point where the canyon narrowed until the wall of it seemed to be leaning together. Those solitary shots were fired by big Harry Bench and Kenyon, of course, and beyond the narrows of the ravine would be the wounded Dave Holman, and the girl.

Now Silver saw the greatest threatening danger—the small silhouette of a man who was climbing the eastern wall of the ravine, working himself up on the jags of a deep crevice. In a few moments, the fellow would be on the upper lip of the canyon cliff, and could destroy the defenders with ease and security.

Silver dismounted, and pressing close to the corner of the rock so that little of his body would show, he made his voice great and thundered:

"Kirby Crossing! Who's there to talk to Jim Silver? I've got news from Tuckaway. The sheriff's on the run to get out here. Buster Wayland has confessed he did the job of robbing the bank. Holman has clean hands. He's cleared."

There was a chorus of surprised shouts, and then a yell in which he recognized the snarling, high-pitched voice of Nellihan:

"He lies! It's a bluff! Why isn't the sheriff here before him? Boys, stand tight. We'll bag the whole lot of them in another minute. Lorens is on top, and we've got the lot of them!"

A yell of triumph ran in on the last of his words, for now the man who climbed the eastern wall had reached the top, and was running forward to gain a better position from which to shoot down into the ravine. That savage yell told Silver that he had come too late to use words. Only his rifle would help him now, and whipping it out of the saddle holster, he lay flat and drew a careful bead. First he ranged his eye down the side of the ravine to estimate the range, then he caught the dark silhouette of the target in his sights, and began to squeeze his hand over the trigger.

At that moment, Lorens disappeared behind some upjutting rock on the verge of the cliff.

Sweat streamed down the face of Silver. But what could he do? If he rushed with Parade, he might escape the gantlet of fire on either side of the ravine, but when he reached his friends in the narrows, he would simply be swallowed in the same trap that held them.

A moment later, the ravine was hushed, and immediately after that, he heard the clang of a rifle, fired from the top of the cliff. That shot had told, for Lorens, in excess of triumph, suddenly leaped to his feet with a yell that rang from far off, coming to the ears of Silver like the cry of a bird of prey from the central sky. It was a fatal mistake for Lorens. In rising to brandish his rifle so that it flashed in the moonlight, a meager, whirling streak of brilliance, he had jumped right into the sights of Silver's gun.

Nellihan's howling voice shrilled a warning, but it was heard too late. Silver fired. And the body of Lorens leaned slowly out. The rifle dropped before him. Then he shot out into the air in a graceful arc, like a high diver, and plunged from the height.

A great yell of rage and of horror came from the men of Kirby Crossing. Before it died out, Silver was in the saddle again and sending Parade down the ravine like a glimmering bolt of lightning.

The watchers were taken totally by surprise. A few turned their guns on him, but the shots they fired were random bullets, before he plunged into the shadows of the narrows. And as he went by, he saw the body of poor Ned Kenyon, spread-eagled behind the rock.

Dead?

He ranged Parade close against the canyon wall beyond the reach of bullets; then he ran forward, stooping low, and gained the side of Kenyon. A faint muttering sound came from the lips of his friend. He turned the limp body, and saw a patch of darkness high on the breast of Kenyon, a patch that grew.

"Arizona?" said Ned Kenyon faintly. "I might 'a' known that you'd get in on the thing before the wind-up. Have they blotted me?"

Silver thumbed the wound. The bullet had entered high on the shoulder, close to the base of the back of the neck; it had ranged forward and come out by the collar bone.

"Take one deep breath—and say one word!" said Silver.

Kenyon obediently breathed and said: "Damn!" clipping his teeth together as he spoke.

Silver sighed with relief. "If that bullet had got the lungs," he said, "there'd be bubbles of blood in your mouth when you talk. Ned, if I can get you out of this trap, you'll live! Try to lift your left arm. No? It's broken, then; the collar bone's broken, at least. But that's nothing. Where are the others?"

He had an answer from behind for that. They heard the crunching of a heavy footfall, and the great bulk of One-eyed Harry cast itself down beside them. He gasped:

"Thank Heaven you're here, Jim. I came back as soon as I got the girl and Holman stowed away in a little canyon that rips back from this here, a short ways down. Holman is raisin' the devil, and tryin' to break away and crawl back here, so's he can die with the rest of us; and the girl's praying for you out loud, Kenyon; and Holman says he never was worth one of your old boots. Who's that out there, looking at the moon?"

For not far in front of the rock there was the body of Lorens, stretched on its back and staring steadily up at the moon, which glinted on the dead eyes.

There was no chance for Silver or Kenyon to answer the question, for the voice of Nellihan, raised to an animal howl, was now urging the men of Kirby Crossing to close in and rush the defenders. And a great, bull voice made answer:

"Where's yourself, Nellihan? Close in and lead up, instead of talkin' from the back row of the church!"

"I'm here!" shouted Nellihan. "Boys, all together, now. Keep shooting as we go in on 'em. And then—"

"Wait a minute!" called Silver. "All you fellows from Kirby Crossing—if you rush us, we've got three rifles to blow the tar out of a good many of you. If Nellihan wants us, I'll stand out and fight him. If he drops me, you can have the rest of them. They'll surrender. If I drop him, you back up and take a rest till the morning. Does that sound fair to you?"

No one answered for a moment, because there was only one man who could speak, and that was Nellihan. Suddenly his long, misshapen body appeared, striding with long steps from out of the shadows near the wall. He was desperate, as Silver knew, for on this night he was playing his last cards to ruin the life of a girl and get his hands on the fortune.

"I'm here," said Nellihan. "Where are you? Stand out here and show us your face. Are you yellow?"

Silver rose and stood out before the eyes of all those enemies. His hands were empty, and so were the hands of Nellihan, who walked straight up to him and glared into his eyes with a hellish malice.

"You've spoiled everything for me. You've smashed every plan, and you've killed Lorens. You won't hang for that, because I guess he's wanted for more than one killing. But you wouldn't have a chance to hang, anyway. Because I'm going to split your wishbone for you to-night, my friend! Are you ready to start?"

Silver looked at him with a shrinking of the flesh. The man seemed neither old nor young. He was a thing of poisonous evil.

"I'm ready," said Silver. "We'll stand back to back, if you want, and walk away till somebody sings out to shoot. Does that suit you, Nellihan?"

Nellihan peered into his face, as though trying to find the source of the mysterious strength that sustained this man in the time of danger.

"Anything suits me," he said. "You're as good as a dead man, right now. Hey, Baldy! Sing out when you think we've walked far enough!"

They stood back to back. Silver, glancing down, saw that his shadow was sloping well out before him. That meant that when he turned, the moon would be in his eyes. But that was a small disadvantage—if only he could subdue the sick shuddering of his flesh, as he thought of this half-human animal, who would soon be whipping a gun from under his coat and turning to fire. To fight men, Silver felt himself capable; but it was impossible to think of Nellihan failing. The devil he served would support him.

"Start!" shouted the voice of "Baldy."

The murmuring of many other voices died down like a wind passing out of trees. Slowly Silver stepped away, straining every nerve to an electric tension.

"Shoot!" screeched the voice of Baldy.

Silver whirled, snatching his gun from beneath his arm. He saw Nellihan drawing a revolver and leaping far to the side at the same instant. Fast as Silver was, that snaky hand had been faster still. The gun in Nellihan's grip exploded. The brief breath of the bullet fanned the face of Silver as he fired in turn, with his gun hardly more than hip-high.

He thought he had missed, and that Nellihan had deliberately fired a bullet into the ground, for his second shot. It seemed almost—as he held his fire, with his man covered—that Nellihan was slowly dropping on one knee to take a more careful aim. But when he had come to one knee, his body continued to collapse, until he lay face down on the ground.

Death had simply laid its numbing hand upon him gradually.

And before this horror ended, or the silence after it had ceased, the ravine was echoing with the beat of the hoofs of horses. Out from the shadows at the upper end of the valley came three riders, and he who galloped in the lead was Sheriff Bert Philips, bringing up the authentic hand of the law, at last.

All was not as simple as Silver had hoped and even expected. It had looked easy enough on that night, when the men of Kirby Crossing gave up the prey that had baffled them so long, and even helped to take care of the two wounded men. There was no trouble afterward about Nellihan or Lorens, either. Because it was clear that Silver had represented law against mob violence. Furthermore, against Lorens, it was discovered, that there were many counts; and when the character of Nellihan was exposed, the world looked on his death as deliverance from a plague.

Ned Kenyon, too, had a simple rôle. When he was well enough to ride, he went into Nevada to get the divorce that was necessary, and he went without any soreness of the heart. He said to Silver:

"The misery just kind of leaked out of me with my blood, after Lorens had sent the slug through me!"

"You're going to be sensible, I hope," said Silver. "You'll take the help that she and Holman want to give you?"

"Well," said Kenyon, "now that I've got over bein' foolish about her, I guess there's something in what she says—that I worked enough to deserve some pay. So I'm goin' to take the coin. She wants to give me a regular cattle king's layout. But I'll stick just to the ten thousand that she wanted to give me in the beginning. Small things are better for small men, Jim, and I never was as big as my inches."

All of these matters went very well, but it was a full six months before Holman was able to shake off the hand of the law. Not that any one doubted his story, now, but there were complications which might never have been solved, had it not been that the governor of the State stepped in to cut all the red tape with a complete pardon.

But Silver was far away in the northland when this happened, and he only heard of it through a letter that had followed him from one forwarding address to another.

It was from David Holman, and he said in part:

> We've put our heads together, but we don't know what to do. We've owed our happiness to three people—one part to One-eyed Harry Bench, and nine parts to Ned Kenyon, and ninety parts to you. Edith has been able to content Harry and Ned. But we are sorry we can't offer you hard cash, or even a ranch. If we could think of anything you need, we'd like to offer it. But a horse and a gun seem to make you a complete man. All that we can give you is gratitude.
>
> Now that I'm free, and the divorce has been granted, we're going to be married quietly and go for a long trip. When we come back, we'll hope that one day you'll drop in on us. And stay the rest of your life, if you find the place comfortable. The best of all, would be to have you at the wedding. You saw Edith at a wedding once before. That was a marriage in the dark. We hope that this one will be in the sun, with not even a shadow on its future, no matter how much wretchedness may be in its past.
>
> When you write to us, if you ever will, we wish that you

could tell us where you are riding. Or do you know yourself,
but simply drift with the wind or let Parade follow his fancy?

It was a cold day, and as Silver read that letter in the little post office
and then crumpled the paper, he echoed that last question in his own mind.
Where was he bound? He could not tell. The ancient melancholy descended
upon him, and he fell into long reflections from which he awakened, suddenly,
remembering that he had left Parade shivering in the street.